Thin Ice
Michael Gerhartz

WingSpan Press

Thin Ice

Copyright © 2011 by Michael Gerhartz

All rights reserved. No part of this book may be used or reproduced, distributed, or transmitted in any form or by any means, or stored in a database or retrieval system without the written permission of the author.

Printed in the United States of America
Published by WingSpan Press, Livermore, CA
www.wingspanpress.com
The WingSpan name, logo and colophon
are the trademarks of WingSpan Publishing.

The following story is a work of fiction. All characters, organizations and events portrayed in this novel are either products of the author's imagination or are used fictitiously.

First Edition 2011

Publisher's Cataloging-in-Publication Data

Gerhartz, Michael.
Thin ice / Michael Gerhartz.
p. cm.
ISBN: 978-1-59594-456-6
1. Global warming—Fiction. 2. Marine biologists—Fiction.
3. Northwest Passage—Fiction.   I. Title.
PR9199.3.G443 T5 2012
810—dc22

2011941262

Special thanks to my friend
Michael MacDonald for his professional advice,
my very special friend Sandra for her eyes,
and, most importantly
to Lauren E. Hardy for all her work and dedication.

Cast of principal characters

Dr. Richard Weber (Expedition leader and scientist)
Renate Kleinfeld (Dr. Richard Weber's common law wife)
Natascha Kleinfeld (Marine Biologist and member of the German expedition team)

Jonathan Brown (US Senator / Chief of Staff)
Carl Miller (personal secretary of Jonathan Brown)
Pierre Dumont (Member of the Canadian Parlament)

Gordon Ramshaw (Member of the Board of Directors of an international oil company, brother of Cathrin Whittaker)

Crew of the research vessel *Northern Explorer*
Captain Sven Goran Rasmussen
First Officer Karl-Heinz Junghans
Second Officer Mika Kankkunen
Astrid Makkinen (Radio Operator)
Vitali Vachenko (Dive Officer and Instructor for the research submersibles *Odin* and *Polar Viking*)
Holger Bloomquist (Instructor for the research submersibles *Odin* and *Polar Viking*)

EuroSec Corporation
Retired Admiral Brian Whittaker (former British NAVY)
Cathrin Whittaker (wife of Brian Whittaker)
Retired General Klaus Schwartze (former German Bundeswehr)
Brigitte Schwartze (Secretary and wife of Klaus Schwartze)

Operation Control and team leaders EuroSec Corporation
Tatjana Volmatovja (former Russian military intelligence)
Ariel Rashid (former close combat instructor for Israeli Special Forces)
Sigrid Schneider (former German BKA = Bundeskriminalamt)
Sean MacLeod (former Scotland Yard Inspector)
Jack MacDonald (former British SAS team leader)
Gunnar Eriksson (former instructor of the Norwegian Navy Special Operations Commando)

EuroSec Corporation Team A
Nick Rehfeld (former German GSG9)
Olaf Magnusson (former Norwegian Navy Special Operations Commando)
Ole-Einar Alsgaard (former Norwegian Navy Special Operations Commando)
Rolf Brengmann (former German Kampfschwimmer)
Oliver Schneider (former German GSG 9)
Shira Hadad (former Israeli Mossad)

Team of American Scientists on board the *Northern Explorer*
Dr. Jospeh Richard (team leader)
Jenna Mason
Frank Garcia
Brian Joice
Nelson Singer

Team of Canadian Scientists on board the *Northern Explorer*
Dr. Markus Habermann (team leader)
Sasha Theriault
Jonathan MacDonald
Marc Thornton

Team of American Mercenaries
Chuck Hogan (team leader)
Robert Tyrell
Russell Greenstein
Martin Cunningham

Central Intelligence Agency
Abigail Sinclair (CIA Special Agent / Head of Security to Jonathan Brown)

EuroSec Corporation Team B
Jack Connory (former British SAS)
Scott O'Melly (former British SAS)
Peter Clarke (former Special Boat Service of the Royal Marines Commando)
John Davies (former Special Boat Service of the Royal Marines Commando)
Ivan Pavlicic (former Russia frogmen)
Yuri Scharapov (former Russia frogmen)

EuroSec Corporation Team C
Markus Brenner (former German GSG 9)
Wolfgang Buhlmann (former German GSG 9)
Dieter Beier (former German Kampfschwimmer)
Manfred Kleinschmitt (former German Kampfschwimmer)
Tom Hart (former British SAS)
Rick Andrews (formar British SAS)

Scotland Yard
Inspector Conolly

Canadian Authorities
Defence Minister Curt Morgan
Admiral Kerman (Commanding Officer of the Canadian Forces Maritime Command MARCOM)
Captain Lambert (Maritime Forces Pacific MARPAC)

Crew of the Canadian *CF142 Arcturus*
Major Josh MacMillan (Pilot)
Major Erin Shields (Co-Pilot)
Warrant Officer Simon Clearwater

Crew of the Russian Nuclear Long Range Attack Submarine, *Akula* Class
Captain Rankow
Vasili (Doctor on board the submarine)
Michail (crew member and rescue diver)
Tatjana (crew member and rescue diver)

Crew of the Russian submarine *K-9, November* Class
Captain Pietrovich
First Officer Alexej Tatamovich

Canadian Customs Officer in Halifax Harbour
Clair MacDonald

Supporting characters
Erika Schmitt (Friend and dive partner of Natascha Kleinfeld)
Andreas Nahle (Friend and dive partner of Natascha Kleinfeld)
Bernd Bresser (Friend and dive partner of Natascha Kleinfeld)
Captain Holger Sorensson (Captain of Norwegian Dive Boat)
Magnus (Icelandic diver)
Björn (Icelandic diver and son of the Icelandic Prime Minister)
General Rashid (Israeli Mossad)
Mario (Marine Biologist and member of the German expedition team, dive partner of Natascha Kleinfeld)
Erika Heynes (News Reporter)
Peter O'Sullivan (News Reporter)
Josh MacKenzie (News Reporter)
Isis (Model working for an American Escort Service)
Rocky (Natascha Kleinfeld's dog)

Prologue

Amundsen Gulf, Beaufort Sea, on board the Russian Nuclear Submarine K-9, November-Class SSBN, 80m below the surface, May 1969

Captain Pietrovich had just entered the control room to relieve his First Officer Aleksey Tatamovich. Although all lights were on, it was never particularly bright inside the submarine. The prevailing drone of the huge generators was the only noise as all eyes rested on Captain Pietrovich.

"What is our depth?"

"Eighty meters, Comrade Captain," *the Diving Officer replied.*

Pietrovich nodded briefly.

"Course and speed?"

"Course is one-six-five at eight knots, Comrade Captain."

"How thick is the ice?"

"Our last measurements showed a thickness of approximately three meters, Comrade Captain."

Reaching for a cup of tea, Captain Pietrovich nodded again. He stirred the tea with a little spoon, watching the lemon slice swirl around. He placed the lemon on the saucer and sipped the tea.

"The reactor?"

"The reactor is operating at seventy percent. All systems are working without a problem, Comrade Captain."

Captain Pietrovich took a few steps towards the table with the navigational charts and studied them.

"Where exactly are we at?"

A young Officer came to his site and placed a ruler on the chart.

"Here, Comrade Captain, approximately twenty-five sea miles northwest of Cape Parry."

"How deep is the sea here?"

"Our sonar is showing us a depth of two hundred and forty two meters, Comrade Captain."

"According to the chart it should be slightly deeper than three hundred meters. You are positive about our exact position?" *the Captain asked cautiously.*

"Yes, Comrade Captain. Please remember that our command has not confirmed the accuracy of these charts."

Captain Pietrovich nodded in agreement, his eyes still on the chart.

"How was the depth contour of the sea floor in the last twelve hours?"

"The seafloor rose constantly from one thousand eight hundred and forty five meters to now two hundred and twenty meters, Comrade Captain."

"Inform me immediately once the depth rises to one hundred and fifty meters.

Keep course at one-six-five and maintain speed at eight knots. Bring the boat up to seventy meters."

"Yes, Comrade Captain. Course at one-six-five, speed eight knots, making new depth of seventy meters," *repeated Aleksey Tatamovich.*

While the crew got to work, Captain Pietrovich walked over to the sonar station.

"Any sonar contacts?"

"Negative, Comrade Captain. Last contact minus four hours. Most likely a small fishing vessel. Distance was twenty-three sea miles west-south-west, at the edge of the ice."

"Comrade Captain! Sea floor rising quickly. Depth is one hundred forty meters!"

The Captain dropped his tea to the floor and ran to his command station.

"Up twenty, blow all ballast tanks, make her depth forty meters, course one-five-zero, new speed fifteen knots," *yelled Captain Pietrovich, while his First Officer repeated his orders.*

Damn underwater mountains! *He thought.* The problem with navigating unmapped territories is that you do not have accurate charts!

"Depth?" *He demanded from his crew.*

"Our depth is seventy meters, Comrade Captain. Sea floor eighty-five meters, still rising, Mountain straight ahead!"

"Full..."*started Captain Pietrovich, but before he could finish his order, the deafening sound of steel smashing into solid rock drowned out any other noise in the submarine. Although K-9 was on its new course, the massive plateau was already too close. The submarine collided amidships with the edge of the mountain and skidded over it on its complete length. Larger stones immediately penetrated the outer pressure hull, destroying all the ballast cells on the starboard side at once. Skidding over the edge, the submarine also lost its starboard propeller with its shaft. K-9 straightened itself up again, still skidding over the now muddy ground of the plateau before it stopped more than 300 meters from the edge. The crippled submarine slowly listed to its starboard side as it came to a final rest.*

Inside, K-9 was in chaos. Within the first seconds of the collision, the complete bow of the submarine was flooded. The watertight compartments failed to close as water burst through the penetrated submarine. It was too late.

Captain Pietrovich groaned as he wiped his hand across his face. He got to his knees before looking at his blood soaked hands in the dim glow of the emergency lights. Suddenly, he felt the rapidly increasing pressure on his ears, and the last thing Captain Pietrovich saw was a black wall of freezing water rushing towards him. The lights went out the same moment he took his last breath.

Within seconds, K-9 was completely flooded. One final scream escaped the broken submarine as the last of the bubbles drifted upward. The sea fell silent.

- 1 -

Present Day

Just off the coast of Kristiansand, Southern Norway, Saturday, May 14th
The last thing the woman saw while she was falling backwards from the boat into the cold waters of the Norwegian coast was the smile on the man's face. The four degree Celsius cold water closed over Natascha Kleinfeld's head and bit her skin with a thousand teeth. She could hardly believe she was only one meter below the surface. Still sinking in the cold water, she could now barely see the man standing on the boat. Her body started to scream for oxygen as she continued to sink into the dark green abyss below her. Natascha turned her back to the surface and reached for the hose looped above her head. She put the regulator in her mouth, exhaled gently, flipped the DSV* to open the loop, and took a couple of guarded breaths from her rebreather*. She repositioned her mask from her forehead into the correct position, rinsed it and pushed the inlet valve from her dry-suit. Immediately, she could hear the rush of the argon* as it expanded between her body and the dry-suit. She could already feel the warmth and positive buoyancy as she began to float back to the surface.

Natascha was upset. With the new group of divers aboard, today of all days this had to happen to her. She had let herself get distracted while putting her fins on and lost her balance, falling into the water.

"Natascha! Everything okay?" Erika Schmitt asked her.

Natascha tipped with her hand on her neoprene hood, the international sign that everything was okay.

"You forgot your fins," Andreas Nahle commented, laughing.

"Oh really?" Natascha snapped back.

"I would like to know what's so funny about that…"

Natascha didn't understand why she was so upset about this. It was now the second week that she spent with her friends and colleagues, and they have been out diving every day since. She admitted that they had a huge pile of gear to test and that many more dives had to be made. But she still didn't understand why this little mishap was so embarrassing for her. It had happened to many divers before and

---

DSV: dive surface valve

Rebreather: Compared to an open circuit, where the diver exhales through the regulator into the water, a rebreather recycles the air used after each breath, filtering the carbon dioxide and adding new oxygen if necessary. This procedure increases the dive time and lowers the risk of decompression sickness.

Argon: Since it carries heat slower away from the human body than normal air, some divers prefer this expensive gas to fill their dry-suits. It gives them a better insulation and they do not waist valuable breathing gas from their normal tanks.

would happen to many more divers in the future. Normally she would be one of the first people to laugh about something like that.

"Would you please give me my fins?" she asked Bernd, who was already geared up and just waiting for Natascha to clear the entrance area so he could jump into the water. Bernd reached down for the fins, but the weight of his own rebreather shifted on his back, and he struggled to keep his balance.

"Wait, I'll give you a hand," Nick said as Bernd grasped the rail.

Until now, Nick Rehfeld, Rolf Brengmann, Olaf Magnusson and Ole-Einar Alsgaard had done what the Captain of their dive boat and Natascha had asked them to do: To wait until Natascha and her group of scientists were in the water and down the buoy line to the wreck. The reason they asked them to wait was that they wanted the clear visibility while shooting some video. Nick and his buddies on the other hand had no problem with that request and were in no rush to get into the water. The wreck of the *Seattle* was resting there for many years and would not disappear in the next few minutes.

On the ten minute trip from the shore to the dive site, Nick and his friends had enough time to look at the gear Natascha and her friends were using.

Not only were they using the latest Swedish dry-suits, they were also using the same type of rebreather. Besides that, Nick's eyes rested jealously on the new High Definition underwater video-camera system with lights. Looking over the gear, Nick decided to ask Natascha, whom he found very attractive, about the gear as soon as he had the opportunity.

But for the moment, he just picked up the fins and handed them down over the rail to Natascha.

"Here they are." He smiled at her, trying to let her know that he also fell in the water before, just like she did.

"Thanks," Natascha replied, this time not as sharply as she had to Andreas. Nick watched how she pulled the stainless steel spring straps over her heels before he sat with his friends again.

While Olaf and Ole-Einar were putting their own double tanks on, Nick and Rolf were observing the remaining three divers from Natascha's group. They were entering the water more smoothly than Natascha did.

Captain Holger Sorensson handed the underwater video-camera system over the rail and noted the time of descent on his clipboard. He watched the underwater lights following down the buoy line, their beams getting weaker and weaker with the depth.

"Quite the gear," noticed Rolf, standing beside Holger watching the descent of the other divers.

"Yes, her name is Natascha Kleinfeld. She just became a Marine Biologist and she will join a huge cold water expedition within a couple weeks. She and her friends are testing some new gear to make sure everything is working properly for the expedition. Her parents have been coming up here for vacation for years. Was the first time today that I saw her falling in the water like that. Must have been embarrassing for her."

Holger looked up and checked out Rolf and his buddies. Both Olaf and Ole-Einar had their double tanks on their shoulders and were walking to the stern of the boat, ready to enter the water. Nick was just getting into his set of double tanks and Rolf took the opportunity to check Olaf and Ole-Einar's gear again. A few minutes later they were finally ready to enter the water, and listened to Holger's last minute briefing about the wreck of the *Seattle* again.

They jumped in one after the other into the water and they regrouped at the buoy. After a final safety check they released the air from their wing bladders and submerged into the green water. Nick waited for his buddies to gain some depth, then turned towards Holger, signaled that everything was okay and lifted his left arm with the release valve. The air was now streaming out of his dry-suit and he began to sink slowly. As soon as he was under the surface, he put his regulator in place, took a deep breath and enjoyed the feeling of the breathing gas streaming into his mouth. Together with Rolf he followed the buoy line down to the wreck. The visibility of almost 15 meters proved that Holger had not exaggerated in his briefing. The water temperature was only 4 degree Celsius, but because of a blue sky and a strong sun with temperatures around 20 degree Celsius, the four had gotten quite hot in their dry-suits while they waited on board. The cold water was actually a relief at the moment.

Nick was still following the buoy line. Below him, with one hand at the rope, he could see Rolf. A little further below, Nick recognized the strong lights from Olaf and Ole-Einar.

After a few minutes descending down into the cold green water, Nick could finally see a dark silhouette below him. First it was just a dark shadow, but with every meter he descended, Nick could see more and more details of the stern of the once mighty ship. Olaf and Ole-Einar were both hovering in the water, waiting for Rolf and Nick. They checked their gauges and noticed only a very weak current at their depth of 21 meters. Once they checked their breathing gas supply, they continued their descent to their agreed maximum depth of 32 meters. The beam of their strong underwater lights revealed an amazing sight. The whole hull of the wreck was covered with sponges and anemones, which provided cover for a countless number of crabs, starfish and mussels. They even spotted a lobster in the wreckage. Swimming around at that depth, Nick was following the beam of his light with his eyes. Looking down, he saw parts of the superstructure of the *Seattle*, which were, according to Holger's briefing, at around 50 meters. Well below that, Nick could see the beam of the video lights from Natascha's group. It seemed like they were diving at the bow 70 meters down. Nick could feel his jealousy rise at the moment he knew this wreck gave so many opportunities for deeper dives. The problem wasn't that Nick or his friends were incapable or uncertified for diving to such depths, it was simply that they lacked the right breathing gas on this dive to go below 32 meters. Reassuring himself that they would be diving the deeper parts of the wreck within the next couple days, Nick concentrated again on his own dive, and followed Rolf around the wreck. They took their time and examined every bit of the wreck at their depth. After almost 45 minutes they started their final ascent back to the surface, where they met Natascha and

Thin Ice

her group at the 5 meter safety stop. Nick asked them if everything was okay and the four of them replied with the okay sign. Natascha let go of the buoy line and drifted with a tiny movement of her fins back into midwater, giving Nick and his friends the opportunity to hold on to the rope. Ole-Einar and Olaf appreciated the gesture and nodded towards her, while Rolf and Nick hovered in the water, just like Natascha did.

While one of her buddies was shooting some video of Natascha, who was hovering perfectly without any motion, Nick noticed that Natascha was looking at him, totally unimpressed by the video-camera. Even when the diver was swimming around her to shoot all the divers at the buoy line, she neither changed her position nor did she take her eyes off Nick.

Rolf signaled Nick that their safety stop was over and together with Ole-Einar and Olaf they finished their ascent. Natascha and her group still had to finish their decompression.

"Wow, I never thought that there would be so much to see," Nick said, swimming back to the ladder of the boat.

"We told you. Did you actually think we'd dive here for years if it wasn't worth it?" Olaf responded and gave his fins to Holger so he could climb the ladder with his double tanks on.

Nick, Rolf and Ole-Einar followed his example.

"Finally some real divers," Holger added happily, once everyone was aboard. "Normally I have to lift those heavy tanks in the boat myself."

He took his clipboard and looked down to the surface.

"Have you seen the other four? They are due any moment."

Rolf and Nick both looked at the water. Holger was right. The closed circuit rebreathers don't release any bubbles and so it was nearly impossible to determine the position of the divers. Beside that, they also seemed to have all lights turned off.

"Yes, we met them at the five meter stop. They've already been there for a while before we arrived, but it shouldn't be much longer now."

"That's why I don't like rebreathers. As long as I can see some bubbles somewhere, I can guess where the divers are," Holger grumbled before he disappeared with his clipboard in the cabin.

Nick and his buddies stowed their gear to make room for the other four divers, who were due back.

Together with Nick, Ole-Einar was watching the surface again.

"That sweetheart seems to be a professional," the Norwegian said.

"Little bit bitchy, but you are right. She seems to know how to dive. There they are," Nick mentioned and pointed to the surface, where the four divers just emerged and signaled that everything was okay.

Holger joined them and Ole-Einar assisted him to lift the heavy video housing out of the water. Nick and his friends made some room and watched as the others came back on the boat.

"Did you get the wolf-eel?" Natascha asked the moment she set her foot on the deck.

"Yes, got it. Even those difficult shots at the bow that you were so eager to get."

"Great. What about the Macro?"

"Should be okay," Bernd assured her, turning his attention now to the camera, checking that everything was fine.

While Holger started the boat and took course towards the shore, Natascha used a towel to dry her hair before she put on a matching Beanie.

"I guess those are standard with those suits. Looks cute," Rolf commented to Nick.

Natascha smiled at them and walked into the cabin where she could get changed.

Only a few minutes later Ole-Einar and Olaf both helped Holger to secure the boat back at the wharf. Due to the low tides, the deck of the boat was now almost 2 meters below the main wharf. While Rolf climbed up the ladder to get the first of two Volkswagen vans, Nick and his two buddies started lifting their gear off the boat. Working together it took them only a few minutes until everything was off the boat and stowed into the two vans. With the weight of all the wet gear the vans were a few centimeters lower to the ground than before.

"Okay, that should be all," Nick noted and jumped back on the deck of the boat.

"Just checking the cabin again to make sure," he added, while Rolf and Olaf took one of the vans and drove off to the Dive Center.

Nick opened the cabin door and looked inside, where he saw Natascha.

While Nick and his buddies were still wearing their thermo dry-suit undergarment, Natascha was already dressed in jeans and a turtleneck. He noticed she was holding her own thermo suit in her hands, inspecting a wet spot on her left leg.

"Did you get wet?" Nick asked in a concerned tone.

"Just a little bit. Must have been the Pee Valve, no big deal," Natascha explained and smiled back at him.

"And before you get any ideas, it's definitely water. I will change it tonight. No problem," she added, still smiling.

Nick nodded towards her and looked at the pile of gear that Natascha's group still had to get off the boat.

"Can we give you a hand with that?" Nick asked.

"It's quite a bit of gear," he added, still looking at the four boxes, each filled with a dry-suit, neoprene hood, mask and a set of fins. The rebreathers and the video housing unit stood separately beside it.

Natascha glanced from their gear to the wharf and back to the gear. She realized that it would be very strenuous to get all the gear off the boat. She raised her eyebrows before exhaling sharply.

"I promise we won't break anything," Nick reassured with his most innocent voice.

"All right," Natascha laughed and looked Nick in his eyes. She couldn't understand why she had hesitated so long. Basically she liked all four of them. She recalled their benevolence. They all stayed on the boat to give them the advantage of being in the water first, helped her with the fins, cared for them underwater and now they even offered to help them unloading the heavy gear.

Beside that, Natascha had already noticed that all four of them seemed to be pretty athletic and didn't have any problems unloading their own heavy double tanks.

"I'm sorry," she smiled at him. "I don't know what's wrong with me today. Must have hit my head on the water a little bit too hard. I'm Natascha," she explained laughing, offering her hand.

"You must have really hit your head. You've already introduced yourself this afternoon when we came on board. But just in case you forgot, I'm Nick," he responded with a smile, shaking her hand and turning towards the Volkswagen van.

"Hey, Ole," he shouted.

"Come back down here. We will give them a hand with their gear."

Ole-Einar jumped down on the boat to help Nick. The Norwegian paused as he spotted Nick admiring Natascha as she climbed up the ladder to the top of the wharf.

"Because of those jeans I can only give her a seven," Ole-Einar said after he reassured himself that only Nick would hear him.

"At least an eight," replied Nick, still looking at Natascha, who now disappeared from his view, while Erika and her boyfriend Andreas walked by. Erika also climbed up the ladder and Nick and Ole-Einar's eyes followed her. They remained silent, cautious of her boyfriend's presence.

"I'd give her a nine," Andreas mentioned to them, looking after his girlfriend. "And I would give Natascha a ten," he added, once he was certain that Erika was out of earshot.

Nick and Ole-Einar both nodded in agreement and together with Andreas they lifted all the gear up and onto the wharf, where Natascha had parked a brand new Mercedes Sprinter. After all the gear was stowed away inside the Cargo van, Nick and Ole-Einar were reading the advertising on the vehicle.

"Not bad to have access to all the gear of a famous international Institute," Nick mentioned, more to himself. Ole-Einar nodded his head in agreement before he entered his older type of Volkswagen van.

"See you tomorrow morning, Holger," Nick shouted to the Captain of their dive boat, who was waving back to them as they were driving off. Ole-Einar followed the Mercedes until they both came to a halt in front of the Dive Center, where they met Rolf and Olaf again, who had already cleaned their gear.

Both had the same befuddled look on their faces once they saw the Mercedes. Because Nick and his group had only arrived in the early afternoon, they had not met Natascha and her crew, who had been on the boat all day.

After they had cleaned their gear, they stored it in a special room so that it could dry. Again they helped Natascha and Erika with their heavy gear before they finally left for their cottage, which was one of several small log homes in a little Resort just outside Kristiansand. Olaf opened the door and they made themselves comfortable in the living room. Attached to the living room were an open kitchen, as well as two bedrooms and a bathroom. It was perfect for four people.

"It was not a bad idea to come here", commented Ole-Einar.

"Yeah, I really like the wreck. Lots of potential there. Once we get settled, we should switch to trimix* and do some deeper dives."

"Yes, this would be the perfect wreck for that. Maybe you could persuade Natascha to take some video of us."

"I actually wouldn't mind taking a video with her," Rolf laughed.

"You are a pig," Nick added.

"Me? You were the one who marked her butt," Rolf laughed, then restarted, "By they way, what are we eating tonight? I'm getting hungry."

"I don't want to start the kitchen now. Let's go somewhere."

"There is a nice place in town. They food is good and they even play some music. I've been there before."

"Okay, let's roll," Nick clapped his hands and got up to take a shower.

On the way to town Ole-Einar recommended to book a table, since the place used to be crowded once the music started to play. Nick, who was fascinated by listening to Olaf talking to his wife in his native Norwegian language on his cell phone, insisted to call the tavern himself to book a table.

"Hm," Nick said, staring at his cell phone after he had just finished the call.

"I either booked a table for four or I just ordered a big round for the entire tavern."

"Neither the one nor the other," Ole-Einar replied laughing. They parked the van a few blocks away and walked into the tavern. The place was indeed crowded. Olaf led the group and talked to a waitress who was obviously not too happy as she looked at the four of them. Olaf pointed Nick out and explained something in Norwegian that Nick didn't understand. He decided to bow to signal that he was sorry for whatever he told her on the phone.

The waitress chuckled and led them to a table for six people instead of four.

"Well, that wasn't too bad," Nick noted, then turned to Olaf, "By the way, what did you call me when you pointed me out?"

"Nothing that I wouldn't have called you in German or English already," he replied in a serious tone and sat down.

"Well, all right then," Nike answered before he sat.

Looking over the menu Nick noticed that the door of the tavern opened once more.

Natascha and Bernd entered the place, both looking around for a free table. Tables that were all occupied. Natascha was disappointed and scanned the tavern. The waitress joined them and Nick could see that she shook her head, pointing to the tables hopelessly. Natascha's initial disappointment soon wore off once she spotted Nick at the far corner waving to her.

Trimix: A special mix of breathing gas for deeper dives. A certain percentage of the nitrogen in the breathing gas mix is replaced with helium to reduce the effects of nitrogen narcosis and to increase the dive time.

Natascha smiled at the offer to join their table, and she could sense that it wasn't just because she was hungry. She waved back.

"Okay guys, move up, give her some space," ordered Nick once he saw that Natascha and Bernd were heading their way.

"You got to be kidding me. You do notice that she's accompanied by her boyfriend?" asked Ole-Einar seriously.

"Relax, Nick killed for less," replied Rolf calmly.

"Why don't you sit with us? Our table is for six anyway. If we get a little bit closer it should be fine," Nick offered once Natascha and Bernd were at the table.

While Natascha and Bernd were grateful for the offer, Rolf leaned towards Olaf.

"And you're absolutely certain that Nick doesn't speak Norwegian? This looks like he planned it," he whispered to his friend.

"Rolf, I can guarantee you that Nick doesn't know Norwegian at all," Olaf replied in a calm voice without taking his eyes from the menu.

"Where are Erika and Andreas?" Rolf asked as soon as Natascha sat beside Nick.

"They're back at the Cottage. They need some privacy tonight," Bernd replied while he studied the menu himself.

"Yes, was about time. They were getting quite difficult to get along with the last couple days," Natascha added, handing the menu back to the waitress and ordered a large salad with a glass of wine.

Nick changed the subject.

"Holger mentioned that you're going on an expedition and that you're testing the gear for that?"

"Yes. I just finished university to become a Marine Biologist and my plan is to take part in an international expedition in the arctic sea this summer," Natascha explained happily.

"The arctic sea? Isn't that a little cold? Why not the Caribbean?" Nick asked.

"Oh, is our little Princess getting cold under water? There is no cold water. It's just a matter of proper underwear," Natascha replied with a tempting smile.

Nick wasn't sure if he should be angry that Natascha called him a little Princess or the fact that his three buddies would call him a Princess from now on. At least he was so shocked that he could not answer immediately.

"Well," Rolf answered slowly, "it's true. Our little Princess does get cold once in a while."

All six of them started laughing but Nick took his knife and pointed it at Rolf.

"Seriously, why in the arctic sea?"

"Well, first of all, I'm very interested in the arctic sea, secondly I can participate for free and finally, it will fit nicely in my résumé."

"What about Erika and Andreas? Are they coming along?"

"No, they're not. I'm the only one from our group here. We all studied and worked on different projects together, but I'm the only one out of the four of us who's going on that expedition."

Bernd exhaled more sharply than he expected and Natascha glanced at him angrily.

"But enough about me. What about you? What are you doing up here?"

"Well, we're on our annual dive trip," Ole-Einar explained while the waitress brought their meals.

"Sort of a tradition. Last year we've been in England and the year before we dove in Italy. This year we decided to come up here. I still have a house just fifty kilometers from here. Olaf also lives nearby."

"How did you happen to know each other?" Natascha asked.

"We all work for the same company," Rolf replied.

"Okay," Natascha commented after she tried her salad. "And what does that company do?"

"International Security, nothing special," Olaf explained quickly.

Natascha looked at the four guys, reached for the dressing and started her salad.

After they had finished their meals, Natascha went to the facilities. Nick observed her coming back to the table. The tight, white turtleneck with stitched, black snowflakes matched her long and naturally curled black hair perfectly.

"Everything okay?" Natascha asked Nick, noticing he was still staring at her after she sat down again.

"Yes, everything's fine. Sorry," he apologized to her, gazing in her dark brown eyes. "Did you fix your dry-suit? I think we have another valve in our tool kit, if you need one."

"Don't worry, it's already fixed," Natascha replied sipping her wine.

"Worse case scenario, I'll put two pounds of cat litter in my dry-suit," she added seriously, while the others cracked up with laughter.

More than an hour later they finally decided that, if they were planning to dive the next morning, it would be the best to call it a night. Nick raised his hand to signal the waitress, but Olaf cut him off.

"It's okay, Princess. With your language skills you might as well make a down payment to this place. Let me handle it."

This time it was Natascha who choked on her wine.

After they paid for a delicious meal, they stepped outside the tavern into a beautiful warm spring evening. Walking down the street to their Volkswagen van Nick was catching up to Natascha, who was walking the same direction.

"Do you think Erika and Andreas are finished?"

"They better be, but it wouldn't be the first time we'd stay up late because of them. We'll see you tomorrow. Have a good night," she waved at him once she reached the passenger side of the Mercedes Sprinter.

"Yeah, you too," Nick replied before he caught up with his buddies, who already had the engine running.

"All right," Nick said as soon as they were off the parking lot.

"Let's brainstorm! What are your thoughts?" he asked his friends.

"I think your Norwegian sucks. You can't tell me you ordered that on purpose."

Rolf laughed so hard that he almost ditched the Volkswagen, but he had to admit that it was the first time he ever saw Nick ordering a salad as a starter and a main course.

"That's not what I'm talking about, I meant her. So, what do you think?" he replied unimpressed by Olaf's insult.

"All right, let's see. Definitely not older than twenty-six. I would guess she is twenty-four or twenty-five. No engagement ring, no wedding ring. She didn't look as if she was wearing one recently either," Olaf explained, then continued with more thought. "Her clothes were expensive. My wife has the same shoes, so I know. Besides that, Bernd was wearing an engagement ring. I noticed that she observed you in her peripherals, Nick," Olaf added and looked at his friend.

"In those pants she's definitely a nine," Ole-Einar recapitulated.

"Okay, so she's officially hot. What about Bernd?"

"I don't think he's her boyfriend. Didn't you notice how she looked at him after the way he reacted because of her participation on that expedition? She didn't seem to be too disappointed that he's not coming with her. And they each paid their own tab."

"Even if he is her boyfriend, all we got to do is to manipulate his rebreather. Do you want us to do it tonight?" Ole-Einar asked Nick as if he would be serious about it.

"Let's wait and see how things turn out. But we can keep that as an option," Nick replied in the same way.

"At least we know where they stay," Rolf interrupted them, "They're still behind us and we're already inside the Resort."

"The other three Cottages are not occupied, one is under renovation, so they must stay right beside our place."

Nick smiled as soon as he noticed that the Mercedes Sprinter came to a halt beside them.

"Which window belongs to Erika and Andreas?" Rolf asked Natascha playfully.

"The one with the closed curtains," she laughed back.

"And just for your information, I usually take my shower around seven."

"Do you mind lending me your camera?" Rolf continued.

"Sorry, have to pass on that one. It belongs to the Institute. I'm not allowed to hand it to someone else," Natascha laughed back and walked to her cottage.

- 2 -

Montana, USA, Monday, May 16th
The huge private hunting lodge was built on a beautiful piece of land. The extravagant furniture reflected the luxurious life-style of its owner, who was sitting with his two guests in the large living room. After a great dinner and a few glasses of good wine they retreated in front of the open fireplace to enjoy a glass of Cognac.

Although it wasn't cold in the lavish log-home, the fire created a degree of comfort.

The British poured another shot of the over one-hundred-year-old Cognac into his glass and looked at it swaying around, before he sat down again in one of the big leather chairs. He never normally met with his American or his Canadian business partner, but the last couple weeks showed some development that made such personal meetings inevitable.

He glanced over the living room, looking at all the trophies mounted on the wall before he looked at his Cognac again.

"How big are the chances that this expedition is going to find our gear?" he asked looking at his two partners who sat opposite of him.

"If they're as good as everybody says, then I'd guess there's a ten percent chance they'll find it," answered the American on his left. He examined the expensive cigar in his hand. A depressive atmosphere soon enveloped the room as they realized their multi-million dollar investment was at risk. Not only would their accounts suffer, but the legal and political consequences would most likely destroy their lives.

"Which expedition team is most likely to find it?" the British continued, looking at his Canadian business partner this time.

"If all my information is correct and in accordance to the permits granted, I'm pretty sure that it'd be the expedition leader himself, Dr. Richard Weber and his team of German scientists. They're the only team conducting underwater surveys in that region and depth," the Canadian replied. He took an envelope out of his jacket, which contained a picture. Without looking at it further, he gave the picture to his British friend. Looking at it, the British saw Dr. Weber just outside his car in front of his house in Germany, looking at the camera that he didn't know was there. In the background the British could see a second person sitting in the passenger seat of the car.

"Permits? Why can't you revoke those permits? Who decided that anyway?" the British asked angrily.

"Canada has always participated in the International Polar Year. I had no control over the people issuing those permits. My hands were tied."

"We can't do anything about the permits now," the American replied. He stood up, walked to the window and looked outside.

"We would only draw some unnecessary attention to us if we try to do something about it. Besides that, how would we explain it? All we can do now is hope they won't find anything. We'll find a way that our area of interest will not be declared a protected area."

"That's right," the Canadian noted.

"Remember that the main part of that area is unreachable for the expedition with their current equipment. They can theoretically survey only a small part of it. Right now, I wouldn't worry too much about it."

"But I do worry about it, Damnnit! It cost my company millions to get where we are right now. We had great difficulties covering up our financial tracks."

"Don't worry, your money is safe," the American tried to calm him.

"What if they find it? The first thing they'll do is go public with it. What then?"

"It depends. Sure, there would be an inquiry and a scandal first, but the project would certainly continue once the dust has settled. Beside that, everybody will profit from this project, even the prosecutors, which in this case would be the government. The whole area is within our territorial waters anyway."

The British still wasn't convinced at all. He got up and walked to the fireplace.

"What if we give that expedition leader a warning? Or should we even consider removing him? How fast could they replace his position for that expedition?" the British asked, staring at the flames.

The American exchanged a quick look with his Canadian friend.

"We thought about that. We'll use the help of a group who've been of great service to us before."

The British nodded slightly.

"What about the Natives up there? From my point of view, we cannot continue as we originally planned, or am I wrong there?"

"We don't have to. This very expedition will solve the problem with the Natives for us."

"How's that?"

"Everything is taking care of. I will personally be there to assure the success of our operation," the American replied, sipping at his Cognac.

Kristiansand, Southern Norway, Monday, May 16th
The two groups had spent the last two days diving the wreck of the Seattle. While Natascha and her group were still testing several configurations of their gear, Nick and his friends simply dove the wreck to enjoy the sight of it. Being comfortable with the layout of the wreck and appreciating the information from Holger and Natascha, they also switched to trimix as a breathing gas and explored the deeper parts of the wreck.

They were still giving Natascha and her crew the advantage of entering the water first. Everybody on board could see that Natascha and Nick grew closer every passing day.

Since both groups planned to leave on the same day, they spent the better part of the last day cleaning their gear and loading the vans. For the evening they had planned a barbeque, since Olaf and Ole-Einar would drive back to their families not far from Kristiansand the next morning. Nick and Rolf planned to start their trip back to Germany in the other Volkswagen late in the next day. By driving through the night, they hoped to avoid any traffic jams around Germany's northern cities.

Erika, Andreas and Bernd decided to leave early the next morning to get the first ferry ride. Natascha on the other hand planned to fly back to Frankfurt in the early afternoon, since she had an important appointment in connection with the expedition in Frankfurt later that day.

Since all her gear was already stowed inside the Mercedes Sprinter she would only travel with one small backpack. Rolf offered to drop her off at the airport.

With all their plans settled, they came together around the campfire later on their last night and enjoyed the evening.

Most of the time they chatted about the last couple days and all the dives they did at the *Seattle*, mixed with some stories of their own mishaps in their diving career. Stories were told about unsuccessful attempts to descend without a weight belt, fins that they forgot on the boat, open zippers on their dry-suits as well as closed tanks. They recalled moments of having jumped off the dive boat while the gear was still attached to a bungee rope, which left the diver hanging midair above the water. They all agreed that they were still happy to be alive. Natascha finished the round with a story of her first encounter with a male sea-leopard, before she tucked her hands in her jacket pocket, watching the flames reach towards the sky.

"By the way, Natascha, would you mind sending us a copy of the video you shot here? You can just send us an unedited DVD," Rolf asked.

"Sure, but it will cost you," she demanded, looking at Rolf.

"Well, I'll gladly give you the five bucks for the DVD and the shipping right now."

"That's not what I meant. I wasn't talking about the money."

"No? What then?" Rolf asked, shrugging his shoulders.

"I'm suggesting that the Princess here could take me out for dinner," Natascha explained and clapped her hands on Nicks leg beside her.

"Deal! Hey, Princess, you'll take that fine lady out for dinner tomorrow," Rolf stated matter-of-factly.

"Okay, I'll take another hit for the team," Nick groaned and looked Natascha in the eyes, smiling happily.

"Well, actually you should have to take Bernd out for dinner. He did most of the video. If you prefer him, that's fine with me," she provoked him further, returning his smile.

"Never mind, I'll manage," Nick smiled, still looking in her eyes.

"I don't want to interrupt you, Princess, but I'm afraid you might not be that lucky after all. Most of the restaurants won't be open until four, and we have to be on the road by then," Ole-Einar interrupted.

"Well, I hope you can cook then," Natascha replied quickly and wriggling her eye-brows, still staring at Nick.

"No problem. We will have the leftovers in the fridge. My specialty," Nick tried to schmooze her.

"What about me? I'm not sure if we have enough for three," Rolf stated seriously.

"You won't be joining us," Natascha and Nick replied simultaneously.

"Oh great, now I'm the one taking a hit for the team. I not only don't have that DVD, no, I won't even get anything to eat any more," Rolf complained, while everybody else laughed.

Natascha was shaking with laughter that she held Nick's hand to prevent falling backwards with the chair. Nick enjoyed the next minutes, but it wasn't because everyone was silent, it was due to the fact that Natascha's warm hand still held his and that he would have a few moments alone with her the next day.

They enjoyed holding hands and every moment they looked deep into each other's eyes, Natascha's smile would turn up in a girlish grin.

Montana, USA, Monday, May 16th

The three men were still in the living room when the housekeeper knocked on the door and entered as the American granted her approval.

"Senor, excuse me, please. Your three o'clock appointment has arrived."

The American stepped away from the window and walked a few steps to the door.

"Ask him to come in, please."

The housekeeper bowed slightly and a few seconds later their guest entered the living room. He was a tall man of approximately 1,90 meters, much younger than the three men in the room, approximately in his late thirties, had his hair cut short in a military style and was wearing a tailored suit that covered a well trained body.

After the housekeeper had closed the door again, the American took the picture of the German Professor and walked over to his guest. He glanced at his eyes and laid the picture on the table in front of them.

"Mr. Hogan," the American greeted as he shook his visitor's hand.

"Can you take care of this person for us?" the American asked, pointing with his finger directly on the picture.

Mr. Hogan glanced at the other two men first, before he took another step towards the table and looked at the picture.

"Certainly. Does it have to look like an accident or do you want to send a message?" Mr. Hogan replied in a cold voice.

The Canadian briefly shrugged about the cold-bloodedness in the voice of this man.

"We will render a warning first. If it is going to be ignored, it will be your turn. It would be very helpful if this person would become the victim of a tragic accident within the next fourteen days of your notification. It should not look like an execution, but the message should be clear."

"Like I said, I don't see any problems. The contact information?"

The American pulled an envelope out of his jacket and gave it to Mr. Hogan.

Mr. Hogan looked at each of the three men first, before he opened it. He read the page with the necessary information without a comment and nodded slightly before looking up again to the men who hired him.

"Who else knows about this?"

"Nobody but the four of us."

"Keep it that way," the visitor demanded and walked to the open fire place in which he threw the contact information.

"Usual payment, gentlemen. Fifty percent now, the other fifty percent after we complete the mission. In the case that we're compromised it will be our decision if we do or do not finish the contract, but we'd still keep the initial payment. Other than that, we want to get paid in Euro this time, not Dollar."

"Don't worry about the money. We will transfer the complete million as soon as you're in Europe. The account number and bank are still the same?"

"Yes," Mr. Hogan replied and turned towards the door, ready to leave.

"Gentlemen, it's a pleasure working with you," he said before he finally left the living room.

The American closed the door behind him and poured another Cognac for his friends and himself. He smiled as he noticed the skeptic look from his British friend.

"Don't worry. Everything is under control. We worked with him before. Mr. Hogan is a very reliable man."

"Well," the British sighed and emptied his glass before he got up, "it's time for me to go now, too. Got to return to London."

His friends reassured him once more that everything was okay as they shook his hand.

The British left the living room, walked through the foyer and finally stepped outside the hunting lodge. He took some deep breaths and walked to his rental car. After he started the car he fastened his seat belt and drove slowly down the driveway until he came to the main gate. The gate opened automatically as he slowly approached it and he successfully turned onto the main street.

Driving down the street toward the airport he couldn't help but think about the future. It was not the huge investment his company had already made that concerned him. He knew perfectly well that not too much could happen to him, even in the case of a public inquiry. Bottom line: the general profits for all parties involved would be way too big, so any government in the world would bend some rules. Well, the Natives would be a problem, but he trusted his American friend that they would take care of them.

His convincing didn't last long as another concern hit him. There was more in this deal for him than the other two could even imagine. And his advantage was that he was the only living person who knew about it. The only other person with that information fell victim to a tragic accident not long ago. The British smiled at the thought.

"I can only hope those two idiots don't blow it," he muttered to himself while thinking about his American and Canadian partner.

He decided to keep playing his role as the worried British and planned to keep his partners in the dark.

Thin Ice

Kristiansand, Southern Norway, Tuesday, May 17th
The next morning Ole-Einar and Olaf stowed their last items into their Volkswagen before they entered the kitchen again, where Nick was examining the contents of the fridge.

"Hey Princess, what's for dinner today?"

"I'm going to kill you if you call me Princess one more time. Why do I have to be accompanied by three idiots, when I meet a great woman?" Nick replied.

"It's funny she's allowed to call you Princess."

"I'm sure she's allowed to do much more than that," Olaf continued.

"Seriously, what are your plans for dinner? There can't be much left."

With a sad expression on his face, Nick held up the last bag of noodles, a little box with two tomatoes and some chocolate mousse.

Shaking his head, Olaf walked by and patted him on the shoulders.

"That chocolate mousse better be very fluffy if you want to lay her with that," the Norwegian commented.

"I'm afraid I'll never get that DVD," Rolf added with disappointment, lying back on the couch and reading his book again.

"I'll impress her with my charm," Nick stated confidently, looking at his buddy.

"You better try the chocolate mousse," Ole-Einar added and followed Olaf outside the cottage.

Nick followed them to wish them a good trip, when Natascha stepped out of her cottage with a garbage bag in hand.

"Hey, Natascha," Ole-Einar shouted. "No need to get fancy with all the make-up. The food doesn't look too promising, but he's really trying hard."

"Too bad," she replied laughing, "that means I don't have to worry about my hair then as well. Have a safe trip. Would be nice seeing you again."

"Oh yeah, would it ever," Olaf whispered under his breath so that she couldn't hear and entered the Volkswagen van.

"All right, see you in London next week. Let's hope that not too much has happened while we were gone," Nick said.

"Yes. I'm really curious if that lady from Mossad* is really going to work with us like they said."

Just five minutes later Nick was back in the kitchen. He was desperately trying to think how he could impress a beautiful woman with just some noodles, two tomatoes and a chocolate mousse'.

Rolf had just finished his book and decided to go for a run to give Nick and Natascha some privacy.

"I think I'll be back around two o'clock," he told his friend.

"Two, really?" Nick moaned, obviously disappointed about the ninety minute timeframe.

Mossad: The supreme institution for intelligence and special assignments as well as the secret intelligence service of the state of Israel

"Give me a break. Do you think I'd run a marathon for the two of you?" Rolf scoffed and stepped outside. He smiled as he saw Natascha coming over.

"I still want that DVD even if you don't like his cooking," he smiled at her and started jogging.

"Don't worry, I'm sure it'll be fine," she laughed and looked after him before she walked into the Cottage.

"Welcome to our little restaurant. May I assist the lady to her table?" Nick asked with a smile.

"You may."

Nick offered her a chair and switched a small LED headlight on that he carefully placed in the middle of the table beside several small spruce twigs.

"Due to some financial cutbacks we had to switch off the light at the end of the tunnel. Instead of a romantic candle I can only offer a LED light."

"I'm impressed," Natascha added with laughter.

"Our special today is old noodles in a tasteless tomato sauce. As an alternative we also have a tasteless tomato sauce that will come with some old noodles. And I would recommend the chocolate mousse for dessert, served with some apple juice," Nick offered and displayed a bottle of apple juice neatly wrapped in a towel as if it was an old bottle of wine.

"Oh my God, I don't have any idea what to choose. I guess I'll take the noodles and a glass of apple juice. For dessert I'll try that famous chocolate mousse," Natascha smiled as she continued their game.

"Very well, my dear."

"Hey, the staff is not allowed to flirt with their costumers."

"Yes, but there's nobody here beside the two of us."

"True enough."

They enjoyed the next ninety minutes chatting and flirting with each other and didn't mind the old noodles at all.

After Natascha had finished her dessert, she emptied her glass of apple juice and looked at Nick.

"Tell me Nick, what do the four of you do for a living? You all seem to be physically fit. Very fit. And this is the first time I ever saw four guys on a man-trip without so much a sip of alcohol."

"Well, you must've been in some bad company before you met us."

"It wasn't that bad. During my time at university, I was only drunk once, which was enough for all the years to come, I might add. And I never did any drugs." Natascha defended herself.

"So you went to all those parties for the boys?"

"Well, let's just say that there was a time, back in my university life, when my father skipped the house arrest and wanted to perform an exorcism with me," Natascha admitted with a shrug of her shoulders as she played with the LED light.

"You were that bad?" Nick asked surprised.

"I'm just kidding, Nick. I was and still am a very decent girl. But you've not answered my question," she smiled at him with a wink.

"Like Ole-Einar told you, we're all working for a company specialized in international security."

"Yes, I know, but that covers a large field of work. Are you valets, bouncers or do you work for the Secret Service," she laughed.

Nick also laughed.

"No, neither. We're more or less consultants for special events and we also provide and develop security plans for other companies and people of special interest."

"So you're talking about Security Systems and even personal protection detail?"

"Sometimes we do that, yes."

"Like in Bodyguard?"

"Well, not exactly like that, but the main idea is the same."

"Does that mean you'd catch a bullet for me?"

"That depends on how large the bullet would be," Nick answered with a smile.

"Oh great, what kind of a bodyguard are you?" Natascha commented laughing, just before Rolf returned from his workout.

"I always thought that size doesn't matter," she asked, now looking at Rolf.

"I also told him that this morning, but he was still nervous. But since you're already on that subject, should I go again?" Rolf asked.

"No," Natascha kept laughing, "it's not what you think. I just wanted to know if he'd catch a bullet for me, but Nick thinks that it depends on the size of it."

"I'd catch a bullet for you," Rolf added without hesitation.

"Seriously?" Natascha asked puzzled.

"Sure, if that means I'd finally get that DVD," Rolf admitted before he closed the bathroom door behind him.

Nick and Natascha both looked at the closed door.

"Well, I better go get ready. I assume that we'll start in about half an hour?"

"Yes, we can drive as soon as Rolf is ready," Nick answered and walked Natascha out.

"I hope you enjoyed your dinner," he smiled on the doorstep.

"Could get used to it," Natascha replied as she hugged him and kissed his cheek.

"Me too," Nick whispered as she entered her cottage.

Twenty minutes later the three of them were in the Volkswagen van driving through Kristiansand, where they looked for signs to guide them to the airport.

"What kind of event is it that you have to go to tonight, anyway?" Rolf asked and glanced at the mirror. He noticed that both Nick and Natascha had been unusually quiet during the last few minutes. It was obvious to Rolf that they both would have loved to spend more time with each other.

"Nothing special. They introduce the German expedition team in Frankfurt this evening. It's just a press conference for one of the major sponsors of the expedition, an international science magazine," she explained but kept looking outside the window, trying to hide her face from Rolf.

After another thirty minutes, Rolf stopped the Volkswagen in front of the airport.

"Okay, here we are," he said and looked at the building.

"Thanks for the ride," Natascha replied and clapped Rolf on his shoulder before she climbed out of the van.

"I'll come inside just to make sure that everything's okay with your flight so you won't be stranded here when we leave," Nick said and looked at Natascha.

Rolf rolled his eyes, while Natascha whispered a thank you to Nick.

"Won't take long," Nick reassured Rolf and closed his door before he walked to the other side of the van.

"Take care, Rolf," Natascha said. "I hope you never have to catch a bullet for me," she added laughing.

"Yes, me too, and good luck with your expedition."

Nick accompanied Natascha to the departure lounge where they checked the information boards for her flight.

"Looks like the flight's on time," she said swallowing harshly.

She tried to avoid eye contact as she looked at the check-in.

"Nobody there either," she said with a broken voice.

Nick nodded and put his hands on her shoulder.

"I would've loved to spend more time with you," he whispered.

"I know, me too."

"Can we meet again before you start your expedition?"

Natascha looked at the check-in again. Her next four weeks were full of appointments.

"Okay, listen, I'll be in Italy for four days in the middle of June to test a new camera. If you're serious about us, I'd like to pay you back for dinner."

"With dessert?" Nick smiled.

Natascha could feel the lump rise in her throat, but her eyes told him everything he wanted to know.

"Okay, let's do this," Nick whispered and wrapped his arms around her. They stood in silence, Nick's arms like bars around her. He didn't want to let her go.

"I hope to see you soon," Natascha choked and kissed him good-bye before she swiftly turned around and walked towards the check-in. She didn't look back.

Nick's eyes followed her and he noticed that she was wiping her eyes.

Damnnit, he thought, *why do I have to fall in love now?*

Once she was behind the check-in, Nick waved to her one last time then turned around and walked back outside, where Rolf waited for him.

- 3 -

**Home Office and Operational Headquarters of *EuroSecCorporation*,
London, Monday, June 6th**
Nick was sitting between Olaf and Ole-Einar at one of the many tables which were arranged in a large u-shape formation in their main conference room. Two seats beside him sat Rolf, who was talking to Oliver Schneider, Rolf's long-time buddy from his time at the German Kampfschwimmer. On their left, the seats were occupied by the members from Team B, which included the former British SAS members Jack Connery and Scott O'Melly as well as Peter Clarke and John Davies. Both Peter and John had served with the Special Boat Service of the Royal Marines Commando before. Two Russian frogmen, Ivan Pavlicic and Yuri Scharapov, completed their team. Beside them sat the members of Team C, with Markus Brenger and Wolfgang Buhlmann, who were both from the German GSG9, like Nick. The other members were the two German Kampfschwimmer Dieter Beier and Manfred Kleinschmitt. Two more former British SAS members, Tom Hart and Rick Andrews, completed their team.

Once a month they had a meeting where all the team members and the members of their operation control had to attend. Various ranks were present in the conference room and all the individual team members were in active duty. Among these active members, Manfred Kleinschmitt was the youngest with just twenty-five years while Jack Connery was their veteran with thirty-four years of age. Nick, like Rolf and Ole-Einar, was twenty-nine years old.

EuroSecCorporation operated exclusively in the private sector and among their clients were also big oil companies located in the Northern Sea and the African Coast. They were in constant alert of terrorist attacks and frequently requested their service. Besides that, *EuroSecCorporation* also provided the security detail for some celebrities as well as specific media-saturated festivities.

While Nick was telling Olaf that he arranged his trip to Italy the next week for a couple days, the members of operation control came into the conference room. They walked with purpose and sat down at the head of the table formation.

The board of directors contained only two people: retired General Klaus Schwartze and retired Admiral Brian Whittaker, who were both in their late fifties.

The remaining members of the operation control were made of six highly qualified and experienced former members of different Special Units and Task Forces.

On the far left side of the table sat Tatjana Volmatovja from Russia and beside her was, with thirty-five years of age, the youngest member of the operation control, Ariel Rashid. He's a former close-combat instructor for the Israeli Special Forces. Nick and the rest of the team were certain he was also working for the Mossad, the legendary Israeli Secret Service. He literally had unlimited access to some very valuable information and no team member dared to ask him about his past. On Ariel's other side sat Sigrid Schneider, formerly from the Bundeskriminalamt in Germany. There were some rumors that she also had close contact to the BND, the German Secret Service, but being a secret service, nobody knew exactly.

The next two chairs were still unoccupied and belonged to retired General Klaus Schwartze as well as retired Admiral Brian Whittaker. The seating order continued with Sean MacLeod, who formerly worked for Scotland Yard. He looked like he would fit better in a Country Club than Special Unit Headquarters.

Next to him sat Jack MacDonald, who used to work as an Instructor for the British SAS. Sitting beside him was Gunnar Eriksson. Not only was he originally from Norway like Olaf and Ole-Einar, he was also their Instructor when they were members of the Mine Diver Command of the Norwegian Navy Special Operations Commando.

Just as Rolf was about to call Nick a Princess again to get his attention, retired General Klaus Schwartze and Brian Whittaker walked into the room and to their chairs. Retired General Klaus Schwartze was standing 1,95 m tall and he exuded an aura of authority that not anyone in this room would question his judgments. His blue eyes were in constant motion and he barely missed a detail. With his great experience came an analytical mind that allowed him, within seconds, to readjust a new crisis and explain his new plan of action.

On the other side, retired Admiral Brian Whittaker was an optical contradiction. Standing only 1,72m he was already shorter than everyone else in the room, including their new guest. However, the retired Admiral's tactical mind and his experience made him the perfect counterpart for retired General Klaus Schwartze to lead this corporation.

Retired Admiral Brian Whittaker still maintained his military crew cut, his gray hair complimenting his weathered face. The contours of his face seemed like it was etched out of concrete making it nearly impossible to read any emotions in his face.

As soon as they had set a foot in the room, all conversation stopped and all eyes rested on the individual who accompanied the two former military officers.

Nick eyed their visitor. He saw a very attractive black haired woman from obvious Middle Eastern heritage. He estimated her age somewhere between 25 and 28 years old and he could not help notice her eyes constantly scanning the room, not missing a single detail. Nick was certain she was reading each pair of eyes that followed her to her seat. Although she was only one of three women in this room, she neither seemed nervous nor uncomfortable.

Klaus Schwartze and Brian Whittaker sat down simultaneously. Brian immediately put his glasses on as he opened a binder. Klaus Schwartze looked at each of his men individually before he looked at some documents that Brian handed to him.

"Good day everyone," he greeted his unit and glanced at his notes again. "So far there's not much happening. British Petroleum asked us for an update on their emergency plans for a hostage situation on one of their oil-rigs in the Northern Sea," he stated and handed the papers over to Gunnar Eriksson.

"Gunnar, I'll trust you with that. They want the usual analysis. How easy it would

Thin Ice

be to get on the rig, how many men the terrorists would need, and most important, how to get it back without polluting all of Northern Europe."

Gunnar took the papers and nodded in agreement while Klaus Schwartze was already looking at the next file that Brian handed him.

"Okay, who's a fan of Manchester United?" he asked after he went over the information.

Peter Clarke of Team B raised his arm so fast that Klaus was afraid he would have dislocated his shoulder.

"Wonderful," Klaus commented and handed the file to Sean MacLeod.

"Sean, this one is for you and Team B. Security detail for the cousin of the Prince of Saudi-Arabia, who's coming for a concert in a few weeks. The Prince has arranged for a tour of the soccer stadium before the event. British Petroleum has recommended us for this."

"I thought we'd watch a good soccer game and look after a VIP, like Shakira or someone else hot," Peter commented and it was obvious that he was very frustrated.

"I never said that," Klaus replied with laughter.

"I only wanted to know who's a fan of Manchester United. By the way, the person you're responsible for is twelve years old and traveling with a fourteen person staff."

Knowing this would be a tedious assignment, the other members of Team B started throwing pencils and paper balls at their colleague.

"Still watching British soccer after the last world cup? Or are you already looking forward to the next qualifier round?" Rolf asked him sardonically over the table.

"Yeah, just in case you forgot. England didn't advance at the last World Cup. What was the score again? Ah right, four to one. Sorry, things like that can happen, but you better get used to it," Rolf added and smiled at Peter, who looked as if he would lunge over the table at any moment.

"Permission to shoot him," Peter snarled back not taking his eyes of Rolf and his German friends.

"Granted!" Sean MacLeod and Jack MacDonald permitted simultaneously. Judging by the fierce look in their eyes, Rolf was certain that they would even supply Peter the bullets.

"Stop it," Klaus interrupted them, before he added that the result of the game did not leave any room for discussions.

"London! Sigrid, that's for you and Team C. After the wedding, the royal family's planning an event with some selected celebrities and lots of press. They're going to have a concert as well. Because of the expected public interest and the large crowds of paparazzi they asked for our input. The evening before the concert, the royal family will host a dinner for the musicians and some VIP's. Enjoy the meal," Klaus explained and handed the file over to Sigrid.

"I assume we'll be involved in some of the festivities. You have my total confidence in this," Brian Whittaker added.

"Okay, Team A!" Brian continued loud.

"Let's see what we got for you. My brother-in-law, Gordon Ramshaw, just got himself a new mansion. He asked us for a security update on his alarm system."

Brian Whittaker's brother-in-law was a leading member of the board of directors of a British oil company and it was not uncommon that he recommended *EuroSecCorporation* to his friends or business partner. Since he has also helped financially to found *EuroSecCorporation*, they normally took great care of his requests.

"Jack and Ariel, I would appreciate it if you'd handle this," Brian said and handed Jack MacDonald the papers.

"As you can all see, we have a guest here today," Brian continued as he rose from his chair and walked beside the woman. She briefly nodded her acknowledgement, still studying the faces of the people in front of her.

"As you all know, not too long ago, we decided to include more female personel for active duty. Therefore, I'm very happy to welcome Shira Hadad to our company. Ariel and Shira know each other from their time in Israel and Shira has been sent to us with highest regards from Tel Aviv. Since Team A has only five members at the moment, Shira will be assigned to them as a member in active status. I expect a cooperative and courteous response. Should I hear one single complaint or unqualified comment, then that certain person will have to directly answer to me."

Just as Brian had finished, Ariel rose from his seat and looked at everyone in the room.

"Since Shira is dear to my heart, I don't believe that it'll be necessary to answer to Mr. Whittaker, since I will personally kill every single person who insults her," the former Israeli close-combat instructor stated in a cold voice.

"Well, that's fine with me," added Klaus Schwartze and looked at Brian who also nodded in agreement.

If there were any sounds occurring in the room, they all ceased and the room fell silent. All humour aside, everyone knew Ariel was resolute with his words.

Since the official business was concluded, Brian and Klaus stood up and left the room, followed by most members of operation control. Ariel spoke to Shira and brought her to Rolf and Nick. Both were still sitting with Olaf, Ole-Einar and Oliver at one table, since their team leader Jack MacDonald wished to speak with them.

"Shalom," Shira said and looked at each of them.

They all greeted her back very politely.

"If I hear the slightest comment, remark or joke about Shira, then that certain person won't even realize how he died," Ariel reminded them seriously before he turned and walked away, refusing them the chance to respond to his warning.

Silence followed Ariel, the five pairs of eyes trailing after him. It was only after they were certain he was out of hearing distance that they turned towards Shira. One thing was certain: nobody in his right mind would make an unqualified comment about a person Ariel cares about.

"Okay, I guess it's now safe to assume we can introduce ourselves without a knife ending up in our throat," Nick started, looking back again to the door Ariel just walked through seconds ago.

"Please me," Shira replied.

"It's *please do*, not *please me*," Rolf corrected with raised eyebrows, before he introduced himself.

Great Conference Room, Hilton Hotel, Berlin, Thursday, June 9th
The conference room offered a great deal of comfort to its occupiers. All the tables were arranged in a way that they formed a large square. Around the tables were enough comfortable chairs for forty people, who could choose from a great selection of refreshments.

Natascha sat right to Dr. Weber and almost thirty other people at the table. Most of them were scientists from different countries and would participate in the upcoming expedition. Some of them were also from the institute that Dr. Weber and Natascha currently worked for. They were therefore in charge of the logistics and finances.

Dr. Weber was reading his thick binder. He knew that this expedition would be by far the largest and most expensive expedition he ever organized, and it would cost much more than they originally estimated. Generally that was no problem. Most expeditions faced higher costs than initially planned, but he still had to explain every single Euro they spent. On top of that, several other institutions from different countries also took part, and it was his responsibility to coordinate their individual programs so all their work was as efficient as possible. The nature of this expedition also created a great political interest. Even though the start of the expedition was still weeks ahead, he had already felt the pressure from some politicians.

Having mastered all those challenges, he was now looking at the latest reports about their research submersibles, and he asked his Russian colleague Dr. Igor Gremchenko if the two Norwegian submersibles were now ready.

"We had some extensive tests in Iceland with them. They are both there at this moment. All tests were satisfying, as well as the emergency procedures. The supplier guaranteed us that all the spare parts would be there in time, and that they can be loaded on the research vessel together with the submersibles."

"Thank you, Igor," Dr. Weber replied and checked that part on his long list.

Sitting beside him, Natascha hardly realized she was drifting from the conversation as she stared at her Blackberry. Natascha and Nick haven't met since Norway, but they called each other on a daily basis. Natascha thought for the moment, unsure what to do. On the one side, she would love to see Nick again, but on the other, she knew perfectly well that she was going on a 14 week expedition soon. That was the one thing she could not ignore, and it was something that would put strains on any relationship.

It's the worst time to fall in love, she thought, reading Nick's message from this morning. He had written that they were working on a huge private mansion outside London, and that their new team member still had difficulties with the language barrier, and thus used very funny phrases.

Natascha paused at another thought. He promised to meet her in Italy where she had to do some final test dives. If he was willing to drive 14 hours to see her, she would have to take the risk and see where it would go from there. This thought offered some comfort, but she still felt unsettled.

"Did you get the new camera housing yet, Natascha?" Dr. Weber asked, looking at this checklist.

"Natascha, did you get the new camera housing?" he repeated, after he had not received an answer the first time. Natascha's reaction was still the same.

She stared at her Blackberry, completely absorbed in the messages he sent. She flicked through her inbox again, making sure she had not accidentally overseen a message from Nick.

Dr. Weber glanced at Natascha and noticed her complete mental absence.

Shaking his head he picked up his own Blackberry, typed the question and sent it to her.

The sound of the new incoming message startled her and she immediately opened it, hoping it was from Nick.

"No, I didn't get it yet," she responded quickly, disappointed the message wasn't from Nick.

"Anything else that needs testing?"

"No, just the housing. The camera arrived last week. The housing should arrive tomorrow."

"Still going to Italy next week?"

"Yes, still planning to go."

"Who's going with you?" Dr. Weber asked, still looking at this checklist.

"I'll be by myself," she replied and sat up straight again.

"And who are you diving with?" he asked, finally looking at the young German. He removed his glasses.

"I'll meet a friend down there. No problem," she assured him, before she returned her attention to her Blackberry.

Dr. Weber looked at her for a few more seconds, his curiosity rising. His attention darted to Dr. Sylvia Gunnardottir from Iceland as her team entered the conference room behind her, completing the group.

As expedition leader, Dr. Weber shook their hands and officially started the conference by asking everybody to silence their cell phones. Natascha reluctantly stowed her Blackberry away and turned her concentration towards the conference.

Estate of Gordon Ramshaw, outside London, Thursday, June 9th
Shira sat at a table in the old mansion with Rolf and together they were examining the blue prints of the building.

"Hey, Nick, what about you? I'm hungry," Rolf shouted at Nick, stretching in his chair.

Nick stood a few meters from the table and had his back turned towards them. His cell phone vibrated and excitement flicked across his eyes. The message grasped his attention and he innocently turned a deaf ear to Rolf.

"Our Princess got mail," Rolf whispered to Ole-Einar with an impish grin.

Without Nick noticing it, Shira got up and stood behind him. She glided to the tip

Thin Ice

of her toes and peeked over his shoulder to read the message. Her eyes lit up as she read: D -126 as well as the GPS coordinates 42 21 58 32 & 10 52 56 93.

"The mystery woman, yes?" she whispered in Nick's ear.

"Jesus, Shira. Are you trying to kill me? Don't ever sneak up on me like that again," he shrieked and almost dropped his cell phone as everybody burst with laughter.

"If I was an assassin, I could have killed you right here and now," she explained calmly and slowly walked back to her teammates.

"Yes, but you're not an assassin," Nick replied and came to the table.

"Well, if you think so," she said and shrugged her shoulders.

"So, what kind of message was that anyway? D minues one-hundred-twenty-six and some GPS coordinates?"

Shira eyed Nick as everyone else did.

"Well, that's none of your business," Nick smiled at her and turned to his laptop on the table.

"Okay, let's have another look at the aerial shots from this place," Ole-Einar said, putting their focus back to their work.

The all regrouped around Nick as he booted up the program.

"Okay, here we are," he noted and zoomed in over the area so they would have a better image of their surroundings.

"There they are!" Shira shouted suddenly, pointing her finger on the *Go To* list of the program. "The same coordinates that have been on your cell phone. Here they are."

Nick closed his eyes with resignation as everyone's interest in the coordinates rose.

"You're sure?" Olaf asked Shira.

"Absolutely polarized," Shira responded triumphantly as everyone else looked at her.

"She meant *absolutely positive*," Ariel corrected, who had also sneaked up close behind Nick.

The German shrieked again.

"The two of you should not sneak up like that!" Nick protested heatedly jumping to his feet.

"Sit down and shut up, Princess," Rolf ordered, pushing his shoulders down forcing him back into his seat.

"Where is it anyway? Doesn't look like England," Olaf mentioned, looking at the computer.

"That's somewhere in Italy," Ariel explained, still standing behind Nick.

"The mystery woman," Shira shouted out excitedly.

"You're having a date with her," she continued and wrapped her arms around Nick with a smile. Rolf and Olaf held Nick's arms down on the arm rest of his chair so he couldn't get up or access the laptop.

Still standing close behind Nick, Shira clicked on the coordinates, and they all watched impatiently as the program took them to the new location. It zoomed in and stopped over a marked building on a small Italian island.

"A cozy restaurant, yes? A romantic place for your date, am I right?" Shira whispered into Nick's ear, whose only hope was that this would be over soon. His teammates examined the shown building and its neighborhood.

"Not bad, Princess, not bad at all," Ole-Einar commented after he had zoomed in over the beach just in front of the marked building.

"That's the reason why you needed another vacation already," Shira stated putting her hands on Nick's shoulder, still standing behind him.

"We just have to figure out what D minus one-hundred-twenty-six means."

While his friends proposed their theories about that message, Nick stared at the laptop in complete silence.

"D could mean Date and minus one-hundred-twenty-six could be a code."

"Could also be the name of the restaurant or a room number in a hotel."

Nick shook his head in silence while Rolf and Olaf held him tight.

Shira wrapped her arms around Nick from behind again and took a closer look at the monitor, where she looked at the building at a higher resolution.

"The building is too small for a hotel and there is barely any parking in front of it," she noted.

"Rolf, what was the most romantic moment between Nick and that mystery woman in Norway?" Ariel asked suddenly.

Rolf and Ole-Einar exchanged some looks.

"As far as I remember, they were only together twice, both times during the last day. First when they had dinner together, and the second was at the airport when he walked with her to the check-in," Rolf shared and looked at Nick. "By the way, I still haven't received that DVD yet," he stated.

Ariel paced behind Nick, his curiosity evident as he tried to put the pieces together. Shira took another look at the surroundings of the hotel.

"How much time did they spend together?" Ariel continued his investigation.

"Well, during the dinner I was gone for almost ninety minutes. For the airport I would say they had a maximum of fifteen minutes. They didn't have much time at the airport. Besides that, they were saying good-bye to each other," Rolf answered.

"That leaves us with the dinner," Olaf mentioned, still holding Nick's arm, who had finally stopped resisting after Ole-Einar placed a roll of duct tape on the table.

"What did they have for dinner?" Ariel asked.

"He cooked some noodles and he tried something with two tomatoes, but it didn't work out. I guess his biggest trump was the dessert. Chocolate mousse," Rolf explained and glanced to Ariel as a smile overcame his features.

"That must be it," Ole-Einar said in triumph.

"D means dessert and minus one-hundred-and-twenty-six could be a countdown," he concluded and picked up a calculator.

"He already knew the coordinates, since they were in his laptop already, but he has just received the message with the countdown. In one-hundred-and-twenty-six hours from now it would be... one second... a quarter after nine in the evening. They are meeting at a restaurant," Ole-Einar said happily and pointed on the laptop.

"Close," Shira whispered in Nick's ear.

"Italy is one hour ahead of us and in t minus one-hundred-and-twenty-six hours, it will be already a quarter after ten, too late for a restaurant. There is also not enough parking in front of the building, so I assume that it's a holiday home. We're on duty all Monday and Nick can leave only early Tuesday morning. Given the distance he has to cover, he'll only be in Italy in the late afternoon to catch the early evening ferry that brings him to this mystery woman. So that would put him on the Island at around nine-thirty and with just enough time to be at that location at ten-fifteen, yes?"

Shira straightened her posture and stepped away from Nick.

"I believe Nick is getting his own private dessert at a quarter after ten right in that building, am I right, yes?" Shira asked him from the opposite side of the table.

"You're just jealous," Nick broke his silence.

"He confesses," Shira shouted happily and clapped her hands.

"Who is this mystery woman anyway?" she continued looking at Rolf, who was still holding Nick.

"Well, you can check her name in the Internet. There should be something. Natascha Kleinfeld."

Shira typed her name into the search engine and had no trouble finding her as a participant for the upcoming expedition.

"Not bad at all," she admitted and let go of Nick as their team leader Jack MacDonald entered the room.

"We have some snacks in the kitchen if you want. Where are we at?"

"We now know where Nick and Natascha will meet next week. Would it be okay if we go down there and wire their room?"

"What? No, you're not allowed to go to Italy to wire their room. What the hell are you doing? I can't walk outside the room for ten minutes. Let's get something to eat and then back to work," Jack ordered and guided them to the kitchen.

Nick, who was walking behind the group, looked at Jack.

"We only have two Israeli specialists for interrogations, and I of all people have to work with them," Nick stated, "that's not fair."

"Why didn't you just keep your mouth shut?" Jack asked and walked by into the kitchen.

Great Conference Room, Hilton Hotel, Berlin, Thursday, June 9th
The conference concluded in the early afternoon, but Natascha felt she spent the entire day in this room. This meeting was about logistical issues only, and she didn't understand why she had to be there in the first place, but Dr. Weber had insisted on her presence. She told everybody that all their tests went without any problems, and that she was just waiting for the camera housing, which she planned to test in a few days.

After Dr. Weber officially announced the end of today's meeting, Natascha stretched and yawned. Dr. Weber rose and shook the hands of the two men who worked with him at the institute.

"I have to step outside for a moment," Natascha mentioned to Dr. Weber and left the room.

"Dr. Weber, could we have a word with you, please? In private?"

"Yes, sure, come this way," the expedition leader replied and lead his two colleagues through a door into a much smaller room with refreshments and snacks.

One of the men made sure that nobody else was watching them, while the other took an envelope out of his jacket.

"You received another threat today, Professor," the one man said carefully.

"So what?" Dr. Weber said and took a bite of a piece of chocolate cake.

"We knew months ago that this would happen. The results of this expedition will be the impeccable proof of global warming and its effect. We know that neither the US, nor Canada or Russia are very happy about this expedition. So, who sent the letter this time?" the expedition leader asked unimpressed.

"We don't know, but we did contact the police."

"What are they thinking?"

"Well, this is actually the first threat that they're taking seriously. All the previous ones were from some idiots, but this one is completely different."

The man gave Dr. Weber a picture that he had just taken out of the envelope.

The picture showed Dr. Weber in front of his private house just seconds after he had left his car. In the background he could see his daughter still sitting in the passenger seat. Without noticing it, Dr. Weber had looked right into the camera when the picture was taken.

"I can't remember looking at a camera," he muttered, more to himself than to them. "This is in front of my house, but how can it be? It's at least four hundred meters down to the main road and our driveway comes up in a loop and has trees on both sides. Whoever took this picture had to be on my property. You're sure this is not altered?"

The two men looked at each other.

"Dr. Weber, the police are sure that this picture was taken with a high resolution scope. Whoever took the picture left the electronic signature of the scope on the picture. It's microscopically small, but detectable. The police didn't find a single fingerprint or DNA sample on the letter, the picture, the envelope or the postage stamp. They also estimate this picture was taken from a distance of around eight hundred meters."

They could see that Dr. Weber was concerned now.

"What about my daughter?" he whispered.

"It's a fact that you're the person in the middle of the picture and it's nearly impossible to recognize your daughter, since she's looking the other way. The police is certain that this picture addresses you only."

"What's our course of action in this matter?"

"We'll arrange some protection for your family and yourself, and then we'll see what the police will uncover. The institute already pressed charges and it'd be a shame if we'd back down from the expedition because of this threat."

"I agree. I've already invested way too much time to resign because of a threat. I'm still not convinced that someone would actually harm me, and I would prefer it if nobody would talk to my family yet. I don't want my wife to panic. I'll talk to them tonight. When did you say the personal protection is going to start?"

"It'll start on the twenty-fourth, until then the police will drive by your place regularly and they'll also be present at the next two public appearances."

Dr. Weber nodded and handed back the picture.

- 4 -

Isola del Giglio, Italy, Wednesday, June 15th
The sun beat through the window characteristically shining bright as Nick lay in bed, the clock ticking passed noon. He found it scary how precise Ariel's and Shira's conclusions had been. He had seriously thought about checking the room for cameras, but he never found the time for it. The reason for that was lying beside him in his arms, sleeping soundly. Despite the heat, Nick enjoyed the warm touch of Natascha's soft skin. Her long and naturally curled hair was completely tousled, but that was no surprise after last night. He enjoyed the smell of her perfume and he let his hand glide over her naked body down to her hips.

Natascha opened her dark-brown eyes slowly and stretched.

"Good Morning," she said sleepy and smiled at him.

"Good Morning, Angel."

"How long were you awake?"

"Just five minutes."

Natascha looked at the sun, turned around and glanced at her watch on the nightstand.

"Oh, we missed the morning dive by more than four hours," she said, but she was neither disappointed nor surprised about that.

She turned back towards Nick, placing her head on his chest as she closed her eyes again, only to bite his chest a few seconds later.

"Ouch, what was that for?" Nick smiled, clapping her bum.

"Just wanted to make sure this is not a dream," she replied, her eyes wearily closed.

Nick turned towards her and during the next half hour they both discovered with great satisfaction, that they were not dreaming. After they took a shower together, they finally decided to go and eat somewhere, but looking for her underwear, Natascha reached a dilemma.

"Do you have any idea where it might be?" she asked him blushing.

"No idea, sorry."

"How could I lose my underwear?" She wondered in embarrassment. Nick smiled a quirky grin and she couldn't help but do the same.

After Natascha was finally dressed, they walked outside and strolled down the street towards a small restaurant located near the beautiful beach. The old white houses were skillfully built very close to each other, offering some shade in the hot summer months. Natascha slipped her hand in his as they walked, enjoying the atmosphere that surrounded the few Italian people. Nick then noticed there were few tourists on the island at this time of year. They sat down at one of the few tables outside the restaurant, and Nick's thoughts wandered to the waitress and the possibility that Shira's working undercover to keep an eye on them.

"Is everything okay?" Natascha asked after she noticed that Nick was glancing over his shoulder frequently.

"Yes, everything's fine," he laughed.

"Believe it or not, but just from reading your last text message, Rolf and the rest of the gang actually figured out when and where we are meeting."

"Really?" Natascha chuckled and ordered pasta.

"Yes, and they threatened me that they would wire our room."

"But they can't do that," Natascha blushed, then second guessed herself, "can they?"

Nick only knew too well that his teammates were more than capable of doing exactly that. If they did wire it, Nick knew it would be impossible to find all the cameras. Just thinking about the possibility that they did watch them last night made goosebumps rise up his neck.

"No, they're not capable of doing something like that," he smiled weakly, unsure if he was reassuring Natascha or himself.

"Besides, they're still in London."

Where else should they be? That's where they have all the necessary gear, he added to himself.

"What's your plan for the next couple days anyway?" Nick changed the subject.

"Well, I didn't get a dive in yesterday because I was waiting for you all day and today we both missed the boat, so we have two days left. It'd be great if we could get at least one dive in with the new housing. I'll be in trouble if it's not working properly or if it's leaking during the expedition. Do you have all your gear with you?" she asked looking at him.

"Yes," Nick nodded with a mouth full of noodles.

Montana, USA, Wednesday, June 15th

The American once again met his British and Canadian friends at his hunting lodge in Montana.

"What's the status on that expedition leader?" the British asked and looked at the grandfather clock in the corner. The gravity of the situation and the severity of the consequences, if the expedition should find their equipment, prompted them to meet more often than they originally planned.

"We issued a warning to Dr. Weber and our men are in Germany, ready, and paid. They've located their mark and are waiting our signal."

"What about the natives up there? Any complications?"

"No, everything is according to plan. There'll be no way it can be traced back to anyone of us," the American reassured his British friend.

"Where's that stuff coming from anyway?" the Canadian was curious.

"Our men used it before with great efficiency. We have more than enough to guarantee a successful operation."

"What about the members of the expedition? All the scientists and the crew members?"

"Like I said before, I'll be personally on board that ship to make sure that everything is following our plan. The participants of the expedition are not our prime target."

"Well," the Canadian said and rose from his chair.

"I still need to know when and from where the container will arrive in Halifax. It'll take me some time to arrange everything with the authorities down there. Do we know when the container is scheduled to arrive?"

"It'll arrive at the end of June so that everything will be ready once the expedition ship arrives in Halifax to pick up the remaining scientists," the American stated and watched the smoke of his cigar swirl through the air.

Isola del Giglio, Italy, Friday, June 17th
After two more long nights, during which neither Nick nor Natascha cared if their room was wired, they had finally managed to get one dive in per day. This was their last day, and after they had some pasta for lunch, they strolled down to the beach and took a sun bath. Natascha opened her top and handed the sun lotion to Nick.

"Do you mind?" she asked him.

Nick squeezed the bottle and applied some lotion on his hands, before he started to massage Natascha's neck. With his hands gliding over her back, he decided to start a subject he avoided for the last couple days.

"I'd really like to see you once more, before you go on your expedition," he finally said, knowing this was something that also bothered Natascha.

She turned around and looked at him.

"What do you mean with *just once*?" She pretended to be upset.

"Well, actually, I wouldn't mind seeing you much more often. I just have no idea how it would work out between us."

"If it's meant to be, than it'll work out somehow," Natascha smiled, though she knew this was a very unsatisfying answer.

Nick looked in her deep brown eyes and passionately kissed her.

"I'd really like to wait for you," he admitted softly, seriously.

"I'd love to come back to you once the expedition is over. Do you think you can wait that long?"

"Well," Nick replied with a smile. "I can still watch the videos from the last two nights, they should be all over the Internet by now."

Natascha chuckled and gently slapped the back of his head, before she turned around, closed her eyes again and told Nick to continue the massage.

**Home Office and Operational Headquarters of *EuroSecCorporation*,
London, Monday, June 20th**
Nick was finally back from his vacation and was sitting together with the other members of Team A in the conference room. While he had been in Italy, the rest of

Thin Ice

the team had successfully finished their job on Mr. Gordon Ramshaw's estate and they were now waiting for a new assignment.

Rolf and Ole-Einar tried halfheartedly to persuade Nick to share some details about his trip to Italy. Nick happily shared the details of the two dives that he and Natascha did together, but beside that he only told them with a big grin that the weather and the food was good.

"A gentleman does not discuss happenings," he closed his defense and leaned back in his chair. His eyes fell on Shira, who had not yet participated in their previous conversation, as she stood up abruptly and walked over towards him.

"We have everything on DVD," she announced in all seriousness and threw a DVD on the table in front of Nick.

Nick's face contorted with disbelief. He stared at the DVD with wide eyes.

"That's a confession," Shira triumphed and sat down again while everybody else was laughing.

"You screwed her, yes?" she asked him with great satisfaction and everybody including Nick started laughing.

"It's *you nailed her*," Oliver corrected Shira without joining in on the humour.

"That's the DVD from Norway," Rolf explained. "Bernd sent it last week."

Nick was relieved, but still speechless.

"That Natascha played you very well," Oliver mentioned freely. He was the only one beside Shira who had not yet met Natascha.

"First of all you cooked dinner for her, even with a nice dessert as I heard, and after that, you spoiled her on a romantic Italian island, just to find out that she didn't have the DVD after all."

They all laughed about this unique presentation.

"Yes, you're right. Never looked at it like that," Nick laughed and glanced at the door.

Retired General Klaus Schwartze, his secretary Brigitte as well as Sigrid Schneider and Ariel Rashid from operation control walked into the room and sat down.

After retired General Klaus Schwartze had greeted them, he immediately came to the subject.

"First of all, I want to forward the comments that I received from Brian's brother-in-law, Mr Gordon Ramshaw. He is very satisfied and appreciates your work," he said and looked at his unit.

"There's a new job coming up. On the twenty-seventh of June, German Dr. Richard Weber is going to lead an international expedition for fourteen weeks from the port of Kiel in Germany into the polar sea. The expedition is part of the world wide activities for the International Polar Year. It focuses on the examination and documentation of global warming and its effect in the arctic regions."

Nick paid extra attention. His boss was talking about Natascha's expedition.

"Several international institutes will take part in this expedition by sending their own team of scientists on board of the research vessel. The interest is big enough for BBC and National Geographic to send their own camera crews to take part as well. During the last couple weeks, the institute employing Dr. Richard Weber received several threats. Some of them were against the complete expedition, some of them were against Dr. Richard Weber himself. It's expected this expedition will prove the human impact on global warming as well as the probable effects caused by it. This is the reason why several nations are not too happy about this expedition. As expedition leader, Dr. Richard Weber is the person with the highest priority for anybody who wants to jeopardize the expedition. Most of the letters they received were simply obtuse, but there was one letter that the German police took very serious. Brigitte, do you have that letter at hand?" he glanced at his secretary, who just inserted a USB stick into a laptop.

"The most critical moment will be when Dr. Richard Weber officially starts the expedition on Saturday, June twenty-fifth at nineteen-hundred during a special event in Berlin. There'll be more than four hundred guests from the business, political and cultural communities and society. The police assume that a hit will most likely happen during this event. We don't believe that it'll be necessary to provide any further protection once the Professor is on board the research vessel and on his way the following Tuesday. It's our job to meet Dr. Weber this Friday, the twenty-fourth at his private home and to accompany him as well as his wife and daughter on the three hundred kilometer trip to Berlin, where we'll also provide security detail during the event. After the festivities, the Professor and his family will stay in a hotel before we take them back to their home on Sunday. On Monday we'll drive the entire family to Kiel, where the research vessel is docked. Team B has already deployed to Kiel and is examining the research vessel itself. Team C is conducting a background check on the crew and all the remaining expediting members. The Captain of the *Northern Explorer*, that's the name of the vessel, is Norwegian by the name of Sven-Goran Rasmussen, a man who has served in the Norwegian Navy. Gunnar Eriksson from operation control is already in contact with him and it seems like the Captain is very reasonable. The same can be said about First Officer Karl-Heinz Junghans from Germany as well as Second Officer Mika Kankkunen from Finland. The Captain has guaranteed total cooperation. Okay, let's focus on our Professor.

"This is the photo they sent him," Klaus Schwartze continued and looked at the screen behind him, where the picture was now clearly visible.

"The picture shows Dr. Richard Weber in front of his house after he got out of his car and coincidentally looked right into the camera. This is the reason why the police is convinced he's the target. The second person is still sitting on the passenger seat, and her face is turned away from the camera. It's interesting that this picture has been taken from a high-resolution scope with an integrated digital camera. Those scopes automatically imprint an electronic signature on each picture. According to that signature, this scope is not available on the free market and it also shows us that the distance to Dr. Weber was a little bit over eight hundred meters. If someone has access to such a scope, it's fair to assume that he has something he can mount it on."

Nick and his friends were looking at the projection of the picture and Nick estimated that Dr. Richard Weber was about 1,90m tall and about fifty years of age. He looked again at the second person in the photo. He could barely hide his shock. Nick glanced over at Rolf and Ole-Einar, but neither of them showed any reaction. Still surprised, Nick was certain he knew the young woman on the passenger seat only too well.

"Excuse me. Who's that person in passenger?" Nick asked his boss and looked back at the image.

Retired General Klaus Schwartze first looked at Nick before he went over his notes.

He finally found the information he was looking for and also looked at the picture.

"The person on the passenger seat is Dr. Weber's daughter. She's a Marine Biologist and a member of his team. Her name is Natascha Kleinfeld."

The following seconds were silent, not even a jotting pen was heard. Everybody was looking at Nick.

Klaus Schwartze made motion to continue, but he noticed each individual in the room lacked attention.

"Is there something I should know?" he finally asked and looked at this team.

"We met Natascha Kleinfeld and three of her friends four weeks ago in Norway. We were diving from the same boat and also stayed at the same resort, but there's something else," Rolf explained and looked at Nick. He wanted to give Nick the opportunity to inform his boss himself.

"Natascha and I met last week in Italy again. We had planned it during our last day in Norway. She told me that her father's a scientist, but she never mentioned he's the expedition leader and had received threats."

Klaus Schwartze took another look at the picture before he turned back to Nick.

"Well, there's a chance that he hasn't told her at that time. Again, the German police are certain that Dr. Weber is the mark, not his daughter. Based on all the facts at hand, I'd come to the same conclusion. Do you have a problem providing security detail for her father?"

"No, I don't have a problem with it," Nick shook his head, "as long as the rest of the team feels the same way. I was just a little bit surprised when I saw the picture," Nick added and looked at his friends who assured him that his relationship with Natascha was no problem for them.

"Have you talked to her since you were back from Italy?" Klaus asked.

"She called me this morning, but she still hasn't mentioned anything about the threats."

"How serious is your relationship with her?" Klaus continued out of interest.

Everybody else in the room turned with mischievous grins towards Nick. They knew he could not go round a straight question from Klaus Schwartze.

"We both take it pretty serious and we want to meet again once she's back," Nick hesitantly admitted. "Can you please tell them to stop staring at me like that?"

"Well, like I said before, I don't see a problem," Klaus Schwartze concluded, ignoring Nick's comment.

"Can you please ask for some more details, Sir? He won't tell us anything and the five of us have a bet running," Rolf requested from his boss.

Nick shook his head and looked at his friend.

"It seems like Shira fits in very well," Klaus noted to Ariel Rashid.

- 5 -

Berlin, Friday June 24th
Chuck Hogan and his friends Martin Cunningham, Sean Greenstein and Robert Tyrell had just returned from a reconnaissance trip and met to discuss their individual observations. They all visited the facility that was housing the event individually, and all four of them resided under fake identities at four different hotels throughout the town. They paid all their bills in cash and only met at places where nobody would ask questions.

"It's impossible to get in the building on the day of the festivities. To get near the great hall alone we'd have to pass one metal detector and one X-Ray machine, both built into a door frame," Martin started with frustration as he looked down to the river. The murky water flowed over the obstructing rocks as he flicked his eyes back to his partners.

"I suggest we wait until our mark leaves the building. I'm pretty sure our mark has to stay until the end of it. That'd be the best opportunity for us," Robert added throwing some bread in the water before he rubbed his hands across his pantleg.

"Do we know which door they'll leave?"

"Yes, it's to our advantage that the building is so old it doesn't have a parking garage inside. All the cars will be parked at the multi-story car park down the street. I found out the organizer has booked the entire car park for that evening. We'll observe all evening, of course. My plan is to wait until our mark is leaving the building. We'll force a mechanical failure on one of the cars in the lane in front of the building, so there'll be a bottleneck. The weather forecast for tomorrow evening is calling for warm temperatures of twenty-five degree Celsius and no wind. I expect our mark'll walk the two hundred meters to the car park rather than wait half an hour for the traffic to flow again. Once our person's on that walk, we'll get active," Chuck explained.

His three friends nodded in agreement. It was not their first job together and they were an accomplished well-trained team.

"Okay," Chuck continued, turning his attention back to his men, "I also called our employer this morning. The money's been wired and everything's okay."

"Employer? I thought we're working for three people?"

"We only get paid from one person, and that makes him the guy who calls the shots," Chuck concluded with a crooked smile.

Private Home of Dr. Richard Weber, Friday, June 24th
Team A arrived in the late morning hours, and Natascha and Nick only exchanged a brief embrace and sneaked in one passionate kiss. Before they settled at the guesthouse, they were meeting with Dr. Richard Weber, his common-law wife, Renate Kleinfeld, and their daughter Natascha in the kitchen.

Dr. Weber explained that he had not received any further threats, but the local police still had reason to believe that something might happen.

Ariel Rashid and Sigrid Schneider had both explained the general procedure of their job, and how they planned to spend the next 72 hours together. Despite Dr. Weber's worriless nature towards the threat, they were satisfied that he was being cooperative. After a strenuous hour and a half they had managed to cover all the details.

"As an expedition leader, what's your exact job during those fourteen weeks?" Sigrid Schneider asked with curiosity.

"Like you said, I'm the expedition leader and therefore responsible that all the scheduled projects are going according to plan. On board the *Northern Explorer* will be several groups of scientists. We have the Russian team with Dr. Igor Gremchenko, the Icelandic team with Dr. Sylvia Gunnardottir, and the American team with Dr. Joseph Richard as well as the Canadian team with Dr. Markus Habermann and our own German team. There will also be two camera crews from the BBC as well as the National Geographic Society present to document the expedition. The goal of the expedition is to prove the human impact on global warming. In order to collect the necessary data, we'll conduct several research projects on board the *Northern Explorer*, and we'll also install several hundred sensors for long-time monitoring.

This will give us the opportunity to monitor and document the melting of the polar ice, the change in ocean currents and water temperatures as well as their influences on the marine wildlife. We'll also be able to determine the amount of green house gases in the northern regions. If we're really lucky, we might even be able to predict some future floods, dry periods and maybe even identify new areas susceptible to hurricanes. But not all nations are happy about this expedition. The United States and especially Canada will experience a huge economic advantage once the North-West Passage is ice free and available for ship transit. Canada will receive a fortune in transit fees and they could build some container ports on each side of the passage. Depending on where ships are heading, we have to consider that the North-West Passage can shorten the normal shipping routes up to seven thousand kilometers. It's not too difficult to imagine the huge financial profits Canada could gain.

If this wasn't enough, there's another advantage. There will be easier access to the oil up there. The thermal frost will be melting, but if the area up there is ice free, they can directly ship their oil. Canada has one of the largest oil fields in the world, but at the moment the costs of getting the oil is extreme and the procedure is exceptionally time-consuming. A new refinery with it's own terminal would flush billions of dollars into the country."

"What about the States?"

"Travelling through the North-West Passage, sooner or later you'll reach Alaska. I'd bet that Canada will get complete strategic control over the Passage if they exclusively sell their oil to America. That way the Americans would satisfy most of their demand for oil without declaring war over it. So I hope you understand that I'm not too surprised that neither the United States nor Canada are doing anything to reduce their emissions. They have no great interest in climate control. The Russians are pretty much the same. Due to the melting ice they'll gain much easier access to the oceans. They also claim a huge portion of the oil underneath the North Pole, since they declare it's in their territory. Bottom line, it's all about the oil.

I was the one who had the idea for this expedition. The reason that the North American countries sent a team on board this vessel is to simply monitor us and ultimately collect evidence against our theories. The same goes for the Russians. They just want to know how far the Americans are. The United States and Canada have invested more money in funding think-tanks to come up with arguments against climate control than they have to reduce their overall emission. Other nations with special interest are Denmark and Norway, but they're not connected to the North-West Passage. This is the reality and I understand why some people aren't taken with this expedition." Dr. Weber concluded as he looked at each of them.

The Professor kept his eyes on his guests as a small pause seperated his thoughts. His lips finally parted as he spoke.

"May I ask who was in Norway?"

Rolf, Nick, Olaf and Ole-Einar raised their hands.

"And who spent some time alone with my daughter in Italy?" he continued seriously.

"Dad," Natascha shouted with objection while Shira, Rolf and the other three all simultaneously pointed their fingers at Nick.

"That would've been me," Nick replied uncomfortably.

"Let it go, Richard," his wife Renate reprimanded lightly with a laugh. She smiled as she turned to one of the cupboards and politely asked if anyone wanted a cup of coffee.

"No, thank you, that's very kind, Miss Kleinfeld. If you don't mind, we'd like to have a look around. We also have to check the security system," Ariel responded freely.

They planned to stay in the guesthouse, which was a much smaller cottage located just behind the main house. They decided upon a three man cycle: one person monitoring the security cameras, while the other two patrolled the outside premises. They all agreed it would be safer for everyone that the family dog, a large 4-year-old male Kuvasz, would stay inside the house.

"Natascha, would you please show our guests around? I'll be in my study," Dr. Weber asked his daughter.

"Certainly," Natascha replied with a smile and stood up.

"Okay, what do you want to see first?"

"We can start right here," Ariel replied, "it doesn't matter to us."

Natascha lead them through the ground floor and into the double garage.

Upon being asked, Natascha explained that the garage door opened simultaneously with the main gate down the driveway as soon as the electric signal was activated from either of the two cars. From there, Natascha walked the crew down into the basement where a small room with the security system was located. Natascha was surprised how much time Ariel spent with it.

"There are only two monitors down here. The footage itself is recorded on a hard drive, which erases itself after five days before it starts all over again. We have a control pad on each floor of the house."

"How do you activate it?"

"Well, we can call in a code outside the house via cellphone to either activate or deactivate it. Inside the house, all you need is a fingerprint scan and to touch the right button. All the panels are connected, so you can't activate the system while someone's still in the house. If this happens, then the display will show you the message. If you ignore the message, or if you override it, then the system will activate itself after fifteen seconds. All alarms are monitored by a company which informs the police directly."

"Does this company have access to the house?" Ariel asked.

"No, all they can do is check it from the outside. But they'll know which sensor has started the alarm. All the exit doors and windows have sensors. There are also some motion sensors inside some of the rooms, as well as in the garage. Once a year the company tests the system. Once the system is armed, our dog normally stays in a safe area of the house."

Ariel wrote down a couple more notes and seemed to be satisfied. Natascha smiled at the team and lead them upstairs. After going through all the rooms, Natascha paused as they stood in front of the door of her ensuite bedroom and walk-in closet.

"I didn't have time to clean up, so...sorry for the mess," she blushed her apology and reluctantly opened the door.

"A solar bear!" Shira shouted the moment she saw the huge white dog jump to its feet and bolt towards them. A burst of laughter thundered through the room and Shira immediately realized her mistake,

"I didn't say it right. It's *polar bear*, right?"

"It's okay, *Rocky*," Natascha calmed her dog with a soft voice as she scratched his ears. "*Rocky*'s the best bodyguard in the world. As long as he's with me, nobody's getting close to me."

"Ha," Shira laughed and elbowed Nick. "Won't be easy after all, yes?"

They all laughed and Rolf stepped inside the room to have a look at the window. Alerted, *Rocky* immediately walked in front of him and growl rumbled from deep within.

"That's exactly the reason why I got that dog for you in the first place," Dr. Richard Weber joined them and their laughter as he continued walking to his daughter.

"So that no strange man can ever enter this room."

Rocky ceased growling as Rolf took a step backwards.

Before Nick realized the imminent threat, he had already taken two steps into the room. *Rocky* stood alert as he did before, a glare flicking across his eyes. He looked at Nick and then to Natascha. Something shifted and he sat down again, ignoring Nick, but monitoring the rest of the group with daring eyes.

"Now that's interesting," Ariel commented while Natascha laughed and warmly wrapped her arms around Nick.

"Traitor," her father mumbled and left the room.

"I guess he senses you mean no harm to me," Natascha smiled and looked at her dog intently watching Nick's friends.

"If the dog would sense what Nick is *really* up to, then he'd bite him for sure. His teeth are at the perfect height for that," Rolf countered and everybody laughed again.

"Well, I don't deny that *Rocky* might not sense that, but he also senses that this would happen with my approval," Natascha answered, still laughing.

"Seriously," Ariel shifted on his feet. "How protective is this dog?"

"He usually sleeps in my room. If I don't tell him that it's okay then I don't believe, anyone other than my parents would be able to get closer than two meters to me."

"What about Nick?" Ariel asked.

"Well, first of all I believe *Rocky* does sense our feelings for each other..." Natascha hesitated feeling the unsatisfying nature of this explanation.

"Yes, and?" Ariel insisted with a smile.

"And just to make sure, I used one of Nick's T-Shirt's from Italy. *Rocky* slept on it all the time... Sorry for that. I got him used to Nick's smell," she admitted and looked at Nick, her arms still wrapped around his neck.

"Would've never thought you could get used to his smell," Ole-Einar commented glancing between Natascha and *Rocky*, and everyone roared with laughter again.

"So you planned to kidnap our little Princess into your room during the nights, yes?" Shira asked Natascha with a fiendish grin.

Natascha just shrugged her shoulders and smiled at her, her eyes sparkling.

"At least I have my T-Shirt back," Nick stated nonchalantly, "what about your bra? Did you ever find it again?" The moment the question slipped from his lips, he wished he could gather the words back again.

Natascha immediately flushed a new shade of red and she hurriedly hid her face into Nick's shoulder.

Olaf's hands raised in triumph.

"Yes, lost underwear. Jackpot! I win the bet!"

Olaf noticed that nobody else shared his laughter and he turned around to see Natascha's father standing in the doorway. Shock and surprise pervaded his disgruntled face, it was obvious that he overheard their last conversation, whether he intended to or not.

It took a moment for the uncomfortable moment to pass before Ariel decided to have a look at the premises. Natascha led them outside and showed their guesthouse, where they finally started to unpack their things.

While Ariel and Sigrid intently worked on a schedule for the next two nights, Rolf started the kitchen. During supper, Ariel explained that Nick, Rolf and Shira would take the first shift and that they would be relieved at approximately 3.00 in the morning.

After supper Nick, Rolf and Shira walked over to the main house where they could overhear a heated discussion coming from the kitchen.

"I'm not sure if this is the right time for something like that," Natascha's father admitted clearly.

"Richard, she's twenty-six years old. She's more than old enough to make that decision herself. And on the plus side, his boss doesn't have a problem with it. It's unusual enough that she's still living at home. She doesn't have to explain anything to us," Renate defended her daughter.

Shira stopped and spread her arms out to stop Rolf and Nick.

"I'm just not sure if it's wise to have him invade your privacy. This is exactly how it started back then when your ex-boyfriend accompanied you on the other expedition."

"Dad, first of all I was much younger then, and we just didn't get along in the end. Secondly, he was the only guy my age on board. On a completely different note, my discretion is my business. I could technically already be pregnant from the last time Nick invaded a few inches into my privacy. I'm old enough and I'm responsible enough to do what I want."

"If she would've only said that an hour ago I would've won the Jackpot," Shira whispered to Nick, who returned her smile with a killing glare.

"Nick's my decision and what does it even matter? He's not even coming on this expedition," Natascha continued with flare.

"I just don't want you to get into some sort of emotional adventure just days before we depart. The last thing we need is a heartbroken marine biologist for the next four months."

"I appreciate your concern, Dad, but I'm old enough and completely certain about our feelings for each other. I'll participate in this expedition and I'll do my best on my assignments to satisfy you and the institute. I'll do all this and Nick will be waiting for me when I get back. And Mom likes him already."

Shira elbowed Nick gently and nodded respectfully.

"Well, I'll be out with *Rocky* if there's nothing else," Natascha concluded the argument and steamed away.

Shira, Rolf and Nick stepped back into the living room as Natascha stormed to the stairs, oblivious of their presence.

"Go with her," Shira ordered Nick, then offered a reassuring smile, "I'll speak with her parents."

Shira watched Nick follow Natascha upstairs, while Rolf went downstairs to monitor the security system.

When Shira entered the kitchen she noticed the argument did not miss a beat without Natascha's input. Her parents continued to argue with heat.

"Richard, you can't tell her anymore whom to date and whom not to. You know perfectly well how intelligent she is, and that she wouldn't do anything stupid. Do you remember our relationship when we were her age? It's pretty much the same. You were on some research trip in the Antarctic for over ten months and I was sitting at my parents place with our daughter. What do you expect? That she's going to marry another scientist who won't be there for her when she needs someone? She's the one who's traveling around the world. She's the one who needs a strong partner who can take care of her. Natascha told me about Nick and I can assure you that it's different this time. You know our daughter. She's not the type who falls in love with the first guy she meets and you know that. And she's right, I actually do like him and I will support them."

"She's even trained the dog not to do anything."

"That was my idea," his wife countered with relentless heat.

"Oh, women," Richard fussed and his attention flicked to the kitchen door where Shira was standing.

"Dr. Weber, I can assure you, that from all the men assigned to your protection, you would want Nick to be the one who penetrates into Natascha."

The appalled expression on their faces caused surprise to flick into Shira's angelic face. She knew she made another large mistake.

"Please excuse my language skills, I still have some difficulties with the new language now and then. What I meant to say was, that Nick is very carefully regarding the privacy of your daughter and that of all men, he's the perfect match for Natascha. I know how serious Nick is about this relationship, and even his boss came to the conclusion that there's no problem with Nick being assigned to the case. Nick is a good person."

"I don't doubt that at all. All I'm saying is that I'm not sure if this is the right time for their relationship to start like this."

"They would not have met, if it isn't the right time. Shalom," Shira acknowledged his point and conclusively bowed before she retreated downstairs to Rolf.

Natascha sat on her bed and was scratching *Rocky*'s ears. She could see *Rocky* frequently look at her and she knew that he could sense her internal battle.

Why does this have to happen to me now? In less then ninety-six hours I'll be on board the Northern Explorer *and on my way to a fourteen-week long trip to the polar sea, and this is the time you unconditionally fall in love. And my father of all people is trying to give me advice after he had left my mother and I alone back then.*

She tried to convince herself that her father only wanted what was best, but she could only find herself agreeing with her mother on this one.

At twenty-six years of age I'm more than old enough, even if I'm still living at home.

Natascha's face scrunched at the thought but having just graduated from university and now working with her father at the Institute, it all just made sense. The Institute was just located a short drive away but despite the economical and environmental advantages, she still found moments she loathes her accommodation situation.

"Hey, Angel," Nick whispered and opened the door. "Can I come in?"

Natascha nodded and wiped tears from her eyes.

Nick approached her slowly and sat on the bed beside her, eyeing *Rocky* who just looked up briefly before he closed his eyes peacefully, enjoying his ear massage again.

"Rolf, Shira and I happened to be outside the kitchen when you had your argument.

We didn't want to sneak up, but we couldn't help to overhear your conversation. We didn't mean to. I'm sorry."

"I know, don't worry. My father cares way too much about me. I'm twenty-six years old. I'm not a teenager any more. If we would have it his way, then I'd marry some rich Professor, to whom he could talk to in the evenings once he's retired."

Natascha rested her head on Nick's shoulder and he impulsively started to run his hand over her hair.

"I'm not a Professor but I can see the difference between a frog and a fish."

"You can actually do that?" Natascha asked him, pretending to be serious.

"Well, I have to get close enough, but yes, I can do that."

She returned her head to his shoulder again and closed her eyes.

"That's more than enough for me. Together we should be able to manage the rest."

Nick chuckled, then asked softly, "can I ask you something?"

"Sure," Natascha whispered back.

"Why'd you tell your father we've already slept together?"

"He's not stupid, and I also wanted to make it clear to him that I'm more than old enough to make my own decisions, and..." Natascha hesitated and glanced at Nick.

"Yes, and?"

"When I was back from Italy, I still couldn't operate the camera housing the way I should, and he knew that we had perfect weather so he guessed right. I think he expected more from me."

Nick looked at her, under *Rocky*'s watchful eyes, and kissed her gently on her forehead.

"I'm sorry they still call you Princess."

"Yes, you really did them a big favor back then," Nick laughed.

"Are you really serious?" Natascha asked suddenly, turning her eyes back to Nick.

"I mean about us."

Nick looked her deep in her eyes, and after a moments pause he continued, "Yes, I'm very serious about us and I'll wait for you and hope you won't run away with a polar bear."

"I love you," she whispered.

"I love you, too."

Natascha's lips met his for a brief moment before she rose to her feet. "I have to take *Rocky* outside. Am I going to see you later on?"

"I have the first shift together with Rolf and Shira until three o'clock."

"If you want, you can sleep up here with me."

"Not that I wouldn't like to, but I don't think it'd be a good idea for the moment. I'm also not sure if I could trust your dog when I sneak into your bedroom in the middle of the night while you're sleeping."

"Good point. At least we'd know then for sure how protective he is."

"Very encouraging," Nick answered and kissed his girlfriend before he went downstairs to meet Rolf and Shira.

"Shira, do you want to go for a walk with Natascha? I think she might want to talk to someone."

"No problem," Shira nodded and walked away.

Rolf glanced at Nick.

"Don't worry, buddy. She'll be back in less than four months, and you can wrap your arms around her again. Nothing is going to happen between now and their departure. Sigrid is certain that everything's okay."

"What kind of feeling does Ariel have?" Nick was curious.

"The same feeling he always has when he's on personal protection detail. Don't worry. Shira already spoke with Natascha's parents."

"Great, now I'm feeling much better," Nick added sarcastically.

"Relax, she almost got all her sentences right this time," Olaf mentioned with a grin.

Container terminal Halifax, Nova Scotia, Canada, Friday, June 24th
Driven by gusts of cold Atlantic wind, the rain was pouring down at the container terminal. Clair MacDonald sat in his costums office and looked at his computer screen where he saw the manifest from the container ship that arrived last night. His computer program was searching the manifest for certain container numbers as well as some companies from the Import- and Export Business which had been caught partaking in criminal activities in the past.

"Let's see, who was stupid enough to send his complete shipment in one single container?" he asked himself and took a sip from his hot coffee he purchased from one of the coffee shops on his way in.

Clair knew only too well that their rate of success was not very high. Most of the criminals, and it didn't matter if they were the small independently run drug dealers or the big companies, split their shipment into several small packages instead of a single large shipment. Typically those small packages were then sent individually on different shipments again. Due to the higher number of parcels with illegal contents, the costums office found many more of those illegal shipments, but the total loss to the dealer was actually smaller since they only lost 10 or 20% of their total shipment. Most of the large shipments of drugs came in under water anyway. The drug dealer basically mounts huge watertight cases with clamps to the hull of a container ship below the water level. Once those ships reach their port of destination, the containers are retrieved during the night from one or two divers either from shore or from a small fishing boat.

Normally we would have to inspect the hull of each damn ship entering the harbor, Clair thought, but he also knew that this was simply impossible. Nevertheless, he was committed to his job and tried as efficiently as he could to find as many illegal shipments as possible.

Today he only found four containers that he wanted to inspect himself. His capable staff would handle the rest.

On the way to the containers, he would also have to stop at a container that had raised the suspicion of one of his staff members. The container belonged to an

American team of scientists, who were scheduled to board the Norwegian research vessel *Northern Explorer* early July here in Halifax to conduct research in the North-West Passage. During the routine X-Ray, one of his staff found a lead-sealed box in this very container, and he was now waiting for Clair to have a closer look.

Clair retrieved the containers manifest, the contact information from the importing company as well as their Canadian contact address from the printer. He briefly glanced through the papers before he walked outside to the car-pool.

One of his friends gave him a ride in a pick-up truck and dropped him off at the container from the American scientist team. Clair closed the pick-up door and ran the short distance to the open container through the rain, where his staff was already waiting for him.

"Damn rain," Clair cursed once he was under the cover of the container and looked around. To his expectation he saw a large amount of scientific gear, including some laptops, survival suits for Polar Regions, as well as four complete new sets of diving gear including tanks. Two of the boxes contained a ROV* and Clair checked the serial numbers with his documents. He even found a rifle, legally stowed away in a special case and also listed with the serial number on his inventory list.

They probably have it because of the polar bears, just in case, he thought and kept checking the contents of the container with his list.

Everything was registered and all numbers were in accordance with his documents. Clair finally turned to the lead-sealed box they could not look into. He read all the *Handle with care! Fragile! Scientific Sensors! Do not open!* stickers and saw two huge locks on it as well. According to his manifest, this box contained thirty underwater sensors.

But why are they stored in a lead-sealed box? He checked the inventory list again and saw a phone number printed at the bottom of it, right beside a note that said to call that number in case of any questions.

For a second Clair thought about calling the number, but he didn't want to look stupid, since everything else in the container was in order. He thought for a moment and recalled this was not a private container. It was from a respected American research company that was not his prime suspect for illegal activities, but his attention was fixed on the phone number.

He recognized it as a number from the Canadian Government.

That means we also take part in the cruise, he thought and looked over the contents of the container again.

Everything was okay, almost perfect.

His many years of experience have taught him that there was no such thing as a perfect manifest. If someone spends so much time to make all the documents so perfect, than they usually have something to hide. His gut feeling let him get suspicious about this lead box, but he did not understand why. He glanced once more at his documents to find out what was supposed to happen to the container.

ROV = Remotely Operated Vehicle

He read that an expedition team under the direction of Dr. Markus Habermann would arrive in time with the research vessel, and that they would then load the contents of the container onto the ship. Until then, the container was suppose to stay at the terminal.

Sent from an American research institute under the order of the American government to a Canadian research institute, again with extra documentation from our own federal government.

The documentation was pure, but he still could not shake his gut feeling. He could feel there was something important missing. He re-read the documentation he held in his hand, flipping through the pages with uncertainty. Something was not right.

"Hey Clair, I'm on my way to get another double-double. If you want, I can drop you off at the other containers on my way back."

"What?" Clair asked and turned around. The rain was still pouring down on the metal container so loud that he had not heard his friend with the pick-up truck.

"Yeah, I might take that ride, damn rain," Clair finally said and turned to his staff.

"Close and seal the container and bring it to it's final position. Everything's fine," he confirmed as he walked towards the pick-up truck.

If Clair MacDonald took another moment and searched the suspicious lead-sealed box, he may have noticed that this container had the potential to destroy half the population of Halifax.

Private Home of Dr. Richard Weber, Saturday, June 25th

The night went without any problems, just like Sigrid had expected it, and everybody was in good spirit during the morning as they prepared to drive to Berlin. For several reasons they decided to use three Range Rover Diesel from the *EuroSecCorporation* since Dr. Weber only owned a small Honda Civic and a Toyota Hybrid. When Ariel stepped into the kitchen, he could hear Dr. Weber on the phone.

"No, I told you that before...And I have not said that either...Well, it's neither my problem nor the problem of my daughter... I really don't care what they're thinking... All right, if you insist...Yes, I'll talk to you as soon as we're in Berlin...Thank you. Good-bye."

Dr. Richard Weber put the wireless phone back on the kitchen table.

"The organizer made a mistake with the seating arrangements," he said and looked at Ariel.

"My family and I are sitting at the main table with the environment minister and his wife, the director of our institute with her husband, as well as the leader from the other international scientists with their respective spouses."

"And where's the problem?" Ariel asked.

Dr. Richard Weber looked at his daughter.

"They arranged a seat for your husband and they now refuse to change it, since it would mess up the seating arrangements. They assured me that they'll get someone to sit beside you."

"I can't allow that," Ariel shook his head.

"I have to know who that person will be and I have to run a complete background check on him first."

"I know who it'll be," Natascha announced with a smile as everyone looked at her. She slipped under Nick's arm as she wrapped her arms around his waist, reeling herself closer to him.

"After all, the person should be my husband and on the plus side, you'd be very close to my father the entire evening. And let's not forget the most important thing. I would not have to listen to some rubbish from a guy who I don't know at all," she explained, briefly pressing her lips against Nick's cheek.

Nick's discomfort was evident as he flicked his attention from Natascha, as she clung to him, to her father and then to Ariel, a crooked smile briefly crossing the Israelis features. "That's perfect. Natascha's right. We can't get anybody closer than that," he agreed.

Dr. Weber nodded in agreement and called back the number to inform them of the solution.

Natascha was smiling happily and hurried upstairs to get dressed.

While Shira, Oliver and Ole-Einar arrived with the SUV's, Nick walked towards Ariel. "You're sure that's okay?" Nick whispered, trying not to be overheard.

"She's right. You're the perfect alternative. Won't get any closer than that. Just don't forget you still have a job to do." Ariel warned sternly, then continued on a new note, "By the way, do have a suit?"

"Ariel, please. You got to be kidding me," Nick laughed nervously.

Ariel knew only to well that Nick hated suits.

"Well, you could always wear a dress instead, Princess," Rolf commented, standing behind Nick, clapping his shoulders.

"This isn't happening," Nick complained, retreating to the guesthouse to get changed.

Twenty minutes later Nick went upstairs and knocked at Natascha's door, but he didn't get an answer. He opened the door a little bit and peeked inside. *Rocky* looked at Nick and then to the bathroom door, before he lay down again. Nick could hear the shower, and he walked into the room and sat down on the bed. His gaze travelled around the room and rested on a picture of the two of them in Italy. He picked up the frame and smiled, before he returned it to its rightful place and let his view glide over the many pictures on the wall. He already noticed the pictures yesterday, but he did not have the chance to take a closer look at them. He stepped closer to the wall and saw several pictures of some fish that he knew, but he also saw some creatures he had never seen before. Among all these shots were also two pictures that Bernd had taken of her at the *Seattle* wreck site in Norway. Nick then walked over to Natascha's desk with the laptop, turned on the music and looked outside the window.

Natascha opened the bathroom door and peeked inside her room.

"Oh, it's you. I thought I heard someone come in." She paused as she noticed what was different about him.

"Whoa, you look so different in a suit."
Nick turned around slowly.
"Very elegant," Natascha commented with laughter.
"Just to let know, I hate suits. This is strictly professional," he complained with a grin.

Natascha threw him a killing glance, followed by her shampoo, before she entered the room.

"Would you prefer if I asked Ariel? He looks handsome."

"You two would not match, and it seems you're changing your mind rather quickly. Just a few minutes ago you wanted me to play husband, and now you're already asking for Ariel."

"Get used to your position," she kissed him and walked towards her closet where she dropped her towel.

"What's the matter?" Natascha asked with a smile, after she noticed that Nick was staring at her.

"It's not the first time you've seen me naked."

"You're right, but the other times you didn't immediately dress again."

"Remember you're just doing your job. No flirting with your costumer. Strictly professional," Natascha joked and moved her body lasciviously to the music.

"Your father's my costumer, not you. Don't forget that. I can flirt with you all day long."

Natascha walked over to Nick and wrapped her arms around him.

"Let's see, since we're officially together, we should also be appropriately dressed."

"That's fine with me. I've never seen you in a dress before, but I also like what you're wearing now," Nick laughed and admired the curves of his girlfriend.

"And you never will see me in a dress," Natascha replied and disappeared in her walk-in closet.

Berlin, Saturday, June 25th

Due to their careful planning the family arrived in time. Ariel, Rolf, Oliver and Ole-Einar had arrived about half an hour before them and coordinated their plans with the local security company that was responsible for the event.

Since there were no new findings regarding the threats, Ariel and Sigrid decided to continue as planned. They informed Dr. Richard Weber as well as Shira, Nick and Olaf, before they finally entered the building.

Oliver waited beside two members of the local security staff at the X-Ray to point his team out.

"Okay, here they come," he told the guards, then explained, "the two younger men as well as the lady with the pony-tail are each carrying a handgun."

The guard nodded, but when Shira walked by, he winced.

Not only did she have her handgun as Olaf had pointed out, she also carried a second revolver concealed at her ankle as well as a knife, which was hidden underneath her belt.

The two guards looked at Oliver.

"She had a difficult childhood," Oliver explained, not sounding very convincing.

The family stepped into the great room and Dr. Richard Weber, who was known to most of the people here, introduced his family to the guests of honor and the team leaders from the international scientist groups. Once in a while some people glanced at Nick, since he was nursing orange juice rather than champagne, but also because Natascha and her mother were known to some of the people, while he was a complete stranger.

At stroke seven, the crowd walked towards their designated tables and sat down. Several short introductions and speeches took place before Dr. Richard Weber was officially introduced and welcomed.

The expedition leader walked to the podium and took the microphone. First he appreciated the support for his expedition and welcomed everybody to the evenings festivities before he turned the subject to the expedition itself. In an aggressive tone he demanded a different course of action to protect the environment.

Nick realized soon that Natascha's father did not agree at all with the current policies and while listening to the speech, Nick was not surprised that Dr. Weber made some enemies in high places.

Looking to his side, he saw that Natascha was fascinated by her father's speech. She tended to lean forward, completely engrossed with every word he spoke. Nick looked around to the other tables and could also see the concerned faces of the other scientists, who sometimes nodded in agreement, while most of the politicians just smiled. It became clear to Nick that this expedition was much more important than he originally thought, and he was proud his girlfriend was a part of it.

While watching the guests at the other tables, he also listened to his little radio receiver which he carried in his ear. Ariel came to the conclusion that there was no immediate risk inside the building. The local security details were well organized and everything was in order.

Nick confirmed and turned his attention to the delicious menu in front of him. He enjoyed the different courses of international cuisine.

His colleagues also enjoyed some refreshments, but there was no comparison to the food Nick was enjoying. They realized that rather quickly, and they decided to make Nick's feast as unpleasant to him as possible. Since Nick could not take the radio receiver out of his ear, they knew that he had to listen to everything they said, so they placed another bet. Winner would be the person who would get Nick either to laugh out loud or to choke on his food. With the rules laid out they now started to tell him one joke after the other and it took all of Nick's willpower to resist making a scene. With everything, willpower has a breaking point. Nick's defence started to unravel. He turned to a new tactic and focused on turning his laughter into a controlled cough.

Calling him a Princess, his friends cheered him on over the radio, while an oblivious Natascha placed her hand on his back.

"Are you okay?" she asked with concern.

"I'm going to kill that miserable cow," Nick whispered harshly to Natascha, her confusion evident.

"Excuse me?"

"Shira told me a dirty joke over the radio and won a bet once I started to laugh."

"Behave yourself, you're not alone," Natascha teased him and laughed.

"Unfortunately not," Nick replied and threw a killing glance to Shira, who was performing a little victory dance up on the balcony.

After the dinner the crowd split in several groups and talked about the expedition and it's outcome. Nick saw his teammate buzzing around him and reassured him that everything was okay. In return, Nick also sent his status messages every two minutes and he finally started to relax. With one arm wrapped around Natascha's waist, she was just introducing him to her former Professor and the Vice President of the institute, which she and her father were working for. *Don't forget to tell them that she calls you a Princess and that Natascha's underwear is still missing,* Shira reminded him just at the same moment he shook hands. He struggled to stay firm to prevent bursting into a fit laughter. He smiled.

After another hour of casual conversations the crowd started to diminish, and they also planned to head to the hotel. As expected, they were some of the last guests, and it was almost midnight when Rolf joined their group.

"Oliver, Ole-Einar and Olaf are on their way to get the SUV's. Ariel and Shira are waiting outside. Whenever you're ready."

Nick nodded and turned towards the family.

"We can go now."

Natascha took Nick's hand, but Nick gently shook his head and walked a few meters ahead of the family. He signaled them to stop a few meters before the exit.

"It's better if you wait inside until the cars arrive. I'll just check with Ariel," Nick explained and stepped outside as Dr. Weber helped his wife into her jacket.

Together with Rolf, Nick stepped beside Ariel and Shira in a warm summer night. There was absolutely no wind and Nick looked around finding nothing suspicious.

"How does it look?" he asked Ariel, who was staring at the crowd in front of them, while Shira scanned the building with her eyes.

"We're being watched. At least two people, but I don't know where they are. One is close by and moving, the other is further away and stationary," the former close-combat instructor stated.

"Are you sure about that?" Nick asked and looked around, still seeing no indication of any threat.

"He wouldn't have said it, if he wasn't sure. I can sense them too," Shira replied harshly and looked at the crowd in front of them. There were at least fifty people in front of the building, and Nick had no idea which of them were a threat. Fortunately, he knew he could trust the instincts of his Israeli friends.

"The family's still inside. Do you want to wait until everybody else is gone?"

"No, I prefer a crowded place. It'll be too easy to identify them otherwise. We move them as soon as the SUV's are here."

Berlin, Saturday, June 25th
Chuck Hogan had Ariel in the crosshairs of his riflescope. He moved the rifle just a little bit and he now saw a woman with a long black ponytail looking directly at him.

Damnnit, he thought. The lights in front of the building were so strong that he could see some details regardless of the 300 meter distance he was away. He had already spotted one bodyguard, one personal driver, as well as the person who was always close by to his mark. It would be very difficult to let this assassination look like an accident. He readjusted his scope and looked at the first Range Rover that now started to drive through the multi-story parking lot.

He picked up his little walkie-talkie.

"Okay, they're yours. Get ready."

Ariel and Shira were still standing in front of the door, when they saw the driver of a luxury sedan getting out of his vehicle.

"How could this happen?" the man shouted and looked at a flat tire.

While the man was still swearing, Ariel looked to the left and already saw three more cars coming to a stand-still in the loading area which was separated with high curbs from the main street. The whole loading area was blocked.

"Shira, we'll walk to our cars, you lead. Rolf and Nick, you stay with the family, I'll trail you. Rover one, two and three, we'll come towards you. Do not drive into the loading area, stay at the street corner to the next side street. One of the cars here has a flat tire and is blocking the lane. Shira, you'll give us the signal once you're at the corner, then we'll follow."

Within two seconds everybody had confirmed their new course of action.

"We'll walk down to the next corner. One of the cars outside has a flat tire and blocks the lane. There's a little traffic jam, nothing serious," Nick told the family.

"Okay, no problem."

Nick was content with the family's lack of nervousness and walked back outside. Shira was already on her way.

She walked down the street towards the next corner and estimated the distance at around 200 meters. Although she had not seen her opponents yet, she was still convinced that someone was watching her. She walked by the cars standing in the loading lane and looked inside, but she could not find the person she was looking for. The Israeli had not even a speck of fear as she solely walked down the street. She was driven to locate her enemy and her eyes actively scanned not only the street in front of her, but also the buildings to her left and right. She was dissatisfied with her result, nothing caught her attention. She even took the time to examine the dark niches in the building, but also to no avail. With her right hand holding her Sig Sauer in her pocket, she walked to one of the "emergency exits only" to find the door closed. Looking up, she could now see the three SUV's arriving at the location. Shira found no sign of any ambush.

You could always trust your instincts, she reassured herself and decided to remain focused. Arriving at the Range Rover's without incident she looked around one more time, before she told Ariel that everything was clear.

"Okay, we can go," Nick announced and together with Rolf they walked the family down the road, knowing that Ariel would follow behind them. Rolf guarded the left side of the family while Nick covered the right. They calculated about 150 meters to their vehicles by now, but did not know that they were only 20 meters from the ambush.

Chuck Hogan monitored their every move through his scope. So far everything went according to his plan. He could only see two bodyguards, but that would not stop his men.

"Okay, go," he ordered in his walkie-talkie.

Walking down the street, Nick noticed two drunken people just outside the emergency exit doors. They were wearing torn jeans and dirty T-Shirts, but Nick wasn't too concerned about them. If they were a threat then Shira would have noticed it just a few minutes ago. Neither Rolf nor Nick knew that Shira had never seen these two men, who used the emergency door to enter the street.

They both stumbled towards them and Nick realized only now, that they were both wearing ski masks.

"Give me your money or we'll kill you," the one guy shouted.

First Nick thought that these perps were joking, but then he saw the blades in their hand. Nick acted fast and pressed his emergency button before the other guy attacked him. In a reflex Nick pushed Natascha back, and he could see the other guy attack Rolf at the same moment. Shira started running towards them. Nick dodged the knife, but his attacker swirled around immediately. It was obvious that they were neither drunk nor after the money. The guy attacked again, and Nick was able to grab his knife hand. Using the attacker's motion, Nick threw the man to the ground where he immediately rolled over and jumped up again to receive a blow to his abdomen. Nick whirled around and placed his second kick at the head, but his accuracy was slightly off. The man fell backwards, rolled over and together with his buddy ran off down the street. Ariel and Shira arrived just a short second later.

"Don't follow them," Ariel shouted and checked on the family.

Together they watched the two attackers disappear behind a corner into a dark alley. Nick still signaled the family to remain still on their position.

That was exactly what Chuck Hogan had waited for.

Chuck adjusted the scope of his rifle one last time and placed his finger on the trigger. His original plan of an armed robbery had failed, but he would still finish the job. Looking through the scope, he could clearly see the head of his mark and his finger rested on the trigger. No wind would temper the flight path of the projectile and his target looked his direction.

Chuck Hogan smiled and pulled the trigger.

"Who were those idiots?" Renate Kleinfeld spluttered, standing slightly behind her spouse as Natascha stood next to him. None of the family members entertained the thought of an assassination.

"Shooter!" Rolf suddenly screamed and jumped in front of Dr. Richard Weber and his family. The projectile hit him mid-air in in the shoulder, whirling him around before he landed facedown on the hard asphalt.

"On the roof, right of the multi-store," Rolf shouted through his clenched teeth, before rolling on his back, holding his shoulder in excruciating pain.

Two of the Range Rover's had already arrived and Nick more or less shoved the entire family on the backseat of the first SUV, before he hopped on the passenger seat. As soon as Nick had closed the door, Ole-Einar drove off as fast as he could, closely followed by Ariel and Olaf in the second SUV.

Shira stayed behind with Rolf, and Oliver strategically parked the third SUV to serve as cover for Rolf.

"You stay with him. Ariel's going to call the police, I'll take a look," Shira shouted and ran towards the building where the shot was fired from.

Oliver looked down to Rolf, who was groaning in pain and checked his shoulder. "Why the hell are you groaning? There isn't even any blood. Let's take your vest off and have a look at what they shot you with."

"You idiot," Rolf barked in between groans. "I've just been shot! I think I reserve the right to groan. I think I broke my collarbone."

Rolf sat upright and took the thin Kevlar vest off.

"Did they hit you in the head too?" Oliver commented after he saw Rolf kissing the vest.

"Oh my God! Rolf's dead! They killed him!" Natascha shouted hysterically, her parents silent with shock. Nick checked the rearview mirror and could see Natascha looking out the back window, while Dr. Richard Weber had one arm securely wrapped around his wife's shoulder.

Ole-Einar ignored the red traffic lights and stop signs and turned onto the autobahn as fast as he could. He looked at Nick who shook his head listening to his radio.

"Rolf did wear a vest, didn't he? Tell me he will survive!" Natascha still shouted, but Nick couldn't reply. He listened intently as Ariel gave them an update.

"Ariel just called in. Rolf's fine. His vest caught the bullet. He may have a fractured collarbone. We'll drive back home immediately."

Natascha and her parent's sighed in relief. Nick was more than glad that his friend and colleague would be okay, but he looked at Ole-Einar. They exchanged worrisome glances, there were too many pieces that didn't fit together.

Although it took them three hours to get to Berlin, it only took them a little over two hours to get back. The teams adrenaline was still pumping as they individually tried to process what had just happened.

"Dr. Weber, would you be so kind and open the main gate with your cellphone for us?" Nick asked once they were in sight of the driveway.

"Of course," Natascha's father replied and punched a code into his cellphone.

"The security system doesn't show any signs of forced entry," he told Nick, who forwarded this information to Ariel.

The two Range Rovers drove up the driveway in front of the house, where Ariel and Olaf got out of the SUV and walked up to the front door.

"Where's the dog?" Ariel asked.

"Garage," Natascha whispered, still in shock.

Ariel opened the door and checked the house together with Olaf. A few minutes later they both stepped outside, their weapons tucked away.

"Everything's fine, there's nobody here," Ariel calmed the family.

Nick opened the rear door of the Range Rover and gave the family a hand. Natascha walked over to the garage and let *Rocky* run loose.

"I'd recommend we all go inside," Ariel suggested and they did as bidden.

After they had all changed into more comfortable clothes, they met in the kitchen again to talk about the event.

Olaf brewed a pot of coffee, while Ariel was on the phone with Sigrid. Since Sigrid worked for the BKA before she joined *EuroSecCorporation*, she had immediately contacted the German police. Normally it was not a big deal to exchange some information. After all, *EuroSecCorporation* was a legitimate and registered company with a very good reputation. It would most likely take some time, but that would be all.

Rolf had been transported to a hospital, where he got his shoulder fixed. Lucky enough, he only suffered from a broken collarbone and Oliver stayed with him. The only person unaccounted for was Shira.

"Do you have any idea where she might be?" Nick asked Ariel, who was neither surprised nor concerned about Shira's disappearance.

"I assume she's doing her job. The fact that the two attackers fooled her won't let her rest now. She'll show up in time and is perfectly capable of taking care of herself. Dr. Weber..." Ariel continued and looked at the Professor.

"Please, Richard will do," Richard said and sat down, still shaking.

Ariel nodded.

"You have to accompany me to Kiel on board the *Northern Explorer* tomorrow morning. We'll have to talk about some things that also require the presence of the Captain as well as his First and Second Officer. It has been arranged that the Board of Directors of your Institute will be there as well. You'll also meet our operation leader, retired General Klaus Schwartze and several other members of our operation control. Are you still following?"

"Yes," Richard replied with a nod.

"I'd like to thank you. Mr. Brengmann had saved my life today. I would've never imagined, that someone would actually shoot at me."

"Rolf only did his job, and he's doing fine. You really don't have to worry about him. The important part is that you and your family are safe and unharmed."

Richard glanced at his wife, who was also shaking.

"Where's Natascha?" Ariel asked.

"I assume she's in her room."

Ariel nodded towards Nick.

Nick found Natascha sitting on her bed. She was now wearing gym pants and a plain T-Shirt. Crawling *Rocky*'s ears, she was staring at the floor.

"They shot at us," she said stunned and looked at her boyfriend.

"Why?"

Nick put an arm around her shoulder.

"Everything's okay. Rolf's going to be fine. He was wearing his vest and he just cracked his collarbone. He'll be here tomorrow."

"Do you remember Norway? When I asked if you'd catch a bullet for me? He did it. He really caught a bullet for my father. I never thought that something like this would happen. What would you have done? Would you have jumped in front of my father as well?"

Nick let his hand glide through her hair and kissed her gently on the forehead.

"If I had seen it, I would've done the same thing, yes," he admitted, although he knew that this was not what Natascha wanted to hear, and he refused to lie to her. He knew perfectly well how Natascha would react once she understood the consequences of it. After all, Nick knew that she was anything but stupid.

She sat up and looked at him.

"Oh my God! You didn't wear a vest tonight. I felt that. You did not wear a vest. What if they hit you instead of Rolf?" she was shocked and her hand covered her mouth with horror.

"But they didn't hit me. Not wearing a vest was the price I paid to sit at your table tonight."

Nick took comfort in Natascha's focus on Rolf. She would be in an even worse state if she pieced that her father, who was standing motionless, was the target, and not Rolf. Nick decided that it would be better to let Natascha believe that it was Rolf and his own life that was in danger tonight.

"Can you please stay with me tonight? I don't want to be alone."

"I don't know, but I'll see what I can do. I have to talk to Ariel first. There are several things that we need to take care of."

Nick stood up and went back to the kitchen, where he met with this remaining team. Everybody told his side of the story and it helped them create a bigger picture. After one hour, Ariel sent Nick back up to Natascha, while Ole-Einar sat in front of the video monitors. Olaf and Ariel would cover the rest of the house and the premises.

The clock ticked just passed 9.00 as Nick awoke. He smiled at Natascha as she slept before he tried to get up as quietly as possible. He recalled how difficult it was for her to get to sleep, but was glad she finally found some after resting in his arms for another hour last night. He could feel her soft hand still in his as he tried to get up. His eyes fell on *Rocky* as he sneaked out of the room, Nick could feel his penetrating gaze follow his every move. Nick hurried downstairs into the kitchen, where he met Richard and Renate, who were sitting at the table and having a cup of coffee.

"Good morning. How did Natascha sleep?" her mother asked worried.

"Good morning. Considering the circumstances I'd say she did okay. She was still very shaky last night but she finally fell asleep. She's still sleeping. How're you doing?"

"I have to admit I underestimated the situation, but I won't step down as expedition leader. Mrs. Schneider and Mr. Rashid will drive with me to the *Northern Explorer* in Kiel in about half an hour, where we'll discuss further actions. I've invested too much in this expedition to quit now."

Nick nodded and looked at Renate Kleinfeld.

"Richard's right. I'm concerned about the safety of my husband and daughter, but if he quits now, then he would do exactly what those criminals want. I came to the decision that it'll make more sense to support them so Richard and Natascha can go on that expedition. My brother will stay with his family here at our place while they're gone. He's a police officer and will take care of me and the house, so I won't be concerned about my safety."

Nick was impressed and poured a cup of coffee for Natascha. He added some milk as well as three cubes of brown sugar before he stirred it.

"Do we finally have a GPS position on our little assassin?" Ole-Einar asked the second he stepped into the kitchen.

"Shira will be back in time. I assume she's following an important lead right now," Ariel mentioned to everybody's surprise.

Nobody heard him come in.

"Mr. Weber, we can go. Rolf and Oliver will arrive shortly. Sigrid will call you later this morning to give you an update. We'll see you tomorrow evening in Kiel," the Israeli explained on his way out.

"Do you want us to call you when Shira's back?" Nick shouted after Ariel, who was already outside.

"That won't be necessary. She won't be coming back here. Don't worry about her," Ariel said as he sat in one of the Range Rovers.

"What'll happen next?" Renate asked Ole-Einar on their way back in the kitchen.

"Well, that depends. If the institute agrees, our protection detail will be extended for the duration of the expedition, but I rather doubt it. We have already two more teams working in Kiel. One team is examining the ship itself above and below the water, and the other team is checking out every person who's going to set a foot on the *Northern Explorer* during the next fourteen weeks. The Captain and his First and Second Officer are working close with us. They're all former navy and know about the situation."

"How high do you personally think are the chances that they'll try a second attempt on the life of my husband?"

"Difficult to say. We're certain they're just hired people, so it all depends on what their original job's are. Once Dr. Weber is on board the *Northern Explorer*, he'll be safe, as far as I'm concerned. With our precautions it'll be impossible to pull another stunt like they did in Berlin. We'll cover every detail," the Norwegian replied.

Nick understood only too well that Renate was worried, and he sympathized with her. He did not want to tell her that it would be absolutely impossible to protect her husband's life if their opponents were ready to die for their mission. At the moment, the entire family thought that Rolf's fast reaction and heroic actions saved the life of Richard Weber. Everybody else knew they had luck in their favour the last night.

Since he had not slept all night, Ole-Einar excused himself and left Nick alone with Natascha's mother.

Nick was still stirring the coffee.

"Three cubes of sugar and lots of milk. She always drinks it like that," she smiled.

"That's how she used to drink it in Italy," Nick explained and sat down at the table. "Mrs. Kleinfeld, I..."

"Please call me Renate, Nick."

Nick smiled, but his discomfort was evident.

"Okay, I just want to say I don't want to create any problems in this very situation. It's just that..."

"Do you love her?" Renate interrupted him.

"Excuse me?"

"A simple question: Do you love my daughter?"

For a few seconds Nick was silent. He never thought she would be so blunt and it took him a second to process the moment. He looked in Renate's face.

"Yes, I do."

"You know she loves you, too?"

"At the moment I'd say she feels the same for me, yes."

"You put that very carefully," Renate smiled. "Natascha and I talked a lot about you when she was back from Italy. Normally she talks to her friends about things like that. You've met Erika in Norway, I assume? Anyway, she only talks to me when she's absolutely serious about a relationship, and this was the second time that she came to me for advice. She told me a lot about Norway and Italy."

Nick's eyes shot up to Renate when he heard Italy.

"Don't worry, she didn't get into the acrobatic details," Renate still smiled.

"I watched both of you last night during the event. I've rarely seen my daughter so happy like she was yesterday evening. The expression on her face, when she was looking at you, the way you were holding her hand and how comfortable she looked when she was in your arm. You were pretty much the same. You could barely keep your eyes off her, even though you should've watched her father. I saw a very happy couple last night, before the shooting, of course," she added and paused for a moment.

"Natascha's very ambitious about this expedition, and she knows there's a lot of pressure on Richard. She'll do anything to help her father, but she needs someone she can trust, and who will support her. If things are not going according to her plan, Natascha needs someone strong to hold on to. She can also be very stubborn, so that certain someone must be strong enough to bring her back down to earth. Although I've only known you for two days I'm already convinced you're the right person for her. I just wish you'd be with her on that ship."

Nick smiled at the compliment.

"Nick, I want you to promise me something," she suddenly started again. "I know Richard's the target, but I want you to promise me that you'll take care of my daughter until she's on that ship."

"I promise you I'll protect her with my life," Nick promised and looked in Renate's eyes.

Renate leaned back and nodded, relieved and satisfied.

"Then go upstairs and wake her up."

Nick smiled, took the coffee and stood up.

"Oh Nick," Renate shouted after Nick, who was already at the stairs. "Don't worry about Richard. He likes you. He just thinks it's bad timing. I'll handle that."

Nick smiled and nodded, then retreated upstairs.

Natascha stirred awake as Nick entered the room. She peeked at him with one eye. "Good morning, I didn't know you do room service," she whispered sleepily.

"All part of the job," Nick replied with a smile and gave her a kiss.

"Three cubes of sugar and lots of milk. Your mother's even sanctioned it."

Natascha smiled and sat up.

"She really likes you."

"Yes, she already told me," Nick went to the curtains and pulled them open. The sunlight brightened the room immediately.

"Your father's already on his way to Kiel together with Olaf and Ariel. They're going to meet the Captain of the research vessel, the board of directors from his institute as well as our operation control to discuss the situation."

"There's not much to discuss," Natascha mentioned and sipped at her coffee.

"My father's invested way too much, he wont quit now. Monday evening he'll walk on the research vessel and so will I."

Nick turned around from the window and looked at Natascha.

"That must be your stubbornness your mother told me about."

"What else did she tell you about me..." she asked and smiled ironically.

"Nothing that you should worry about."

"Yeah, and that's exactly what makes me worry," she replied and went into the bathroom and closed the door.

While Natascha was taking a shower, Nick looked outside the window and saw a Range Rover coming up the driveway. Behind the windshield he could recognize Rolf and Oliver, but Shira was not with them.

Nick knocked at the bathroom door.

"You can come in," Natascha answered and dried herself off.

"Rolf and Oliver just arrived. I'm downstairs," he glanced through a small opening.

"I'll be there in a minute."

Running down the stairs, Nick could already hear Renate, who struggled to find words that would thank him enough. Once she was finished, Nick stepped into the kitchen and gave his friend a hug.

"Great to see you, buddy."

"Yeah, I was lucky. Could've been much worst," Rolf said and raised his right arm as it rested in a sling.

"Any news from Shira?"

"No. Once you drove off she immediately started running towards the shooter. That was the last time we've seen or heard from her. The police only arrived five minutes later. Doesn't look like there were any witnesses, but there may be a surveillance tape from the emergency exit. Sigrid's already on it and she's working with the police. The only thing we're sure about at the moment, is that the two guys with the knife and the shooter were working together. "

"Do you still have your vest?"

"No, the police took it as evidence. After I took it off, we could see that the projectile was totally deformed, but it was something small. Not really the first choice for a such a distance."

"What did they say in the hospital?"

"Ah, wasn't that bad. Just got a hairline fracture in my collarbone. The sling is more or less a precaution. The police was also okay. I gave my statement and they helped me as much as possible. Sigrid is taking care of the rest. How are things here?"

"Ariel and Olaf are on their way to the research vessel with Dr. Weber. Operation control and Klaus will also be there to discuss things. There's nothing else going on here. Did you hear anything in the local news this morning?"

"No, but I assume something will appear in the newspaper on Monday," Rolf finished mentioning, as Natascha flew down the stairs and wrapped her arms around him.

"Oh my God, Rolf. I thought you were dead!"

"That was also my first thought when they hit me," he said and returned the hug. They paused for a moment and Rolf continued. "It's not that I don't like being hugged by you, but my shoulder really hurts," he half-laughed and pushed her gently away after a few seconds.

- 6 -

**Conference Room on the research vessel *Northern Explorer*,
Kiel, Sunday, June 26th**

Captain Sven-Goran Rasmussen sat at the head of the table, looking at his pipe, still in thoughts. To his left sat his First Officer Karl-Heinz Junghans, while his Second Officer Mika Kankkunen sat on his right. Looking at them from the opposite side of the white table were retired General Klaus Schwartze, Ariel Rashid as well as Gunnar Eriksson from operation control. The other individuals who joined them were Dr. Richard Weber, and two members from the management of the institute. Representing Team A was Olaf. Their individual team leaders also represented Team B, responsible for the safety onboard the ship, and Team C, responsible for the background check of all the people on board, the *Northern Explorer*.

Retired General Klaus Schwartze had introduced all the people before Ariel took over. The Israeli covered the events of the past twenty-four hours and came to the conclusion that the assassins had not expected to meet such resistance.

Scott O'Melly from Team B stated they had finished the inspection of the *Northern Explorer* and the ship's hull was free of any mines or other types of explosive devices. Closing the initial assessment was Wolfgang Buhlmann from Team C, who reassured everybody that no one onboard the research vessel had any criminal history or additional causes for concern.

That's if none of them uses an alias, he thought about the little problem they had at hand. He had already told Ariel about it, but he didn't say it in this round. Retired General Klaus Schwartze looked at Dr. Richard Weber, who was just talking to his two colleagues from the institute, before he turned towards the Captain.

"I would like to inform everybody that I still plan to lead this expedition. I'd prefer it if my daughter wouldn't take part in it, but I can't exclude her from the expedition like this. I also won't be a able to find a replacement for her in time. But as far as I understand, we all believe that I'm the target and not my daughter. I'd also like to take this opportunity to officially express my gratitude towards Klaus Schwartze and his employees, who have saved my life last night. If my institute agrees with me, I'd still like to lead this expedition."

Retired General Klaus Schwartze acknowledged his thanks, then he looked at Dr. Weber's superior. The man on Dr. Weber's left was cleaning his glasses.

"Can you guarantee the safety of our Professor onboard this research vessel?" he asked worried.

"No, we'll never be able to guarantee someone's safety," Ariel responded shortly, before he explained. "If someone really wants to eliminate Dr. Weber, and if they've received the proper training and the proper technical equipment they need, then that person or group will succeed. Dr. Weber's location, whether he be at home, at the institute, onboard a ship or even under water, would be completely irrelevant. All we can do is minimize the risk and try to make it very difficult for the other side to get close enough to him. I personally believe that onboard of this ship we have a very good chance to keep everything under control. There is only limited space and staff on the ship, which reduces the available options for the assassins. But in order to keep the risk low, I'd have to be onboard the ship with one of our teams for the duration of the expedition. If you agree to these conditions, we should be able to reduce the risk to a minimum, but I'm still unable to guarantee his safety."

Dr. Weber looked down at the table and thought about what Ariel had just said.

Captain Rasmussen slowly took a puff from his pipe, then he looked up, eyeing everyone in turn.

"So what you're trying to tell me is that there's now a risk that a group of assassins will try to kill the expedition leader during the next fourteen weeks? Maybe even on my ship? And they plan to do that so the expedition will either be stopped or at least interrupted?"

"Given the circumstances and evidence so far, it's a fact that the goal of last night's assassination attempt was either to stop Dr. Weber from leading the expedition, or to stop the expedition itself. At the moment I believe that Dr. Weber himself was the target and not the expedition. However, their first attempt was a complete failure. We now have to find out if the other side is still planning to eliminate Dr. Weber. This could be the case if they still want to interrupt this expedition. On the other side there might be a chance that those hired professionals have already been paid to finish their job, and there's no more contact between the assassins and the people who hired them. Another option might be that the assassins want everybody to know that last night was just a mishap, but that they're very capable of finishing the job. In their line of work, a good reputation is very important. But after last night's failure they also might drop the whole plan and simply leave us alone. For the moment we just do not know," Klaus Schwartze explained.

"How high would you estimate the risk for the *Northern Explorer*?"

"Well, you know that my men have checked the vessels hull for explosives. However, I personally don't believe that any government-driven group in the world would attack a ship of this size directly. Not with the mission that this ship is about to carry out. The media interest is simply too much of a risk to handle. Everything would have to look like an accident, but even then they would have to make sure that most of the people would have more than enough time to get off the ship. I don't see a bigger risk for the ship or anybody else onboard, from those assassins than from icebergs."

"How many people would you need onboard the ship? How would they operate?"

"We'd bring one of our teams on board, consisting of five people under my command. So, including me, we're talking about five men and one woman. In order for this to work, I would need direct access to you as well as the opportunity to send or receive a coded message via satellite at any time, day or night. All the members of our team are former members of special military units, mostly divers. They know their way on a ship. We can introduce them as general security staff. Each of my men and myself will carry a 9mm handgun."

"What would be your position during the expedition?"

"I'll come up with something," Ariel smiled.

"How many cabins would you need?" the First Officer asked.

"Two should be fine, if we can get three people in one cabin."

"We do have two cabins available, that shouldn't be a problem."

Everybody looked at the Captain, who was still staring at his pipe. It would be his final decision that would determine the course of any future action.

He took another puff and watched the smoke rising up.

"All right," he finally said. "I didn't spend twenty-five years with the Royal Norwegian Navy just to duck my head. Tell me what you need, and you'll get it. Karl-Heinz, inform the cook that we'll accommodate six more people and that he should check the supplies. Fourteen weeks are a long time."

The Captain stood up and leaned on the table, resting on his hands.

"Mr. Schwartze, Mr. Rashid, as Captain of the research vessel *Northern Explorer* I will grant you permission to accompany the expedition leader Dr. Richard with one of your special units during the duration of the expedition onboard the *Northern Explorer*. Furthermore I'll allow you to carry handguns and to use them for the purpose of your assignment only. I also authorize, that you and your team will be granted access to all of our available communication equipment under the condition, that you clear all your activities with me first. In addition to that I also want to receive a personal update every twenty four hours. I also allow you, if necessary, unrestricted access to all areas and compartments of the ship after consulting either with me, or Mr. Junghans, or Mr. Kankkunen. And lastly, I reserve the right to throw every person overboard myself, if they jeopardize either the safety of the people onboard or the safety of the ship. Are those conditions acceptable?"

"Absolutely, Captain Rasmussen," Ariel replied with a grin.

"And I thought this would just be another boring trip into cold waters," the Captain groaned and sat down again.

Berlin Airport, Sunday, June 26th
Sitting in his chair in the business class, Chuck Hogan waited for the American Airline Jet to take off for its journey to New York. He ignored the welcome drink and didn't take any notice of the other passengers who walked by. Staring outside the small window, his thoughts were still at the events from last night.

How could I be so stupid? he asked himself repeatedly and shook his head. During the preparation of this operation, he relied on some information provided by his employer. *The institute might have hired some security,* he recalled the words spoken to him on the phone, but he knew better now.

The people protecting Dr. Weber weren't just overly ambitious doorman or bouncers, they were professionals trained in close combat. Including the driver from the SUV's he had counted a total of seven bodyguards. The woman with the pony-tail even ran in his direction once he had fired the shot.

Seven! he repeatedly told himself. His information had said something about one, maybe two. That would not have been a problem. But the two bodyguards last night not only blasted the assassination attempt itself, they also kicked the butts of his own two men, who were equipped with a blade. And even with the rifle he couldn't finish the job himself. He had rarely seen such a well organized unit. Chuck could hardly control the frustration that continuously overcame him.

If possible it should look like an accident. Maybe like a robbery went wrong. How could I not check the information my employer gave me? Why didn't I do my own research?

For the first time he had to admit it as a complete failure. Not only that the primary plan was crossed, even his back-up plan didn't work out.

Why did I shoot with that ammo?

The moment he decided to use that caliber he had second guessed himself about the efficiency of the bullet over that distance.

There's no point crying about last night. I failed and I have to report it. The next time we will be better prepared, much better.

Looking at his watch he eventually picked up the glass and sipped back some of the champagne.

A final check on his Blackberry showed him that his friends had already arrived in France and Italy, from where they would fly back to the United States as well.

Private Home of Dr. Richard Weber, Sunday, June 26th

Together with Natascha and her mother, Nick, Rolf, Olaf and Ole-Einar were sitting at the table. Renate and Natascha demanded that the four men would have dinner with them. Having bestowed this plan upon them, they had spent the better part of the afternoon in the kitchen and were now having dinner. Rolf struggled to hide his handicap and discomfort as he tried to cut his food with the edge of his fork. To no avail, Rolf's frustration increased. Being right-handed Rolf had great difficulties and Natascha noticed. With a smile, she was more than happy to help him cut the meat.

Rolf's appreciation of her gesture was evident as a smile spread across his face, but Nick and the rest of the crew already started to make comments. They reassured Natascha that Rolf was actually doing fine and constantly reminded her that Rolf was not nearly in so much pain as he was letting on. Sitting between Rolf and Nick, Natascha didn't want to hear anything about that. Ignoring the jokes from her friends, she insisted on helping Rolf with his food and continued to do so. Since she was in a bad mood all afternoon already, nobody argued with her. Everybody realized that Nick's upcoming departure was taking a toll on her. Even when Nick's cellphone rang, she just ignored him and turned to her dessert.

Nick excused himself and went outside the kitchen to take the call. Five minutes later he returned and stood just inside the kitchen.

"That was Ariel. The expedition will continue as planned, with Dr. Weber as expedition leader," Nick announced and Renate Kleinfeld nodded her head in agreement.

"He also said that your father doesn't want you to come along," Nick told

Natascha, who inhaled deeply with retort. "But he also knows that you won't change your mind, and since you insist on coming anyway, he's expecting you tomorrow afternoon in Kiel," Nick added quickly before Natascha could start her protest. Natascha's contempt vanished, and she relaxed as she took another spoon of chocolate pudding.

"Well, I expected that," Renate Kleinfeld commented.

"Klaus and Ariel also decided that we'll board the research vessel tomorrow afternoon. Our protection detail has been extended for the duration of this expedition."

"Well, I didn't expect that," Ole-Einar said surprised, and Natascha choked on her pudding.

"Wasn't our call. Ariel recommended it, and the representative from the institute jumped at it without hesitation," Nick shrugged his shoulders and padded Natascha's back, as she spluttered out her coughs.

"What did the Captain say after he found out we're boarding his ship?"

"He seems to be all right. Former Royal Norwegian Navy. Was Captain on one of Norwegians largest battle ships. He gave us full power on the ship, providing that we keep him informed. Ariel had to promise him that he can throw all dirt bags overboard himself. We'll operate under different positions, such as ship security, or normal personnel, but also as assistants to the German team," Nick explained.

"Does that mean our Princess will carry all your diving gear for you now?" Rolf asked Natascha, who had just regained control over herself again.

"That's exactly what it means," she shouted and jumped up to hug and kiss Nick, as he was just sitting down. Natascha's lips met his and his hand missed the chair as she bowled into him. Being caught completely off guard, Nick lost his balance and fell to the floor. Natascha laughed as she landed on top of him, her arms still wrapped around him as she kissed him passionately. The others burst with laughter, under their frivolous behaviour

"At least I have a very good explanation why I'm hurt. But I would really like to see Schwartz's face when you tell him how you just injured yourself in the line of duty," Rolf laughed.

Finally Natascha stopped and she helped Nick up, who was lying half underneath the table by now.

"Sorry, it just came over me. I couldn't resist," Natascha apologized and sat down again between Nick and Rolf.

She turned her attention back. "Is everything okay with your food? Did you like it? Do you want me to cut your pudding as well?" she asked Rolf and was in a much better mood than before.

After a long night Natascha and Nick didn't hear the alarm clock the next morning. It took Renate's loud knocking to even stir them to consciousness. Nick was thankful she had woken them up instead of one of his teammates. After they all had breakfast, it was finally time to say good-bye. Rolf decided to stay with Renate Kleinfeld until her brother arrived. Loading the Range Rover, Nick and Olaf gave Natascha and her mother some privacy, before Nick also shook Renate's hand.

With Renate in tears, Nick had to promise her, he would take care of her daughter and husband. Natascha wrapped her arms around Rolf to express her gratitude once more and said good-bye. Nick was relieved there was a miracle that night for Rolf. Though to think that he was in so much pain the night before as he tried to cut his own steak, was a marvel in itself. Now he didn't seem to have any difficulty as he wrapped his arms around Natascha, holding her tight.

Finally they got into the Range Rover and drove off.

Halfway into their four hour drive, Natascha finally relaxed. She could hear the others in deep discussion but her thoughts were elsewhere as she looked outside the window and maintained her silence. Her hand came up and she quickly wiped the tears out of her eyes and became her normal self again. Stepping outside the Range Rover in front of the *Northern Explorer*, Natascha's excitement came in bursts as she walked to the gangway.

"Whoa, now I understand why Ariel wanted us all onboard this ship. This is huge," Nick marveled and the three of them were looking at the superstructure of the research vessel. Resting at the dock, the *Northern Explorer* was several stories high and equipped with a huge crane and even a helicopter deck. Their eyes followed the ship over its complete length and after having spotted the antennas they recognized that the ship was also equipped with the latest technology. Olaf also spotted two 8m long Zodiacs that looked very tiny on the ship's deck. Looking at the rescue rafts, Nick assumed that the ship was capable of being host to more than one hundred people.

Ten minutes later Nick walked behind Natascha along a corridor.

"My cabin is right beside my father's. Each cabin has two beds and a little bathroom. Originally it was planned that I have my cabin for myself, since there are not that many women onboard. I don't see any reason why you shouldn't be able to live in my cabin." Natascha reasoned, her eyes on the floor. She turned her attention back up to Nick, and added with a seductive smile. "After all, you are my personal assistant."

"You already sound as if we're in a long-time relationship," Nick added, who's four-person-cabin was one deck below.

"Get used to it. I doubt you'll prefer sleeping two meters below me with Olaf and Ole-Einar, over sleeping in the same bed, twenty centimeters beside me. But if you do not want to, that's fine with me. I'll have better luck finding another man on board a ship in fourteen weeks than you another woman," she added, still smiling seductively.

"You won't get rid of me that easy. I'm taking my job as your personal assistant very serious," Nick replied and clapped her on her bum.

"I really hope so," she laughed and stopped in front of a cabin door.

She opened the door and stepped inside. The inside of the cabin was a complete contrast to the cold, white steel walls they just walked along. The cabin was relatively large with two single beds positioned at the inside walls. A heavy carpet covered the floor and below the watertight window was a small desk with Internet access and a phone. The walls itself were covered with a material that looked like wood panels and there was even a small TV in the one corner. Based on this first impression, Nick found this cabin quite cozy. Nick followed Natascha inside, and he saw that her personal luggage was standing in the middle of the room. It had already been delivered last week. Smiling all over her face Natascha looked around and at the two beds. Her smile vanished the moment she saw the other woman sleeping in the second bed. They could only see the long black hair since she had turned her back towards them.

Natascha turned to Nick and shrugged her shoulders in disappointment. Nick also failed at hiding his disappointment, and he returned his gaze to the woman in the bed, who now turned around to look at the people who woke her up.

Nick could not believe his eyes.

"Shira?"

"Shalom," Shira said sleepily and sat up.

Montana, USA, Monday, June 27th

It was the first time that Chuck Hogan had to report a complete failure, and voicing it just made him feel that much worse. Judging by the expression on the faces of his employers, he assumed they felt the same.

"I'll take the blame for this failure, but the information you provided me was wrong. Your information about the security detail was an assumption. It was not based on facts."

"What do you mean? Are you trying to tell me that your men can't handle some parking attendants?" the Canadian asked.

"I'm not sure how much you know about these parking attendants. You might be surprised to learn that there were seven, I repeat, seven, perfectly trained specialists to protect our target. And the fact that it should rather look like an accident instead of an execution didn't help us at all. But I admit that it was my mistake. I should have never relied on information gathered from people who are comfortably sitting behind their desk."

"Enough, that won't help us," the American interrupted.

"We trusted our source and our information wasn't correct. That was neither intended nor could we expect them to be wrong. Mr. Hogan, I understand that all your people are back in the United States?" the American continued.

"Yes, the last one arrived this morning."

"You're certain that nobody identified you and your men?"

"Absolutely."

"The *Northern Explorer* is scheduled to arrive in Reykjavik around the first or second of July, where she will stay docked for several days. Send your people up to Iceland and try to figure out if there's still a way we can make this look like an accident. We cannot afford an execution style killing anymore, it's too late for that. But I still think we can achieve our goal if you finish the mission."

Chuck Hogan nodded and left the room.

Thin Ice

On board the research vessel *Northern Explorer*,
Kiel, Monday, June 27th
Together with his First and Second Officer, Captain Sven-Goran Rasmussen had called for a meeting with Ariel Rashid and his men as well as with the expedition leader Dr. Weber. Just as he wanted to introduce everybody, Natascha opened the door and entered.

"My apologies I'm late."

"Captain Rasmussen, I want to introduce my daughter Natascha Kleinfeld. She's aware of the situation."

"Very well," the Captain replied and stood up.

"I would like to welcome you on board the research vessel *Northern Explorer*. As a former Norwegian icebreaker the ship still holds the highest certifications regarding operations in ice. With a length of eighty nine meters, the ships displacement is about five thousand tons. The draught under full capacity is eleven meters while she is twenty one meters wide. Compared to the famous *Titanic* we are still capable to float with six flooded compartments. Maximum speed is around eighteen knots, our average speed across the Atlantic Ocean will be fourteen knots. The *Northern Explorer* is equipped with the latest navigations and communications technology, and her safety equipment is also up to date. We have our own helicopter deck as well as a stationary decompression chamber and even a well stocked store. In our medical department are two specialized physicians, who are available twenty four - seven. On my left side you see my First Officer Karl-Heinz Junghans and to my right is my Second Officer Mika Kankkunen. Together we have more than thirty years of experience in navigating the polar sea. On board the *Northern Explorer* are also fifteen more members of my staff, twenty-four crew members as well as fifty-two scientists. In addition to that, we are also host to six members of two different international scientific film crews. Your unit will be housed in the only two remaining cabins. On board the ship you will be officially assigned to different positions. Mr. Rashid will explain to you the details. Are there any questions so far?"

Everybody shook their head.

"I would now like to show you our detailed route." Captain Rasmussen turned around and looked at a big screen that was now showing their simulated route through the polar sea.

"As long as we don't get a storm, we'll leave Kiel tomorrow morning and set course for Iceland. With the current weather forecast I predict we'll arrive in Reykjavik during the morning hours of the second of July. In Reykjavik we'll welcome the Icelandic expedition team with Dr. Sylvia Gunnardottir. We'll also take the two research submersibles *Polar Viking* and *Odin* on board. There will be several events and festivities in Iceland, and two teams of scientists will conduct some studies at the continental shelf in Silfra Creek. On the sixth of July we will continue our journey towards Halifax, in Nova Scotia, Canada, where we'll pick up the American team with Dr. Joseph Richard and the Canadian group with Dr. Markus Habermann with their respective gear. We will leave Halifax in the early evening hours on the twelfth to be off Cape Breton's south-east coast in the early morning hours of the thirteenth. A group of Marine Biology students from a local university will come on board and take a tour on our ship. They'll stay on board the *Northern Explorer* during the short trip up the east coast until we're just off Louisbourg, Cape Breton, where your German group has scheduled two dives. The university students will leave the research vessel there and we'll set course north, through the Belle Isle Strait and west of Newfoundland, where we'll turn into the Labrador current. That's where the first scientific projects will start. We will then follow the coast of Labrador through Baffin Bay, to cross the polar circle. North of Baffin Island we will turn westward to follow the traditional route of the North-West-Passage. First we cross the Lancaster Sound, before we stay north of Somerset Island to get into Peel Sound. From there we continue south along the Bellot Strait, until we reach King William Island, where we turn westward again into the Victoria Strait. We follow along Cambridge Bay through the Coronation Gulf until we finally reach Paulatuk. That's where the North-West-Passage enters the Beaufort Sea. The expedition officially ends in Paulatuk, and all the scientists are flying out from there. After about seven days in Paulatuk we'll take the same route back, but this time it'll take much less time. Under normal circumstances we wouldn't need more than twenty days for this journey, but since this is an expedition we're in no rush. Are there any questions regarding our route?"

Everybody shook their heads again.

"You all found your cabins?"

"Yes, everything is okay, thank you."

"Are the women in the team satisfied? I assume you have the two person cabin?" the Captain asked Natascha and Shira with a smile.

"Couldn't be happier," Natascha smiled back.

"I want to be informed immediately if you or any other woman on board this ship is being harassed by any men on board."

"Would that be before or after I throw that person under board?" Shira asked.

"It's *over board*, not *under board*," Natascha explained and smiled genuinely.

"Ius Primae Noctae," the Second Officer Mika Kankkunen whispered to the First Officer. But unfortunately for him, it was one of those things that everybody heard.

Captain Rasmussen turned towards him.

"You can keep those stupid comments to yourself. I want you to apologize at once," he shouted at him.

"It's okay, Captain," Natascha interjected, in an attempt to calm him down.

"He's a little too late for that anyway. And I doubt he'd even survive the night," she countered with a clear understanding of what Mika Kankkunen tried to whisper privately.

Captain Rasmussen nodded towards her, then threw a killing glance to his Second Officer before he left the room. Mika's discomfort was evident as he stood up and walked over to Natascha, "Mrs. Kleinfeld..."

"You can call me Natascha," she smiled at him.

"I want to apologize for my comment. I didn't intend to make a sexual remark."

"Of course you did. You just said it a little bit too loud. Don't worry, I'm a mature adult and this is not my first expedition on sea. But I'll have you know that I'm already in a very happy relationship, and that I don't plan to change that."

"Certainly," Mika said and bowed, before he turned around and walked outside.
Nick and Ariel stepped beside Natascha.
"Primae Noctae?" asked Nick.
"The right of the first night," Shira translated.
Nick raised his eyebrows and looked after Mika, who had just left.
"You've never told me something so sweet," Natascha smiled at Nick.
"What do you mean?" Nick asked puzzled.
"I mean that you should let it go. This is a ship, that's normal. Nothing to worry about," Natascha eased his worry.
"But he doesn't know you at all."
"Yes, but didn't you mark my butt when we first met in Norway?"
"It was meant as a compliment," Nick defended himself muttering.
Natascha gave him a stern look, but still smiled.
"I gave you the highest score," Nick desperately continued to defend himself.
"Yes, but only after Italy, once you had insider information," Ole-Einar interjected, stabbing Nick in the back.
Natascha's mouth fell open and she threw Nick a harsh scowl. But before Natascha could walk around the table to attack Nick, Ariel interrupted.
"Okay, like the Captain said, we'll all be working different jobs. So, listen carefully."

The next day the *Northern Explorer* started her journey as scheduled. Nick shared his cabin with Olaf and Ole-Einar, while Oliver and Ariel occupied the second cabin. The whole team had spent the remaining afternoon of the previous day to purchase some appropriate clothing for their trip. After five hours at sea, Captain Rasmussen ordered everybody new on board to participate in several different safety drills. Among other drills, they had to put on a survival suit within sixty seconds and reach the open deck. Oliver, Olaf and Ole-Einar as former Navy divers were especially used to such exercises and had lots of fun. Natascha and her father had already acquired their qualifications earlier in the spring, so Natascha enjoyed watching and cheering for her boys. During their transit to Iceland, Dr. Weber spent most of his time talking to the other team leaders either in the meeting room or in one of the several cabins, which had been transformed into research labs. Natascha took the opportunity to check their gear and to set the ROV up. Nick, who had been assigned under loud Princess cheers as Natascha's and Dr. Weber's personal assistant, helped her with the task.
Only one person was required at the moment to stay with Dr. Weber and Nick was happy that he could also look after Natascha.
On Friday evening they could already see Iceland on the horizon, and they would arrive in Reykjavik the next morning, just as the Captain had said. There had not been any incidents during the last couple days. Even the Second Officer was very friendly and kept his distance from both Natascha and Shira. Nick expected this to be the direct aftermath of a conversation that the Captain had with his Second Officer. Natascha didn't care about the Second Officer. She had already forgotten the incident and her already good spirit rose even higher when she realized that Nick had

to basically carry out her orders. On occasion Natascha would humorously tease him by snapping her fingers immediately after asking him to do something. Nick usually obeyed, but he also explained to her with explicit details how he could kill her with a simple O-Ring remover in seven different ways.

Natascha woke up early in the morning and found herself alone in her cabin after glancing at Shira's bed. Listening to the sound of the shower running, Natascha knew that her new Israeli friend had been up for a while. After a few minutes Shira came out of the little bathroom and walked to one of the small closets in which she had stowed her items.

"Good Morning," she addressed happily with a big smile.

"Good Morning, Shira," Natascha replied sleepily. She was not used to getting up at five in the morning, but Shira insisted on her usual routine.

"Shira, can I ask you something?"

"Sure," the Israeli replied as she pulled a sweater over her head.

"I'll be busy the next three days getting acquainted with the two submersibles once they're on board. Nick's going to have a half day off Tuesday afternoon, and we're planning to dive at Silfra Crack. That's the ravine between the Eurasian and American continental shelf. Do you have any plans for that evening yet?" Natascha asked and looked at Shira apologetically.

"Already? It's only been a week," Shira replied with a knowing smile.

"We see each other all day, and we're not allowed to let anybody else know about us. This is actually quite difficult for me," Natascha tried to defend herself.

"Don't worry, I understand. I won't be back before midnight on that very Tuesday. I'll be enjoying that nice bottle of wine I just won from the other three," Shira laughed and tied her shoes.

Natascha rolled her eyes in laughter.

"How are you and Ariel managing your relationship anyway? I mean, you see each other all the time now, and you don't show your feelings for each other at all. At least not as Nick and I do, but it's very obvious that there's more. I just don't understand. Do you meet somewhere secretly? Not that it's any of my business, but if the two of you want some privacy, I don't mind staying out of the cabin for a few hours. Just let me know. I have plenty of jobs to do."

Shira struggled to hide her humorous smile, but finally busted out laughing.

"No, that's okay, thank you. You're right, Ariel and I do have a relationship. But it's a very special relationship, and we're happy the way it is. Don't worry about us, okay? Let me know if there's anything else I can do for you," Shira answered and walked to the cabin door.

"Thank you Shira, I owe you."

"The way it looks right now, I assume this won't be the last time you'll ask me for that special favor," Shira winked at her on her way out.

"I hope so," Natascha muttered more to herself, before she got up and took a shower.

Only fifteen minutes later she walked outside the cabin and downstairs to the deck below. After a few meters down the corridor she stopped at Nick's cabin and knocked at the door.

"It's me, Natascha."

"Come in," Ole-Einar said and opened the door.

So far, Ole-Einar, Olaf and Nick managed to squeeze in a ninety-minute workout in the ships gym every morning. Ole-Einar just got dressed while Nick was still taking a shower.

"Good morning, boys."

"Good morning, Natascha."

"Hey, Princess. You have a visitor," shouted Olaf without looking up from his laptop.

"Stop calling him that," Natascha hissed and slapped Olaf on the back of his head.

"You're the one who started it," Olaf argued.

"Who is it?" Nick shouted from the bathroom.

"It's your superior, your beloved mistress, your precious lady," Ole-Einar shouted back.

Nick walked out of the bathroom, a towel wrapped around his waist.

"Oh, it's you," he said, aiming for disappointment. "I thought you were the cute Norwegian lady from the radio room."

Natascha glared at him with an open mouth, but before she could respond, Nick pulled her into his arms and embracing her with a long passionate kiss.

"You better behave, otherwise you'll be carrying my gear from one spot to the other all day," Natascha warned him, before she kissed him again.

"Oh, and how would that be different from the last couple days?" Nick countered.

"Would the two of you just stop, please? You know this is not fair," Olaf interrupted them.

Natascha let go of Nick and looked at Olaf.

"I'm sorry. Why don't you talk to the Norwegian girl from the radio room? She seems very nice."

"Ole-Einar and I are both happily married already," Olaf mentioned and held up his hand to show his wedding ring.

"The international sign of a broken man," Ole-Einar added and showed his wedding ring as well.

Natascha shrugged her shoulders and wrapped her arms around Nick again.

"I spoke to Shira about Tuesday evening. It won't be a problem."

"What won't be a problem?" Olaf asked.

Natascha gave Nick another kiss before she turned back to the door.

"If you get turned on just by watching me kissing him, then I think it's best if I don't say anything about Tuesday evening," she winked at Olaf and left the cabin with a smile.

"Why didn't I give her those damn fins back in Norway?" Ole-Einar shouted, once Natascha was gone and threw his T-Shirt on his bunk.

Reykjavik harbor, Iceland, Monday, July 4th,
Chuck Hogan and Robert Tyrell had spent the last couple days in Reykjavik following their mark to different events and festivities. They came to the conclusion that it would be very difficult to make their next assassination attempt look like an accident. Checking out the harbor and the area where the *Northern Explorer* was docked, it became clear to them that it would be impossible to get on board the ship. The risk of being detected was simply too high. On one of the festivities they were able to overhear some conversation, and it seemed that their streak of bad luck finally caught a break. Knowing that Tuesday might be the only chance to finish their mission, they walked back to the hotel and worked on a plan.

On board the *Northern Explorer*, Reykjavik, Tuesday, July 5th,
The two little submersibles *Polar Viking* and *Odin* were stowed safely on the aft deck of the *Northern Explorer*. Natascha and her father had spent the last three days under the watchful eyes of Senior Dive Officer Vitali Vachenko participating in an introduction course on how to operate the submersibles. It was Tuesday afternoon, and Nick had the afternoon off. Together with Natascha, they stood on the main deck and were looking at the activities in the harbor. Nick wrapped his arms around her waist a little tighter as the sunlight shimmered across the water accentuating the beautiful afternoon. The sun somehow made the 20 degree Celsius temperature that much more bearable.

The last couple days Nick had voluntarily stayed on board, while all the other members of his team had accompanied Dr. Richard Weber and Natascha to the different festivities and events on shore. Natascha had the feeling that Nick was sometimes uncomfortable when his friends saw him together with her. Natascha on the other hand, had suggested staying on board the ship with him during those events, but the fact that she was the daughter of the expedition leader required her presence on all those evenings. Today they finally had the chance to spend some quality time off board the ship and away from the others. They still planned to dive between the two continental shelves at Silfra Crack. Natascha would take the opportunity to test the underwater housing one more time. Something she did not have the time for when they were in Italy.

"Shall we go?" Nick asked and Natascha nodded.

They both went down to storage magazine, where Natascha started to assemble her closed circuit rebreather. Not having his own gear on board, Nick was allowed to use Dr. Weber's gear, who did not really plan to get into the water unless it was absolutely necessary. Compared to Natascha's, her father's gear was old school. Nick lifted the set of double tanks on the table and started to check the breathing gas and the regulators.

"Thirty-two percent," he said after a while, looking at his gas analyzer.

Since he had done pretty much nothing else the last couple days than checking the gear, the two independent regulators worked perfectly. Satisfied, Nick disassembled his unit and stowed all the gear in a big bag. He then watched Natascha preparing her closed circuit rebreather for the dive. Since it was much more complex than a normal open circuit system, it took Natascha much longer to check the whole unit. Once she was done, she attached the black cover back on the unit. Nick took her rebreather and carried it down on the dock. When Nick was back, Natascha had already changed into her thermo dry-suit underwear, and she had also packed her own bag with her dry-suit, fins, hood, dry-gloves, underwater lights and mask. Carrying the camera housing herself, Nick was carrying the two dive bags and put them beside the rebreather on the concrete of the dock. Looking up, Nick could see Shira and Dr. Weber standing at the rail and waving at him. Knowing that they would keep an eye on the gear, Nick walked back on board the research vessel to get changed. They had arranged that an employee of the local dive shop would come and pick them up.

Dressed in her warm thermo underwear, Natascha stepped beside Shira and looked at her father, who was talking on a cell phone. After a few minutes, Dr. Richard Weber signaled his daughter to come over.

"Your mother," he said and handed her the cell phone.

Natascha happily took the phone and saw a white minivan drive up and stop beside the dive gear. Reading the advertising on the vehicle, she knew that it was their dive guide. Natascha turned around and walked out of the wind, so that she could understand her mother better. The driver got out of the minivan and looked at the two sets of gear. Shira watched the man and also saw a second person with a hooded sweatshirt. To protect himself from the wind, the second man had the hood pulled over his head and shook hands with the driver before they started to talk to each other.

Maybe an old friend, Shira thought.

"Natascha, is this the dive shop that's suppose to take you out?"

Natascha glanced over the rail and nodded towards Shira, before she turned around again, listening to her mother.

Shira watched how the two people loaded the gear into the minivan. While the driver was lifting the gear, the guy with the hooded sweatshirt secured it inside. After everything was stowed away, the two men shook hands, and after a few more words the guy with the hooded sweatshirt disappeared.

Shira's attention was drawn toward Nick now, who walked beside them, dressed in the thermo jumpsuit of Natascha's father. The jumpsuit was a few centimeters too long, but much too tight in the shoulders and it was obvious that it squeezed a bit.

Natascha and Shira could not refrain from giggling.

"You're looking hot, Princess," Shira commented.

Nick simply gave her the finger as he walked down the ramp unfazed, where the minivan was waiting. Natascha finished the phone call and said good-bye to her father and, with an appreciative smile, Shira. Seconds later she and Nick were sitting in the minivan and on their way to the dive site.

"I'm Magnus. You spoke to me on the phone," the driver introduced himself. Natascha and Nick introduced themselves and thanked him for loading the gear.

"No big deal. Oh, by the way, you'll have some prominent company today. Bjorn is the son of the Premier Minister and he'll be joining us. He owns the other rebreather in the back. He's a long time costumer of ours. Very experienced. I'd suggest you relax a little bit. It'll take us a little over an hour to get there. It'll give you a great opportunity to take in the landscape."

Home Office and Operational Headquarters of *EuroSecCorporation*, London, Tuesday, July 5th

Sigrid Schneider had just arrived with the latest findings of the investigation from Berlin. After finishing his talk with Sigrid, retired General Klaus Schwartze walked over to the office of his long time friend, retired Admiral Brian Whittaker. Inside the office were not only Brian Whittaker, but also his wife Catherine and her brother Gordon Ramshaw, whom they had worked for a few weeks ago. All three were laughing.

"Good morning, Catherine. Hello Gordon," Klaus greeted them, before he looked at Brian.

"Sigrid just arrived with the latest information. Maybe you should have a look at it."

"Of course," Brian answered and followed his friend.

"I'll be back in about half an hour, just wait," he called back to his wife on his way out.

Two minutes later, Klaus and Brian sat down at their usual positions in their conference room. With them were all the members of operation control as well as Rolf, whose arm was still in a sling. Looking up at the monitor, they could see both Ariel and Shira, who were communicating to them via satellite connection from the *Northern Explorer*'s radio room.

After Klaus and Brian sat down, Sigrid immediately started to share her newest information.

"Well, I want to be honest. The cooperation with the police in Berlin was not the best, but they were willing to share some information. At this point I'd like to show you the facts we have at hand. The police believe's that we're dealing with a total of four assassins. I'm going to talk you through this. The moment the family was ready to get outside the building, a technical mishap caused the cars in front of the building to back-up. Later investigations showed that a nine millimeter projectile fired from close distance caused the flat tire. Since nobody heard the shot, we assume that the person used a silencer. The police did not find any shell casing. I didn't see the surveillance video myself, but Berlin told me that the person responsible for the mishap knew the position of the cameras and was out of view. Having successfully blocked the lane, the assassins now waited for the Weber family to walk down the street to their SUV's. Shira walked ahead of them and checked the short route. Not seeing anything suspicious, she informed Ariel that the street was safe. At this time, there was no way that she could have seen the two assassins, since they were still hiding behind the door of an emergency exit. Shira actually checked that door from the outside, but it was, as expected, closed and can only be opened from the inside.

Once Nick and Rolf were close enough with the family, someone must have signaled them over a radio. The two assassins left the building and pretended to be drunk. Getting closer they successfully covered their faces with ski masks and draw a knife, demanding the money of the family. Without waiting for a reaction, they immediately attacked their biggest threat, Rolf and Nick, who were both positioned between the family and the attackers. Rolf and Nick could successfully defend the attackers, who ran away just in time before Ariel and Shira arrived at the scene. While everybody else was looking at the two fleeing attackers, Rolf glanced towards the SUV's in the other direction. Somehow he noticed a muzzle flash from a rifle and jumped in front of the family. The projectile, a small caliber hollow point would have hit him right in the shoulder, if he would have not carried his Kevlar vest. Let that be a lesson to all of you. The energy of the projectile fractured his collarbone on impact. In the meantime, Nick pushed the entire family in the back of one of our SUV's and took off, closely followed by a second SUV which provided some cover. Our third SUV parked close to Rolf to cover him, and Shira immediately started running towards the shooter who was positioned, as Rolf told everybody, on a roof of a building beside the multi-story parking lot. Does anybody have a question so far?"

"So far everything is clear, but now let's address some of the ambiguity," Brian Whittaker said and looked at Rolf.

"Rolf, what can you tell us about the two attackers?"

"Nick and I are convinced that they were not drunk. They staggered towards us and they also babbled, but their coordination was perfect. So were their knife handling and close-combat fighting skills. Those two were professionals. They wore torn jeans and dirty T-Shirts. But my attacker was also wearing light combat boots. They both used identical knives, the same type we used back in the Special Forces. I didn't smell any liquor at all and they both moved much too fast for bumbling drunks. Besides that I'm sure that my attacker had perfectly manicured fingernails and clean hands. I noticed a tattoo on his lower arm, but I can't remember what it was. Those weren't drunks, they were professionals."

"Sigrid, what do we know about the shooter?"

"Shira was able to find his nest. He had a great view over the main entrance as well as the emergency exit in the back. From there he could also see the complete route that our cars had to take from the parking lot to the entrance. It was an excellent position. The distance to Rolf was one-hundred-and-eighty-five meters, declining just eighteen meters over the whole distance. Almost a straight shot. The only reason why Rolf was able to see the muzzle flash was because of the lights. Just a few minutes before the shot was fired, every second streetlight in the area was automatically switched off. It's part of an energy saving program during the hours of low traffic. This was unknown to the shooter. Regarding the projectile I have to come to the conclusion that taking the shot was only plan B. The police also agrees that the whole attempt should have looked like a robbery gone bad. The reason they failed is most likely from bad reconnaissance and the fact that they totally underestimated the abilities of our people."

"What do we know about their identities?" Klaus Schwartze asked.

"Not much. At all times they stayed out of camera covered areas. There is, however, one promising shot from the camera monitoring the emergency exit. Once the two dirt bags were hiding behind the emergency door, they automatically started a motion-controlled camera. We could isolate one frame in which the camera recorded a tattoo on the lower left arm from one of the attackers. I assume that's the guy who attacked Rolf."

Sigrid used the remote control and zoomed into a still picture. It was a black and white shot of a simple tattoo, which looked like a combination of a few numbers and some initial letters.

Brian asked Sigrid to zoom in closer until he could clearly read the tattoo.

"Oh my God," he said and looked in several concerned faces.

Reykjavik, Iceland, Tuesday, July 5th

Chuck Hogan steered his rental car on the edges of the parking lot of the local hospital. By coming here he was hoping to find out if their new plan to finish the job was successful or not. Walking over the parking lot, he went over the plan again, and he was satisfied that Robert had been able to arrange everything. Nothing could go wrong this time, and nobody would expect any foul play.

What a waste, he thought, walking inside the hospital and thinking about his mark.

Home Office and Operational Headquarters of *EuroSecCorporation*, London, Tuesday, July 5th

All eyes rested on the tattoo. Everybody recognized that the tattoo was showing the blood type of its bearer.

"We're dealing with former special forces or mercenaries," Klaus said what everybody already knew.

"That'll totally change the situation and all our previous assumptions, Sir," Ariel commented via satellite, speaking for the first time during this meeting. All eyes were now on the screen, from which the Israeli was talking to them.

"If they're really former members of a special force, then we have to reconsider one very important issue in this whole matter. Sigrid, can you show us the picture with the flight path of the projectile, please?"

Sigrid took the remote and only four seconds later, everybody was looking at the picture Ariel was referring to.

"We now have to assume, that all four of them are professionally trained. That also means, that the shooter is a high precision marksman. The flight path of the bullet is almost ideal. No wind and no other factors that would temper with the flight of the projectile. I have to agree, that the selected ammunition was not perfect for this kind of shot. It rather looks to me like a last minute decision for a back-up plan, and that this ammunition was the only thing available at such short notice. Nevertheless, in the hands of a trained sharp shooter it's more than enough. Have a close look at the flight path. We know exactly where the shooter was. Now check out the position of Dr. Weber. He's standing right beside Natascha. When Rolf jumped in front of them, the projectile hits him in his shoulder. Rolf measures one meter ninety-five, Dr. Weber one meter ninety-two. If I want to shoot someone with that ammunition over this given distance, I'd always aim for the head. Especially once I know that my target is protected by several people and probably even wearing a vest," Shira continued Ariel's theory.

"The shot was too low to hit the head. He would have hit him in the chest," Klaus Schwartze acknowledged.

"Oh God," Sigrid commented and clicked on the remote control until she saw the picture from the warning. Richard Weber stood outside his car and his daughter sat on the passenger seat.

"Dr. Weber has never been the target," Shira explained.

"His daughter Natascha Kleinfeld, one meter seventy-four tall," Ariel continued.

"She's the target!"

Thingvellier National Park, Silfra Crack, Iceland, Tuesday, July 5th
Nick and Natascha were actually diving the ravine between the two continental plates. As expected, the visibility was endless, and together they were gliding through the ice-cold water. They turned towards one of the walls and examined the ravine that divided the Eurasian continental plate from the American. Natascha and Nick both enjoyed the silence between those two vertical walls, which was only disrupted by the exhale bubbles from Nick's open circuit scuba unit.

Sinking down just above the bottom in about 18 meters of depth, they even saw some fish, swimming effortlessly in the mild current created by underground wells.

Natascha was constantly taking pictures, and Nick was afraid that she would be the person to fill a 16GB chip in record time. Before the dive she had promised the film crew from National Geographic some pictures. Fascinated by such clear water, they followed the walls towards the lake. Although they were both very experienced divers, they had never experienced such great visibility in open water conditions.

The electric sensors in Natascha's self-regulating closed circuit rebreather permanently checked the contents of her breathing gas. Only a few more minutes and the high level of carbon dioxide would make a diving accident unavoidable.

Home Office and Operational Headquarters of *EuroSecCorporation*,
London, Tuesday, July 5th
Retired Admiral Brian Whittaker shook his head in disbelief and went back into his office. His wife Catherine and his brother-in-law Gordon Ramshaw were still waiting.

"I'm sorry I kept you waiting so long. I'm afraid you'll have to go for dinner without me," he apologized.

"Did something happen?" Gordon Ramshaw asked concerned.

"We just found out that we spent the last couple days protecting the wrong person," Brian explained, still shaking his head.

"Are you talking about the Professor?" Catherine asked.

"Yes. Can you imagine? Those bastards weren't after him after all," Brian continued and went over some notes on his desk.

"But who were they after?" Gordon asked.

"His daughter. On the twenty-fifth of June, one of our men already caught a bullet, when he jumped in front of the Professor. We just found out, that they did not aim at the Professor, but at his daughter, who was standing next to him. We were lucky. If you want to excuse me now, I have to go back to the meeting," Brian apologized again and left his office with some notes.

"Well, I guess I can get ready then," Catherine said and stood up.

Her brother nodded at her, still thinking about Brian's comments.

"Since when are they protecting a Professor?" he asked.

"Oh, this is because of that big international polar sea expedition. There was a serious threat against the expedition leader, and his institute decided to hire our company. One of our staff has a friend in the institute. He remembered her and contacted us. I'll just go and get my jacket."

"Yes, sure. Would it be okay if I just use your phone here? I left my cell phone in my car and I have to call the office."

"Certainly," Catherine replied and pointed at Brian's phone.

"Use Brian's. You just have to select a free line."

"Thank you," Gordon said and watched his sister walked out of the office. Seconds later he picked up the phone .

Thingvellier National Park, Silfra Crack, Iceland, Tuesday, July 5th
The steel deck was the perfect entry spot for Silfra Crack, and Magnus was patiently sitting on it and waited for his four guests to finish their dive. Today he did not find it necessary to enter the water himself.

Two of his guests had already spent hundreds of dives together in this ravine and almost knew it better than he did. The other very experienced couple were a marine biologist and her boyfriend.

Nevertheless, Magnus was wearing his dry-suit. He wanted to be prepared, just in case something would go wrong. After about half an hour he believed that both teams must be on their way back already. Since three of them were using rebreathers, and only one was using an open circuit unit, he lost track of the bubbles after a while. To reassure himself, he put his fins on and slid into the cold water. Once in the water, he rinsed his mask and put it on, before he looked under water. Due to the great visibility he could normally see his divers from a great distance. He glanced around, and it was not the cold water that let his blood freeze. Just one meter above the bottom, in approximately seventeen meters of depth, he recognized the black cover of his guest's rebreather. The different stickers as well as Natascha's name on it, made it very easy to identify. Its user was gently drifting on the side but didn't move at all. The dive buddy didn't know what to do and constantly signaled for help to the other two divers.

Goddamn rebreathers! I can't see any bubbles! Magnus cursed. He wondered why the dive buddy wasn't reacting. Magnus looked to the other two divers and noticed that they now recognized the situation.

Come on...swim towards them...Bring them up!

Finally one of the other divers rushed towards the casualty. Magnus decided to get out of the water and to put his own gear on to assist the divers back out.

Just when Nick and Natascha turned around to dive back the ravine, they both noticed the emergency signal one of the other divers was giving with his dive light. Nick looked at Natascha, but she could not see what was going on just thirty meters in front of them.

Nick used his own dive light to signal if everything was okay. He wanted to make sure that the other dive team was not in an exercise, although he was sure, they did not mention it before the dive.

Once the other diver only answered with another hectic emergency signal again, Nick realized that something was horribly wrong. He briefly looked at Natascha and rushed off to the other team. Getting closer he could see that Bjorn was now drifting on his side, obviously unconscious. Nick was not sure if he was still breathing. Once he reached him, he noticed that Bjorn had his eyes closed. Without wasting another second, Nick got hold of Bjorn and started the emergency ascent. Natascha, who had just arrived seconds after Nick, quickly checked the instruments on her unit and assisted Nick on their way to the surface.

As soon as they reached the surface, Nick started to take Bjorn's gear off, while Natascha signaled for help. Luckily they were only a few meters from the steel platform, and in less than a minute Magnus and Nick had Bjorn back to the exit point.

"What happened?" Magnus shouted and looked at Tomas, Bjorn's dive buddy.

"I don't know. He just didn't react to my signals any more. First I thought he was concentrating on his buoyancy, so close above the ground and with a different rebreather."

Nick walked up the stairs with his double tanks. Once at the top step he turned around and pulled Bjorn up to the dry part of the deck. Kneeling down, Nick was checking for any vital signs, while Magnus was running to the minivan to get the oxygen unit.

"I can't feel any pulse with my gloves, but I think he's still breathing," Nick said and made room for Magnus, who was not wearing gloves.

"Weak pulse and barely breathing," Magnus diagnosed and put the oxygen mask on Bjorn's face. After they were sure that Bjorn was breathing on his own, Nick took his gear off and helped Natascha and Tomas to get to the platform. They were still in the water and holding on to the gear that Bjorn had used. Natascha took her gear off as well and kneeled beside Bjorn, securing his breathing mask and checking his vital signs. While Magnus was calling an ambulance, Nick took the emergency sheet out of the oxygen unit, checked his watch and started the timetable.

After a few minutes Bjorn regained consciousness again and was breathing normally. His heartbeat had also recovered just shortly after he was breathing pure oxygen. Knowing that Bjorn was doing okay, Natascha thought about what went wrong. When they arrived at the dive-shop, Magnus had introduced them to Bjorn, the twenty-three year old son of the Icelandic Prime Minister. Bjorn was a passionate tech-diver and used a different rebreather than Natascha. As a tech-diver it was normal that he showed a great interest in Natascha's rebreather, and he asked her if she would mind swapping the gear for this dive. Under normal circumstances, divers using a rebreather never let anybody else use their gear, but Bjorn showed Natascha that he just replaced the complete breathing loop and that the counter lounges had been disinfected after the last dive. Natascha was also interested in diving Bjorn's rebreather. After a few minutes of begging, Bjorn even promised Natascha, that Iceland would be forever in her debt.

Convinced that his gear was clean, she agreed and they both explained their gear to each other. Once at the dive site, they double-checked their units again, and Nick and Natascha finally entered the water a few minutes after Bjorn and Tomas.

Forty minutes after the accident, Bjorn sat in the rear of an ambulance and was still breathing oxygen. He had full memory of the accident until seconds before his black out, and he once more thanked Nick for his fast rescue. Natascha felt guilty of the accident, since he was using her gear, but Bjorn waved all her apologies aside. He made it clear that he was the only one to blame, and that it was nobody else's fault. While he thanked Nick once more, Natascha walked to her rebreather to take a closer look.

"Any idea what happened?" Nick asked and stepped beside her.

Natascha shook her head.

"I almost killed him," she whispered, her eyes filling with tears.

"Come here, Angel," Nick whispered back and hugged her closely.

"You know that's not true. You both checked your unit more than once. All the instruments worked flawlessly. It wasn't your fault."

"We just lifted the cover for a quick check inside. We just checked the breathing loop and the tanks and the instruments. I should have opened the cover completely," she sobbed.

"Listen, nobody checks their gear as precisely as you do. You have done so many dives with that unit without any problems."

"I still must have missed something."

Magnus walked over to them and looked at the ambulance.

"Carbon dioxide poisoning. He was lucky you were not too far away. If he was deeper and had to do some deco, then it could have turned ugly. Any idea what went wrong with your rebreather? Maybe old scrubber?"

Natascha wiped some tears out of her eyes and shook her head.

"I just opened a new box this morning. Our storage room is under lock and key, and my father is the only one who has the key. The scrubber can't be old. I assembled the unit in the storage room and checked it thoroughly. Everything was fine. After that I didn't take the cover off."

Natascha removed the huge black cover and her mouth dropped in shock.

"Everything seems to be in order," Magnus commented, looking over Natascha's shoulder.

"Nick, do you remember that small good luck charm that you bought for me in Italy?"

Nick remembered the little plush orca key chain. He joked that it would be her good luck charm for the expedition, and that she would have to carry it all the time.

"Yes, why?"

"I glued it to the inside of the cover. It's gone. That means that someone had opened the cover from my unit, after I closed it."

"Are you sure?" Nick asked concerned.

"Absolutely. Here, look. You can see where it was glued. I took special care," she said and looked at Nick.

"Well, I certainly didn't open your rebreather."

"I know it wasn't you," Natascha snapped back.

"Maybe it was your friend?" Magnus tried to help.

"What friend?" Natascha asked, ignoring Nick's cell phone as it started ringing.

"Well, that guy at the ship. The one who helped me load all your gear in the van."

"We didn't ask anybody to help us with the gear." Natascha said angrily.

"He told me that he's a member of the crew, and that you and Nick would take a couple more minutes. He said, that you asked him to help load the gear."

"Was he alone with my rebreather?" Natascha asked unnerved and glanced at Nick, who was still ignoring his cell phone.

"Well, now that I think about it," Magnus said and walked towards the Minivan. "He might have spent a few minutes with your rebreather. He told me he would tie down the gear, what he actually did. I also remember, he didn't mention Nick's name. He said 'Natascha and her friend,' that's strange."

Magnus opened both rear doors and took a look inside. Natascha immediately found the little plush Orca behind a wooden sheet. It must have fell behind it, while the guy manipulated her unit. She picked her good luck charm up and turned around to show it to Nick, who was now finally on the phone.

"Nobody from our team and nobody on board of the ship would ever touch my rebreather without my presence. I made that pretty clear to everyone," she said to Nick.

Nick put his cell phone away.

"That was Shira. We have a problem, Natascha. This was not a diving accident after all."

Nick took Natascha aside and told her, that after careful consideration of all facts, she was the target of the assassins, not her father. Since he did not want to upset her even further, he did not share the details that had lead to their conclusion.

"Well, that doesn't surprise me anymore," she barked and walked a few steps away.

"I'm still going to continue. I don't care what my father says. Everybody is on board anyway. Nothing will change," she shouted angrily.

"I don't disagree with you, and nobody said anything about quitting. Not your father, not your mother, not Ariel and I didn't say anything either."

Natascha walked towards Nick and wrapped her arms around him.

"I'm sorry, I didn't mean it."

Nick kissed her on her forehead.

"I know, but we really have to go now," he whispered back.

While Magnus was loading his emergency gear back in the minivan, Nick and Natascha walked over to the ambulance to bid farewell to Bjorn.

"How are you doing?"

Bjorn nodded and gave him the thumbs up, since he was still breathing from an oxygen mask.

"We just found out that someone had tempered with Natascha's rebreather this morning. Once we're back, we'll have a closer look at what he did. If you want, we can give you a call or send you an e-mail," Nick explained.

Bjorn nodded again and took the mask off.

"I'm certain it wasn't your fault. You have saved my life today, Nick. If there's anything I can do for you in the future, just let me know, okay? I owe you big time."

Nick nodded and shook his hand, while Natascha gave him a hug, not without apologizing once more.

Reykjavik, Iceland, Tuesday, July 5th
Chuck Hogan sat in the lounge of the local hospital and was reading the newspaper, while his partner Robert Tyrell was monitoring the *Northern Explorer*. Both were eager to find out if today's attempt on their marks life had been successful or not. Chuck Hogan noticed that an ambulance had rushed away from the hospital under all signals. He did not speak or understand the local language that well, but he was certain he heard someone talking about a diving accident. Without any particular expression on his face, he still pretended he was reading the local newspaper, although he didn't understand a single word. But since there was a picture of the research vessel beside the article, he was sure the story had something to do with the expedition. Once in a while he looked up from the newspaper and through the glass doors where he could see the driveway leading to the emergency unit. It felt like hours since the ambulance had left, but he finally spotted the vehicle driving up the driveway, this time much slower than it left.

Maybe it has worked after all, he thought. He admitted that their plan was anything but perfect, but when they had learned the previous evening that their mark was planning to go diving today, they decided to take the chance. The former member of an American special unit put the newspaper back to the other magazines

Thin Ice

on the table and walked outside. He watched his steps and made sure that he was not spotted by any of the security cameras he saw when he came in. He stayed clear of hospital staff and covered his face to prevent identification, as he walked up to the emergency unit. As he approached the vehicle, he realized, that he did not have to go any further. The person, whom the paramedics were caring for was definitely not Natascha Kleinfeld. He identified the man to be in his early twenties as he walked by breathing from a portable oxygen unit. Once he and the two paramedics walked into the hospital, Chuck walked over to the driver.

"Excuse me please," he said in English.

"A very good friend of mine was diving this morning and I heard the rumor of a diving accident. Could you please tell me if she is..."

"Don't worry," the driver replied in English, but with a strong Icelandic dialect. "You did hear right, there was a diving accident, but this diver here suffered from carbon dioxide poisoning. He was lucky, that his buddy reacted in time. A little bit longer and with a less observant buddy, and this could have turned ugly."

"Oh, thank you. Well, let's hope he'll get better soon. I'm glad it wasn't my friend," Chuck answered and turned away.

Chuck knew that the likelihood that two divers would have the identical diving accident in the same day, was very slim. As soon as he had reached his car, he took his cell phone out of his pocket and called Robert Tyrell.

"Take a guess who has just arrived at the ship," Robert asked him with a sarcastic tone.

"I know, they must have swapped their units. The diver in the ambulance suffered from carbon dioxide poisoning. "

"So it did work, it's just that the wrong person was using the unit. Nothing we could have done about that. She didn't even look like she had a headache."

"Okay, we'll meet at the airport. We tried our best, and at the moment there's nothing else we can do. I assume they'll figure out soon enough what's going on," Chuck Hogan said and flicked his cellphone shut with a click. Hesitating for a second, he flipped it open again and looked at the display. He thought he had noticed a reminder of a new message on the display and he was right. To avoid drawing any attention inside the hospital, he had turned off his cell phone, that way he didn't hear the new message arriving. He punched in his pin code and held the unit to his ear.

After listening to the message, he immediately erased it.

Great, you could have told us that before, he thought and got in the car.

- 8 -

On board the *Northern Explorer*, Reykjavik, Tuesday, July 5th
Together with her father, Ariel, the Captain and all other members of Team A, Natascha was sitting in the meeting room on board the research vessel. While Shira was furious that she witnessed the assassinator sabotage the equipment and did nothing to prevent it, Natascha stared blankly, her elbows on the table and her head resting in her hands.

"Did you find out how he manipulated your rebreather?" Ariel asked.

Natascha looked at him from the corner of her eyes.

"He tampered with the scrubber and the sensors. Pretty easy, pretty fast, pretty effective."

"If we still assume that the assassin is a former member of a special force with underwater demolition training, then he knew how to manipulate Natascha's unit quickly and effectively," Nick explained.

Ariel, who was not a diver himself, trusted Nick's statement.

"How are we going to proceed?" the Captain asked as he cleaned his pipe.

"We proceed as planned. The only thing that's changed for us, is that we now have to protect Natascha instead of Dr. Weber. Since Natascha is his personal assistant, our security measures will remain the same. The assassin was definitely not from the ship. I also don't believe that he set foot on the vessel, however we will still search the whole ship, including the underwater hull. We will remind the guards to remain alert. The dive guide looked at pictures from all the people on board, but he was positive that the person is not among them. For the moment I'd suggest that either Shira or Nick stay at Natascha's side. That's what we did before and that way we won't draw much attention. Natascha, have you told anybody else about the accident?"

Natascha shook her head.

"I called my wife," Dr. Weber said.

"Don't worry. She's fine. She supports any decision you make," he told Natascha who looked at him.

"How do you feel, Natascha?" Ariel asked.

Natascha straightened up and still shook her head in disbelief.

"I don't know. On the one side I feel stupid, because Bjorn was in an accident with my gear. On the other side I also know that it wasn't my fault. How could I know? Fact is, this was a very efficient way to get me killed very slowly."

Natascha was now in rage and Nick placed a hand on her shoulder.

"I'm wondering why I'm their target. The police didn't think so, you didn't think so and luckily Rolf caught a bullet that was meant to hit me in the head. What good would it be, if I were dead?"

"The goal in Berlin was to put enough pressure on your father so that he would

Thin Ice

not go on this expedition. For them, he seems to be, and I'm sorry to tell you this, too important, impossible to kill him in an open street. It is fact, that the whole thing should look like a robbery gone wrong. Taking the shot was a back-up plan. However, the expedition is finally on its way, and today's attempt on your life showed us, that they're still serious. It also showed us something else. At this point, whether you're alive or dead won't stop this expedition any more. So they either wanted to demonstrate that they're no rookies, or they're after you for a different reason, which I doubt. However, I don't believe that they can attack you while you're on board this vessel and on sea. On a good note, we now know that you're the target, we'll concentrate on you," Ariel explained and looked at the Captain, who looked back at him in return.

Ariel began again, "Captain Rasmussen. How many people are responsible for the submersibles?"

"Their trials are over, and they're secured on deck. Our Diving Officer Vitali Vachenko is the only person responsible for them now. Natascha was a co-pilot on most of the tests during the last three days, and everything was fine. I doubt someone manipulated the submersibles. We actually have two of our security cameras pointing at them at all times, just in case. But like I said, I don't think there's any chance that someone from outside the ship could have tampered with the submersibles."

"Excellent," Ariel replied.

"Before we return to our stations, I'd like to have a word with Natascha. Richard, Shira and Nick, you may stay if you wish. That would be all. Thanks."

The remaining people stood up and left the meeting room. Natascha smiled, as each expressed their support on their way out.

Ariel waited until the door was closed.

"Natascha, I know that you're shaken-up at the moment, and I want you to know that this is completely normal. I understand that…"

"Listen, Ariel," Natascha interrupted him freely. "I admit that I was shocked earlier this afternoon, but I'm fine, trust me. Rolf caught the bullet in Berlin, and Nick was there today to save the day, okay? I'm pretty sure that Nick would've noticed it in time, if I had used my unit today. I'm not too worried about the gear. It's all under lock and key, and absolutely nobody has access to it. Nick is at my side all day, and Shira shares the cabin with me during the night. There's really no chance for me to wander off by myself to get into any trouble on this ship. I'm fine, okay?"

Ariel and Shira smiled at each other.

"Very well. I still have to ask you some more personal questions, just in case we have to identify you, let's say in the unlikely event of an abduction. I don't like to be fooled by a woman with too much make-up."

"Who's saying anything about an abduction?" Natascha asked surprised, her eyes widening.

"Nobody, but trust me. If I ask you about something, then I have a very good reason for that." Ariel paused for a moment, withholding the real reason for the questions, then prompted.

"So, do you have any special identification marks? A birthmark or a scar?"

Natascha looked at her father.

"I do have a little scar on my right elbow. Not much, just two stitches. Fell with the bicycle when I was a kid," Natascha explained and pulled up the sleeve of her sweater. Everybody looked at the tiny scar.

"Oh, and I have a pierced belly button," she continued and showed the piercing.

"Do you take any medications?" Ariel continued.

"Only the pill," Natascha mentioned and looked at Nick.

"Anything else?"

"No, not that I know of. Can I go now? I have to go to the bathroom," Natascha asked and rose from her chair, hurriedly.

"I'll take you to your cabin, if that's fine," her father asked and looked at Ariel, who nodded in agreement.

Once the door was shut again, Ariel looked at Nick.

"What do you think? How did she handle it?"

"Well, shortly after the accident she was shocked. Once I told her that she's the actual mark, and that this was not a diving accident, she became upset. Better that way than being paranoid. I think she'll do fine. I'll talk to her later."

"Shira, what do you think?"

"It won't throw her off track. She's too stubborn for that."

"Do you know anything else about her that might help us? Identification marks?"

"She has a small tattoo on her bum," Shira tried to remember with closed eyes. "She must have forgotten to mention it. I just saw it the other day, after she had taken a shower. It looked like a fish," she explained and was squeezing her eyes tighter as she tried to remember more details.

Ariel looked at Nick.

"It's a little dolphin, blue in color. It's placed on her right hip and it's looking to the right, about five centimeters long."

Ariel looked at Shira, who was now staring at Nick, obviously impressed by his observational skills.

"You're getting old, Shira," Ariel teased her.

"Remarkable," she acknowledged and smiled at Nick.

"Hey, I'm just doing my job," Nick defended himself smiling.

"Go to her cabin. Talk to her. Let me know, if there's something wrong."

Nick nodded towards his superior and stood up.

"Tell Natascha that I'll stay up this night and that I won't be back before the morning," Shira whispered, winking her eye.

Nick walked down the corridor. In front of Natascha's cabin, he met Dr. Richard Weber, who just closed the door behind him.

"How's she doing?" Nick whispered.

"Well, I'm actually surprised at how well she's doing. She either blocked it out, or her stubbornness has taken over and she defies the odds. Not sure. Are Shira and Ariel still in the meeting room? I wanted to ask them something."

"Yes, they're still there. Shira just opened a nice bottle of wine. Maybe you want to accompany them?"

"Yes, why not? Are you going to stay with her until Shira's back?"

"Yes, but as long as she locks the cabin from the inside, not even we can get to her. She's absolutely safe in there."

Richard nodded in agreement and gave Nick a pat on his back, when he walked by.

Nick watched as Richard walked down the corridor, and only after he had disappeared, Nick knocked at Natascha's door.

"Yes? Who is it?"

"It's me, Nick."

Nick could hear Natascha unlocking the door, before she opened it.

"It's good that you keep it closed all the time. How are you doing?"

"Ah, not sure. This is the second lucky escape. First it was Rolf, and today it was sheer coincidence that I swapped my gear with Bjorn. I'm not sure how I would have reacted to that poisoning. "

"I'm sure you would have noticed it in time," Nick tried to comfort his girlfriend.

"Not necessarily," Natascha replied and threw herself onto the bed.

Nick sat down beside her and started to massage her neck and shoulder.

"Listen to me, Angel. I'll not allow anything to happen to you now, okay? We'll all take special care of you from now on. We all know that the guys responsible for this never set foot on this ship. You heard the Captain. We turned the whole ship inside out without finding anybody. Those guys are not on this ship."

Whether it was Nick's massaging skills or the comfort of his words, Natascha's eyes closed and a smile flicked at her lips.

"I know. Little lower," she whispered and waved with her hand behind her back.

Nick let his hands glide down her back further.

"You're sure you're all right?"

"Yes, I'm just afraid that something will happen to you, instead of me."

"Listen, nothing's going to happen any more. Neither to you, nor to me or anybody else, okay?"

"Okay, " She whispered silently, turning her head to the other side, "keep massaging."

Nick continued and extended his massage to other body parts, which Natascha obviously enjoyed with closed eyes.

Nick startled as she suddenly jumped up and looked at her watch.

"We have about an hour and half left before Shira will be back," she stammered and hurriedly undressed.

"Don't worry. Shira won't be back before tomorrow morning. We have all night for us."

It was hardly a moment later that they were both in bed again

Dr. Weber walked back to the meeting room, where he met Ariel and Shira. They were both sitting in front of an excellent bottle of wine and were accompanied by Ole-Einar and Olaf.

"Nick's with her. She's fine," Richard informed and sat beside the Norwegian.

Shira smiled at him and offered him a glass, while Ariel just nodded.

"Here, try the local wine. It is delicious."

Richard appreciated the gesture and lifted the glass up, swirling it around with scrutiny. Content, he took his first sip. "Indeed, it is excellent. Where did you find it?"

"I won a bet," Shira explained and looked at Olaf and Ole-Einar.

"Mr. Rashid, I know that you and your men are doing your best to provide us with as much security as possible, and I would never question your qualifications, but I have to admit that I'm concerned for the life of my daughter," he changed the subject suddenly.

"You'd be a bad father if you weren't."

"What happens if one of those lunatics gets their hands on one of the submersibles?" the expedition leader asked and looked in the faces around him.

"Like I said before, there's always the chance that something might happen. So far, we know that it's impossible for the assassins to get on board the ship. They had to manipulate the diving gear in the middle of the pier, something that would never had happened if we knew back then what we know now. If they had a chance to get on board and manipulate one of the submersibles, they would have done it. But they didn't have that chance. We have a twenty four hour video surveillance for both submersibles for tonight. We also have two guards at the gangway. They can't get on board the ship. Tomorrow, during daylight, we will load the submersibles back into their storage containers, which will be locked and monitored with cameras. We just have to disassemble the lights. I will personally keep the only key. Both submersibles will undergo a triple check before any dive anyway. Nobody, who is not involved in the dive itself, will get near them. They're as safe as they can be."

"I hope you're right," Dr. Richard Weber replied and emptied his glass.

He thanked everybody once more and headed for his cabin.

On his way through the corridors, he met some of the other expedition leaders, who wanted to ask him something, but he put them off until the next morning.

He opened the door to his cabin. As expedition leader, he occupied the cabin just by himself. Once he had locked the door, he sat down at his desk and started to play some classical music from the stereo. He relaxed, closed his eyes for a moment and waited for the computer to start up. After a few minutes, he concentrated again and filled out the expedition logbook. Once he was finished, he read his report again and looked at the tasks scheduled for the next few days. Although it was a very emotional day for him, he was very tired. He was now awake for almost 24 hours, and he could barely concentrate. Once more he leaned back and closed his eyes.

What kind of a father are you anyway? He asked himself with frustration. *When your daughter was born, you were on an expedition for your dissertation. Your twenty-one year old girlfriend was at home alone and had just given birth to your daughter and you were in the Antarctic examining fish.*

He would never forget the call that Renate had made over satellite back then. The Captain of the research vessel on that expedition had called him over the intercom to the bridge, where the Captain had given him the phone with a broad smile.

Everything went fine, no complications, Renate's father had told him. *Beside the irrelevant fact that you were on the other side of the earth at that point, everything was perfect.*

He wasn't able to talk to Renate back then, only three days later he had a chance to speak to her. Once he heard Natascha crying on the phone, he could not hold back his tears and words were unable to form. The lump in his throat he felt back then returned. He swallowed harshly at the memory.

He remembered it clearly, as if it was yesterday, when Renate had asked him if he would come back to them.

When you had left for the expedition back then, you even didn't know that she was pregnant.

Richard had noticed Renate's uncertainty about their relationship the moment she told him that she was pregnant. Although he had immediately promised her that he would come back and care for them, Renate had never lost that uncertainty. Maybe that was the reason why they never got married and Natascha kept her mother's name.

During these important nine months, you haven't been with your wife. You've even missed the birth of your one and only daughter. Not for one hour, no, you missed it by about eighteen-thousand kilometers and two months. And now, twenty-six years later, you're again on board a ship, leading an expedition. And you have even managed to drag your only daughter into this mess, too. We've not even left Iceland, and your daughter has already survived two attacks just by sheer luck. Two attacks on her life, just so that you would not lead this expedition, and here you are.

But even if I would have stepped down two weeks ago, this expedition would have still taken place, he argued with himself. *That's true, but they wouldn't have shot at your daughter's head. And they wouldn't have tried to poison her, so that she would drown slowly.*

Richard closed his eyes and tried to relax. He concentrated on the music, but his mind was still rattling.

And on top of that you have been against the only person who made your daughter happy in these difficult times. The only support that she has in this moment, since you have to lead the expedition.

And of all your qualities, she has to get your stubbornness. You could have convinced any other person, that it would have been safer not to take part in this expedition, but with your own daughter, you didn't even try. You have even been too much of a coward to tell her yourself, that you didn't want her in this journey. You had left this task to her new boyfriend.

Yes, but she would have insisted to come anyway, he continued his argument with himself.

So what? You are the expedition leader. One word and she would have been off this expedition. There were enough other scientists, who could perfectly execute her duties and who were equally qualified but with even more experience.

Yes, but she would have never talked to me again, he kept arguing.

Maybe, but her life would not be in mortal danger.

Richard opened his eyes and wiped a tear away. He looked around, turned the computer off, leaned back in his comfortable chair and closed his eyes once more. Seconds later he was asleep.

Richard kneeled on the boardwalk in Berlin, looking at his daughter. Natascha was lying in his arms, a gunshot wound on her forehead. Her blood was running over his hands and he was looking up. Ariel and Shira were both holding Nick, who wanted to get to Natascha. Richard looked back at his daughter. She looked back out of her dead, lifeless eyes, accusing him.

"Why me, Daddy? It's your expedition, not mine. Why did they shoot me and not you? Why are you with me, when I die? Where have you been, when I was born? Why did you ask me if I wanted do accompany you on this expedition, when you knew that I wouldn't say no? Is this expedition so much more important to you than my life?

Richard woke up with a scream and looked around in his cabin.

He was still sitting in his chair, but two hours had already past. He turned the CD player off, went into the bathroom and splashed some water in his face. Cleaning his face he looked at the mirror.

All I wanted for my daughter was for her to be happy.

For the first time this evening, he did not argue with himself.

When Nick looked at his watch at 5.30 the next morning, Natascha was still sound asleep, her head resting on his shoulder. Nick gently kissed her forehead, but she didn't react.

After yesterday's incident, Nick felt helpless, even vulnerable, and he had shared his feelings with Ariel. He knew that they could do little against a sniper operating from a long distance away, but this was different. Although Shira had even seen the assassin yesterday, he was still capable to manipulate the rebreather right in front of the ship in a very effective way. Even with the team's conclusion that it was not a well-planned operation but rather an opportunistic action, it still unnerved him. The thought that it would have been a very effective method if the dive was deeper and not so many other divers were around, made him feel that luck was the basis to Natascha's survival. Nick pondered how they gathered the intel about the dive, then concluded that they must have picked it up when they were trailing Natascha during the events. The fact that they knew how to manipulate a rebreather fast and efficient, did not surprise anybody.

Considering all this, and everything they learned from the Berlin incident, Nick was certain that they were dealing with professionals. Professionals, who were determined to finish their job, which was to eliminate Natascha. And it was obvious they were careful enough to consider patience and jump at the first good opportunity that would present itself. Knowing that time wasn't an issue for the other side, and

Thin Ice

the fact that they had already followed them from Europe to Iceland, Nick was afraid Natascha's luck would run out. But something else was clear for Nick. So far it had been impossible for the assassins to set foot on the ship.

Nick's weak smile turned serious as he looked at his still sleeping girlfriend. He gently kissed her once more. It was now quarter-to-six, and Shira would walk into the cabin any minute now, dead tired, demanding a few hours of much needed rest.

When Natascha rolled over in her sleep, Nick attempted to gently slide his arm out from underneath her head. Still asleep, Natascha rolled over again and clasped his arm.

"Not yet," she mumbled.

"I have to go, Angel. Shira will be here any minute and I have to get to my position," he whispered back.

"Just five more minutes," she mumbled, still sleepy, her eyes having not yet opened.

The temptation was hard to resist, but Nick reluctantly got up, put his clothes on and started to gather her clothes from the floor. He quickly surveyed the floor again to make sure he had everything, then placed it all on the chair. Leaning down again, he kissed her one more time, but Natascha was already fast asleep again.

"I love you, Angel," he whispered and looked at her, when he heard a noise at the door. Nick got up and unlocked the door for Shira.

"Good Morning," Nick greeted her.

"Good Morning," Shira whispered back, after she noticed that Natascha was still sleeping.

"Are you tired?"

"No, not really. I stayed in Ariel's cabin. Oliver stayed up all night monitoring the gangway. Everything's fine. How did she sleep?" Shira asked, her eyes trailing back to Natascha.

Nick also looked at his girlfriend, and with a smile he straightened the blanket again, but Natascha didn't notice that either.

"Well, as far as I can tell, she slept very well. We should try not to wake her up."

"I'll lay down for a few more minutes. We have an appointment with the harbor authorities at eight," Shira whispered.

"Is Ariel in the mess?"

"Yes, he wants to supervise the loading of the submersibles into the container later this morning."

Nick nodded towards Shira and left the cabin. Walking down the corridor, he could hear Shira locking the door from the inside again. Two minutes later, Nick was sitting together with Ariel in the canteen. They enjoyed the peaceful early morning and had breakfast together. Beside them only ten other people were sitting scattered at different tables.

"How did she sleep?"

"Good. Any news from England or Germany?"

"Not yet. We're trying to find out the nationality of the assassins in Germany. Did you recognize anything when they spoke? A dialect maybe?"

"No," Nick replied and shook his head.

"They only said a few words and that sounded pretty normal to me. Did we catch anything on video from the guy who manipulated Natascha's gear yesterday?"

"No, at least not on our systems. Shira will talk to the harbor authorities this morning. Maybe we're lucky and their cameras caught something, but I rather doubt it. We spoke to Natascha's mother. Everything is fine there. Richard seems to have a much harder time dealing with this, than he wants to let on. It seems to me that he's blaming himself for the assassins targeting his daughter."

"Do you think they'll try again?" Nick asked, looking at his friend. He hid the worry from his voice, though it was evident in his eyes.

Ariel took a sip from his tea before he answered. He looked in his cup and glanced to the attractive Norwegian from the radio room, who was just sitting two tables away. Placing the cup back on the table, he smiled at Astrid, who returned the gesture, before he returned his attention to Nick.

"Nick, you know as well as I do, that Natascha has been very lucky the last two times. I can only hope that you'll be there again if they should try it once more. Since Berlin they know, that she has heavier protection than they expected. So far we're certain that the assassins are former members of a special command. You know that they are very good at what they are doing. Although I have to admit that I don't see the immediate connection behind their actions. On the one side, we're dealing with former special forces who try everything to let their attempt look like an accident. But everything they did has not been very effective yet. I doubt they want to send us a message or anything else. The fact that they tried another attempt on Natascha's life yesterday makes me believe, that it's not the delay of the expedition, but rather Natascha herself is the target. It seems to me, that they want to use Natascha to gain control over her father. Maybe they want him to do something special, or maybe they want him to refrain from doing a certain task or whatever. Regardless, his reaction yesterday showed clearly that he has no idea about it."

"What do we know about him? Did we check him out?"

Ariel waved his concern aside.

"I checked him out and have followed his life back to the day he was born. He is a very solid person and does not give any reason for concern. If he carries a secret, then neither I nor Shira and her old employer found out about it. That would be very unusual for a scientist in his position. We just have to be better than them, and we have to control our emotions."

Nick knew only too well, that his final words were aimed at him. Looking in Ariel's cold eyes only confirmed his suspicions.

Nick nodded, to make it clear, that he had understood.

"What are we going to do today?"

"The Captain wants to cast the lines in two hours. Once we're on the open sea, we will load the submersible back in its shipping container. I will keep the only key and seal the locks. They will have a presentation tonight for the crew member in the

Thin Ice

mess hall. A few scientists will present their work and show some videos and pictures. Might be interesting. As far as I know, Natascha has also prepared something."

"Yes, Richard has given her an assignment. I saw her working on it on the computer."

"Stay close to her. Do not make it to obvious that the two of you are together," Ariel said and stood up. The Israeli went and cleared his tray away, not without smiling to the beautiful Norwegian once more.

Heathrow International Airport, London, Wednesday July 6th
While Robert Tyrell flew directly back to the States, Chuck Hogan had taken the longer route and flew to London first. Although he had received clear and straight instructions regarding contacting his employer, he had to inform him personally about what happened in Iceland. He used the time and sat down in a little Bistro with free Internet access. Drinking a coffee, he surfed the Internet and checked the latest news around the world. Finally, after he was certain that no one was watching him, he started his real search. It took less than a second and the search engine provided him with the web page of *EuroSecCorporation*. The website confirmed the information he had received in Reykjavik. The former member of the special forces visited all the different pages of the website, getting all the information he wanted. Once he was done, he checked for other security companies on the internet to cover his tracks. After that, he erased the search history of the computer and left the Bistro to get to their meeting point.

So he was now sitting in another Café, drinking a much better coffee than he had in the Bistro, and waited for his employer.

Chuck looked to the clock and his attention suddenly shifted to the crowd of travelers coming towards him. The British contact emerged from the crowd and they shook hands like old friends. The British ordered another coffee and they talked about the British weather and the latest politics.

"How was your business trip?" the British finally asked.

"Well, it could have been better. The contract fell through. Our business partner had changed their protocol on a short notice and did not take part in the actual negotiations. We received the necessary information regarding this matter too late. But it's good that we now finally have all the information we need."

"Did you talk to the Americans?"

"No, not yet."

"Our business partner found out that we preferably deal with their junior partners, instead of the seniors," the British added with a concerned look.

"Yes, I received your message. I believe they had to come to this conclusion after our last meeting with the junior partner."

"Yes, obviously. We'll continue as planned. The North Americans will try to get you and your team on board of this ship. You and your men will do exactly that, just as we have discussed previously. We should meet again in a few days to discuss the details."

The British leaned back and took a USB stick out of his pocket. Looking at it, he gave it to Chuck.

"All the information and plans are on this drive. Couldn't e-mail it to you. Make sure you don't lose it. One week from now, I'll know what's possible and what's not. It is very important that the North American's do not find out about our agreement. We will stay in contact," the British said and left.

Chuck Hogan's eyes followed the British contact until he disappeared in the crowd of travelers. He thumbed through his pocket and put some money on the table and walked to his gate.

On board the *Northern Explorer*, Reykjavik, Wednesday July 6th
Natascha got up around 8.00 o'clock and stepped in the shower. The running water prompted Shira's weary eyes to open. She noticed the clock and realized she had fallen asleep for another hour. She sprung out of bed and planned to visit the harbor authorities as soon as they were open. Once Natascha was dressed, Shira accompanied her for breakfast.

"What are going to do this morning?" Natascha asked her friend, still tired and sipping her tea.

"I'll go to the harbor authorities after breakfast. Maybe their cameras caught a glimpse of our terrorist." Shira noticed how Natascha winced and decided not to bother to conceal the concern in her voice, as she looked at her with new eyes.

"Are you okay?"

"Don't start with this again. I'm fine, I will survive."

"Well, that's the whole point of our job," Shira explained and laughed.

"Yes, I know, but what can possibly happen to me on board this ship? I mean, I can't spend all day being locked up in my cabin."

"I don't believe you're in danger right now. Nobody can get on board here in Iceland. The security precautions from the Icelandic authorities are excellent. It's important that you don't worry too much. I want you to know I'll always be there for you, if you want to talk or need any help, okay?"

A weak smile turned Natascha's lips as she nodded her appreciation, "I need to find my father. We want to load the submersible today."

They both got up and cleared their tray. After Shira had dropped Natascha off at one of the meeting rooms, the young Israeli left the ship and walked to the harbor authorities.

About one hour later, Ariel sat in the bridge, where Captain Rasmussen gave his final orders to set sail again. Sitting at a table in the rear area, Ariel was looking at the video footage from last night. Due to their thermo- and motion-activated infrared video system, it was nearly impossible to enter the ship undetected, especially with Oliver at guard, looking at the gangway. Nick, Ole-Einar and Olaf spent the last two hours inspecting the hull of the ship below the waterline. Due to the sheer size of the *Northern Explorer*, it took a few minutes to report that everything was fine. The First Officer had finished his checklist and reported all stations and engines ready to operate. Captain Rasmussen ordered the gangway to be hauled back on the ship and called the harbor authorities over the radio. They cleared the previously filed course and warned all the other ships and boats in the area. The Icelandic harbor authorities confirmed the research vessel that their shipping channel was free and wished them a safe trip.

"The *Northern Explorer* appreciates your hospitality," the Captain finished their conversation. He checked the two radar screens, only to see a free fairway for the next six miles.

"Is the gangway on board and secured?" He asked his crew.

"Gangway on board and secured."

"Cast all lines."

The First Officer repeated the Captains order over a little Walkie-Talkie and looked outside the window. A crew of three people, both at the bow and the stern, were pulling in the heavy lines. As soon as the lines were clear of the water, they signaled back and Captain Rasmussen gave order to sail.

"Helmsman, bow- and stern thruster. Get us clear of the quay wall."

"Aye, aye, Captain. Bow- and stern thruster."

The helmsman used two joysticks at the same time and Ariel, who watched this maneuver, noticed how the *Northern Explorer* silently glided laterally from the quay wall.

"Only bow thruster. Turn the bow forty-five degrees into the channel. Watch our stern. The tide wants to push us back to the quay."

"Aye, aye, Captain. Only bow thruster. Eyes at the stern."

The huge research vessel silently swung into the shipping lane.

"All engines slow ahead. Watch for fishing boat."

"All engines slow ahead. Being on look-out for surface contacts."

"Constantly check our depth here in the harbor, especially at the exit of the shipping lane."

"Aye, aye, Captain. According to our charts, we'll have enough water below our keel."

"Yes, the famous last words of the helmsman. I don't care about the chart. I want you to check the sonar all the time."

"Yes, Captain."

Slowly, the *Northern Explorer* made her way through the shipping channel, ready to enter the Atlantic Ocean.

Ariel, who had monitored the maneuver with great interest, looked up to Shira, who had just entered the bridge a few seconds ago.

"Did you find something?" he asked her as she stood beside him.

"No, the person seemed to know exactly where the cameras were positioned. He knew we'd get suspicious if they manipulated the cameras, so they located surveillance free areas. When he was in camera sight, he was always wearing his hood. It's impossible to see his face. When I saw him from the ship yesterday, he kept his back to me so nobody on board the ship would be able to identify him. I hoped for more luck with the harbor authorities camera's but the guy was smarter."

Ariel's mannerisms lacked all sense of surprise after hearing Shira's update.

"Yeah, I was afraid that would be the case. Something doesn't seem right. If they're really this determined to kill either Natascha or Richard, they could have done it a long time ago. That mistake in Berlin just shows their arrogance. Why do they want to make it look like an accident? Somewhere out there is the guy who hired these people, and that guy is worried about something. I have no idea what that might be. Where's Natascha anyway?"

"We had breakfast together. After that I accompanied her to her father, where she still is. I just checked in with her on my way up. Where are the boys?"

"Nick, Ole-Einar and Olaf are just changing. They inspected the hull underwater, but they didn't find anything. Oliver was up all night and is now sleeping. Did you get a chance to talk to her?"

"We talked, but not much. It looks like she's handling it well, given the circumstances. I made it known she can always talk to me. What about Nick?"

Shira asked, lowering her voice to make sure the crew on the bridge could not hear her.

"Nick's worried something will happen to her. And he's even more worried that it'll happen when he's with her. I told him this morning that he has to control himself a little bit more."

"Do you think he can do that?"

"He doesn't have a choice. Otherwise he'll leave this ship as soon as we're in Halifax," Ariel whispered back and turned his attention to the Captain now.

"Captain Rasmussen, could you please call me as soon as we can store that submersible?"

Captain Rasmussen held up the binoculars to continue monitoring the shipping channel as he replied.

"Give us another hour. We'll be on the open sea by then. I don't want my Helmsman running over fishing boats because of activities on deck."

Ariel nodded his agreement and went to the radio room nearby, where he connected his laptop to the satellite feed.

"Good Morning, Astrid," the Israeli greeted the attractive Norwegian.

"Good Morning," she replied and smiled at him.

"Can I upload a message to the satellite, please?"

"Sure, why not. Let me know if you need help."

Astrid turned her attention back to her two computer screens, as Shira caught up with the scene in front of her. Her eyes turned sharply towards her countryman.

Ariel smiled innocently and shrugged his shoulders.

"Tell the boys I want them on deck to load the submersible in one hour, please."

"Sure," Shira replied displeased, her glare never faltering as she closed the door on her way out.

A few minutes later she stood in front of the cabin that Nick shared with Ole-Einar and Olaf. Without knocking, she opened the door and walked in. While Nick was still in the shower, Ole-Einar was standing nude in the cabin. Olaf was already dressed and lay in his bunk.

"Normal women knock on the door before they enter a men's chamber," Ole-Einar complained and dressed quickly.

Shira just shrugged her shoulders carelessly.

"Ariel wants the submersible stored in one hour. He wants all three of you to meet him on the deck and help."

Ole-Einar nodded and at stroke 10.00, Ole-Einar, Olaf and Nick met Ariel and Dr. Richard Weber at the two submersibles on the deck. They discussed, that from this moment forward, one of the two submersibles was only assigned to Natascha and her father.

Ole-Einar walked around the submersible and took a closer look at the rail system the submersible used to slide back into the container.

"Okay, the only things that have to come off are the lights. After that we should be able to push that can back just the way it is," the Norwegian said after he had inspected the system.

"I want to remind you, that the lights themselves costs more than eighty-thousand Euro. Please be careful with it."

"Does that mean we're not allowed to use a hammer?" Olaf asked with a serious grin. "Just kidding," he added quickly, after noticing the displeased scowl that clouded the expedition leader's face.

Using utmost care, the submersible and its light system was stowed away around noon. Ariel locked the container, sealed the locks and put both keys in his pocket.

"One less object we have to monitor."

Natascha spent the rest of the afternoon working on her project focused on the behavioral science of Sharks that was due in the evening. It was more of an information session for the crew members, but she knew most of the scientists would prefer this to the usual movie presentation.

After Nick and his buddies had cleaned their dive gear from the morning dive, Nick walked to Natascha's cabin. He knocked at the door, said his name and smiled as the door unlocked.

"Hi, everything okay?" he asked Natascha and kissed her on the forehead.

"Yes, I just don't know what I should say tonight. It should be easy material for the crew, but I don't want to embarrass myself in front of other scientists. I don't want them to believe my father's the only reason I'm on this expedition."

Nick and Shira exchanged an exasperated if-those-are-all-your-problems look, before he returned his attention back to his girlfriend. He smiled before he continued.

"What are you talking about anyway?"

"Well, I guess you've noticed there was a paper in the canteen where crew members could choose from a list of topics. I offered to talk about Orcas, Sea Leopards and Sand Sharks. Unfortunately, the majority had chosen Sand Sharks, and my father wants me to talk about them for an hour. My problem is, that the guy from the Icelandic team is also talking about sharks before me, so I better come up with something unique."

"Is there anything unique with Sand Sharks?" Shira asked, as she quickly disembled her whole gun in just three seconds.

"Yes, actually there is. They were the first sharks where scientists could monitor a special breeding behavior. "

"Now we're talking," Nick commented with a sheepish grin, but both women ignored him.

"While they copulate, the male shark bites the female shark on her belly. The female then falls in a state of rigor for most of the breeding act and up to one hour afterwards, she lays motionless on her back. And Nick, there's no need for comments."

Nick raised his eyebrows, but he held his silence as he glanced to Shira for support. To his dismay, she was smiling.

Natascha further explained, that because of this breeding behavior, it was possible for scientists to study sharks in captivity without seducing and stressing the animals.

"From there I plan to switch over to the Great White Shark, where scientists recently noticed a similar behavior. That should be enough then."

"Well, I find that very interesting," Nick tried to compliment Natascha. With his luck she ignored him again and, without saying a word, went into the bathroom.

Nick paused a moment as perplexity engulfed him. He turned to Shira and waited for an explanation.

"She thinks you share intimate details with the other guys," Shira whispered quietly, once she was certain Natascha was out of earshot.

"What? I've never done that!" Nick hissed back loudly, the shock overbearing his senses.

Shira held up her hand and continued before Nick could spurt further protest.

"I'm going to talk to her. You better go now. Let me handle this."

Nick stood up and shook his head in disbelief as he left the cabin.

Minutes later he met Ariel in the radio room, where the Israeli was flirting with Astrid.

"Any news?" Nick interrupted willingly.

"No, everything is quiet."

"I just spoke to Oliver. He'll go to the presentation tonight and I'll spend the evening on the bridge. I've already seen Natascha's presentation on her computer. It's interesting."

Judging the way Ariel looked at him, Nick knew he was already suspicious.

"That's fine with me, but make sure you're there on time."

Nick nodded and retreated to his cabin, where he met Olaf and Ole-Einar.

"Everything all right?" Ole-Einar asked, completely unable to excuse Nick's odd behaviour.

"No. Natascha thinks I'm sharing intimate details with you guys and has decided not to talk to me anymore," Nick explained and threw himself in his bunk.

Ole-Einar and Olaf both looked puzzled.

"We can tell her that's not true. Why would she think something like that?"

"How should I know? Shira already wants to talk to her."

Ole-Einar shrugged his shoulders and got up.

"Time to get ready if we want to get a bite to eat before the presentation."

Olaf rose to his feet also, expecting Nick to do the same.

"Go ahead, I'm not hungry," Nick informed coldly.

"I switched with Oliver for tonight and I'll go up to the bridge in a few minutes."

"Whatever you say," Olaf shrugged and closed the door on his way out. He and Ole-Einar knew it would be pointless to talk to Nick now.

A few minutes later in the canteen, they sat beside Ariel. Shira and Natascha followed just a minute later. While Shira joined their table, Natascha chose to sit at another table. She sat with the Second Officer and two other crew members and immediately started a conversation.

Shira and the others concealed their surprise but could sense it among the group, as they all looked at Natascha. With no comment they turned back to their plates.

Ariel wiped his mouth with a napkin and smiled at Shira. His eyes scanned the canteen and noticed Dr. Richard Weber together with most of the members of the German team at another table.

"Is there something I should know?" he asked, still smiling.

Shira took a deep breath and pushed her fork through her food.

"She thinks Nick is telling intimate details about their relationship," she whispered, without looking up at Ariel.

"Did Nick share some intimate details about their relationship?" Ariel asked everybody, still smiling.

"No, since he got back from Italy he's never mentioned anything to us."

"Did he say something that would explain her behavior?"

Everybody shook their head, avoiding eye contact with Ariel.

"Great," Ariel continued, not breaking his smile even though he angrily threw his napkin on his plate.

"Our protecte doesn't talk to the one person who was close-by each time there was a problem, anymore. And after two failed assassination attempts."

The others now realized the gravity of the situation.

"Shira. Have you talked to her?" Ariel asked.

"Yes, but she didn't pay any attention. She doubts Nick shares the same values in their relationship."

"But she still realizes that Nick has a job to do?"

For the first time in this conversation, Shira looked Ariel in his eyes.

"Listen Ariel, I know damn well what kind of job Nick has to do. I tried to explain it to her and you know that. It's not my fault," she snapped at him.

Ariel still smiled and looked around. He spotted Astrid as she walked by winking to him.

Ariel winked back.

"You're all going to the presentation?"

Everybody nodded as an answer.

"Do you want us to talk to Natascha?" Olaf asked his superior.

"No, I'll take care of that myself."

Montana, USA, Friday, Wednesday July 6th
Everything about the estate seemed to stay the same, unharmed, unaltered, though important matters did the opposite. The American was sitting with his Canadian friend in the huge living room in front of the open fire. They both watched the golden liquid swirl in their glasses before they took a sip.

"I found out the *Northern Explorer* will arrive as scheduled on the eleventh of July in Halifax. Is everything clear?"

"As far as I know, everything's clear. I don't have any information that would indicate anything else," the Canadian replied and nodded.

"Do you know why it failed again in Iceland?"

The American shrugged his shoulder.

"There's no way to get on board the ship. They even checked the hull underwater for mines. There was only one gangway, and they had that one under constant surveillance. Anyone who doesn't belong to the crew did not get on board the ship. Our men overheard a conversation during one of these events, that our target was planning a private dive in Iceland. They actually found a pretty good way to let it look like an accident again. It was just sheer coincidence that the girl got away. Anyway, there's nothing we can do about that now."

"Do you think Chuck and his men will work with the other?"

"They're driven by money. I don't think that there'll be a problem. If everything goes according to our plan, then Chuck and his guys won't have to get active."

On board the *Northern Explorer*, North Atlantic, Sunday, July 10th
The last three days went by without any serious incident. Following Ariel's instructions, Nick kept his distance from Natascha, who spent most her time checking some gear or planning the details of her upcoming submersible excursions. Toward Nick's colleagues she remained friendly, but cool. With just Shira she spoke like everything was normal. Natascha even tried to avoid Ariel as much as possible. She knew she was no rhetorical match for him in case of an argument. The only person she totally ignored was Nick.

Being by herself in the storage magazine for the German diving gear, she was just assembling her underwater light. She inspected the O-Rings from the akku pack as well as the cable leading to the separate light head itself. Her thoughts however switched from her father, who had already given her an I-told-you-that-this-would-happen look, to Nick.

She thought about it a moment, and realized she lacked a solid reason why she was so upset with him. She could not believe he told anything to his friends. And even if he did, what was the big problem? None of his colleagues made any embarrassing comments, and since Iceland they were even more helpful and friendlier than ever. Natascha's thoughts suddenly raced in a violent pattern. *Maybe it's because I have to take the initiative all the time. I had to ask him, if he wanted to go diving with me in Iceland. I always have to ask him first. He never suggests anything.*

Natascha hardly smiled when she found the root of her bad mood. She questioned their relationship, because she felt that Nick was not returning her feelings.

You know damn well that it's not a pleasure cruise, and that he's taking his job very seriously. He took the first step when he drove all the way down to Italy, just to see you. And every unscheduled activity off the ship is very dangerous, and since Iceland it's only possible at great expense. Besides that, we're in the middle of the Atlantic. And where exactly do you want him to take you here on board this ship? To a romantic candle-light dinner in the engine room? But why is he not giving me a little something? Because he can't buy any flowers on this ship and Ariel has ordered him not to make your relationship too obvious. Why does it matter? Every time he's alone with you, he tells you how much he loves you.

Before Natascha realized what she did, she threw the little wrench against the steel wall of the room, from where it clanged as it fell to the floor. She could suddenly feel her anger burning, as she was abruptly ripped from her thoughts. She hated it, when her stubbornness was losing an argument with her common sense.

Two seconds later Ole-Einar, who was just working in the storage room next door, was standing behind Natascha.

"Is everything okay?" he asked, his eyes scanning the room.

Natascha rolled her eyes and took a deep breath.

"Yes, everything's fine. The wrench just slipped," she lied and was surprised to see the gun in Ole-Einar's hand.

"Okay," Ole-Einar said finally, still scanning the room. After he was convinced nobody else was in the room, he smiled back at her and returned to his duties.

Natascha knew Ole-Einar did not believe her, but she couldn't tell if she cared. She got on her knees and picked up the wrench. Once she turned back to her underwater light, she could feel her heart beating in her throat. Shira seemed to have emerged out of nowhere.

"Jesus, you scared me," Natascha said after she caught a breath.

"Ariel wants to talk to you. Now," Shira explained coldly, then left.

"Ariel? Why?" Natascha asked taking a few steps towards her, only knowing too well the reason why he wanted to talk to her.

"You'll know soon enough, in our cabin," Shira shouted back from the end of the corridor.

Five minutes later Natascha was sitting on her bed in her cabin. Shira was standing at the table. Since Natascha did not know what to say, she decided that it was better to remain silent.

Someone knocked at the cabin door, and a few seconds later Ariel came in.

Natascha greeted him with a smile and shrugged her shoulders.

"You wanted to talk to me?"

"Yes, indeed. I do want to talk to you," Ariel said, polite as always, as he closed the door.

"I want you to tell me what the problem is between you and Nick."

"There is no problem, it's..."

"Don't lie to me, Natascha." Ariel interrupted her, almost whispering.

"I want to know what the problem is between you and Nick, or our entire team will leave this ship tomorrow morning in Halifax at once."

Natascha swallowed hard. Although she always assured everybody that she was fine, she could not deny that she felt much safer in the presence of Ariel and his team. She survived two attempts on her life while under their watchful eye. Both times, Nick had been with her. Hoping for some support, Natascha looked to Shira.

"Don't look at me, Natascha. I've told you several times that Nick didn't tell anyone any details about your relationship. I also told you that you can talk to me if you want to. You ignored both."

Knowing Shira was telling the truth, it was Natascha who felt hurt.

"And how can I be certain he didn't say something? There are always those stupid bets going on between you. He must have said something."

"The guys had some bets running, and I was also involved. That's true. But think about this, Natascha. At your house in Germany, when we first met, it was you who told us about Nick's T-Shirt. You started the whole subject there. That was one bet. During that event in Berlin we had another bet. But that had absolutely nothing to do with you at all. And you were the one who had asked me in Iceland, if I could spend the evening somewhere else, not Nick. Nick has not told anything. And when you were preparing your presentation, you jumped all over him. He came up here to help you."

"But I have the feeling that I always start things. He never takes the initiative. I suggested him to accompany me to this event in Berlin. In Iceland he rather stayed on board the ship, instead of coming with me to the event. I even had to ask him if he wanted to go diving with me. Everything comes from me," Natascha burst furiously.

"Natascha, I'm not sure if you realize how much responsibility Nick has," Ariel explained. "When we were assigned to this case, he immediately asked us if there would be problem because the two of you were dating. Back then he already knew, that it could get complicated. Your idea to let Nick accompany you to Berlin came so quick, that no one else had a chance to think about an alternative. The reason why he wasn't all too happy about that, was the fact that he couldn't wear a vest, a little detail that might have saved Rolf's life. And there were several reasons that he didn't want to go with you to the event in Iceland. First of all, he wanted to give his team members the opportunity to get off the ship, since the two of you had already planned to go diving, and because his friends did not have the opportunity to visit their girlfriend during the night. But there was another reason. I ordered him to stay on board. It was his turn to take the shift on the bridge that night. The fact that he had concerns about your diving trip is simple. Although we didn't know at the time that they were after you, he was still the only one responsible for you during that time. He's afraid to lose you, and he has to stay focused. Besides that, he has to make sure that you stay focused as well. I have supported your relationship from the beginning. I assigned him to you as your personal assistant, so you could spend more time together. I could have given him Oliver's job or Olaf's. I allowed the two of you to go diving in Iceland. I also didn't object when he visited you during the night, something that is against all rules in our business. I'm not sure about your feelings for him, but I know how he feels about you. This was the only thing he told me. You have to tell me if you can deal with this situation. Otherwise I have to draw the consequences from it."

Natascha was thinking hard, but she could not find a way to counter Ariel.

Her stubbornness was still refusing to reason.

"I know you're responsible for my safety, and you're all doing an excellent job, so that I can do my work and have as much freedom as possible. For that I'm really grateful. And I would appreciate it even more, if you and your team would not leave this ship tomorrow morning," Natascha finally said, with an apologizing look.

Ariel stared at her for several seconds and could see she was getting more and more nervous.

"Did I say something wrong?" she finally asked.

"No, you didn't. But you didn't say anything that I didn't know already. Nevertheless you still haven't answered my question."

Natascha raised her arms and exhaled sharply.

"There's no point," Ariel mentioned to Shira and turned to the door.

"Tell Nick that he'll be leaving this ship tomorrow morning. I'm going to the Captain and will inform London that he'll be flying back tomorrow morning. Tell Nick that I want to talk to him. I'll be on the bridge."

Ariel stooped over Natascha and without another word, he left the cabin and closed the door.

Natascha was stunned. Her eyes stayed on the door, hoping he would come back and change his order. Shira got up from the bunk and Natascha's eyes darted towards her as she turned to the door.

"Lock the door behind me. I'll be back in a minute," she instructed on her way out.

Natascha reluctantly flopped back on her bed and stared at the ceiling. Now it was final, Nick would have to leave the ship the next morning, regardless if he wanted to or not. And she could not do anything about it. If he would leave the ship the next morning because of her behavior towards him, then that would also definitely be the end of their relationship. She closed her eyes and tried to concentrate, but too many thoughts were spinning in her head. She would never wake up beside him in the morning, never again holding his hand. The entire time she considered themselves a perfect match. They were always laughing together and even shared the same hobby. They had never had an argument before, and Natascha had actually started to think that she might have found her partner for life. Closing her eyes again for several minutes, she tried to focus, but she wasn't able to think straight. The only thing she saw were memories of the time she had spent together with Nick in Norway, Italy, Iceland and on board this ship. Tears filled her eyes as she recalled those memories for the next few moments. Suddenly she jumped up and opened the door. Her thoughts were erratic and her actions mirrored it, but it seemed right.

Jesus, I'm so stupid, she thought and ran down the corridor towards the stairs. Taking two steps at a time, she ran upstairs towards the bridge. On her last turn she collided with one of the Russian scientists and pushed him aside. After a quick apology, she finally stood in front of the only obstacle that rested between her and saving her relationship, the bridge door. Totally exhausted, she knocked and waited for a response. The Second Officer Mika Kankkunen, with whom she had enjoyed dinner a few days ago, opened the door.

"Natascha, is everything okay?" he asked her, his concern obvious.

"Yes. Is Ariel in there? I have to talk to him," she explained, still catching her breath.

"Did something happen? You're panting," Mika asked.

"No, nothing happened. I just have to talk to Ariel. Now," Natascha snapped back.

"He's with Nick and Shira in the radio room. I don't think you should disturb them. It seems to be very important."

Shaking her head in frustration, Natascha pushed the Second Officer aside and walked to the radio room. When she opened the door, she saw both Ariel and Shira talking to Nick, who was standing in the middle of the room. Astrid was sitting at her station, staring at her computer screen, pretending not to catch any of the conversation.

They all looked at Natascha and Mika, who had just caught up to her.

"My apologies but she just squeezed by," the Second Officer apologized.

Ariel looked at Natascha, while Nick turned away from her and stared at the floor.

"Is everything okay?" Ariel asked in his typical calm way.

"Yes, everything's fine," Natascha replied aggravated.

"Then please wait outside until we're finished here. Won't take much longer," Ariel said and turned his attention back to Nick.

"Okay, fine. Nothing is all right," Natascha snapped angrily and walked into the radio room, slamming the door shut behind her. She looked at everybody individually and walked directly in front of Nick and looked him in his eyes.

"I love you and you know that. I became besotted with you the moment, you sat foot on that dive boat in Norway. I only fell into the water, because I got distracted watching you. I convinced my friends to continue diving that wreck only, even though we had other plans. I even convinced them to drive home separately. In Italy I risked my participation in this expedition, because I didn't get nearly as much done as I was supposed to, and for what I drove down there in the first place. I started to train our dog the moment you told me, that you'd come to our house to provide security for my father. I did recommend you to accompany me in Berlin, before anybody else could say something and without knowing that it would put you at a higher risk. It was the first time I really enjoyed such an evening, and it was only because you were there with me. Here in Iceland I had the best dive of my life, and I had it with you. I'll never

Thin Ice

forget that. I don't know how I could think that you said something to the other guys. Ariel and Shira are right. I know you didn't say anything, and I know that in all your decisions you only wanted what was best for me. I have never felt so great in my life before than I do when I'm with you. I want to be with you."

Holding Nicks hand, Natascha turned around and threw both Ariel and Shira a challenging look. The room was silent.

"If Nick is leaving this ship tomorrow morning, then I'll be going with him," Natascha stated with finality.

Captain Rasmussen interrupted suddenly, entering the room.

"Is everything okay? Somebody slammed the door in my Second Officer's face. His nose is bleeding. I heard loud voices."

"Actually it was only one loud voice," Ariel corrected the Captain, before he convinced him that everything was fine. The Captain nodded, taking this moment for his chance to leave, and closed the door behind him.

"If Nick tells you to cover, will you do so?" Ariel asked Natascha seriously.

"Yes, I will," Natascha nodded and squeezed Nick's hand further.

"If Nick tells you to throw yourself on the floor and hide, will you?"

Natascha nodded again, squeezing Nick's hand even more.

"And if Nick is lying on the floor bleeding, and he tells you to run away for your own good, will you do so?"

Natascha swallowed hard, squeezing Nick's hand as tight as she could, and looked back and forth between Nick and Ariel.

"If...I...have to," Natascha stuttered, completely appalled by the question, as she tried to shake the image from her head.

"Will you do it if he tells you to?" Ariel repeated calmly.

"Yes, I will," Natascha whispered, her fingernails digging deep into Nicks arm.

Shira and Ariel looked at each other.

"What to you think, Shira?"

Shira shrugged her shoulders.

"That's fine with me."

Ariel looked back at Nick and Natascha.

"Very well. But you promise me, you'll stick to those rules."

"I promise."

Ariel raised his arms and waved his blessing.

A flutter bounded in her stomach and a smile burst across her face as Natascha kissed Nick intensely.

"You fell in the water, because I distracted you?" Nick smirked.

Natascha nodded impatiently, her smile unfading before she kissed him again.

"Okay, that's enough," Ariel interrupted them.

"Get out of here. And apologize to the Second Officer for breaking his nose."

Even the fact that she had to apologize to Mika did not dampen Natascha's spirit. A new flame of passion burned through her as she just nodded again and left the radio room. Her hand tightened around Nicks.

Ariel followed them with his eye and shook his head.

"Can someone please explain to me what the reason was for all this drama?" He asked.

"Drama?" Shira asked. "From what movie did you get that whole *lying on the floor bleeding, and he tells you to run for cover* episode?"

"Can't remember, but I waited years to say it," Ariel smiled.

"You really were going to send Nick home tomorrow morning, weren't you?" Shira asked solemnly.

"I didn't plan to, but if it had to be done, I would have sent him home, yes. I'm just not sure how much longer I could've played this scenario. I was afraid she got lost on her way up. Women!" Ariel complained and turned back to his laptop. It wasn't a moment later Shira slapped him up the side of the head.

- 9 -

On board the *Northern Explorer*, North Atlantic, Monday, July 11th
Driven by strong wind, the cold rain pelted down on the *Northern Explorer* as she battled heavy seas on her way to Halifax harbor.

Captain Rasmussen was standing on the bridge and had contacted Halifax Traffic Control. Considering the weather conditions and the poor visibility, the Norwegian had asked for a pilot boat. Waiting for the guide, he ordered the *Northern Explorer* in a big circle.

"The entrance to the harbor under good conditions is very tricky. The tide is harsh, stay in the shipping channel! There's more metal on the bottom of this harbor than in a steel plant. I don't plan on getting acquaintanted with those ladies," the Norwegian skipper explained to his helmsman.

Due to the rain, the visibility was reduced to less than one hundred meters. Nevertheless, the four radar screens showed a steady flow of ship traffic.

Scanning the horizon with his binoculars, he could finally see the huge container ship, whose course he had been following on the radar screen for the last hour. Closing the angle to the container ship, he could now see the radar signature of the little pilot boat, as it approached them under the cover of the container ship.

"About time," the Captain muttered and picked up the radio.

Ten minutes later they were following the pilot boat to the harbor entrance.

In the meantime, Nick, Natascha and his friends were all sitting in the mess for breakfast. While Natascha, Ole-Einar, Olaf and Oliver were well rested and in good spirits, Nick, Shira and Ariel had barely slept a wink, since the ship was tossed back and forth by the violent waves. Just as Nick scooped the last mouthful of his breakfast, the Captain's voice came over the speakers, announcing that they would make port in Halifax within the next hour.

Dr. Weber walked over to their table, wished them a good morning and sat down. "We'll most likely face very strict regulations and inspections by Canada Costums and Immigration, just in case someone wants to go off board in Halifax. After two-thousand-and-one the Americans and the Canadians have tightened their security precautions. There are no events scheduled anyway, just a little hint from the Canadians. Although they tolerate our mission, they're not very enthusiastic about it and won't support it."

"Well, we can't change that," Ariel replied and looked around.

He noticed that the next two tables were both occupied.

"I suggest we continue this conservation in one of the meeting rooms," Ariel suggested and rose from his chair, leading the group outside.

Five minutes later, they were all sitting in one of the many cabins that had been transformed to serve the many needs of the scientists.

Richard Weber waited until everybody was seated.

"I recommend we all stay on board during the next three days here in Halifax, unless it's absolutely necessary. That'll allow us to relax a little bit. Once we head back into the sea on the thirteenth, we'll only have three days left before we start with the first examinations. If everything goes as planned, we will have traveled through the Belle Isle Strait northwest of Newfoundland and entered the Labrador Current."

"Are there any changes regarding the American and Canadian scientists? Any last minute replacements?" Ariel asked.

Richard Weber shook his head and went over his clipboard.

"At least none that I'm aware of. I'm pretty sure that someone would have informed me about any substitutions. The Captain was very particular with that."

"Do you actually know all the members from the American and Canadian scientific teams?"

"Can't say that I actually know all of them personally. The Canadian group is lead by Dr. Markus Habermann, a scientist from one of the bigger universities here. The team leader for the American group is Dr. Joseph Richard. They're the only two I've met during the conferences regarding this expedition."

"Do you know their particular tasks?"

"Well, since I am the expedition leader, they have to coordinate all their activities with me. According to the Canadians, they're mainly interested in the melting of the polar ice. I assume that they foremost want to know how much longer it'll take before they can use the North-West-Passage for commercials ship traffic. They also indicated, that they want to do some sporadic tests around Newfoundland to figure out if the codfish stocks have recovered. Originally that wasn't planned, but it's on our way anyway. We scheduled two days for those studies. As far as I know, some of the Canadian funding came from the fishing industry. They put some pressure on them, that in exchange for their funding, they expect some positive results supporting a new catching quota. After all the fish stocks were decimated by the bottom trawlers a couple years ago, Newfoundland had lost most of its fishing industry."

"What about the Americans?"

The expedition leader waved his concern aside.

"They're even less interested in it than the Canadians. I'm surprised they're taking part at all. They only confirmed their participation a few days before the deadline, and this was after they ignored several of my invitations. Officially they're interested in the melting polar ice. Unofficially, they want to know when they can use the North-West-Passage, since they consider it an open trade route, and not Canadian waters. Their other interest is, how fast they can gain access to the oil underneath the North Pole and how much it'll cost them. And finally, I'm pretty sure they want to know what we're doing up there, so they can react to anything we come up with. They plan to install various underwater sensors over the complete course of our expedition. Those sensors are used to record and transmit water temperature, current and some other factors."

"What about the individual members of the two groups? Do you know any of them?"

Again, Natascha's father just shook his head.

"No, but that's not unusual. I only know the team leaders from the other groups, but not the individual scientists."

Ariel seemed to be satisfied and addressed his team.

"I'm going to ask the Captain if there are any personnel changes. Maybe a new crew member or a replacement for a scientist. I'm going to check the list of people who will come on board today and compare it with the names of the people who actually walk over the gangway. Ole-Einar and Nick, you'll make sure that no one, whose name is not listed, will set foot on this ship. I want both of you at the gangway. Olaf, you'll cover our security cameras. Just like in Iceland. Oliver, I'd like you to continue your night shifts on the bridge for a couple more days, if you do not mind. We will rotate the shift soon. I also want a fingerprint and a picture from each member of the Canadian as well as the American team. Shira, that's your part."

"Is there something I can do?" Dr. Weber offered.

"Just keep me informed about anything you notice."

"What about me?" Natascha asked, alternating her attention from Nick to Ariel.

"Stay away from the strange men," Ariel replied seriously without offering any eye-contact.

Natascha looked at Nick.

"Is this your idea?" She asked and pointed at Ariel.

"No, but I couldn't agree more," Nick said with a smile.

He and the rest of the team couldn't refrain from laughing.

"Make sure you're always close to one of us. Do not walk alone inside the ship and stay away from the newcomers for at least today, and until we know if they really are who they claim to be. If you want, you can come up to the radio room. From there you have a great view over anything that's going on and you can keep me company," Ariel said.

"And Astrid," Shira smiled and threw Ariel a piercing glance, while the others chuckled.

Ariel stared at Shira with vicious eyes, before he officially dismissed his team.

Shira waited until everyone had left the room and finally started. "Is there something going on between you and Astrid?"

"Nothing that should concern you. Everything's going according to my plan," Ariel informed, smiling confidently.

"Does the rest of the team know?"

"Like I said, everything is going according to my plan," Ariel winked and went to the Captain.

Nick and Ole-Einar had put their rain gear on and were watching the final procedures to secure the only gangway to the wharf. The rain was still pouring down. Although it was summer, it was only 15 degrees Celsius, and the cold wind was blowing strong from the northeast. Since there was no sign of any relief, both hoped Ariel would relieve them, so they wouldn't have to spend all day in this miserable weather. Ole-Einar looked once more at his clipboard with the list of names from the Americans and Canadians.

"So, if I read this right, the Americans will also get their own container on board. They're going to unload all their gear and send the container back off the ship. The Canadian gear is on a pallet. Other than that we'll get a delivery of general cargo. Eight pallets with food, four pallets with storage tanks for helium, argon and oxygen as well as two pallets with various spare parts," the Norwegian explained.

"Will somebody come aboard to help unloading?" Nick asked.

Ole-Einar looked at his clipboard again.

"It doesn't look like it, but I'll check with the Captain."

Ole-Einar turned around and activated the little Walkie-Talkie. While Ole-Einar spoke to the Captain, Nick had a chance to look over the harbor. He could see how the Canadians installed a fence over the complete length of the ship. They also put up a little shack, which they obviously used as a guardhouse. Nick noticed before, that the research vessel was berthed in the industrial part of the harbor, far away from any traffic. Although Nick found those precautions a little bit extreme, he could see a huge advantage for them: it would be almost impossible to get on board the ship without being detected.

"According to the Captain, there's no one else coming on board except the two expedition teams," Ole-Einar told Nick, who was still looking over the harbor.

"What about him?" Nick asked and pointed towards a heavily overweight man, who was now coming up the gangway. Looking at the uniform, he could see that he was from the Immigration Office. Once he was standing in front of Nick and Ole-Einar, he was already out of breath.

"Good Day. I have to talk to your Captain. I had informed him over the radio."

"Your name, please," the Norwegian asked, looking down at the much shorter man.

"Immigration Canada," he replied loud, struggling to ease his breathing.

Nick turned away and rolled his eyes. He had not expected to be on collision course so early.

With his most serious face, Ole-Einar activated his Walkie-Talkie and called the Captain once more.

As soon as the Captain replied, Ole-Einar started to report in his Norwegian language.

"Captain, we have a very heavy and out of shape Mr. Immigration Canada who wants to talk to you. He claims that he has an appointment. I can bring him up, but I'm not to be held responsible if he gets a heart attack."

Nick understood most of it and had to turn away from the officer for fear of bursting out in laughter. The Canadian was still breathing heavily, and although the sky was covered with dark clouds and the heavy rain, he was still wearing sunglasses.

"If you would follow me, I can bring you up," Ole-Einar told the Immigration Officer and handed Nick the clipboard. Nick looked after them, and he noticed that his Norwegian friend took a much longer way to the bridge, which included two

Thin Ice

more set of stairs. Ole-Einar always took two steps at once, and Nick smiled as the Canadian struggled to keep up. Ripples of laughter soon pried through his lips as he shook his head and looked up to the radio room where Natascha was sitting.

She and Astrid had lots of fun looking out the windows following the activities on deck. They both looked at Nick, who now stood alone in the pouring rain. She felt bad, that he had to stay in this miserable cold weather.

"Have the two of you been dating for a long time?" Astrid asked, after she noticed Natascha was looking at Nick through the binoculars.

"What? Oh, yes," Natascha replied and put the binoculars down. She totally forgot that Astrid was there yesterday evening, when she threatened to leave the ship with Nick.

"Technically we've only dated a few weeks, but I think he might be the one."

Natascha looked at Astrid, who was now peeking out the window.

"What about you and Ariel? Is there something going on?"

Astrid shrugged her shoulders and smiled.

"Don't know. I find him very attractive, but as far as I can tell, he's already together with Shira. They're definitely very close. What kind of relationship do they have anyway?"

Natascha shook her head.

"I have no idea, really. I share my cabin with her, but I have never seen them together. If they are dating, then they are a very ascetic couple."

"I somehow like him. He is always very nice to me, very friendly. Not one stupid comment, totally opposite from the rest of the crew. He's very interested in what I'm doing here and I can talk with him about anything. He's somehow… I don't know… mystical."

You can say that again, Natascha thought, but decided to keep her comment to herself and just smiled instead.

"How well do you know Ariel?" Astrid asked.

"Well, not that good. I know that he's Nick's superior. And I know that I don't want him to be pissed at me."

"Is he leaving you and Nick alone?"

"Generally yes. After all, he is still his boss," Natascha explained and looked through the binoculars at a group of four people coming up the gangway.

"It's kind of a difficult situation we're in, and he tries to please everybody."

"Yes, I already figured that out. He told me a little bit. After he set up his headquarters here in the radio room, the Captain told me that he's officially my apprentice. That sounded a little bit kinky to me, since I didn't know anything about that before. Ariel seems to know more about communication electronics than I do. What about you and Nick? Is everything okay now?"

"Yes, we spoke for a few hours in my cabin last night. Do many people know that we're together?"

"Well, I overhear many conversations and Ariel has already told me some background information. The Captain ordered me to keep my mouth shut. I assume the officers know what's going on between you and Nick, but I don't know about the rest of the crew or the scientists. Does it have to be a secret?"

"I don't know. It doesn't make a difference to me if they know or not. I guess we would have to ask Ariel for that," Natascha replied and picked up the binoculars again to check out the newcomers.

"Someone among them who's worth a sin?" Astrid asked and peeked out the window again.

"Hard to tell under all that rain gear," Natascha answered seriously, before they exchanged a quick glance with each other and burst out in laughter.

Ariel and Shira suddenly appeared in the radio room.

"Nick has just radioed in that the Canadian team has arrived. Immigration Canada has told us that those, who want to go off board, have to report to that little shack down there first. Everybody is required to carry their passport. I suggest we do not leave the ship. Natascha, I recommend you to stay on board."

Natascha nodded in agreement and took another peek at Nick, who was walking up and down at the gangway to stay warm.

Just a few minutes after the Canadian scientific team arrived, the Americans showed up. So far, there were no personnel changes and the loading of the container also went flawlessly. Ole-Einar escorted the Immigration Officer off the ship and joined Nick, who was still shaking his head.

"I would not have given him mouth to mouth if he collapsed on the stairway," Nick laughed.

The Americans had just taken their personal stuff to their designated cabins and returned to unload the container that stood just a few meters away from Nick and his friend.

"And? Did something interesting happen?" Ole-Einar asked.

"Did you know that some women are named Sasha over here?"

"We have more women on board?" Ole-Einar exclaimed with excitement.

"Yep, we do. Two more. One Jenna and one Sasha."

" How do they look?"

"Hey, leave me alone. I'm not saying anything about that anymore," Nick retorted and looked up to radio room, unable to see anybody.

"So, how do they look?" Ole-Einar asked again, totally unimpressed by Nick's reaction.

"With all that rain gear, not more than a five."

"You're biased," the Norwegian hissed.

One of the crew members had just showed both the Canadians and the Americans their designated storage rooms, and they started to unload their gear.

"How far are they with the unloading of the supplies and the Canadian gear?" Nick asked.

Ole-Einar pointed to the little crane, which was normally used to lift the submersibles. It was just swinging a pallet with several boxes on the deck.

"They are just unloading the Canadian gear now. Only things missing after that

Thin Ice

are the supplies, the storage bottles with oxygen and helium as well as the spare parts. Shouldn't be much longer before we can get out of here."

Nick looked at the guy who had introduced himself as Dr. Joseph Richard, the American team leader. He just opened the container and gave instructions about the storage of their items.

While some of the Americans already carried some of the gear to their storage room, Nick went over to have a look inside, but he could not see anything suspicious.

"Nothing special," Nick told his friend as soon he was back.

The rain and the wind suddenly gusted, and the rain struck harder as it flowed down their gear. Nick looked at the Canadians, who were still trying to open the straps that held their boxes together. Once they were free, they worked quickly to get their gear inside.

While three of the men were each carrying a hard plastic box, Sasha Theriault, the only female Canadian scientist, stayed behind to open more straps.

Nick was curious and walked over to find out if there was anything unusual with those boxes.

"Hey, just want to make sure everything is on board. The dock workers are still down there, so now would be a good time to let them know if something's missing."

"Yes, thank you, but everything's here. We just want to get it off the deck as fast as possible," she answered and winked at Nick flirtatiously.

"Why are women always winking at you?" Ole-Einar asked as soon as Nick was back. "You're not that goodlooking."

"You could've gone over there as well as I did," Nick shrugged.

Against Ole-Einar's previous assumption, it took all afternoon until everything was loaded on the research vessel. Both Ole-Einar and Nick were so cold, that shivers were now chattering their teeth. Unfortunately there was still gear and supplies on the ships deck, so they could not leave the gangway. They did not want to take the chance that someone might slip on board the ship.

It was late afternoon when the last pallet was loaded, and they could finally leave their post. The gangway was now under video surveillance.

Nick and Ole-Einar went to their own storage room, took their rain gear off and hang it up so it could dry. The Norwegian muttered a series of complaints about the Canadian dockworkers, who had taken several long breaks during the day, leaving everything the way it was. Nicks hands were still shivering when Natascha and Shira joined them.

"You're completely frozen!" Natascha gasped when she looked at Nick.

"Welcome to Canada," Nick muttered under his breath.

Ole-Einar told Nick that he would take the first shower. Walking down the corridor, they could still hear him swearing at the dockworkers in his Norwegian tongue.

"Any news?" Shira asked.

"No, the people who were registered came aboard. I checked their passports. Seven Men, two women. Other than that, I've learned several new Norwegian curse words. Why is Ole-Einar taking a shower first? It always takes him an hour!" Nick complained suddenly on his way to the cabin.

"Just grab a few dry clothes. You can take a shower in our cabin," Natascha offered.

Nick looked at Shira, who nodded her agreement.

Home Office and Operational Headquarters of *EuroSecCorporation*, London, Monday, July 11th

Gordon Ramshaw was chatting with his sister, Catherine. Both were sitting in her office and waiting for retired Admiral Brian Whittaker to accompany them to lunch. They acquired the habit of having lunch together once a week.

The retired Admiral was still laughing when he came back from a meeting.

"So, everything's okay. We can leave any minute now. Just give me a moment, I have to check something on my desk," Brian announced and went through the door to his own office.

"Do you know who shot your man?" Gordon asked his brother-in-law.

Brian looked up briefly, before he continued to go over some papers on his desk.

"No, not really. We have some ideas and a direction to look at, but definitely no names or faces. Why? Did you hear something?"

"No, it is just that this is the first time I ever heard something like that. I'm not sure, but maybe your man has been in my house?"

Brian stopped and thought for a moment, looking at his wife.

"Yes, that's true," Catherine said.

"Rolf was indeed at your place. Have you met him?"

Gordon shook his head.

"Not really. I just shook everybody's hand in the morning before I left for work."

Brian nodded, looked at his watch and then at this wife.

"How does it look for this afternoon? How much time do we have?"

"We're fine as long as we're back at fifteen-hundred," his wife answered and looked at retired General Klaus Schwartze, who had just joined them.

"Brian, can you come to my office please? I have to show you something. Catherine, maybe you can come as well. It's about the report from last week. Nothing special, but I would like to finish it today."

"I'll wait here," Gordon said and looked after the others on their way out.

Five minutes later Brian and Catherine came back. Gordon just hung Brian's phone up.

"Just called my office," he said.

"No problem," Brian replied and took his jacket. "Let's go, I'm hungry."

On board the *Northern Explorer*, North Atlantic, Monday July 11th

Expedition Leader Dr. Weber had called for a special meeting after supper to welcome the last two expedition teams. Shortly before eight o'clock in the evening, all scientists and most of the crew and personnel had gathered in the canteen.

Together with Astrid, Nick and the other members from his team, Natascha was sitting at a table close to the door and listening to her father. Directly beside them were the German scientists. Since most people on board still believed that Ariel and his crew were part of the German team, he still wanted them to be close to each other. Dr. Weber asked the Captain to allow a spontaneous party to welcome their fellow scientists. Captain Rasmussen gave his consent, but only under the condition that nobody would commit mutiny and take the ship somewhere south and warm. He also insisted in the limited consumption of liquor.

Since Nick and his friends barely drank any liquor, they didn't care for those rules that much. Although they believed that Natascha was in no great danger at the moment, Ariel still insisted on the basic safety precautions. Therefore they occupied the two tables closest to the exit, and Natascha was only allowed to dance with Nick or one of his friends or with someone from the German scientists. Since Natascha had taken dance lessons during her university time, she didn't want to miss a chance. Ariel reminded her once more not to accept any open drinks from anybody, something he had already told her back in Kiel as a general precaution. Just to make sure, they decided two of the guys would always be close to her.

Nick had offered Oliver to relieve him from the radio room after an hour, so he could spend some time at the party. But Olaf insisted that he would relieve Oliver, claiming that he didn't feel well enough to hang around. He ducked out of the room before he admitted to Nick that Natascha had asked him for that favor.

While Natascha danced wildly with Oliver, Nick took the chance and looked for his teammate. He spotted Shira, who was chatting with the three male American scientists, and he was convinced, she was trying to find out more about them.

Nick watched Shira's movements and knew, even from this distance, that she was careful with her words. He suddenly looked to Ole-Einar as he elbowed him and nodded towards the bar. Nick followed his friend's eyes and saw Sasha Theriault, the lone female Canadian scientist standing in plain view. Looking at her, Nick had to admit that she was actually quite attractive without the rain gear. Her long blond hair almost reached down to her hips, and the snug jeans and T-Shirt showed a very athletic body as it hugged the right places.

"I would have to give her an eight in those jeans," Ole-Einar said and looked at Nick.

"Yeah, Nick. What score would you give her?" Natascha whispered in her boyfriend's ear. Neither Ole-Einar nor Nick had noticed Natascha standing right behind them, as they admired the attractive woman. Astrid, who had been talking to Natascha, choked on her drink.

"Not more then a seven," Nick answered matter-of-factly, pretending he neither heard nor noticed Natascha.

"Liar," she whispered in his ear, smiling wide.

"What marks are they giving?" Astrid asked after she managed to clear her throat.

"They're grading the butts of other women. Imagine that," Natascha explained.

Nick and Ole-Einar both turned towards them.

"It's not what you think," Ole-Einar defended, dead serious.

"No, of course it isn't. I'm sure it's just a professional scientific assessment of her gender specific anatomies," Natascha laughed and wrapped her arms tightly around Nick.

"What mark did you give me back in Norway?" she asked and looked Nick deep in his eyes, searching for his answer.

"You actually graded your own girlfriend's bum?" Astrid was shocked.

"Technically speaking, they weren't dating at that time," Ole-Einar stepped in on the defensive again.

"I gave you an eight in Norway and after Italy, a ten," Nick said as if he was explaining a scientific project.

"Why first an eight and then a ten?" Astrid asked curiously.

"Because when he met with Natascha in Italy, he nai…"

"Ole!" Nick interrupted, slapping his arm sharply.

"Ole-Einar was going to say that Nick has seen me only in a dry-suit, thermo underwear or my jeans in Norway, but since Nick and I had performed the coitus in Italy, he had suddenly gained classified information and changed his mind," Natascha explained in a more noble way than the Norwegian did.

Still hugging her boyfriend, the young German scientist glanced at Sasha.

"A seven, you said," she whispered with consideration.

"Maximum, maybe only a six point five," Nick reassured his girlfriend.

"I'm going to kill you if you ever get some classified information from her," Natascha whispered seriously, but so that only Nick could hear.

"Don't worry. I'm holding all the classified information I'm ever going to need, right here. Everything else is off limits," Nick whispered back and kissed her nose.

"And we won't change that."

"Did you mark my bum as well?" Astrid asked seriously and looked at her fellow countryman.

"I can't say anything about that," Ole-Einar replied with his poker face.

"Of course they did. They just don't want to admit it," Natascha said and turned to Astrid.

"Yeah, sure. As if the two of you never looked at other men," Nick retorted.

"Yes. Who knows what you're giving grades for!" Oliver helped his friends.

Natascha shrugged her shoulders seductively and looked over the crowd.

"That's our secret," she stated, before turning back to Nick again.

"Sometimes it could be worth a sin," she smiled as she gazed into his eyes.

"You do remember you're not allowed to hang out with other men, right?" Nick reminded her with a wide grin.

"You really like that, don't you?"

"Oh yeah, I really do. It looks like you're stuck with me."

Natascha blew him a kiss and asked Oliver to dance with her again.

"And by the way, Mr. Rehfeld, once we're back in Germany, you're going to learn how to dance," she finally whispered to him, before she disappeared with Oliver again.

While Oliver and Natascha danced, Nick and Ole-Einar noticed that Sasha was coming towards them. The Canadian scientist stopped once she had recognized them and walked over to introduce herself. When Natascha and Oliver came back about fifteen minutes later, Nick and Ole-Einar were still talking to Sasha.

Natascha walked over to Nick, threw her arms around his neck and kissed him passionately.

"What's the rush?" Nick asked, taking a deep breath.

Natascha glanced over his shoulders at Sasha, who was watching them from the corner of her eye.

"I'm marking my territory," Natascha whispered sternly.

For the next morning, Ariel called a meeting in Natascha's and Shira's cabin. While Natascha was more or less unsuccessful in her attempts to pick up some clothes, Ariel looked at his clipboard with the names from the American and Canadian team members.

"We've already checked their names back in Germany the moment we got the assignment. Everything was okay," Shira explained.

Shira and Ariel were convinced, that the assassin, or assassins, would have most likely infiltrated either the Canadian or the American team. But at the moment, they weren't even sure if there was even the risk of another attempt on Natascha's life. As soon as the *Northern Explorer* had left Kiel, Ariel and Shira had conducted a detailed background check on all people on board this ship.

Ariel checked his clipboard and flipped through the individual pages. The profile of each person on board was on a single page. The American scientists all ranged between twenty-five and forty-five years of age, only their team leader, Dr. Joseph Richard was in the mid-fifties. With the Canadians it was the total opposite. Team leader Dr. Markus Habermann was only thirty-two years old and the oldest member of the team. The two male scientists were in their late twenties, while Sasha Theriault was in her mid-twenties.

"As far as I'm concerned, the Americans don't look like former members of a special unit to me," Shira said, looking at the picture of one of them.

Two of the American scientists were indeed obviously out of shape, and Ariel had serious doubts they would have qualified for a special unit fifteen or twenty years ago.

"I checked the personnel files from the Americans this morning," Shira continued and took the clipboard.

"I can't find any indication, that they had ever been a member of a special unit. I'm more concerned about the Canadians. All four of them seem to be at least physically fit. So far we still lack any evidence, that the assassin from Berlin was actually American. All we know is that they spoke English, most likely from North America."

"Nick, you're certain that none of them were in Berlin?"

"Absolutely. They were wearing masks, but I could still see enough to be certain they were neither from the American nor the Canadian team. I paid special attention when they boarded the ship. They were definitely not from the American team, they're all too short for that. The guys in Berlin were much taller and in much better shape. The Canadians do fit that bill. But again, we don't know if the guys from Berlin are Americans. They had the tattoo from the Navy Seals, but we all agreed that they're all mercenaries and not regular soldiers anymore. Therefore there might also be any different english speaking nation as well as Canadians involved. Who knows?"

"We would need their fingerprints to be sure," Ariel said, looking at the pages on his clipboard.

"What about a DNA test? All we need is some hair. Much easier to get," Natascha suggested hopefully.

"That's true," Shira agreed and looked at Ariel.

"Shira and Natascha, you will not pull any hair from any male and especially not from any female person on board this ship, regardless how much you want to. What are we suppose to do with the hair anyway? Fax them to London?" Ariel exhorted the two women.

"But could we not get some…just in case…?" Natascha whispered, still hoping she would get the chance.

Ariel glanced at her over his clipboard.

"For the last time, Natascha: No hair pulling!"

"Okay, okay," Natascha slinked, disappointed.

"We can only use fingerprints. Those we can scan and send to London. Shira, have you already figured something out?"

Shira smiled and took her backpack. She opened it and pulled a bag with two glass bottles and another bag with a single glass out.

"The glass is from Frank Garcia and the bottles are from Nelson Singer and Brian Joice. There might be some other fingerprints as well, but their fingerprints will definitely be on it. I'll meet with Dr. Joseph Richard and Jenna Mason this afternoon. Shouldn't be a problem to invite them for a cup of coffee and get their prints as well. That will take care of the American team members," Shira explained and enjoyed the recognition that they showed her.

"Great, well done, Shira," Ariel acknowledged and looked at the guys in the team. "And what have you figured out so far?" he asked and looked at each individual.

They all looked at each other, but they had nothing to show.

"Any fingerprints?" Ariel asked specifically.

Olaf raised his hands in an apologetic gesture.

"While all of you enjoyed an excessive party, I dodged the bullet for the team and performed my duty on the bridge as ordered."

"Traitor," Ole-Einar growled.

"Well, Ole-Einar, Nick? Have you found something out?"

Both looked at each other, but their situation had still not improved at all.

"Oliver, anything you want to add?"

"Actually I didn't spend too much time on the party. I only danced with Natascha for a few minutes," Oliver tried to defend himself and looked at Natascha, just like everybody else did now.

"Don't look at me," Natascha whined.

"I'm officially prohibited to get near any other men except the ones in this room," she added to her excuse, knowing perfectly well that she was not responsible for any of those tasks.

"Okay, I want to have fingerprints from every Canadian team member and from the two remaining Americans at eight o'clock this evening in my cabin. I'm serious about this," Ariel said and left the cabin at once.

Ole-Einar's surprise rose with his eyebrows as he looked at the door.

"What's eating his apples? Did Astrid turn him down last night?"

"Ariel has a strange feeling. So have I. It has nothing to do with Astrid. Something is wrong, but we both don't know yet what this might be. I suggest we really try to get those fingerprints by tonight," Shira defended her countryman.

"And how are we suppose to do that?" Olaf snapped back.

"Why don't you watch them during supper? All the drinks here are served in glasses. If not, try to invite at least Sasha to a drink. Try to improvise, it's not that difficult."

They all got up and left the cabin with defeat.

"Oh Nick, could you please do me favor?" Natascha called after her boyfriend, who stopped in the door with his buddies.

"Yes, why not? What is it?" Nick asked.

"Could you please get me something from the little store?"

"Sure, what do you want?"

"Well, you know...what all girls need once in a while..."she whispered and rolled her eyes.

"Okay, I'll do my best," Nick responded in complete surprise, not exactly sure, how he should master the task his girlfriend just gave him. He slipped out the door quickly.

"Why was he so down about this? I only asked him for a little favor... I thought that would take his thoughts away from Ariel," Natascha asked Shira the moment they were alone.

"Well, we'll see later," Shira answered and smiled, not sharing her suspicion with Natascha.

"Do you really think that my life is still in danger?"

"I don't know, Natascha. After Iceland, Ariel and I were convinced that it was all over, but something is wrong here. Ariel is sensing it and so am I. Listen to me, Natascha. As long as we're not one hundred percent certain about the identities of the American and Canadian scientists, I don't want you near them, okay? Can you promise me that?"

Natascha fell backwards on her bed and took a couple of deep breaths.

"Why can't they just leave me alone? It doesn't even make any sense! Who would benefit from my death anyway?"

"Nobody, but if the contract is paid and the contacts are broken off, then they won't stop until they succeed."

"Great. You really know how to raise my spirit."

Montana, USA, Tuesday, July 12th

"Can I offer you a drink, Mr. Hogan?" the American asked relaxed.

"No, thank you."

While the two North Americans were sitting in their comfortable leather armchairs as usual, Chuck Hogan was standing at the window looking outside.

"Mr. Hogan, I want you to know that it's no longer necessary, that you and your men go after the girl. The expedition is already on their way, and it wouldn't help us anymore. Another attempt would only stir up much more unwanted attention. But you can keep all the money, there's no problem there. Can you agree to these terms?"

Mr. Hogan turned around and raised his eyebrows.

"According to my information, it was your British friend who paid us. As far as I'm concerned, it's his money and his decision."

The American and the Canadian briefly exchanged looks, then the American got up and walked over to the assassin.

"Mr. Hogan, unfortunately our British friend is unavailable today, but I can assure you we're talking on his behalf. Forget the daughter of that Professor. We have some much more important tasks ahead of us."

Chuck Hogan shrugged his shoulders and sat in another armchair.

"On board the *Northern Explorer* is another group of people, who are representing our interests. Would you and your men have a problem working with them?"

"It depends. What exactly is their job and who would be leading?"

The American smiled. Now that he had Chuck's general interest in this matter, he was sure he could get him to agree.

"During this expedition, you and your men will accompany my Canadian friend here and myself on board the research vessel. We'll personally oversee one of our operations up there. We only need you for the unlikely event that something doesn't go according to our plan."

"Will your other group know who we are?"

"Well, we worked with some of them before, and we know all of them personally. Officially we'll be introduced to them on board this ship for the first time. I'm not sure if you've worked with them or met them before."

"Do you know their real names?" Chuck asked.

The Canadian unfolded a little note and read out some names.

Chuck Hogan listened carefully, but he kept a straight face and shook his head.

"No, I don't know any of these names. I will double check with my guys. What exactly is the job of that team?"

"It's a need to know basis. All you have to do, is to make sure that nothing will happen to the two of us. That's all."

"What's the likelihood that something's going to happen?"

For the first time, the Canadian now took part in the conversation.

"If all goes well, then nobody will ever know what has really happened."

Chuck looked at the Canadian, but he wasn't convinced. He experienced these so called "foolproof" plans that ended quite the contrary much too often.

"What about the European group providing the security detail for that chick?"

"Like I said, if everything goes according to our plan, no one will learn about this operation. No shots will be fired and there won't be any casualties as long as we are on board. It'll be a completely normal day on board that research vessel."

"What's your personal security detail for that trip? Who else is coming?"

"I'll only be accompanied by my private secretary. He's also responsible for my security. Carl's worked for me almost ten years now. He knows everything and is very reliable. Normally he's more than capable of protecting me on his own."

Chuck nodded and noticed the Canadian's nervousness.

"I'm just thinking about something," the Canadian said, promptly.

"Is there any risk that those members of the European group will recognize your men?"

"No, I don't think so," Chuck shook his head.

Chuck Hogan did not consider it necessary to reveal his source for that. The instructions from his British employee were straightforward in this matter.

"Very well then. We'll get back to you in a couple of weeks," the American finally said and stood up.

Chuck Hogan nodded, rose from his chair and shook both hands before he left.

As soon as he was outside the house and walking down the driveway to his rental car, he stole a deep breath. He hoped his matter-of-fact behaviour concealed his surprise, when they revealed the names. He reflected back to the moment and was certain both the American and the Canadian did not notice. Once he reached the rental car, he sat behind the wheel and shook his head in disbelief. He was actually looking forward to see his sister again.

On board the *Northern Explorer*, Halifax harbor, Nova Scotia,
Tuesday, July 12th

Together with Ole-Einar and Olaf, Nick stood in a corner of the little store and all three were looking at the small shelf with the products in question. Nobody knew exactly what to look for.

"How could she expect me to pick the right ones?" Nick complained to his friends.

"Well, look at it this way. A couple is only officially dating when the man has to buy these certain items." Ole-Einar smiled, holding two products in his hand.

"Whatever you do, you're screwed anyway."

"Here, get those. Can't do much wrong with them," Olaf recommended, trying to help Nick as best as he could.

Although Olaf and Ole-Einar had promised him their support on this devious mission, they abandoned Nick rather quickly, once he made his way to the cashier to pay for them. With this task successfully behind them, they concentrated on the more important mission handed down to them by Ariel.

Trying to get some fingerprints, Nick, Ole-Einar and Olaf had monitored the Canadian scientists during supper. Having finished their own meal already, the two Norwegian and one German were now waiting for the Canadians to leave the mess. They had to wait a couple more minutes than expected, but the Canadians finally got up and left. Nick, Ole-Einar and Olaf were happy when they noticed that none of the Canadians bothered with returning their tray. The two Norwegians promptly walked by their table and picked up their trays.

Just a few minutes later, all three knocked at Shira's and Natascha's cabin. After they had identified themselves, Shira opened the door and let them in.

Natascha sat in front of her laptop and was planning her first official dive as a submersible pilot. It was scheduled, that she would operate the submersible *Odin* for the first time as lead pilot on July 20th. Holger Bloomquist, who was her lead instructor for the submersible, would be the 2nd pilot. While Holger would evaluate Natascha under water, the leading Dive Officer, Vitali Vachenko, would follow the dive closely from the diving station on board the research vessel. Each of the participants in this particular course had been issued a laptop with a simulation software, on which Natascha spent hours practicing. Since the Canadians were planning to start their research in front of Newfoundland on the 19th and 20th of July together with the Americans, Vitali had decided this would be the perfect time for Natascha to follow up on her practical training.

Vitali and Holger had both given Natascha the task to plan the entire dive herself, and she was performing that specific dive profile on the simulator again and again.

"Anything new?" she asked and looked up briefly when Ole-Einar and Olaf entered the cabin.

"We might get lucky and have the fingerprints from the Canadians," Ole-Einar said and closed the door behind him.

"Let's see," Shira ordered.

Olaf pulled a plastic bag with four knives from underneath his sweater.

"I think we would have drawn to much attention, if we left with several glasses, but I'm sure nobody noticed us taking the knives."

Shira walked over to her locker and took a small hard plastic expedition case. She opened it, put on some latex gloves and examined each knife with hawk eyes.

"Yes, I think that'll be enough. I assume you don't know who was using which knife?"

"No, we didn't get the chance."

Curiosity got the best of Natascha and she watched closely, as Shira carefully applied some powdered black graphite on the handles with a fine brush. Once Shira saw that some of the graphite stuck to the metal, she had to smile. She then took an adhesive strap and pressed it carefully on the fingerprint. Satisfied she gathered the evidence, she then prepared a white sheet of coated paper, pulled the adhesive strap off the knife and carefully pressed it on the paper again. She examined the full fingerprint as if it was a masterpiece. She repeated that procedure three more times and ended up with four different fingerprints.

"Okay, I'll go up to the bridge and scan them in. Ariel can send them to London and Israel to check them out. Did you touch the knives with your fingers?"

"No, we used napkins for that."

"Well done," Natascha approved and looked at Nick. "Did you get me what I asked you for?" she asked and clapped her hands with excitement.

Thin Ice

"Well, you could've been a little bit more specific, but I did my best," Nick replied apologetically and handed her a small bag with a box of tampons.

"What's this?" Natascha asked puzzled, her excitement faded.

"Well, wasn't that what you asked me for? *What all girls need once in a while?*" Nick defended himself, and both Shira and Natascha couldn't restrain their laughter.

"Oh Nick, I'm so sorry. I wanted you to bring me some chocolate, not tampons," Natascha explained, laughing so hard they could barely understand her.

"Oh God, you guys always have to think about that, don't you?" she added, still laughing hysterically.

"Well, if you want I can still get you some chocolate," Nick offered, his nervous grin swirling with embarassment and relief upon knowing, that his next shopping trip would be much easier.

"Guys are just priceless," Natascha added and sat up, wiping a tear out of her eyes before she looked at Olaf and Ole-Einar.

"As a reward you can both use my submersible simulator. But don't do anything stupid, okay? Shira, I'll come with you. I want to see what my father's doing."

Shira and Natascha left the cabin together with Nick, while Ole-Einar and Olaf sat down and started the simulator again.

- 10 -

On board the *Northern Explorer*, two miles off the coast off Petit de Grat, Cape Breton, Nova Scotia, Wednesday, July 13th

It was early in the morning, but Natascha and Dr. Weber were already standing at the rail and looked at the eight Marine Biology students from the local university. The students excitement was evident as their plans to spend the day on the *Northern Explorer* was finally happening. Since the research vessel was too big to approach the local harbor, Oliver and Nick had picked them up with one of the RIB's* at the local government wharf. It took them only a few minutes, before they were back at the research vessel and made their way up the gangway. Ole-Einar and Olaf greeted them at the ships deck and checked their picture ID with the names on their clipboard and collected the liability release forms. The group finally stood on the deck and looked around.

"Welcome on board the *Northern Explorer*," Dr. Weber welcomed his guests and asked them to follow him to one of the presentation rooms, where Natascha gave them a detailed overview about their expedition. Her father noticed immediately, how well Natascha and the students connected to each other, and he let her answer most of the questions. The students were accompanied by a local German diver, who was their dive instructor and who guided them on field trips. He and his Canadian buddy were also their dive guides for today's dive.

The first dive would take them to the remains of an irish wreck, which the two divers had rediscovered just recently. During their extensive documentation, the local divers had placed a memorial plaque in memory of the two hundred forty eight people who had lost their lives back in 1834. The second dive would take them to the remains of a historic french wreck, which rested in a depth of just six meters on the muddy bottom of the harbor in front of the historical Fortress of Louisbourg. The ship sank during the second British siege of the fortress and still had several cannons, anchors and cannon balls clearly visible. Both wrecks were part of an exploration project from one of the Swedish companies who had supplied some of the dive gear for the German scientists team. In return, Dr. Richard Weber had agreed to take some video footage of both wrecks for them.

After one hour in the presentation room, the *Northern Explorer* was already on it's way north again, and Natascha lead the group on deck to show them *Odin* and *Polar Viking*.

"Was my speech that boring? One almost fell asleep." Natascha asked the German dive instructor in their mother tongue, so that the student's could not understand.

RIB = Rigid Inflatable Bottom, a modern type of zodiac, usually used by military or other government agencies.

Thin Ice

"No, not at all. They're actually very excited about this, but they also like to party a lot. In general I have to say, that they're some of my best students I ever had," the German laughed on their way back to visit the onboard labs. After they had all taken turns using the different microscopes and learned how they set up their cold water tanks that would keep any species they collect, Natascha lead the group to the dive storage room.

"Whoa," their German guest said, once he saw the several scooters, two rebreathers and all the other gear.

"Yes, we got extremely lucky with the funding for this expedition. All new gear. The whole nine yards," Natascha explained and showed them around.

"I'm actually using the same fins, suit and regs. How do they work for you?"

"Loving them so far, no issues at all."

"My buddy won't like those fins," the German instructor said with a smile before they left the storage room, but Natascha simply shrugged her shoulders and smiled back.

"So, what's the detailed dive plan anyway?" Dr. Richard Weber asked their German dive guide as everybody took a snack break in the mess.

"Well, if the Gods are with us, we'll meet my buddy at the dive site. When we're about one and a half hours away, I'll call him and he'll come with his zodiac to the dive site. Everything's already loaded. I only have to get dressed on this ship. I will give you the coordinates, and we will use one of your RIB's to get there. We will dive the irish wreck first, since she's over thirty meters deep. After we're done with her, we'll drive with the RIB into Louisbourg harbor, where we'll meet my buddy again. He has to trailer his zodiac after the first dive, but with the RIB it will only take us a few minutes to get there. We'll pick him up at the wharf, and from there we will be at the french wreck within five minutes. Once we're done, you can taxi the students back to Louisbourg. The van that dropped us off this morning will be up there by then."

"Sounds easy enough for me. I'll tell the Captain," Dr. Weber said and rose from his chair.

While Natascha spoke with the university students, their German guest had a great conversation with Nick and Ole-Einar.

"I think I got to call my buddy," he looked at this watch and picked his cell phone up. While Natascha's father would personally entertain their guests, Natascha, her dive buddy and fellow scientist Mario, Nick and their German dive guide went downstairs to get ready. Ole-Einar and Oliver would launch the RIB in the meantime. As everything flowed according to plan, they were all sitting in the RIB only a few minutes later, which Ole-Einar piloted. He looked at the GPS coordinates that he punched in and scanned the horizon for the second dive guide in his smaller zodiac.

"Over there," Nick shouted over the sound of the outboard engines and pointed at a small dot on the water, almost a mile away.

"It doesn't look like anybody's in the zodiac. Do you think he's okay?" Natascha asked and stood up, concerned that their Canadian dive guide might have a problem.

"Ah, don't worry. He's not that tall. He is perfectly fine," their German dive guide informed them without even looking at his buddy's zodiac. As they got closer, they could see that it was completely packed with dive gear, and the single person inside it was lying on top of one of the side walls, his ball cap deep in his face. Natascha smiled as he was obviously sleeping.

"You're late, like always," he yelled at his German friend as soon as the larger RIB idled closer. He got up to catch the line and greet the other divers in a much more polite professional voice.

"We installed a little buoy here yesterday. You should tie to it and I'll tie my zodiac to yours. That will be best."

Within a minute, the two boats were calmly floating on the surface and after shaking everybody's hand, the Canadian guide started his detailed dive briefing.

"I know that my buddy here has already told you all about this dive site, but since he's a complete moron, I'll give you a now detailed briefing," he continued.

Although the two friends went on like this, it didn't take long before they all disappeared below the water. After one hour, Natascha and Mario were the first to be back on the surface, since they had a shorter decompression time because of their rebreathers. They took off their gear in the water, and Ole-Einar lifted the gear back in the RIB. Not long after they were back in the RIB, the other divers ascended and they loaded all the gear in the larger zodiac. As agreed on in their dive planning, their Canadian guide left to trailer his zodiac and to meet up with them again at the Louisbourg wharf, while the powerful RIB drove around the shoreline.

"That's a nice memorial plaque. Right beside the anchor. The video should be awesome," Natascha said to her German dive guide in her native language.

"Yes, we thought it was the perfect spot. Actually quite the story until the plaque was finally there. Thirty-two meters is not too deep, it's just so difficult to get to. Best thing is with a small zodiac, since it's so close to the rocks. Or you scooter around the point, but it's quite the distance. Remember the little canyon we went through before we got to the old bell stand in twenty meters?"

"Yes, I do."

"Well, if you keep going, you'll get to a second shipwreck that is in much better shape. You can dive it from the shore, it's only fifteen meters deep, but we don't have time today."

"Too bad. Sounds like a great spot for diving."

"There is one site where you can dive two wrecks in one dive, if you carry double tanks. First wreck is over eighty meters long, three dimensional, all steel, completely covered with anemones. Tons of fish, and just twenty meters deep. Those students are loving it," the German screamed over the loud outboard engine.

"Seems like we have to come back one day," Natascha smiled at him.

Without much further delay, they picked up their Canadian guide. While Natascha, Nick and Mario started to fill out the necessary paperwork for the second dive, the Canadian dive guide and his German friend were getting into another verbal dispute because the German didn't bring his own certification card. While they were exchanging their usual obscenities, Natascha and her friends couldn't help shaking their heads. Nevertheless, just minutes later they rolled from the RIB and back into the water, where Mario shot some nice footage of Natascha shining her light at the cannons, the anchors and the many cannon balls. They spent the better part of an hour at this wreck, before they climbed back on the zodiac. With enough daylight left, they drove by the nearby Fortress of Louisbourg to have a closer look at the magnificent historic site. Just a few minutes later, they dropped their two new friends off at the wharf and Nick, Ole-Einar and Mario helped them to unload their gear. It turned out the university students had already been dropped off by the second RIB, and they also came down to help. After they bid farewell to each other, Ole-Einar steered the RIB away from the wharf. Natascha was still waving at them, and she could see the two of them starting another argument. Natascha, Mario and Nick looked at each other and laughed.

"When you meet them for the first time, someone will actually think they don't like each other. Who calls his dive buddy *short, bald and ugly*?" Natascha asked.

"I would," Nick replied and looked at Natascha with a wide smile.

"But only if I'm not diving with you," he added hastily after he saw the look on her face.

"Yes, I would do that, too. I'm more impressed by the fact that his buddy simply said he isn't ugly," Mario commented laughing.

"You remember those two old guys from the muppet show? That's who they remind me of," Natascha told Nick, curling her hand in his, while Ole-Einar drove back full speed to the *Northern Explorer,* which waited in safer waters just off the coast.

Home Office and Operational Headquarters of *EuroSecCorporation*, London Friday, July 15th

Sigrid Schneider sat together with her colleague Sean MacLeod in his office. Before long, they matched all the fingerprints to the Canadian and American scientists. While Sigrid had reactivated some old contacts in Germany to check names and fingerprints, Sean MacLeod went straight back to his former employee, Scotland Yard, to call in a favor. Brigitte Schwartze, retired General Klaus Schwartze's wife, even double-checked the names against the database in Europol. The only flaw in their process was the fact that all their data was based on European Intelligence. They did not have access to the American files. As long as the Canadians or Americans were not wanted by international arrest warrant, it would be difficult to confirm their real background and identity.

Sigrid leaned back in her chair and checked the list of names once more.

Dr. Joseph Richard, Jenna Mason, Frank Garcia, Nelson Singer and Brian Joice were the American scientists. Dr. Markus Habermann, Jonathan MacDonald, Marc Thornton and Sasha Theriault were the Canadian scientists. Sigrid followed the live's of those scientist back as far as she could. She managed to trace them back to the first day of school, and continued through elementary and high school up to university and all their jobs after that. She recognized them in several pictures from their high school and university years. As far as she could tell, there was nothing to worry about. She put all her findings in a little report and sent it via satellite to Ariel. Another copy of her findings would go into the case file after Klaus Schwartze and Brian Whittaker read it.

Gulf of St Lawrence, west of Newfoundland, on board the *Northern Explorer*, North Atlantic, Tuesday, July 19th
It was only seven o' clock in the morning, but Nick already knocked at Natascha's door. After he had identified himself, Shira opened the door and let him in.
"Good morning."
"Good morning. Is Natascha still showering?"
"Yes, but she should be finished any moment. I'm going up to the mess," Shira said and went outside.
"Do you need much longer?" Nick shouted at Natascha.
"No, will be there in a minute," Natascha shouted back.
For another fifteen minutes, Nick thought and sat down at her table. He started the computer and activated the simulation. Just five minutes later he was the virtual pilot of the research submersible. Except for Shira and Ariel, every team member had spent some time with the simulator the last three days, most times without Natascha checking on them. Still assigned as Natascha's personal assistant, Nick spent most of his time with her and Dr. Richard Weber. Ole-Einar and Oliver took turns in their regular security details, while Olaf had taken the night shifts from Oliver. They had agreed to take one-week turns in the night shifts.

Natascha and her father took part in the daily classroom sessions for their pilot course. Although Richard was already a certified pilot for several other research submersibles, he did not have the qualification for this particular model. So he decided to hit the books again along with the other trainees. Nick and Ole-Einar both took the chance to sit in during the morning classroom sessions.

In the afternoon they normally practiced what they learned in the morning. *Odin*, which was assigned to the German team only, stayed in its storage container for that purpose. They had enough lights to conduct all the necessary safety checks, and beside that, they only had to close both container doors to simulate a complete electrical failure. Natascha had already done several dives on board *Odin* during the three days in Iceland, but back then she was only the co-pilot. However, the safety regulations clearly stated that each of the two pilots had to be fully certified, just in case something happened to one of them.

Nick tried to remember what he learned during the last classroom session and looked at the simulated cockpit on the computer monitor. He maneuvered the little submersible about ten meters above the ocean bottom and tried hard to control the speed and the position. From his previous virtual excursions, he knew the ocean bottom would raise to a solid wall right in front of him any moment. Trying to concentrate on the task ahead, Nick heard the bathroom door open.

Natascha came out of the bathroom, wrapped in a large towel. On her way to her closet, she hugged Nick from behind and gave him a kiss.
"Good morning," she whispered.
"Good morning, Angel. I love you," Nick replied, his eyes glued to the monitor.

Thin Ice

"I love you too."
She kissed him once more and walked over to her closet.
"Watch the current. Use the thruster to stabilize yourself and reduce the speed. You're still to fast."
"Thank you," Nick said and looked at her with appreciation. Natascha was turned to her closest and quickly retrieved her towel from the floor the moment it fell. One second later she heard the well-known simulated noise of a submersible colliding into the rock wall at high speed.
"I told you you're to fast. Did you not see the rock wall?" Natascha asked without turning around.
"No, I didn't. Somehow I didn't see the rock wall, but you need to know it's all your fault," Nick laughed as he admired his girlfriend.
Natascha turned around and threw the towel at him.

Chuck Hogan's house, Boston, USA, Tuesday, July 19th
Chuck leaned back in his chair, closed his eyes for a few seconds, took a deep breath and stretched. After a moment, he looked back at his computer. At this point, his complete operation was at a stand-still. The operation was simply not doable the way they had planned it. He stood up, had a glass of orange juice and went back to his desk. Once more he activated the detailed drawings of the *Northern Explorer* and it's gear. His attention was focused on the air compressor that could fill all kinds of gas mixes.
Okay, trimix is no problem. They also have plenty of helium on board. Oxygen is also no problem since they have their own decompression chamber, he thought.
The *Northern Explorer* also had two modern diving helmets, equipped with two way communication as well as one hundred and fifty meters of breathing hose for each unit.
One hundred and fifty meters, Chuck thought and grasped a piece of paper. He drew the expected water depth and added the approximate horizontal distance.
If we can anchor at the right position, then those one hundred and fifty meters will be more than enough.
He looked at more of the ships details and noticed, that the research vessel was equipped with new air driven underwater tools, as well as all the gear required to weld or cut steel and metal. For an arctic research vessel of her size, this was actually standard equipment.
That should save us a lot of breathing gas and time at least for our first phase of the operation.
Chuck opened another file which showed him the details of the two submersibles. Flying over the general technical specifications, he found out that both submersibles were certified to an operational depth of two hundred and fifty meters.
I don't even want to go that deep. Seventy meters are more than enough. I'm more interested in how much weight they can both lift under water.
Chuck found the information just seconds later and looked at the grappler.
Would make sense if we attach a cable to those babies underwater. We can move

them underwater, but once we get them to the surface, they'd be too heavy. If we can hook a cable to them on the bottom, then we can use the cable winch from the research vessel. That's no problem at all.

Chuck made some notes of the technical details on a sheet of paper and returned to the drawings of the *Northern Explorer*. From the Internet, he had downloaded the details and public information about this expedition, as well as its daily logbook. The American carefully read the information and wrote down the total number of people on board, how many of them were scientists and how many crew personnel. He also paid attention to the section on which the individual scientists introduced themselves. He rubbed his eyes and looked back at the screen. Disappointed, yet hardly surprised, he did not find any information about the *EuroSecCorporation* and their people on board.

After the little mishap in Iceland, I'm pretty sure they're still on board. I counted seven back then in Berlin. I doubt there are going to be less people now.

Chuck zoomed in to some of the drawings, then he focused again on his own task.

If we always have two divers under water and one person on board, who is monitoring the dive and the breathing gas, then that would leave us with one person to deal with the crew. That way we would be able to do one dive in the morning and one in the afternoon. But what are we doing with our hostages who are still on board? At least six or seven of them are former member of Special Forces, and they will all carry weapons. Besides that, they know the ship inside out by now, and they have the support from the Captain and the crew.

Chuck got out of his chair and paced the room with thought. Regardless of whatever angle he looked at, he always came to the same result: he would need more men. His eyes opened wide as it suddenly struck him like lightning. He took his cell phone and smiled as he dialed the number of a satellite phone. Only seconds later, he could hear the voice of a woman, though not very clear and with lots of interferences, but he immediately recognized her.

"Hello?"

"Hi sister, how are you doing? Do you have a moment?"

On board the *Northern Explorer*, Gulf of St Lawrence, west of Newfoundland, North Atlantic, Tuesday, July 19th

The *Northern Explorer* lay at anchor as Captain Rasmussen, Ariel and Shira entered one of the classrooms where the students were meeting. Holger Bloomquist and the leading Dive Officer Vitali Vachenko stood in front of the room, and the students pulled out their laptops with the simulation program as instructed.

"We'll stay with them for the rest of the afternoon. If you want, you can leave now. We'll see you at supper time," Ariel mentioned to Nick, while Holger told everybody that he wanted the submersibles called by their name or addressed as "submersible" rather than the wrong identification as a "U-Boat." His frustration was evident, as he stressed this important point.

"We'll be in the gym for the next two hours," Nick whispered to Ariel and left the classroom quietly with Ole-Einar, who closed the door behind him.

Holger Bloomquist explained how to connect the laptops to the main unit on the front desk.

"The trick with this simulation is pretty easy. Each simulation program has it's own hidden protocol unit, and only Vitali and I have access to them. That way, we can examine each individual test run. It's much easier for us to find out which student has some accumulated needs. You don't have any access to that protocol unit without our passwords. We can make sure that students do not temper with the simulation protocol and therefore not only put their own life, but also the life of their co-pilot, at risk later on."

Oh no, Natascha suddenly gasped as she scanned the room with concern, *Nick crashed the sub this morning!* She tried to calm her worry and seemed to be successful with the thought, that this little mishap was the only mistake in the ten hours she spent on the simulator. She started to work on her explanation of the crash with as much decency as she could.

She activated the program and followed Holger's instructions. Seconds later, Holger and Vitali were checking out the individual protocols from their students on their main computer in front of the class. Every now and then, one of them pointed on the monitor and made some notes, but generally they seemed to be pleased.

Suddenly Holger shook his head and pointed something out on the monitor.

Natascha did not know why, but her stomach churned at the sight. Her suspicion was confirmed when both Holger and Vitali briefly looked at her and asked her to stay at the end of the class. With her blood running cold, Natascha now noticed that even Captain Rasmussen walked over to the computer and looked at the monitor himself.

The Captain had taken the liberty to check out the protocol data from this classroom.

"I want to know that the people, who are driving circles around my propeller in a pile of steel, are capable and know what they're doing."

Now Captain Rasmussen shook his head in disapproval together with Holger and Vitali. Natascha's eyes suddenly darted to her father, as he went over to have a look for himself. Her heart raced as Richard went over the protocol and also shook his head slightly. Natascha picked up on his nonverbal gesture and her heart sank.

"Natascha, we have a problem with your protocol," Holger finally said.

"Yes, I know, the protocol has recorded a crash this morning, but I can explain it," she said hastily.

"Well, the protocol does not record the time and date, but I'm more concerned about your general performance. According to this protocol, you've spent more than fourteen hours with the simulator. Generally I can say you have improved a lot, that you have a great knowledge about the physics of the submersible, and that you have showed a great technical interest. Nonetheless, you have made some crucial mistakes in this simulation. You have lost *Odin* twice in a depth of over one thousand meters because you have completely ignored the maximum operational depth. Three times you have performed a buoyant emergency ascent from over six hundred meters of depth without any reason at all. And three times you collided with *Odin* at maximum speed at the rock wall, and once more at low speed. But between all those chaotic dives, you also had some very good performances. It looks to me that you absolutely carelessly and unnecessarily tried to push *Odin* over its limit. Based on this protocol, I can't let you participate in any further pilot training. Can you explain that in any way?"

Natascha's shock turned to a vicious scowl as she stared at her instructors in complete disbelief.

"I don't know how…wait a second. Over fourteen hours you said?"

Vitali checked the monitor again, with all other eyes resting on the young German woman.

"Fourteen hours and eighteen minutes, to be precise."

"There is no way that I spent…," Natascha stopped and closed her eyes.

I'm going to kill them all! She took a couple of deep breaths and looked up to her instructors again.

"I can explain that, give me five minutes," she said calmly as she got out of her chair. She turned around and looked furiously at Ariel.

"Where are…"

"Gym," Ariel interrupted her.

"I'm coming with you," Ariel added, but Natascha was already on her way.

Without looking back or slowing down, she rushed through the corridors and downstairs to the gym with determination.

Ariel was at a slight jog to keep up with her.

"Listen, Natascha. I'm sure they didn't know you could get in trouble for that."

"I've told them they could use the simulator. I never asked them to spend several hours with it to let me look like a complete idiot in front of my father and the instructors!"

"I'm sure they can explain all this," Ariel tried to calm her down.

"And that's exactly what they're going to do right now," Natascha snapped back with finality. She was silent as she continued towards the gym. Her breath was harsh and her anger made her move stiffly. She hurriedly opened the gym door and looked around to see only a few people were working out. Natascha spotted Nick, Ole-Einar and Oliver in one corner at the bench press and walked over to them.

"Who messed around with the simulation program?" She snapped at them.

Ole-Einar wiped some sweat from his face and looked up at her from the bench.

"We all played with the simulator, but you allowed…"

"I told you that you can try the simulator if you're careful. I didn't ask you to spend four hours with it to make a complete idiot out of me in front of my father, the Captain and the other instructors!"

Nick looked at Ole-Einar and Oliver. Beside the one mishap this morning, Nick had only used the simulator with Natascha. With this lone fact, it only offered little comfort as he recalled the mishap this morning.

Ole-Einar looked unhappily to the floor, working on an apology.

"Listen Natascha. We're sorry. We can explain it."

"And that's exactly what you're going to do right now," Natascha shouted at them. "Right now?" Oliver asked and looked at the bench press.

Still glaring at them, Natascha pointed her finger to the door. The three guys moved quickly to their feet, knowing her gesture could have been a lot worse. They scurried to the door and walked off like dogs with their tail between their legs, as they slowly made their way to the classroom. Natascha lead their way and Ariel fought his burst of laughter.

A few minutes later, Natascha opened the door to the classroom, a furious scowl still evident. As soon as the three guys arrived at the door, she pointed into the classroom, still emitting her eerie silence.

With their heads down, Nick, Ole-Einar and Oliver walked into the classroom and sat down. Ariel closed the door and joined Shira, who's smile quivered across her lips.

Holger, Vitali, Captain Rasmussen and Natascha's father all looked at the three guys. "Those three gentlemen would like to give an explanation," Natascha said and walked over to the main computer. She wiped her hair out of her face and oriented herself on the screen. After a few seconds she had found the information she was looking for.

"Twice a total loss in over one thousand meters of depth, exceeding the maximum operational depth of two hundred and fifty meters and under total ignorance of all warning signals and manual override of the automatic security valves. Who of you hobby pilots is responsible for that?"

Ole-Einar and Oliver both raised their hands, while all the instructors behind Natascha started to chuckle.

"Three times uncontrolled emergency ascent due to ditching the ballast weights and one hundred percent blown trim cells. Manual override of the automatic overpressure relief valves. Three times total loss due to ruptured trim cells." Natascha didn't ask, she only threw them a killing glance.

Ole-Einar and Oliver raised their hands again.

"Olaf was responsible for the third loss," Oliver whispered.

"What did you say? Olaf was the third crash test dummy?" Natascha snapped.

Oliver just nodded his head, still looking at the floor.

"Three times collision under water with a solid rock wall in one hundred and eighty meters of depth with the maximum speed of six knots. Twice total loss due to a ruptured pressure hull, one total loss due to ruptured trim cells."

Leaning on the table and resting on her hands, Natascha only glared at them again and Ole-Einar and Oliver also both raised their hands.

"Olaf also caused the third accident here," Ole-Einar whispered.

Natascha looked down at the monitor and checked the data from the accident this morning. She turned around and looked at Holger and Vitali.

"The last accident is from this morning. Nick was using the simulator under my direct supervision, but I had distracted him unintentionally. Normally that would not have happened."

She turned around to face Ole-Einar and Oliver again and suddenly all her anger was gone.

"When I told you that you could try the simulator, did you not think that I would look really bad if you mess with the program? You all know how hard I'm working to become a pilot. Why would you do this?"

Ole-Einar and Oliver already felt uneasy a few minutes ago when Natascha was shouting at them, but it was nothing compared to the miserable feeling they had now. Natascha's eyes filled with tears,

"Okay, everybody listen," Ole-Einar abruptly stood up, the sight unbearable.

"We take full responsibility for all the accidents that Natascha just mentioned. Natascha didn't know what we were doing with the simulator. All she knew was that we would spend a few minutes with the program, but she had no idea that we did several independent dives on the simulator. Yes, we did crash the submersible on purpose, because we wanted to see how the simulator would react to it. But it has never been our intention, that Natascha would get any disadvantage in her training because of this. I don't think that it would be fair to exclude Natascha from any further training just because…my friends and I weren't responsible enough."

Holger and Vitali both looked at the Captain, while Shira bit her tongue, still fighting her laughter.

"Okay, Natascha. If you want, you can perform another simulation right now in our presence. If that simulation is as good as the other perfect simulations that you had on the simulator here, then I wouldn't see any problems and you can certainly continue your training. Captain Rasmussen?" Holger said and turned to the Captain.

Captain Rasmussen straightened up, held his hands behind his back and glared at Ole-Einar.

"A fellow country-man of all people. I'd suggest you come up with something special as an apology to Ms. Kleinfeld. If I'd have it my way, you'd swab the deck. Keelhauling you would also be an interesting alternative, but I'm afraid it'd be problematic, given the actual water temperature and the length of the ship. I leave that to your superior." Captain Rasmussen turned his attention to Holger.

"I trust your judgment, Holger. I'm confident with Natascha's performance."

Captain Rasmussen left the classroom and told Ariel that he could find him on the bridge.

"Can we leave now?" Ole-Einar whispered.

"Why? Wasn't that enough already?" Shira asked and finally burst into laughter.

Ole-Einar and Oliver both left the room under Ariel's disapproving glance.

Without a word, Nick turned around and followed his friends.

"Nick, can you please wait a minute?" Natascha shouted after him.

She took him by the hand and walked outside the classroom with him, where she waited until Ole-Einar and Oliver were both out of hearing distance.

"I'm sorry you were stuck in the group with the others and that I yelled at you. I know you didn't cause any of those accidents, but I was really upset with the other two."

"Well, I did crash the submersible this morning," Nick reminded with defeat, but really hoped Natascha would feel better.

His girlfriend rolled her eyes.

"Yes, you did collide with the wall this morning, but I wasn't completely innocent either. Normally you wouldn't get distracted in a submersible or under water the way you got this morning."

"Too bad," Nick said and smiled.

"You're a pig," Natascha whispered and laughed.

He hugged her closely for a moment and gave her a kiss.

"I'm sorry the guys caused you so much trouble."

"It's okay, they explained it in the end."

Nick kissed his girlfriend once more and went back to the gym, where he found his two friends. Both were sitting at the bench press, their heads still down.

"I have an idea," Nick said to cheer up their spirit.

Chuck Hogan's house, Boston, USA, Tuesday, July 19th

Oh my God! That can't be true, Chuck Hogan thought and closed his eyes for a moment, after he had ended the call. He almost spoke for over an hour with his sister. Although they both only described all their actions and planned operations, they both knew without a doubt, what they wanted from each other. His sister assured him that she would talk to the rest of her team. The only determining factor would be a matter of cost. If Chuck could arrange that they were paid enough, then there wouldn't be any problems. Fact was that he knew all the team members, and they also knew him. But Chuck did not think that it was necessary to tell that to the American and the Canadian. They planned that they would still act as if the two groups would not know each other.

With her team, we finally have enough people. That's enough to keep the complete operation under control.

He opened his eyes again and dialed a number in London.

"Listen, we have a serious problem, but I also have the solution. We have to talk."

On board the *Northern Explorer*, Gulf of St Lawrence, west of Newfoundland, North Atlantic, Wednesday, July 20th

Like usual, Astrid was sitting in the radio room since eight o'clock in the morning. The *Northern Explorer* was now at the entrance to the Gulf of St Lawrence, a heavily frequented shipping lane used by oil tankers and cargo ships on their way to the Canadian Province of Quebec. There was a lot of radio traffic this morning. Ariel came into the radio room, connected his laptop to the satellite and started it, not without wishing Astrid a "Good Morning."

"Anything interesting on the radio?" he asked her.

Astrid shook her head. "No, not really. There is a lot of steel under way, but everything's fine. I just have to report our position and activities every hour and to each ship that comes within twenty miles."

Ariel nodded to her and thanked her. After he launched his program and checked the satellite for any new messages, he got up and walked over to the window.

On the deck, Dr. Richard Weber was standing together with Nick, Ole-Einar and Oliver at the foredeck. The *Northern Explorer* was still at anchor and both the Americans and the Canadians were doing some research using the two eight meter long RIB's.

Natascha and her instructor Holger Bloomquist were on board the submersible *Odin* and at the moment around one hundred meters below the surface. It was the first time that Natascha was piloting the little research vessel by herself in such deep waters. She could still feel the nervousness she had all morning.

On board the *Northern Explorer*, Shira was sitting together with leading Dive Officer Vitali Vachenko in the dive control room, which was located on the main deck directly beside the decompression chamber. From the dive control room they could manage the air compressor, mix the necessary breathing gasses and most importantly, they could communicate with either the divers or the submersibles. Vitali and Shira were sitting in front of the large panel with all kinds of communication equipment as well as gauges and dial knobs, and together they followed Natascha's performance in *Odin*.

Vitali scribbled on his decades old clipboard in front of him as he kept a detailed record of the dive.

One hundred and four meters below them, Natascha was fighting the cold temperature with her thermo jump-suit, which she normally used under her dry-suit, and Nicks woolen beanie. Naturally she always cared about her appearance, even on a long expedition, but for the moment she was just happy to be warm.

"Okay, Natascha. How does the bottom look down there?" she heard Vitalis voice over the radio clearly, but not loud.

Natascha stretched a little bit and looked outside the huge plexiglas window. With her left hand she operated a little joystick and changed the angle of the strong underwater lights.

"We're about five meters above the ocean floor. I can see lots of mud and sand. Not much going on down here."

"Okay Natascha. I now want you to check all your systems again. Give me a triple check," she heard Vitali telling her.

"Okay, I confirm. Triple check, all systems."

Natascha turned her head to her left and looked at her own clipboard, which she had temporarily mounted to the frame at her eye level with a simple magnet. She took the clipboard and put it on her lap. Checking all the gauges, she filled out the checklist. Every pilot had their own clipboard and Natascha had glued the little Orca, which she had received from Nick as a gift, on hers.

She went over her checklist one last time and asked Holger if she had forgotten something.

"No, so far everything is fine. Are you ready for your first emergency exercise?"

Natascha took a deep breath and looked over the instrument panel.

"Okay, more ready than I'll ever be. Maybe a little emergency exercise for the beginning?" she asked with a tempting smile.

"Don't worry. Later on, when you're on your own, you can also choose the type and the moment of the emergency you will encounter," Holger countered sarcastically and pressed the radio button.

"Okay, Vitali, we now start emergency exercise number one. All stations, all stations, all stations. This is *Odin, Odin, Odin*. Emergency exercise number one."

"This is *Northern Explorer*. I confirm, emergency exercise number one, number one, number one. Good luck."

"What exactly is exercise number one?" Shira asked Vitali.

"Exercise number one is pretty simple. It's an all systems down due to a complete loss of the primary power source. Nothing special. All Natascha has to do, is to activate the emergency battery and perform a safety check. Once everything is up and running again, she has to identify the mistake and make a decision whether she can fix the problem or to abort the dive."

Being slightly overwhelmed about all the tasks involved in a simple exercise, Shira raised her eyebrows.

Vitali pushed the radio button on his panel.

"Okay, Natascha. Whenever you're ready."

One hundred meters below, Natascha sat up straight and took another breath.

"Okay, I'm ready."

"Just assume I'm not here. But I want you to tell me every individual step before you actually do something. Should you become scared at any point or if you don't know what to do, then just let me know and I'll take over. Agree?"

"Agree."

Holger turned around and activated some switches.

The anticipation made her nervousness spike. She noticed Holger straighten up in his seat and she waited. A few seconds passed and nothing changed.

She took a deep breath to settle her beating heart.

So many things happened in such a short time that Natascha was not sure which happened first. The sum of the batteries suddenly died and the lights flickered for a view seconds before everything went black.

Natascha was sitting in total darkness, not even the emergency lights were working.

The only thing she could hear was her heartbeat in her ears as she took a few deep breaths. Although she knew that basically nothing could happen, she had to admit, her nervousness increased.

She tried to find the pocket in her thermo jumpsuit, but Holger noticed it right away and his voice pierced the silence.

"I know you have a little LED headlight in there. And that's not a bad idea at all, and under normal circumstances it would be really helpful now. But I have to insist that you do this exercise in total darkness."

Would have been too easy, Natascha grimaced, but glad he could not see.

"Okay," she finally said more to herself.

"It looks to me that we've just experienced a complete power loss to all our systems. First I will use my right hand to find the main battery switch at the main switchboard over our heads. I will then turn the two main batteries off, before I switch to the back-up system."

"Okay, that sounds great so far," Holger encouraged her and the young German scientist reached over. Natascha reached in the darkness, her hand drifting more to the right as she reached up quickly. Instead of reaching the switchboard, her finger moved quickly and poked Holger's eye.

"Oh my God, I'm so sorry! That was an accident," Natascha apologized immediately.

"I believe the switch is more to the left," Holger groaned as his hand shot to his left eye, rubbing the pain and tears away.

Being more careful, Natascha found the main battery switch and turned it to the OFF position.

"Okay, all batteries are off now. I'll now turn the switch for the emergency batteries one position clockwise, without trying to injure my instructor any further," Natascha explained her next move calmly.

Holger could not help but laugh, despite the pain that pulsed his eye.

"Yes, that's the way to do it. I wish they'd all be so careful," he said.

Natascha turned the switch clockwise and waited until she heard the familiar sum of the batteries again. A few seconds later, the LED lights flashed back on and Natascha was now able to see everything again.

"I'm really sorry about your eye. I thought the switch was further to the right," she apologized once more and looked at Holger.

Holger waved her off, but he still kept his left eye closed.

"Okay, I'll now report the power loss to the surface and start to check all the individual systems."

"Yes, that's correct."

Natascha called Vitali on board the *Northern Explorer* and reported their situation, before she took her clipboard again.

"Okay, according to our gauges, I can't find any particular error. So my conclusion would be, that we have a problem with our main power source. I would inform our support vessel about this. Since we're already on the back-up batteries, I would now immediately end the dive and return to surface in a normal controlled ascent using the thrusters."

"Good. That would wrap it up. You can now switch back to the main batteries and tell Vitali that the exercise is over."

Natascha switched back to the main batteries and called the *Northern Explorer* over the radio again.

"*Northern Explorer, Northern Explorer, Northern Explorer*, this is *Odin, Odin, Odin*. Our emergency exercise is over. I repeat, our emergency exercise is over and we'll continue our dive as scheduled."

"This is *Northern Explorer.* I confirm that the emergency exercise is over and that you continue your dive. Roger that. Anything special?"

Natascha thought for a moment and glanced at Holger, who was still wiping tears of his eye.

"Is Shira with you, Vitali?" Natascha asked.

Vitali and Shira looked at each other.

"That's positive. She is sitting beside me," Vitali answered.

"Tell her that she'd be proud of me."

Shira frowned and looked at Vitali, not knowing what Natascha was referring to.

Down in the submersible, Holger checked all systems once more and checked them on his own clipboard.

"Okay Natascha. I think we can try the hydrophone once more."

Natascha nodded and looked to her left, where she found the switch for this highly sensible equipment.

"First I will bring *Odin* up to a depth of fifty meters. After that, I will activate the hydrophone and check if it's working properly. After that, I'll lower its cable to about thirty meters below *Odin* to reduce the recording of any unwanted noises caused by the submersibles batteries and thrusters. We can finally start recording then," Natascha explained her next steps.

"Yes, that sounds good. You can use the thrusters to bring *Odin* up to fifty meters."

Ariel was on the bridge of the research vessel and looked at one of the four radar screens. He had identified the two zodiacs used by both the Canadians and Americans, and he was very satisfied to see that they were actually operating in the area they had indicated, while Natascha had taken *Odin* in the complete opposite direction.

Captain Rasmussen walked beside him.

"Is everything the way it should be?" he asked.

"Generally yes. At the moment everything seems to be under control."

"Ms. Kleinfeld had definitely put your men back into their places yesterday," the Norwegian Captain added with a smile.

"Yes, that's true," Ariel laughed. "Normally it takes at least a three star general to get that expression on their faces. But I've been told they came up with something really unique as an apology. As far as I'm concerned, I don't think that any further actions in that matter are necessary."

Captain Rasmussen nodded in agreement, still smiling.

"The Canadians?" he asked and looked on the radar screen.

Ariel pointed out one of the two little green dots.

The Captain nodded again and sat back in his comfortable chair, looking out the window.

One hour later, Natascha maneuvered *Odin* back to the *Northern Explorer* and surfaced right beside the research vessel. She found it very unusual to look through the huge domed plexiglas window. Due to its low center of gravity, *Odin* was still partially submerged in the water, and Natascha was still afraid that she would get wet feet. At the surface, the little submersible was not very maneuverable, but Natascha had surfaced close enough in the lee side of the research vessel. Together with Holger, she could see a small zodiac with two crew members coming to them. One of them was in a dry-suit and jumped on *Odin* to install the lifting cable to *Odin*'s frame. Once he had secured the huge snap, he signaled Natascha through the window that everything was fine. Natascha turned off all systems, excluding the radio.

Fifteen minutes later *Odin* landed safe and sound on the foredeck of the *Northern Explorer*. The hatch opened with a loud smack and, beaming with joy, Natascha climbed out of the submersible. Her father was already waiting for her and gave her a big hug.

"Congratulation, this was your first dive in a submersible as a pilot."

"Thank you," Natascha beamed happily and kissed her father on his cheek.

While Natascha reconstructed the emergency exercise for her father again, Nick, Ole-Einar and Oliver already started to disassemble the huge underwater lights and prepared *Odin* to be stowed away in the container again. The two zodiacs used by the Americans and Canadians would soon occupy the room on the foredeck.

Natascha and Holger went to the dive control room where they met with Vitali and Shira.

"Congratulation Natascha. That was really good for the first time," Vitali smiled.

His smile froze on his face as soon as he saw Holger's eye.

"What in God's name happened to you?"

Natascha blushed.

"The moment I turned the lights off down there, Natascha tried to poke my eye out with her finger."

Vitali and Shira both laughed.

"After I saw you yelling at your three friends yesterday I'm not surprised at all. I'm just concerned what you will do to our poor Holger once you get to the more complex emergency exercises," Vitali said and laughed.

"Well, we will have to wait and see. I'll go and change. We will still meet at six this evening for the debriefing?"

"Yes, 18.00 it is."

Natascha thanked once more and walked with Shira to her cabin.

On their way to the cabin they both saw the zodiac with the Canadians coming back to the research vessel at high speed. Natascha stopped for a moment and watched them sternly.

"Relax, Natascha. Look at it this way. Without them, Nick wouldn't be on board."

Natascha looked over to Nick, who was just carrying one of *Odin*'s underwater lights in the container with Oliver.

"That's true. Would be pretty boring without you and the guys," Natascha laughed.

A few minutes later, they both stood in front of their cabin door. Before Natascha could open the door, Shira got in front of her and looked at her seriously.

"Listen Natascha. The boys are feeling really bad because of that simulator thing and they really have a bad conscience and want to apologize to you. Nick had a nice

Thin Ice

idea, but I'm not so sure if they executed that idea the way Nick had planned it. But I can guarantee you that they really tried their best."

Although Shira had planned to remain serious, she could not help herself and burst into laughter before she opened the door.

Natascha looked around and immediately noticed the huge chocolate cake, which was standing on the little table in the middle of the room. Leaning against it was a letter sized sheet of paper with a professional drawn cartoon.

It showed a woman with long black hair wearing a Captain's hat, and who was standing on top of the cunning tower of a surfaced submarine. Natascha recognized, that this character obviously was meant to portray her. In this cartoon, Natascha was also wearing pink slippers, and her left foot rested on top of the head of a man who was standing on the submarine's deck. This male character was wearing a sweater with the German flag as well as the capital letter "N" on it. Beside that, the character, which definitely portrayed Nick, was also wearing a long skirt as well as a little tiara, still clearly recognizable underneath Natascha's slipper. In his hands, Nick's character was holding three ropes, each tied to another male character. While all three of those characters were wearing a sweater with the capital letter "O", two of the sweaters also showed the Norwegian flag, while the other sweater showed the German flag. Another thing that the three characters of Olaf, Ole-Einar and Oliver had in common was that they were getting keelhauled by Nick's character.

Natascha picked the cartoon up and burst into laughter with Shira. She laughed so hard that she had to lay down on her bed. It took Natascha several minutes before she gained some control again and she had tears running down her cheeks. She wiped the tears out her face and sat up again.

"And this was Nick's idea?" she looked at Shira.

"Nick had actually suggested that you are the one person with the ropes and that you're keelhauling all four of them. As far as I know, he doesn't know that Olaf has changed the cartoon into this. I know Nick hasn't seen it yet."

Natascha was still laughing when she stood up again to place the cartoon beside the cake again.

"Where did they get the cake? It looks delicious. There's no way they made this one themselves."

"No, they didn't make it. They had to pay a lot of money to the cook for this one."

"Well, I suggest we try it once I'm back from my debriefing. Those four are really amazing," Natascha laughed again and walked into the bathroom to get changed.

After both the Canadian and the American team were back on board, and the two RIB's safely tied to the deck, Captain Rasmussen ordered the research vessel back on it's course. Without delay, the *Northern Explorer* continued her journey north.

The evening debriefing for the submersible pilots in training didn't take too long. All four them had shown exceptional results. Dr. Richard Weber was very proud of his daughter and asked her to listen to her audio recordings from the hydrophone.

Natascha decided that they would attack the cake at 19.00 in their cabin. To support her and Shira in this difficult task, she had invited not only the four culprits, but also Ariel and of course her father. She knew that it would get a little bit cramped in the cabin, but she was convinced that it wouldn't be problem.

With Shira resting on her bed, Natascha and her father were listening to the audio recording. While Natascha was concentrating on the recording, her father was sitting beside her, still amused about the cartoon.

Richard put down the cartoon and showed her at the laptop how to filter out any unwanted interferences.

"Can you hear this noise here? That's the sound of the engine from the *Northern Explorer*. If you use this filter here, you can reduce that frequency altogether. And this sound here are *Odin*'s batteries. Although the hydrophone is designed in such way that it doesn't record any sound that is immediately on top of it, it's still sensitive enough to record all the traces of those sound sources. But we can also eliminate them if we use this filter here," Natascha's father explained and showed her how to change the settings on the computer, so they wouldn't hear any mechanical interference any more.

"Okay, with the two loudest interferences sources gone, we can hear now the two zodiacs as well as one of the container ships. We can also filter them out without losing too much of the recording, but the traffic in those waterways here is way too high to get anything really useful out of this. You will notice the difference as soon as we're in the North-West Passage and away from all the commercial shipping lanes," Richard explained and sat back stretching.

Since they expected their guests any moment now, Shira sat up and looked at them.

"What range does this hydrant have anyway?" she asked.

Both Richard and Natascha had to laugh for a moment.

"It's called a hydrophone, Shira," Richard explained. "The hydrophone itself has technically an unlimited range. The quality of the recording depends more on the intensity and the frequency of the source. This unit here is the most powerful and sensitive unit available outside military applications. Do you hear this sound here?" Richard asked and played a certain sequence of the recording.

Shira nodded.

"This is one of the many container ships. It's definitely over thirty sea miles away. Water is about eight hundred times more denser than air, which means that it carries sound waves much faster and over a much greater distance than air does. You usually use a specially designed computer for the analysis. With a little bit of experience, you can actually determine with a high grade of certainty from which distance and direction the individual sound waves are coming from. Technically it is no different to what all the Navy's have been doing all the time. On this computer here we are just practicing to recognize different sounds, that's about as accurate as they get."

Someone knocked at the door and Ariel identified himself.

"Someone told me that there's some free chocolate cake here?" Astrid asked and peeked in the cabin.

"Yes, there is. Prepared from the chef himself," Natascha explained and offered them to sit anywhere they wanted.

Thin Ice

"Is that true?" Astrid asked and sat down on a chair. "Sven made this one? He usually only makes a cake for a round birthday starting with your fifties, for anniversaries or on special holidays. That must've cost them tons of money," Astrid explained, still impressed with the cake.

"It was their own fault," Natascha said and shrugged her shoulders.

"Here, have a look at this. That's their idea of an *I'm sorry I screwed up* card," Natascha added before she handed Astrid the cartoon.

Astrid and Ariel both burst into laughter the moment they saw the cartoon. They almost didn't hear the knocking on the door shortly before Nick and the remaining members of the team stepped in.

Nick found his way to Natascha, wrapped his arms around her and gave her a huge kiss.

"Congratulation to your first successful trip as main submersible pilot. I'm happy you did so well," he explained.

"Yes, considering that I was just one step away from getting kicked out of the program, it wasn't too bad. Your cartoon is first class. Was it really your idea?" she asked.

"Yes, it was my idea," Nick answered.

"Do you think the cartoon reflects the situation realistically?" Natascha asked innocently.

Nick thought for a while.

"Well, I do think everybody in this cartoon is in the position they deserve. After all, I did cause one of the accidents on your simulator. I would have explained your instructors how you distracted me, but you didn't give me the chance."

"Insignificant details. All I want to know is if you really identify yourself with the position your cartoon character is in. I would think it unfair if the other three talked you into that. After all, you weren't as bad as they were. You didn't have to give yourself that position just because of me," Natascha said with the most innocent look she could master.

Behind Nick's back, the other three were smirking.

"Listen, I caused one of the accidents and I'm in the exact position I deserve in this cartoon ," Nick explained, still unaware of what was really going on.

Natascha closed her eyes for a few seconds to enjoy the moment, while everybody else except Nick started to laugh.

"I hope you all bear witness about what had just happened until the end of our lives," Natascha said and finally handed the cartoon to Nick.

Nick's eyes widened in shock and disbelief, but then he had to laugh as well.

"Are you all nuts?" he asked and looked at his friends.

"This is not the how we discussed it. I was suppose to be with you under the sub. Why am I wearing a skirt and a crown? Are those really slippers on your feet?" Nick continued, taking in the details.

Still laughing about Nick, they all volunteered to testify on the back side of the cartoon that Nick had officially accepted his position under Natascha's slipper.

"You can frame that for your wedding. That would take care of all eventualities for the rest of your life," Ole-Einar explained and padded Nick on the shoulder.

"I have the right to protest," Nick said.

"Yeah, right. A man having a right to protest. Dream on, brother. Just seconds ago you admitted that you belong in this position. There's no back paddling now," Nick's Norwegian friend explained.

"Okay, enough with the cartoon before Nick changes his mind," Natascha laughed and took the cartoon from Nick. After she placed it in the drawer of her table, she turned her attention towards the masterpiece of a chocolate cake.

"Does someone have a knife so we can actually cut the cake?" Natascha asked and everybody looked around.

Shira moved suddenly and pulled a knife from her belt.

"It's not usually meant to cut cake, but it will do. And don't worry, it's a new one," she explained after she saw the worried look on Ariel's face.

"You should get one as well," she added and looked at Natascha, who had also given her a puzzled look.

"Not sure about that. Even unarmed, Natascha's very dangerous. I heard she injured her instructor today pretty bad," Ole-Einar commented.

"Yes, I think it's safe to say that Sasha would really appreciate it, if we don't give you any weapons. What's your deal with her anyway?" Olaf asked.

Natascha looked at Nick and shrugged her shoulders in innocence.

"It's one of those women things. She shows way too much interest in Nick," Natascha explained calmly.

"You're jealous?" Nick asked surprised.

"Well, the watchful eye can indeed detect that they both have a great deal in common," Shira answered.

"Really? I can't detect them," Nick commented seriously, not knowing that he started to dig himself another hole.

"Both are marine biologists, about the same age and are very attractive. You also marked both their butts the first time you met each of them. Except the color of their hair, they actually do have quite a lot in common," Shira explained.

Nick looked to the ceiling and pretended to be thinking hard.

"Well, now that you mention it, she is indeed pretty hot. Maybe I should visit her later tonight," he said and looked at Shira.

Natascha's mouth fell wide open and she threw herself on Nick to punch and bite him.

"You're so not going to visit her," she hissed, still punching her boyfriend.

"As long as I'm not allowed to get close to other men, you'll keep your hands and other body parts away from this God-only-knows-what-she-is."

"Relax, I saw her yesterday at the bow. She was standing there talking for over an hour to someone on her cell phone. She seems to be longing for someone," Astrid mentioned and hoped to help Nick.

"She's on board this ship until October and I prohibit seduction," Natascha argued with relentless attack.

"But I'm not even interested in her. She's so not my type," Nick defended himself from under Natascha.

"Really?" Natascha asked and sat up surprised. "She's not your type?" she asked and wiped her hair out of her face.

"No, she isn't. I don't like good looking marine biologists who are alone on a research vessel for several weeks."

Natascha's jaw dropped down again, while the others all started laughing.

"Oh!" she screamed, before she launched another attack on her boyfriend. "Completely the wrong answer," she hissed and landed on Nick again.

Nick let her fight for a few second before he held her tight and had her promise him she would behave and let him eat cake.

"But only if you stay away from her. I don't want to hear that you even got close to her," she demanded.

"I promise," Nick said and rolled his eyes.

"If you don't want to hear that I got close with her, then I'll simply not tell you about it. Problem solved," Nick answered with a smirk, convinced that he had Natascha under control.

Natascha proved him wrong and her next attack was even more furious. She only stopped after she had made Nick promise her several times, that he would stay away from Sasha.

Still not trusting him completely, Natascha sat up again and continued to watch Nick, who was still laying on the bed.

"Oh, Nick, there's something else I wanted to ask you to do," Ariel mentioned, enjoying his piece of cake before he continued.

"I want you to get close to Sasha. Use your charm, ask her out, meet her, spend some time with her alone. Do whatever you have to do to find out what they are up to," Ariel said and looked at Nick with a wide grin.

Nick, who was just trying to sit up, looked horrified as he glanced from Natascha to Ariel. Natascha took the opportunity and launched another surprise attack at Nick.

"You're so not going to do this," she hissed and continued the attack on her boyfriend.

"Why are you attacking me? That was his idea, not mine," Nick tried to defend himself and held her tight.

Realizing that she couldn't free herself, Natascha glanced at Nick.

"That's true, but I'm too much of a chicken to attack him," she explained.

"Okay kids, let it go," Shira said and handed each of them a piece of cake.

- 11 -

London, Friday, July 22nd
Chuck Hogan and his British friend and client followed the little path that led the two of them through the century old forest on the estate.

"If we want to continue with our project as planned, then we do need the assistance and support from my sister and her group on board the ship. At the moment, we simply have to assume that *EuroSecCorporation* still has five to seven people on board the research vessel. If this is the case, then every single member of that group will not only be armed, but also able to use those weapons very efficiently. I also believe they have the total cooperation of the Captain and the entire crew. If they know how to do their job, and I'm certain that they do, then they're also using several surveillance cameras. There's no way we can eliminate this security force and take over the whole ship with just four people, without any of them sending a radio message. We need more people. Just the diving operation itself will need too many people at the moment."

"And everybody in your sister's group can dive that deep?"

"No, they actually can't. They're not trained for the type of diving that we need, but they can control the ship during the dives. There is something else," Chuck paused for a second before he looked at his client.

"Do you know the details about the job my sister's group is about to do?"

"All I know is that they're responsible for our investments protection, and that all the evidence in this operation leads back to the expedition. But I don't know the details of their assignment."

Chuck stopped walking.

His British client turned around after a few steps and looked at the American assassin.

"Chuck, I can assure you, that I don't know the details of their assignment. Neither the American nor the Canadian was willing to inform me about that. I decided to keep playing the role of the concerned money bag and didn't pursue this matter any further. I've been in this business for years, I've done my homework."

Chuck stepped closer to the British and during the next few minutes, he told him the details that his sister had told him just a few days ago. Once he finished, Chuck could see that his friend's face was pale. The British took a few steps and sat down on an old bank at the side of the path.

"Oh my God! I didn't know that," he muttered and looked over a little pond.

"But, on the other hand, what other choice is there?" he continued after he rearranged his thoughts.

"Has your sister mentioned how much time they have?" he asked.

"Well, fact is, they have to keep their time frame, since both the American as well as the Canadian will be on board the ship by then to supervise that part of the operation," Chuck answered and sat beside the British.

"According to my sister, we have ten days. That will give us eight days for the actual diving operation. After that, I presume the authorities will get nervous."

"Do you think that eight days are enough?"

"Let me put it this way. It'd be in all our interest that we don't run into any complications at all. I spent some more time and studied the blue prints and the layout again. I also considered the conditions up there. If all my information is correct, then most of it will be covered in mud and in decent condition. That means we should not have too much trouble to cut it open. Once we're in, the rest shouldn't be a problem."

"What have you told your sister?"

"Just enough to make sure that she knows what she is up against," Chuck explained and shrugged his shoulders.

"I haven't told her any details. She is not the one I'm concerned about."

"What about the other members of her group?"

"I spoke to her again yesterday. The other members of her group are willing to work with us, but it will cost you."

The British got up and paced the path for a moment. He knew this would cost him a lot of extra money.

"How much are we talking about?" he finally asked with consideration.

"Twenty five million dollars," Chuck calmly stated, then added slowly, "for each of them."

"Twenty five million for each? Are they crazy? My research showed there are only three of them. The cost to get them just up to the boat is equal to the value of one of them."

"Which also means that you have two more to sell. That is still way over four hundred million dollars. You have to remember that we'll turn into the most wanted terrorists on this planet the moment we pull this stunt off. After this operation, we have to disappear forever. We need the support from my sister and her group, otherwise I can't guarantee any success. It's not like we're just going out to a nice weekend fishing trip," Chuck defended his demands.

The British sat down again and watched the birds flutter in the pond, though Chuck knew their actions were furthest from his mind.

"What about the ship's crew?"

"We'll only get active once all the expedition members are off the ship. The expedition leader and his German team will stay longer, and they'll still be on board once we're up there. We can't change that. As far as the crew and the officers are concerned, they will meet the same fate as the natives up there. It's unfortunate, but it's our only option."

"Okay, that means we still have eight weeks left. Let's make sure we don't draw too much attention until then," the British said and got up.

"When are you planning to met that Russian?" he asked Chuck on the way back to his estate.

"I've arranged to meet him in the middle of August. Once I speak to him, I'll be able to plan the final details."

On board the *Northern Explorer*, just east off the Labrador Coast, Saturday, July 23rd
The dark green water glimmered under the bright lights of *Odin*, but the visibility was the usual ten meters. Natascha was very focused behind the plexiglas dome where she was monitoring the two divers as they conducted scientific research in a depth of sixty meters. Natascha looked nervously from her wristwatch back up to the divers and exhaled sharply. According to the plan, they would end their work in this depth within the next two minutes before following the ground up to the shallower depth of forty meters, where they would continue their studies.

"Relax, everything is fine. They have plenty of time left," her father told her. Richard was sitting to Natascha's left side and he watched the two divers calmly.

"They're still taking pictures when they should actually spend some time preparing their ascent," Natascha argued when she saw the huge underwater camera strobes flashing.

Both divers finally turned toward the submersible and signaled that everything was okay, and that they would now start their ascent along the bottom to a depth of forty meters. Natascha was irritated and pointed demonstratively on her watch, before she signaled that everything was okay. The two divers clipped the underwater camera with it's light system to the submersible's frame and carefully placed the bottom samples in a box that was mounted just below the plexiglas dome. With their hands now free, they double-checked their gas supply and the partial pressure of the oxygen in their closed circuit rebreathers. Satisfied with the levels, each of them unclipped one of the large scooters from the frame. Richard piloted *Odin* a little bit closer to the divers, who were now relying on *Odin*'s lights for visibility. Once they had clipped the scooter to their crotch strap, they signaled each other and activated the trigger mechanism to follow the ground. Still irritated about her teammates, Natascha shook her head and marked the time on her clipboard. Richard followed the two divers in a short distance. He had to run at almost full speed to keep up with the lithium-ion battery powered scooters. Both divers could only be seen by their powerful HID dive lights.

"I know I have asked you a thousand times, but have you had any problems with those rebreathers in Norway?"

Natascha looked up from her clipboard and shook her head.

"No, we never had any problems in the cold water with them. Everything was fine."

They followed the two divers until they had reached a depth of forty meters. As soon as they stopped, Natascha leaned forward and looked out the plexiglas dome. The bottom was not as muddy as the deeper waters, and Natascha could actually recognize some starfish, crabs and mussels. She smiled at the moment she noticed the sunlight was able to penetrate the green water into this depth. No wonder visibility

Thin Ice

was so much better. Natascha looked up to the instrument panel and activated the hydrophone once more.

"You never know what might be out there," she said more to herself, and marked the time down while her father nodded in approval. Since both divers had clipped their light heads to their harness, they relied on *Odin*'s lights. Natascha turned the four huge HID lights on and watched, how both divers carefully clipped the scooters back to *Odin*, before they took the camera and the sample kit again. Natascha leaned back in her seat and Richard told her the exact depth, water temperature and current, which she jotted down on her clipboard. Outside *Odin*, one scientific diver was taking pictures, while the other marine biologist was taking bottom samples, which he stored in specifically marked sample flasks.

"How much longer do they need?" Natascha asked impatiently after a long fifteen minutes.

"Relax, Natascha. They have two more stops ahead of them. What's the rush? We have much more air than they do and we're dry and relatively warm," Richard tried to calm his daughter.

"Yes, but we don't have a toilet in here. Why is there never a toilet in these submersibles? Does no one ever realize that there could be a woman on board? My bladder is not the size of a pillow case," Natascha muttered.

"You should mention this in one of your reports. Maybe no one has even thought about this."

"I actually did mention it in my oral exam, when Vitali asked me about the several determining factors of the total dive time of these submersibles."

Richard laughed and smiled at his daughter warmly.

The next few minutes both Natascha and Richard remained silent as they watched the divers prepare to move on to the next site. This time, Richard let Natascha navigate *Odin*, after all, he wanted his daughter to get as much experience on them as possible. While Natascha also had to bring up *Odin* to almost maximum speed to follow the two divers, Richard was giving a brief update with their new depth to the *Northern Explorer*.

The visibility was much worse at the twenty meter stop, but they had also much more ambient sunlight. Natascha turned two of the huge HID lights off and she even had to dim the other two. The water was filled with plankton and unicellular organisms. Both Richard and Natascha enjoyed the sight of so much life in the water, and no one spoke a word until one of the divers looked at them and pointed to some larger shadows in the distance. A few seconds later, Natascha and her father could recognize several seals swim towards them, their curiosity getting the better of them as they inspected the intruders in their territory. Since both divers used closed circuit rebreathers, no loud exhale bubbles left their system. This was a huge advantage to get so much closer to marine animals compared to a traditional open circuit system. While both divers concentrated on their work again after a few minutes, Natascha and Richard were still watching the seals playing around. By now, no less than four seals were playing in the immediate area around *Odin*. One seal had almost lost all fear, and it wasn't intimated at all any more by this huge strange object. First it looked at it's reflection in the glass, then it started to examine the plexiglas dome itself, before it finally looked inside.

"He seems to like you," Richard noticed happily.

Natascha leaned forward and smiled at the seal.

"Listen Natascha, there's something I wanted to ask you."

"Oh oh, I know this tone," Natascha answered and sat back, still smiling at the marine mammal.

"The other evening in your cabin, when we had your cake, Ole-Einar mentioned something about a wedding. Is there anything to it?"

Natascha gave it a laugh and looked at her father now.

"No, don't worry, dad. There's absolutely nothing to it. Nick and I have never even mentioned this subject. We're in no rush, believe me. I won't even think about something like that during this expedition. Although I have to admit that I really love Nick a lot, and I can picture him as my future husband. But I really haven't thought too much about it, I promise you," Natascha said and looked back at the seal again. Natascha paused and looked back at her father and laughed.

"Or do you insist that we get married right away? We could ask the Captain if it's so important for you."

"No, that's okay. There is no rush on my side," Richard answered, also laughing.

"Yes. And what do you think of Nick, anyway?"

Richard sat up in his chair and thought hard on a diversion.

"Your mother really likes him," he answered.

"Yes, I know that. She told me that several times, but I'm asking you," Natascha insisted, still laughing.

Just before Richard could answer, one of the scientific divers knocked at the plexiglas dome and signaled that they had accomplished all their scheduled work. According to their dive plan, they would scooter all the way back to the *Northern Explorer* in a depth of ten meters first, before they would perform their last deco stop in a depth of three meters, all the while being closely accompanied by *Odin*. Although the research vessel was almost three quarters of a sea mile away, this distance was no problem for the powerful scooters. To reduce their water resistance, both scientific divers had clipped the tanks they didn't need any more to *Odin*.

Natascha started to follow the two divers.

"Saved by the bell," she commented on her father, who was on the radio giving an update to the *Northern Explorer*. He glanced at her from the corner of his eyes, and Natascha noticed, that he was telling Vitali way too much information, just to avoid their previous subject.

Like before, Natascha piloted the little research submersible and followed the two divers. It didn't take too long before they could recognize the huge black shadow of the *Northern Explorer*'s underwater hull.

"Let's go around the ship and have a look at the hull. Captain Rasmussen had asked me for this favor once in a while. That way our divers will also have enough time to get out of the water first," Richard said.

"Okay, you're the boss," Natascha said and navigated *Odin* closer to the hull.

"So? Did you come up with an answer yet?"

"About Nick?"

"Yes, about Nick. That's his name. You can actually appreciate that I've taken the time to ask you. You know very well that I'm mature enough to decide that myself."

"Yeah yeah, a grown up woman, I know. I think he's all right. After the expedition you'll see how the two of you get along."

"Yes, we will see," Natascha claimed and turned on all four lights again to have a closer look at the huge propeller.

Twenty minutes later they were floating on the surface and a little zodiac was standing close by. The wind had increased during their dive, and the man on the zodiac needed several attempts to connect the lifting cable to *Odin*'s frame. He finally gave the thumbs up and jumped back into the water, where he was picked up by the zodiac.

Natascha turned off all systems, except the communication device, and just a few minutes later, she opened the hatch and climbed out of the submersible. Ole-Einar and Olaf were already standing by and immediately started to disassemble the dive lights.

"Everything went well?" Oliver asked.

"Yes," Natascha replied quickly and ran to the nearest bathroom.

Later in the evening, the *Northern Explorer* was at anchor in a protected bay off the coast of Labrador. While the waves were getting higher and higher on the open sea, nobody noticed anything but the strong winds in this protected bay.

Nick was sitting in the radio room, checking the monitors and he reassured himself, that he had not missed any new messages from London. Since they sent the fingerprints from the American and Canadian scientist a couple days ago, they had only transmitted their usual status signals, just to notify the guys in London that they were all right. In return, they had just received the daily updates, and the latest news. Nick checked once more and there was still nothing new.

It was now Nick's turn to work the week long night shift up in the radio room to watch the monitors and any incoming messages. It was the most boring job he had done so far. The only upside was, that Astrid was also on night shift. With her, he had at least someone to talk to who knew about them. That way he didn't have to be too careful about what he said. Beside them, Second Officer Mika Kankkunen was the only other informed person on duty.

Nick was telling Astrid about their vacation in Norway, when they heard someone knocking at the door.

Just a moment later, Shira and Natascha entered the radio room.

Natascha greeted her boyfriend with a kiss and looked at the monitors.

"Anything interesting on TV tonight?" she asked him.

"This, my dear, is the most boring reality show you can imagine. There's not even any advertising in it."

"I'm sorry you all have to spend the nights up here just because of me," Natascha apologized warmly.

"It's not because of you, Natascha. It's because of them," Nick explained pointedly, then asked, "Don't worry, it could be worse. Are you all right?"

"I can't sleep. I'm not even tired, but Ma didn't want me to come up her alone," Natascha explained and looked at Shira, who could barely keep her eyes open.

"That's true. But Ma is tired and going back to her bed now," Shira answered and turned around to walk back to her cabin.

"At least I can go to the bathroom by myself," Natascha commented a few seconds after Shira had closed the door behind her.

"Hey, don't be so harsh on her. She's just doing her job and I'm glad she's so serious about it. I wouldn't have let you wander off by yourselves either," Nick defended his Israeli friend.

"Yeah, I know. I didn't mean to be rude. I know she's very professional. And I really do like her a lot."

"Only two and a half months and everything will be over."

Natascha nodded and started her laptop.

"Is it okay if I listen to our hydrophone recordings from today?" she asked Astrid, who was also looking very tired.

"Yes, knock yourself out. There's no radio traffic anyway. Just one fishing trawler and a coast guard boat."

Natascha used the hydrophone only for a few minutes today and she was determined to identify the individual sounds that she recorded earlier.

"You can actually identify what that is?" Nick asked surprised.

"Yes, we can hear the four seals. Do you hear this noise here?"

Nick leaned forward a little bit and concentrated on the frequency that Natascha played back again.

"Yes, I can hear it. What is it?"

"Those are the magnetic valves from the rebreathers. And this sound here are the generators from the *Northern Explorer*. I just haven't figured out what this one here is," Natascha explained and played another frequency which lasted only a few seconds.

"Perhaps a container ship or one of those tankers, but for some reason it sounds a little bit different."

"Do you know where it came from? How far away is it?"

"I'm not really sure. The noise from *Northern Explorer*'s generators are almost completely overlapping it. I think it might be from the same direction. The length of the sound waves is completely different. I'm not even sure if we can still hear all those container ships and tankers further south."

"Do you have another recording of a container ship? One that you know is from a container ship?"

"Yes, I should have one here," Natascha said and navigated through the menu before she started another frequency.

"Here. This is definitely a container ship on it's way east from the St Lawrence."

The three of them listened to the steady monotone sound caused by a gigantic single propeller with four blades. After a few seconds, they all agreed that this was not identical to the other recording.

"Well, according to this, it's definitely not a container ship. Who knows, maybe it was just another fishing vessel. I'm going to ask Dad tomorrow morning," Natascha stated with irritation and shut down her laptop.

On board the *Northern Explorer*, Clyde, east of the Labrador Coast, Thursday, August 4th

Myriads of unicellular organisms reflected the shine of Natascha's powerful HID canister light, while she descended down a buoy rope into the black depth below her. Just as she passed thirty meters, she could barely see the glimmer of *Odin*'s four strong HID lights far below her. The Icelandic dive team had found the remains of a wooden fishing vessel during yesterdays ROV operation. Since it was a habitat for many fish and largely covered with sponges and anemones, the Icelandic scientists had attached a buoy to it. Earlier this morning, Richard decided that he wanted to take a closer look and to spent more time with this wreck. The video footage from the ROV revealed that the wreck was resting on its side on the soft muddy bottom, and it would be nearly impossible to get close to it with *Odin* without stirring up all the sediment. Natascha decided to dive the wreck together with another diver from the German team. After a detailed briefing, her father had piloted *Odin* around the wreck and informed Natascha that there were no hazards like fishing nets or ropes visible from his position. With her father standing by in the little research submersible, Natascha and her buddy finally went into the water.

Reaching a depth of forty meters and one hand close to the buoy line, Natascha could now clearly recognize *Odin* below her, and she continued her descent. Every three meters she turned around and checked her dive buddy as well as her instruments. At sixty meters they finally reached *Odin*. The young German scientist signaled her father that everything was okay, before she clipped off her bail-out gas* to *Odin*'s frame. While her buddy was taking the underwater video system, Natascha had a closer look at the wreck. She let the shine of her dive light wander over the stern area of the twenty meter long wooden hull. All the white and orange colored anemones shone in the light and Natascha could see some cod-fish dart for cover underneath the wreck. After Natascha had convinced herself that there weren't any fishing nets or ropes or anything else she could get entangled in, she slowly swam closer to the wreck. She showed her dive buddy all the animals and sections she was interested in, and he took the detailed video footage of it. Later this evening they would watch the video and spend much more time identifying and counting the individual species. That procedure allowed them to spend more time at the wreck. Natascha even requested some macro footage of some anemones, since she wasn't sure if those species were supposed to be in these cold waters. Due to the rich nutrient water, most of the anemones had a diameter of almost forty centimeters.

Bail-Out gas: As a redundancy, divers using a rebreather usually carry enough breathing gas with them in an open circuit configuration to end the dive safely or to render assistance to their dive buddy in case of a rebreather malfunction.

Natascha looked over the hull, and she regretted the fact that her bottom time at this wreck was limited to a short twenty minutes.

Once in a while she also spotted some star fish as they also called this wreck their home. With the utmost care and minimal fin movement, she looked under a part of the hull, with just centimeters to spare between both her rebreather and the hull as well as her body and the ground.

What are you doing here? You're not even suppose to be that far north, she said to a crab that was running away as fast as it's little legs could carry it out of the light. Natascha reached out her right arm, signaling her buddy that she wanted the camera, while her father was knocking on *Odin*'s plexiglas dome to show his disapproval towards his daughter squeezing into this tight space.

Ignoring her father, Natascha insisted on the camera and took some video of the little crab as well as her dive computer, which showed an unusually high water temperature of six degree Celsius.

After they neared the maximum allowable bottom time, Natascha clipped the video-camera back to the submersible and loaded herself again with all her bail-out gas. Her father asked her if everything was okay and after a last check of her instruments, Natascha formed a circle with her thumb and index finger.

She swam to the buoy rope and finally started her ascent towards her first decompression stop.

Two hours later, she was safe and sound back in her cabin, and after a more or less cold shower* she was waiting for Ole-Einar to pick her up for supper.

With Ole-Einar in time, she was now sitting together with Nick and her father at a table and enjoyed her salad. It was already after 20.00, and they were lucky they got any food at all.

"Didn't you get cold?" Ole-Einar asked.

"No, I was actually wearing my electrically heated vest. The water was too warm anyway. We had six degree Celsius down there."

"Well, not sure if I would call six degree Celsius too warm during a two hour dive," her Norwegian friend replied.

"I know, but it's true. This time of the year the water should only be around three or four degrees. It actually wouldn't surprise me at all if we found some species down there again, that do not belong there," Richard explained.

"You don't expect tropical fish, do you?" Ole-Einar asked.

"No," Natascha explained. "We won't see any tropical fish down there, but more and more often we find species that have their natural habitat much further south in warmer waters. Some of them follow the gulf stream up north and migrate along the coast into regions they have never been seen in before. Even a change in the water temperature as less as two degree Celsius can make a huge difference to some of the species. You can also notice more and more often that this severely interferes with the reproduction cycle of several species of fish. I'm pretty sure that I've seen at least one little crab today that definitely does not belong up here in the north. Due to rising temperatures, the water gets warmer and warmer and more dominant species are migrating north. This is a huge threat to the fragile cold water ecosystems."

Thin Ice

Both Nick and Ole-Einar were silent as they thought about what the young German scientist had just explained to them.

"I asked both the Americans and the Canadians about their findings," Richard continued. "Their research has also revealed that the water temperature is an average two degrees Celsius higher in most areas than normal. Actually they're conducting some very interesting research in the deeper areas with their gear."

"Do you have the feeling they're competent and know what they're doing?" Nick asked.

"As far as I can tell, they indeed seem to know what they're doing. I haven't had any in depth discussions about their work yet, but as expedition leader I also can't ignore them. I'm meeting all the team leaders several times a week and so far, I must say, everything seems to be okay. The Americans and the Canadians concentrate on their temperature study only, but that's also not unusual. There are actually some expeditions, where nothing else is done but this. You don't even have to be a marine biologist for that."

"Is Shira in the radio room?" Nick asked after a few moments of silence.

"I'm not sure. She said she wanted to go to the gym first. Dad and I will watch the video later on in our cabin. Are you coming over this evening?"

Shira had also decided to take the night shift in the radio room for one week. This would give her the opportunity to get some space again between her and Natascha. Natascha supported her decision, but mostly because Nick could spent the nights with her during that week.

"Yes, I'll come over later. First I have to perform my duties as your personal assistant and clean your dive gear," Nick mentioned playfully with a contemptuous tone.

"Oh, I love you so much," Natascha replied with a big smirk on her face.

Ole-Einar posed a cough, but the word *Princess* still clearly audible.

Nick stood up, not without showing a very rude hand gesture towards his girlfriend and picked up his tray.

"And don't lose an o-ring again. I'll deduct it from your salary, if you do," she shouted after him, so that everybody else could hear them as well.

Nick turned around and threw her a killing glance.

"Don't you think you're pushing it a little bit too far?" Richard asked in a concerned voice.

"No, it's okay. Nick knows very well that we have already cleaned our gear. He's just going to double check if everything is all right. That's all."

Nevertheless, it took over two hours before Nick entered Natascha's cabin.

"Have you found something interesting? Any new species?"

After longer dives with excessive nitrogen built up, it is not recommended to take a hot shower or use the sauna, since the nitrogen bubbles in the body tissues can expand their size due to the higher temperature. This can cause the nitrogen bubbles to block nerve cells as well as the blood flow = decompression sickness

"Yes, so far we found two species that supposedly live much further south. In total, we could identify over one hundred different species on this wreck. Most of it little critters, but it's still amazing how many different animals this little shipwreck gives a habitat. Where have you been, anyway? I started to get worried," Natascha said and looked at her boyfriend.

"Your gear was so dirty that it took me forever to clean it. And I lost another o-ring that I had to find. It took me over an hour," Nick explained seriously.

"Liar," Natascha countered, stepping closer to him.

"I know for certain my gear was clean. I cleaned it myself," she explained, her face just centimeters away from his.

"Okay, you win. I can't stand the pressure of your interrogation any more. I went to the gym with the guys and we met Sasha there. She was wearing one of those tight aerobic shirts and pants. I couldn't leave," Nick continued, still trying to remain serious while he watched Natascha.

"Don't push it. Shira's not here tonight to help you."

Nick kissed his girlfriend.

"Don't worry. I was your faithful boyfriend. You can ask the guys if you don't believe me."

"Yeah, sure, like I'd believe them," Natascha said and went to the bathroom.

"Shira was also in the gym. Ariel was occupied in the radio room, so she stayed a little bit longer. You can ask her."

"Don't worry, you know I trust you. Just going to brush my teeth. And I can smell that you just took a shower."

"Yes, took me quite a while. Her perfume was very resistant," Nick said and barely dodged the shampoo bottle Natascha had launched at him.

While Natascha got ready in the bathroom, Nick took his clothes off and laid down on the bed. Two minutes later Natascha entered the room again, wearing nothing but her underwear. She slowly stripped out of it and Nick was certain he would have lost another submersible, if he would have been on the simulator right now.

"Are you still thinking about Sasha?" Natascha asked in her most seductive voice.

Nick wanted to say something, but he decided against it and simply pulled his girlfriend into the bed.

The next morning Natascha and Nick spent a few hours running a thorough inspection of Natascha's rebreather as well as of one of the ROV's. After their experience in Iceland, Natascha was even more careful when she packed a new scrubber or checked on the electronics. They spent the afternoon watching the video from the wreck and tried to identify more species. Ole-Einar and Oliver helped with the maintenance of *Odin*, but this task was performed by Vitali, the lead Dive Officer as well as Holger, so nobody was concerned there. It was not until supper, that the entire group met at their usual table. Even Shira sat down, before she went up to the radio room for the night shift.

"Haven't seen you at all today," Natascha mentioned and looked at her Israeli friend.

Thin Ice

Both Natascha and Nick had left her cabin before Shira came back from her previous night shift.

"That's strange," Oliver noted seriously.

"And why is that strange?" Natascha asked back, well aware, that they would start to pick at her and Nick.

"Well, usually it's just Nick who's stealing himself out of women's cabins in the early morning hours. You actually could have stayed," Oliver continued without looking up.

Natascha threw him a reproachful look.

"Yes, I heard that he was even a little bit later yesterday evening for your date than scheduled. Must have gotten busy in the gym," Ole-Einar continued on Natascha's other side, sounding as serious as Oliver.

"Spent lots of time under the shower to clean himself up again," Oliver added.

"Keep agitating. I totally trust him," Natascha said.

"And that you can do," Shira said, while she prepared her bread.

"I watched him in the gym. Nick was as strong as a German toad," the Israeli stated firmly.

Everybody burst into laughter.

"Did I get that wrong again?" Shira asked and looked up.

"It's *German oak*, not *German toad*. A toad is a type of frog," Natascha explained, still giggling.

"And," Natascha continued with a more serious voice, "Nick knows very well why he's together with me. So, with this being officially said for the record, I'll have to go. Got to meet with Dad and the guys from National Geographic. They want to see the video from that little shipwreck. Can I go alone, Ma?" Natascha asked and looked at Shira.

"No, you can't go alone. And you'll be in bed by stroke ten," Shira replied rigidly, while everybody started to laugh again.

Natascha got up and looked at Nick.

"Did you hear that? She wants us in bed again by ten."

"Does that mean you'll dig out your pleasure root again this evening?" Ole-Einar asked calmly, as Nick choked on his drink. Everybody else continued laughing.

Natascha stepped behind Ole-Einar and wrapped her arms around him.

"Well, I very much hope so. Why don't you think about us, when you're working in your own garden tonight?" Natascha countered.

"We don't call that a vegetable. With us, it's much more robust, more like a tool. It has nothing to do with vegetables," the Norwegian continued in his typical calm voice, not stopping to prepare another piece of bread.

"It's too bad then that I'm technically untalented, and that, as a Vegetarian, I really like vegetables," Natascha laughed before she returned her tray.

- 12 -

Severodvinsk, Russia, Sunday, August 14th
Chuck Hogan traveled all morning long on the M8 towards Severodvinsk at the White Sea. A few days ago he had entered Russia from Scandinavia, and he purchased a used Lada Niva in one of the small Russian villages just behind the border. He paid cash in Euro, since the former owner of the vehicle did prefer the European currency over the American dollar.

After he spent the last two days on more or less disastrous concrete roads, he was now enjoying the relatively good conditions on the M8.

It had taken him over four weeks to finally organize this meeting, and he was hoping, that the information he was about to gather was worth the money and the effort he had put into it. Being guided by a used GPS system, he also orientated himself with the help of the road signs until he finally reached the town itself. While the typical standardized buildings for the Russian middle class have dominated the landscape outside the town, Severodvinsk itself was a clear demonstration of the ever growing rift between the rich and poor people inside Russia. The city itself presented itself like any other modern western city, but Severodvinsk could not deny its past in the outskirts or even in some of the side roads off the main city. Chuck could easily spot the typical remains of poverty in many abandoned buildings caused by the communistic regime over the last couple decades. Today, Severodvinsk was still home to one of the most important shipyards for the Russian naval forces, even after the time of the Cold War, when countless mighty and powerful Russian nuclear submarines were built in nearby Sevmash, was finished. Today, they concentrated their efforts to dismantle the old submarines so as to use the parts to keep the remaining submarines of the North Fleet more or less operational.

Under the guidance of his GPS, Chuck followed the main road through the city north towards the harbor area. He knew, that he would need a written permit from the Russian security police FSP to gain access to Sevmash itself, but that was not his goal. The person he was interested in was living about fifty kilometers outside the town. He looked at his watch and noticed he had another hour and a half to spare, before his meeting with the Russian woman.

To make sure he knew his meeting point, Chuck parked his car a few blocks away and took a little walk over to the marketplace, where he was suppose to meet his contact. He looked for any signs of an ambush and came to the conclusion, that he might as well continue his observation from inside one of the restaurants.

While enjoying his meal, he reassured himself that nobody was watching him. Without tipping the waitress too much to avoid any attention, he left a couple bills on the table and returned to his car. He sat behind the wheel and started reading a Russian newspaper. Another glance on his wristwatch told him his Russian contact was almost

Thin Ice

ten minutes late by now. Chuck assumed the other person was also checking out the area and kept his nervousness at bay. He decided to give it another thirty minutes, when he saw the person on the other side of the marketplace. A young, blond haired woman walked towards his Lada. Chuck took his gun in his right hand and concealed it under the folded newspaper, while he winded down the window. As the Russian came closer, Chuck recognized she was also at the same restaurant just a few minutes ago. Chuck had not expected his contact to be that attractive and he put his smile on.

She walked up to the drivers window and watched Chuck closely.

"Can you tell me how late it is?" she finally asked.

Chuck gave her the completely wrong time.

The Russian checked her own watch and nodded slightly, not without glancing up and down the road.

"Do you want to go for a drive?" she asked.

"If it's not too late for it, sure," Chuck answered in perfect Russian.

The woman walked around the little Lada Niva, as Chuck stowed the newspaper with the gun in the area between his seat and the drivers door. He watched how the woman took her seat beside him.

Without any further comment, Chuck started the car and followed her instructions outside of town. Chuck noticed she sent him in several circles through the city as she checked her mirror the entire time. Convinced that no one was following them, she finally guided Chuck over some gravel roads closer to their actual destination. After another few kilometers, the Russian pointed out another dirt road to their left, leading to an old farmhouse in the distance. Chuck nodded and steered the Lada into the driveway. Minutes later, her turned the Lada around to face the gravel road again and turned it off. He waited for the Russian to leave the car first so he could conceal his gun under his jacket.

"My uncle is waiting inside for you. Follow me," she said and led the way.

"We'll meet outside. At this table over there," Chuck demanded and pointed at a table on the porch. He would not set foot in an unknown house as long as he did not know what was inside.

The woman hesitated for a moment and looked at him.

"Okay. You can wait here. I'll go get him."

While she disappeared inside the house, Chuck noticed two little children peek out the door and laugh at him. Chuck smiled and waved at them. Both kids giggled and ran back inside the house.

The young Russian woman came out, followed closely by a much older man. Chuck guessed he was in his mid-seventies, even though he looked much older. The old man slowly walked to the table and sat down with a load moan.

"Good evening," Chuck greeted in perfect Russian.

The old man returned the greeting and watched his visitor closely, as he offered him a seat with the wave of his hand.

Chuck sat on the bench opposite the man and also watched the Russian for several minutes in silence.

"It's my understanding that you started to work in the shipyard in Sevmash and Severodvinsk in nineteen-fifty-eight?" Chuck finally broke the silence.

"Yes, that's correct."

"And you remember the information I asked you about?"

"Yes, I do remember."

"Do you think it's technically possible?" Chuck continued.

Instead of answering, the Russian simply shrugged his shoulders and watched some chickens run around.

Chuck reached into his jacket and took two envelopes out. He placed one of the envelopes on the table. The Russian woman quickly picked it up and counted the money inside.

"That's only fifty thousand. We agreed on one hundred thousand," she demanded quickly.

"You'll get the second half the moment I get the information I'm looking for," Chuck replied coldly and showed her the second envelope.

The old Russian man shrugged his shoulders again, looked at the money and started to tell Chuck everything he needed to know.

Two hours later, Chuck rose from the table and gave the woman the second envelope with another fifty thousand Euro. After the woman had counted the money, she accompanied him back to his car.

"What do you want to do with them anyway?" she asked just out of curiosity.

Instead of answering her, Chuck took his sunglasses off and gave her a cold stare.

"Never mind. I don't want to know," the Russian quickly said.

Chuck nodded and got into his vehicle. He started the car, opened the window and waved the Russian good-bye.

"It's in your best interest that your uncle hasn't lied to me. Should that be the case, I'd unfortunately have to come back with my friends. It would be a shame for the kids," he said and took off.

- 13 -

On board the *Northern Explorer*, Coronation Gulf, Monday, September 19th
Without any complications, the *Northern Explorer* continued its journey through the North-West Passage. The only time they encountered packed ice was at the most northern part of their route in Lancaster Sound as well as in Peel Sound. During their travels, they were fortunate enough to have the chance to watch some polar bears actively hunt for seals, without having to leave the research vessel. Almost at the end of their route, the *Northern Explorer* was now laying at anchor just off Coppermine. The last of the scientists who were scheduled to leave the expedition just departed the ship and began their journey home by plane. As far as Ariel and his team was concerned, the last couple weeks turned out to be the most uneventful job they ever had. Both the American and Canadian scientists continued their studies and neither their work nor their behavior rose any suspicion. Furthermore, Ariel was convinced that no one else on board the ship knew about the incidents in Berlin and Reykjavik, except for those who he personally briefed. He and Shira even considered terminating their mission and depart the research vessel here in Coppermine, but Natascha turned a deaf ear. After a long and intense discussion between Natascha and Ariel, the Captain himself asked Ariel to stay for the last three weeks.

Content with the fact that the team was here to stay, Natascha turned her attention back to her task. She glanced at her father, certain he was watching her, but his attention was elsewhere. She maneuvered *Odin* through the dark waters, wary of the rocky bottom that rested twenty minutes below the *Northern Explorer*, at a depth of one hundred and fifty meters. Her thoughts wandered, and she suddenly imagined what it would be like down here without *Odin*'s four powerful HID lights. She shuddered at the thought.

"What's the water temperature?" Natascha asked, breaking the silence.

"Four degrees Celsius. Still too warm. The water in the North-West Passage was at least one degree Celsius warmer than usual. The sensors from our North American scientists confirm this. Do you remember what Captain Rasmussen said the other day? He said that, according to the Canadian Ice Report, this year was the season with the least ice."

Natascha nodded and added the water temperature in a column on her clipboard.

She followed her father's gaze and watched as their divers collected the bottom samples consisting of anemones and cold water sponges. After a moment, Natascha leaned back and stretched as far as the little research submersible permitted her.

"Are you okay?" Richard asked his daughter.

"Yes, fine. I just needed a stretch, I'm a little stiff," she replied and returned her concentration to her instruments.

Her father watched her for several more seconds. He noticed, and Shira confirmed his observation, that there's something odd about her. His hand rubbed his lips, as he tried to place his finger on it.

"Shall we turn on the hydrophone?" the young German scientist asked her father, without taking her eyes off the instruments.

"Yes, why not. Go ahead," he gave his okay.

Natascha pushed several buttons and was satisfied once she saw some green LED lights blinking. She marked the time and the depth in her clipboard. Together with her father, they listened to the hydrophone for the next several minutes. Nothing interesting was happening for a few moments, when suddenly several loud clicks and whistles broke the silence.

"Belugas. They must have been behind the inlet and are now coming our way," Natascha assumed and looked at the instruments for the hydrophone.

Richard leaned towards the speaker and concentrated on the noise.

"Those aren't belugas. Those are orcas," he noted.

"Orcas? Are you sure? Do they even travel this far north?" Natascha asked in disbelief.

"Yes, they do actually. You should know, they migrate as far north as the Polar Sea. Several years ago there was actually a research done on a pod of orcas who hunted in the Beaufort Sea. From an oceanographic point of view, we're in that Sea. Some of the orcas follow the melting ice towards the east during the summer, before they travel back west around Alaska in the fall."

The clicks and whistles intensified so much so that Natascha actually leaned forward to look up towards the surface.

"No, you won't see them. We're way too deep and way too far away, it's amazing we can hear them at all. I assume they're a few sea-miles away. Let's get back to the *Northern Explorer* and see if we can launch a zodiac. We should be able to watch them from one of the RIB's," Richard said and contacted the *Northern Explorer* to share the news as Natascha turned *Odin* around.

Despite the excitement, it took them another hour before *Odin* was back safe on the front deck of the research vessel.

While Nick and Oliver both started to work on *Odin*'s lights immediately, Natascha and her father were already intercepted by some other German scientists.

"We've just spotted the orcas and we can launch the RIB any time now. Do you want to go?"

"Yes, I'm just going to the bathroom and will get my dry-suit. I'll be back in ten minutes. Someone should go and get Shira. She'd love to see them up close," Natascha said on her way below deck.

Driven by it's twin 150 horsepower engines, the RIB was flying over the calm water less than twenty minutes later. Natascha sat beside her father in the middle of the zodiac. The German scientists were both wearing their dry-suits, and together they held on to the video-camera housing. Behind them sat Nick and Shira. While Nick was wearing a survival suit, Shira used Natascha's back up dry-suit. She was so excited to finally see huge marine mammals, Natascha was surprised the Israeli managed to stay onboard. Ole-Einar shrugged his shoulder under his survival suit as he piloted the RIB. He zipped across the water as Natascha's body stiffened. She would have been nervous, but knew he was well-trained from his time with the Norwegian Mine Diver Command.

Everyone braced themselves and it was Natascha who discovered the group of five orcas in the large bay to their left. She pointed her arm in the direction and Ole-Einar altered the course and reduced speed significantly.

"Ole, take us around in a huge semi-circle and see if you can get us a little bit closer. It seems like they're resting in that bay over there. We have to give them some room to access the open water, just in case they want to avoid us," Natascha ordered excitedly.

The Norwegian reduced the speed even further and stopped the zodiac just over one hundred meters away from the orcas. The animals were still resting inside the bay and didn't seem to be too uncomfortable with the RIB so close by. Richard took his binoculars and scanned the water when he noticed some movement on the shore.

He adjusted the binoculars and could see four Inuvialuit standing in the distance waving at them. Richard smiled and waved back as Ole-Einar stopped the engines to give the marine mammals more time to adjust to their visitors.

"I can count five animals, four adults and one calf," Richard identified and handed the binoculars to Shira.

Natascha was using the camera to get a closer look. Over the next twenty minutes, they could see the orcas were generally interested in their new visitors, but they did not come any closer than one hundred meters.

"They're not getting any closer because of the calf. They're too careful," Natascha said.

"Can't we get closer?" Shira asked.

"No, we'd put too much stress on them. The moment we get closer, they'll escape. It would tire out the calf. I'll try to snorkel over to them," Natascha explained and picked up her fins, mask and snorkel before she carefully slid over the side of the zodiac and into the water. Richard handed her the camera housing.

"Could you wait here for me? My plan is to drift with the current directly to them. I'll shoot some video as I drift by. You can pick me up at the inlet over there," Natascha explained to Ole-Einar, pointing in the distance.

Ole-Einar nodded and watched as Natascha drifted in the mild current away from the zodiac and towards the group of orcas. Nick jealously followed his girlfriend with his eyes, since she was the only one who actually thought to bring a mask, snorkel and a pair of fins. Natascha quickly noticed that the current was stronger than she had originally expected, and she could now see three adult orcas watching her very closely. Despite the caution, none of the animals showed any signs they would swim away within the next few minutes. Using the fins, Natascha adjusted her course. Her plan was still to drift by the orcas in a distance of several meters. Keeping that distance, Natascha hoped they would not see her as a threat. She also hoped she would trigger their curiosity and they would come a little bit closer to check her out. Natascha tried to control her breathing and not concentrate too much on the orcas, since she was sure they would sense her excitement. Keeping to this plan, the young German scientist noticed that the visibility in this little bay was excellent, and she could see the first shadows under water from as far as thirty meters away. With a slight movement of her fins, she stopped and turned on the video-camera. She could hear the clicks and whistles herself now, knowing very well that the marine mammals were trying to determine with what kind of creature they were dealing with. After a little while they must have come to the conclusion that Natascha was no threat to them or their calf. Curiosity got the best of them and one of the older animals left the pod and swam closer to her. By the size and the shape of the back fin, Natascha was certain that it was a mature bull. The eight meter long orca slowly swam around Natascha, before it returned to its family.

Natascha rose her head out of the water and looked back to the zodiac, which was almost three hundred meters away by now. The current took her much further along the shore than she had anticipated. Natascha couldn't believe her eyes when she looked at the orcas again. It was now the adult female together with its calf, that started to swim towards her. Just a few meters away now, Natascha estimated the size at about six meters for the adult, while the calf was about half the size or even a little less.

Natascha could feel her heart racing with excitement as she watched them closely through the cameras monitor and followed their every move. Several times, she double checked that the camera was actually recording. The little calf and its mother had lost all fear. Both were swimming as close as they could to Natascha. After the calf had seen it's own reflection in the dome port, it started to examine the housing. Several times it even nudged the dome port with it's nose, curious to see what it's reflection would do. Natascha couldn't hold back and reached out with her hand to touch the calf. The adult orca positioned itself between the calf and Natascha. Her surprise overwhelmed her, as she reached to touch her as well. She could feel tears of joy fill her eyes. She watched everything, absorbed every detail, to remember this moment forever.

It was not a moment longer, when her peaceful encounter with these majestic animals was disturbed by the roar of the two outboard engines revving up. The same moment, the clicks and whistles also changed and within seconds, both animals were back to their family over forty meters away. Natascha's excitement was quickly consumed by the fierce lick of anger as she turned around to look at the zodiac.

No wonder they got scared! Natascha screamed inwardly, and her anger intensified when she saw everyone on the zodiac were frantically waving their arms. Before a string of curses could form, she noticed they were not only waving at her, but pointing at something beside her. The moment the realization hit, she could also hear the sound of heavy breathing. Natascha turned around a little bit further and her blood froze. Only ten meters away from her was a fully grown polar bear, with it's eyes locked as it swam towards her. Paralyzed with fear, Natascha could do nothing but feel an uncomfortable lump rise in her throat. Panic rose inside her. Her heart raced to a new beat. The zodiac was still over two hundred meters away, and she knew very well, that she would never make it to shore either. Natascha wanted to scream, but no sound left her lungs. The bear was now only five meters away, it's eyes still set on her. Natascha could clearly distinguish the heavy breathing, and she could see every little detail in the massive creatures head, as it's open jaws and long yellow teeth surged towards her. With the polar bear just two meters away, Natascha thought to raise the large aluminum video-camera housing as a shield, but her arms refused to move.

At the moment the sharp menacing teeth were to strike, she closed her eyes. Her dispair caused them to open again to see that the bear stopped, turned around and swam back to shore as fast as it could. The beast faced her and growled before it darted away.

Natascha swallowed the fear as it clawed up her throat. The tension was harsh, and she tried to understand what happened. Shock made her turn around. Her eyes blinked quickly as she saw the adult female orca just one meter behind her, it's mouth wide as it watched the polar bear. Natascha's eyes were captivated by the sight in front of her. She looked right into the open mouth with it's enormous conic teeth and huge rose-colored tongue, but she could not sense any fear.

With the polar bear a safe distance away, the orca looked at Natascha for several seconds before it swam back to its family once more.

Natascha swallowed and turned around to locate the zodiac, but all she could see was that they were floating in the distance. Both Nick and Ole-Einar worked on the outboard engines. She registered the panic on the RIB, but knew it was not the same. Gaining control over her body for the first time, Natascha picked up the video-camera and started to swim the short distance to the shore. Her knees were still shaking, when she more or less crawled out of the water and sat down beside one of the larger rocks. Looking at the opposite side of the bay, she could see the polar bear on the shore trotting away. She was finally safe from it.

Natascha closed her eyes and tried to regain control over her breathing. It took her several seconds before she noticed the four Inuvialuit standing right beside her. All four of them smiled at her, and Natascha tried to smile back, but her quivering was insistent. The older Inuvialuit woman said something in her native tongue, but Natascha shook her head apologetically. She looked at the youngest member of the group, a teenage boy.

"My grandmother says the whale sensed you're not alone. That's why she brought the calf along at the beginning, before it came back to protect you and the young," the teenage Inuvialuit said in a strong accent.

Natascha was able to manage a faint smile, but she didn't know how to respond.

Before she could do anything else, she noticed that the zodiac finally arrived at the shore. Still shaking, she tried to stand up, but two of the Inuvialuit quickly grabbed her before she fell over. The teenage boy picked up the video-camera and handed it to her.

"Thanks," Natascha stammered and carefully walked the few meters to the water, checking her shoulder to see the polar bear was still in a safe distance away. Natascha swam the short distance to the zodiac and handed the camera up to Shira, and Nick and Ole-Einar helped her back in.

She fought to catch her breath, as she watched how Ole-Einar turned the zodiac around to drive slowly back towards the *Northern Explorer*. When Natascha saw the four Inuvialuit again, the pressure finally left her and she started to cry. It was not until now that the she realized, that everybody on the boat was talking to her, and her father was holding her shoulders tight with his arm.

"Oh my God, Natascha! Are you okay?" her father asked with great concern.

"Yes, I think I'm okay," she stammered quickly, then added. "I'm still shaking, but I'm fine."

"Are you sure?" Nick asked and took her hand.

"Yes, I'm fine, thanks. Where did this bear come from anyway? I didn't notice it at all."

"It suddenly came over that promontory on the other side of the bay. We couldn't see it. I assume it was watching the whales. The bear charged at you the moment it saw you. We were all screaming our lungs out," Natascha's father explained.

"Yes, if it wouldn't have been for the orca, I would've most likely got some live footage from inside a polar bear," Natascha said, finally smiling again.

"I thought the orca would kill you," Shira admitted, completely upset.

"No, orcas don't attack humans," Richard explained. He tried for a smile as he continued. "It was unbelievable. As soon as the orca brought it's calf back to safety, it dove under the water and it came up right behind you just two seconds later. I bet that polar bear got a scare out of that one!"

Natascha flashed at her father.

"And you actually believe the bear got scared? How do you think I felt? I see all of you waving and the moment I turn around, I see nothing else but it's huge head and it's black eyes darting towards me. I could even see the teeth! I was like paralyzed. I couldn't do anything. All I knew was that I wouldn't make it to the zodiac. I never even thought about the whales and the shore any more." Natascha admitted hurriedly, the adrenaline that pumped ignited her memory.

"What did you yell at me anyway?"

"That completely depended on who was shouting," Ole-Einar explained in his calm voice before he continued.

"Shira was only screaming *Oh my God, Oh my God* and looked for her pistol at the same time, but it was under her dry-suit. Your father was yelling as loud as he could that you should swim towards the orcas, but the most remarkable thing was what your beloved boyfriend suggested. Nick was shouting that you should swim towards the shore. He obviously thought the polar bear would get scared once you swam towards him," Ole-Einar explained with a smile, and Natascha's eyes darted to Nick, growing wide.

"I meant the other shore," Nick defended himself.

Natascha smiled and looked back towards the promontory, where the polar bear was standing on it's rear legs, watching them drive by.

"And you're sure that you're okay?" Shira asked, still nervous.

Natascha smiled at her Israeli friend.

"Well, I think I may need some fresh underwear," she admitted and for the first time since the attack, everybody was laughing.

"I know that this might sound rude right now, but is there a chance you have any of this on video?" her father asked.

"Yes, I double checked the camera twice while I was with the orcas. You should be able see some footage about how your daughter was two seconds away from getting eaten by a polar bear," Natascha replied easily.

"Great, we'll watch that later this evening," her father said and went to sit down.

"Why did it take you so long to get me anyway?" Natascha turned to Nick.

"If Captain Ahab here wouldn't have hit that huge rock over there, we would've actually caught up to you much sooner," Nick added and pointed to the outboard engines. One engine was still tilted up and it's propeller was completely torn off. It was only now, that Natascha noticed they were not driving very fast and the whole zodiac was vibrating wildly, as Ole-Einar muttered something about inaccurate charts and faulty sounders.

The news about Natascha being attacked by a full grown polar bear spread in no time. Everyone on the *Northern Explorer* could feel the excitement and fear as the rumors rippled through the ship. As soon as they were back on board, many people came and asked Natascha how she was feeling and if there was anything they could do for her. Nick and Shira couldn't help to notice that even the American and Canadian scientists showed deep sympathies towards her. Even the Captain took his time and visited Natascha personally in her cabin to show his support and to ask the same question. Natascha appreciated his concern and reassured him that she was fine and was in no need of anything at the moment.

Later on that evening, most of the scientist and some of the crew member met in one of the larger conference rooms on board the ship to have a look at the video footage.

While Natascha was connecting the camera to the beamer, she could see that even the members from National Geographic came to watch this.

The first part of the video wasn't bad at all. It clearly showed the three different orcas and how they examined Natascha. Especially the part with young orca looking at it's own reflection in the dome port was cause for many *oh's* and *ah's*. The next thing for everyone to see was simply how the two mammals disappeared, and how the sound of their whistle and clicks changed, as well as the sound of the high revving outboard engines. The next few minutes of video footage weren't that great at all. During the whole ordeal, Natascha must have pointed the camera to the ground, but for a few seconds, two huge white paws were visible as they plowed through the water.

"Sorry," Natascha said loudly and stopped the camera, knowing there was nothing else exciting, then commented, "The next time I'm getting eaten by a polar bear I'll make sure to get some better video footage of it."

Most of the people laughed, before they rose from their seats to leave to the room. Before each person left, they clapped Natascha on her shoulder to offer their support once more.

"So," Nick said and looked at Natascha.

"Are you coming or do you need a couple more minutes?"

"I think I'll need the minutes. Dad and I want to go over today's audio recording from the hydrophone," Natascha replied as she disconnected the camera.

Since Shira had already left the room, Nick sat down on one of the chairs and used the camera to watch the footage again.

Richard had already started the audio recording and was just waiting for Natascha to sit beside him. For the next few minutes, all that could be heard were the clicks and whistles from the orcas.

"Right now, this is the moment when the orcas swim around the island towards the bay. Do you hear the difference? Do you notice how much better we can hear them now?" Richard asked and looked at his daughter, who nodded.

Richard used the computer software to filter most of the whistles and clicks out. He wanted to hear what was recorded in the background.

"Maybe there's a second group somewhere and they're communicating with each other," he explained and filtered out some more frequencies.

The only thing they could hear now was a very weak and distant sound of some propeller noise, which only lasted for a few seconds.

Nick recognized it at once and looked up. He noticed that no one else seemed to be bothered by the noise.

"Can you play that propeller noise again, please? The one at the end," he asked Richard and got up from his chair.

"This one here?" Richard asked back and played the sequence once more.

"I guess it's a fishing boat. Some of the Natives are using them up here. We hear them once in a while," Natascha's father explained.

"Isn't that the same sound we heard before?" Nick asked and looked at Natascha.

She shrugged, exchanged a glance with her father and looked back at Nick.

"Remember the one noise a couple weeks ago during my nightshift? The one we listened to that evening sounded exactly like this one here," Nick added and looked at the monitor.

"Yes, I remember, but that could've also been a fishing vessel," Natascha replied.

"Can the computer show you if the two sounds are identical?" Nick asked unimpressed.

"Yes, we can, but like Natascha said, it's most likely a fishing boat," Richard said and let his finger fly over the keyboard.

"When did you previously hear the sound?" Richard asked.

"Sometime in late July. It was a Saturday," Nick answered.

Richard looked at the list of sound files on the monitor.

"Here it is," Natascha said and pointed at one of the files.

"When we were off the Labrador coast."

Richard activated the sequence and compared it with the other sound file on the computer. Both sound profiles were identical.

"Very interesting," Nick said, stepping behind Natascha's chair.

"What are the odds that two fishing vessels have the exact same sound profile?"

"Well, if it's the same type of boat and engine that's so commonly used up here, then the chances are pretty high that they have the same sound signature."

"Do you remember if you heard that noise on other recordings as well?" Nick asked and looked at Natascha.

His girlfriend leaned back and looked at him.

"I actually think we heard it several times. I just didn't pay too much attention to it. Just give me one moment here," she said and turned towards the computer again.

She opened the audio logbook and tried to look for this sequence. After several minutes and as many unsuccessful attempts to locate it, Richard took the keyboard away from his frustrated daughter, who was now cursing at the program.

"Pounding your fingers on the keyboard won't help you find the files either, Natascha," Richard reprimanded and opened the search function again.

Under less than a minute, Richard had identified the specific sequence and established a short list.

"Okay, here it is. First time we heard it was on Saturday, July twenty-third, just east of the Labrador coast. That was the recording we just listened to. The second time we heard it in front of Clyde, also Labrador, after that we recorded it in the Lancaster Sound, in the Admiralty Inlet, twice in the Franklin Strait, once in the Victoria Strait and finally today in the Coronation Strait," Richard explained.

Natascha analyzed each of the sound sequences.

"They're all absolutely identical," Richard said.

Natascha looked up to Nick.

"We had pack ice during two of those excursions in *Odin*. There's no way that this could've been a fishing vessel," Nick stated.

"What about the Coast Guard? Aren't they out on patrol up here? I mean, just because we don't see any ships from the *Northern Explorer* doesn't mean we can't hear them on the hydrophone. The range of the hydrophone up here in the north is huge," Natascha said.

"I don't know. I'm pretty sure we would've known if there was another ship in the area that's big enough to make it through the North-West Passage," Nick said in a concerned tone and looked at the monitor.

"So you think there's a problem?" Natascha asked. "What is it?"

"I'm not sure. Just a feeling. I want to tell Ariel about it," Nick said and picked up the phone.

Just a few minutes later, Ariel and Shira were standing beside Nick. Natascha explained what they had found out during the last thirty minutes and played the sound several times.

Ariel was at a complete loss.

"No idea," the Israeli said and shrugged his shoulders.

"Nick, please call Ole-Einar and Olaf up here. I want them to listen to it."

Five more minutes and all the members of their team were listening to the sound.

Ole-Einar had received some training at a sonar station before he joined the Norwegian Navy Special Forces.

He focused while Richard repeatedly played the sound.

"Well, I have to admit this sounds strange," the Norwegian said and looked at Ariel. The expression in Ariel's face told him he was not satisfied with his answer.

"If I had to bet some money on it, I'd say it's a fishing boat, but something isn't right. If this is a fishing boat, we'd hear the turbulences created by the boat moving through the water. Sorry, but this is the best I can do. It has been a while since I listened to something like that. We could ask the skipper. He is a naval veteran. Maybe he knows more."

Ariel nodded toward Shira who immediately left the room, just to show up a few minutes later with Captain Rasmussen.

Natascha rose from her chair and offered it to Captain Rasmussen. The Captain had also asked his First Officer Karl-Heinz Junghans to accompany him, and the two of them repeatedly listened to the sound.

"How often have you recorded this sound signature?" the Captain asked and looked at Dr. Richard Weber.

Natascha walked over to a chart and showed the Captain when and where they had recorded the sound.

"Those include the recordings from both *Odin* and *Polar Viking*," the young German scientist explained.

The Captain nodded and asked Richard to play the recording once more.

"And? What do you think?" Captain Rasmussen asked his First Officer.

First Officer Karl-Heinz Junghans shook his head.

"I'm sorry, I have to pass on this one. The only thing I'm certain about is that this is not a fishing vessel. It's definitely moving, but there are no turbulences from the surface," he confirmed Ole-Einars assumption.

Captain Rasmussen nodded in approval and looked at Dr. Richard Weber again.

"Can you play it twice as fast?" the Norwegian skipper asked.

Richard changed the menu and played the sound with twice the speed.

"Hm, I might be wrong, but I think we're dealing with a submarine here," Captain Rasmussen said. He leaned forward, closed his eyes and asked Richard to play it again several more times.

"Seven blades on the propeller...most likely Russian....definitely only one screw, which also means that it's not a *Typhoon*....hm, this one here...yes, that might be it," the Norwegian said, opening his eyes as he leaned back in his chair. He exchanged a glance with Ariel and Dr. Richard Weber.

"I might be wrong, but my guess is that we're accompanied by a Russian *Akula.*"

"An *Akula*?" Natascha asked puzzled.

The former naval veteran looked at her.

"Yes. The Russian *Akula*'s are long range nuclear submarines, around one hundred and thirteen meters long, which makes them a little bit longer than the *Northern Explorer*. Under water they can reach a top speed of thirty five knots. They're one

Thin Ice

of the newer type of submarines from the Russians, and the *Akula*'s are one of the few models they actually keep running. The reason for that is they're the Russian counterpart to the American *Los Angeles* class. Most Navy's agree that the *Akula*'s are among the best long range nuclear submarines in the world. They were especially designed to be as silent as possible. I assume that the sub is following us within one or two sea miles. In naval terms, that's pretty close, especially in the North-West Passage. Although the NATO has several sonar surveillance systems installed around North America, I doubt it'll detect it. If the Russian skipper keeps his *Akula* always close to the *Northern Explorer*, then it will be nearly impossible to hear it. As soon as we stop or as soon as we drop our anchor, the Russian skipper will stop all engines and go on the ground. The sound we're hearing there might be because of the shallow water we were in when you recorded him with the hydrophone. He can't simply stop and roll over in shallow water. To maneuver his submarine around, he'll most likely go silent and stay below five knots. If he makes any noise at all, it would most likely sound like a fishing boat. They can spend up to ten months under water, but this is also only determined by the amount of provisions they carry. The *Northern Explorer* is such a noisy ship, I'm sure they could hear us even in Moscow if they wanted to."

"And what do they want here?" Natascha asked, fearing there might be a nuclear submarine out there to hunt her as well.

The Captain looked at each of them.

"Don't worry. They're not after you. If they were after you, they would have finished their job a long time ago. I assume they're just interested in what we're doing here. I think they just want to make sure that neither the Canadians nor the Americans are doing anything stupid in regards to the oil up here."

Captain Rasmussen rose from his chair and looked at Ariel.

"I was convinced right from the beginning that we would be accompanied by at least one nuclear submarine. I'm not too worried about it. If you don't need me any longer, I'll be back at the helm."

The Captain said good-bye and left the room together with his First Officer.

Ariel waited until the First Officer had closed the door behind him, then he turned to Dr. Richard Weber.

"Could you give me a copy of the isolated sequence only? I want to do some research with it."

"What about us?" Oliver wanted to know from his Israeli superior.

"Does this change anything for us?

Ariel shrugged his shoulders.

"I agree with the Captain. If a one hundred meter long nuclear attack submarine would be interested in Natascha or Richard, I'm sure we would've noticed that by now. I just want to make sure," Ariel explained and put the USB drive, that Richard handed to him, in his pocket and left the room.

Later that evening Natascha was lying in her bed, staring at the ceiling of her cabin as Shira brushed her teeth. When the young Israeli went to bed a few minutes later, she wished her German friend a good night, but Natascha didn't respond at all.

"Natascha!" Shira said, this time almost shouting.

"What?" Natascha jumped and looked at her.

"You don't have to worry about this submarine, Natascha. It's normal. They're just following us," Shira said in her attempt to calm Natascha down.

Natascha turned on her side and looked at Shira for a long while without saying anything.

"It's not the submarine I'm thinking about," Natascha finally said and started to tell Shira about the Inuvialuit family she had met earlier that day.

Home Office and Operational Headquarters of *EuroSecCorporation*, London, Thursday, 22nd September

Brigitte Schwartze sat behind her desk in her office and picked up the phone at the second buzz. After the caller had introduced himself, Brigitte passed the call through to retired Admiral Brian Whittaker.

"Hi Lawrence, you old dog. How are you doing? Are they still bugging you up there in Faslane?" Brian greeted his old friend.

"Hm, it could be better. At least they're keeping all those young foxes away from me. I'm now teaching in the simulation room. That cold and damp climate in a sub is not good for my old bones any more. And I'm getting way too old to handle the stress when one of those wannabe skippers is trying to pilot a sub through the loch. No, I'm done with that. How are you doing?"

"Well, now that the people I'm working with are actually listening when I say something, I feel much better. I can't complain. I assume you got my message?"

"Yes, I got it. I listened to it this morning and checked out our databank. The sound is not very clear. Was it recorded by one of our subs?"

"No, we have an assignment on a research vessel in the Polar Sea and they recorded it with a hydrophone. Some of our guys recorded it over a period of several weeks. The Norwegian skipper is an old naval veteran. He assumes this sound is from a Russian sub that's following them. He even went so far as to guess that it's an *Akula*. Single prop, seven blades," retired Admiral Brian Whittaker explained.

"Well, for a scientific recording the quality isn't too bad. I made my best three sonar officers listen to it independently, and they all confirmed what your Viking was thinking. Our computer gave me a ninety-eight percent likelihood that it's a third generation *Akula*. The Russians are calling it *Bar Class, Project nine-seven-one*. The remaining two percent are lost in the fact, that the recording is not from our gear, but from a scientific hydrophone. I think your men should give that cunning old Norwegian fox a cigar."

"Very well. Thank you very much. That's some good information towards the end of the week."

"Brian, should we be concerned?"

"No, I don't think so. They're just following a research vessel in the North-West Passage. Nothing that immediately affects us."

"A Russian nuclear long range attack submarine inside Canadian waters? I might be wrong, but the last time I checked, Canada was still a NATO member and pretty close to Great Britain. I took the liberty and checked on the Russian subs. At the moment, there are only two *Akula*'s active. One is suppose to be on routine patrol in the Barents Sea, while the other is running some test trial after it had received some major upgrades. After the *Kursk* disaster, the Russians planned to build their own submarine that they can send pretty quickly to render assistance. The upgrade included a universal docking station for a smaller type rescue sub. Of course you could also load that sub with a special forces unit and bring them close to shore, but we don't have too many details. But we do know that this *Akula* is not carrying any ICBM's * at the moment."

"Well, like I said, I don't think we should be concerned about this. They're most likely just keeping an eye on the research vessel. My men just wanted to be sure. I owe you one. You let me know the next time you're in town."

"I will. Given the fact that they don't carry any ICBM's and they're most likely not going to deploy a handful of soldiers at the north pole, I'll agree with you and won't report it for now. Otherwise all hell'll break loose. I'll be seeing you. Goodbye."

Retired Admiral Brian Whittaker pressed the button on his phone to end the call and walked over to Klaus Schwartze's office.

Without saying a word, Brian sat in the comfortable chair at his desk, leaned back, and closed his eyes as he put his feet on the second chair.

"I assume there's something you want to tell me?" Klaus asked calmly, without even looking up from the report he just read.

"Yes, there is indeed something I want to tell you. I just spoke to my old friend in Faslane, and he has confirmed that this propeller sound is in fact from a nuclear Russian submarine that's following the *Northern Explorer*. Good thing is, that the sub seems to be used as a rescue tool now and that it's not carrying any ICBM's. "

Klaus looked up and shrugged his shoulders.

"So what? We assumed right from the beginning that the Russians would follow them. The Americans are most likely crawling around somewhere as well. Maybe the Russians are just testing some new gear? You said it yourself, they're not carrying any ICBM's. What do you want to do?"

"I know they're not interested in us. But bear with me here for a moment. We have one Israeli who's leading a team of former Special Force veterans from three different nations on a Norwegian research vessel in Canadian waters to protect a German citizen, while he's being closely followed and watched by a nuclear Russian attack submarine. Am I the only one who can see the potential for an international crisis here?"

For the first time during their conversation, Klaus put the report down. Not even looking at his friend and partner, he reached for the phone instead.

"Maybe we should call BBC. It's going to be a company outing for them if something happens up there," Klaus muttered and picked up the phone.

ICBM: Inter Continental Ballistic Missile

Brian rose from his chair and shook his head.

"I knew you wouldn't take me serious," he said and went for the door.

"Again it's up to the British to save the world," he added on his way to his own office.

Brian sat behind his desk and wrote a quick note for Ariel, which Brigitte sent just a few minutes later via satellite to the *Northern Explorer*.

On board the *Northern Explorer*, Dolphin and Union Strait, north off Cape Young, Thursday, September 22nd

Shira sat in the radio room and looked at Ariel's computer, which was just downloading a message from the satellite, when Ariel and Astrid returned from their breakfast.

"We got mail," Shira announced and looked up.

"What is it? Something important?"

Shira printed the message and read it out loud, before she handed the page to the Israeli.

"Your skipper was right. Ninety-eight percent third generation Russian Akula. *Most likely unarmed. No need to panic. PS: Don't screw up!!! Whittaker."*

Ariel smiled and looked for the Captain. He found him in the company of Dr. Weber, Natascha and Nick in the cabin that was used to plan all the dives with both *Odin* and *Polar Viking*. Dr. Weber was just discussing the locations for the remaining dives with the research submersibles. Ariel refused to interrupt them and stood beside Nick.

"So, is everything okay?" the young German asked his Israeli friend.

"The Captain was right. Third generation Russian *Akula*."

"What's the boss saying?"

"It's no reason to get excited and that we must not screw it up," Ariel said with a smile.

"Okay," Nick replied, also smiling about retired Admiral Whittaker's choice of words.

Two minutes later, Ariel informed Captain Rasmussen about the news, but Captain Rasmussen lacked any and all concern for the matter. Natascha and her father were still studying the charts to find the best location for the next couple dives.

"I got an idea," Natascha said and jumped up, after she overheard Ariel.

"What's the minimum depth that this Russian sub can operate without being seen on the surface?" she asked enthusiastically.

Captain Rasmussen wondered where this question would lead her.

"It'd mostly depend on the speed it's traveling at. Why?"

Natascha walked around the little table and pointed at a certain location on the charts.

"Just a few hours ago we came through the Duke of York Archipel. According to these charts, it's pretty shallow there. If this Russian submarine is following us in a distance, it'll come through there later today. All we have to do is block the shipping channel to force it to the surface. Then we would know for sure!"

Natascha had not even finished her last sentence when she noticed, by the expression on the faces of the others, that she just said something very embarrassing.

"Well, if I give it a second thought," she more or less whispered and looked back at the chart to avoid their faces, "then I think that it'd not be the best idea if an unarmed Norwegian research vessel, which is occupied in an international expedition in Canadian waters, tries to force an armed to the teeth Russian nuclear attack submarine to ascend. We probably shouldn't push our luck," she added with a smile and looked at everyone.

"Let's put it this way. If our radar wasn't mistaken, and I actually tend to believe that it's in good working order, then the Russian followed us within a quarter of a sea mile through the Archipel on periscope depth. Their periscope was nearly invisible in our wash. Although I have to admit that I could detect a sense of adventure in your suggestion, I'm not overly disappointed that we have missed our chance," Captain Rasmussen replied with a fatherly smile.

"Thank you very much, that was very kind. I assume it's safe to say that, if I were a member of your crew, I'd be scrubbing the deck by now," Natascha added apologetically.

"You're assuming right. That would indeed be safe to say. If anybody else needs me, I'm on the bridge. Dr. Weber, can you please promise me to keep your daughter away from the rudder, just in case there's no one at the helm?" the Norwegian said and winked before he left.

Natascha gathered her notes and swung the backpack on her back on the way out.

"Can we just forget what I just said in there?" Natascha asked her father.

Richard burst into laughter.

"Well, I can try. I was actually convinced that you wouldn't need another rush of adrenalin after your polar bear encounter. Just promise me you don't plan to attack that *Akula* with *Odin*."

"I'm pretty sure all of those plans would shatter the moment I see that submarine for the first time underwater," she promised.

"Very well then. Are you stopping by later on? I want to discuss the details of our remaining *Odin* dives with you. We also have to see which projects aren't finished yet. I'll meet the other team leaders at ten. You can sit in if you want," the expedition leader said.

"That's okay, but I won't be able to make it to the ten o'clock meeting. There's something else I have to do," his daughter replied.

While Richard walked to the cabin, Nick dropped Natascha off at the doctors quarters, before he went back to his own cabin himself.

Natascha spent the next half hour with the doctor. Knowing that both the American and Canadian scientists were still out with the two RIB's, she slowly walked back to her cabin alone and completely lost in thought.

Shira was lying on her bed and waited until Natascha had closed the door behind her.

"Did you had a chance to see the doctor?"

"Yes, I did, but he's saying that he can't diagnose anything at this moment. He doesn't have the necessary gear."

"How do you feel about it?"

Natascha flopped on her bed and looked at the ceiling.

"I have absolutely no clue. I haven't had my period for a while now, but that happened to me before on my first expedition as well. But I think this time it's different."

"Did you tell anybody?"

Natascha turned on her side and looked at Shira.

"No I didn't," the young German woman said and shook her head. "Why should I tell anybody? I don't even know if it's actually true or not. Maybe I completely misunderstood the whole thing she said. I just don't know if I should still dive or not."

"Do you want to tell him?" Shira asked.

Natascha didn't know what happened to her, but suddenly tears were running down her alread red cheeks. She tried to force them back even now, but knew there was no use.

"What am I going to do if he doesn't want to? We barely know each other, we don't live together and I have no idea how this could work!" Natascha sobbed and reluctantly sat up.

Shira hurried over to her bed. The Israeli took Natascha in her arms to comfort her.

"Natascha, you know very well that he loves you. He won't reject you. The two of you spent more time together in the last few months, than most other couples do in their first year. You two are the perfect match. There won't be any problems, Natascha," Shira comforted, but Natascha was reluctant to calm down.

"I have to tell my father that I can't dive any more. I won't know for sure for the remaining three weeks of the expedition, but I can't risk anything. He was against it right from the beginning and he was right," Natascha sobbed.

"But you can still work with the submersibles, right?" Shira tried to support her.

Natascha nodded, still sobbing.

"Yes, I can still work with them, but there are two more deep dives that I'm scheduled to do, and I'm the only one in our team beside Mario who's certified to dive that deep."

"Just wait and see what happens. Maybe the weather won't be the best. Don't worry about that right now. Maybe one of the other scientists can do the dive for you. Aren't there some deep divers among them?"

Natascha thought for a moment.

"That's true. Both the Icelandic and the Russian team have at least one deep diver that I know about."

Natascha blew her nose and wiped some tears out of her face before she continued.

"I've no idea how to tell Nick. We never talked about something like this. What am I going to do?" Natascha sobbed and started to cry again.

"Most important thing is that you talk to Nick about this as soon as possible. It just takes too much time before you know for sure. And maybe there isn't even anything to be concerned about after all. I can assure you that Nick's the last person who would abandon you. Don't be sad. Everything'll work out just fine."

"Are you sure?" Natascha asked sobbing and put her head on Shira's shoulder.

"Yes, I'm sure."

"Thanks," Natascha whispered and was thankful Shira was with her. For Natascha, Shira was not only a very good friend, but the German also looked up to her as if she was her older sister. Shira was silent as she held her in her arms.

- 14 -

**On board the *Northern Explorer*, Dolphin and Union Strait,
north off Cape Young, Thursday, September 22nd**

It was early in the evening, but Natascha asked Nick for a little walk. They both stood at the ship's bow and looked at the sunset. The air was much colder in the last couple days, and the temperature was just below the freezing mark. Natascha was wearing a wind jacket and Nick's black woolen beanie. It was the same beanie she always wore when she was researching with *Odin*. Though Natascha was never slow to admit that there was more comfort and safety woven in this one item than in the product itself.

Nick stood behind her and wrapped his arms tightly around her, as they watched the sun slowly set on this cloudless evening. The water's surface was flat as glass and reflected the last sunlight of the day.

"I love you, Angel," Nick whispered into Natascha's ears, at the same moment the sun finally dipped into the horizon.

So far so good, Natascha thought, and her eyes filled with tears again. She concentrated to push her feelings aside as she fixed her attention at the horizon.

"I wish you were with me when I was with the orcas," she whispered.

"Yes, I would've loved to experience that, except the polar bear."

"That little orca and it's mother were so sweet. There was so much love in their eyes."

"Yes," Nick whispered and kissed Natascha on the head.

Natascha didn't know how to tell him. She spent all afternoon thinking about how to break the news to him, but all her well prepared sentences were gone or simply appeared to be silly to her. Without knowing what she was doing, she spun around and looked Nick in the eyes.

Nick was caught by surprise and smiled at her.

"Nick, when I was on shore that day, do you remember the Inuvialuit family that came over to me? There was that old woman with them. I don't know how old she is, but I have the feeling that she's a very wise person."

Natascha stopped and watched to see if Nick was taking this as a joke, but he wasn't.

"She said something to me. Do you know what she said?" Natascha asked.

"No, how could I?" Nick answered, with a weak laugh.

Natascha had never mentioned that part to Nick until now and took a deep breath.

"She said that the female orca knew that I was not alone in the water. That it would've also been the reason they accepted me, and the reason the female orca came over to me with the calf. And it was the reason that she protected me and my young from the polar bear," Natascha finally said and took another breath.

For the next few seconds, Nick looked at her speechless.

"And you believe now…"

"I don't know," she quickly interrupted him.

"Fact is, and this is documented, that dolphins and other marine mammals can detect if a human is pregnant, even if the woman herself doesn't know," Natascha hastily explained.

"And you really believe now…" Nick asked again, still shocked.

"I'm not sure, but I think I'm pregnant," Natascha finally said and could feel the stress leave her shoulders. She heaved a wobbily sigh as her eyes filled with tears again. Before she had the chance to reel them back in one spurt, and the rest flowed uncontrollably.

Nick smiled, but he could not find the right words. He pulled her in close, and embraced her much differently than he used to. He refused to let go as he told her how much he loved her and repeatedly pressed kisses on her head. Natascha soon noticed the tears in his eyes.

"Hey, I'm the woman. Why are you crying?"

Nick wanted to say something, but he could only shake his head and embraced her even tighter.

Many moments passed, and Nick could feel the cold wind finally reach his skin. "How certain are you?"

"Well, that's the catch. I'm not certain at all. I mean, what the woman said and the whale's behavior perfectly match together, but I went to the doctor this morning. He couldn't diagnose anything, but he also doesn't have the right gear. It was not in Italy, I would definitely know that by now. I also rule out that one night in Germany at my place, just a feeling that I have. I think the earliest that it could have happened, would be the one night in Iceland. That would be eleven weeks ago and I think that I would notice something by now, but I'm not sure. Another opportunity would be the week when Shira took the night shifts, but that was just six weeks ago. So, really, I'm not sure if I'm pregnant or not. I feel dizzy in the morning sometimes, but that doesn't have to mean anything. And during my first expedition I also didn't get my period in time, but it's way overdue by now."

"Have you told anybody?"

Natascha shook her head.

"No, I haven't. The only one who knows is Shira. I just had to talk to her about it, because I…" Natascha avoided his eyes and looked at the floor.

"Because you didn't know how I would react?" Nick finished her sentence.

Natascha started crying again and threw herself on Nick, hugging him.

"Angel, I love you. How could you think I wouldn't be happy about it?" he whispered.

"Don't know," Natascha sobbed, barely understandable.

"I don't know what I shall do alone," she added, still sobbing.

"You're not going to do anything alone. I'll always be with you," Nick said and kissed her again.

"The expedition will be over in three weeks and then we'll leave this ship together and we'll plan our future together. And if you really are pregnant, then this is wonderful and we'll have a happy, healthy boy and you'll be a fantastic mother," Nick whispered to comfort his girlfriend.

"Daughter," Natascha sobbed and rose her head to look at her boyfriend.

"We'll have a daughter," she added whispering.

"It doesn't matter if it's a boy or a girl. As long as our son is healthy."

Natascha smiled and they kissed.

"What about your parents? Did you tell them yet?" Nick asked after a while.

Natascha took a couple deep breaths and shook her head.

"No, they don't know. I mean, there's no reason for immediate panic. I'm not even sure if I'm pregnant. I was just so horrified that you'd break up with me. Dad won't be happy for sure. He predicted something like this would happen from the beginning."

Suddenly Natascha looked Nick in his eyes and all humour aside, she continued. "Listen, I don't know if my father has told you anything about that. I don't want you to think that I'd jump into bed with the first person the moment I'm on a ship. I'm not…"

Nick interrupted her before she really got started.

"Your father hasn't said anything like that. I trust you. You know that. Fact is that we have to tell your father. I don't want you to do any more dives. What about your mother?"

"You're going with me to my father?" Natascha asked and threw herself into another hug, tears running down her cheeks again.

"Of course I'm coming with you. After all, it's also my son," Nick said.

"Daughter," Natascha kept sobbing.

Nick released his arms from her hips and looked into her eyes.

"This is my son, isn't it?" he joked.

"This is not the time for jokes," Natascha flashed at him.

"So, what about your mother?"

"She doesn't know anything. If I'm going to tell her now, then she'll worry for no reason. I think we should wait until we know for sure before I tell her. Do you have to tell anyone?"

"Well, I think I can't avoid telling Ariel about it. I can't see that Shira will say anything about it. I wouldn't recommend saying anything to the boys until we're one hundred percent sure. Otherwise we'll have to listen to *there's a little pleasure root growing in your garden* for the next three weeks."

Natascha couldn't help but laugh.

"I love you," she whispered softly.

"Well, I suggest we go to your father now."

Nick took her hand and together they walked back towards the superstructure.

"Am I really the father?"

Natascha clapped him on the back of his head.

"The more I think about it, the more uncertain I get," she returned.

"You're a miserable cow."

"Hey you, don't call your girlfriend a miserable cow just ten minutes after she confesses."

The visit with Natascha's father didn't take long. They found Dr. Richard Weber in his cabin, and Natascha was glad, that Nick sat beside her holding her hand, as she explained the reason behind their unannounced visit.

After being shocked for the first few moments, Richard promised them his support.

"Very well," Natascha's father stated. "It's not that I'm not happy for you, Natascha, but you have just caught me completely by surprise. If I understand this correctly, then you're not even sure if you're pregnant. I'll leave it up to you when and how you inform your mother about it, but I don't want you to send her a simple e-mail, understood? As far as this expedition goes, you won't dive any more. I'll talk to the Icelandic as well as the Russian, I'm pretty sure they'll help us out. I also leave it up to you if you want to continue to work with the research submersibles or not. You have asked me about my opinion on this matter and I'll give it to you. I don't doubt your feelings for each other, but I'd be much happier if the two of you would've known each other a little bit longer. But after all, you're my daughter, and I love you more than anything else, and you'll get all the support I can give. Just let me know if you're pregnant or not as soon as you know. I don't want to hear it from the ship's boy, okay?"

"Thank you, Dad," Natascha whispered, fighting her emotions again.

"It's okay, darling. Come over here and give your old father a hug."

Natascha walked around the table and hugged her father.

Nick smiled as he watched the Professor sook up to his daughter.

"Okay, all we got to do now is tell Ariel," Natascha said relieved and looked at Nick.

"Yes. I just don't know where he is."

"I'm going to ask Shira. She should know where he is," Natascha said and went to her cabin next door.

"Nick, could you please come here for a moment?" Dr. Richard Weber asked suddenly.

Nick stepped back into Natascha's father's cabin and closed the door behind him.

"Listen Nick, I'm not sure if you know that I wasn't with Natascha's mother during her pregnancy and the birth of our only daughter, because I was stuck on a research vessel in the Antarctic for ten months. By the first time I saw my daughter, she was already two months old. It almost broke mine and Renate's heart. I know about your feelings for my daughter and I don't question them, but I want you to look me into my eyes and promise me that you'll not abandon her. I want you to promise me that you'll be a better father than I was, and that you'll be there for your child no matter how it turns out between you and my daughter."

Nick walked closer to Richard.

"I'm going to promise you as I promised Natascha's mother, that I'll take care of your daughter. I'll do anything to make sure that she and, if she is pregnant, our child will be happy."

Richard nodded and gave Nick a hug.

Just as Richard had released Nick from his hug, Natascha came into the cabin again. She was in a much better mood than one hour ago.

"Shira said that Ariel is in the gym. Let's go," she mentioned and took Nick's hand.

"I'm coming," Nick said and Richard looked after them until they reached the end of the corridor and disappeared downstairs.

Although it wasn't late in the evening, they were not surprised to find Ariel alone in the ship's gym. He was sitting on the floor and it seemed that he was meditating.

Nick carefully walked over to him. He didn't want to disturb him, but Ariel had already noticed their arrival and opened his eyes.

"What's going on? There must be a good reason for the two of you to look for me in the gym."

Natascha and Nick sat in front of Ariel and looked at him.

"There's a slight chance that Natascha's pregnant. Therefore she won't be diving any more for the rest of the expedition, but she still might use the research submersible. We'll most likely not know for sure within the next three weeks if she is pregnant, since the doctor lacks the necessary gear on board. I thought you should know the reason why she's not diving any more. Only Shira and Richard know about this besides us and I'd appreciate it if the boys don't hear about it," Nick said and stood up again.

Natascha gave him a puzzled look as she looked up to him from the floor where she sat.

"That's it? That easy?"

She glanced between Ariel and Nick with surprise. Ariel had his eyes fixed on Nick and he was silent.

"Yes, what did you expect?" Nick shrugged and looked at his girlfriend.

"He's my boss. That was a conversation between men. Doesn't have to be complicated," Nick explained.

Still irritated, Natascha stood up and looked at Ariel, who had not shown any reaction yet. Whatever Natascha had expected, this was not it.

"Well, if this is all, we'll go then, okay?" Natascha stated, condescendingly.

Ariel looked at her, but still maintained his silence.

Nick and Natascha turned around and were almost at the door, when they heard Ariel's voice behind them.

"Nick, I want to talk to you later. Alone."

Nick and Natascha turned around and looked at him again.

Natascha noticed that Nick nodded remorsefully.

"If you want to say something to Nick, you might as well say it to me," Natascha almost shouted and walked in front of Nick, as if she was protecting him.

"Listen Natascha. This is not that simple…" Nick returned.

"Why not? This is both our business," Natascha burst.

"There's a reason why Ariel wants to talk to me alone and he's right," Nick explained.

"Oh, there's a reason, yes? Then what?" Natascha asked aggressively.

"Okay, if you want, you can listen," Ariel said calmly, and Natascha turned around again to face the Israeli as he spoke.

"Nick, I don't question anything on the emotional level, and you know very well that I've supported this relationship from the very beginning. You've ignored all the rules and I've always looked the other way. Fact is, we had an agreement and you didn't stick to it. I want you to think about it. If you should find out within the next three weeks if you're pregnant, I would have to know. This is all I have to say about this matter."

"What agreement?" Natascha asked and looked between the Israeli and Nick.

"Nick can explain. I thought he's telling you everything anyway," Ariel said and closed his eyes again, a clear sign that this conversation was over for him.

Natascha started to walk towards him, but Nick grabbed her arm and guided her out of the gym. After a few steps outside the gym, Natascha pulled her arm free from his grasp and stopped.

"What agreement?" she demanded and looked at him.

"Before I explain, I want you to know that everything that happened between us, happened because I really love you, okay?" Nick reassured calmly. "It may sound childish, but it's not really very helpful in our job, when there's an intimate relationship between the guard and his client. Remember that we met and fell in love before the institute hired us. When we started the protection detail, everybody was under the assumption that your father was the target and that we were only hired for the one weekend in Berlin. Back then, nobody thought that there'd be a problem if the two of us would see each other during those three days. After it was decided that we were boarding the ship, I had to promise Ariel not to rush things with you. Ariel knew that he could not separate us on this ship against our will, so he decided to support us, so that everything was under control. Fact is, he would have not taken me along if Rolf was not shot. Ariel's biggest concern was that you would not trust or like him. He tried to avoid that at all cost. Once we found out that you are the actual target, he wanted me as close to you as possible, since he knew that of all our people you would trust me most. He knew that you would trust me with things you would never tell anyone else. To be fair to the other team members, he had asked me not to rush it with the sex. Ole-Einar and Olaf are both married and Oliver is in a relationship as well. Ariel didn't want any tension among us while we're on a ship for several months. As for your safety, I had to promise him that we would be careful as long as we're responsible for you. That was the agreement I had with him. He used our relationship to make your life as easy and as safe as possible."

"Have you or Shira told him anything that I confided you with?" Natascha snapped.

"No. I did not tell him anything private about us. Remember he almost kicked me off the ship in Halifax because our relationship was getting in the way. I also doubt that Shira said anything to him. Natascha, you know how I feel about you and you know that I'm not in an easy position. Ariel only wants what's best for you and he's completely right to be pissed at me."

Natascha thought for a while about what Nick had just told her and looked at the door to the gym.

"I hate that he's always right," she finally muttered and took Nick's hand as they went back to her cabin.

Natascha carefully opened her cabin door, but Shira was still reading a book in her bed.

"How did it go?" the Israeli asked.

"Actually, the longer the evening went, the easier it got," Natascha answered and took her clothes off for the night.

Nick sat down on Natascha's bed.

"What did Ariel say?"

Nick looked at her.

"What do you think he said?" Nick sighed.

Shira closed her book and looked at Natascha, who was just brushing her teeth.

"Just enough so that you feel miserable and that you both know that he's right. Am I right?" she asked with a smile.

"Precisely. He does all that in six sentences."

Shira gave it a laugh and noticed Natascha closed the bathroom door behind her.

"Yes, I believe that. He was always good at that. Do you agree with him?" the Israeli asked.

"There's nothing to disagree. I know he's right. But you also know the position I'm in. And you know how Natascha might think about it. Do me a favor and explain it to her again, okay?"

Shira nodded and looked at the closed bathroom door again.

"Other than that, everything is fine between you and Natascha?"

"Yes, as far as I know."

"Her father?"

"Much better than she expected. No problem at all." Nick hastily sighed, "Let's just be realistic here for a moment, we don't even know if she's pregnant."

"You know you have to marry her," the Israeli demanded.

"Easy, slow down. First off, let's just be pregnant. After that, we'll see where we go from there. Our religion is not as demanding as yours," Nick defended himself with a smile.

"Cold hands?" Shira asked with a smile.

"It's *cold feet*," Nick corrected his Israeli friend the same moment Natascha walked back into the cabin in her pajamas.

"So, what are your plans?" Shira asked as Natascha walked to her bed.

"Well, I think we agree on the general direction. We just have to work out some details," Natascha said and sat beside Nick, kissing his cheek.

"Assuming you're indeed pregnant. Do you already know what you'll do once the baby is born?" Shira asked.

Natascha wrapped her arms around Nick and looked at him for a few seconds before she answered.

"Assuming that I'm really pregnant, then we'd give our daughter everything she needs to be happy once she's born."

Shira was impressed and nodded, before she looked at Nick.

"Assuming that you're really pregnant, I suggest that once our son is born, you should lose all that extra weight and get back to work. We could need that extra money," Nick said as seriously as he could.

While Shira immediately burst into laughter, Natascha's mouth dropped wide open.

Although Nick appealed several times that it could not be good for the unborn child to experience how it's father was getting beaten up by it's mother, Nick received what Shira and Natascha simply called justice. After a while, Nick was holding his girlfriend tight and he didn't dare to release her until she promised him she would not attack him any more.

Being serious again, they both agreed to wait until they would know for sure. There was really nothing they could do before then anyway.

Since it was now almost midnight, Nick decided to head down to his own cabin to get some sleep. Natascha followed him to the cabin door, where she hugged him again.

"I love you," she whispered to Nick.

"Love you, too," Nick whispered back and kissed her goodnight.

Montana, USA, Thursday, September 29th

While his three friends stayed in the nearby town, Chuck visited his American and Canadian clients.

"If everything goes according to plan, we'll fly to Anchorage on Saturday, October 8th. From there we'll take a smaller plane to get to Inuvik, where two helicopters will be waiting for us. We'll use them for our flight to Paulatuk, where we will refuel and continue directly to the *Northern Explorer*, but we'll only use one helicopter to get to the research vessel. The other helicopter will stay in Paulatuk on stand-by. Is everything okay on your end?" the American asked.

Chuck shrugged his shoulders.

"We received very detailed orders from you. We'll just be there as babysitters in case you need us."

"I know I asked you this before, but are you absolutely certain that the Germans won't recognize your men?"

" I have very reliable information that they have no idea what we look like. I'm not worried about them. How long do you plan to stay on board the research vessel?"

"It should not take us any longer than the better part of a day. We decided, that you and your men will stay a little bit longer to make sure that there are no complications."

"We keep one of the helicopters?"

"Yes, that's the plan. The *Northern Explorer* is several miles off shore and has it's own helipad. According to their internet log book, most of the scientists will have already left the ship when we come. That means, they don't need the helipad the entire time to taxi back and forth. You mentioned earlier that your men can fly the helicopter?"

"Yes, that's correct. I'd prefer to operate our helicopter ourselves, so we don't have to worry about the pilot."

"That won't be a problem. We'll make the arrangements later today. Once we left the ship we will leave the second helicopter refueled and ready for you in Inuvik, just in case."

Chuck nodded and sat down in the chesterfield to enjoy his drink. So far everything was going as planned.

On board the *Northern Explorer*, Amundsen Gulf, Darnley Bay, Thursday, October 6th

The *Northern Explorer* was laying several miles off the coast of Paulatuk on her last scheduled stop at anchor. The expedition was, as far as Dr. Richard Weber was concerned, a complete success. They had been able to do all the scheduled tasks and no one got injured. Besides that, it seemed that the threat against his daughter's life was no longer acute after the failed assassination attempt in Iceland. Although he never really believed that his daughter's, or his own, life was at risk at any time on board the ship, he really appreciated the presence of Ariel and his team, who planned to stay with them until the end of the expedition. The fact that his daughter might be pregnant also brightened his mood after the had slept over it. From then on he had asked her during the following days at least three times a day if she knew anything new. Natascha always said no and had to promise her father, that his name was on the top of the list of people she would notify as soon as she knew. It took Richard lots of willpower not to tell Renate, but he respected Natascha's wish to tell her mother herself at the right time.

For the first of the two scheduled deep dives, the Icelandic scientist took Natascha's part. She had accompanied the dive together with her father in *Odin,* and she was actually quite relieved about the support she received from her father in her situation. The problem was now the second deep dive. Since both the Russian and the Icelandic divers would fly out the very next morning, they both couldn't do the dive for safety reasons. Under these circumstances it seemed very difficult to organize the dive. In the end, Nick volunteered to take Natascha's part for this dive.

"I don't want to be rude my little pumpkin, but you're not a marine biologist," Natascha explained.

"No, but I can shine the lights, shoot some video and assist Mario. He's quiet capable of doing the tasks himself."

"That's true," Natascha said after she entertained the thought for a few seconds.

"But you've never been down so deep with a rebreather," she continued, still not convinced that this would be the best solution.

"That's right. With a rebreather I was only down to sixty meters, but I can use an open circuit configuration. I used your father's gear before."

Natascha knew that Nick was right.

Since the runway at Paulatuk's airport was only 1200 meters long, only small planes could start and land there to fly the scientists out. All the gear would remain on the research vessel for several more weeks until it's arrival back in Germany. Only there would the scientists be able to unload their gear.

"The boys also mentioned that they wouldn't mind helping you out, but since I somehow feel responsible for you being unable to do this dive, I want to do it."

"*Somehow responsible*? Do they know why I'm not diving?" Natascha asked, alarmed.

"No, they assume you're on your period."

"They've no idea," Natascha whispered with a smile.

"Okay, I'll talk to Dad. You're sure my father's gear is okay?"

"Ole-Einar and Olaf are just checking it. Can't see anything being wrong with it. I'll go over to them now. Oliver will be with you in a moment."

Three hours later Natascha and her father were both sitting inside *Odin* and they watched the two divers in the murky water in front them. Although Natascha was a little bit nervous at the beginning, she finally relaxed when she noticed that Nick was up for the task, and that the dive went without any complications so far. Both divers just reached their last deco stop. Natascha watched as Mario checked the partial pressure of the oxygen in his rebreather and made a note on her clipboard, while Nick unclipped another half empty tank from his harness to clip it to *Odin*'s frame. Although he was still carrying the large double tanks on his back, he was breathing from a single tank under his left arm. After Natascha had also marked Nick's gas change down on her clipboard, she saw that both divers were now pretty relaxed and just hovering beside the buoy line. The young German scientist finally leaned back in her seat.

"So you'll move in with him once the expedition is over?" Dr. Weber asked his daughter.

"Yes, that's the plan," Natascha replied, biting her lip.

"Does he know?"

"Does he know what?" Natascha asked curiously and smiled at her father.

"That you can neither cook nor bake at all," her father laughed.

"That's so not true," Natascha shouted. Then paused as she defended herself, "I can cook…certain meals…if I have to…"

"Darling, the last time I checked, you could barely boil water," Richard laughed.

"Well…I'm a scientist…not a cook," Natascha said defiantly and laughed.

"Yes, I can see how all those dive courses and dance lessons are going to pay off now."

"I remember you signed me up for those dive courses, Dad," Natascha laughed.

"True enough," Richard shrugged his shoulders.

"But what about all those dance lessons you took beside the diving?"

"Well...I needed something else to do back in the university," Natascha continued, knowing very well that she could not win this argument.

"I should've done that exorcism with you. That would have straightened you out and you might would have learned how to cook. A hungry husband is not a happy husband."

"Hear, hear, calling him my husband now, are you? " Natascha laughed, entertaining the thought longer than she expected.

"You know it, don't you?" Richard asked after a few moments of silence.

"Yes, I know," Natascha whispered, defeated.

"Then say it, please. For the record," her father insisted.

"Okay, I'll say it....you're right...I should know how to cook at my age...are you happy now?" Natascha mumbled.

"Now I'm happy. See, that wasn't too difficult."

Natascha turned to her father and stuck her tongue out.

"I saw that. I can't believe I didn't do that exorcism back then," he whispered without looking at his daughter.

"But Dad, you love me the way I am," Natascha enthusiastically proclaimed and clapped her father on his shoulder.

"If you would've done that exorcism back then, I would probably be working in a boring lab, dating a banker or a doctor and know how to cook instead of how to dance..."

"Yes, what a horrible thought," her father whispered wryly.

"And I would have such a boring life and I wouldn't have a piercing or my little tattoo and all that," Natascha continued and saw her father eyes widen in surprise.

"You have a tattoo? And please define *all that*," he asked totally shocked.

"Ah, I think it's time for our check again," Natascha changed the subject, winked at her father and picked up her clipboard, still smiling.

She looked at the instruments and gauges as her father offered her some numbers to document in their designated tables.

"Do you know where you're going to live?"

"No, Dad, we don't. I think it'll be London. His company owns several little houses in a little village about thirty kilometers outside London. They rent them out to their employees at a special price. Both Ole-Einar's and Olaf's families are living there for the most part of the year. Nick is sharing one house with a couple other employees, but they have other small houses available for rent as well," Natascha explained while she concentrated on her checklist. She remembered that both Ole-Einar's and Olaf's families spent time both in England as well as Norway.

"London also," Richard said, defeated.

Natascha immediately knew he would prefer if she would stay at home for the next few months.

"Do you know where to find some work there? I could make some calls and talk to some institutes, if you want me to."

"Thanks, but I don't think I have to worry about that right now. But that actually might be very helpful," Natascha replied and tensely watched how Mario checked his instruments again to signal that everything was okay. Natascha noted the time in the dive log on her clipboard and signaled back.

"Did you came up with a name yet?"

"Dad, slow down. I'm not even sure if I'm pregnant. The only thing I know is that my period is overdue, and that an old woman told me something in her own language, and I don't even know if I really understood what she meant. That polar bear encounter was a little bit stressful, and I had to express my feelings. That my period is overdue is something I already experienced on my previous expedition. Nick and I talked about it several times and we agree on almost everything. When this is all over, we'll go to a doctor to find out what's going on. After that, I'll move in with him. And if I'm really pregnant, we'll start to worry about it then."

"Okay, just let us pretend for a moment that you *are* pregnant. I don't want to sound patronizing, but is Nick making enough money to support the family by himself?"

Natascha didn't look at her father, and although she knew that he only wanted what was best for her, her tone was getting much colder.

"It will be enough. Your daughter won't starve."

"Don't you think it would make more sense if you live with us…"

"Father! I'm twenty-six years old! I'll go my own way from now on and I'll go this way with Nick. I will not stay at your house, especially not if I'm expecting Nick's child," she cut him off with much irritation. She paused and restarted again gently, "We want to live our own life, Dad. You and Mom are always welcome, but it's our life now. You have to respect that. I know you only want what's best for me, and that you want to help us. But by helping me you can't fix what you've neglected to do with Mom back then," Natascha hadn't even finished the sentence when she already regretted it. She didn't want to hurt her father.

She could feel the remorse instantly set in. She paused in the silence and looked to her father and placed a hand on his shoulder.

"Listen Dad. I'm really sorry. I didn't mean to say it like this."

"Yes, Natascha, you did. And you're right. I was on a research vessel in the Antarctic for ten months when your mother found out she was pregnant with you. I missed the entire pregnancy and your birth. The first time I saw you was when you were two months old and you started screaming the moment I picked you up. You and your mother had to live at her parents place for the first year because I didn't have any money to support you. I simply don't want you to experience what your mother had to go through back then…"

"But Dad, everything's fine. Nick will be with me," Natascha reassured her father.

"How can you be so sure? Look at him right now," Richard said and pointed to the plexiglas dome.

"He's been on this ship for months now, exactly like me. What if there's another assignment like this?"

"He can refuse such assignments if he's a father to a little child. He could even do normal day hours for a while. His company is very flexible to support the families. We spoke with Ariel about it. There are several fathers of young family's employed. He'll still make enough money. And if I'm not pregnant I'll start working as well, and then we won't have any issues. I'll be fine, Dad. You just have to get used to the fact, that your twenty-six year old baby is finally starting to walk on her own. Besides, we're not too far away..." Natascha said, her hand resting on his shoulder.

Richard wanted to say something, but he couldn't speak and just shook his head.

"Trust me, Dad. Nick's the right man for me. I'm happy with him."

Her smile quickly faded when she looked out the dome. Her blood froze as she watched Nick repeatedly shaking. For fear of the worst, Natascha could not help but scream, "Oh my God!"

She looked at Mario, who was obviously enjoying this scenario. He signaled to Natascha that everything was okay. Not convinced, Natascha shrugged her shoulders and pointed at Nick. Mario swam to Nick and tapped him on the shoulder. Nick turned towards *Odin* and also signaled that he was okay. Nick could see his girlfriend's perplexity and he took out his wet notes and wrote a message. He held the wet notes to the plexiglas dome. Still concerned, Natascha leaned forward to get a better look at it.

"*Got to pee real bad. Tell your Dad I'm sorry if I ruin his suit,*" Natascha read out loud and started to laugh.

"Well, most of the time he's presentable," Natascha laughed and looked at Nick's dry-suit. It had no urine dump valve built into it and Natascha demonstratively shrugged her shoulders and picked up her thermo jug with tea.

With a diabolical smile she opened the jug and knocked at the plexiglas to get Nick's attention again. Mario and Nick both turned towards her.

Natascha showed the jug and poured the tea into the cup over a height of almost forty centimeters, all the while smiling seductively.

While Mario started to laugh out loud, Nick showed his girlfriend a very rude hand gesture, before he turned the other way.

"You didn't learn that from me," Richard was appalled when he saw what his daughter did.

"You learn stuff like that during your practicum. Now he can experience himself what I always had to go through," she simply explained.

"I should've done that exorcism when I had the chance," Richard whispered, then started on a new note, "Does Nick know about your tattoo?"

Natascha smiled at him and raised her eyebrows.

"Never mind," Richard mumbled.

One hour later, *Odin* was back on board the research vessel. Nick had managed to avoid a hygenic accident, but he had to relieve himself over the side of the zodiac at the first chance. Minutes later he climbed out of the zodiac on the deck of the

Northern Explorer. Natascha was already waiting for him and immediately noticed he looked much calmer and much more relieved.

"You're such a miserable cow. Two more minutes and I would've peed in your father's suit."

Natascha laughed and warmly embraced him.

"Relax, nothing happened. Is everything else okay?"

"Yes, no problems. I'm just going to change."

Nick walked to the storage magazine and took the suit off, before he went to get the remaining gear. He disassembled and cleaned everything and, once he was finished, went to see Ariel in the radio room.

"Has the helicopter arrived yet?" Nick asked.

Ariel picked up a little parcel and threw it to Nick.

"Good luck," the Israeli wished him and winked.

"Thanks," Nick said and turned around to leave.

Nick was glad his apology to Ariel was accepted, and that their relatonship was not ruined because of the recent potential development. This moment alone helped Nick realize it would take a lot more than a pregnancy, or pregnancy scare, to tarnish their relationship. Before he put too much thought into it, he turned into the galley, where he handed the little parcel to the cook. Feeling great, he went to his own cabin where he finally changed into some other clothes.

Shortly before seven o'clock, Nick walked into the conference room. He noticed he was the last to arrive at the table for the debriefing of the last dive. Upon spotting him, Mario picked up a bottle of water as he looked at Nick. He let the water pour down from a height into his glass. Everybody else in the room started laughing.

"Yeah, keep laughing," Nick smiled as he reached his seat.

"Next time I'm taking your dry-suit and I will pee in it."

"We just finished. Are you hungry? I think I have to grab a bite," Natascha said and stretched on her chair looking at Nick.

"Yes, whenever you're ready."

Natascha got up from her chair and noticed that the three guys didn't say anything when she said good-bye.

"Did I say something? Is everything okay?" Natascha was concerned and looked into her friends faces. They didn't show any reaction, but Shira was kind enough to give the explanation.

"While you were diving, the boys received an e-mail from Peter Clarke, who works for Team B. He wrote that we're missing a huge backstage job on Shakira's concert this Saturday because we're still on your protection detail. They're a little peeved at the moment," Shira laughed, completely ignoring the fact that her three friends were in hearing distance.

Natascha looked at them and shrugged her shoulders before she turned around.

"*I'm on tonight and my hips don't lie...*" she started to sing one of Shakira's songs as she moved her hips almost the same way as the Columbian singer on her way out.

Nick muttered some apologies before he closed the door behind them.

"You do realize they can shoot you..." he reminded his girlfriend.

"Ah, they won't do that...hopefully," Natascha replied as Nick took her hand and led the way.

"Where are we going?" Natascha asked suddenly when Nick led her past the stairs they would normally take to get to the mess.

"Surprise! Follow me," her boyfriend enthused and kept walking.

"The guys didn't draw another cartoon because of your dive today, did they?" Natascha joked.

"No, they would never do something like that."

Moments later they stood in front of Natascha's cabin.

"Not that I don't want to, but I'm really hungry and I'm afraid that Shira might come back any moment," Natascha said matter-of-factly.

"We'll see," Nick smiled and opened the cabin door.

Natascha immediately perked at the smell of good food. She looked at the table and what she saw completely surprised her. Nick closed the door and while Natascha sat down at the little table, Nick started her laptop and played some music.

Nick unveiled the bowl and Natascha was even more surprised when she spotted the pasta.

"That's my favorite pasta. Where did you get that?" she laughed.

Nick shrugged his shoulders and lit a candle he had taken out of one of the emergency kits.

"I told you, it's a surprise."

He opened a bottle of apple juice and filled two glasses.

"Just like Norway," Natascha laughed and started to eat.

"Yeah, except that this pasta here tastes good," Nick added and sat down.

"Hm, did I miss something?" Natascha asked after a few seconds.

"We haven't dated for a year, we don't know if I'm pregnant, and if you would want to break up with me, you wouldn't have paid the cook so much money."

"Maybe it's just because I love you," Nick laughed.

Natascha smiled at him and they both finished their meal.

"Dessert?" Nick asked with a grin.

Natascha nodded impatiently and watched as Nick uncovered two small bowls.

"Chocolate mousse," Natascha laughed and looked at the decorated dessert.

"I'm not sure if I should eat that this late in the evening," Natascha said and ran her hand over her flat stomach as she looked at Nick.

When Nick showed no reaction, Natascha looked at the dessert again. It was only now that she recognized the details of this masterpiece. The décor showed two large and one very tiny orca. All three of them were connected to each other with a rope in their mouth.

"Oh Nick, they're so sweet," Natascha whispered, her voice catching in her throat.

Her hand came to her mouth as she examined his impressive artwork.

"I can't eat this. This is way too nice."

"Angel, it's chocolate," Nick rolled his eyes.

"Hm...good point," Natascha laughed and started to eat around the orcas.

Thin Ice

When she tried to push the spoon through the rope, she noticed there was something in the mousse. She picked it up and could see a tiny golden necklace. Natascha put the spoon on the table and pulled out the necklace with her fingers, until she saw the ring hanging from it. She sat there speechless and looked at the ring.

Nick took the necklace, cleaned it in a glass of water, dried it off and showed it to Natascha again.

"Oh my God, this is so beautiful," she whispered through her tight throat.

Under Natascha's watchful eyes, Nick took the ring off the necklace, and reached for her hand. He carefully slid the ring on her ring finger as he kneeled in front of her.

"Oh my God!" Natascha cried, tears welling in her eyes. Passion overcame her and she fought to contain her excitement, the rush, the flood of emotion that flowed through her. Her heart beat fleetingly and with fear it would leap from it's cage she swiftly threw herself on Nick before he could say a word. They both fell to the floor and Natascha ungracefully landed on top of him.

"Yes, I do, I do!" she urgently whispered between kisses. Her sobbing laughter of excitement and shock subsided as he curled her hair behind her ear, looking deep in her eyes.

Natascha bit her lip as the unbelievable moment caught up with her. A smile flashed across her lips before she fervently pressed them into his. Nick could sense the formalities dwindle and it was hardly a moment before he curled her small frame under his.

Their effervescent love and passion fuelled their desires as Nick carefully rubbed his hand along her cheek. They would cherish this moment forever as all other cares were forgotten like the morning mist. Their future together was just beginning, but neither of them knew that in just forty-eight hours all of it would change.

- 15 -

**On board the *Northern Explorer*, Amundsen Gulf, Darnley Bay,
Saturday, October 8th**
The helicopter idled and the pilot patiently waited for the last two people to board. Although it was only eight o'clock in the morning, it was his last departure for the day from the *Northern Explorer*. He taxied several scientists to Paulatuk, from where they would continue their flight in a little plane to Inuvik. A yawn escaped his lips as he watched the farewells.

Dr. Richard Weber stood with Natascha and Shira on the deck of the research vessel. Natascha just released Mario from their brief hug. He was the last German scientist besides Natascha and her father to leave the ship.

"We'll catch up in Germany. Have a good flight!" Natascha yelled over the deafening sound of the helicopter blades as they chopped through the wind.

"Thanks, and congratulations!" Mario winked and nodded to the shiny ring that hung around her neck. The news about Nick's and Natascha's engagement had traveled extremely fast among the Germans.

"Thank you very much, Mario. You did an excellent job," Dr. Richard Weber complimented, shaking his hand.

Mario smiled easily and climbed in the helicopter. Within seconds it took off and flew towards the shore.

Natascha turned around and looked at her father.

"So, we almost have the ship to ourselves."

"Yes, only four Americans left on board. Their team leader already left," the expedition leader commented.

Natascha took her ring and put it underneath her sweater.

"Too bad it doesn't fit," Shira noticed, nodding towards the ring.

"Yes. Nick said the only shop where he could get a ring in time was in Inuvik. He's very sad it doesn't fit, but that's not so important to me. I told him not to worry. I'm happy the way it is," Natascha admitted freely and kept walking.

Shira nodded with a smile, but her feet slowed. Her eyes fell from Natascha as she left the deck. Whether she was conscious of it or not, Shira stepped towards the railing, her thoughts taunting her.

Her hand slowly reached her neck, where she fumbled a trinket from under her sweater. Shira could feel her pulse quicken as she unveiled the ring from around her neck. Her eyes filled with tears and she could feel the knot rise in her throat. Her eyes darted away from the ring and to the horizon. The Israeli's hand tightened under the memory.

"Don't be mad with her. It's not her fault," Ariel appeared behind her unannounced. He placed both hands on her shoulder.

Hastily, Shira veiled the ring under her collar, and with a few brushes with the back of her hand, she wiped her eyes clear.

"Natascha must've seen it by now. Have you told her?"

Shira stared at the horizon and slowly shook her head, almost unnoticeable.

"Well, Ariel, for a few days I had really forgotten it. I was so happy for her. I was so happy *with* her," Shira corrected herself, whispering.

"Then we were in that zodiac and that polar bear came after her. Back then I remembered how fast death can get you."

"You could've told her. It would have helped," Ariel whispered and turned away.

"I think Natascha has enough things to worry about herself. She doesn't have to worry about my problems as well."

Ariel slightly turned to her, but knew the subject was over for the young Israeli woman. He shook his head slowly, regrettably.

"Do you want to come? We want to have a look at the Canadians' storage room," Ariel asked on his way back to the door.

The Canadian scientists departed the ship earlier this morning and they locked and sealed their storage room. Whether it was protocol or common sense, Ariel ordered his men to make sure they didn't leave anything that could harm them. Shira spent the most part of the morning with Dr. Richard Weber and Natascha to say goodbye to the departing scientists.

"Yes, I'm coming," she said finally with a last look at the horizon, before she turned and followed Ariel inside the ship.

Nick and Ole-Einar were already in front of the storage room and professionally removed the seal.

"It's locked," the Norwegian said.

Ariel nodded and searched for the master key in his pockets.

"I must have left it in the cabin," he said angrily.

Shira pushed him aside and managed to draw a little lock-pick out of her belt.

Within seconds she opened the door.

Inundated with Nick's and Ole-Einar's admiration, she just shrugged her shoulders and stepped into the storage room.

"Okay, let's see what we got," Nick exhaled sharply and scanned the area before he started his search.

After a quick thirty minutes, Ariel was convinced the storage room posed no threat to them.

"I think we can fly home tomorrow without any problems," Ariel said, while Shira locked the door and fixed the seal within a minute.

"Yes, that would be nice," Nick commented on his Israeli friend.

"Ha, keep dreaming, buddy. Your life is over. There'll be a completely different world waiting for you back there. Your problems are just about to begin," Ole-Einar picked on his German friend with a laugh.

"Don't be silly, Ole. Natascha and I are getting along really well."

"That'll change the minute she finds out how and where we celebrate your bachelor party. What were you thinking proposing in her cabin? Are you completely out of your mind? Do you have no sense for romance? I booked a weekend at a spa for my girlfriend and me. And what do you do! Have supper in her cabin. You're lucky she didn't kick you out. What's the rush anyway?"

"First of all, I had my reasons to ask her before our departure. And secondly, where do you suppose I should've taken her on the ship? A romantic picnic in the engine room?" Nick scoffed, then stated pointedly, "She liked it and she said yes, that's the most important part."

"Yeah, chocolate mousse and jewelry, works all the time..."

Amundsen Gulf, Darnley Bay, Saturday, October 8th

The visibility underwater was less than two meters, but the two divers didn't care. They had been dive buddies for years and, like so many times before, they had their minds set on their task. Nothing would stop them in the early hours of this Saturday morning, not the bad visibility and not the freezing cold water. Determined to fulfill their mission, they used the powerful scooters to follow the new oil pipeline that they located in no time. The pipeline was brand new and not in operation at the moment. The leading diver was pulling a canister behind him. The bucket sized device was secured with many lines and shackles to the divers harness. Being pulled by the scooters, the divers patiently watched the pipeline to locate the right spot. They finally stopped in a depth of about forty meters and they worked with the utmost care. It took them almost twenty minutes before they were both satisfied and turned around to dive back along the pipeline to where they came from.

In exactly ten days, the chemical process, which started the moment the canister came into contact with the cold salt water, would release the canister's contents, which would then raise to the surface. Without the canister, it didn't take them long before they could see the anchor line from their zodiac. Since they performed their necessary deco stops on the way back along the pipeline, they ascended without incident. Once at the surface, they took their gear off in the water and handed it to the two remaining people in the zodiac. Without a word, they pulled the heavy double steel tanks and the scooters on board and made some room for their friends. While the two divers silently swung into the zodiac, the engine spluttered to a start as the forth person secured the anchor. In complete silence, the four people drove back to the *Northern Explorer*.

Amundsen Gulf, Darnley Bay, on board the *Northern Explorer*, Saturday, October 8th

Although everything inside her fought to hold on, to embrace him for a moment longer, Shira let go of her friend. She kissed him one last time and his hand slipped from hers as he ran to the bus that waited for him. Her heart slowed under the anguish of his departure. She saw her fiancé step into the bus and run to the back seat, from where he waved her good-bye as the bus rolled away. The same moment Shira blew him a kiss, the bus exploded in an orange fire ball. The flames licked up to the sky as the shockwave threw Shira back off her feet and viciously to the ground. Her hand ran along her face as the heat scorched her skin and metal crashed down from the heavens. The bus was a burning inferno. She hurried to her feet, and tried to run to the vehicle, tried to help her fiancé, but the heat tore at her flesh. Shira was numb, her body ached and twitched under the pain from the cuts she sustained from the glass. Shards shimmered in her flesh as blood ran down her face. The pain she felt was of a different nature. Again and again she pushed herself further to reach the wreckage, to embrace her love. The heat, the flames, the screams suddenly stopped as she fell to the pavement.

Shira burst forward from her bed, her hands gripping her sheets as a scream emitted from deep within. Her eyes perceived the image before her. Papers crunched beside her and she recognized the personal files of the Americans. The warriness that provoked her to double check the files returned like it had never left. She tried to piece it together, but the shocking images of her fiancé's tragedy replayed. Though this was her typical nightmare, the pain never ceased. Her hand subconsciously rose to her neck. Still confused, Shira looked around before she noticed Natascha's concern.

"Are you okay?" Natascha asked slowly, concernedly.

"Yes, yes, I'm fine," Shira appeased her and sorted the pages of the personal files that were scattered over her bed.

"I must've dozed off and somehow got scared," the Israeli explained halfheartedly. concentrating on the files.

Natascha knew this was not the case and she could see from her peripherals that Shira held on to her ring that hung around her neck before she replaced it under her sweater. Natascha considered saying something but soon decided against it. Curiosity was getting the best of her, but she knew one thing for certain. Natascha knew this was the sixth time since they were sharing a cabin that Shira woke up screaming. Every time Natascha woke up too, but now, Natascha was convinced that it was always the same dream. She offered to talk to her several times, but Shira always refused.

Since Shira didn't offer any indication that it was any different now, Natascha turned her focus back to her report, while Shira continued to study the American personal files.

After a few minutes, the Israeli put the files down in frustration.

Natascha turned around and looked at her.

"Why are you so upset? Do you still believe that someone's after me?"

Through all the excitement during the last couple days, with getting engaged to Nick and her potential pregnancy, Natascha had almost forgotten the fact that there was someone out there coming after her.

"As long as we're assigned to protect you, I'd be a fool to think otherwise," Shira explained.

"Well, if you say so. I don't think I have to worry about it anymore. If there's really someone on board this ship who wants to harm me, then that person is running out of time. And, besides all that, the Canadian scientists left the ship this morning. I didn't even show up to say good-bye to them. The only other scientists on board are the Americans, and even their team leader has already left the ship."

Shira didn't respond and looked at her notes again.

"They all have the same education, went to the same university and they even worked for the same company. We checked everything several times, but we didn't find anything. Nothing at all," Shira explained frustrated.

"Maybe the reason you didn't find anything is simply because there's nothing to be found. But I have to admit, it is unusual they all went to the same university."

"Maybe not so. They're all from the same State. Two of them even received some rewards for exceptional academic achievements."

"That's not that unusual. As a Marine Biologist you concentrate on a few courses only."

"Is Chemistry one of them?"

"Chemistry?" Natascha frowned and looked at Shira.

"Well, it's not a major course for it, but they might have taken it for an extra credit."

Shira kept reading in the file, looking for some additional information.

"It says here that Nelson Singer was best in his year in Chemistry and that he had received an award for that."

"Maybe he studied Chemistry before he decided to become a Marine Biologist."

"But he only studied for five years all together and he had Chemistry as his major."

"He had chemistry as his major? What about Marine Biology?" Natascha asked and looked puzzled while Shira checked the other files.

"All four team members had Chemistry as their major. Their team leader has a doctorate in Chemistry."

Natascha started thinking. She remembered that her father told her that he didn't know the American team leader that well, and that someone didn't have to be a Marine Biologist in order to place some temperature sensors.

"Has any of them graduated as an actual Marine Biologist?" the young German woman wanted to know.

Shira compared the files and shook her head in disbelief.

"It's unbelievable. None them has a degree in Marine Biology. When they double checked their background in London they only checked if something stood out in their life, but they didn't check the details of their education. It says they all took a little bit of Marine Biology, but they all graduated as Chemists."

Shira stood up and went for the door.

"Where are you going? The Americans are not on board. They're just doing their last dive and will leave tomorrow morning."

"I have to talk to Ariel," Shira said and left the cabin.

"Lock the door," the Israeli said on her way out.

Natascha locked the door and lay on her bed.

Just five minutes ago she had been convinced that everything was fine, but an odd sensation suddenly overcame her as a knot inexplicably twisted her stomach.

A few minutes later, Shira found Ariel in the radio room and told him their new discovery. Ariel looked at the personal files himself before he looked at Shira.

"But London had checked them all out."

"Yes, they did, and there's nothing wrong with them. Their complete academic history is spotless. They had even studied Marine Biology for a little while. I just find it strange that none of them has graduated as a Marine Biologist and that they're all Chemists."

"What do we know about the company they're working for?"

"According to London it's a well renowned institute that also employs Marine Biologists among other occupations."

"Among other occupations?"

"Yes, they also employ Biologists, Chemists and Technicians. The exact job position of the American team members was not listed. London couldn't find anything wrong."

Ariel took his satellite phone and dialed a number.

"What are you doing?" Shira asked.

"Something I should have done weeks ago," Ariel explained.

Seconds later Ariel was talking in Hebrew.

While Ariel and Shira patiently waited for his phone to ring, the *Northern Explorer* was contacted over the radio by a helicopter. Astrid informed Captain Rasmussen about the radio contact and confirmed their position as well as the weather and wind conditions.

"Who was this?" Ariel asked the Norwegian when his satellite phone rang.

Ariel looked at the number, activated it and answered shortly in Hebrew. The conversation was over in a few short minutes. Ariel stored the satellite phone in it's pouch on his belt and closed his eyes for a second.

"What's wrong?" Shira asked.

"Their company doesn't only employ Marine Biologists, Technicians and Chemists. Until a few years ago they were one of the major contractors for the production of components for both biological and chemical weapons. Some of their research money came directly from some CIA black accounts."

"Do you think they're after Natascha? We're certain none of them were in Berlin."

"I don't know, but I'm only satisfied when we're off this ship and far away from those Americans," Ariel answered, eyeing the little dark dot on the horizon that approached quickly.

"Shira, send a message to London and don't mind stepping on their toes. I have to talk to the Captain. Astrid, what helicopter is coming over there. This is not the air taxi."

"They're visitors for Captain Rasmussen. Politicians and a film crew of four," the Norwegian answered.

"Politicians? Out here?" Ariel asked and looked at Astrid, who just shrugged her shoulders.

Ariel rose from his chair and walked to the helm. Captain Rasmussen harshly exchanged Ariel's greetings while he put his uniform jacket on. The First and Second

Officer were already waiting for him. With a distasteful look Captain Rasmussen looked outside the window to watch the helicopter complete its landing approach to the helipad.

"They announced their visit this morning. Politicians. Don't give a damn about what we're doing here and they're now showing up to take pictures," he grumbled on his way out.

"Captain, if you may have a minute," Ariel stopped him.

Captain Rasmussen looked out the window and back to Ariel, "What can I do for you?"

Ariel informed him in a few sentences about their new findings.

"And you didn't notice that any sooner? Do you see an increased threat level because of that?"

"No, I don't think Natascha's in any more danger than before, but we'll keep our eyes open for the next twenty-four hours."

The Captain nodded and left, escorted by his First and Second Officer, to the bridge.

Home Office and Operational Headquarters of *EuroSecCorporation*, London, Saturday, October 8th

When they did not have a team on active duty, no one worked at their main office at *EuroSecCorporation* during the weekend. In these situations they would usually redirect any incoming calls to one member of their operation control. Since two of their teams were on an assignment at a huge concert, retired General Klaus Schwartze, his wife and secretary Brigitte, and retired Admiral Brian Whittaker all sat in their respective offices. They each fought their own battles in the hopeless war against mountains of paperwork on this late Saturday evening.

Brigitte Schwartze flipped through some files. A frown coursed her brow as she checked the phone bills from the last three months. She noticed two unusual calls to the same number that she could not identify. Even when she checked the companies address book, she could not find this specific number. It was company policy to identify and document any phone call that ever left the building, not only for security reasons but also for legal issues. Brigitte activated a program in her computer and checked the call list. It took her less than a minute to find out the exact date and time and from which phone the call was made. She followed the call to it's destination. A few moments later she had gathered all the information she needed and wrote them down on a piece of paper. She picked up the phone bill and walked over to Brian's office, where he was accompanied by Klaus as they read some files.

"I know secretiveness runs through Ariel's veins, but I'd really appreciate it if he would inform me when he's using a new satellite phone."

"What are you talking about, Brigitte?" Klaus asked and looked at his wife.

"Ariel only uses the company satellite phone."

Brigitte showed him the phone bill with the number.

"Obviously not," the secretary defended herself and looked at the two former military officers.

"This satellite phone number was called twice from your phone. First time was on Tuesday, July fifth when the call was received in Iceland, and the second call was on Monday, July eleventh, where the call was boosted over a cell tower in Boston. Ariel was in Reykjavik on the fifth as well as in Halifax on the eleventh. That call might very well have come from that Boston cell tower."

Brian's eyebrows rose as he looked at Brigitte's notes. Preoccupied by the news that Brigette delivered, he did not glance up when he heard the sound of an incoming e-mail arrive on Klaus' computer. Klaus opened Shira's message.

"Damnnit, we screwed up on the background check of the American scientists."

"What? How? Why?" Brian asked, suddenly looking up from the phone bill.

"The American scientists are not Marine Biologists. Shira went through their files again and it was Miss Kleinfeld who noticed that the courses they took in university are not exactly part of the Marine Biology program. They studied some of it, but they all graduated as Chemists. Ariel called for some information from Tel Aviv and they found out that the company who employs them used to produce components for chemical and biological weapons, among other things. Part of their research budget came directly from some government black accounts, CIA most likely. How could we miss that?" Klaus informed, flustered. His embarassment and shame was evident as he exchanged a glance with his wife.

"That's pretty simple to miss," his wife explained. "All our research is based on the available European information. Don't forget we're not a government agency. We can only ask favors to get partial information from data that's available within Europol, Interpol, Great Britain, Norway and Germany, but we never had any access to American data. How could we? Our best resource in such matters is Tel Aviv, but Ariel is on board the ship himself."

"We should have thought about that. There's no excuse for missing crucial detail," Brian stated and he looked at the phone bill and Brigitte's notes again. Something didn't feel right and he thought hard to figure it out.

"Klaus, ask Shira if Ariel has a second satellite phone and if any of our guys knows this satellite phone number here... But technically that can't be. Both calls came from my phone and I definitely can't remember ever calling this number. What did we do during those calls anyway, Brigitte?" Brian asked, his eyes locked on the phone number.

Brigitte went into her office, checked her computer and came back over again.

"This is strange. On Tuesday, July fifth, we had our debriefing about the incident in Berlin. We had a video conference call with both Ariel and Shira on board the research vessel and Ariel had used the satellite phone as a receiver to guarantee a secure line. By the time this call was placed, you were in the other room talking to Ariel and Shira on the other phone. The second call from Monday, July eleventh was immediately after your meeting with that event organizer regarding the concerts."

Brian leaned back in his leather chair.

"I definitely did not talk to Ariel or anybody else on the ship that Tuesday, except for the video conference. And I do remember that other meeting very well. I didn't call anyone afterwards. Who else is using my phone?" Brian asked.

"Nobody," Brigitte stated.

"What did I do on those two days after the video conference and the meeting?" Brigitte checked his schedule.

"Both times you met with your wife and your brother-in-law for dinner."

"That's right, I remember. Wait a second. If I'm not completely wrong, then Gordon used my phone to call his office on those two days. I remember because I once showed him how to place an outside call."

"Well, problem solved. Send him the invoice over five pounds for calling a satellite phone from your desk and we can call it a day," Klaus stated with finality, returning his attention to his emails.

"No, we're not calling it a day," Brian proclaimed and theatrically rose his hand. "That dog told me both times that he called his office. Why did he call someone in Iceland, when our boys are in Reykjavik? And why did he place a call that could have easily been received in Nova Scotia, when our boys were in Halifax? Gordon's company has no business in Iceland. Why did he lie to me about this? Why?" he whispered, asking himself more than the others.

Klaus looked at the computer again to read another incoming message.

"From Shira again. She says it's definitely not a satellite phone they're using. She also thinks it's possible that a signal can be boosted from a cell tower in Boston to get to Halifax, but she believes it's very unlikely. I wouldn't disagree with her on that one," Klaus commented.

"Brigitte, please do me a favor and get my beloved brother-in-law on the phone."

While Brigitte walked out of the office, Brian leaned back and looked at the ceiling. His brilliant mind started to create a theory.

On board the *Northern Explorer*, Amundsen Gulf, Darnley Bay, Saturday, October 8th

Captain Rasmussen stood with his two officers on deck and waited for his guests to come to him.

"Good day, Captain. I'm United States Senator Jonathan Brown. This gentleman here is my assistant, Carl Miller. My apologies for the short notice about our visit. I hope we didn't cause any complications."

"No, not at all," Captain Rasmussen greeted coldly and shook US Senator Brown's hand before he turned toward the second man.

"Good day, Captain. My name's Pierre Dumont. I'm a member of the Canadian Parliament and I had some previous business in this area. Senator Brown and I are old friends and thought we could take the opportunity to pay you a visit," MP Dumont introduced himself with a smile.

Captain Rasmussen nodded and looked at the four remaining men as they climbed out of the helicopter.

Senator Brown noticed Captain Rasmussen contemptuously examined the camera crew.

"Yes, I know," the Senator commented freely.

"They're the film crew we mentioned. They've accompanied us for a week now and they want to shoot some footage about this expedition as well. I hope you don't mind, but if it's a problem for you..."

"It's no problem," Captain Rasmussen nodded and asked his guests to follow him to the wardroom.

Ariel smiled at the two politicians as they walked by, then returned his attention to the four men who pulled their gear from the chopper.

Just a few minutes later, Senator Brown and MP Dumont sat together with Captain Rasmussen and his First and Second Officer in the wardroom.

"I'm devastated we could not visit your expedition any time sooner. We would've really liked to meet and talk to the other scientists. My Canadian colleague and I traveled all this distance to show how much our countries care about our climate. Unfortunately, our schedules didn't allow us to visit you sooner on board this magnificent research boat to support your mission."

"Too bad," Captain Rasmussen muttered impassively.

"I can only agree with what my dear friend, Senator Brown just said. We think it's very important for our country to take a leading role in the international climate politics. It's my understanding that there are just a few scientists on board?"

"Yes, that's correct," Captain Rasmussen replied. "If you would have arrived two days sooner, you could've met most of the scientists. Unfortunately, there are now only four American scientists as well as seven members of the German group and our expedition leader himself, Dr. Weber, on board this ship."

Senator Brown checked his watch. It was almost noon.

"I know this may sound strange, but would it be possible to stay over dinner to talk to the remaining scientists? They could tell us about their observations during this expedition. I would also like to ask for permission for the film crew to stay until this evening to shoot some footage and have some interviews. They'd leave your boat tonight with our own helicopter. Would that be possible?" Senator Brown asked politely.

Captain Rasmussen knew there was no reason to decline this request.

"No, I don't see a problem there. Please feel welcome on board the *Northern Explorer*. I'll make all the necessary arrangements. My First and Second Officer will be at your service until dinner is served in about twenty minutes."

Captain Rasmussen rose from his chair and left the wardroom together with Ariel.

"A bunch of hypocrites they are. They don't give a damn about what's been going on during the last couple months on this ship. Do you think it'll be a problem to have Dr. Weber and his daughter at the same table with them?"

"I can't see a way to keep the expedition leader away from their table. The Senator specifically asked for the entire team. As long as they don't ask Ole-Einar any biological details, I don't see a problem."

"Very well. The quicker they're off my ship the better," Captain Rasmussen said and rushed to the helm.

Ariel walked into the radio room where Shira gave him the latest update about her conversation with retired General Klaus Schwartze.

"That's strange, but I don't know that number at all. Anything else?" he asked.

Shira shook her head.

"Okay, gather the troops. We'll meet in five minutes in their cabin. I want to explain the situation to them."

Shira nodded and hurried off the bridge, already calling the others on their little radio.

Ariel sat behind his laptop and, lost in thoughts, stared at the horizon.

"What are you thinking?" Astrid asked.

"I need a new password. There's more going on today than in the last two months," the Israeli replied and looked at her.

Astrid smiled at him. Looking at her, Ariel smiled back, entered a new password and wrote a little report for London.

After Shira picked Natascha up, they both went to Nick's cabin where they met the four guys. Natascha walked in and everybody except Nick threw her a withering look.

"What did I do now? Are you still mad at me because you're stuck here with me instead of being at the concert?" Natascha asked with a crooked grin.

In silence, Oliver pointed at the laptop they were all looking at. Their British friend and colleague Peter Clarke from Team B had sent them several videos from their backstage job in London. Natascha could see Shakira fooling around with some people. She guessed they were Nick's colleagues.

Natascha took a tissue and walked to Ole-Einar.

"My little boy is drooling, wait a second, I'm going to make it all better and clean you up," Natascha cooed jokingly and wiped his face with the tissue.

"Natascha!" Nick pulled his girlfriend back. "That guy can bench press over four hundred pounds. You really don't want to piss him off."

Nick stood between Natascha and Ole-Einar, who had shown absolutely no reaction.

The door opened again and Ariel and Dr. Richard Weber stepped in.

"Okay, I have an update," Ariel started immediately after Oliver turned the laptop off.

"Earlier this morning Natascha and Shira found out that all the American scientists are Chemists and not Marine Biologists. I called Israel and they did a thorough background check on the institute that officially employs all the American scientists. We discovered that their institute indeed employs Marine Biologists as well as Chemists and other scientists, but they have also manufactured components for chemical as well as biological weapons. They were partly funded by black accounts. We also know for certain that some of their employees are working either very closely with, or maybe even for, the CIA. Richard, how unusual is it that on this expedition the scientists are Chemists and not Marine Biologists?"

Richard sat at the little table and looked up from the personal files he had just studied.

"Well, it's a little strange that none of them is a graduated Marine Biologist, but not entirely unusual. Being a Marine Biologist has never been a prerequisite in order to participate in this expedition. Their job description was very clear: To sink and install some sensors to measure the water temperature and current. It wasn't exactly rocket science and any decent university student with a little bit of technical understanding could have done this. They had executed all the jobs they had planned to do to my complete satisfaction. I also want to mention that I personally have a hard time to believe that a group will wait three months just to get active in their last twenty-four hours on board," the expedition leader explained.

Ariel nodded his agreement.

"Okay, this number here belongs to a satellite phone," the Israeli continued and read out the number.

"Does anybody here know this number?"

Everybody shook their head.

"Here's the latest news. We do have sitting US Senator Jonathan Brown, his assistant Carl Miller, and a Member of the Canadian Parliament, Pierre Dumont, on board the ship. They arrived with a film crew of four, who are shooting some video about the Senator, the MP and this expedition. I believe this is just a PR project for them, since the campaign for the presidential election has already started. Captain Rasmussen had agreed to their request to have dinner with the remaining scientists. Richard, I assume you have no issues sitting at their table?"

Richard shrugged his shoulders.

"No, not really. The expedition's already over and they're only interested in our findings as long as they're on board this ship and as long as their camera is running. As soon as they're back in the helicopter they don't give a damn."

"Is it normal to visit an expedition after it's literally over?" Ariel asked.

Richard shook his head again.

"The timing is not that bad. Logistically it's actually the only time they could've visited us, since Paulatuk is relatively easy to reach compared to the rest of the North West Passage. It was also probably the only time it did fit in their schedule. When an expedition is almost over, they can get first hand information about it, which they can use in their election campaign. So really their timing isn't unusual at all. It's also normal that they show up on such short notice."

"What about me?" Natascha asked.

"I don't think there's a problem for you to sit with them at the table. Shira, can you please send an update to London and ask them if they found out anything about that satellite phone number?"

Just in time for dinner, Dr. Richard Weber led his team in the wardroom. The four remaining American scientists already sat around the table and were chatting to Senator Brown. They finished their last scheduled dive this morning and would leave the *Northern Explorer* tomorrow. Their team leader already flew out earlier this morning. Captain Rasmussen introduced Dr. Richard Weber and his daughter. Nick watched the four cameramen, but he couldn't see anything suspicious. He noticed that all four of them were wearing light combat boots, but it was not unusual to wear something like that when someone was out in the field. Senator Brown and MP Dumont walked around the table and shook Dr. Weber's and Natascha's hand. They insisted to sit right beside them.

During the dinner Senator Brown asked for some information regarding the expedition. He was very interested in any preliminary results. Dr. Weber answered the questions to his best knowledge. Shortly after the dinner, MP Pierre Dumont turned towards Captain Rasmussen.

"Would it be possible to get a tour of this boat and the submarines?"

Captain Rasmussen quickly looked at Ariel, who, barely noticeable, nodded his agreement.

"Of course. If you would please follow me," Captain Rasmussen answered and rose from his chair. He led the small group to the bridge, where they also visited the radio room. From there, Captain Rasmussen led them to the dive control room.

Dive Officer Vitali Vachenko unlocked the door, turned on the light and let them in.

"Can you please explain to us what we're looking at?" one of the cameramen asked and Nick had the impression that he was their leader.

Vitali Vachenko stepped in front of the group and pointed towards the panels behind him.

"Most of the time we work with only one underwater team on board this ship. In case of emergency repairs, we can also operate two underwater teams simultaneously. With this intercom here, we can communicate back and forth with every diver underwater who's using one of our four diving helmets. The communication system works both ways, that means that both the diver and the person at the intercom can listen and talk to each other. As for the connection, we're using a simple telephone line, which is part of the umbilical cord that connects the diving helmet with it's surface supply. We also use wireless transmission to communicate with our two submersibles.

At this gas panel, we can mix all the required breathing gas for our divers, regardless if they're using the hard hat or an open circuit. Depending on the depth of the dive, our divers have to breathe up to three different gas mixtures. If they're using the dive helmet, they have a different hose for each breathing gas. Underwater they simply select the right gas with a simple switch. All the gas flow to any of the individual hoses of the umbilical cord is monitored with both an oxygen as well as a helium sensor, so we can always guarantee the right mix for the depth. With this system, we can operate in a depth of up to one hundred meters. We also use the same panel to mix the breathing gas for open circuit scuba dives.

Over here you can see our control panel for any work that has to be done underwater. We have two very big welders with all the necessary gear as well as a large selection of air driven underwater tools for any repair or salvage operations. The *Northern Explorer* also has two large air compressors which operate completely independently from each other. Each compressor has a filling capacity of over two thousand liters of air a minute."

"How deep was the deepest dive during this expedition?" the cameraman asked and looked at Dr. Richard Weber.

Maybe a diver himself, Nick thought.

Dr. Richard Weber had to think for a second.

"If I remember correctly, our deepest dive with a closed circuit rebreather was around seventy meters. With a traditional open circuit system the deepest dive was around sixty meters. Although we have all the gear to dive that deep, not all the scientists are qualified to dive that deep."

"Do you still have divers on board who are qualified to dive that deep?" the cameraman wanted to know.

"Well, as far as I know, everybody in this little German group is actually qualified to dive that depth. It's just not always necessary to penetrate such depths. If you'd follow me to our research submersibles, please..." Dr. Richard Weber asked and led them to the two submersibles.

The group gathered around *Odin* and *Polar Viking* and Senator Brown carefully knocked at the several centimeters thick plexiglas dome.

"What you can see here is one of our one-atmosphere research submersibles. The maximum operational depth is two hundred and fifty meters, but their test pressure is over four times that depth. Each research submersible has triple redundancy and just enough space for two pilots. Inside, the pilot can control those hydraulic arms to perform several tasks underwater with a joystick," Vitali explained.

"Very interesting. How long does it take before someone can operate one of those submersibles?" the leader of the camera crew asked and took a closer look at *Odin*.

Dr. Richard Weber looked at his daughter.

"My daughter has just finished her course to become a pilot during this expedition. After around twenty-five dive hours she's now certified to operate one of those submersibles as the main pilot. The more experience you have, the better you are."

The cameraman looked commendably at Natascha.

**Home Office and Operational Headquarters of *EuroSecCorporation*,
London, Saturday, October 8th**

Brigitte Schwartze placed the receiver back on her phone and walked into Brian Whittaker's office.

"I couldn't reach Brian in his office or his town apartment. After a while I finally got his assistant on the phone. He told me that he's out at his mansion for the weekend and that he doesn't want to be disturbed unless it's an emergency. Do you want me to call him anyway?"

Brian checked the time on his watch and looked at Klaus, who nodded.

It was already late in the evening, and Brian was asking himself why he had the urge to talk to his brother-in-law as soon as possible.

"Yes, call him. Tell him that it's important and that he has to come to our office as soon as possible. If he asks why, tell him that I said it's important."

Brigitte nodded and looked up Gordon's private phone number.

On board the *Northern Explorer*, Amundsen Gulf, Darnley Bay, Saturday, October 8th

"Is that true? You're already a submarine captain?" Senator Brown asked and looked at the young German scientist.

"Well, I'm trying my best," Natascha replied and smiled at him, trying as best she could to hide her contempt. *And it's called a submersible pilot, you idiot,* she thought, but didn't say the comment out loud though her smile faltered.

"What a shame that such a beautiful young lady disappears in the blackness of the ocean," Senator Brown tried what he thought was his best flirting tactic.

"If one actually considers that over sixty percent of our planet is underwater and that we don't know much about it, it's not a shame at all," Natascha replied and nodded to thank him for the compliment.

That was one of the most stupid harassing comments I ever heard, she thought and briefly looked at Nick, who was watching one of the cameramen.

"How long would it take you to get one of those submersibles ready and in the water?" the cameraman asked.

"Well, *Odin* is generally ready within two hours. The timeframe between the individual dives is mostly determined by the status of the batteries. Since we have two identical submersibles, we're fortunate to always have one submersible ready to go. While one submersible is underwater, we can recharge the batteries and do all the checks on the second submersible. At the moment, both *Odin* and *Polar Viking* are fully operational," Dr. Richard Weber said and walked around *Odin*.

"In need, we could have one of those submersibles underwater within the next thirty minutes," he added and let his hand glide over the plexiglas dome.

Senator Brown joined the German scientist and took a closer look at *Odin*. He had not planned to ask, but he was really interested in it.

"Would it be to blunt to ask for a test ride? Would it be possible? During a test ride I could make my own picture about this pristine underwater world," Senator Brown asked.

It took Dr. Richard Weber several seconds to understand what Senator Brown had just asked him and he finally looked more or less helpless at Captain Rasmussen and even at Natascha.

"Well, I don't know. I have no idea how it'll fit in our schedule. There's really not much to see in this area either," Richard explained, without sounding to convincing.

"As far as I was told, the *Northern Explorer* is scheduled to lay at anchor at this location for another seventy-two hours. Your expedition is officially over. I'm begging you, just a little round trip. I don't want to go deep. Just a little glimpse at your work."

Richard Weber looked at Ariel, who once nodded almost unnoticeably.

"Captain Rasmussen?" Richard Weber asked.

The Norwegian Captain looked at Dr. Richard Weber.

"You're the expedition leader. They're your submersibles," the Captain Rasmussen answered.

"Dr. Weber, please. I release you of all responsibility and I sign any waiver you want me to," the American politician pushed.

"Okay, if you really insist. Come with me, please. We'll get you something more suitable to wear. It can get a little cold down there. I'll also give you some general rules and guidelines in case of an emergency," Richard said and nodded to Vitali Vachenko, who already climbed up on top of *Odin* to perform the safety check. Ole-Einar and Olaf connected the lifting cable and checked the lights on Vitali's command.

"Would it also be possible that Miss Kleinfeld drives the submarine?"

"Excuse me?" Dr. Weber asked puzzled and turned towards the Senator.

"I asked if it would be possible that Miss Kleinfeld could drive the submarine. I completely trust your daughter's capabilities as a submarine captain."

"Sure, no problem," Natascha responded quickly, not leaving a moment to realize what she had just gotten herself into. She kept her attention fixed on the Senator, avoiding the punishing looks from both Ariel and Nick, and most definitely her father.

"I'll go get changed," she finally said and walked away.

Nick caught up on her after a few meters.

"Natascha, why in God's name do you want to do this? Let your father take him down there."

"I don't know why I said it. It just kind of slipped out before I could even think about it. Maybe because he made that stupid flirting comment," she said on her way to her cabin.

"I think it's best if you just take him down there for a few minutes and drive a couple circles around the ship. It isn't deep here and…"

"Listen, Nick," Natascha opened the door and turned around to put her arms around him.

"I don't know why I volunteered to take him down there, but you're not really trying to tell me that a sitting US Senator poses a threat to me, are you?"

"No, I don't think so," Nick said after a few seconds and followed Natascha inside the cabin.

Natascha changed and closed the zipper from her thermo overall, before she put on Nick's woolen beanie. She gave her boyfriend another hug and kissed him.

"Don't worry. I won't be long, and if he says anything stupid, I'll start flooding *Odin*. Down there I'm in control," she whispered in his ear.

"Promise me you'll be careful, okay?"

"Always," she whispered, planting another kiss on his cheek before they left the cabin together.

Five minutes later, she and Nick stood on the deck and saw that *Odin* was ready to go. The Senator stood with her father beside the submersible and was also wearing a thermo overall that was a little bit too big for him.

"Ready if you are," Natascha walked up to him.

Senator Brown was noticeably nervous and simply nodded before he climbed up the ladder after Natascha.

"What if he's grading her butt..." Ole-Einar whispered to Nick.

"Then not even his bodyguard will be able to protect him," Nick replied louder, but in a much more serious tone that completely surprised Ole-Einar.

Inside the submersible Natascha glided into her seat and watched Senator Brown as he clumsily flopped into his chair. The camera crew recorded everything and Natascha fought to hide her smile.

"Okay, here we are. I just want to give you a little introduction to *Odin*."

The Senator looked at her in anticipation. Natascha could clearly see how nervous the American politician was when *Odin* was lifted off the ground and over the side of the *Northern Explorer*.

Natascha pointed to a microphone with a built in button. She picked it up and pressed the button on it's side.

"This button on this microphone is the most important thing for you in here. It's our connection to the surface," Natascha handed the microphone to the Senator, who's hand brushed hers.

"As for everything else inside this submersible you keep your fingers away. Otherwise it could lead to some very serious consequences. In case of an emergency, all you have to do is to activate this microphone and everybody in the dive control room can listen to what's going on down here."

Senator Brown immediately realized the rules that Natascha had established and nodded nervously.

"Are there any questions?" she asked in a cold tone, while the Senator waved into the camera and shook his head.

"Okay, let's go," she said and watched as *Odin* broke through the surface.

- 16 -

Home Office and Operational Headquarters of *EuroSecCorporation*, London, Saturday, October 8th

It was pouring rain when Gordon Ramshaw parked his dark green Jaguar in the parking lot just in front of *EuroSecCorporation*'s building. With a quick look at the multi-storey building Gordon saw lights shining in at least three offices on the floor that was home to the corporation.

I hope there's nothing wrong with one of our rigs, Gordon thought, but immediately discarded the worry. *No, if there was something wrong on one of our rigs, I would definitely know it before they would.*

He cut the engine and reached for his hat as he opened the drivers door. The wind was so strong that he had to keep a hand on his hat. He quickly slammed the car door and rushed to the entrance of the building. As soon as he had left the Jaguar, he cursed his brother-in-law for calling him into their office at this time of the night.

He walked to the main door and saw that only a few people were still in the gym that just opened on the lower floor a couple months ago. Walking by the gym, Gordon stopped in front of another security door at the end of the hallway. He pushed the button beside the name plate. He looked at the *EuroSecCorporation* plate as he waited to be buzzed in. Gordon knew that someone upstairs would see him now on their computer screen. It was just a few seconds later that someone activated the electrical contact to open the door. With another curse on his lips, Gordon entered and took the elevator on his right. With the push of a button, the elevator was on it's way up. Once out of the elevator, Gordon walked through the large glass door.

"Good evening, Gordon. You can go straight in. Brian and Klaus are in conference room one," Brigitte greeted him.

"Good evening," he grumbled.

"They better have a damn good reason to call me this late on a Saturday night," he continued and walked to the conference room where Klaus and Brian were sitting, looking over some notes and a time sheet.

"Good evening, Gordon. I appreciate that you found the time for us on this Saturday evening. Thank you," Brian said and stood up.

"Good evening. Is there something wrong with one of our oil rigs?" Gordon asked nervously.

"No, not that we know of. It's about those two phone calls you placed from Brian's office earlier this year," Klaus explained.

"Phone calls? You make me drive over an hour from my mansion to your office in this pissing rain to talk to me about the two phone calls? Are you out of your mind?"

Gordon turned away as he whisked his jacket off and paced the room with heat.

How much do they know? Did I make a mistake? he asked himself agitatedly.

Brian and Klaus were silent as they watched him.

"The number you called belongs to a satellite phone. It's not registered to one of your offices," Brian explained and waited for a reaction.

"Excuse me? You're checking up on me, now? No, that number's not registered to one of our offices. It's the private number of one of my foremen, who I called twice from your office. Where's the problem?"

"The problem is that we currently find ourselves in a situation where we stumbled over that number, and I have the feeling that you're not entirely honest with us. We'll call one of our own men with some instructions, and after that, we'll call the number you dialed from my office. Then we'll see what happens." Brian explained.

"And what does my man have to do with any of your people?" Gordon asked.

"That's exactly what we're trying to find out," Klaus said and watched as Gordon sat down in one of the chairs and shrugged his shoulders.

On board the research submersible *Odin*, Amundsen Gulf, Darnley Bay, Saturday, October 8th

Natascha navigated *Odin* away from the *Northern Explorer* at a forty five degree angle to the shore. The amount of time she's been down here, she realized she has never been in this area before and took the opportunity to look around. Their depth was only around thirty meters and Natascha explained to Senator Brown the different species of animals they could see through the Plexiglas.

"Those over there are anemones. They are filter feeders," she explained as they coasted just two meters above the muddy bottom.

Senator Brown turned out to be an interested listener and he asked several questions about the symbiosis among different species. Natascha was actually surprised that the Senator showed such a great interest, and she willingly explained everything he wanted to know and why it was so important for this region.

They were now reaching a dive time of almost thirty minutes and the bottom soon became mud, without any visible life.

"Hm, that doesn't look good," Natascha commented and leaned forward to have a better view of the bottom.

"What is it?" the Senator wanted to know.

"The bottom doesn't look very good. Doesn't seem to be much life down there."

"Hm, that is bad," the Senator replied, half-heartedly.

"No, what's actually bad is that in a few years most of this region will look like this," Natascha informed with frustration. She realized that this was her chance to talk to a Senator, who lacked the liberty to walk away from the conversation.

"If we don't change the way we consume energy soon, then we'll face consequences that are beyond our imagination," she gave it a try.

"Hm," the Senator nodded and looked outside.

"We almost didn't have any ice at all in the North-West Passage. The water is way too warm. All the ice is melting and many species are losing their habitat."

Thin Ice

"Well, that's unfortunate," the Senator said coldly and still watching the sea floor.

"I know that your country and Canada can't wait for the North-West Passage to be ice free to cash in on transit fees and to have easy access to the oil, but do you think it's really worth it?"

"Is it really worth what?"

"To drive so many species to extinction. You can't deny that all the ice is melting."

"No, I don't deny it. I'm just not completely convinced that we're the reason for it. There was always a cycle between ice ages and warmer periods. Our scientists believe that we're just at the start of a warmer period. It happens all the time. Greenland is called Greenland for a reason."

"So you're telling me that you don't believe in global warming?"

"Oh, I do believe in it. The facts are out there. I'm just not totally sure if it's our fault that it happens."

"Well, I agree that there is a cycle between ice ages and warmer periods. When I look back in time, I can see the population on this little planet jump from a few hundred million people, who reached an average age of around fifty years to seven billion people, who all grow almost eighty years old. With them came the industrial development with all it's pollution. Factories, cars, planes, ships, coal operated or bio mass power stations, everything. All those people have to eat something, which results into overfishing and clear cutting. I think we're way out of balance."

"Well, maybe. What do you suggest? Kill most of the people? Stop having an industry? Without an industry, people will die, not only because of hunger. We need the industry for food, medications and for transports, among many other things. It's not that simple."

"I'm not saying that we should kill people, we have more than enough wars going on to manage the population. At this time we simply can't afford a coal plant or a bio mass plant to produce power. I'm just saying that we have to find a much better balance. Humour me a minute. What's your most precious resource, Senator Brown?" Natascha asked.

"What? What do you mean?"

"Please, just answer the question. We're underwater. No one will ever hear about this conversation, and if so, you can always deny everything. So please, what's the most precious resource and why?"

Senator Brown wasn't sure if he should answer, but since they gave him the opportunity of this experience, he decided to do so.

"Well, at the moment, our most precious resource is not gold. It's oil. Oil creates millions of jobs and it doesn't only keep our cars or even a research vessel running," he smiled at Natascha, "but also the industry itself. Oil is necessary in everything from plastic, food and up to medications. The taxes on gasoline keep most modern countries alive. Yes, I know what you want to say, but sometimes it's necessary to go to war over it to control it. Without control over the oil, the world would be in chaos. Take the oil away, and the world as you know it wouldn't be the same any more in just six months. So, what do you think is the most precious resource?" Senator Brown returned the question with satisfaction.

"Simple," Natascha said without looking up from her instruments.

"It's fresh water. Take clean drinking water away for two weeks, and life on earth as *you* know it won't exist any more. Beats your six months without oil by twenty-two weeks," she argued and winked at him. "At the moment, Canada alone is using four liters of fresh water to get one liter of oil. They're spending hundreds of thousands of dollars every year to control a seal population that they believe threatens their fish stocks. All the seals together eat less than five percent of the fish that's discarded as unwanted bycatch by the North Atlantic fishing fleet. Instead of renewable energy, governments all over the world are investing in bio mass or coal plants. All I'm saying is that we're way out of balance and that we should use our resources better," Natascha said and noticed that they were now under water for almost forty minutes.

"I think we better turn around." Natascha freely interrupted herself. "Thank you for listening anyway."

"You're welcome," the Senator replied calmly as Natascha leaned forward and looked at a darker shadow some distance away. The Senator watched her and noticed they were not ascending. The concern grew in his voice,

"Is something wrong?"

"No, everything's fine. I just want to have a look at that shadow over there, then we'll turn around. Looks unusual," Natascha commented and accelerated *Odin* a little bit.

That looks like a long pipe, Natascha thought with wonder, which soon turned to frustration.

"I think we better turn around now. We've been gone a while now. I'm sure my assistant is getting nervous..." Senator Brown muttered.

"Just one second. I just want to know what it is."

Natascha leaned forward and turned the other two underwater lights on.

"I really, really, think we should turn around now. This looks very dangerous to me. We can get entangled in it," the Senator stammered and the panic in his voice increased.

It took Natascha only a few more seconds before she recognized what was causing the shadow.

"That's a pipeline," she whispered more to herself. Her frustration and shock increased as her brow furrowed.

"That's a pipeline!" Natascha said again, this time much louder and with heat.

"That explains the dead seafloor. The ships who installed the pipeline used thrusters to keep their positions. That's what's caused all the damage. But there's an application out there to protect this area. Pipelines are prohibited!" she explained, her anger rising. She activated *Odin*'s video-camera with her left hand.

"Miss Kleinfeld. This looks dangerous. I have to insists that you turn around now," Senator Brown was shaking.

Natascha completely ignored the politician and followed the pipeline from a safe distance. The heat from her anger boiled in her veins and she could feel it rising up her neck. *A pipeline! Right in the middle of the protected area! How is that possible?* she asked herself.

She kept following the pipeline and completely ignored Senator Brown as his requests soon turned to orders. Natascha turned a deaf ear to his stern voice as she saw another unusual shadow right on top of the pipeline. She maneuvered *Odin* a little bit closer and she could see a canister the size of a bucket floating over the pipeline. It was attached with some rope leading to a complicated looking mechanism to the pipeline.

Natascha brought the little submersible up close and leaned as far forward she could manage, her face just centimeters away from the plexiglas.

"Miss Kleinfeld, I have to insist that we do turn around right now. I don't think that it's a good idea to be that close," the politician almost begged.

"Did you know about this? Is this the reason you and your Canadian friend came all the way up here? To make sure we haven't found your pipeline?" Natascha asked coldly and sat back in her seat, still looking at the canister. She surprised herself by keeping her voice calm despite the aggravation she was feeling. The canister sat only a few meters away from *Odin* as they floated over the pipeline.

"What on earth is this canister?" Natascha asked aloud and looked from the canister to the Senator. Leaning forward again, she couldn't see any markings on the canister, but she could see that the ropes were brand new, which meant that the canister must have been installed within the last couple days.

This means it must have been someone from the ship. But who? And why? The only thing someone would attach to an underwater pipeline would be explosives. But they would have attached that right at the pipeline, not one meter above. But if this is really something explosive, then this can be a huge threat to the Northern Explorer *and the people in Paulatuk,* Natascha thought quickly.

She hurriedly gathered her ideas together, devising a plan of action. She decided that it would be best to take the canister back to the *Northern Explorer*. She was convinced that if it was really something dangerous, Ariel and his friends would most certainly be able to disarm it. Without thinking about it much further, Natascha activated the joystick and reached with *Odin*'s hydraulic arm for the canister.

"Oh my God, don't touch that! You'll kill us all!" Senator Brown screamed so loud that Natascha actually pulled her hand back from the joystick in shock. The hydraulic arm stopped less than fifty centimeters away from the canister and remained motionless.

On board the *Northern Explorer*, Amundsen Gulf, Darnley Bay, Saturday, October 8th

Ariel stood together with all the other people in the dive control room and watched the instruments. So far everything on *Odin* seemed to be fine.

"Gentlemen, if you don't mind, but we're needed on the bridge. Feel free to come up if you need me," Captain Rasmussen finally said and left the dive control room with his two officers. MP Pierre Dumont as well as Senator Brown's assistant, Carl Miller, followed him up. Not being dressed for the cold temperatures outside, they could feel the chill and quickly preferred the warmth from inside the ship. The remaining people in the dive control room were the four American scientists, the four men camera crew, Ariel with his complete team as well as Dr. Richard Weber and the only remaining Dive Officer on board the research vessel, Vitali Vachenko.

Ariel monitored his people and noticed how Nick kept a fixed eye on one of the cameramen. Ariel walked over to him and lead him outside.

"Is something wrong?" the Israeli asked.

Nick shook his head.

"I'm not sure. I have the feeling that I've seen that guy before, but I can't place him."

Ariel looked at the cameraman, but there was no familiarity.

Before Ariel could say anything, his satellite phone rang. Ariel took it from his belt and looked at the display.

"London," he said to Nick before he answered the call. Nick went back inside.

Home Office and Operational Headquarters of *EuroSecCorporation*, London, Saturday, October 8th

Klaus Schwartze spoke with Ariel on the satellite phone and shared his plan. It turned out that, according to Ariel, this was the perfect time to execute the plan. With Ariel still on the line, Klaus looked at Brian and nodded. Brian looked at his brother-in-law and activated his own phone. First he punched in a code so that his Caller ID was blocked, after that he dialed the satellite phone number that Gordon Ramshaw had dialed from the same phone. Standing at the table, retired Admiral Brian Whittaker listened to the speakerphone, his hands resting by the phone. During the seconds it took to establish a connection, Brian Whittaker was watching his brother-in-law closely. Finally they could hear the peep that signaled them that the satellite phone was ringing. Once… twice…three times…four times…five times. Finally, someone answered.

"Yes, Gordon, what is it?" Chuck Hogan said at the other end of the connection.

On board the *Northern Explorer*, Amundsen Gulf, Darnley Bay, Saturday, October 8th

Ariel had carefully listened to the plan and the Israeli was now carefully watching the four American scientists as well as the four cameramen, when he heard a phone buzzing. One of the cameramen took a satellite phone out of his jacket pocket and walked outside. Ariel watched him leaving and counted how often the phone rang.

Once…twice…three times…four times…five times.

Once in safe distance from the other people, the cameraman finally answered the call.

"Yes, Gordon, what is it?" Chuck Hogan asked, but he didn't get a reply. "Gordon? Are you there?" the American mercenary asked again and checked the signal bar on his satellite phone.

Chuck Hogan stared at the display. The signal strength was good and he and Gordon had agreed to only contact each other in case of an emergency. Besides that fact, Gordon was the only person beside his sister who knew this number.

Still confused, the man who had tried to kill Natascha twice, held the phone back to his ear.

"Gordon? Can you hear me?" he asked again, this time much louder.

Although the connection was still active, he didn't get an answer. Chuck Hogan felt that something must have gone wrong and his instinct told him to turn around.

Just three meters away from him was Ariel, holding his own satellite phone to his ear in one hand and a 9mm Sig Sauer in the other. Ariel's eyes were cold as ice, and Chuck knew the Israeli would shoot him without hesitation.

Chuck closed his satellite phone and demonstratively stretched his hands away from him. No one else had noticed anything yet, but Chuck knew that this could change any second. He kept his eyes fixed on Ariel as he was about to tell Klaus what happened, but before he could say a word, he heard a female voice behind him.

"I'll blow your brains out if you say one goddamn word," the woman whispered, but still loud enough for Ariel to understand her and her seriousness. Ariel froze. He knew that Jenna Mason, the American scientist, stood just a few meters behind him.

Chuck Hogan took his own gun and aimed it at Ariel's head.

"Close your phone and drop it," Jenna commanded.

Without having the chance to inform retired General Klaus Schwartze in London about what was going on, Ariel disconnected the call and dropped the satellite phone on the deck.

"And now you'll put down your gun on the floor very slowly, and don't say a word," the American scientist continued.

Ariel searched his brain for any plan of action, any solution, but could not find a way out. He decided to obey. The Israeli glimpsed over his shoulder and could see Jenna standing about four meters behind him, just out of reach for any counter. The silencer on her weapon was unwavering, a clear indication that he was dealing with professionals.

"Walk three steps forward, kneel down and put your hands behind your head. Palms facing up. One false movement and you're history," she continued to command coldly.

Ariel did as he was told, and he could hear Jenna pick up both his satellite phone and gun. Chuck stepped behind Ariel, placed one foot firmly in the back of his knee and pulled two heavy duty plastic tie wraps with metal clips out from underneath his belt. While Jenna stood a safe distance beside Ariel and held her aim at this head, Chuck used the two tie wraps to bind Ariel's hands together behind his back. Chuck fed one tie wrap aroundAriel's belt so he couldn't move his hands at all. With the Israeli bound up defenseless, Chuck started to search him. He found another little revolver as well as a knife and stowed both items under his belt.

"Okay, let's go," Chuck commanded and helped Ariel to his feet before he violently pushed him towards the dive control room.

On board the research submersible *Odin*, Amundsen Gulf, Darnley Bay, Saturday, October 8th

Natascha was completely stunned about the aggression in Senator Brown's voice and looked at him. What she saw shocked her even more. US Senator Jonathan Brown had no interest in the canister at the pipeline. Instead he was looking at Natascha over his little revolver.

"What the hell is wrong with you?" the Senator asked, knowing very well that the communication to the *Northern Explorer* wasn't activated.

"I told you several times to turn around, I even asked you nicely, but no, you didn't listen. Why didn't you listen to me? We now have a problem at our hands and I'm telling you for the last time: Turn around and get us back to the ship. And don't even think about using the radio. Understood?"

The horrification pervaded Natascha's features and she couldn't think clearly. Optimising on the opportunity to talk some sense into a politician who could hopefully change the environmental situation, she just realized she was alone with a gun pointed at her. Without saying anything, she simply nodded.

"Okay then, take us away from this canister very slowly. Should you get that stupid idea to rip it off the pipeline, then you should know that you'll be responsible for the death of every living organism within a three mile radius."

Natascha's face paled and she felt nauseous as she maneuvered *Odin* backwards and away from the pipeline with shaking hands.

Terrified, the thought to contact help over the radio never crossed her mind.

How did he know what's inside the canister? Natascha asked herself. All this didn't make any sense.

Home Office and Operational Headquarters of *EuroSecCorporation*, London, Saturday, October 8th

Retired Admiral Brian Whittaker disconnected the call and briefly glimpsed at Klaus before he returned his fixed gaze on Gordon Ramshaw.

Klaus knitted his brow.

"Ariel? Are you still there? Ariel, can you hear me?" he asked, but he didn't get an answer. Instead, Klaus heard how the connection was cut off a few seconds later.

"What did he say?" retired Admiral Brian Whittaker asked, without taking his eyes of Gordon.

"That's the exact problem. After someone answered the call after the fifth ring, Ariel simply said *Yes*. That means this person in question, who just answered this satellite phone, is on board the *Northern Explorer* at this very moment. After that the connection was cut off."

"Excuse me?" Brian Whittaker asked and briefly looked at Klaus before he kept watching Gordon Ramshaw, who sat motionless in his chair.

"Ariel has confirmed the presence of this person on board the ship, but he didn't get the chance to say anything else. I didn't hear any suspicious background noise before the line went dead. No fighting, no shots fired, nothing."

"Maybe they had to improvise and neutralize the other person. We'll call again in a few minutes," Brian said.

"I'm going to send a message to the *Northern Explorer* anyway. Just in case," Klaus said and pulled the keyboard over.

Brian was still watching his brother-in-law.

"So, Gordon. Is there anything you want to tell us?"

"I have no idea what the hell you're talking about," the British said, still trying to convince them that he had no hand in this.

Brian Whittaker hit his fist on the table so hard that Gordon Ramshaw started.

"For God's sake, Gordon," Brian yelled at him. "We're not that stupid. You lied to me twice about who you called. You used my phone twice to speak to a person who was in Iceland at the same time there was an attempt on the life of a young woman who we're paid to protect. The same person who followed our men to Canada's east coast, and now this person is on board the same ship as my men and the person we have to protect. Something just went wrong up there. I have no idea how deep you are involved in this, but may God have mercy on your soul if anything happens to that girl or any of my men. I can guarantee you that."

Gordon slowly rose from his chair and took both his jacket and his hat before he faced his brother-in-law.

"I think that you have the wrong man," he said calmly and went for the door. "You seem to have forgotten whom you have to thank for all this. I wish you a nice evening."

Before he could reach the door he heard the cock of a gun.

Gordon turned around and looked right down the barrel of a gun.

"Brian, you can't be serious!" Gordon yelled.

"My men are on a ship, most likely together with a professional assassin. So long as I don't know how much you're involved in this, and so long as I don't know if my men and this woman are safe, you're not going anywhere," Brian ordered and his voice left no room for any doubt.

"You'll sit down in your chair again, while we call Scotland Yard. And once they're here you'll tell us in every detail what's going on out there."

Gordon slowly raised his arms and sat back down in his chair, not without throwing a hateful look at Brian as his scowl burned into his forehead.

On board the research submersible *Odin*, Amundsen Gulf, Darnley Bay, Saturday, October 8th

Natascha piloted *Odin* back to the *Northern Explorer*. Her heart was racing with every passing minute. It had been twenty minutes since the last word spoken. Her mind worked hard to find a way out of this. Under the stress of the gun pointing at her, she could feel the need for a solution becoming more demanding as time ticked by.

I could flood Odin. No, I would need both hands for that and it takes lots of time. Besides that, I'm too far away from the Northern Explorer and the water is way too cold. What if I simulate a complete system failure? The alarm will sound on the ship and they'll definitely come and get me, but that still won't take care of the gun in his hand.

Whatever idea Natascha had, she didn't come up with a solution. Suddenly she realized that she actually didn't have to do anything. Sooner or later they would be back on board the *Northern Explorer*, and she could not believe that the Senator would have any support back on the ship, except from his assistant. Thinking of him, Natascha could not see him being a match for Ariel and his boys. Looking back, Natascha knew that she accidentally found both the pipeline and that canister, and she also knew that the Senator had knowledge of both them. Until now, Senator Brown had also done nothing to inform anyone else on board the ship.

Does he actually believe he can step out of this sub and pretend that nothing has happened? That there's no pipeline and no canister and that he didn't point that gun at me? Is he actually that stupid?

Although Natascha found herself in an anything but perfect position, she was convinced that the Senator's reaction was very impulsive and a faint smile flicked across her lips.

As soon as we're back on board I'll watch my boys rip you apart.

On board the *Northern Explorer*, Amundsen Gulf, Darnley Bay, Saturday, October 8th

Using Ariel as a living shield, Chuck Hogan walked from the deck back into the dive control room. Besides the presence of Ariel's entire team, there were the American scientists Frank Garcia, Nelson Singer and Brian Joice as well as Dr. Richard Weber and the Vitali Vachenko gathered around the table. It was Vitali who noticed first that something was wrong.

"What the hell is..." he started, but he never had the chance to finish his sentence.

With the sound reduced by the silencer to a mere *plop,* both 9mm projectiles fired from Chuck's gun hit Vitali right in his heart. Leading Dive Officer Vitali Vachenko was dead before he hit the floor.

"The first person who moves, or says a word, will be killed immediately. Going to *Phase B* immediately," Jenna Mason commanded with a certain authority and pointed her gun at the Germans, while Chuck Hogan threw Ariel on the floor.

Nick and his friends looked at each other when they realized that not only the other three cameramen pointed guns at them, but also the remaining three American scientists. Outnumbered eight to five and in a crossfire position, they had no choice but to obey. Anything else would be suicidal.

"Jenna, are those all of the Germans?" Chuck asked his sister.

"Yes, those are all of them. You'll now kneel down right where you are and you'll keep your hands reaching up far above your head. The first person who does something else or says a word will die," Jenna commanded.

Nick and his friends looked at each other, but knowing they lacked an alternative, they followed her orders.

"Next you'll lay down on your belly and stretch both arms out sideways, palms up. The first person to make a sound or reaches for a weapon will die."

After Nick and his colleagues had followed Jenna's order, they were individually searched for weapons and tied the same way as Ariel.

"Where can we bring them?" Chuck asked and looked at this sister.

She leaned towards her brother and whispered something in his ear, but Nick noticed that Chuck didn't agree with her.

"No, we need them later on. We can't weld the door to their cabin. We have to bring all of them into one cabin, otherwise we'll lose too many people guarding them," he whispered back to his sister.

Jenna pointed at Shira and kept whispering to Chuck, but Nick struggled to understand her this time.

"Okay," Chuck nodded and looked at his hostages.

"We'll help you to get up. You'll go to Shira's cabin. Sean, Robert, you two lead and make sure that no one else sees you. You know what to do," Chuck commanded and the little group started walking.

Nick walked behind Shira the same route he had taken so many times during the last couple weeks. Suddenly it struck him like lightning.

Natascha! Nick stopped, but Jenna immediately hit him in his neck with her gun. Nick collapsed on his knees and tears shot from his eyes. With his eyes closed, he could do nothing but concentrate on the pain. He took a couple deep breaths as his head throbbed aggressively.

"If you stop one more time I'll blow your brains out. Get moving," Jenna hissed at the German.

Without another word they continued their way to Shira's and Natascha's cabin. Nick noticed one of the American scientists always walked a fair distance ahead of them to make sure the hallways were clear and that no other crew member would accidentally run into them. It didn't take too long before Jenna searched the cabin and the little bathroom. Everything that could be used as a weapon or a tool or communication devices were put in one of Natascha's backpacks. After that, Jenna ordered Nick and his friends to lay down on the floor, where their ankles were tied with some additional tie wraps to their hands. That way it was impossible for them to stand up.

"We'll keep one guard in front of the closed door. If we hear anything that resembles a morse code or something else to warn the remaining crew, then we'll execute all of you right away. Is this clear?"

Representing his people Ariel nodded and Jenna turned the lights off and locked the cabin door from the outside.

Nick could hear how Ole-Einar hissed a curse in Norwegian, but Nick's thoughts were with Natascha. After all, they lost and the others finally succeeded.

Home Office and Operational Headquarters of *EuroSecCorporation*, London, Saturday, October 8th

Retired Admiral Brian Whittaker fixed his eyes on Gordon Ramshaw, who didn't break his look. Although Brian had placed the gun right in front of him on the table, Gordon knew that his brother-in-law would not hesitate for a second to pick it back up and to even use it, should the need be.

In the meantime, retired General Klaus Schwartze had contacted Scotland Yard, while his wife and secretary Brigitte called all available members from operation control. Her first call went to Sean MacLeod, who used to work in the anti terrorism department of Scotland Yard before he joined *EuroSecCorporation*. He answered the phone at the second ring and was already on his way. Within thirty minutes Tatjana Volmatovja, Sigrid Schneider, Sean MacLeod, Jack MacDonald and Gunner Eriksson represented the available members of their operation control in their big conference room. While Klaus Schwartze was still on the phone, all eyes rested on Gordon Ramshaw, who was, after all, Brian Whittaker's brother-in-law and the financial force that started *EuroSecCorporation* off the ground.

Brian Whittaker walked up and down, looking back and forth from his watch to Gordon Ramshaw. The officers from Scotland Yard should be there any moment. Until they were present, he had ordered everybody to silence.

On board the research submersible *Odin*, Amundsen Gulf, Darnley Bay, Saturday, October 8th

Though Natascha could feel the retort, she managed to hold her silence for the next ten minutes. Her anxiety rose once she realized they were only five minutes away from the *Northern Explorer* and it was time to contact the ship. It was not until now that she also realized there was complete radio silence, something that was completely against their briefing. Not knowing why, Natascha tensed and shifted in her seat.

"Nervous?" US Senator Brown asked coolly.

"Not as nervous as you're going to be once we're back on board. I can't even imagine how you plan to get away with this," the young German scientist said with disgust.

"You see, that's the good thing. You don't even have to imagine. I'll do all the thinking. That's what the American government pays me money for. Don't worry. Everything is fine."

Natascha's fury quickly returned. How he could speak so coolly, so crookedly only seemed to increase her aggrivation. Her thoughts spilled over one another, so many words for such a difficult situation but little time to say them. She harshly bit her tongue once she recalled all the lessons that Shira taught her over countless conversations. Over and over the young Israeli informed Natascha on what to do should she be taken hostage. Back then Natascha was convinced that she would have forgotten all of it by now, but even though she remembered it, her surprise stemmed from the fact that she had a clear head in this moment. She replayed Shira's words, and focused her concentration on *Odin* and the fact that Nick and his friends were waiting for her on the *Northern Explorer*. Natascha's throat clenched as another fierce string of retorts swarmed her thoughts. She stole a deep breath as she spotted the *Northern Explorer*'s hull in the distance.

"I have to contact the *Northern Explorer* now over the radio. We depend on their assistance to get us back on board," the young German explained tensely.

"Go ahead, beautiful, but remember: If I were you, I wouldn't try anything stupid. You seem to be very bright, so that shouldn't be too difficult. I really like you," the Senator calmly said and smiled at her.

Natascha swallowed hard and reached for the microphone.

"*Northern Explorer, Northern Explorer, Northern Explorer,* this is *Odin, Odin, Odin.*"

No reaction, except a few clicks. Natascha frowned as more clicks followed. It seemed like someone was trying several buttons in the dive control room. It couldn't be Vitali.

"Yes, I hear you. Get back to the surface. We'll get you back on deck somehow. Had to move to *Phase B* already. Everything under control."

Natascha's frown intensified as she mulled over his message. It lacked any sense and she looked at the speaker in disbelief. The one thing confirmed was that it was not Vitali. She struggled to understand what was meant by *Phase B*. Natascha looked from the speakerphone up to Senator Jonathan Brown, who was clearly relieved. He smiled and shrugged his shoulders.

"I told you not to worry. You heard what he said. Everything is under control," the Senator smirked arrogantly.

Approximately thirty minutes later *Odin* was back on the deck of the *Northern Explorer*. Natascha looked irritated through the plexiglas dome and noticed that two of the American scientists helped to get them back. There was no sight of her father, Nick or any of her friends.

The moment *Odin* touched the deck, Natascha jumped out of her seat, opened the hatch and climbed out. She swivelled around on her heel once her feet met the deck and her breath escaped her lungs as she stared down the barrel of another gun.

"How'd it go?" Martin Cunningham asked, and Natascha recognized him as one of the cameramen. He pointed with his gun as he ordered her forward.

"Let's go. To the dive control room."

Natascha righted herself and slowly walked by the American and into the dive control room. She opened the door and was immediately horrified at the sight. Her stomach churned as she registered Vitali Vachenko laying face down in a pool of his own blood.

"Oh my God!" Natascha screamed, her hand flying to her mouth. She swallowed violently, trying to maintain her composure.

Senator Brown just walked into the room and his eyes fell to the dead Dive Officer. Natascha noticed that the Senator lacked surprise and showed no reaction at all.

"What happened?"

"Slight change of plan. We had to switch to *Phase B* a little bit sooner. One of the Germans seemed to have discovered something. We're not sure about what it was, but we're checking it out now. We had to act fast."

"Any problems?" the Senator asked, concern evident in his voice.

"No, we have everything under control. We have the whole unit under control."

While the Senator just nodded in satisfaction, Natascha felt the complete opposite.

One of the Germans! That has to be either Nick or Oliver!

But Natascha wasn't even sure if the Americans knew all the different nationalities of Nick's friends.

They have the whole unit under control. Have they shot someone else? What about my father? What about Nick?

For the first time in the last couple months, Natascha could feel her usefulness dwindling as her helplessness increased rapidly every passing moment. After two unsuccessful assassination attempts, she finally seemed to run out of luck now.

"What about the Captain and his officers? What about the crew?" the Senator wanted to know.

"Chuck and the others are just on their way to the bridge. I'm making sure that no one runs into the dead body here. As soon as you and your Canadian friend have left the ship, we'll take over the command."

"Perfect. Don't leave her out of your sight," Senator Brown nodded, then looked at Natascha, before he turned to the bridge.

While US Senator Brown was on his way to the bridge, Ariel and his friends tried to assess their situation. They knew there was an armed guard in front of their cabin. Ariel could see the shadow of two legs in the light that seeped in from the bottom of the door. As long as they whispered to each other, their guard would not hear anything. Although Jenna had closed the curtain to cover the window, some light still made it inside the cabin.

"Okay, has anyone noticed if they left a radio or a microphone here to monitor our conversation?" he whispered, but everybody just looked at him and shook their head.

"No, I watched Jenna the entire time. She was the only one in the cabin. I'm sure she didn't place a bug," Shira said.

"How many people are we dealing with?"

"Four cameramen and the four American scientists make at least eight people," Oliver whispered helpfully.

"Why did they lock us up together?" Ole-Einar questioned quietly.

"I'm not sure," Ariel commented, confused.

"From what I heard, they still need us for something. Jenna wanted to lock us up separately and weld the cabin doors to the frame, but their boss didn't agree," the Israeli continued.

"But what do they want from us?" the Norwegian asked.

"Two things," Shira whispered.

"They either need us to do some dirty work for them or it has to look like we're the ones who killed the whole crew in the end. That would hardly be possible if we sit inside separate cabins with their doors welded from the outside," Shira shared her theory.

"You think they're going to kill everybody?"

"Do they have another choice? They already killed Vitali and there are two high ranking politicians on board. They're following a plan," the Israeli woman whispered to Ole-Einar.

"But who the hell are those guys?" Oliver spoke up again.

"I think I recognize one of them," Nick whispered, finally taking part in the conversation. "I believe they're the guys from Berlin. When the one guy searched me for weapons, I noticed his tattoo. Those are the guys who are after Natascha."

For the next few seconds silence muted their lips.

"But that doesn't make any sense," Ole-Einar stated suddenly from the other side of the room.

"Yes, and I'm sure that's in Natascha's favour," Nick replied honestly, though there was little comfort in such truth.

Home Office and Operational Headquarters of *EuroSecCorporation*, London, Saturday, October 8th

It was very late on Saturday night, but this did not hinder the two Scotland Yard officers to arrive immediately. It turned out that Sean MacLeod knew both of them very well and Brian Whittaker let Sean handle the introductions.

Inspector Conolly finally nodded and looked from Gordon Ramshaw to retired Admiral Brian Whittaker.

"Inspector Conolly," Brian said and pointed at two chairs.

"Are you familiar with the area of responsibility of our company *EuroSecCorporation*?" the retired Admiral promptly asked.

"I have a few ideas, but in order to save some valuable time I suggest you give me and my colleague here a quick overview," Inspector Conolly answered.

"Very well," Brian Whittaker nodded and reached with his hand towards his colleague, retired General Klaus Schwartze.

"Together with my good friend and former colleague we founded *EuroSecCorporation* back in two-thousand-and-two. The security business was booming after *9/11* and there were many black sheep on the market. First we started as free lance consultants, before we founded our own company. We recognized that there was an enormous demand for consultation in regards to security as well as the installation of security systems. Another big part of the business back then was the training and education of staff members and employees of high target facilities, like airports, oil rigs, sport stadiums, exhibition arenas, you name it. In order to achieve the required manpower, we started to hire specialists from all over Europe. Every single one of our employees used to work for the government of their respective nation and passed an intense security and background check. It was very important for us to hire only decorated and experienced people and not some wild guns. After a while we specialized on the assessment of security risks for large events or objects as well as the protection of oil rigs and personal protection detail not only for celebrities but occasionally the royal family. All of our employees have the privilege to carry handguns within European borders. We're an entirely private company and we don't work for a government agency and we don't follow any government orders. However, once in a while we do work in cooperation with the government and sometimes we even do consulting jobs for the government. Is this explanation satisfying or do you have any questions?" Brian Whittaker asked shortly.

Inspector Conolly shook his head and Brian Whittaker continued. "The gentleman in that chair is my brother-in-law, Gordon Ramshaw. Mr. Ramshaw originally provided us with the necessary financial support to start the company, but he received complete financial compensation plus interest several years ago and there are no financial ties between him and our company whatsoever. Furthermore, as you may very well be aware of, Mr. Ramshaw is a member of the board of one of the world's leading oil companies. Until recently, we sometimes worked for both Mr. Ramshaw as well as his oil company, but it was always strictly business. Mr. Ramshaw never had any insider knowledge of our other jobs."

Brian paused for a moment and glanced at Gordon before he looked back at Inspector Conolly.

"Let me now explain our current situation. On Tuesday, June fourteenth we were contacted by a German scientific institute with the request to provide personal protection detail for one of their Professors during an international event in Berlin later that month."

Klaus Schwartze started a presentation and everybody could see the pictures on the big screen.

"The person in question was Dr. Richard Weber, a German Professor and leader of an international team of scientists on a polar expedition through the North-West Passage. The institute received several threats by mail against the Professor as well as the expedition itself. One threat was considered serious and it contained this photograph." He pointed to the photo as it popped up on the screen. "Our research confirmed the original threat assessment from the German police and we agreed to provide personal protection detail in agreement with the local police. A background check revealed that Dr. Richard Weber would not only step on the feet of the American, Canadian and Russian government, but also the feet of several big oil companies, like Mr Ramshaw's. At the end of the international event in Berlin, unknown people executed a carefully planned and well prepared assassination attempt on the life of Dr. Weber's daughter. I'll explain in a second why. At the time we were dealing with at least three well-trained people and they even used a distraction to carry out their plan. Two of the assassins pretended to be drunks who simply wanted to rob the Professor and his family at knife point. We assume that the original plan was that either the Professor or his daughter were suppose to get fatally injured during the failed robbery. However, two of our men successfully fought them off, but they did not pursue them once they ran away. This moment of confusion was optimized on by a third person, a sniper who had his position almost two hundred meters away. Coincidentally one of our men saw the muzzle flash and threw himself in front of the family. The projectile hit him in his bullet resistant vest and he only suffered a minor injury while the family was unharmed. We followed protocol and successfully evacuated the family before we notified the local authorities. At this point and time, we were still convinced that Dr. Weber himself was the target. During a meeting with the board of the institute on the following day, the institute asked us to extend the personal protection detail for the duration of the expedition. This happened in agreement with the skipper of the research vessel *Northern Explorer*, a former Norwegian naval officer, Captain Rasmussen, as well as his two officers. Without any further incident, Dr. Weber, together with his daughter Natascha Kleinfeld, boarded the research vessel with one of our teams assigned to their protection. During a scheduled event in Reykjavik, one of our men went diving with Natascha Kleinfeld on their day off. Just minutes before the dive, Miss Kleinfeld coincidentally swapped her scuba gear with another diver, who suffered a severe accident during the dive. Both Miss Kleinfeld as well as the other diver were very experienced with their dive gear. It was sheer luck and a well coordinated rescue attempt that saved the life of the young diver. Miss Kleinfeld herself did not get harmed in any way. Inspecting her gear immediately after the incident, Miss Kleinfeld noticed that her unit had been manipulated in a way that required detailed knowledge of this type of gear's technology. At the same time, we were actually debriefing the Berlin incident here in this very room. Our research revealed that the two robbers were actually former members of some special forces. Both had their blood type tattooed on their arms, something that was caught by one of the security cameras. This fact made us nervous, since we now knew that we were dealing with professionals. So we looked at the flight path of the projectile again and we found out, that, considering all circumstances, Dr. Richard Weber was not the intended target, but his daughter Natascha Kleinfeld. Based on this new information we informed both our men on board the research vessel as well as the institute and we concentrated our protection detail now on Miss Kleinfeld. Since that second failed assassination attempt on her life on Tuesday, July fifth, no further attempt has been performed. At this moment Dr. Richard Weber, his daughter Natascha Kleinfeld as well as six of our men are on board the research vessel *Northern Explorer*. They are currently at anchor at Darnley Bay, Amundsen Gulf, a few miles off the coast of Paulatuk, at the western entrance of the North-West Passage. Can you follow me so far?"

"So far everything's clear," Inspector Conolly nodded and looked up from his notes, knowing there was more to come.

"Until today, it was common practice that my brother-in-law, Mr. Gordon Ramshaw met with my wife and I once a week for dinner. In most cases, he picked us up here at this building. When we went over our phone bill, we discovered that Mr. Ramshaw placed two calls to a satellite phone from my office phone. He first called a person in Reykjavik at the same time the second assassination attempt took place in Iceland. His second call a few days later went to the same satellite phone, but this time the signal was boosted by a cell tower in Boston. At this time, our men were in Halifax. Technically there's a chance that the call could still be received in Nova Scotia. When I asked Mr. Ramshaw about the nature of the two calls, he denied the true nature, first claiming that he had called his office, then changed his story to calling a foreman in the field. Careful as we are, we wanted to be sure and contacted our men on the research vessel. It's interesting to know that the research vessel was host to two politicians today. First politician is sitting US Senator Jonathan Brown and the second politician is a member of the Canadian Parliament, Pierre Dumont. Nervous as we are and with our own man successfully on the phone, we also called the number of the satellite phone that Mr. Ramshaw dialed from my office. Somebody at the other end picked up the phone and our man on board the research vessel confirmed that this mystery person is on board the ship. Immediately after that, we lost contact and haven't heard anything since. We were not capable to contact our unit either with the satellite phone or over the computer. Our last contact was over one hour ago," Brian Whittaker concluded.

Inspector Conolly looked from his assistant, who was still taking notes, to Gordon Ramshaw and rose from his chair. He looked back and forth between Gordon and Brian as he walked around in the office, thinking hard.

"And you're now thinking that…" he started, but didn't finish.

"That's exactly what I'm thinking. I think we currently have a hostage situation on board a Norwegian research vessel within Canadian waters on our hands. I also think that an American and a Canadian politician are somehow either actively or passively involved in it and maybe even still on board. At this moment and considering all the facts, I also have to presume that Mr. Gordon Ramshaw is somehow involved in it as well, but we have no idea how many people we're dealing with here."

On board the *Northern Explorer*, Amundsen Gulf, Darnley Bay, Saturday, October 8th

US Senator Jonathan Brown stepped into *Northern Explorer's* bridge. He quickly scanned the room and saw Captain Rasmussen, his First and Second Officer and the two Navigation Officer's under the watchful eyes of Chuck and Jenna.

"Senator Brown, how was your trip?" Chuck Hogan asked the Senator enthusiastically. The Captain and crew that were present were calm and resumed their duties. It was clear to the Senator that no one on the bridge noticed what happened in the dive control room half an hour earlier.

"It was actually very exciting and it exceeded all my expectations. Miss Kleinfeld is an excellent submarine captain. She just went to change back into some normal clothes. Captain Rasmussen, let me take this opportunity to express my gratitude for being such a great host on such short notice. Thank you very much, but I believe we've abused your hospitality more than enough already. I think it's time for us to get back to shore," Senator Brown said and walked over to the Captain.

Captain Rasmussen nodded and shook both the politicians hands.

"Anytime, Senator. One can only hope that you don't forget what you have seen today too soon," Captain Rasmussen commented and winked at the American politician.

"No, we won't. Although we're politicians, deep inside we're still human. Thank you once again," MP Pierre Dumont replied and left the bridge together with Senator Brown and his assistant Carl Miller.

Chuck Hogan and Jenna Mason followed them out.

"So, everything is going according to our plan so far, that's great. Make sure there are no complications. Do you remember your initial contract regarding the Professor's daughter?" Senator Brown asked Chuck once he was sure that no one else could hear them.

"Of course I remember," the American mercenary answered when they were just a few meters away from the dive control room.

Thin Ice

"Maybe you should fulfill your contract. She knows too much," Senator Brown informed, not without thinking of the young attractive German scientist.

Chuck Hogan simply nodded and opened the door to the dive control room. Martin Cunningham briefly looked to Chuck before he continued to watch Natascha, who was still shocked by the murder of Vitali Vachenko.

Senator Brown only took one step inside the dive control room. The last thing he wanted to do was ruin his expensive shoes with blood. He turned to Natascha. "Listen, I'm really sorry you got dragged into this. I'm sure you would've had a wonderful career under different circumstances, but unfortunately you've seen a little bit too much, and I'm afraid I can't trust you. Please don't take this personal," Senator Brown simply explained before he turned towards Chuck.

"Make sure nobody knows what happened, okay? And make sure there's no blood on the floor when you're done."

"Don't worry, we know what we have to do. This is not our first rodeo. Everything will be fine. Martin, you can fly our guests back to shore. Check the second helicopter and make sure it's refueled before you come back. Wouldn't hurt to refuel that helicopter as well, just in case. Once you're done, you come back right away."

"Okay, I think we should really get going now. Make sure everything goes according to our plan," the Canadian politician added nervously.

"Pierre is right. It's time."

Natascha had no idea where this hatred came from as it built up inside her. Whether it was the arrogance or the cold bloodedness that the two politicians demonstrated, it didn't matter. She resolutely walked over and stopped just a meter away from them.

"Who the hell do you think you are? You can't kill all those people here just because of this stupid oil! Hundreds of people are living in this area and there are people on board this ship. Why are you doing this? For goddamn oil?" Natascha yelled and took another step towards the Senator before she glared at the three mercenaries in turn.

"You can't let that happen. You can't kill all those innocent people for those two politicians. That doesn't make any sense! You don't have to do that," she appealed at Chuck Hogan, Martin Cunningham and Jenna Mason.

"You have no idea," Senator Brown whispered calmly. "You have absolutely no clue how the world is functioning at this time and age. Without oil the earth would stop spinning. What do you think is powering this research vessel over these waters? Sun and love, maybe? What rubbish. The United States of America and Canada rely on the arctic oil, that is a fact. It's the foundation for our industry, for our economy. It's the foundation of our freedom and our way of life. Without this oil up here, both the United States and Canada would lose most of the things they stand for. We're already at war because of the oil and there will be more war. Renewable energies, what a stupid idea, so excuse me if I'm laughing. Neither the sun nor the wind creates any jobs or any wealth. Oil has done this for decades. Oil has created jobs for our citizens, it has created wealth for them and it gave them the opportunity to live the way of life they want to. Down here there's enough oil for Canada and the United States for the next twenty years. That means jobs and wealth for the region as well as much needed revenue for our countries. And at what cost? A few drunk Eskimos don't get a protected area and have to move their totempole somewhere else. Trust me, once the oil flows, the people will be thanking us," Senator Brown yelled back, his face just centimeters away from Natascha's. His breath was as rank as his spluttered words. He could not believe his sudden outburst, and he tried to manage the anger that burned through his veins.

Natascha was appalled and she wasted no energy in hiding this fact. The shock of his words was like lightning to a tree. His words struck her ears with heat, and she could feel the fire of anger burn within her as her heart raced with unfathomable speed. Her breath came in quick short gasps, her thoughts tumbling one over the other as she suddenly thrust her knee up into the Senator's groin. Senator Brown immediately fell to the deck, his cry resounding through the room as he curled on the floor. It took Natascha a second to realize what happened and in that same instant she involuntarily staggered to the ground and landed on her side. She could taste the blood as her hand rushed to the sudden pain. Chuck returned his open hand to his side as she threw him a hateful glare.

A muffled groan escaped her lips as she caressed her face. She was hardly surprised when she returned her eyes to Chuck that she saw Jenna aiming a gun at her just a short distance away.

"Don't shoot her, Jenna," Chuck Hogan yelled angrily, then added coolly, "We need her later on."

Reluctantly, Natascha followed Jenna's order and rolled on her stomach, just to have her hands tied behind her back. The American checked her for weapons, but, as expected, didn't find anything.

Senator Brown was back on his knees, but still gasping for air. Pierre Dumont and Chuck went over to him and helped him to get back to his feet.

"It seems she doesn't share your opinion," Chuck Hogan commented freely.

"That bitch," Senator Jonathan Brown groaned and accepted Carl Miller's assistance.

"Let's get out of here," he whispered in agonizing pain.

Martin Cunningham escorted the two politicians and Carl Miller to the helicopter.

Chuck looked after them and noticed the camera they had used to film the Senator as he climbed into the research vessel earlier. It was still mounted on a tripod not far away and Chuck could see the red light suggesting it was still recording. Someone must have simply forgotten to turn it off. Chuck walked over to the camera, stopped it and his first thought was to throw the whole thing overboard, but then he had a better idea. He took the camera and brought it to the Senator, who was sitting inside the helicopter.

"Here, a little souvenir. Might be worth a lot of money someday. See it as the last chance to watch that lovely Marine Biologist," Chuck Hogan smirked.

"By the way, I think I have to lock up most of the crew. There are far more people still on board this ship than I expected, but I have a plan. Don't worry."

US Senator Jonathan Brown took the camera, nodded and threw a last hated look at Natascha, who was rose to her feet with Jenna's assistance.

Chuck walked back to Natascha and Jenna and they watched the helicopter take off. Just a few minutes later, he was out of sight.

Perfect. They're finally out of my way. Time to get to the real plan, Chuck thought and smiled at this sister.

"Okay, let's go. To the bridge. Don't do anything stupid. Kneeing one of America's top politicians was a really bad idea," Chuck commanded and pushed Natascha in front of him.

With Jenna leading the way to make sure no one else would see them, Chuck walked into the bridge, holding Natascha beside him. With a quick look around he could see Captain Rasmussen, his First and Second Officer, the two Navigation Officers as well as Astrid, who had just joined them to pour herself a cup of coffee.

"Captain Rasmussen. Can I ask you something?" Chuck said in a normal tone.

The Norwegian skipper looked up from some documents and was puzzled to see Natascha, who was not only still in her thermo overall, but who harboured a bloody lip.

"Natascha, what happened to you?" Captain Rasmussen asked, ignoring Chuck. His eyes were fixed on the young German scientist.

"Captain Rasmussen, who's in command of this ship?" Chuck Hogan asked again in a much more demanding tone.

Instead of answering, the Norwegian naval veteran was fixed on Natascha, who only looked at Chuck, her fear clearly visible on her face.

"Excuse me? What did you say?" he finally asked perplexed.

Frustrated, Chuck immediately pulled his gun and shot First Office Karl-Heinz Junghans right in the head.

"I asked who's in command of this ship, Captain Rasmussen," Chuck repeated harshly, emphasizing Captain Rasmussen's name and title.

The Norwegian Captain was stunned and looked at this dead First Officer. By the time he returned his attention to Chuck, he was staring right up the silencer of Chuck Hogan's gun, while Jenna brought up her own gun to the back of Natascha's head, smiling wickedly.

Silence engulfed the bridge, shock pervaded the essence of every crew member hindering them from uttering a single word.

"You of course. You are in command of this ship," Captain Rasmussen stated finally, feeding the response Chuck Hogan wanted to hear all along.

- 17 -

Home Office and Operational Headquarters of *EuroSecCorporation*,
London, Sunday, October 9th

Although is was now well past midnight, everybody inside the conference room was still very much awake. Inspector Conolly from Scotland Yard confirmed Brian Whittaker's theory. He was also convinced that this was not a coincidence, especially since Gordon Ramshaw refused to identify the person he called twice from Brian's office. The content of Gordon's only words consisted of a request for the presence of his lawyers.

"Mr. Ramshaw, after careful consideration of all available facts, you're now a suspect of being involved in an internationally criminal operation, which has it's goal to liquidate at least one innocent citizen. I can guarantee you that every judge in London would quickly say the word *terrorist* if I call him this early on Sunday morning to present him the facts at hand. Chasing a person through three countries over two continents with the help of paid mercenaries usually falls under that category. Calling the judge now would save you time and money and ultimately many pointless discussions with your non-accessible lawyers now that you are labelled a terrorist. At the moment, there's just a suspicion, and I'll give you thirty minutes to rethink your position. After that, I'll not only call the judge, but also the American and Canadian authorities. If you still decide not to cooperate, you'll be held responsible and charged with being an accessory to all crimes committed by those people up to that time as well as from then on. That would include, as far as I remember, two attempted murders. Mr. Ramshaw, do you understand what I just told you?" Inspector Conolly asked.

Gordon Ramshaw maintained his silence and kept his attention fixed on the floor as he fearfully searched for a solution.

"Mr. Whittaker, can we talk somewhere?" Inspector Conolly asked briskly.

"Of course," the retired Admiral answered and pointed to the door, before he led the way to his office.

Together with Klaus Schwartze and Sean MacLeod from operation control, Inspector Conolly followed him, while his assistant stayed with Gordon Ramshaw.

"Is there anything else that you need to tell me that couldn't be said in the presence of your brother-in-law? Do you have any further details from your investigations that might help us?" the officer from Scotland Yard asked.

Brian offered him a chair, as well as a cigar and his choice of scotch and coffee, before he sat down himself.

"No, Inspector Conolly. Like I said before, we're not a government agency and we have no authority whatsoever to prosecute criminals. We also don't have access to any data, so our information is limited at best. However, we're one hundred percent certain of the facts we presented to you tonight, otherwise we wouldn't have contacted you. We were obliged to inform the Icelandic authorities, but we have no knowledge about their investigation. We would love to know the names of the people who traveled to and from Iceland during the time of the second assassination attempt. If we have access to the data, we can then compare those names with the names of people who traveled to Germany and Berlin during the time of the first assassination attempt. With a little bit of luck, we will be able to find out if someone was in the Boston area or in Nova Scotia as well. With all that information, we would have something to run with to identify the person at the other end of the satellite phone. But until then our hands are tied by the law," Brian Whittaker explained and he made it no secret that he was very frustrated with the fact that they could not act as they wanted to.

On board the *Northern Explorer*, Amundsen Gulf, Darnley Bay, Saturday, October 8th

With everybody still in shock, Chuck Hogan took a little radio out of his pocket and called his friend Robert Tyrell and two of the American scientists to the bridge. Together they would have much better control over their hostages. Robert Tyrell walked by the dead body of the First Officer and impassively looked at it before he stopped beside Chuck.

"What happened? I thought we wanted to avoid things like that," he asked, pointing to the lifeless body.

"It had to be done. I had to set an example," Chuck said coldly, briskly.

Natascha shivered with fear as she listened to the two cold-blooded mercenaries. She never experienced such callousness. She closed her eyes for a moment, trying to shake their conversation from her head. Her thoughts soon rested on Nick, her father, and the rest of the team. She had no idea where they were. She clenched her fists at the thought and opened her eyes again with hope. She looked to the other hostages, searching for any faith in the situation. She fought the tears when all she could detect was their blank terrified faces.

"Captain Rasmussen," Chuck calmly said and looked at the Captain.

"I'll now establish the rules of our further cooperation. If I'm going to ask you a direct question, then I expect a prompt and straight answer. Do you understand this?"

"Yes, I do."

Chuck slowly walked over to Astrid, who tried to shy away, but her back touched the wall before she made it one meter away. Chuck touched her hair and looked back at the Captain while Astrid sobbed in fear.

"If you should lie to me, or if I get the simple feeling that you may lie to me, or in the case that you try to trick me, or you're not completely honest with me, I can guarantee you that I'll shoot your beloved radio operator in the knee with a large caliber gun. Do you understand this?" Chuck asked calmly as Astrid collapsed to her knees sobbing. She subconsciously covered her knees with fear.

The Captain swallowed hard, but looking at his First Officer's corpse, he didn't doubt Chuck Hogan for a second.

"Yes, I do understand. We'll all do as you say."

"Very well. That didn't take too long. First, I need you to announce this message here over the speakers to the last corner of this ship. And trust me when I'm telling you that your radio operator will appreciate that you follow this message to the letter," Chuck Hogan commanded before he gave the Captain a piece of paper. Together with the Captain, Chuck walked over to the communication panel. Captain Rasmussen picked up his glasses and looked at the message, before he followed Chuck's order.

As soon as the Captain had finished his announcement, Chuck nodded to Robert Tyrell, who immediately left the bridge with Sean Greenstein. Jenna Mason took two monitors from the surveillance system out of the radio room and installed them on a table beside the communication panel.

Natascha spent much of her time focusing on good thoughts, things that would help keep herself under control, but the moment she looked at the dead body of the First Officer she felt her nausea return. She fought the images that replayed in her mind, but nothing was shaking it. She exhaustively leaned back against the wall and sat down with her eyes closed. She swallowed hard and took a couple deep breaths. Feeling a little better, she opened her eyes again after a few minutes. When she looked around she noticed that nothing changed, except the picture on the monitors. Both cameras showed two different doors. Natascha was certain the first door lead to the large conference room. The second monitor showed a guard standing in front of a simple cabin door. Natascha looked closer and identified the cabin number as her own. Hopeful she may have retrieved something useful, Natascha glanced back to the first monitor when something moved towards the conference room. Her jaw dropped slowly as the blood froze in her veins..

Home Office and Operational Headquarters of *EuroSecCorporation*, London, Sunday, October 9th

"Mr. Whittaker, Mr. Schwartze, as you know I have the highest respect for you, your men and your company, and I know from my old friend here that the service your company provides is highly regarded. At this time our options are limited. The research vessel is, as far as I understand, in Canadian waters. That means we have to notify the Canadian authorities. Another big problem is that there were two politicians on board the ship and we have no idea what role they're playing. It might be just a coincidence, they might be taken hostage, they might have left the ship unharmed or they might even run the show. We simply don't know, so we have to inform both the American and the Canadian authorities about that fact and I'll do my best to find out the whereabouts of those two politicians. As soon as we have some hard data and some facts in our hands, we have to immediately contact the Norwegian and the German authorities, since they are their citizens. If there is an operation, it would be under the command of the Canadians, there's no way around that. Just to get everybody moving and on the same page it will take us at least twenty four hours since it's a weekend. That would be our best case scenario."

Thin Ice

"I know. Hope for the best and plan for the worst. My gut feeling somehow tells me that both the American and Canadian politician are in on this and that they're pulling off something big. I'm having a hard time believing that a sitting US Senator and a Member of the Canadian Parliament are flying thousands of kilometers just for a photo op. Let's say they are involved in this. My biggest issue is that they'll have everything organized in such a way that no one over there will get out of their chair until everything is over."

"Would you really go that far to accuse a sitting US Senator and a member of the Canadian Parliament based on your gut feeling?"

"Maybe, maybe not, but in my position you develop a certain feeling for certain situations. Klaus and I are used to analyzing all options," Brian explained before he leaned forward in his chair.

"Damnnit," he cursed and slammed his fist on the table.

"We need more information. Does my brother-in-law know those two politicians. If so, how does he know them? Why? From where? What are they doing? Why are they on a research vessel thousands of kilometers away from their work? Why are they traveling to the research vessel with the person who has always been at the same place and time of two unsuccessful assassination attempts? Why the hell did we lose contact with our team the moment they confirmed the presence of that guy? And why in God's name can we not get them back on the phone?" Brian Whittaker continued with frustration.

Inspector Conolly sipped his coffee and looked at the floor. He only knew too well the helpless feeling Brian Whittaker had just described.

"Listen Mr. Whittaker. I know how feel right now, but you also know that your company is in no legal position to prosecute anybody in this matter. I'll get back to Scotland Yard and arrange everything. I will recommend to appoint you as our liaison officer, since your in-depth knowledge in this case will most certainly help us. But before I go I have some questions about your men on board that ship."

"Of course," Klaus Schwartze said and handed him a file, while Brian shouted to Brigitte to get him on the next flight to Canada.

"Five men, one woman. All former members of military Special Forces. Well-trained and well-equipped. Before we hired them we thoroughly checked them out. They're more brain than muscles. We can't use any loose cannons," retired General Klaus Schwartze explained.

Inspector Conolly looked at the details of those six people.

"And you've now lost all contact with them for over three hours?" he finally asked and swallowed.

"That, my dear Inspector, is the reason why I'm so nervous. In order to neutralize them you need a well-trained group of specialists who have some balls." Klaus sighed then continued, "Many specialists."

On board the *Northern Explorer*, Amundsen Gulf, Darnley Bay, Saturday, October 8th

Natascha's eyes widened as she watched the events unfold on the first monitor. She closed and reopened her eyes to be sure she was not imagining anything. Two masked men welded the door from the conference room permanently to the door frame. It was clear that no one inside was meant to survive whatever was going on.

Is Nick in there? What about my father? The very thought unnerved her more than she already was. Natascha didn't know what had happened to them or where they were. The sudden panic twisted her stomach in knots. She fought the constraint as fear gripped her tightly, but her battle was already lost when her eyes filled with tears and, still looking at the monitor, she started to sob.

This is not going to help you! This is not going to help them! Pull yourself together, you can do this! she demanded from herself. Natascha closed her eyes to concentrate and took some deep breaths before she turned on her knees to stand up again. She moved her wrists for comfort, but they were still tightly bound behind her back. Satisfied that she made it to her feet, she felt much better.

Okay, there's no point sitting here and crying all the time. What can I do to help them? What would Nick and them do? They would most likely wait for an opportunity to overpower them and that would be the end of it. Wait, they're all trained and much stronger, and they're a team. What would Shira do? Bad example, she would most likely be the first one to kick someone's butt. What would she do if she was alone? Information. That's the key. Information is important. If I want to help my boys then I need information.

Natascha took a couple more deep breaths and opened her eyes.

Okay, what do I see? The Captain, the Second Officer, Astrid and two Navigation Officers who are always on the bridge.

The young German's observation was interrupted by two men who came back to the bridge. Natascha identified them as those who had just welded the door to the frame.

"And? How many are safely locked away?" Chuck demanded to know.

"Thirty-two," Sean Greenstein replied and pulled his ski mask off. It was only now that Natascha realized that they were wearing the official work overalls of the German scientists. Sean ran his hand through his hair and added, "They have enough supplies for the seven days."

Chuck picked up a list with all the names of the people still on board.

"Thirty-two locked away, two dead and six up here with us. Well done, Captain. You didn't try to trick me, that means I won't shoot your radio operator's knee. Keep co-operating and there won't be a need for any unnecessary harm," the assassin said before he finally turned his attention towards Natascha again.

"My apologies for keeping you waiting so long, but I first had to make sure the ship is under our control," he mentioned and waved at Nelson Garcia from the American scientist team.

"Take her away and lock her up. Don't touch her, we need her later on," he commanded matter-of-factly.

Without rendering any resistance, Natascha let Nelson grab her arm and push her out the door.

If I was useless to them, then I'd already be dead by now. That means they need me for something. They don't want me dead and they don't want to rape me and that Senator is going to think about me for a while. Could be worse. Natascha told herself with comfort and her thoughts drifted once more to her father and her friends, leaving an unusual pain in her heart.

Ariel and the others immediately stopped whispering the moment they noticed that someone opened their door and turned the light on. Squinting under the sudden illumination, they watched as Nelson Garcia pushed Natascha inside the cabin. With her hands still tied behind her back, she immediately lost balance and tripped over Ariel before she landed on Ole-Einar, who yelled in pain. Nelson left and locked the cabin door once more.

Natascha rolled from Ole-Einar on her knees and stood up.

"I'm sorry," she sobbed and looked at Ole-Einar.

"Natascha, quiet, or they'll come back," Shira hissed.

Natascha controlled herself as best she could and just realized that both her father and Nick were also in the cabin. She kneeled down beside her father, tears streaming down her cheeks.

"Dad, are you okay?" she choked out her whisper.

"Yes, I'm okay," her father painfully groaned, since the position they were tied in was not the most comfortable one. Despite his own situation he was happy to see his daughter not only alive, but also unharmed.

"How are you Natascha. What did they do to you?" Nick asked after he rolled on his side to get a better look at her.

Natascha leaned down and gave him a kiss.

"I'm fine, they didn't do anything."

"You're bleeding. What happened?"

"That was in the dive control room, just before they took me to the bridge."

"You were on the bridge? What did you see?" Ariel asked hopeful.

"Yes," Natascha whispered carefully and was proud of herself. She knew gathering information was the best idea.

"I saw the Captain, the First and Second Officer, Astrid and the two Navigation Officers. Oh my God, I forgot. Vitali! He's dead! He is lying in the dive control room. And they shot the First Officer," she stammered, tears immediately running down her face again.

"Not so loud," Shira hissed at her.

"Sorry," Natascha apologized and closed her eyes for a second to regain control.

"Okay, back to the bridge. Those were the only hostages I've seen up there. Okay, just let me think here for a second, I want to be sure I don't mix it up."

Natascha closed her eyes again and took a couple seconds to recall what she saw just minutes earlier.

"Okay, now I got it in the right order. When I got back with that stupid Senator, one of the cameramen waited for me with a gun. He lead me to the dive control room where I saw Vitali. They killed Vitali," Natascha cried and fought to maintain control.

"We know, that was their leader just before they overpowered us," Shira explained in a sad voice.

Natascha took a couple deep breaths and continued.

"Okay, I had to stay in the dive control room and that cameraman was guarding me, while the Senator left. I assume he went to the bridge, but I'm not sure. A few minutes later, he came back with Jenna and this other cameraman. His name is Chuck and he's their leader. The Canadian politician was also with them and that assistant as well. The Senator then told Chuck to make sure that everything goes according to plan."

"Both politicians are in on this?" Ariel asked and was stunned.

"Big time. They discovered an oil field close by. During the dive with the Senator I found a brand new pipeline. Later in the dive control room the Senator yelled at me and told me some weird stuff, so I rammed my knee in his balls…"

"You did what?" Nick interrupted suddenly, the shock overpowering his tone.

"Not so loud!" Ariel hissed at his friend.

"I rammed my knees in his nuts. He deserved it, you should have heard the rubbish he was saying," Natascha defended herself.

Nick shook his head in disbelief.

"What happened next?" Ole-Einar questioned impatiently.

"After I did that, Chuck slapped me in the face, I got scared and fell down. That's why my lip is bleeding. Jenna wanted to shoot me, but Chuck told her they need me for something later on. She tied my hands behind my back and searched me for any weapons. One of Chuck's guys flew the two politicians and their assistant out with the helicopter. I think they have a second helicopter in Paulatuk as well and Chuck told his guy to come back as soon as he refills both helicopters. After that, Chuck and Jenna brought me up to the bridge, where Chuck shot the First Officer to demonstrate that he's in control. The First Officer didn't do anything, he just stood there and looked at him when he got shot. After that Chuck ordered the Captain to announce that all crew members had to get into the conference room."

"Yes, we did hear that."

"After that I could see that two of them checked with the personnel list that everybody was inside that conference room. They were wearing ski masks and the coveralls from our scientists and they welded the watertight door to the frame. But I also heard them saying that they have food for the next couple days. Jenna took both monitors with your security cameras and reinstalled them on the bridge. One camera shows them the welded door from the conference room, the other camera shows them this door, but you also have a guard standing in front of it," Natascha finished her observation.

"Do you still have anything with you?" Shira asked.

"I had a ballpoint pen, but I think I lost it in the control room when I fell," Natascha shook her head sadly.

"Did they call eachother by name or did they use code words?" Shira asked hurriedly.

"No, as far as I could hear, they're on a first name basis," Natascha explained and shook her head.

Shira threw Ariel a concerned look. They had a very serious problem.

Being satisfied with what he saw, Chuck Hogan looked up from the monitors and out the windows to watch Martin Cunningham. Martin had just landed the refueled helicopter safely on the helipad and told Chuck that the politicians were safely on their way back to Inuvik.

Chuck nodded and turned around to signal his sister to follow him outside.

"Okay Jenna, time for us to move on. I know there are two Dive Officers on the ship, and I know from the personnel list that they're not with the other hostages. One is dead, but I need you to tell me who the second Dive Officer is," the American asked and looked at his sister, who shook her head in disbelief.

"Chuck, there's no other Dive Officer on board this ship. The other Dive Officer has left the ship two days ago. Vitali was the only other. Of all the people in there, you had to shoot him!" his sister snapped at him.

For a moment Chuck thought that someone had punched him in the face. He had not thought about this.

"Shit, that doesn't help us," he whispered and turned around to go back to the bridge. Once inside, he looked at Captain Rasmussen.

"Captain, I want to inform you that the rules of our cooperation are still in effect. I will not hesitate for even a second to shoot your lovely radio operator in the knee if you lie to me, if I get the feeling that you lie to me or if you trick me. Is this still understood?" Chuck Hogan repeated the rules, knowing very well that no one present on the bridge would have forgotten them. For Chuck it was more the mind game behind it, to constantly remind them of the horrific consequences should they not do as he said.

"Yes, I do understand," Captain Rasmussen replied with a broken voice.

"Very well. I'm in need of a person capable to operate the gas panels for the surface supplied diving gear for a dive to a depth of seventy two meters. Who's capable of doing this?"

"Excuse me?" the Captain asked and obviously didn't understand.

"You heard me right. Who can operate the gas panels for a surface supplied dive to a depth of seventy-two meters. I know you have two Dive Officers for that purpose. Unfortunately one of them is on his way back home and the other one is regrettably dead. So, who else can do this?"

"Vitali is dead? Oh my God," Captain Rasmussen stammered and his eyes fell to the floor with concentration. He struggled to find a name as the rest of his crew behind him sobbed at the news. Captain Rasmussen's thoughts betrayed him as he could only think about Vitali.

Chuck walked determinedly towards Astrid, who started to scream once she saw him coming for her. Her back against the wall and her eyes closed, she crouched on the floor and cried. Chuck pulled Astrid by her hair down on the floor and turned her onto her belly before he pressed his gun in the back of her knee. He sharply looked back up to Captain Rasmussen.

"It depends on how long you want to stay in that depth, I suppose. It's not only about operating the gas panel right, it's also about mixing the right breathing gas," Captain Rasmussen finally stammered.

"Who else can do it?" Chuck asked in a dangerous voice and cocked his gun.

"Listen! I didn't lie and I didn't trick you. To operate the gas panel correctly is not the easiest thing. I believe there are two more people who can do it, but I beg you to take the gun away. It's not necessary."

"Who else?" Chuck asked unimpressed.

"I assume Dr. Weber and his daughter might be able to do it."

Chuck thought about this answer for a few seconds and finally let go of Astrid, who simply curled up and cried.

"Why those two?"

"Well, that depends on the depth of the dive. I do know they're both certified to dive that deep, although Dr. Weber doesn't dive that deep anymore himself, but Natascha does. That's why they both know what kind of breathing gas they need for such dives and how to mix it. To operate the gas panel itself is one thing, but to mix the right breathing gas is a completely different thing and you need to know how to do it."

Chuck considered what the Norwegian skipper had just told him and paced the room before he finally stopped in front of the monitors. He didn't see it first, but then he noticed the light was turned on in Shira's cabin.

"Jenna!" he called his sister.

Jenna walked over the moment she heard the tone in his voice.

"What is it?" she asked and also looked at the monitor.

"Why is the light on in that cabin? I specifically said that they should not have any lights on."

"I don't know," Jenna shook her head and picked up her little radio.

"Brian," she called the guard at the cabin door.

"Yes?"

"Brian, is the light on in the cabin?"

"Yes, Nelson turned it on when he brought the woman down here," Brian explained and shrugged his shoulders, looking at the camera.

Infuriated by Nelson's stupidity, Jenna turned away from the monitor, while Chuck hissed a curse and grabbed the radio from his sister.

"You idiots put her in the same cabin with the others? You were suppose to put her in the cabin next door. Bring both the woman and her father on the bridge. Now!" Chuck yelled at Brian and threw the radio on a chair, not even waiting for a response.

He walked over to a window and stared outside for a while. His frustration was getting the better of him. His temper cooled the longer he looked out the window. He turned around again after a moment.

"Okay, sister. Time to move to *Phase C*."

- 18 -

Inside Shira's and Natascha's cabin, on board the *Northern Explorer*, Amundsen Gulf, Darnley Bay, Saturday, October 8th

"Okay, let's summarize. We have to assume that there are at least eight hostage-takers. Everybody else from the crew is locked up, so I don't think that there are any sleepers anywhere. We know that the four American scientists work for a company which produced components for both chemical and biological weapons and that this company received some money from CIA black accounts. Worst case scenario, all eight of them are former Special Forces and now members of CIA Black Ops. That would explain why the two politicians are involved in this. If they're really pulling strings, then we'll be entirely on our own, since they will most likely make sure that nothing of this ever gets public. Even if some alarm bells are ringing somewhere, it would take them at least twenty-four hours before they get here. I think it's safe to say that both politicians will be safely back in their office in time to convince everybody who's nervous that there's nothing wrong up here. So, bottom line we're dealing with eight bad guys and we're locked inside a cabin with only one door, video surveillance and a guard. Does anyone have a weapon?" Ariel whispered.

Everybody shook their head, before the Israeli continued.

"Okay, we also know that they don't hesitate to kill and that they're willing to kill a large number of people to get what they want, otherwise they wouldn't have locked them up. They even went so far as to make sure that everybody thinks that it was us who locked them up."

"Do you really think that the crew believes it's us who locked them up?" Dr. Weber asked abhorred by the very idea.

"Yes, that's only if they ever see the light of day again. Once they've been locked away for several days in a small room, all they remember are the guys wearing German coveralls. They'll swear that it was us who locked them up. But they don't want them to starve to death. They're planning something else. Something that'll cover up their tracks. Since they allow everybody to listen in on their discussions and since they're calling each other by their first name, we're already dead as far as they are concerned. Our only hope is the fact that my phone call to the office got interrupted. But there are two things I don't know: Why are we still alive and how do they plan to kill everybody?" the Israeli wondered.

"Well," Shira whispered and continued the theory. "Sooner or later someone will investigate what happened on the ship. Even if they're planning to sink it, there's no water up here deep enough to prohibit them from investigating it. They've already welded one door to the frame. The Investigators will know right away that this was a crime. Given the number of dead people, this'll clearly be considered a terrorist attack.

And in the unlikely event that there are any survivors, they'll tell the Investigators that we're the terrorists, otherwise they wouldn't have used our coveralls."

"That would make sense," Ariel agreed.

"But we still don't know how they want to kill us..." Shira trailed, her theory unable to fill the gap.

"Oh my God!" Natascha gasped as she rose to her knees.

"I know what they want to do. They..."

But before Natascha could tell them, the cabin door opened and two of the hostage-takers walked in.

"Shut up! The first one who says a word will be executed. Let's go," Brian said and helped Natascha up. He pushed her in front of him and outside the cabin, where Jenna was already waiting. Next, Brian stepped over Nick and cut Dr. Richard Weber's legs free. Since Richard had trouble with the blood circulation in his legs, Brian had to help him up and out of the cabin. As soon as they retrieved their two hostages from the cabin, Jenna walked in and put the infrared surveillance camera on the little table.

"How's the picture?" she asked over her radio.

"Little bit more to the left, yes, that's better," someone radioed back.

"And you keep your mouth shut," she said on her way out as she turned the light off and locked the door.

Ariel shook his head in resignation.

Nelson and Jenna pushed Natascha and her father into the bridge. The only good thing for Natascha at the moment was the fact that everybody was still alive, although it was clear that Astrid was an emotional wreck.

Chuck Hogan turned towards the two Germans.

"Dr. Weber. I do have a question for you. Are you and your daughter capable to operate the gas panel in the dive control room for a dive to seventy-two meters with a bottom time of around forty-five minutes?"

"Excuse me?" Richard asked clueless.

Chuck walked towards one of the windows and looked outside again.

"Captain Rasmussen, would you please be so kind to explain to Dr. Weber the rules of our cooperation?" the American mercenary asked politely.

With a hateful glare, the Norwegian Captain turned his attention from Chuck Hogan back to the floor in resignation.

"Should we lie to him, or even if he suspects us of lying to him, or if we try to trick him or if we're trying to withhold some valuable information, he'll not hesitate to shoot Astrid in her knee," Captain Rasmussen said tiredly.

Natascha's father was shocked at the cruelty, but it also explained the emotional state Astrid was in. Knowing the rules, he thought about the original question.

"Well, a bottom time of forty-five minutes for a surface supplied dive in such a depth is very long and it would require a huge amount of breathing gas for the decompression. Given the water temperature, anything longer than twenty minutes would be a physiological nightmare," the German Professor explained.

"Does that mean you could control and execute such a dive with the available gear on board?" Chuck asked pointedly.

Dr. Richard Weber thought for a second.

"Yes, I think I'd be able to run the gas panel if I get the chance to read the manual before the dive."

"Perfect. Miss Kleinfeld, I couldn't help but noticed that you're not using the same family name as your father. Do you have a special reason for that? Do you question your father's feelings for you?"

Natascha had decided not to fall for his mind games. After she had seen Astrid, Natascha did not want to give him the pleasure of breaking her. She didn't answer his question and looked at him disgusted.

"Do you really want Astrid to suffer tremendous pain so far away from any medical help?"

"No, I don't," Natascha snapped at him. "The reason I don't carry my fathers last name is none of your goddamn business. I trust my father."

"Excellent. You have to trust him since you'll be diving that deep," the American finally said.

The shock hit Natascha quickly. *I can't dive. I'm most certainly pregnant!* Natascha couldn't say anything. The emotions and the shock she felt completely overwhelmed her.

"My daughter can't do this dive. She's the only one who can calculate the decompression on the go if something goes wrong and the dive takes longer than planned. There's a reason why this gas panel has to be operated by two different people."

"This sounds like you're trying to trick me," Chuck calmly said and briskly walked towards Astrid. She immediately screamed again and tried to crawl away.

"No! I didn't try to trick you!" Dr. Richard Weber shouted.

"Fact is, I haven't done such deep dives for years, and I don't have the time and skills anymore to get back into multigas decompression dives. My daughter is the only one who has the knowledge about this. Besides that, the gas panel has to be operated by two people to eliminate individual mistakes."

Chuck stopped, just one meter away from Astrid. He seemed to be thinking. He remembered the gas mixing panel and the control panel and he admitted that it would be very complicated for a single person to operate it. One tiny mistake in the calculations could have horrible consequences for the diver. He would need someone who could dive that deep without running the risk that Natascha and her father would try to kill them by issuing the wrong breathing gas.

It has to be someone they care about, Chuck thought.

Suddenly he knew the answer and he smiled before he looked at the Professor again.

"Okay, I believe you. I do have another question. This morning I asked you how deep your divers can operate and you told me that all remaining divers from your group are qualified to dive seventy meters deep. Do you remember telling me that?" Chuck asked and demonstratively looked at Astrid.

Dr. Richard Weber felt the nausea in his stomach when Chuck slowly started to walk towards the Norwegian woman again.

"It's true," Natascha blurted before he took another step.

"Four of the guys in my cabin can dive that deep."

Natascha looked at her father for support. She knew that at least Nick, Ole-Einar, Oliver as well as Olaf were trained to dive that deep, but for Natascha it was also the only chance to get one of them out of the cabin.

Chuck nodded and seemed to be satisfied. Then, without asking or saying anything, he pinned Astrid down to the floor with his knee and pressed his gun to the back of her leg.

"My final question," Chuck shouted over Astrid's hysterical screams, "Those six people in your cabin aren't scientists, are they?"

Scotland Yard,
London, Sunday, October 9th

Looking at his watch, Sean MacLeod yawned and stretched. It was already five in the morning by now and he sat together with Inspector Conolly in the interrogation room. At the opposite side of the table sat Gordon Ramshaw. His only statement was that he had confirmed his own identity and that he insisted on the presence of his lawyers. Since then, he had not said a word and simply sipped at the coffee that was offered to him. Without showing his frustration, Inspector Conolly rose from his chair and left the room closely followed by Sean MacLeod. They went through the door next to them and walked into the observation room, from where they watched Gordon Ramshaw through the one-way-mirror window. Gordon still seemed to be completely unimpressed as he drank his coffee.

"How long can you hold him without officially pressing charges against him?" Sean asked his former colleague.

"Not much longer, I'm afraid. You know the law. Not much has changed since you left us. If we don't catch a break soon, we'll have a problem."

Sean poured two more cups of coffee for his friend and himself when Inspector Conolly's assistant walked in. She was holding up a file and seemed to be very pleased with what she found.

"It took us a while, but since we concentrated on Reykjavik first, we saved a lot of time. We found out that only four people traveled to both Berlin as well as Reykjavik during the times when both assassination attempts took place. I'm taking a wild guess but I'm sure we can skip the first person. He's seventy-two years old, lives in Frankfurt and visits his two sons, who live in Berlin and Iceland. We could follow his travel patterns back for the last twelve years and he checks out to be okay. The second person is a British woman in her late forties. She extensively used her credit card on both trips. Both times she went shopping and she used her card to pay for pretty much everything. According to the paper trail she left, she wasn't even near your people at the time in question. That leaves us with two Americans. Two guys by the name of Chuck Hogan and Robert Tyrell. It's interesting that both of them were on the same American Airlines flight from Boston to Frankfurt, from where they flew separately to Berlin two days later, but within thirty minutes of each other. Just twenty-four hours after the assassination attempt, Chuck Hogan takes the same route back, while Robert Tyrell takes his flight back to Boston from Paris. During their complete time in Germany, they never paid anything with a credit card, not a room, not a rental car, they even didn't withdraw cash with those credit cards. Same thing for Iceland. Both took the same flight from Boston to Reykjavik with Iceland Air and spent the next five days in Reykjavik without using their credit cards once to rent a car or pay for some food or a hotel. After the attack, they take the next flight out of Iceland and here's the interesting part. While Robert Tyrell takes the first flight back to Boston, Chuck Hogan travels to London Heathrow first, before he boards a first class flight with American Airlines back to Boston just three hours after his arrival."

"He was here in London?" Sean MacLeod asked in disbelief.

"Yes, but he was only here for a few hours on Wednesday, July sixth, arriving from Reykjavik at seven fourty five in the morning and leaving for Boston at eleven fifteen just three and a half hours later."

"Impossible to do something outside the airport within this time frame. He flew with two different airlines, so he had to check in again. He most likely traveled with carry-on luggage only, but still impossible," Inspector Conolly said and looked up and through the window at Gordon Ramshaw.

"We got even more. Once we knew that he was in London, we concentrated on the airport. One of our computer specialists found his credit card. Since they're mercenaries, I doubt they have access to the latest phony passports. That explains why they travel under their own name, but as soon as they're at their destination, they disappear. When our computer specialist followed Chuck Hogan's credit card, he found out that Mr. Hogan used his credit card that morning from eight fourty eight to nine eightteen at a local internet café. We checked the server and found the websites he visited. He started with a few American newspapers from the Boston area, with a particular interest in the sport section. After that he googled if he could find anything in the Icelandic media about the incident up there, but he didn't spend much time there. Once he was done with that, he checked the online logbook and diary of the expedition to see if he could find something there. Finally he searched for London based security companies. Although *EuroSecCorporation* is only listed on third position, he visited your website first and he looked at each individual page. He almost spent ten minutes on your website. After that he opened the website from three other security companies, but he spent less than a minute on their sites. His interest was definitely set on your company. I would say he's our man."

"Thank you very much. That was excellent work, Shelley. Please stay on it and keep pushing. Have we heard something from our Canadian or American friends?"

"No, but I have arranged that any call will be directly forwarded to you," Shelley said on her way out.

"Thank you again, Shelley," Inspector Conolly called after her, while Shelley closed the door behind her.

"That was really impressive," Sean MacLeod admitted to his friend and looked at the door Shelley left before he called Klaus Schwartze.

"Yes, she really is one of our best people. That's why I wanted to have her on board. Okay, we're in much better shape now. I assume we'll know much more about those two gentlemen within the next thirty minutes. Now we just have to find out what exactly this Hogan guy did here in Heathrow. He didn't come here to check the news in an internet café. I'm sure he was here to meet someone," Inspector Conolly said and fell silent the moment Sean gave his update to Klaus Schwartze.

"Brian Whittaker is on his way to the airport. He'll leave in one hour with the first flight to New York and from there he'll go on to Canada," Sean MacLeod explained after he finished his call.

Putting his cell phone back in it's belt pouch, Sean noticed the little box with Gordon Ramshaw's belongings. He walked over to the table and looked at them.

"Do you mind?" he asked Inspector Conolly, who shook his head and walked towards him to have a closer look himself.

Sean went through the belongings and picked up a well used blackberry and reactivated it. Luckily for him, it was not turned off and did not require any password.

"Well, we got to get lucky once in a while," Sean mumbled and activated the menu. It did not take him long to find the satellite number.

"It's saved under *Eddy*. No last name, no company name, nothing."

Sean continued to navigate through the menu and opened the scheduler. As he had expected, Mr. Ramshaw's scheduler didn't show any free time. Using the buttons, Sean MacLeod went back to the morning hours of Wednesday, July 6th.

"Interesting. The morning of the sixth is empty. It only says *Terminal two, Gate D*. I wouldn't be surprised if this is where he met Chuck Hogan," Sean said.

Inspector Conolly looked at Gordon and back at the display. Before he could say anything, the Blackberry went active and started vibrating. Both Sean MacLeod and Inspector Conolly looked at the device as if they were holding a hand grenade. The display simply read *Eddy* as well as the satellite phone number.

Knowing that this call came from someone on board the *Northern Explorer*, Sean MacLeod swallowed hard. He glanced at Inspector Conolly, accepted the call and activated the speaker.

**On board the *Northern Explorer*, Amundsen Gulf, Darnley Bay,
Saturday, October 8th**
Although her hands were still tied behind her back, Natascha ran to Astrid to help her, but Jenna pulled her back by her hair the moment she started running. Screaming out in pain, Natascha fell to her knees and could do nothing but watch Chuck kneel on her, pressing his gun in the back of the knee of the screaming Norwegian woman.

"So? What is the answer? Three…Two…One…," Chuck asked and cocked his gun again.

"It's true," Natascha shouted in pain, her eyes filling with tears.

"They're employees of a security company that our institute hired to protect me and my father. They used to work for the military before that and four of them are technical divers. Please let go of her, I beg you. We'll do what you want," Natascha begged, her voice shaking.

"What about the other two? Are they not technical divers?"

"No, they're not."

"Were they members of a military special unit?"

"Yes, as far as I know," Natascha sobbed and lowered her head. She felt guilty of betraying her friends, but for her it seemed to be the only way to help Astrid at this moment. Natascha was hoping that they would eventually forgive her.

Although Natascha crouched on the floor, she looked up at Chuck and Astrid. It seemed to her that Chuck wasn't surprised about her answers at all. Relieved that Chuck finally released Astrid, Natascha stood up again.

"Very well. I just wanted to make sure you're playing by my rules. I already knew all that and we also found their weapons. Captain Rasmussen?" Chuck said and turned around to face the Norwegian.

"Yes?"

"How long would it take for the *Northern Explorer* to be under way?"

Captain Rasmussen walked over to the control panel and checked some gauges.

"We could go slow ahead within thirty minutes," he explained.

"Perfect," Chuck Hogan said and gave Captain Rasmussen a piece of paper.

"Pull anchor and maneuver the ship to exactly this position. Once there, make sure that we hold that position and that we don't drift away. It's not only in your best interest that you master this," Chuck added and demonstratively looked at Astrid again.

Captain Rasmussen took the paper with the coordinates and punched them into the navigation computer.

"We can be there in approximately two hours," he explained and looked up from the monitor.

"Excellent. You can go ahead right away. Don't forget what will happen if you try to trick me."

"Astrid will have to radio in a message," Captain Rasmussen said.

"Why is that?" Chuck asked distrustful.

"Because the *Northern Explorer* is over eighty meters long and with that size we're simply not allowed to cross the shipping channel at free will. Although this is the North-West Passage it doesn't mean that the rules of the sea don't apply up here. We're still registered at this anchorage for the next three days with both Traffic Control as well as the Coast Guard. If we pull anchor and cross the official shipping lane just to drop anchor over thirty miles north, then this is not a problem. But we do have to notify them and file a new navigational plan. It was one of the conditions prior this expedition. Any little incident can be enough for the Canadian Coast Guard to come out and inspect this ship thoroughly. This expedition and this research vessel is only tolerated in Canadian waters, but we're not welcome. And for that reason, my radio operator has to call in our new navigation plan, and I would prefer if she could do that without having a gun pressed at her," the Captain explained, eyeing Chuck's weapon.

Chuck thought for a moment before he looked at Astrid.

"Okay, but if you still want to be able to walk, I really recommend you don't try anything stupid. Do you understand me?"

Chuck had no trouble intimidating Astrid.

Astrid was ghostly pale, exhausted and shaken as she nodded. She tried to stand up but her legs shook violently with fear.

"Let go of me!" Natascha snapped at Jenna and walked over to Astrid. Kneeling down, Natascha allowed Astrid to hold on to her shoulder for support, while Chuck called for another guy on his radio.

Without raising any suspicion, Natascha moved Astrid away from the others. Looking for support, Astrid held on to Natascha and let her head rest on the young German's shoulder. This was Natascha's only chance.

"The politicians are behind it, there are eight hostage-takers, four of them are the American scientists. Ariel's team is locked up but okay. Try Ariel's computer," Natascha whispered as carefully as she could, making sure that her mouth was covered by Astrid's hair.

Just seconds later, Nelson came over and grasped Astrid's arm and pushed her away from Natascha and into the radio room. Still shaking, Astrid sat down on her chair and looked at the computer in front of her. Nelson took a few steps backwards and took position at the door. Astrid selected the right channel and called Traffic Control, but she knew that it was pointless to tell them anything about what was happening. They were too far away to help in time. The Norwegian told them the new navigation plan as well as the new coordinates for their next anchorage. While she waited for the confirmation, Astrid looked at Ariel's laptop, which was within arms reach. She saw the green power light and thought feverishly.

Natascha mentioned something about a special force unit. Ariel did several background checks from this computer and he spoke Hebrew. Maybe he's still online. Astrid thought and gave a quick look at Nelson, who only halfheartedly guarded her with his back turned towards her.

Astrid shifted with her chair so much that the chair hit the table. Nelson immediately spun around and looked at her.

"I'm sorry," Astrid said and pushed her chair back a little bit, before she looked at the monitor again.

"Will take a few minutes. We'll get a written confirmation for the new navigation plan. Once it's in I have to verify it," Astrid lied.

Nelson just nodded and turned his back towards her again. He was much more interested in what was going on on the bridge.

Astrid looked at Ariel's laptop. Since Ariel used a mouse, bumping the table was enough for the laptop to activate itself again.

She had a hard time showing no reaction when she noticed that it was still in the message mode and pulled the laptop closer.

"What are you doing?" Nelson turned around, but didn't come any closer.

"We have a redundant system. The laptop is connected with the main computer. The last two days we had several system crashes and we're using the laptop as a back-up. If I don't update it manually, it will automatically send an emergency signal to the Coast Guard when there's another system crash. Same idea as an EPIRB," Astrid explained and tried to sound as convincing as possible.

If he comes over now to check it out, I'm dead, she thought.

"What the hell is an EPRIB?" Nelson asked, spelling the letters wrong.

"It's called an emergency personal radio indicator beacon. As soon as it's activated it will send it's current position to a satellite."

Nelson thought for a second and decided to believe her before he looked back at the bridge.

Idiot! Astrid thought and concentrated on Ariel's laptop.

On the bridge Chuck stepped closer to Natascha and her father. Jenna watched the Captain and the remaining three people on the bridge, while two of their men were outside on the deck preparing the anchor winches.

"Let's go. We'll go to the dive control room," Chuck commanded and pushed both of them ahead of him.

At the door to the dive control room Chuck asked them to stop so that he could untie their hands. Both Natascha and Richard massaged their wrists to increase the blood circulation to their hands. Chuck opened the door and turned the lights on.

The moment Natascha saw Vitali Vachenko's dead body on the ground, her eyes instantly filled with tears and she kneeled down beside him.

"Don't waste your valuable time, he's dead," Chuck said bitterly.

Natascha swallowed hard and closed his eyes as best she could. It was the least she could do for her instructor.

Chuck looked at both the gas and the control panel, before he turned towards Natascha and Richard.

"Okay, listen carefully, here's the situation. We have to do several dives with the surface supplied gear to a depth of maximum seventy-two meters. You said that we can operate with a bottom time of around twenty minutes?"

Natascha looked at her father before she answered.

"Generally yes. Definitely not longer than twenty-five. It all depends on how many dives you're planning."

"Well, we do have four divers at our disposal. They will dive around the clock, which means that they'll probably dive up to two times a day, considering the decompression they have to do."

Natascha had to swallow. She knew that this would end in a disaster.

"They need enough surface interval between the dives, otherwise they won't be able to dive that profile."

"Really? We'll deal with that problem at that time. I'm a little bit on a tight schedule here," Chuck said ironically.

"What about the canister that's at the pipeline?" Natascha asked quickly, immediately regretting what she said.

It was the first time she saw Chuck completely shocked.

"What do you know about that canister?" Chuck whispered.

It was the most dangerous tone Natascha had heard from that man yet. "You saw it when you were down there with the Senator, correct?"

Natascha nodded. Fear rose in her and she couldn't help but curse herself for being so stupid.

"What did he tell you? What did the Senator tell you about it?" Chuck demanded and stepped closer to Natascha.

Natascha had a hard time not to panic. Chuck was standing right in front of her.

"All he said was that I mustn't touch the canister if I didn't want to be responsible for the death of any organism within a three miles radius…"Natascha whispered slowly, honestly.

"The Senator's an idiot. It has a far greater range than that." Chuck simply said.

"But…"

"Shut up. I don't want to hear anything about the canister. Back to the dives. You have two hours to come up with a dive profile."

"What are they doing down there? It would be helpful to know to set the partial pressure for the oxygen."

"They will do some hard work."

"Hard work? How many dives are we talking about?" Natascha asked, fear raising in her again.

Chuck thought for a few moments.

"When everything goes as planned, we're looking at around twenty dives," he said.

"Twenty?" Natascha shouted in disbelief.

"Yes, twenty. Is that a problem?"

"Yes, that's a problem!" Natascha answered heatedly, still shocked about the number of dives.

"I already told you that I don't care if they die of decompression sickness at the end of the operation."

"I know you don't care about my friends. Fact is that we don't have enough breathing gas for so many technical dives with surface supply," Natascha snapped at the American.

Chuck reached for his gun and aimed at Richard's knee. To her own surprise, Natascha remained completely calm.

"Shooting my father in the knee won't do anything to help your questionable mission to succeed. The reason why we don't have enough breathing gas for such a number of technical dives is simple. We're at the end of the expedition, not at the beginning. During the last two months we did hundreds of technical dives. And just in case you haven't noticed it, but we're in the middle of nowhere up here. Our storage tanks for oxygen, helium and argon are almost empty and it would take days to get new breathing gas."

It was the second time within minutes that Natascha saw Chuck completely shocked. She wanted to throw some idle words at him, but decided against it. Chuck lowered his gun and paced the room again.

"How much gas do we still have?" he asked seriously.

Natascha shrugged her shoulders and walked over to Vitali's desk. She picked up Vitali's clipboard, which the dead Russian had always carried with him, and walked over to the gas panel. The young German opened a few valves, checked the gauges and wrote a couple numbers down. After that she sat at the table and concentrated for the next few minutes.

"If everything goes well, I'd estimate we may have enough gas for around ten, but definitely not more than twelve dives," she said and shook her head.

Chuck cursed. He realized this was something he completely ignored in his planning. Back then he looked at the ships gas supply *before* the expedition, but Natascha was right. The expedition was over, after hundreds of dives. Desperately looking for a solution, he turned around and saw *Odin* outside.

"What about those?" he asked and pointed out the door. "Those are one atmosphere submersibles, correct?"

Natascha nodded.

"Yes, that's correct. They only need compressed air and have an on board oxygen unit."

"Would it be possible to do around eight dives with surface supplied helmets and the rest with the closed circuit rebreathers?"

Natascha looked at her notes.

"Technically possible, yes…We would have enough gas for that, but…."

"What? What is it now?" Chuck barked at her.

Natascha noticed that his temper was rising.

"The problem is that the other four divers don't have that much experience with a closed circuit system. They dive open circuit systems mostly. They all dove rebreathers before, but never that deep," Natascha explained with fear in her voice.

"Then let's hope you give them a great crash course once it's time. Let's go, we go back to the bridge. Don't forget your paper. You have two hours to come up with a dive plan for four people for the next three days. You and I will do the first dive in one of those submersibles as soon as we're on location, so I can get an idea of what's going on. They'll do as many dives as possible with the rebreather first, while we watch and assist them from the submersible. The last eight dives will be with the dive helmet, do you understand that?" Chuck hissed.

Natascha simply nodded, frightened to say any words.

"Then get your butt moving," the American commanded, pushing her forward.

In the radio room Astrid stared at the laptop and tried to conceal her disappointment. At the moment she pressed the first button, the laptop required a password. The only bright side was that it did not require another fingerprint scan, but just the password protection alone would be an impregnable barrier.

Just this morning he told me he needed a new password. He even told me that he came up with one. Think, Astrid, think. What could it be?

Astrid closed her eyes and tried to remember. She knew that Ariel only used the index- as well as the middle fingers of both hands. He only used his left pinky finger to press the *shift* key. Beside that, he was not a fast writer.

Remember! What did you talk about this morning? What did you say that could have inspired him?

The Norwegian concentrated hard and the only thing she did remember was the fact that Ariel was a former member of a military special force. The chance that he would select something simple was very slim.

But maybe that's the reason why he did pick something simple.

Astrid's thoughts countered. Concentrating back to her morse code class, she was certain that the password had ten digits. She also remembered that it started with a capital letter, since Ariel had first pressed the *shift* key with his left pinky finger.

What did we talk about this morning? We took turns to guess each others birthday.

Despite her situation, Astrid had to smile at the little flirting that had gone on between them this morning.

He wrote the first four letters with his left hand, the next one with his right hand and the sixth letter again with his left hand. First two were in the middle row of the keyboard, the next three in the upper row and the last letter was in middle row again, followed by four numbers, starting with a "one".

If there was one thing Astrid could rely on, then it was her photographic memory. Convinced that her memory was correct, she opened her eyes and look at the laptop again.

"How long does this take?" Nelson Singer interrupted her concentration from the door.

"Won't take much longer. The computer is just downloading the confirmation for the new navigation plan. Once it's done, I just have to confirm that we have received it, but I have to wait for the download to be finished first, since I do need the new number. Maybe five minutes," Astrid lied.

Nelson nodded and turned his attention back to the bridge, where Chuck, Natascha and Dr. Richard Weber had just arrived. While Natascha and her father had to sit down at a table, Astrid could see Chuck walk back outside again, holding his satellite phone in his hand. Lucky for her, Chuck didn't care about her. Astrid knew Chuck wouldn't buy her lies as easy as Nelson did. Knowing that her time at the computer was running out, she focused again at the keyboard.

No, that can't be it. That would be too simple, wouldn't it? Astrid asked herself.

Astrid entered her first name and her year of birth and pressed the enter key. Holding her breath she was relieved when the password was accepted and thanked Ariel as she released a sigh of relief. She glimpsed at Nelson, who still didn't pay too much attention to what she was doing and checked the laptop again. The laptop was still in the message program, similar to a normal e-mail program. All messages received were from the same company and all messages sent also went to that company.

Okay, keep it short and simple. Those are pros. Ariel sent them a detailed update this morning. Astrid thought and started typing.

"Ship under control of 8 hostage-takers (4 of them are the former American scientists, 4 came with the politicians). 2 crew members executed, both politicians *involved, but no longer on the ship, Ariel and team alive, but locked up, no idea about what is going on, do not reply to this, new position is..."*

Astrid looked for the little piece of paper with the new coordinates and entered them to her message. She wrote her name and position under the message and pressed the *Send* button. The next few seconds she waited patiently for the confirmation that the message had successfully been sent. Once she received it, she deleted all the messages on the laptop and powered down the unit. Once she closed it, she exhaled in relief. If someone else wanted to use the laptop, they would need Ariel's fingerprint, and Astrid was convinced that no one would be able to read what she had just written.

To keep her cover intact, she added a few meaningless lines to the main computer.

"I'm done," the young Norwegian finally said and rose from her chair.

Nelson walked over to her and checked all the messages she had written for the Radio Traffic, but he could not detect anything suspicious.

"Okay, back to the bridge."

Home Office and Operational Headquarters of *EuroSecCorporation*, London, Sunday, October 9th

Convinced that the speaker was activated, Sean MacLeod placed the blackberry back on the table.

"Yes, what is it?" Sean said shrugging his shoulders as he looked at Inspector Conolly. He hoped that by using the speaker, his voice would not sound suspicious.

Almost certain that it was Chuck Hogan who just called them, all they could do was hope he would fall for it.

"Did you call me today? The Germans got suspicious about something," the caller finally said, believing that he was talking to Gordon Ramshaw and not Sean MacLeod.

"No, I didn't. What about the others?" Sean asked and tried to keep his talking to a minimum.

"So far everything goes according to plan. Just started *Phase C*."

All or nothing, thought Sean MacLeod.

"What about the politicians, Chuck?"

Silence. Sean bit his lip nervously. He may have said too much by not only mentioning the politicians, but also by calling the other person *Chuck*.

"They're already gone, as you planned it, but they're both nervous. They told me several times to make sure that everything goes according to plan. Well, I got to go," Chuck said and disconnected the call.

"Okay, now we know for sure. Both politicians are involved and Chuck Hogan and Robert Tyrell are our men," Sean MacLeod stated with a weak smile.

"Could be possible that he got suspicious," Inspector Conolly commented.

"Maybe, but I had to take that risk. Look at the information we got from him," Sean MacLeod said and called Klaus Schwartze.

While Sean gave his superior the news, Shelley came back into their room.

"We got some information about those two politicians. According to their office, both had been on an official visit to the *Northern Explorer* and they both left the research vessel as planned and are back to their offices. That's all we know about their whereabouts for the moment. I have two guys working on their full background, in the meantime I'll see what I dig up about that Chuck Hogan and Robert Tyrell character," she said and immediately left again.

"Thank you Shelley," Inspector Conolly said and his eyes rested on the sheet of paper she just gave him.

Sean MacLeod finished his phone call and looked at this former colleague.

"Both politicians had indeed been on board that ship and according to the tower in Inuvik they're on their way back. Okay, it really looks like they're involved in this. Let's see what our friend Gordon Ramshaw has to say about this." Inspector Conolly suggested and went for the door.

Just as he went to open the door, Sean's phone rang.

Sean saw Klaus Schwartze's number on the display.

"Yes, what is it?" he answered the call immediately.

Sean listened for the next two minutes and made a few notes before he ended the call.

"Excellent," he said and read the notes again.

"What happened?" .

"Believe it or not, but we've just received a satellite message from our laptop on the *Northern Explorer*. It was sent from the radio operator, a woman by the name of Astrid Makkinen. Listen to this. According to her message, the ship is under the control of eight hostage-takers. Four of them are the American scientists from the expedition, the other four came with the two politicians. At least two members of the crew were executed. She made it clear that both politicians are behind this and that they have both left the ship again. Our people seem to be okay, but they're locked up somewhere. She doesn't know what they're planning, but they're on their way to a new location. She gave us the new coordinates. Isn't that something?"

"Well, I do need a copy of the original message. What else do you got?"

"Klaus is already sending you that message. We also have the four names from the American scientists. We checked them out, but they turned out clean. However the company they're working for is dirty. Biological and chemical weapon components and CIA black accounts. Klaus is sending you everything we got. Should be here any moment."

"Very well. Shelley will get it as soon as it arrives. Okay, let's see what Mr. Ramshaw has to say about all that." Inspector Conolly said and led the way.

On board the *Northern Explorer*, Amundsen Gulf, Darnley Bay, Saturday, October 8th

Together with her father, Natascha was sitting at the chart table and tried not only to plan the dives but also to fit them into the tight dive schedule. She also tried to calculate the exact amount of breathing gas they would use for the eight surface supplied dives at the end. With both elbows on the table, her head rested in her hands and she focused on the piece of paper in front of her.

What can I do to help the others? How can I get them out of that cabin? You can't do anything by yourself, you need to think. They're suppose to do some work for them. That means they have to take them out of the cabin and untie them sooner or later. All you can do is concentrate on a decent dive plan so they have a clear head. Without that, they have no chance at all!

Richard Weber knew how hard his daughter concentrated and he took the chance to read the user manual for the gas panel.

Natascha leaned back, angrily took the piece of paper, crumpled it up and threw it into the garbage bin.

"I can't work like this!" She snapped suddenly, her hands thrown up in the air with frustration. "I need my computer. I have a program for this on my laptop."

She found Chuck Hogan standing beside Captain Rasmussen, looking at some digital charts.

"If you want me to come up with a detailed dive plan for four people for several multi gas decompression dives, then I do need my laptop. I have a program to calculate the correct volume of gas for mixing all their breathing gas. Without using the laptop I can't guarantee they won't get bent*," Natascha shouted louder.

Chuck Hogan looked up and his eyes rested on Natascha.

"I told you before, I don't care if they suffer from the decompression sickness at the end, I want…"

"I know you don't give a damn about them. Fact is that a diver who suffers from the symptoms of decompression sickness cannot dive any more. Same thing for a diver who has way too much nitrogen in his body because his surface interval between two dives wasn't long enough. So, give me my laptop and I'll write you your stupid dive plan," Natascha hissed.

Chuck thought for a second about what the young German had just said, but he finally smiled. He took Natascha's and Shira's backpack that Jenna took out of their cabin, and retrieved her laptop out of it. He turned it on and erased all her internet accounts.

"What's the name of the program?"

"It's a *Numbers* file, it's on the desktop."

Chuck looked at the program and opened it. He clicked through the different menus to make sure that Natascha could not send any messages with it, before he brought it over to her. The American placed the computer in front of the young German.

"Here you are," he smiled at her.

"Thanks," Natascha snarled back ironically and looked at her laptop.

With a quick movement Chuck pulled her head back by her hair.

"The Bents": another name for the decompression sickness injury. If someone suffers from DCS, divers say that the person got "bent".

"Should I notice you're using a different program than this, then I'll personally make sure that Astrid's blood is all over your face. Do I make myself clear?"

Natascha fought against the pain and her eyes filled with tears. She could feel a scream rip up her throat but she refused to release it, to give Chuck the pleasure. She hurriedly nodded as best as she could.

"You have ninety minutes," he hissed at her and released her from his painful grip.

Chuck walked back over to the helm, from where he could oversee everything and ordered Nelson to make sure that Natascha didn't use any other program.

Without hesitation, Nelson walked over and stood behind Natascha. With Chuck being so close, he didn't want to disappoint him.

Turning her head, Natascha glimpsed at Nelson and shook her head in disappointment. From all the American scientists, Nelson was the one who had shown real sympathy for her after the polar bear attack. Natascha was angry she even believed him back then. She looked him in the eyes to let him know how disappointed she was, before she turned back to her laptop to plan the dives.

Home Office and Operational Headquarters of *EuroSecCorporation*, London, Sunday, October 9th

Inspector Conolly almost lost it. Gordon Ramshaw didn't show any reaction, not even when they confronted him with the names of Chuck Hogan and Robert Tyrell. His reaction was always the same.

"Given the fact that you have not officially charged me with a crime yet, it's fair to assume that you have absolutely nothing against me. If you release me right now, I might even consider not pressing charges against your stupid company and Scotland Yard."

Inspector Conolly and Sean MacLeod left the interrogation room and went back to the observation room again, from where they both watched Mr. Ramshaw through the window.

"Don't you think you could find a judge who would take him into custody until we know for sure what's going on?"

"That's going to be difficult. I hate to say it, but our biggest problem is the fact that a sitting US Senator as well as a member of the Canadian parliament seem to be involved in this. We're just waiting for some statements from their offices, but I can already tell you that both statements will say that everything is fine. Radio contact to the *Northern Explorer* is a technical nightmare. Even if we do get them on the radio, we're still dealing with pros. They will handle all the radio traffic themselves. All they got to do is to tell us that everything is fine, and we're back at square one. If the new coordinates are correct, then the *Northern Explorer* will be out of sight from the shore within the next ninety minutes. All we have for hard fact is one simple e-mail from a radio operator named Astrid Makkinen and a disconnected call from your man. Everything else is circumstantial at the moment. If I call a judge to tell him the facts, then he has to base his decision on a single satellite message, in which Astrid accuses a sitting US Senator as well as a member of the Canadian parliament to be terrorists. I'm not sure if I can find a judge who's willing to risk an international crisis with our two greatest allies based on that single satellite message. Gordon Ramshaw knows very well, that the clock is running out on us."

Sean knew that his friend was right.

"Yeah, I know. They probably want to talk to the Prime Minister first. Maybe he's going to ask the Arch Bishop or even the Queen for advice," Sean said frustrated and dialed Klaus Schwartze's number.

Klaus answered the call after the first ring and listened to the latest developments.

By now, Klaus sent most of his people home to get some well needed sleep, so they could start fresh again later in the day.

Klaus added the latest developments in the presentation program together with their times and projected them to the board.

He focused on the presentation for a few moments before he called his wife and secretary.

Brigitte walked in his office, shaking her head in disbelief.

"I still can't believe that Gordon is involved in this," Brigitte said to her husband and looked at him tiredly.

"Darling, please do me favor before you drive home…"Klaus started.

"I won't go home. I want to stay, you need me here. I took a little nap in our recovery room, I'm fine."

Klaus looked at his wife, but he didn't say anything. He knew she was right.

"Fine. Could you please bring me the phone number from Ariel's father? I think it's about time that I inform him."

"His private number or his office number?" Brigitte asked on her way out.

"As far as I know, we only have his office number. Just bring me the number we got on file, I'll call him myself."

Less than two minutes later, Brigitte gave him the phone number.

Klaus looked at his watch and realized that it was almost seven o'clock in the morning in Tel Aviv.

He anxiously dialed the number that would connect him directly with the office of Ariel's father.

After the second ring someone picked up the phone.

"Shalom, this is retired General Klaus Schwartze from *EuroSecCorporation*. I'd like to talk to General Rashid in the matter of the sixth November two-thousand-and-two," Klaus greeted his interlocutor in English.

Silence.

The 6th November 2002 was the day when Klaus Schwartze had officially hired Ariel Rashid for *EuroSecCorporation*. Klaus and Brian knew at that point that Ariel was not only a close-combat instructor for the Israelian military special forces, but that he was also very loyal to the Mossad, the legendary Israelian secret service. The same secret service where his father worked in the rank of a general. Back then, they agreed that they would indicate a call of the utmost importance by mentioning the date 6th November 2002.

"One moment please, General Rashid is on his way."

"Thank you," Klaus said and heard he was transferred to a secure line.

Seconds later he heard how General Rashid picked up the phone.

"Shalom my friend. What can I do for you?" General Rashid greeted the German.

Klaus exchanged the greetings and reassured himself that the line was secure, before he told General Rashid in just a few sentences what had happened in the North-West Passage. He even mentioned the Russian submarine, something they had not told Scotland Yard, and he assured the Israeli that they would forward all the information to a contact person who worked at the Israeli embassy.

"This is indeed troublesome. I'll make the necessary arrangements and see what we can do. I will personally keep you updated. And you're sure about my son? You haven't heard from him?"

"Yes, General Rashid, I'm sure. The last contact was interrupted, after that we only received that message from Astrid, sent from your son's laptop."

"This is quite unusual for him. What about my daughter? Have you heard from Shira?"

On board the *Northern Explorer*, Amundsen Gulf, Darnley Bay, Saturday, October 8th

Natascha sat in front of her laptop and looked at the screen. She created two different dive plans. Based on the more conservative dive plan she now calculated the total volume of gas they would need. While she was working her schedule, she was looking for an opportunity to give her friends an advantage over the attackers, but she knew she couldn't take the risk. Once Nick and the others were using a surface supplied diving helmet under water, they completely relied on the surface support crew, no matter what. Natascha realized that those were not the best circumstances for any counter measures.

By now the *Northern Explorer* reached it's new location and Chuck walked over to the Captain.

"I want the ship at exactly the position I told you. It's in your interest that this ship doesn't change it's position in the tides or the currents. Your lovely radio operator won't appreciate any unnecessary waste of time," he threatened the Norwegian as he saw the research vessel slowly move past their new location.

"I know what you want and I'd appreciate it if you'd let me do my job. In order to secure the ship in one position, I have to use all four anchors," Captain Rasmussen replied without taking his eyes from the control panel.

Chuck kept watching Captain Rasmussen, but the Captain did an excellent job, and half an hour later, the *Northern Explorer* was resting motionless on the water.

Martin Cunningham walked over to Chuck and Jenna and his eyes fell on Natascha.

"How do you know she's not lying to you about the divers?" he whispered.

"She won't. She cares about them. She's too afraid to do anything stupid," Chuck explained.

"I don't know. She didn't sound too scared to me. She's still pretty snappy. If you want, we can break her for you…would be fun…" Martin smiled at Chuck.

"She must not be harmed, you idiot. I need her to be afraid of me. She's useless to me once she's suicidal. Nobody touches her!" Chuck hissed back aggressively.

Martin's smile faded and he watched Natascha instead.

"Who do you want to go diving first once the two of you are back on board?" Martin asked after a few minutes.

Chuck turned around and also looked at Natascha. He had not thought about that yet.

Just a few meters away from him, Natascha set at the table, her left elbow resting on the edge, her head resting in her hand as her right hand played with the engagement ring on her necklace. Natascha was totally focused on the dive plan.

"Jenna, do you know if she has a boyfriend here on board?" Chuck whispered to his sister.

Jenna also turned around and all three of them were watching Natascha now.

"I remember she stuck her tongue into some guy's throat during the welcome party in Halifax, but I can't remember who it was. I didn't have any contact with them. You didn't see the guy back in Iceland?"

"No, couldn't take the risk," Chuck shook his head.

Natascha didn't notice anything about the conversation behind her back and was still staring at the sheets of papers in front of her. She continued to fiddle with her necklace, lost in detailed thoughts as she looked from one paper to the next. Her concentration was so fixed she didn't notice the screensaver on her laptop activate itself.

"Bingo!" Jenna whispered as soon as she spotted the picture on Natascha's laptop.

It was already after midnight when the research submersible *Polar Viking* swung over *Northern Explorer*'s railing. Natascha shifted in her seat as she stole a quick glance to Chuck who sat beside her in the submersible. She could see he was nervous, but was sure he would never admit it. Dr. Richard Weber nervously sat in the dive control room, closely guarded by Jenna Mason.

Chuck's attention darted upwards when he heard Nelson jump from the little zodiac onto *Polar Viking*. He stifled his nervous sigh as the American scientist disconnected the lifting cable.

Natascha navigated the research submersible as it slowly drifted away from the research vessel.

"Okay, you can go down along the buoy rope we dropped. That's where we'll start our search from," Chuck commanded and pointed at the huge buoy, that measured almost one and a half meters in diameter. Natascha steered *Polar Viking* towards Chuck's marker as it floated in front of them.

The young German reconsidered her options again, but in the best case scenario she would only be able to get rid of one person, and she would need a lot of luck for that. But even if the hypothetical plot was to pan out and she got away, she would not be able to escape the freezing water. She surveyed the horizon again, hoping to see a spit of land that was much closer. Her hand rubbed across her face as she acknowledged her inachievable plan as just that. There was no one to run to for safety.

She breathed a wobbly sigh as she thought of her security, her friends, her family. Natascha knew it was out of the question to abandon them, regardless of the success of her escape plans.

It was in a mere moment that she felt the stress of the last hours dawn on her. She could feel her shoulders getting heavy with hopelessness. She tried to remember the last time she felt safe. The only image that came in her mind was Nick. It was not even twenty-four hours ago that she was the most happiest girl on the planet. She never believed that life could change so drastically in such short a time, that even her happiness, that was just a day ago, would be such a distant memory.

She pushed her depressive thoughts aside and focused on the feeling she had when Nick proposed. Their future, their anticipation to find out if she was indeed pregnant, filled her heart with excitement. But it was not the same. That same blissful moment she shared with Nick was just a memory now.

Natascha cursed under her breath as she concentrated on navigating the submersible. She swallowed, exhaled deeply and took her check list.

"Any problems?" Chuck asked.

"No, everything's perfect," Natascha snapped tiredly.

"Relax. The sooner you get us to the bottom and find what I'm looking for, the faster we're back on the ship. As a reward, you and your father can get something to eat and a couple of hours of sleep. We have some long days ahead of us."

Natascha looked at Chuck in disbelief.

"What's the matter? Do you think I'm a barbarian? Let's go, we can't lose any more time," the American reminded her as he turned his attention back out the plexiglas dome.

Natascha shook her head and went over the check-list with the outmost care. It was the first time that she and her father prepared one of the submersibles without Vitali's or Holger's supervision. With a desperate look at Nick's little good luck charm Natascha navigated *Polar Viking* a little bit closer to the buoy. With her hand adjusting the joystick swiftly, the two thrusters on top of *Polar Viking* came to life and seconds later the little research submersible dipped under the surface.

"Why don't you turn on the lights?" Chuck demanded eagerly.

"The large underwater lights need the cold water to keep them cool. I'm going to switch them on once we're five meters below the surface," Natascha whispered exhaustively.

Chuck nodded and was satisfied once two of the four lights lit up.

This is completely crazy. The last few weeks we did everything possible so I'm only operating one submersible, so we know there was no mechanical manipulation. Now I'm sitting here, taking this lunatic for a ride. Natascha thought and shook her head furiously. Chuck anxiously looked outside the plexiglas dome. He knew they weren't that deep, but his mission made him anxious to find what he was looking for.

"Did you shoot at me back in Berlin?" Natascha asked suddenly, her suspicion prompting her curiosity. The moment she asked she was not sure if she wanted to know. She then thought of the powerful revenge that would satisfy the pain that tortured her. Natascha knew if her friends ever got free they would keep searching for her fail assassin.

"Yes I did. Don't take it personal, it was strictly business. That has nothing to do with you as a person. After all, I think I could really like you," Chuck explained casually, without even looking at her.

Natascha shook her head in disbelief. She never thought he would be so carefree, so willing to admit his failed attempts. A wave of hatred, something she never felt before, rose inside her. Her hands tightened as she steered the submersible. She fought alongside her willpower to keep her attention focused. There would be no use in her attacking him. She recalled how fast he moved when he struck her. The sheer memory made her lip sting.

"You can hardly contain it, can you?" Chuck whispered, without even turning his attention to her. His eyes were fixed out the plexiglas dome as he eagerly scanned the water, anxiously waiting to see the bottom. They were now over forty meters deep, but all that Chuck could see when he looked outside the window was complete darkness. "Just so you know. I was also there in Reykjavik. You got lucky back then. It should have looked like an accident. It really would have too. Personally, I prefer a different approach. I had a few ideas about you, but it wasn't my call. Business is business. But like I said before, don't take this personal."

Natascha looked to the side and took a couple deep breaths to ignore his provocation. It helped that she could see the reflection of the bottom underneath her. She checked the depth gauge and they were at sixty two meters.

"Okay, now turn on the sonar," Chuck ordered anxiously.

Natascha looked at the instrument panel. Although *Polar Viking* and *Odin* were technically identical, a few switches were located differently. She found the switch she was looking for and activated the sonar.

"If you tell me what I'm looking for, I might actually be able to find it," Natascha said bitterly.

"A submarine, darling. I'm looking for an over forty year-old nuclear Russian submarine."

- 19 -

Scotland Yard, London, Sunday, October 9th
While Inspector Conolly was watching Gordon Ramshaw through the window, he sipped at his coffee. He knew he had no choice. He either had to call a judge and officially charge Gordon Ramshaw with a crime or he would have to let him go.

They were unable to learn anything about Chuck Hogan or Robert Tyrell during the last hours and Inspector Conolly shook his head when his assistant Shelley walked in again.

"We found out that Gordon Ramshaw flew twice to the United States this summer for private reasons. First time was from the fourteenth of May until the seventeenth and the second time was from the thirteenth of June until the sixteenth. According to his scheduler, he had no business obligations whatsoever during that time. Both times he used his credit card to rent a car to drive to Montana. He used the same credit card all the time, gas stations, hotel, you name it. It's also interesting that we found another credit card trail for the same time period. This trail started in Boston. Although it's not the credit card that Chuck Hogan used to get to Berlin and Iceland, it's still registered on his name."

"Why Montana?" Sean MacLeod asked.

"This is were it gets really interesting. US Senator Jonathan Brown owns a private hunting lodge in Montana. We weren't able to find out if Senator Brown was at the lodge during those two time periods, but we're trying to figure it out. We also found something else. Chuck Hogan was in London from the nineteenth to the twenty third of July. According to Mr. Ramshaw's scheduler, he didn't work on Friday, the twenty second of July," Shelley reported enthusiastically.

Sean MacLeod immediately briefed Klaus over the phone, when Inspector Conolly's phone rang.

"Yes, Conolly here. What is it?...Excuse me?...Who wants to see me?...Now?...She's already here? Okay, bring her up."

Still puzzled, Inspector Conolly looked at his phone and turned to Sean.

"Now it's getting interesting. I'm getting a visitor from the American embassy. It looks like we stirred up a hornet's nest. Checking out Chuck Hogan obviously rang some bells over there," Inspector Conolly said and guzzled down the rest of his coffee, before he looked at his old friend and colleague.

"Listen, Sean, please don't take this personal, but there's no legal ground that you can be present during this conversation, okay? I suggest you take a few minutes and get some breakfast. I promise you I'll fill you in once I'm done."

"Yes, I was afraid you'd say that," Sean said and went for the cafeteria.

He had some breakfast and read the Sunday newspaper. After about one hour his phone rang and Sean went back to the observation room as fast as he could.

He found both Inspector Conolly as well as his assistant Shelley with a pile of papers in front of them. Sean sat at their table and looked at them in anticipation.

"We just had a visit from our American liaison officer. They're officially on our trail over there. The name Chuck Hogan rings a few alarm bells in certain spots. According to our liaison officer, Chuck Hogan was indeed once a member of the Navy Seals. Together with his Seal buddies Robert Tyrell, Martin Cunningham and Sean Greenstein, they had their own unique clique within the team. Unfortunately they had a very bad experience on one mission during the second gulf war and they all resigned their duties. But instead of going home, they stayed in Iraq and worked for a security company in Bagdad. They got greedy and started their own operations. They introduce themselves as independent consultants and specialized on highly paid private jobs of questionable moral and legitimate grounds. According to their former Seal buddies, they're very experienced, very loyal and very dangerous mercenaries with an extremely low level of morality and literally no awareness for wrong doing. They're keeping an eye on him. I showed our liaison officer our cards and told her about the politicians."

"And? What did she say?" Sean asked. He already noticed that Inspector Conolly had some bad news.

"US Senator Jonathan Brown is on top of a very short list for a very important job in the White House if his party gets the Oval Office back. In order to get the job he's looking at, you have to be extremely well connected with all the agencies. It has been made very clear to me in more or less drastic words, that Senator Brown is quite untouchable at the moment. I was told flat out that all investigations in his direction won't go anywhere. As far as Chuck Hogan and his guys are concerned, they're willing to have a look at the ship, but they're also going to handle this with kids gloves. Reason for that is their present relationship with Canada. The Canadian Dollar is very strong compared to the American right now and they don't want to risk any tensions with the Canadians since their economy is not the best. As arrogant as the Americans are, they don't want to expose the Canadians in their own back yard, especially if there is a Canadian politician involved."

"As long as they don't go on board the ship, no one can confirm our suspicion," Sean said, knowing very well he didn't say something new.

"That's correct, Sean, but I can't change it. We have to find a different way. Our liaison officer told me that once Chuck Hogan has been paid, he's going to finish the job."

"Okay, off the record. How likely do you think it is, after considering everything we know, that Chuck Hogan and his men are responsible for the assassination attempts and for what is going on on that ship?" Sean asked his old friend.

"I'd say it's over ninety-nine percent. We found out that Gordon Ramshaw ordered a wire transfer for one million Euro from one of his private accounts to a Swiss account, just after he got back from Montana this spring. Was the first time in his life that he did this. We lost the money in Switzerland."

Before Inspector Connolly could say anything more, Sean suddenly jumped from his chair and rushed into the interrogation room. Bursting through the door with utmost rage, he grabbed Gordon Ramshaw by his sweater and pulled him from his chair.

"Have you already paid Chuck Hogan? Did he get all the money! Can you reverse the transaction?" Sean yelled at him and pushed him backwards against the wall.

"Are you out of your mind? I have no idea what you are talking about!" Gordon Ramshaw yelled back and broke free from Sean's grip.

Inspector Conolly hurried into the interrogation room and haphazardly separated both of them.

"Mr. Ramshaw, sit back down. You'll have to stay a little bit longer. The judge is looking at your case right now, but I can already assure you that we'll press several charges against you. If there's anything you can do to avoid someone getting hurt, this would be the time for it," Inspector Conolly bluffed. It was his last chance to get Gordon Ramshaw to cooperate.

Gordon pulled his temper in check and picked the chair up and sat down at the table again. He calmly looked back up to them.

"I have nothing to say. I didn't do anything wrong."

On board the *Northern Explorer*, Amundsen Gulf, Darnley Bay, Sunday, October 9th

It was eight in the morning and Chuck Hogan stood by his word. After they were back on board the ship in the early morning hours, Natascha and her father were locked up in a cabin with nothing else but a single bed, an adjacent bathroom and enough to eat and to drink. They were both way too frightened to even entertain the thought of escape.

After a few restless hours of interrupted sleep, the young German scientist stood now in one of the two little conference rooms and followed Chuck's order to prepare breakfast for herself, her father and the four divers.

The American gave her strict orders that none of the four divers was allowed to use any knives or forks. Under Nelson's watchful eyes Natascha prepared some bread as well as some cereal, before Chuck himself took away the forks and knives. Chuck counted the utensils as Natascha placed the food on the table. She brushed the burning tears from her eyes and tried to avoid the thought of this moment for so long, but there was nothing she could do. Her eyes drifted up to her rebreather. Her brow furrowed with fear. She knew she had to explain this contraption to her four friends within the next hour.

This is complete insanity! she could not help but yell at herself. Since there was no one else to argue with that wasn't threatening her life, her inner battle continued.

She feared something would happen to one of the divers and she was convinced it would be without a doubt her fault if something would go wrong. Just when the young German wiped her tears off her face for the second time, Jenna opened the door and escorted Nick, Ole-Einar, Oliver and Olaf into the room. Robert Tyrell followed them in and closed the door.

Natascha barely glimpsed at them, before she concentrated on her rebreather again.

Don't show any emotions! Shira had told her. *The moment you let them control your emotions, they control you and you don't have chance.*

Although she didn't want to, she couldn't help but look at them. Their hands were now tied in front of them and all four of them struggled with their coordination. The side effects of being tied up in an uncomfortable position for hours burned their joints.

"Good morning," Chuck greeted the four overenthusiastically.

"You're allowed, one after the other, to step forward and get something to eat and to drink. I think you understand we can't allow you to use any silverware, so my apologies for that. Before we start, I want to take the time to tell you the rules of our cooperation, since they are very important. As you have noticed by now, you have neither been executed nor locked up with the remaining crew of the ship. Considering your personal military history, I'm sure you're wondering why this is the case. The reason for that is simple. Seventy meters below the surface is something that I need rather urgently and our job is to recover it. If you now please focus your attention to the monitor on my left, you'll see one of your wireless surveillance cameras beside it. At the other end of that camera is one of my men. As soon as he's under the impression that the four of you are trying to trick me, or if you try something else stupid, or if I don't check in with him in certain time intervals with certain passwords, he will immediately execute your two non-diving and therefore completely useless friends in a very painful way. I'm sure you have noticed that we brought both of them to a different location on board this really huge ship this morning. Natascha, darling, do you believe me when I say that we'll execute the others or do you think I'm bluffing?"

Natascha tried to fight it, but despite her might, tears were streaming down her face as she shook her head.

"Please do as he says," she sobbed and finally looked at her friends.

"You see, the lovely Natascha is fully aware of the situation. So, do you understand the rules?"

Nick and the others nodded their heads.

"Then you're now allowed, one after the other, to eat something and in the meantime, listen carefully," Chuck commanded.

While Nick and his friends ate everything Natascha had prepared for them, Chuck started a presentation on a computer.

"A little over forty years ago, a Russian submarine sunk at this very spot. Thanks to Natascha's outstanding abilities with a submersible, we found the wreck of this U-Boat in a depth of seventy-one meters last night," Chuck explained and showed some blueprints on the presentation.

"We're talking about one of the first fully functional Russian SSBN submarines. I assume you have all seen the movie *K19- The Widowmaker* with Harrison Ford. The submarine in that movie was a Hotel-Class submarine. The U-Boat below our feet is *Project 658*, a modified version of the Hotel-Class, which we call November-Class. It was built in nineteen-hundred-sixty-eight in Severodvinsk before it was stationed in Poljarnij. The U-Boat itself is one hundred and nineteen meters long, nine point two meters wide and had a draught of seven point three meters. It's displacement was around four thousand and eighty tons on the surface and around five thousand tons once it was submerged. All U-Boats of the November-Class had a crew of one hundred and four and could operate in depths down to two hundred and forty meters, but they were tested to a depth of three hundred meters. The submarines got their power from two nuclear reactors with one hundred and ninety MWT each, which powered two steam turbines with over seventeen thousand horsepower to run the two propellers. They also had four torpedo tubes with 533mm as well as four torpedo tubes with 400mm. They didn't build that many U-Boats from the November-Class. Some sources are writing about eight units, some sources mention nine. The ninth submarine of the November-Class, K-9, is exactly seventy meters below this research vessel right now. This is the point where you enter the game."

Ole-Einar had detailed knowledge about submarines and he even heard the stories about this phantom sub.

"What makes you so sure that this is a November-Class and not one of the Hotel-Class submarines?" the Norwegian asked, shrugging his shoulders.

"With Natascha's help, I could identify the submarine last night based on the torpedo tubes and the propeller, but most likely because of the cunning tower, which is further aft on the November-Class than it is on the Hotel-Class. Looking at the damage down there, it seems as if K-9 had collided with the solid rock ridge just four hundred meters away from here. Although the outer pressure hull is almost completely corroded away, it's not difficult to imagine the force with which the submarine hit the rock. I already found a large area which will allow you to penetrate the wreck," Chuck explained and pointed on some pictures that Natascha had taken with *Polar Viking* last night.

"In this area is not only the outer pressure hull gone, but also the noise barrier as well as the inner pressure hull. The total area is several square meters, so penetration should be easy for you."

Chuck gave them a few minutes to take the pictures in, before he came to the important part.

"As soon as we're done here, the first diver will descend down the line that Natascha installed last night with the little submersible. Using this rebreather here, you'll penetrate the wreck through this opening here. From there it's only twenty meters to your actual goal. Worst case scenario, you'll find three closed bulkheads, which you have to cut open. Once you're behind the first closed bulkhead, internal damage should be minimal and your progress should be rather rapid. Technically not too difficult at all. While you're working inside the wreck, the lovely Natascha and I will be outside in one of the submersibles and I'll be watching you. If you should need the welding gear to cut through the bulkheads, you simply let us know and we radio it in. If you decide to do anything stupid down there, rest assured I'll notice it. The moment I suspect any foul play, I'll radio my friend here and your two non-diving and therefore completely useless friends will be wrapped in chains and down there with you before you're even at your first decompression stop. Do you understand?"

Everybody nodded. They knew Chuck wasn't bluffing.

Thin Ice

"What are we supposed to do once we're through those bulkheads? What are we looking for?" Nick asked seriously.

"He wants the warheads," Ole-Einar told his friend calmly.

"All Russian November-Class submarines carried three SS-N4 ICBM's. They had nuclear warheads. He wants the forty year old nuclear warheads," the Norwegian explained.

"You see, that wasn't too difficult after all," Chuck smiled devilishly.

- 20 -

Scotland Yard, London, Sunday, October 9th
It was almost noon but Gordon Ramshaw was still sitting in the interrogation room. He was convinced he would have been a free man again earlier this morning. He never thought he left any clues that would connect him directly with what was going on in the Arctic at this very moment. But now he became more nervous with every passing minute. Despite the fact that the deadline had come and gone over five hours ago, they still kept him in custody. That could only mean that the judge in charge knew something that Gordon didn't.

Still lost in his thoughts, the door to the interrogation room flew open and a smiling Inspector Conolly entered, closely followed by his assistant.

It was Shelley who told him the news.

"Mr. Gordon Ramshaw, you're now an official suspect for two accounts of the attempted murder for hire as well as an official suspect in a supposedly hostage-taking with terrorist background on board a Norwegian research vessel. Based on those charges you're now officially under arrest and a full investigation will take place immediately. Because of the immediate risk for the life and the wellbeing of the people on board the research vessel, you're hereby denied any contact to any other person than your interrogators. Because of the possibility of a terrorist nature of this crime, you're denied any means of personal communication, whether they are electronically, non-electronically or by telephone. Your current state of custody will at least be in effect until we have positive confirmation about the situation on board the Norwegian research vessel *"Northern Explorer"*. Do you understand this?"

Gordon rested his head in his hands and took a deep breath. He had a serious problem.

On board the *Northern Explorer*, Amundsen Gulf, Darnley Bay, Sunday, October 9th
Her legs shaking, Natascha stood in front of her friends. What otherwise could have been a funny lecture with lots of laughter, turned into a quick introduction of a highly dangerous operation. It bothered her a lot not to make eye-contact with her friends, and the young German scientist fought more than once to keep her emotions and her exhaustion under control. For her, it was simply too much to deal with.

"Okay, unfortunately we don't have enough breathing gas to do all the dives with the helmet gear and on open circuit," Natascha whispered and tried to concentrate on her briefing. She took a slow wavering breath before she continued again.

"Whoever is going to do the first dive will descend down the rope of the marker buoy, which will bring you more or less directly to the crack in the outer and inner hull of the submarine. Last night the visibility was around ten meters, the water temperature is a constant four degrees Celsius. You'll all use my own rebreather. The most important thing is to monitor your instruments and the sensors. Always make sure you have the right partial pressure for the oxygen. I'll take care of the oxygen sensors and the solenoid after every dive myself. You all know how to flush the unit and how you manually adjust your oxygen content. There's no difference to the units you used back in your days. With this unit, you'll hear a clicking noise underwater once in a while. It's the sound of the valve that's regulating the oxygen in your breathing mix. It's completely normal..."

Natascha went on for another thirty minutes, then she focused on the upcoming dive.

"During the rebreather dives you'll take the drop down video-camera from the research submersible and you'll position it beside you. That way he can monitor your activities down there," Natascha said disgusted, before she continued.

"All our gas supply is limited. I'll give everybody a bottle with Argon, but I doubt it will be enough for all the dives. Even if you limit the use of Argon, you won't have any left at the end of the dives and you'll most likely get cold. You can't use my heated undergarment, since your dry-suits don't have the connections and it won't fit you anyway. It's important that you stick to the dive profile. I don't have any room for safety, so please listen carefully. We'll lower you in the water with the boom. In our current position, we can pretty much lower you right beside the buoy. You descend down the buoy line and you'll reach the maximum depth of seventy-one meters after around six minutes. Your bottom time down there is a maximum of twenty three minutes. Please do me the favor and start ascending immediately after that, okay?" Natascha swallowed hard. She thought for a moment, worried she would forget something.

"The way I had to calculate the dive, you'll have zero room for mistakes. I wrote down your decompression obligations in my wet notes, including some alternate profiles. While you're down there, you can clip all your spare tanks to the submersible, but you have to carry all your tanks with you during the ascent because we won't stay with you in the water the entire time, okay?" Natascha finished, her voice breaking.

During the briefing Natascha kept her eyes on her notes, but her four friends could clearly see her suffering. Her heart thudded quickly as the moment caught up with her.

"I'm so sorry!" she sobbed, falling back to the wall where she slid to the floor. Her anguish burned through her as her tearless sobs singed her eyes red. She buried her face in her hands with defeat.

Chuck briefly glanced at her unimpressed, before he looked at the four guys, enthusiastically.

"Okay. Who's up first?"

New York, International Airport, Sunday, October 9th
Retired Admiral Brian Whittaker stood in a corner of the airport and spoke to his friend and partner Klaus Schwartze on the phone.

"Ah, so he's now officially in custody, but he hasn't said anything yet. Well, that will come as soon as he realizes he won't get access to a lawyer. Anything new from our guys?...Nothing at all? That's bad. You spoke with Tel Aviv?....That's good, very good....Okay, no problem. Do you know where I have to go from here?...What do you mean, they haven't gotten back to you?...Does that mean they just believe their politicians?...Of course they make sure that the ship is still answering any radio calls...Jesus Christ, this is unbelievable. Well, keep me updated. I'll stay here for the moment."

Brian looked at this phone and ended the call furiously.

We had contact with the politician in question as well as the research ship. They insured us that everything was okay. We don't believe there's an emergency. For crying out loud, at least send someone up there to take a look! Brian thought angrily.

He never tolerated such incompetence. If their enemies were indeed so highly organized as he feared, no one here would suspect anything until they personally set a foot on board that research vessel. He also didn't like the fact that the Canadians reacted very slowly. Despite all that, Klaus promised him to update the Canadians with the latest information as soon as he would get them. Maybe they would send a team to the *Northern Explorer* after all.

Brian Whittaker shook his head and picked up his suitcase.

Well, we still have one ace up our sleeve, he smiled.

On board the *Northern Explorer*, Amundsen Gulf, Darnley Bay, Sunday, October 9th

Nobody said a word. They all looked at Natascha, who crouched on the floor and cried. Nick wanted to go to her, take her in his arms to comfort her, but he knew very well that Chuck would stop him just centimeters away from her, just to increase her suffering. Like his friends, Nick concentrated on not paying any attention to Natascha. He fought his urges that prompted him in two directions. The two options he would love to do the most, soothe Natascha and attack Chuck, were improbable. Instead he turned his cold eyes up to Chuck, certain to never forget a single detail in his face.

"No volunteers? What a pity. Natascha, would you please explain to our four incredibly stupid heroes what's going to happen to Astrid, after they sacrifice their two non-diving and useless friends?"

Natascha sobbed and tried to catch a breath.

Within a split second, Chuck grabbed Natascha's hair and viciously pulled her up to her feet. Overwhelmed with pain and shock, Natascha screamed.

"Please do as he says! He's not only going to kill Ariel and Shira, he's going to shoot Astrid in her knee."

Smiling arrogantly, Jenna slowly walked over to Natascha and gently, almost like a sister, stroked her hair. With a careful motion, Jenna pulled out Natascha's necklace and looked at the ring.

Nick swallowed hard.

"Nick, if you want to do your friends and the lovely Astrid a life-saving favor, then I suggest you get your ass in the water," Chuck barked at him and picked up his radio.

"Russell, if I don't tell you within the next twenty minutes that the diver is in the water, you can execute the two hostages before you shoot the radio operator in the knee. Make sure it's painful. Do you copy?" Chuck asked over the radio, his eyes resting on Nick.

"Copy that," Russell answered after a few seconds.

"Okay," Nick agreed. There was nothing he could do at the moment.

"I'm going. Where is the dive gear?"

"Great! I knew you'd be reasonable."

While Robert and Jenna locked Ole-Einar, Oliver and Olaf up in the cabin, Nick changed into the dry-suit in front of the dive control room. The two corpses of Vitali Vachenko and the First Officer Karl-Heinz Junghans were still on the deck. Nick assumed the Americans would later put a weight belt around them and throw them over board. Nick was certain that the terrorists simply lacked the time to do it yet. His eyes fell on the bin with the dive gear, which Natascha had to prepare. Like always, Nick was using the gear from Natascha's father. He didn't take long to get dressed and after a few minutes he closed the zipper on his dry-suit. While Chuck already concentrated on *Odin*, Nelson kept his eyes on Nick. Inside the dive control room was Dr. Richard Weber, who just performed the safety check for the submersible. Nick slowly looked around and he was seriously considering his options. Nelson didn't pay too much attention to him, and Nick was sure he could overpower him, disarm him and use him as a shield before Chuck would turn around to face him. To verify his plot, Nick turned around and was disappointed when he saw Jenna carefully watching him from the top of the staircase, three meters above him, one hand at her pistol. Pretending as if nothing happened, Nick turned around and tried to adjust his neck seal. Since Nick was diving a dry-suit with integrated dry gloves, he struggled in adjusting it.

Natascha came up to him and helped him with the silicone seal, when their eyes met.

"I'm so sorry Nick. I...I don't have a choice."

"It's okay, Angel. We'll get out if this. Love you," Nick whispered carefully.

"I love you, too."

Natascha didn't want to raise too much attention and stepped back as soon as the silicone neck seal was resting flat against his skin.

She handed Nick the neoprene hood.

"There's a container with gas at the pipeline. I've seen it and the Senator knew about it. That's how they want to do it," she whispered as she tucked the neoprene hood into the warm neck collar of the dry-suit.

The young German scientist wasn't even sure why she said it, then wondered if it was her own free-will to go against Chuck's direct orders.

"Okay," Nick whispered back and nodded, before he walked to the rebreather.

Under Chuck's watchful eyes Natascha helped Nick put on the rebreather.

"Remember it can take up to several minutes before you notice you have an O2 leak. Always keep a close eye on your sensors and the gauges. Should you notice an increase in your breathing rate, or if you're feeling unusually warm, you might have Carbondioxide poisoning. When that happens, you have to bail out immediately, okay? Down there you can stow all the bail out gas at the submersible, like before, okay?"

Nick listened carefully and nodded.

"Okay, time for Romeo to hit the water," Jenna ordered briskly.

Natascha did a final check on the rebreather and brushed a kiss on Nick's lips.

"Sorry," she whispered again.

"Okay, enough of this romantic stuff. Come one, get your ass in the water. We lost more than enough time already," Chuck commanded and pulled Natascha away from her fiancée.

Natascha glanced back quickly, then climbed up the ladder and into *Odin*, closely followed by Chuck.

Nick watched as the woman he loved entered the submersible with that terrorist. His blood boiled and he knew that not even the cold water would passify it. He could see Natascha glance at him through the plexiglas dome as they were hoisted over the reeling and down to the water. As soon as *Odin* was released, Nick secured himself to the cable and only seconds later, he was in the water.

Montana, USA, Sunday, October 9th

Sitting behind his desk, Jonathan Brown stared at the phone right in front of him. Although he just got home not too long ago, he knew he was in trouble. The Senator picked up the phone and dialed the number of his Canadian friend and partner Pierre Dumont. It took a little while before the Canadian picked up.

"Hello Pierre, how are you doing?" Jonathan asked matter-of-factly.

"Can't complain. How about yourself? Something strange happened, actually. I just received a call from our intelligence service. According to them, they received a message that there's a hostage situation on this research vessel we were just on. Did they call you too?"

Pierre spoke as casual as he could manage. There was the possibility that their phones were wired.

"Yes, I just hung up the phone before I called you. Our people obviously got the same phone call. I believe there's some idiot from the opposition behind it who wants to make a fool out of us before the election campaign picks up. Did you hear any details about it?"

"No, not at all. I was only told that the message originated from Great Britain. A local company obviously has some personnel on the research ship and it seems like they've lost contact with them. You know how the Brits are. As soon as they have some sour milk in their tea, they're getting the weirdest ideas. All I could tell them was that I found it a little bit too cold up there. I told them everything else seemed to be perfectly normal to me. I even showed them the video about us and the Captain. They seemed to be happy after that. Did they tell you something about England?"

"No, all they told me was that they received a tip, but they didn't tell me the source."

"Hmm, that doesn't make any sense. Like you said, most likely an idiot from the opposition. I'll see you in two weeks?"

"Yes, two weeks. Take care," Jonathan finished and hung up the phone.

From England. That means we have a problem with Gordon Ramshaw.

The Senator closed his eyes for a moment and rose from his chair. Trying to think up a quick solution, he paced his huge office. He stopped suddenly and pressed a button on the intercom system.

"Carl, can you please come over for a moment?" he called for his assistant.

Just seconds later, Carl entered the office and closed the door behind him.

"Carl, I have to know as soon as possible and without raising any suspicion if the British are interrogating Gordon Ramshaw. If this should be the case, then we need someone to make sure that he's not talking too much. Do we have someone over there we can rely on?"

"That's going to take some time. I first have to find out if and where he is under arrest. The rest won't be a problem if we can get close to him. We have two people over there that we can trust."

Jonathan Brown looked at his assistant and thought about what he just heard.

"Okay," the Senator said after a few seconds.

"Make the necessary arrangements. There's absolutely no room for errors in this one, do you understand?"

Carl nodded and left the office, while Jonathan walked towards the window.

His thoughts were with the research vessel. Looking back, he knew it was a really stupid idea to talk the expedition leader into that underwater tour in the submersible.

Without that tour, the young German marine biologist would have never discovered the pipeline or the canister with the gas. There was nothing the Senator could do about that now and that worried him. It clearly showed his involvement in this matter.

He took comfort in the fact that if everything went according to his plan, then the Captain and his crew were already executed and all remaining people were safely locked away. The German scientists would be somewhere on the ocean floor and Chuck and his team would already be on their way back.

Did we make a mistake somewhere?

Nervously, the Senator shifted his weight from one foot to the other. He wasn't sure if Chuck could even imagine the significance of this project for the United States and Canada for the near future. If everything would go as planned the first signs of a mass mortality in and around Paulatuk would be reported within the next few days. Until the appropriate forces would finally arrive at the scene, the gas would have evaporated without leaving any traces or survivors. Even thorough autopsies would only show light traces of methane, but not enough to suspect any foul play. Alarmed by these circumstances, the Canadians would then find the *Northern Explorer* at anchor at it's current position just off shore. The complete crew would also be found dead. Pulling some strings, the final result of the investigation would reveal that the scientist around Dr. Weber had released a gigantic methane gas bubble while they took some bottom samples. Slowly and unstoppable, the methane would have escaped the ground and entered the atmosphere. While the crew and their Captain heroically tried to save as many lives as possible, the German scientists, lead by the expedition leader himself, tried to cover everything up and flee. Not to be deemed responsible, they even used weapons to overpower and lock away the crew, leaving them to their certain death. With this being the official finding of the investigation, it would also mean the end for all those stupid and unnecessary expeditions to save the world. To secure the area and to avoid any further catastrophe, a team of American and Canadian specialists would fly out to work there around the clock. During their mission they would find this enormous oil reservoir, and it would be Jonathan Brown who seals the deal with a Canadian politician by the name of Pierre Dumont, that would result in a joint venture for both countries to get the oil. This would secure the American oil demands for the next ten years. If he would personally announce this message during the final stage of the election campaign, all the promises from the opposition would go up into smoke. The expectation of a low oil price and economic independence, even for just a few years, would give them a landslide win during the election and complete control.

For one moment, Senator Jonathan Brown remembered the conversation he had with Natascha inside the submersible. His detailed futuristic plans in riding and for the sister countries paused as he recalled her energetically make her point.

He barked a short laugh.

Although he was convinced that she was a very attractive and capable Marine Biologist, she didn't know anything about world politics. What meaning did a few hundred people have compared to billions of barrels of oil?

Jonathan Brown poured himself a generous drink and thought about the gas. He hoped the calculations of the company were right. Certain American government agencies already used that gas with great success, but that was years ago and the gas was now old. The Senator wanted to be sure about it's deadliness and so it had been tested again in a war zone, and the results were as deadly as they had been years ago.

With closed eyes, the Senator enjoyed the Whiskey running down his throat. If everything would go well, and knowing there was no reason to believe otherwise, he would just be at the beginning of a very successful career. His thoughts brought him back to Natascha, his eyes still closed.

Thinking about her, the first thing that came to mind was her beauty, her enthusiasm. But after just a short moment his lip twitched at the memory of her striking him. Senator Brown flicked opened his eyes again and concentrated on the tasks that lay ahead of him. He was hoping the streak of bad luck ended here and now.

On board the *Northern Explorer*, Amundsen Gulf, Darnley Bay, Sunday, October 9th

Nick entered the water just a few meters away from the marker buoy. Without any trouble he swam to it and held on to the rope. He secured the two cables from the welder as well as a bucket with tools and welding rods to a cable eye around the buoy line. The welder cables and the tool buckets would be carefully lowered down along the buoy line as soon as Nick would descend. After he made sure that nothing could fall out of the bucket, Nick let some air out of his dry-suit and buoyancy compensator. Slowly he sank along the rope into the deep black waters below. All he could see was the buoy rope, guiding him deeper and deeper under water.

Suddenly, as he reached a depth of about fifteen meters, everything went bright. Nick turned around and saw both Natascha and Chuck in *Odin*, just a few meters away from him. Without stopping, Nick continued his descent in the ice cold water. Reaching a depth of thirty meters, Natascha turned the lights on and off. The young German scientist wanted to remind her fiancée to check his instruments and the partial pressure of the Oxygen. Nick checked his gear and signaled that everything was fine. Natascha nodded in relief and made a note in the dive log, before she smiled at Nick.

"I hope I'm not going to ruin any wedding plans," Chuck commented sarcastically and smiled at his hostage.

"At the moment, I don't believe Nick and I will actually live long enough to get married," Natascha hissed back coldly.

"Usually I'd say you have a very negative attitude, but in this specific scenario, I'm afraid you're right. One can only hope you've practiced enough for your wedding night. It would be a real shame otherwise," he winked at her, laughing at his own idle comment.

Natascha ignored him and signaled Nick to check the instruments again. Nick checked his gauge and looked at the display on his wrist. He adjusted the oxygen content in his breathing mix and continued his descent shortly after. Although he was over forty meters deep now, he had little visibility below him. He looked hopelessly in complete darkness.

Only after he passed the sixty meters mark, he noticed a slightly brighter contrast on the bottom. Once he reached sixty five meters, he could clearly see the muddy bottom and the wreckage of K-9. What was left from the outer pressure hull was completely covered in anemones. After Nick orientated himself, he had to admit Chuck was right. The buoy rope led him directly to the huge crack in the outer and inner pressure hull, which allowed him for easy penetration. Nick tried to see some more details of the crack and the area behind it in *Odin*'s light, but the angle of the submersible was not the best. All he could see was a dark hole with sharp metal edges. Nick swam slowly to *Odin* and picked up the cable controlled video-camera and dive light. It took Nick some effort to unwind the cable from the drum on his way to the wreck and Natascha turned both the camera as well as the light on. When Nick arrived back at the crack, he picked up the camera with it's light and shone inside the opening. What he saw was typical for a disaster of this magnitude.

Nick guessed the actual chaos would start around three meters behind the crack. Back then, almost everything had been ripped out of it's anchorage by the massive force of the impact. Especially in this area, where the actual collision happened, the damage was the worst. Immediately behind the opening, Nick noticed several loose cables and wires, but also a maze of pipes and an overturned shelf which made any penetration impossible. It was just this morning that Nick wondered how Chuck got his hands on the plans of this type of submarine. Nick was glad that he spent the time to study them. This would help him a lot with his orientation.

Nick looked at what was now the bottom of the inside of the submarine and he could see a thick layer of fine sediment. This meant that the visibility would automatically turn to zero the moment he entered the wreck to start working. The fact that there was absolutely no current inside the wreck that could have carried away any loose sediment didn't help him either. He gave himself another minute to memorize what he saw before he penetrated the crack.

Natascha shifted nervously on her seat while she looked at her stop watch. Nick was already down here six minutes. Usually, Nick would have been excited to be the first one to dive such a wreck after all these years, but now he was simply focusing to give his best on this job. This would be the only way to decrease the risk of his friends or Natascha's life.

First Nick wanted to see if there was anything he could move without using the tools. He reached for the first pipe and pulled at it, but it resisted. Since he was already down here for eight minutes, Nick decided it was now time to use the welder to cut his way in. He turned around and swam to the buoy line.

Before he disconnected the two welding cables, he tugged four welding rods under the bungee of his gauges on his wrist. Due to the heavy weight of the cables, it took a lot of effort to drag the cables all the way to the submarine, but after eleven minutes in this depth, he finally managed it. This gave him an additional twelve minutes to do some efficient work. At this rate, Nick feared they would need weeks to finish the job.

Inside *Odin* Natascha radioed her father to start the welder, then she checked her watch again. Beside her, Chuck was extraordinarily calm. His view switched permanently between the monitor with the camera feed and through the Plexiglas dome to the actual wreckage. A sudden and continuous stream of air bubbles mixed with sediment showed Chuck that Nick had started to cut a passage inside the submarine. Just from seeing the camera feed on the monitor, Chuck realized how big the damage was. All he could do was hope that the damage further inside the submarine was not as bad as in the immediate collision area.

After Nick used three welding rods, he cleared the pipes and the cables he just cut to the outside of the wreck. Nick examined his work and guessed he gained one meter in total, but due to the bad visibility, he wasn't sure. His plan was to secure the welding cables in the wreck and he also had to take the camera and light back out. Determined to finish his work, Nick entered the wreck again.

Natascha looked at her watch. Twenty-one minutes. It was time for Nick to start his long ascent back to the surface. Ninety seconds left.

Come on! Don't do this to me! Natascha begged silently.

Sixty seconds of bottom time left. Natascha turned all of *Odin*'s lights off and on.

Finally she saw Nick swimming out of the wreckage. Her fiancé carried the video-camera and the underwater light back to *Odin*, where Natascha unmistakeably signaled him to start his ascent immediately.

As soon as the cable from the video-camera was clear of the submarine wreck, Nick started to swim towards the buoy rope, already ascending.

While Natascha maneuvered *Odin* away from the bottom, she looked outside the Plexiglas and monitored the video and light cable. As soon as it hung freely, she activated a switch and both the light and the video were winched back in. Minutes later she met Nick at his first decompression stop.

Nick constantly checked the partial pressure from his oxygen and he also monitored the countdown on his OLED bottom timer closely. While he was waiting for the bottom timer to count down the last minute for this particular stop, he double checked Natascha's wet notes with his decompression schedule again. After he put them back in his leg pockets, he checked his bottom timer and ascended to his next decompression stop. Natascha followed him closely and she stayed with him until Nick was at his stop in nine meters of depth. Knowing that Nick would not need the extra gas from the tanks that were stowed at *Odin*, she waved at Nick and brought *Odin* to the surface. Two of Chuck's men were already waiting for them in a little zodiac and just minutes later, the little research submersible was back on board the research ship.

As soon as *Odin* touched the deck, Natascha opened the outer hatch and left the submersible before Chuck could say a thing. She hurriedly climbed down the ladder, jumped on the deck half way and ran to the rail where she was looking for any signs of Nick. Just a few minutes later, Nick surfaced and signaled that everything was okay.

Natascha smiled at him.

When she finally turned around, her eyes fell to the deck where the two dead bodies rested. She gulped back the nausea as it rose from her stomach. Her hand covered her mouth to keep her stomach in check. Chuck noticed her reaction and also looked the two dead bodies, before he looked around.

"Nelson! Take another man and get rid of those bodies. Tie a weight belt around them and cut them open, so they won't float up again. I want them off the deck immediately!"

With a worried expression Chuck's eyes darted to the clear sky. He didn't expect any planes to fly low enough to actually see what was going on, but the risk was enough for a fright. Chuck knew no one had any knowledge of what was happening on the ship, but it was a high unnecessary risk leaving them lying around.

Natascha turned away and watched closely as Nick was hoisted back on board the *Northern Explorer*.

Fortunately this dive has turned out good for Nick, Natascha thought, and tried to fight herself but her concern got the best of her, *At least this one did...*

The next twenty-four hours bore the same routine. The moment Nick was back on board the ship, he was searched for anything that he might have taken out of the wreck to use as a weapon. After that, Nick had to tell Chuck in every detail what he saw inside the submarine before they locked him up in a separate cabin. By now, all four divers were locked in separate cabins on the same floor. The floor was under video surveillance and a guard was always present. Each cabin had it's own toilet and they all got enough to drink and to eat. The only two things the four friends did not have was a way to communicate with each other or a way out of their cabins.

After Nick was locked away, Natascha cleaned the rebreather and, if necessary, topped off the tanks and changed the solenoid. In the meantime, her father concentrated on the submersibles. He checked the one that had just been used and prepared the second submersible for the next dive. All he had to do was go through the checklist and connect the batteries to the charger. As soon as everything was ready to go, the next diver had to go into the water. After one day, all this went into a rhythm and Natascha concentrated so hard on her tasks that she did not have to consciously keep her emotions in check. This efficiency allowed them to do four dives a day, something that Natascha would have deemed to be terribly negligent.

Natascha always helped their friends get into their suit and to adjust the straps of the rebreather, and she could not avoid the eye contact. She was looking for any sign of hope, but she wasn't sure if or what they wanted to tell her. After helping each diver, she was only certain about one thing: they would not go down without a fight.

Home Office and Operational Headquarters of *EuroSecCorporation*, London, Tuesday, October 11th

Retired General Klaus Schwartze almost went mad. He had spent the last several hours on the phone talking to the Canadian authorities, but with no result. They insisted on their position, that the Canadian politician in question had been on a scheduled visit on the research vessel and that he returned safe and sound to his office. Based on that, the Canadians did not see any other reason for a kidnapping on board the *Northern Explorer*. They also tried to assure Klaus that they indeed had contacted the *Northern Explorer* both with radio and satellite telephone. Both the radio operator as well as the Captain himself had assured them that everything was fine. When Klaus asked about the current radio silence, he was told that the research vessel was, after all, in arctic waters and not in London city. The unscheduled change of position was explained by the fact that the German expedition leader himself wanted to perform some additional surveys at a different location. They also promised Klaus that they would keep a close eye on the ship and it's activities. The ship's presence was deemed to be more of a hindrance since those additional surveys were not part of their original permits. The Canadian's lacked the enthusiasm of the scientists taking part in the expedition, declaring these new surveys as pointless as the expedition entirely. Furthermore, Klaus was told that Canada was seriously considering pressing charges against the German expedition leader, something that would certainly have a negative impact on all future expeditions.

"That's perfect! If that's the case I suggest you fly up there and take the German expedition leader and all of his team members in custody," Klaus suggested, but the Canadian just hung up the phone without further comment.

At least it was pretty clear now that the Canadians were no longer interested in this matter. Klaus was really skeptical that something could change that. The former General rammed the phone back on it's station and rose to his feet.

The Canadians don't want to help us, Gordon Ramshaw is not saying a single word and insists on his innocence and Brian sits in New York and will most certainly run amok if nothing happens soon!

Klaus Schwartze knew he was running out of options. He even called some people in Paulatuk over satellite and asked about the *Northern Explorer*, but the research vessel was too far off the coast and out of sight. Even if they were able to go out with a fishing vessel, all they would see would be the hull of the ship. The importance of this matter was what was happening in the ship.

The retired General placed another call to the person in charge of the local airport in Paulatuk and asked if someone was able to fly out and take some pictures of the ship. It didn't matter how much money he offered, they could not find the only pilot.

After all those failures, Klaus could do nothing else but to sit tight and wait. Something his stubbornness refused him to do.

Scotland Yard, London, Wednesday, October 12th

Gordon Ramshaw knew he had a serious problem. For over three and a half days he was sitting in this cell inside Scotland Yard. They prohibited him to contact a lawyer or anyone else. Scotland Yard also briefed his company about his whereabouts. He lacked information on what they told them, but he knew his position on the board was in jeopardy. But that wasn't even his biggest concern. By now, he was convinced that the investigators had somehow found some evidence, that not only came back to him, but also connected him with his partners and the research vessel.

Jonathan Brown, Pierre Dumont and Chuck Hogan.

Over and over again, these same names repeated.

How much do they know? What evidence do they have against me? the British constantly asked himself.

Gordon regretted not knowing more about his North American friends. He lacked confidence in his partners, and knew they would, could, and just might use him as their scapegoat. Sure, their first contact was years ago, and it was a fact that they had hired his company to build the pipeline. At the current stage of their election campaign, it would simply be too dangerous for an American or Canadian company to build the pipeline. But Gordon did it. Nobody got suspicious or asked any questions and nothing leaked to the public. Considering all this, he knew he could trust them somehow.

If I'm going down, they're going with me!

Those were the words that Gordon had told them before they started this venture, but the more Gordon thought about it, the more he was convinced that the two politicians were not his problem. They had too much to lose themselves. He was now more concerned about Chuck Hogan. Although Chuck and his men were cold-blooded mercenaries, Gordon knew little about him. Another reason struck his concern to new heights. Chuck was relying on the help of four more people. People, who Chuck obviously trusted, but Gordon didn't know so much as their names. On top of all this, there was still the main reason why Chuck was on board that research vessel. Dealing with weapon grade nuclear material was an international crime, and many agencies were scouting the black market and the internet for that. Maybe they had left a clue or a trace of evidence somewhere.

Gordon Ramshaw wasn't sure about it, but he did remember the exact words of the police officer at the point of his official arrest. He was a suspect, not more. But also nothing less.

Gordon sat upright on his little bed, when he heard the little window in the cell door open.

"Mr. Ramshaw?"

"What is it?" he answered briskly.

The window was closed again and Gordon listened as someone unlocked the two locks on the door. When the door opened, Gordon could see not only his cell guard, but also two more plain clothed officers he had not seen before.

"Mr. Ramshaw, if you would please come with us. Someone from the Central Intelligence Agency would like to talk to you."

This was the first interrogation since last Sunday and Gordon looked suspiciously from one officer to the other.

Someone from the CIA wants to talk to me after official hours? What the hell are they doing here?

Gordon's exhaustion got the better of him as he merely shrugged his shoulders, rose to his feet and followed the two officers out of his cell.

On board the *Northern Explorer*, Amundsen Gulf, Darnley Bay, Wednesday, October 12th

Natascha knelt on the deck beside Nick. She could see her reflection in his mask. He wasn't moving. Her heart raced and her stomach twisted in knots as she took the diving helmet off his head. Her soul ached and her breath escaped her. She stole short quick gasps as his lifeless eyes stared at her. His face was pale. She struggled to find a heart beat. Tears struck her cheek as she pulled him into her. Her eyes shot up to the sky, her rage and sorrow escaping her with a bloody wail. Her eyes returned to the deck where she saw Chuck and his men standing beside a rocket. They all pointed their fingers and laughed at her.

"I told you he's not the right one," *Her father simply stated, standing a short distance from her. Shira and Ariel stood on a staircase, but they didn't say anything. Chuck suddenly came over, grabbed her arm and pulled her on her feet. Under the loud laughter of his men, he pushed her towards them.*

"She's all yours. Have some fun," *the American laughed wildly.*

Natascha woke up with a scream. Her heart raced and she could feel the beads of sweat on her brow. She found herself sitting in the tiny bed. It had been days now that she had this same nightmare. Everything she knew was gone, those she thought would help couldn't.

She rubbed her face and looked down to her father, who was sleeping on the floor beside the bed this night. Despite Natascha's scream, he did not wake up.

The bed was simply too small for two people to sleep comfortably in it. They tried it the first night, but it didn't work. After that, they decided it would make more sense, if they took turns sleeping on the floor.

Completely exhausted, Natascha rose to her feet and sneaked into the little bath room. Beside some toilet paper, there was nothing else she could use for hygiene purposes. She washed the tears from her face and looked in the mirror.

This is not going to end well! she told her reflection.

For several minutes, Natascha stared at her image and never imagined she could look so horrible. Her face was pale and her eyes had deep black rims, her hair was dirty and a complete mess. She stared into her own eyes and could see her own sorry, unhidden and dark. She ran her fingers through her hair in hopes to fix the dishevelled mess. With no luck, she suddenly wished for a shower.

For all the cares that suddenly overcame her, dreaming of a long warm shower was the only desire. She supposed this was because of her nervousness of being separated from Shira and Ariel caused her to endure a deep panic. Natascha didn't even know if they were alive or not. Her father told her he always saw someone take food towards the storage rooms while Chuck and Natascha were under water. It could be, that the two Israeli were locked up down there. The lack of knowing made her queasy. Natascha's concern soon scurried to the bridge. She had no contact with any of the officers or Astrid since they started the diving operation. She had absolutely no idea about their condition. The young Norwegian radio operator had already been under enormous psychological stress and Natascha feared she would no longer be able to handle any more of it.

The young German scientist exhaustedly looked back up in the mirror again.

They're not going to break you. Sooner or later, they'll make a mistake and once they do, I'm ready.

Just a few hours later, Natascha sat in the submersible again. Olaf just finished his first shift underwater and was on his way back to the surface and already at his decompression. Chuck wanted to make sure that everything went according to his plan and ordered Natascha to stay at the wreck of the Russian submarine for a few more minutes. All four divers made great progress inside the inner pressure hull of the submarine, and it was possible to see much more from the outside now. Although Olaf's work during the last twenty minutes stirred up a lot of sediment, Chuck insisted that Natascha brought *Odin* closer to the crack in the submarines hull.

"Get a little bit closer. I can't really see how it looks in the inside," he ordered briskly.

"We can't get any closer. If I'm not careful, our skids will hook into one of those pipes. If that's the case, we have to wait until the next diver comes down here. Worst case scenario we might even damage one of the props from the thruster, then we have a real problem. I can't get any closer," Natascha snapped at the American terrorist.

Involuntarily a shiver descended Natascha's spine at the look that Chuck threw at her. She was afraid he would hit her any moment now, but she was lucky it had not come to such an escalation yet. Slowly the American looked back outside the plexiglas.

"They've scattered the pieces everywhere," he yelled at the four divers.

Natascha looked at the wreckage and the immediate area in front of the crack herself. Chuck was right. The whole area close to the entrance to the submarine's outer pressure hull was scattered with several metal pipes, electric cable, a metal shelf, chairs, a table and many more items she could not identify from this distance. Every diver cleared the submarine from the debris of their previous work. First Natascha was under the impression that they simply wanted to show how much they accomplished during their dive, and it was just now that she realized what they had really done.

They placed those items like this on purpose. That way I can't get any closer to the wreck and Chuck has to rely on this stupid underwater camera, if he wants to see something. They also left the pieces large enough and wedged them into each other so I can't move them with the submersible. My boys have a plan!

Scotland Yard, London, Wednesday, October 12th
The bright light fulfilled it's purpose as Gordon Ramshaw squinted his eyes to see around the light. The British knew the light was supposed to make him uncomfortable and he rubbed his hand over his eyes, before he opened them again. He was waiting for over fifteen minutes in the interrogation room.

Something is different with this room! he noted and looked around. He noticed several distinguishing features.

No mirror and no cameras.

Before he could think more about it, his attention darted to the door as it was being unlocked.

Inspector Conolly entered the interrogation room, closely followed by a woman. Gordon estimated the woman to be in her mid-thirties and he found her, under the circumstances, quite attractive. An evaluation which was, according to the looks that she gave him, only one-sided. Gordon looked deep into her eyes, but the hollow pits of her soul was deterring. He returned his attention to Inspector Conolly.

"Mr. Ramshaw, this is Special Agent Sinclair from the CIA. She has a few questions for you."

Gordon Ramshaw shrugged his shoulders and watched as Special Agent Sinclair turned towards Inspector Conolly.

"Inspector Conolly, would it be possible to speak alone with Mr. Ramshaw," she asked in a tone that made her request sound more like a demand.

The Scotland Yard Inspector was obviously surprised, and Gordon couldn't help but notice, Inspector Conolly did not know Special Agent Sinclair's intentions.

The Inspector looked from Sinclair to Gordon.

"Why do you want to talk to him alone?" he asked, his voice mirroring his surprise.

"I'm sorry, but I can't tell you right now. Should I get any information that benefits your investigation, I'll let you know immediately."

Gordon noticed Inspector Conolly's discomfort as he eyed the Agent carefully. He reluctantly agreed to her terms.

"Very well, then. I'll be waiting in my office for you. I definitely want you to stop by once you're finished here. I don't think it's necessary, but there will be two guards in front of this door at all times. If there are any problems or if you need anything, just let them know. Okay?"

Special Agent Sinclair nodded and only turned her attention to Gordon when Inspector Conolly closed the door behind him.

For the first time she smiled at Gordon, sat opposite him and placed her little suitcase on the table. Still in silence, she popped the lid open and took some files out. Her attention was set on the files as she thumbed through some of the pages.

Gordon could feel his patience wearing thin, but knew this was a tactic. He refused to become uncomfortable under her silence. He spied out her elegant wristwatch and noticed it had been fifteen minutes and she still had not said a single word. He examined her closely as she read the file, completely ignoring him.

Well, that's fine with me. I have nothing else on the go tonight anyway, Gordon told himself and leaned back in his chair.

"Mr. Ramshaw," Special Agent Sinclair suddenly started. It was the precise moment Gordon moved for the first time since Special Agent Sinclair was in the room.

"My British colleagues informed me that just recently you've had personal contact as well as some telephone contact with several American citizens, amongst them a politician. Is that correct?"

"I didn't know it's illegal to contact Americans, and yes, in my field of work, someone has contact to politicians, even American politicians."

Special Agent Sinclair stared at him for several seconds before she started her interrogation. Gordon only told her what everybody else already knew. He wasted several minutes telling her about himself and his position in the company. From there on he continued to talk in detail about completely irrelevant conferences and meetings in the United States, which had absolutely nothing to do with the situation at hand and were completely legal.

Special Agent Sinclair listened carefully and took plenty of notes. She also followed up on the subjects of those conferences and on the people who took part in those. Since neither the results of those conferences nor the identity of the participating people were a secret, Gordon did not see a reason why he shouldn't lead the young American woman even further away from the initial subject.

Gordon was convinced, that before long, he fed her with so many irrelevant and unimportant details that Special Agent Sinclair would question why she was here in the first place.

After two hours, he could feel his success.

The CIA Special Agent put her pen down and with a wheeze, she leaned back. Shaking her head, she looked at her notes.

"I think I could use a coffee," she said more to herself and called for the guards.

Immediately the door was opened and a young guard entered the interrogation room.

"I'm sorry to bother you with this, but would it be too much to ask you for a cup of coffee, please?"

"No problem, Ma'am. I'll get you a cup right away. Milk? Sugar?" the guard asked politely.

"No, thank you. Black please."

The guard nodded and turned around to leave the interrogation room.

Special Agent Sinclair briefly looked at Gordon and turned back to the guard, who just turned to lock the door again.

"Can you please bring two cups?" she smiled apologetically, hopefully, "Thank you!"

On board the *Northern Explorer*, Amundsen Gulf, Darnley Bay, Wednesday, October 12th

By the time Chuck and Natascha were back at the surface, Olaf was already on the deck of the *Northern Explorer*, taking his dry-suit off. As soon as Chuck left the submersible he walked over to Olaf.

"How far are you down there?"

The Norwegian looked at him with deep hatred.

"We successfully cleaned the first compartment and I assume that according to the blueprints we only have two more meters to go until we reach the missile silo. The damage should be minimum in there, since there's nothing in them but the missiles."

"I have the feeling you're wasting a great deal of time down there by cutting out things that don't need to be removed in the first place," the American shouted at him suddenly.

Natascha jump with fear when she heard Chuck. Obviously the mercenary had come to the same conclusion as the young German scientist.

Before Olaf responded, he slowly took a towel to dry his hair.

"I don't know what your personal experience is when it comes to the recovery of nuclear warheads out of a submarine wreck in over seventy meters in arctic waters, but I can guarantee you that it gets pretty damn tight down there when you plan to move three warheads in zero visibility through a mangled submarine. If we could have done this without much room, we would have gone through the outer hatches, but unfortunately it's not that simple. I suggest you go down there and do it yourself, if this is not fast enough for you."

Olaf threw his towel on top of his dive gear and turned away from Chuck frustrated. The Norwegian knew that he irritated Chuck, but he didn't care. Although he could see Chuck moving, Olaf could not react in time. Chuck's fist and pistol hit the Norwegian in the neck. Olaf yelled out in pain and sank to his knees.

Natascha couldn't restrain her own scream as her hands quickly rushed to her mouth with shock. She immediately rushed towards her friend to help him, but Jenna stepped in her way with an arrogant smile.

"Escort this idiot back to his cabin and bring the next diver up. Make sure they do not see each other," Chuck barked his order. One of his men quickly approached the superstructure, ignoring Olaf's tender moans.

**Home Office and Operational Headquarters of *EuroSecCorporation*,
London, Wednesday, October 12th**
Retired General Klaus Schwartze sat behind his desk. His elbows on the table and his chin resting on his hand, he looked at the clock on his desk. It was almost six in the evening. He frustratedly stared at the piece of paper in front of him. He skimmed his notes again. All the information from the last sixty hours was compiled on one sheet of paper. He furiously looked for more details, but there was nothing else added to it. The only real news was that a Special Agent of the Central Intelligence Agency was interrogating Gordon Ramshaw at this very moment. Klaus hoped Gordon would tell her something useful, but he wouldn't bet on it. Another quick look at the clock told him that his friend and colleague Brian Whittaker would call him within the next five minutes just to ask him the same questions he had asked him the last three days. All that Klaus could report, was that there was nothing to report. Klaus could understand Brian's frustration only too well. While the retired General was at least directly involved in the stream of information, Brian could do nothing but sit in New York and wait. It was no surprise that the former Admiral felt the situation becoming more insufferable by the minute. On top of that they still didn't have any radio contact with the *Northern Explorer*. With that his men were somewhere in the Artic without displaying any sign of life for what has now been over ninety-six hours. This was a fact he was really concerned about. During such a mission it was very unusual for someone to not check in at the agreed time. If they were going to be five minutes late, they would need a very good explanation for it, but the fact that he did not hear from his men for several days now, almost drove him insane.

Like many times before, his eyes looked for the last confirmed contact with the *Northern Explorer*. The message from a radio operator by the name of Astrid Makkinen was so few words but still detailed. Her message clearly described the situation they were dealing with. The former General knew about the circumstances and in his opinion, there were only two explanations why he had not heard from his team. They were either still alive but under complete physical control of the enemy or they were already dead. Usually situation one would eventually result in situation two. It was only a matter of time. Time that neither his team nor Klaus himself had. The ringing of the phone interrupted his thoughts and although Klaus knew that it was Brian, he double-checked the display. The caller identification was blocked, another sign that it was Brian, since he never rid himself of that habit. Klaus straightened up and picked up the phone. He heard the voice before he could say anything.

"Good evening, General Schwartze. This is General Rashid in Israel. We have something for you."

**On board the *Northern Explorer*, Amundsen Gulf, Darnley Bay,
Wednesday, October 12th**
Since the attack on Olaf, Natascha refused to speak to Chuck. Prior to the attack, she voluntarily provided some useful information, but only because she thought it would help Nick and his friends do their jobs. Whether consciously or otherwise, she

only spoke to Chuck when he asked her something, and when she did, she was very brisk.

Without a word she serviced the rebreather and had to use the last scrubber. After that she helped Oliver in his dry-suit and the gear. Like so many times before, she leaned forward to adjust both his neck seal and his neoprene hood. Even the slightest leak could have serious consequences due to the combination of the total dive time and the low water temperature.

"Chuck hit Olaf, but he's okay," Natascha whispered as she fixed his neoprene hood and the warm neck collar.

Oliver slightly nodded, but he didn't say a word.

Natascha helped him to his feet and made sure the rebreather was working properly.

"Hey, it's time. We wasted enough time today. Let's move it," Chuck yelled at them.

"Everything's going to be fine, okay? Stay focused," Oliver winked at Natascha with a smile, offering a taste of hope.

As much as Natascha wanted to, she couldn't really believe him. All she could manage was to force a smile, before she turned away from him. On her way to the submersible she wiped a tear from her cheek. Completely exhausted, she slowly climbed down into the submersible and sat beside Chuck. She exchanged a quick glance with her father as they went over the checklist together. The young German let out a yawn as they submerged into the cold arctic waters.

Something that would have been an exciting and interesting adventure under different circumstances was now nothing more than a dangerous operation.

Like before, Oliver descended along the rope of the marker buoy into the black depth with Natascha shining the submersible lights at him. Down at the bottom Oliver took the cable controlled underwater camera and light and swam towards the wreck of the Russian U-Boat. On his short swim he passed a collection of pipes and cables that Olaf removed and placed outside the wreck earlier this morning. Oliver looked at them and stopped for a second. By looking at the items, the young German was hoping to get an idea how it would look inside the wreck. Oliver gazed at the opening in the outer hull of the U-Boat as he glided into the wreck. As he expected, the visibility inside the wreck was the same if not worse. This was a direct result of Olaf's work earlier this morning. The fine sediment was everywhere in the water and Oliver could barely see anything. His left hand followed the cables from the welder, while he used his right hand in front of him, waiting to make contact with whatever would be in his way. He finally reached the wall to the next compartment. According to the blue prints, it was only two more meters to the missile silo. Oliver examined the wall carefully with his right hand, satisfied that he didn't find anything sharp enough to obstruct his work or pose as a hazard to himself. He carefully checked the floor in the same way. In this depth and with such low water temperatures he could not risk to cut,or puncture his suit. Since the visibility was already ruined, he didn't care about the sediment he stirred up. He could feel some longer items. Apparently he found four short pipes or heavy cables. Making sure that no one else would damage their suit on those, the young German diver decided to move them outside. Carefully he picked them up and noticed they were neither corroded in any way nor had any marine growth on them. Their ends also felt different than normal pipes. Since he couldn't see, he relied on his sense of touch, but he still could not figure out what he was holding. All he was certain about was that they were not pipes. Curious about what he found, he held one end close to his mask. His heart instantly raced,

Oh my God! I didn't know! I didn't mean to disturb you. I'm sorry! Oliver apologized inwardly as he held a human femur bone. Although he knew he was inside a grave of over one hundred sailors, the first real contact with some remains was still unexpected and frightful. This would also mean that they would most likely find more human remains from now on. As dignified as possible, Oliver put the remains down and out of his way. He did not want to take them out of the U-Boat. This was their grave and this was where they should remain. Oliver positioned them in a way the other divers would see the remains of the Russian sailor on their way in. That way, they would at least know what to expect and they could prepare themselves as good as possible. After he overcame his initial shock he looked at his dive computer. The OLED display showed him a remaining bottom time of only sixteen minutes. Without thinking about the human remains any further, he installed a cutting rod and started to work. After the first rod burned down, Oliver waited a few moments to get an idea of what he accomplished. With a little bit of luck he could see a more or less straight cut of about forty centimeters. Using a loose wire he reassured himself that he cut right through the thick wall. He quickly installed the next cutting rod. His process was falling into a rapid routine as the next two cutting rods worked flawlessly.

The gas that was released during the chemical reaction of the cutting formed a rather large bubble directly over Oliver. Without realizing, the gas obstructed the sight of loose cable loops and produced a constant shower of rusty particles. Satisfied with his work, Oliver checked his dive computer. Twenty-one minutes. It was time to start the ascent.

Just outside the wreck of the U-Boat, Natascha sat inside *Odin* and her nervousness increased by the second. Usually the divers started after eighteen minutes to move the items they had just cut, outside the wreck. Especially since they had to take both the camera and the light with them out of the wreck. But Oliver was now inside the wreck for twenty minutes and she still couldn't see any sign of him.

For the third time within a minute she checked her wrist watch and swallowed hard.

Twenty-one minutes and still no sign of Oliver.

"Come on", she whispered impatiently. Her instincts told her that something inside the wreck of the Russian U-Boat was wrong.

"What is it? Don't tell me you have something going with him as well?" Chuck mocked.

Natascha ignored this comment, refusing to offer him the slightest reaction.

Oliver just finished his work and was, given the circumstances, more or less satisfied. After he convinced himself that he did not create any hazardous areas for his friends, he pushed himself off the bottom to turn around. Startled he didn't move, he swallowed slowly and tried again. With no avail, Oliver tried to keep his panic in check. Very slowly and carefully he turned back to his original direction and he noticed he had more movement this way. His nervousness subsided for the moment, but he knew he was no step further than he was before.

His anxiety returned on a new level. He hurriedly looked at his computer again. Twenty-two minutes. No matter what, he had to get out of this wreck now. Trying to avoid getting caught up again he tried to turn the other direction. Not noticing any resistance, he thanked God and picked up the underwater camera and reached for the light. Just centimeters before his fingers touched the light, something yanked at this gear and pulled him back into the bowels of the wreck. Oliver gasped with fright as the light went out.

Scotland Yard, London, Wednesday, October 12th

While Special Agent Sinclair waited for her coffee, she silently went over her notes one more time.

That's a very strange interrogation technique. This way it will take some time before I make a mistake, Gordon thought hopefully.

The door opened and an officer carrying two cups of black coffee entered the room.

"Here's the coffee," the man smiled and placed the tray with the two cups, some milk and several little bags of sweetener on the table.

"Oh, thank you very much. That's very kind of you," Special Agent Sinclair replied and followed the officer with her gaze as he left the interrogation room.

Once the door was closed again, she opened her little executive case and, under Gordon's watchful eyes, took her own small bottle of sweetener out of it.

"I'm allergic to all those cheap chemical copies and use my own brand," she explained and dropped two little dollops in her coffee.

"Can I offer you some as well?" she asked and looked at Gordon.

The British frowned at the offer.

She really has no clue about interrogations.

"Yes, why not? If you can spare one or two, please."

He watched carefully as Special Agent Sinclair pressed the same button on the little dispenser, before he stirred his coffee.

It can't be a drug, she's drinking that stuff herself right in front of me.

Gordon waited and watched carefully as Special Agent Abigail Sinclair drank from her coffee, before he finally took the first sip from his own.

"Well, Mr. Ramshaw," the American finally continued. "Let's get back to that meeting in Boston. What did you do immediately after the conference?"

It took Gordon some effort not to smile or even laugh. Slowly he put his cup back on the table and started to tell details from a meeting that had absolutely nothing to do with the situation up north.

On board the *Northern Explorer*, Amundsen Gulf, Darnley Bay, Wednesday, October 12th

By now the twenty-three minute mark has come and gone and Natascha repeatedly turned the cable controlled underwater light on and off. There was still no reaction.

"Come on, Oliver," she shouted in sudden panic.

Twenty-four minutes and still no sign of Oliver. Again and again, the young German scientist turned the underwater light on and off, while she closely watched the monitor from the underwater camera. The visibility inside the pressure hull of the wreck was so horrible she could not see anything.

Inside the wreck of the U-Boat Oliver fought against the panic that slowly started to rise inside him. He closed his eyes, forced himself to calm down and took a few deep breaths.

Don't panic now. It can't be a big problem. You have more than enough gas with you and outside on Odin *is all the spare gas you need. Everything is okay. Before I will be at my first deco stop, Natascha will have figured out an emergency decompression. Everything is going to be fine. Okay, try to find out why you can't move.*

Carefully Oliver reached back over his shoulder as far as he could. He was hoping to feel what he was entangled in, but all he could sense was the housing and the valves from his rebreather.

Okay, when you came in here earlier, you saw an old electric cable, that was hanging in a loop from the ceiling. That must be it. My gear is somehow stuck in that cable. Because of the bubbles I created when I cut through that wall I didn't see that cable any more. That's the reason I'm stuck. It's no problem.

Oliver took another couple deep breaths and tried to free himself again. When this second attempt didn't work either, Oliver realized he had to do something different. Although he didn't want to he checked his dive computer again. Twenty-six minutes, three minutes over the scheduled bottom time.

Okay, time for plan B, Oliver encouraged himself and started to remove the rebreather.

Not far away from him Natascha looked at her wrist watch again. Twenty-six minutes, and still no sign of Oliver. Her panic rose incredibly. She continued to switch the underwater light on and off, her only way of communication, but she didn't get any reaction from inside the wreck.

"Why's he not coming out?" Chuck asked seriously without getting an answer.

Natascha carefully maneuvered *Odin* closer to the wreck, but as much as she tried, she couldn't peek inside.

Frightened, she looked at the monitor again, but she couldn't even see shadows. The fine sediment had reduced the visibility effectively down to nothing. Another quick look at her watch, twenty-seven minutes. Oliver was four minutes over the scheduled bottom time. It was now certain that Oliver would need the spare gas that was secured outside on *Odin*'s frame. Since all the divers used Natascha's dive computer, they could only use it as a bottom timer. Natascha checked her notes for a new decompression schedule for Oliver, but she realized that she was wasting her time so long as Oliver was inside this wreck. Twenty-eight minutes. For a second she could see the sudden movement of a fin on the monitor. That was it.

In front of the underwater camera Oliver was fighting for his life. He had taken the rebreather off, but because of the bad visibility he could not see where his gear was stuck. His bottom timer, which he had carried around his wrist, was also gone and he was pulling with all his strength at the rebreather, but it remained stuck.

Okay, stay calm. Stop yanking at the gear. Control your breathing. All you have to do is to swim outside and to the submersible. There's enough breathing gas there for the complete decompression. Relax, control your breathing and leave that stupid rebreather here before you swim outside. Natascha's already waiting for me. It's not more than twenty-five meters. No problem with fins.

To prepare for his escape he let all the air out of his dry suit. He did not want to risk losing control over his buoyancy once he was outside the wreck. Unfortunately he did not notice he accidentally altered with the manual controls of the rebreather during his attempts to free it. The gas he was breathing was a complete different mixture and not suited for these depths, something Oliver wasn't aware of. He still tried to control his breathing, but somehow he couldn't manage it. His breathing rate was still way too high and he tried to fight against the rising panic inside him. With his eyes closed he saw the bones again and he could feel his pulse in his temples. The moment he reopened them, the bones sprang to life and formed a sailor in Russian uniform. The banging in his temples grew stronger and stronger and throbbed as a painful headache. The Russian sailor came towards him and tried to reach for him. His headache grew unbearable. Although the water was just over the freezing point, Oliver could feel his temperature rise. He opened his eyes again and all he could see were flashes of light drifting through the complete darkness, then he saw more Russian sailors. They started to dance in front of him and Oliver's head burst with pain, igniting his confusion to scream. Finally Oliver spit out the mouthpiece of the breathing loop and swam outside the U-boat as fast as he could.

Even when he had his eyes closed, he could clearly see all the Russian sailors to his left and his right, chasing him away from their grave. Finally he was outside the wreck and Oliver opened his eyes again. He saw a bright light just in front of him and he stopped. His survival instincts and his training as a former German Kampfschwimmer took over. All he had to do was get to that light. There he would find the lifesaving breathing gas that his body needed so desperately at this moment. In a last effort Oliver reached the submersible. His pulse hammered inside his head as if someone punched him with iron fists. Every string in his body screamed for oxygen. The ghosts of the Russian sailors were standing beside him now and they watched him silently as he reached for a tank. Without knowing it, he opened the tank valve and put the regulator in his mouth. Oliver could hear someone calling his name in the distance and he wondered how this was possible, but the hammering in his temples and the pain in his head prohibited him from thinking clearly. As his name was called he could also hear knocking on something in the distance, but he didn't care.

One of the Russian sailors came closer towards him and reached out with his hand, inviting Oliver. Finally he noticed the flow of the breathing gas. Oliver took a deep breath, then another and another. The Russian sailor took his hand and smiled at him. His pain was finally ceasing as the light got brighter and brighter. It was only a few more breaths until he was completely engulfed in the alluring white light.

"Oliver!" Natascha screamed and hammered with both her fists on the plexiglas dome. She knew something went horribly wrong, but the moment she saw Oliver coming out of the U-Boat without the dive gear her blood froze.

"Oliver! The other tank! That's the wrong tank!" she frantically screamed but he could not hear her. Natascha immediately realized Oliver couldn't think rationally anymore and she just watched as he reached for the first tank he could get.

"Oliver! Oliver! You have to take the other tank! That's the wrong tank, Oliver!"

Natascha still repeated frantically, pounding her fists harder against the plexiglas. Her attempts were good, but there was nothing she could do. Less than one meter away she helplessly witnessed her friend breathe one-hundred-percent pure oxygen. Oliver knew full well this could only be used to a depth of six meters during the decompression. But his conscience was muddled. The moment Oliver took his third breath he started to cramp uncontrollably. The green regulator fell out of his mouth and only seconds later he sank peacefully to the sea floor, establishing his final resting place.

Petrified Natascha sat in her seat, covering her face with both hands. She couldn't control herself any longer and her tears were running down her face. She didn't want to look outside and see the body of her dead friend any more.

Chuck sat silently beside her. During the complete tragedy, which had not taken longer than a minute, he did not say a single word. Although he had absolutely no problem taking a human life, he found himself swallowing hard and taking some deep breaths. Oliver had been his enemy and he would have been executed sooner or later anyway, but that did not mean that Chuck did not respect him and his training. The mercenary immediately thought about his problem and what he had to do next. Oliver was gone and in his situation it was much more merciful for him to drown down here instead of performing an uncontrolled emergency ascent. Chuck decided he wanted to get back to the surface as quick as possible. The second rebreather had to be checked and prepared and the next diver had to continue their mission. Other than that, Chuck had no idea how it looked inside the wreck of the Russian U-Boat and what happened. Fact was that Oliver left the wreck without the rebreather and Chuck knew he wouldn't have done so without a very good reason. The loss of the diver did not so much concern Chuck, but the loss of a day nerved him. There were now only three divers to do the work of four, making their diving breaks much shorter.

The American knew he had to give Natascha some time now. As much as he wanted to get back to the surface, he knew he relied heavily on the young German scientist down here. If he pushed her too far now, there was a risk that she would do something stupid; something that could end deadly for the both of them. After a while he turned on the underwater light and the camera again attempting to see anything inside the wreck, but it was impossible. Oliver's fight for his life had stirred up more sediment as ever before and it was impossible to see anything. Chuck orientated himself at the instruments and spotted the switch for the winch. He activated it, but after two seconds the winch stopped automatically. Both the underwater camera and the light were stuck inside the wreck.

Chuck swallowed hard.

They were stuck.

- 21 -

**Home Office and Operational Headquarters of *EuroSecCorporation*,
London, Wednesday, October 12th**

"What do you have?" Klaus Schwartze asked, his disbelief evident as his face widened at General Rashid's words.

"We have a few satellite images from that area from last Sunday. There were no clouds at the time, we were lucky. I just sent them to your computer. Can you confirm you received them? I'll guide you through them."

Klaus activated the speakerphone, put his phone down and turned towards his computer. In his Inbox he found the new message with two attached pictures.

Within seconds he saved them to his hard drive and opened them anxiously.

"Okay, I got them. What am I looking at?" he finally asked his Israeli friend.

"The first picture shows the area around Paulatuk from an altitude of one hundred kilometers. In the center of the picture you can see a little image. That's the research vessel *Northern Explorer*. Picture number two shows the *Northern Explorer* from an altitude of only two hundred and fifty meters. Can you recognize it?"

With heavy concentration Klaus looked at the monitor.

"Yes, I can clearly see it. Looks normal. Helicopter on the deck and a boom lift that reaches over the rail. I assume this is during a diving operation. I can't see any signs of a hostage situation. What are those two objects right beside the life raft?" Klaus asked and tried to zoom into the image to take a closer look.

General Rashid did not have to give him the explanation.

"Wait a second. I got it. Those are two bodies."

"Unfortunately you're correct, as always. Those are indeed two dead bodies. Our experts altered the resolution a little bit. At least with one of the dead bodies we're certain he's wearing the white uniform of an officer. Unfortunately, we can't read the name tag at this time, but we're working on that as well."

Klaus was thinking. Something still did not seem right. The two dead bodies were a disturbing and disastrous sign that the vessel was experiencing a high level of violence. Klaus looked closely at the image again.

Why is the officer wearing his uniform? He thought for a quick moment. He knew that during an expedition they were usually dressed casually, except on special occasions. Curiosity suddenly clicked.

"General Rashid. Do you believe that it's possible that the officer was killed while the politicians were still on board?"

General Rashid paused a moment, "Well why not? That would explain why he's wearing his uniform. By the time we took this picture both politicians had officially left the *Northern Explorer*, but we don't know when the two men were executed. All we know for certain is that on Sunday, October ninth at zero-nine-fifty-four two dead bodies lay on the deck of the research vessel."

"Yes, you're correct."

"What do you plan to do now?"

"Well, we still don't have any news from the research vessel itself and still have no contact with our unit. Brian is in New York, since the Canadians are still refusing to inspect the vessel. I'm planning to light their asses on fire today. I'm also thinking it wouldn't be a bad idea to contact both the German and Norwegian Ambassador to put some weight behind it."

Klaus fell silent for a few seconds before he continued in a much softer tone.

"General Rashid, how do you feel about Israel being officially involved in this?"

In his position Klaus knew only to well about the latest tensions between the American and the Israelian government in regards to the political situation in the middle east.

"My dear friend, we both know about the military background of my son and my daughter. If the people behind this operation are really politicians, then we can be certain they have an iron clad story and that they have several back-up stories. It'd be devastating for me if I lose one of my children in this horrible situation, but it would really break my heart if some political wannabe paints them as terrorist scapegoats." General Rashid paused a moment with further thought, "What options do you have?"

"We're prepared for this scenario. I respect your position and will keep you informed. I appreciate all your help. Thank you very much, my friend."

"My pleasure. I'll call again tomorrow morning ten-hundred. Shalom."

The moment Klaus disconnected the line, his wife and secretary Brigitte entered his office.

"I have Brian on line one. He wants me to tell you that you better be talking to either one of our guys on the ship or to the Queen of England. He's very indignant about the fact that you're ignoring his call."

"Yes, I know, but I just have the right thing for him," Klaus replied with a tense smile. He turned his attention back to the phone and activated the line.

On board the *Northern Explorer*, Amundsen Gulf, Darnley Bay, Wednesday, October 12th

In disbelief Chuck stared out the plexiglas dome. Shock overcame him as the images registered and engrained the horror in his memory. Oliver's last moment was graphic, worse than most other things he had seen. But his concern grew as he looked at the Russian U-boat. The cable from both the underwater camera and light slacked as soon as the winch stopped. The submersible gently drifted closer to the sunken submarine and Chuck watched as the cables loosened. Nervously he looked over to the young German scientist, whose face was buried deeply in her hands, completely horrified of Oliver's unexpected death.

"We're stuck," the American told her with a trace of panic in his voice.

Natascha's shoulders shook violently as a new wave of fear, shock and blame overcame her. She cried unrestrainedly, her sobs darkening to deep choking moans. The vicious images replayed in her mind, his lifeless body drifting to the depths of the dark abyss of the ocean, claiming another loved soul. She cursed herself for being so lucky to escape her impending doom twice. It was only a matter of time fate would pull it's graceful hand away.

Blame coursed through her veins with every thought, boiling her rage from deep within. If she wouldn't have gone to this expedition then Oliver would still be alive. It was only now that she realized she was the only one who was voluntarily on the vessel. The only reason Nick and his friends had to deal with this situation was because of her. Sure, at the beginning everybody believed they had to protect her father, but since Iceland everyone knew she was the actual target. Her eyes flicked open furiously, the cause of all of this was sitting right beside her.

No! It's not your fault Oliver's dead. It's their fault! Oliver was with you for over three months and nothing happened to him. It's not your fault! she told herself repeatedly.

Her thoughts quickly drifted to the past, cycling around the memories with Oliver. It was always him she danced with. Nick never mentioned anything about it.

As long as you're coming home with me afterwards, you can dance as much as you want with him. Nick told her one day, knowing how much she enjoyed dancing.

Natascha shook her head as she realized her trivial thoughts. Nothing could change what just happened. Oliver's lifeless body rested just a few meters in front of her.

After all it didn't take too long. He didn't suffer much.

Natascha was gripped with fear when she thought about the slight possibility Oliver could have survived an uncontrolled emergency ascent to the surface. The inevitable outcome would have been the same, except that it would have been much more painful for her friend.

Okay! You got to be strong now. The last thing Oliver wanted was for you to suffer a mental breakdown now...But he certainly didn't want to die either! Her inner voice yelled at her.

Once we're back on the Northern Explorer *something has to happen. You have to be strong for that. They can't get away with this. You don't let them ruin your life!* she told herself again and again.

"Hey, I said we're stuck!" Chuck yelled at her loudly. His fear was evident, though much more controlled than the first time.

Tiredly, Natascha wiped some tears from her face and looked outside. Her eyes followed the cable for the underwater camera and light. For a moment she considered the different options.

"Do something," the American commanded in his usual aggressive tone.

Emotionally exhausted, Natascha looked at him. His impressions accentuated his nervousness as he refused to remove his fixed attention from the cable.

You goddamned bastard! Natascha thought and stared at him silently.

Without even looking at the instrument board she pushed a button. Immediately after they heard a little mechanical release that disconnected the cable winch, the monitor turned black as a *lost signal* message warned them. The cable winch slowly sank to the ocean floor.

Natascha took a few more seconds to check all the systems before she brought *Odin* back to the surface.

Scotland Yard, London, Wednesday, October 12th
It was almost ten in the evening and Special Agent Sinclair went over her notes once more.

I'm going to eat my hat if she can find anything useful in that, Gordon thought pridefully. He spent the last two hours telling her completely irrelevant details about some legitimate business trips in the United States. He knew she would follow up on his travel patterns, just to find out if he missed any details. The moment she realized there was nothing to be found she would come back to him. He knew this was for certain. She would not come back empty handed, though. Gordon could easily guess that she would compare his statement with his credit card charges. Fortunately, these would only lead her to a few dinners with different business partners in different restaurants. None of this could be actually tied to the situation up north. If she concentrated on those unimportant details, she would waste several days investigating a dead end trail. He knew just several days of unproductive investigations would get him out of this.

He looked up and watched Special Agent Sinclair closely as she packed her notes into her executive case.

"Well then, Mr. Ramshaw, I think I have enough information for today. It might be possible we have to continue this interrogation at a later date."

"My pleasure," Gordon replied emotionlessly and watched as she left the interrogation room.

Shortly after the two guards escorted him back to his cell and he sat down on his bed.

He couldn't help himself and a smile spread across his face.

Well, that's a first. They're either playing a game I don't know or they're complete idiots. Either way they didn't get anything useful from me today.

His confidence in the events of the interrogation prohibited his satisfaction from leaving his face. He laid back on his bed with a wonderous sigh. For a moment he closed his eyes. The warmth of such satisfaction reignited something he had not felt in a long while. Whether it was the heat of the room or his own contentedness that triggered his blood to a degree of comfort he had never experienced, he didn't care. Knowing the clock was ticking, he removed his clothes and went to bed.

On board the *Northern Explorer*, Amundsen Gulf, Darnley Bay, Wednesday, October 12th
On the deck of the *Northern Explorer* Natascha stood at the rail and stared at the water, lost in thought. Her father stood beside her, one arm over his daughter's shoulder. Natascha stammered uncontrollably about the events that transpired at the wreck, it took Richard several moments to piece it all together. The horror contorted his face,

Thin Ice

but he could only imagine the emotions his daughter was struggling with. Without saying a word Natascha still stared at the surface where Oliver found his final resting place in seventy meters depth.

She could remember Chuck's harsh words, his very aggressive reaction, at her suggestion to recover Oliver's body with *Odin*. His aggression only suggested it would obviously not fit within his great plan.

First Vitali, then the First Officer and now Oliver.

Natascha shook her head in disbelief. She could feel her energy leaving her each day, today taking the worst of it. She struggled to grasp her motivation to continue, and found her faith in her team. Natascha knew Ariel and his team would be able to rescue them all.

But how could they do that? They always work in a team. Oliver was a crucial member of their team. Now he's dead and they don't even know about it. Natascha struggled to admit Oliver's fate to herself, but knew she had to tell them, they had to know. *The team will find out during their next dive. My rebreather's still inside the wreck and there's still the chance they're going to find him.*

"Okay, move on. Get yourself together," she heard Chucks aggressive command bellow from behind her.

Slowly the young German turned around.

"Where's the second rebreather?" the American demanded.

"It's in our storage room," she replied in a broken voice, barely understandable. She returned her gaze to the water again.

"Then move your ass and get it. It's not going to help you if you're just standing their crying your eyes out. Nelson, go with her," Chuck ordered with finality, and turned away.

Nelson Singer walked over to her and Natascha followed his demand and walked over the deck to the stairs that led them below to their storage room. Slowly and without even realizing where she was going, Natascha led Nelson past the American's and Canadian's storage room before she stopped in front of the locked door of her storage room. While Nelson took a set of keys and tried different ones to open the door, Natascha noticed something at the end of the walkway. Her surprise overcame her. One of the American scientists sat guard in front of a door and Natascha knew immediately where they kept Ariel and Shira. Even better, the fact that someone was guarding that door also meant that both of them were still alive. Without attracting any attention Natascha looked away and watched as Nelson finally opened the door. She followed him inside and turned on the light. The second rebreather was secured to the wall and Natascha placed it on the table. While she took the cover off she remembered she took the scrubber out of this unit during her last inspection. She slowly realized she had a serious problem. The last usable scrubber was in her own rebreather, which was now out of reach in over seventy meters inside the wreck of the Russian U-Boat. Even if they were able to recover the unit, the scrubber would be completely useless by then. Natascha swallowed hard and walked over to the closet just to confirm her suspicion. The rebreather needed the scrubber to filter the breathing gas after it was exhaled and without any scrubber the rebreather could not function.

"What's the problem?" Nelson asked irately.

Although he tried to put some authority in his voice Natascha could clearly notice how nervous the young American was himself.

"We don't have any scrubbers. The last cartridge is down inside the wreck," Natascha stammered quietly, swallowing hard as she thought of Chuck's reaction.

"Okay, well, nothing we can do about that. Let's go back on deck," Nelson ordered and escorted Natascha outside.

She knew the faster they moved, the sooner they would reach Chuck. Even with each step she could already feel her apprehension increase drastically.

"What's the problem. Where's the rebreather?" Chuck asked in a dangerously low tone.

"The unit's still in the storage room. She says there's no more scrubbers left," Nelson replied to his boss.

Natascha was too scared to look at Chuck and stared at the water instead. Every second she expected him to beat her. She saw his sudden movement, closed her eyes and started, but there was no pain. When she opened her eyes she realized Chuck simply walked by her on his way to the storage room to check it himself.

When he came back to the deck several minutes later he could barely control himself.

"She's right. Goddamnnit. Okay, change of plans. They have to use the helmet gear from now on. It's going to be their problem if they have to breath air at the end."

Although Natascha was convinced nothing could shock her any more, she just learned better.

"Let's go. We don't have much time left," Chuck commanded impatiently.

"Do you really believe her?" Jenna asked her brother, shocked.

"I couldn't find any and there was barely any left when we started. Bring up the Norwegian. He'll go next."

Home Office and Operational Headquarters of *EuroSecCorporation*, London, Wednesday, October 12th

Klaus just finished his conversation with Brian, who yelled out his euphoria and was already looking for the next flight to Ottawa. Although it was already late at night, the work just started for Klaus. First he contacted the German Embassy as well as the Bundesnachrichtendienst and the Norwegian Embassy. The retired General was quite happy he had Gunnar Eriksson, a former and well respected Norwegian Officer in his staff. Gunnar was the best person to brief the Norwegian Ambassador correctly and with the necessary emphasis in regards to the significance of this matter. It turned out that not only the Bundesnachrichtendienst, but also the German and the Norwegian Embassy were far more interested in this situation than the Canadian's and they all promised their utmost support. They agreed it would be best for Brian Whittaker to meet both the Norwegian and the German Ambassador's in Canada to offer them details himself once more. After, they would officially inform the authorities together.

Klaus was convinced the Canadians would not sit idly the moment they would hear the involvement of foreign countries.

**On board the *Northern Explorer*, Amundsen Gulf, Darnley Bay,
Wednesday, October 12th**

Natascha was unsure whether she liked the idea of her friends going to the wreck without her safe eyes watching them from *Odin*. Since the future dives had to be done with the surface supplied diving helmet, it was no longer necessary for Chuck to go down to monitor the diving activities underwater. Both diving helmets had a little cable operated underwater video-camera mounted to their site. The video signal could be seen in real time on a monitor in the dive control room.

The very thought of telling her Norwegian friend made Natascha's throat clench with fear and shock. Her tears suddenly sprung as she helped Ole-Einar with the neck seal. Overwhelmed with emotion and the images that reflectively occupied her thoughts, she told him what had happened to Oliver and that his body was still outside the wreck. Ole-Einar looked at Natascha in shock. He did not expect such news, and dreaded the day that it would happen. While the young German flung her arms around his neck with an exhaustive cry, Ole-Einar threw a hateful glance at Chuck. He hated that the American had his back turned to him.

"Shira and Ariel are in the Russian's storage room," Natascha whispered barely audible and let go of Ole-Einar as Jenna stepped closer to them.

Although the Norwegian had not shown any reaction, Natascha was convinced he understood her. With a swift movement Ole-Einar put the helmet on his head and Natascha latched it to the neck dam.

After they checked the communication system, Natascha helped Ole-Einar towards the basket that would swing him over the rail. Only a few minutes later the Norwegian disappeared into the depths of the arctic water.

Natascha watched his descent for as long as she could see him, fearing the worst. Knowing he was not going to come back up for a while, she walked back towards the dive control room.

Fortunately, the two-way communication system allowed them to talk to Ole-Einar at all times to recieve updates. During the descent the Norwegian looked at his bottom timer, so that Chuck and the other people in the dive control room could always see his actual depth. The two-way communication system was also very helpful to remind Ole-Einar when he had to switch breathing gas. All he had to do was adjust the gas select switch that was secured to his harness. Although Ole-Einars descent went as planned, Natascha still asked him about any symptoms. The Norwegian was the most experienced diver of them all and he had no issues. Just minutes after he started his descent he reached the bottom. Knowing about the task ahead of him, he decided to dive without fins and was now hopping towards the wreck. Inside the dive control room Chuck noticed that Ole-Einar continuously scanned the area around the wreck. The Norwegian was obviously looking for Oliver's body, but he assumed the tide carried him away.

"I need more hose," Ole-Einar demanded just before he was ready to enter the wreck.

Natascha confirmed his message and directed the Norwegian's command towards Nelson, who stood by the rail to make sure the umbilical hose did not get caught up in anything.

Seventy meters below, Ole-Einar climbed into the wreck of the U-Boat and immediately found the rebreather. This was Natascha's and her father's least concern when they were focused on the breathing gas. Satisfied to see he was breathing the right mixture, they returned to the monitor.

As if spellbound, Chuck followed Ole-Einar's work with great detail on the monitor. It mattered greatly to him that every diving helmet had a video-camera mounted to it's side. Even in the low visibility Chuck could see relatively well with this camera system. Inside the wreck Ole-Einar had no issues to free the rebreather from the cable. He carefully took it outside, where he positioned it together with the underwater light and camera system from the submersible. With those items out of his way, he made his way back into the U-Boat wreck to continue with his work.

Without any interruptions, he was able to cut the entire wall that separated them from the access room to the missiles. The moment the heavy wall fell inside, the visibility improved immediately. Since this part of the Wreck was not exposed to the damaged area, no sediment settled but a cloud of loose sediment followed the Norwegian into the wreck.

"I'm now in the access room to the missiles. The access door is locked."

Half-heartedly Ole-Einar tried to open the heavily corroded latches, but he couldn't move them. He looked at the door and the wall itself.

"The wall is in pretty good condition. It shouldn't take too long to cut it out in one big piece. That would give us the space we need. I got to go now."

Ole-Einar turned around and made his way back through the wreck.

"We got to be careful. I can see the remains of at least five sailors. May they rest in peace," he added barely audible.

Chuck neither cared nor was he interested in the remains of the Russian sailors. All he cared about was that he was only one day away from reaching his goal.

Without any problems Ole-Einar ascended to his first decompression stop, which he finished as planned.

After him, Olaf was the next diver in the water. Natascha managed to tell him not only about Oliver, but also about Ariel and Shira's whereabouts without anyone else noticing it. Olaf's dive went without any complications as well and he was able to provide a free passage to the missiles. He confirmed the presence of three missiles and started his ascent.

After Olaf was locked up in his room again, Chuck took his notes and checked the information again that he obtained from the old Russian. He was hoping for the Russians sake that he did not lie to him. If he told him the truth back in Severodvinsk, then that Russian was one of the few living people who had seen K-9 from the inside. Not even that, but he had also been an expert on the SS-N4 missiles and Chuck had detailed instructions on how to retrieve the nuclear warheads without heavy machinery. Chuck would have preferred if the more experienced Ole-Einar would perform the next and most important dive, but the Norwegian had already dove today and couldn't dive again for a few hours. Nick was the only one left who could dive today.

While Natascha inspected the diving helmet with extra caution for the next dive, Chuck explained to Nick in every detail what he expected from him.

"Do you understand this?" the American asked.

"Yes," Nick replied briskly and closed the zipper on his dry suit before he and Chuck simultaneously looked at Natascha. Nicks fiancée briefly tried to smile, but it soon twitched into broken sobs. Natascha quickly sopped up her tears with the sleeve of her sweater. Nick exhaled sharply, fighting his urge to embrace her closely.

Chuck abruptly leaned towards him, "If you screw this thing up, or if you plan to do something stupid down there with them, then I'll personally make sure you hear your girlfriend's screams as my men rape her over and over and over again. Once they're finished with her I'll humanely shoot her in the knee, tie a chain around her and send her down the buoy line before you've even reach your last decompression stop. Do you understand me?" he whispered harshly into Nick's ear.

Nick's eyes rolled dark with fury. His blood boiled immediately as the vivid images pervaded his imagination. His vision sharpened as he stared coldly into Chuck's serious eyes. He held his silence under the deep short breaths consumed by his rage.

Not knowing what was going on Natascha walked over and interrupted them.

"We're ready," she stammered, eyeing both men seperately.

"Very well. Help our Romeo into his helmet, will you?"

Nick rose to his feet and Natascha adjusted the neck seal and the neck dam for him.

"Shira and Ariel are in the Russian storage room. Oliver's dead."

Tears instantaneously ran down her face as she uttered her news to him. Sharing her knowledge was now in few short sentences, though the pain was more than she could bare. Her briskness, and almost matter-of-fact approach to the matter, made her worry he did not understand her. She eyed him closely, waiting for his reaction but nothing came. She thought to whisper it again, but instead additional words escaped her quivering lips.

"You be careful down there, okay? I love you."

"Love you, too. Stay strong, it's not over yet."

"Hey, enough of this whispering. Let's go," Jenna interrupted them, pushing Natascha away from Nick.

Nick put the helmet on and Natascha was only allowed a quick check-up on the closing mechanism. The communication system worked flawlessly and to offer encouragement to Natascha, Nick walked towards the lifting basket without hesitation. He entered the contraption, locked the door and signaled he was ready to be lowered to the water.

Without looking back he focused on the surface and finally swam the few meters to the marker buoy. He let the air out of his dry suit and started his descent. His eyes rested on the bottom timer that he carried on his right wrist. Ten meters...twenty meters...thirty meters. The light from the surface was fading as he sank deeper into the water. Using the light from his helmet that offered little illumination, he finally switched the breathing gas for the first time. Nick had a few problems equalizing, but he managed to continue. After eight minutes he could see the long cylindrical silhouette of the Russian U-Boat wreck underneath him. About five meters over the bottom Nick let go of the rope and swam towards it. His eyes fell on the rebreather and he stopped.

"You don't have to look for him any more, Nick. He's already gone," he heard Natascha's shaking voice inside his helmet.

"I need more hose," Nick demanded bitterly and pulled the umbilical hose behind him as he entered the wreck. The first compartment had little visibility due to the stirred sediment, but it improved the further he made it into the wreck. Eventually he saw the three missiles right in front of him.

"Okay, remember what I told you a few minutes ago," Chuck warned him eagerly.

"Okay," Nick answered, his voice barely recognizable under the helium scrambler, but at least he did not sound like Mickey Mouse any more.

With Chuck guiding him through every single step, Nick started to work. A quick glance at his bottom timer told him he already spent eighteen minutes down here. He gave himself another two minutes and was almost done.

On board the *Northern Explorer* Jenna walked up behind her brother and together they watched Nick's work closely on the monitor.

"Do you think he'll manage?" she asked curiously.

"He better. I gave him a special motivational speech," Chuck grinned and nodded towards Natascha, who was unaware of the conversation. Jenna looked at the young German scientist and smiled back at her brother.

"How's our timeline looking? We have to be on our way in thirty-six hours at the latest. I don't like sitting on a time bomb."

"Relax sister, everything's going to be okay. The gas from the pipeline can't harm us here and we'll release the gas on the ventilation system for the crew when we get off the vessel. It's in a frozen form right now and by the time we release it, we'll have two hours to get away. But we're good in time, sister. No more than four dives and we'll be done."

Chuck noticed Natascha's eyes darted to him at his last sentence. His eyes narrowed and he didn't acknowledge Nick when he told them he was starting his way out of the submarine now.

Chuck looked back at the monitor and was satisfied to see Nick accomplished more than he hoped for.

"Natascha," Chuck barked and rose from his chair.

"How many more dives do we have enough breathing gas for?" he asked in his usual aggressive, low voice.

Natascha shimmied in front of the gas panel and covered the gauges with her body.

"I asked you something. How many more dives do we have enough breathing gas for?" the American asked threateningly.

Natascha refused to reply, but Chuck noticed she burst in tears.

"Stop crying and answer my goddamn question! How many dives?!"

"After this dive, maybe one more, maximum two," Natascha sobbed involuntarily.

It took a couple seconds before Chuck realized what the young German admitted.

"What did you say? We don't have any more breathing gas?"

Natascha nodded and closed her eyes. Panic and fear rose inside her.

Screaming in anger Chuck took his chair and threw it out of the dive control room. He followed it into the cool air. This was a better place for him to think.

There'll either be a miracle during the next two dives or they have to dive on air only. Damnnit! We can't dive on normal air. They're either so narced they won't realize what they're doing or the oxygen will kill them. There has to be a different way. Only three more dives. Only three!

Chuck stared at the water and got an idea. Quickly he turned around and walked back to the dive control room, where he faced Natascha.

"Where's your decompression schedule?"

Natascha's fear of the angry American peaked as she handed him her notes immediately. Together with Jenna, they went over the dive profile.

"We're wasting sixty-two minutes per dive for the decompression. If we use that gas more efficiently, we might be able to get enough bottom time for a third dive. Ole-Einar is the most experienced and efficient diver. He's going to do the next dive with the regular decompression. After him, Olaf will go into the water. We can turn his breathing gas off the moment he's out of the wreck. He'll be followed again by Ole-Einar. That way we have enough breathing gas for the bottom time for those last two dives. The rest doesn't matter."

Natascha stared at Chuck in shock, but it was her father who reacted first.

"You can't do this! Without decompression they will both die!"

"I don't care! I have more important things to take care of. Take him away," Chuck ordered as the Professor approached him. Nelson took Richard's arm and escorted him out.

"You're going to kill them all," Natascha whispered and stared at Chuck in disbelief.

"Did you really expect something else?" he asked emotionlessly, before he turned to Frank and Brian from the American expedition team.

"We don't need him any more. I'll let you know the moment he's outside the wreck. As soon as he's out, you can start pulling him up," he ordered in his usual tone.

But I still need him! Natascha screamed inwardly, her anxiety fluttering her heart at an unbearable pace.

"You can't do this! You can't torture them to death like that! They did everything you want!" she screamed furiously, storming towards Chuck.

Jenna hurriedly stepped behind her and pulled her back to her knees by her hair. A different scream ripped up Natascha's throat as Jenna pulled harder.

Chuck looked at her with amusement.

"You know what Jenna? I just got an idea how we can save even more breathing gas."

With a few steps he came to Natascha and violently pulled her back on her feet by her hair. He pushed her in front of him and towards the mixing panel. Although Natascha was screaming out loud for pain and tried to resist, she didn't stand a chance against the mercenary.

Slowly Chuck took Natascha's hand and placed it on the main valve for the umbilical hose.

"Do you think he'd forgive you if he knew of this?" he whispered into her ear.

"No, please don't do this!" Natascha screamed, her voice quaking violently, her legs shaking. "I love him! I need him!"

Unimpressed by Natascha's screaming, Chuck still pressed her hand onto the main valve. Natascha tried to fight him with all her strength, but her resistance was effortless under his grasp. Chuck forced her hand and the valve all the way down until it closed and interrupted the flow of the breathing gas.

"No!" Natascha screamed, crumpling to the floor. Her stomach churned violently, her eyes burning red with tears as the pain twisted her heart in an indescribable knot. Her sobs turned to violent moans, her throat closing over her vocals as she fought the nausea that overwhelmed her. She broke out in a fluctuating sweat, the floor spinning in front of her.

Chuck smiled devilishly to his sister, knowing full well that Nick had only enough breathing gas for the next three minutes and he wasn't even out of the wreck yet.

Laughing loud, Jenna placed herself between Natascha and the valve, while Chuck looked at the monitor and the communication system.

"Sit down, enjoy the program. He's still breathing", Chuck laughed at Natascha.

Over seventy meters down below Nick checked his bottom timer and had no knowledge of the situation inside the dive control room. He just left the wreck and swam towards the buoy rope. On his way out of the wreck he came to the conclusion that both Ole-Einar as well as Olaf would know about Oliver's fate and the whereabouts of their Israeli teammates. He knew they were running out of time. They had to do something soon.

"I'm starting my ascent now. Everything's okay."

At the surface, Chuck leaned back in his chair before he stood up. He walked to the door to let the two American's monitoring the umbilical hose know when to pull Nick up. His attention darted back to the room when he heard Natascha rush to the microphone.

"Nick! They turned your air off! They want to pull you...!" Natascha couldn't finish her warning. Her breath escaped her as she felt abrupt pressure push into her back, forcing her forward into the floor. Without resisting any further, Chuck stood over her and pulled her up to her feet. She gasped for air as he pushed her outside to the rail. Jenna followed the two of them and stood guard. Natascha could hear Chuck yelling at her, but she was unable to grasp the words he was saying. He held her against the railing, the cold metal pushing into her ribs as he violently held her head to look at the water. Natascha did not notice her pain, the tears, the burning sensation that scorched her soul. She knew her one and only love would be pulled back on board, his lifeless body staring at her with sorrow and shame knowing he did not keep his promise.

Down at the wreck Nick stared up towards the surface, fear darting across his eyes, his heart racing. He did everything right, what made him deserve this? So many fearful questions filled his mind, though he knew no answers would come. The only thing he knew was that someone turned off his breathing gas. He feared the inevitable tug of the cord that would pull him up to the surface. He struggled to think of a way out of this situation, but no immediate solutions followed. He could not do anything about it. He knew Natascha was in serious trouble right now and that she had absolutely no reason to lie to him. The vicious truth only meant that there was most likely a fight on board the vessel at this very moment. He struggled for the truth and knew his teams retaliation would not happen without him. This made him fear the events occuring on board.

Maybe they had to improvise or the situation presented itself suddenly.

Whatever it was, he was stuck down here and his personal situation got worse by the second. Nick closed his eyes quickly only to reopen them a moment later. It was getting more difficult to breathe. Thinking about it, he cursed Chuck once more for not letting him have a bail-out tank with him.

Nick waited, hoping the gas would be turned back on. He took slow deep breaths as the difficulty to breathe increased.

Come on guys! Hurry up. I'm not going to last much longer! Don't do this to me! Nick panicked suddenly.

Whatever was happening on board the ship, Nick decided he didn't want to give them the pleasure of watching him die. His hand curled in a fist at the thought. Natascha suddenly came to mind. His hand reached up and he ripped the video cable out of the camera. The last thing he wanted her to see was his dying moment.

Nick concentrated on his breathing, though he feared it was getting worse. He swallowed hard and could feel the headache starting.

The throbbing increased rapidly and his body screamed for oxygen. He forced himself to concentrate. Natascha appeared in front of his inner eye, he saw her laughing, saw how she smiled at him for the first time in Norway. How she took his hand at the bonfire that one evening and how she gazed deep in his eyes. He recalled her alluring, temptuous gesture leading him into the bedroom in Italy. His senses peaked, he could feel his hand running through her hair, the smell of her perfume, the softness of her skin. He could see her carefree spirit.

Nick tried for another breath, but nothing happened. There was no gas left in the umbilical hose. Panic immediately rose inside him. The memories of Natascha laughing flew by faster and faster. Memories of Iceland, her reaction to his proposal, he could even hear her laughter. His headache grew unbearable. His head throbbed violently, rattling the images of his bride to a fizzling memory. Every fiber of his body burned up like a fire, viciously consuming the little energy he struggled to keep. Suddenly his instincts took over and his hands reached up and removed the helmet. Only for a second Nick noticed the freezing water nip at him. He blinked quickly, certain he was seeing things, but it was real. There was a ghost. He saw one come straight at him, arms reaching out to welcome him, to escort him. Without knowing it, Nick raised his arms. He wanted to go with the ghost, and reached for his hand. A smile twitched across Nick's lips as the light filled his vision. He could feel the peace that suddenly overcame him. He knew everything was going to be fine now.

On the deck of the *Northern Explorer* Natascha stopped struggling inside Chuck's firm grip. They stood at the rail and Natascha was forced to witness the two American's pull the umbilical hose to the surface as fast as they could. While the others were laughing, Natascha's voice cracked as her throat closed over her scream to silence. She couldn't cry or resist. Things moved like pictures, snapshots of time that would change everything. She could feel it, she could feel she lost him. First Oliver, now Nick. Of all the people, it had to be Nick. The first man she really loved. The first man who accepted her the way she was. The first man that ever loved her back.

She stared blankly at the ocean, refusing to acknowledge the inevitable. Her thoughts darted to their time together, when she saw him for the first time in Norway, the dinner he cooked for her, their time in Italy, the dive they did together in Iceland, his proposal. All that meant nothing any more. Nick was attached to the other end of the umbilical hose and they pulled him out of a depth of over seventy meters.

Their arms moved fluidly as they grasped the cord, pulling in unison, their pace increasing. Natascha knew Nick had absolutely no chance of survival.

I wish you're already dead. I love you. Please forgive me. Natascha started at this thought and tears burst from her ducts when she saw the five meter mark on the umbilical hose.

Her heart pounded in her ears, her throat closed tighter as, just seconds later, she saw the helmet break through the surface. There was no sign of Nick. A loud scream burst through her burning throat, everything zoomed into reality, bursting in bright colours as her heart bore the truth. She collapsed to the deck through Chuck's tight grip, their laughter filling her ears as they pulled the helmet on board. Her greatest fear exposed itself in front of her with wide open arms, the truth, the reality, the very detail of her new life was forever gone. Nick was dead.

- 22 -

Home Office and Operational Headquarters of *EuroSecCorporation*, London, Thursday, October 13th
Klaus Schwartze sat behind his desk and discussed the results of last nights briefing with Gunnar Eriksson. Both the German's as well as the Norwegian's spent the better part of the night reviewing the available evidence. The retired General planned to send Gunnar as a liaison officer to the Norwegian embassy. Just when Klaus took a sip of his coffee the phone rang. Klaus placed the cup on its plate and looked at his watch. It was stroke ten.

"I assume that's going to be Tel Aviv," the retired General noted to Gunnar and picked up the phone.

"Good morning, General Rashid. Klaus Schwartze here. What's the news, my friend?"

"Good morning, Klaus. Sean MacLeod here. I just stopped by Scotland Yard to find out if there was anything new. They just found Gordon Ramshaw in his cell five minutes ago. He's dead."

On board the *Northern Explorer*, Amundsen Gulf, Darnley Bay, Thursday, October 13th
The moment they recovered the empty helmet and harness the previous day, Natascha fought the truth, to believe that something so horrible could really be true. She lost more than she could bare, the final straw was pulled. At first Chuck was under the impression that she was tricking him, but even when he threatened and yelled at her, she didn't show any reaction. Natascha had a complete physical and emotional collapse and even Chuck realized she did not simulate. Her eyes moved slow, her thoughts lost to the abyss of nothingness. She was floating between the realms, unable to reel herself down to the ground.

All she could hear was her father having an argument with both Chuck and Jenna. She could hear his angry voice yelling at them, but she didn't understand a single word he said. Without resisting, she let Jenna and Nelson pull her on her feet before they escorted her to an empty cabin.

She walked aimlessly, willingly going where they needed her to go. She perceived her movements, though she was unable to define where she was going. The only thing she did register was that she was one deck below where Olaf, Ole-Einar and her father were usually kept.

The moment they closed the door she was already curled up on the floor, staring into the corner. Tears streamed down her face, but she didn't bother wiping them away. Her thoughts roamed sporadically, nothing registering as she stared blankly, lifelessly.

First she survived two assassination attempts and an attack from a grown polar bear. She discovered a huge amount of nerve gas, which was enough to kill an entire city. She happened upon the dead body of her teacher and mentor Vitali, before she had to witness how this lunatic irrationally executed the First Officer. She watched as Oliver breathed from the wrong gas, unknowingly killing himself just one meter away from her. But all this meant nothing compared to Nick's certain death. Nick, her love, her fiancé, her husband, her baby's father. Her eyes stung with unbearable grief. She could feel a wave of nausea overwhelm her. Her head sank to her crossed arms. She knew there was no way out for her, or anyone. There was no hope of liberation.

Natascha's head rose when the sound of the door opening interrupted her grief. She recognized Astrid, who brought her something to eat. Behind her, Nelson was guarding the door. Astrid approached her German friend, kneeling beside her, only to wrap her arms around her.

"I'm so sorry," the Norwegian whispered, her voice cracking. She had a strong desire to tell her that everything was going to be alright, but she knew any level of lies would not do her any good. The false hope she would ensure her would only make it worse. There was no hope. The hope they all embraced was gone and worthless now. Too many people died for that. It took Astrid all her willpower to control her own emotions and she tried to offer the little strength she had left to Natascha.

Natascha sobbed uncontrollably under Astrid's contact. She tried to say something to her, but the only word that she understood was Nick's name.

"Let it all out, Natascha. It's okay," she whispered her support as she stroked Natascha's hair.

Nelson watched as Astrid consoled her. After a few moments he got nervous. He actually really liked Natascha and having this happen to her was uncomfortable to watch. Nelson was the youngest of the American scientists but nevertheless he agreed without hesitation to his new assignment when Jenna asked him. The only difference between him and the rest was that he was not that cold-blooded yet.

"Okay, that's enough. We have to go," he commanded as best he could.

Astrid let go of Natascha, kissed her on the forehead and smiled at her.

"Try to be strong, okay? You're not alone."

Astrid stood up and Nelson escorted her back outside, where Ole-Einar just finished his dive. The Norwegian did not know that this was the last dive with enough breathing gas for the complete decompression. Since he kept strictly to the dive plan and the decompression obligations he was also symptom free.

Astrid could overhear them. It seemed that Ole-Einar just confirmed Chuck that all three warheads were in a different compartment of the U-Boat and that they could start winching them up in the next dive. When Ole-Einar asked Chuck where Natascha was, the American simply told him that Natascha wasn't feeling well. Astrid couldn't get any more information, but she was convinced that Ole-Einar mentioned *warheads*.

Scotland Yard, London, Thursday, October 13th
Retired General Klaus Schwartze stood beside Sean MacLeod and Inspector Conolly

inside Gordon Ramshaw's cell. Together they looked at Gordon, whose lifeless body lay on the bed. A physician was just performing an initial examination.

"I suspect a sudden heart attack. Maybe the stress was too much for him. An autopsy will definitely tell me more. As far as I can venture an opinion at this point, I'd rule out foulplay. But like I said, once I'm done with the autopsy I'll know more."

The physician took his little bag and left the cell.

Klaus took another step towards the corpse and looked at it carefully.

"Did you find any medications when you searched his mansion and his office?"

"No, we didn't. Mr. Ramshaw didn't take any meds. Immediately after we laid official charges against him we had one of our medical officers examine him. The medical officer attested an overall condition of great health. We have his attest in the files. Do you suspect he killed himself?"

"Gordon? Killing himself? How? He didn't hang himself with his tie or with his shoe laces. He also didn't cut his arteries. Without a drug cocktail or some poison he would certainly not be able to create a heart attack. Did he seem to be depressed during the last couple hours?"

"Depressed? On the contrary. He seemed to be in complete control, but I wasn't present during his interrogation with Special Agent Abigail Sinclair from the CIA."

Klaus looked up at Inspector Conolly.

"Did someone check her out?"

"My assistant is talking to Langley as we speak. All I know for the moment is that they confirm her identity and her involvement in this case."

"Did someone check her bag before she talked to Gordon?"

Inspector Conolly stared at Klaus in disbelief.

"Do you really want to tell me that you suspect the CIA to kill a suspect right in front of our eyes? Why should they do that?" Inspector Conolly asked, but he already knew the answer.

"The Central Intelligence Agency has executed many people if it helped their agenda. If there really is, as I suspect, a high ranking politician involved in this, I wouldn't be surprised if Abigail Sinclair poisoned Gordon yesterday. We mustn't forget that the CIA used black accounts to finance the company that now has four people on the ship."

"Yes, that's true. But how did she do it?"

"What do I know? Maybe a handshake. There are hundreds of different ways."

"They had coffee together," the same officer who brought them the coffee mentioned.

Inspector Conolly looked at him in a mixture of disbelief and frustration.

"Excuse me. What did you just say? They did what?"

"They had a cup of coffee together. Black, if I'm not mistaken."

Klaus shrugged his shoulders.

"That's it. She poisoned him."

Inspector Conolly still stared angrily at the guard when Klaus walked by and patted him on the shoulder.

"Don't worry about it. She would've found a way."

Inspector Conolly looked from the guard to Klaus.

"Do you have any idea what to look for during the autopsy?"

"It doesn't matter. Look at the company they worked for. You won't find anything. It'll look like a stress induced heart attack. Natural death, no foulplay," Klaus finished and called Brian over his cell phone.

- 23 -

On board the Russian nuclear long range attack Submarine, *Akula* Class, Amundsen Gulf, Darnley Bay, Thursday, October 13th
Even with his eyes closed Nick could still see the bright light. Slowly he opened his eyes and stared at a dark grey metal ceiling. He could still see the ghost in front of him. Now there were two, even three. They all smiled at him, but he was way too weak to give a reaction. His headache was completely gone and Nick noticed that he was breathing from an oxygen mask.
That's a strange feeling. I always thought that being dead would feel different.
Nick also noticed that it wasn't really that warm. After a few more seconds he realized that he neither wore the dry-suit nor the thermo underwear any more. Both items were completely soaked and laid on the metal floor in front of his bed.
Not that bad after all, but I always imagined heaven would look different than this.
Suddenly he registered a voice. One of the ghosts was talking to him, but Nick couldn't understand him.
Since when do ghosts speak Russian?
Suddenly the ghost spoke to him in English, then even some broken German.
"Hey, Towaritsch! Can you hear me? Understand me?"
Still weak, Nick simply nodded.
"Very well. How many finger?"
Nick looked at the hand of the ghost and counted three fingers being stretched away.
"Three," Nick whispered and noticed that the ghost nodded satisfied.
Never thought that the entry exam for heaven would be that easy.
"Towaritsch, we did find you outside. You not dead and me not Sankt Peter. Me doctor. Me Russian."
Nick frowned and he could hear the other people in the room laughing.
What does he mean? I'm not dead? How can that be?
It seemed as if the Russian could read his mind.
"You on Russian submarine. We have ten men support submersible, to bring help to sunken submarines. We were watching you and your men. When we see that you have problem, we come to rescue you. We maybe twenty, maybe thirty meters away from you when you take helmet off. Then we knew that something wrong on big ship. We did recover you and you're now in pressure chamber inside support submersible. You maybe unconscious for eight or nine minutes, but without air you only less then two minutes. You not have problems. In two hours we'll be done with decompression. We are good."
The Russian smiled at Nick and patted him on the shoulder.

Nick thanked him and closed his eyes again. Satisfied, he noticed he didn't really feel any pain at all in his body. He took a deep breath thinking that the nitrogen bubbles inside his body did not form to a life-threatening size. Slowly and carefully Nick moved his arms and his legs, one at a time. He was still scared to feel the itching pain or the typical feeling of numbness in one or more of his joints. But nothing happened. Glad that he didn't feel any pain, he tried to sit up. The Russian didn't stop him. Slowly Nick looked around. Beside the doctor there was another man and a woman inside the pressure chamber.

"You were the ones who rescued me from the water?" Nick asked the two.

Obviously neither of them understood his German and the doctor translated for them. They both nodded to him.

"Thank you. I owe you one."

"Their names are Mikhail and Tatjana. When you took off helmet, you damaged neck seal. Lots of water inside suit. We had to take off suit and everything."

Nick looked down at him and it was only now that he noticed that he was completely naked under the grey blanket.

The Russian doctor looked at Tatjana.

"That was the only reason she volunteered. She on board of submarine for long time," the Russian said in German.

Judging by the surprised expression in Tatjanas face, Nick assumed she had not understood a word the Russian just said.

Nick had to laugh.

"My name's Nick," he finally said and offered the Russian doctor his hand.

"Vasili."

Nick shook everybody's hand and thanked them personally once more.

A few moments later some dry clothes for him arrived through an air lock.

Carefully Nick stood up and put the clothes on, before he laid back on the bed again.

"Nick. What you and your men are doing is not right. They are our people out there. Let them rest in peace. What's going on ship anyway? We heard shots a couple days ago. We can understand something, but not everything."

Nick leaned back, looked at his new friends, closed his eyes for a few seconds and with a deep breath he started to tell them everything.

Montana, USA, Thursday, October 13th

US Senator Jonathan Brown leaned back in his leather chair and looked at the cigar he just lit. He reached for the whiskey bottle to pour himself a generous drink. With a knowledgeable look he examined the yellow liquid before he enjoyed a sip.

His secretary Carl Miller still stood in front of him, but he didn't say anything.

"And you're certain about that? Gordon Ramshaw is dead?"

"Yes, he's dead. We just got confirmation from London."

"And it's certain that he didn't say anything?"

"Yes, it is. The British are still looking for a needle in the haystack."

"Great!"

Thin Ice

The Senator took a deep puff from his cigar, leaned back again and closed his eyes.

The untimely death of Gordon Ramshaw wasn't originally planned, but it didn't bother him either. That way he could hire an American company to get the oil to America. Now he would not have to cut the British a deal. The best part of this was that the British couldn't even sue him, since all they had done so far was highly illegal and there was no written agreement.

US Senator had to laugh out loud. This was exactly how he preferred his business.

On board the Russian nuclear long range attack Submarine, *Akula* **Class, Amundsen Gulf, Darnley Bay, Thursday, October 13th**
Knowing that he depended on the assistance from the Russian's and given the fact that they saved his life, Nick decided to be honest and to put all the facts on the table. He simply lacked the time to leave any details out. If they learned about them later, they would probably not trust him when he needed them most. So he started with their dive trip to Norway and he just wanted to introduce them the rest of his team when Visali interrupted him.

"Not so fast, I can't remember. Too many names."

Visali pressed a button at the communication panel and as far as Nick could understand him, he was asking for the Captain.

"We already docked at big submarine. I'll translate for my Captain."

Just a few minutes later the Captain and two of his officers stood by and listened to Nick's story over the communication system.

It took him about forty minutes to tell everything that happened. Once he was finished Visali, Tatjana and Mikhail stared at him in disbelief. Nick could overhear the Captain yelling at one of his officers.

"What is that about?" Nick asked and looked at Vasili, but the Russian tiredly waved his hand.

"Captain angry that research vessel heard us. It was Victor who maneuvered submarine at surface."

"It's not his fault. We heard your submarine several times. Our Captain even identified it correctly as an *Akula*. But we could only hear you with the use of the sensitive hydrophones. Otherwise we couldn't."

Vasili translated and Nick could hear everybody laughing.

"What's so funny about that?" Nick wanted to know.

"They are laughing about sonar officer. He's new. Not very smart yet. So, what's your plan?"

Not knowing exactly how to tell his Russian friend his plan, Nick's eyes dropped to the floor.

"I have to get back on board the *Northern Explorer*. If I don't go back, then my friend's and especially my fiancée won't survive this. I don't have a choice."

Looking in Nick's eyes, Vasili could see how determined the German was.

"You would die for them?"

"They would do the same for me," Nick nodded affirmative. "Besides that, I was convinced I'm already dead. When I woke up, my first thought was that I was in heaven," Nick laughed nervously.

Vasili translated and while everybody else laughed, Tatjana blushed and turned her face away.

"What did you tell her?" Nick asked and looked from Vasili to Tatjana.

"I told them you thought that Tatjana is an angel. Didn't know the other words. This is same meaning," Vasili explained calmly.

Nick wanted to reply something, but he didn't want to waste any more time and decided against it.

"Can I talk to Captain Rankow personally? I depend on your help and I can't lose any more time."

Vasili shrugged his shoulders and forwarded Nicks request over the communication system to Captain Rankow.

"Decompression done in forty five minutes. Captain waiting for you."

Although Nick was not totally satisfied with this answer, he knew he had to finish the decompression first. If he did not complete his decompression properly, he would have no chance to succeed. He knew he would get serious signs of decompression sickness within the next few hours if he would go back to the *Northern Explorer* now. The best plan would not be worth anything. Besides that, the three other Russian's were with him in decompression. Nick simply had to wait. Reluctant, he lay back and started to think. First of all he had to convince the Russian Captain to help him. Not only that, he also had to come up with a pretty good idea on what he wanted to do once he was actually back on board the research vessel. The next forty five minutes would definitely not be boring.

Ottawa, Department of National Defence, Thursday, October 13th
Although he just wore a tailored suit instead of the uniform of a highly decorated Admiral, Brian Whittaker stormed down the corridor of the Canadian Department of National Defence like he did during the best times of his career. The determination in his face itself was enough to make everybody from the janitor all the way up to a young Captain jump out of his way and to look after him in disbelief. In Brian's wake were both the German and the Norwegian Ambassador. They both had an adjutant with them.

Determined and ready to use force if he had to, Brian walked into the outer office.

"Good Morning. We have an appointment for zero-nine-hundred," he snarled at the person behind the desk.

The young man knew who the visitors were and froze under their penetrating eyes.

"That would be today at zero-nine-hundred, if you don't mind," Brian added in a low voice and stared at the poor guy.

"Yes, of course. One moment, please." The adjutant rose from behind his desk, opened the door to the office and announced the visitors.

"You can come in now, Sir."

Without losing another word, Brian walked by the adjutant, still having the two ambassadors in his wake.

"Good Morning, Mr. Whittaker. I'm so glad to see you again. I'm not sure if you remember, but we actually met a couple..."

"Good Morning, Curt. My apology I interrupted you, but we both know we met a couple years ago and you also know who these gentlemen behind me are. Now, since we've already lost more than enough time due to your hesitant actions, I suggest we skip the formalities and get straight to the point."

This was the first time someone had spoken to the Canadian Defence Minister like that. Not only that, but the expression on his face also made it very clear that it had never happened in his own office. With his mouth wide open, he stared at retired Admiral Brian Whittaker, who was completely unimpressed by the Defence Minister.

Brian opened his attaché case and presented the two enlarged satellite images from the *Northern Explorer*. Without a comment he placed them on the desk side by side and pointed out the two dead bodies.

"You're looking at two satellite images that show the research vessel *Northern Explorer* just a few sea miles north of Paulatuk inside Canadian waters. Both images were taken in the early morning hours of October ninth. The two people who are lying on the deck are not taking a sun bath. Several factors show us that this is not the case. Number one would be the outside air temperature of only five degree Celsius at that time. Second would be the fact that they're both fully dressed, in one case the person is dressed in the uniform of an officer. Third would be the fact that both people are dead. That scenario actually fits very well to the fact that we have received our last scheduled satellite transmission from our team on board this ship on Saturday, October eighth. That very same day, just a few hours later, we received an authenticated electronic message from the radio operator of this research vessel over one of our communication channels. In this message the radio operator was literally crying for help and confirms that the *Northern Explorer* is under the control of eight hostage takers. She also stated that they had already executed two people," Brian explained and pointed at the picture again before he continued.

"The radio operator also voiced her concern that both politicians are involved in this situation and that they have already left the vessel." Brian presented a copy of Astrid's message and handed it to the Defence Minister.

"Brian, I understand your concern, but I've personally contacted the two politicians in question just two days ago. Our people were able to get radio contact to a female person on board this research vessel. I wouldn't be surprised if that person would be this Astrid Makkinen. She didn't tell us about any problems. I can assure you that everything is fine."

Brian slammed his fist on the table.

"Goddammit, Curt! I'm sick of this bullshit! On this research vessel is a group of former special soldiers of Norwegian and German nationality. Their job is to protect one single person, a completely legal operation. If this unit misses a scheduled status report for twenty four hours, then something is not okay. If I don't hear from my boys in five days, then that means that something went wrong. Terribly wrong! Especially if I have a satellite image with two dead bodies and an e-mail with a detailed description and an outcry for help. Eight terrorists have taken control over the *Northern Explorer*, at least with the knowledge of the politicians and most likely after they left. And what do you have? Nothing! You heard a voice over the radio. Did you see if they pressed a gun to her head when they forced her to say that? No, you did not. Did you send a reconnaissance plane up there for a close-up inspection? No, you did not! Did you send a frigate up there for a personal inspection? No, you did not! Oh, I'm sorry. I forgot. You don't even have military presence up there. So, let us ignore all this bullshit and let's talk about facts. Within the next five minutes you can either arrange for a reconnaissance plane to fly up there to contact the *Northern Explorer* or you can explain to both the Norwegian and the German Ambassador why Canada is not taking some solid evidence about possible terrorist activities in their freezer seriously. Should you opt for door number two, then I want you to know that both Germany and Norway are sending out their own special forces while you're talking to their respective ambassadors. We'll contact the research vessel today, and we'll do it either with or without your help. It's your call."

The Defence Minister was silent. His shock was evident as his jaw hung loose. Never in his years of service has anyone dared to talk down to him like this before. However a quick look at the Norwegian and German Ambassador showed him a similar determination. Nevertheless he was not willing to accept this kind of behaviour in his own office.

"Mr. Whittaker," he replied, no longer on a first names basis.

"I'm well aware of your former military career. Nonetheless I'm not totally convinced you realize who you are talking to. I'll file a formal complaint about your behaviour."

"Very well. If you read my file thoroughly you must've noticed that the only person I have to report to is my wife. You must've also noticed that I'm no longer with the British Navy. And just in case you're wondering about the blacked out parts in my file, I want you to know that I'm having tea with her Majesty once a month since I got back from the Falklands. I presume you understand that there's a very good reason for that. So, if you want to file a formal complaint about me with her Majesty of England, the Queen, then please be my bloody guest," Brian explained calmly. "And if you don't have her number, her outer office is on speed dial two. Speed dial one is my wife. Do you want me to dial for you?" Brian asked and offered his cell phone seriously.

The Defence Minister quickly realized he could not threaten Brian and took another look at the satellite image and the e-mail.

"All right then. Even if I make a complete idiot out of myself," he muttered and finally picked up the phone. He just spoke for a few minutes. After he finished he looked back at Brian and the two ambassadors.

"I just spoke to MARCOM, the Canadian Forces Maritime Command. I'm going to escort you to their headquarters. If it turns out that you're creating all this fuss for nothing, then I expect an official and personal apology from you, Mr. Whittaker."

Brian nodded and packed the images back in his attaché case.

"You'll get that as soon as one of my men has personally briefed me on the situation on board. Until then I expect to be informed about every little detail."

The Defence Minister nodded, took his coat and led his guests out of his office.

On board the Russian nuclear long range attack Submarine, *Akula* **Class, Amundsen Gulf, Darnley Bay, Thursday, October 13th**

Immediately after the doctor gave his approval, Nick was escorted to the command center of the Russian nuclear submarine. Since there was nothing else available, he wore the casual uniform of a Russian sailor. Although the uniform fit very well, Nick was not very comfortable wearing it.

He followed Vasili into the command centre.

"Please tell him first that I want to say thank you for saving my life and that I really feel sorry for working at the wreck of K9. I also want to apologize for disturbing the peace of your lost comrades and for wearing your uniform."

Vasili listened carefully to Nick and nodded in appreciation before he translated. The Captain listened motionless, but he carefully watched Nick and nodded several times to honour the respect that Nick had shown towards him and his lost comrades before he answered.

"Captain Rankow accepts your apology. He says thank you for your respect towards our dead comrades."

Nick already explained why they had to work on the wreck and that it had not been their decision.

Now comes the difficult part.

Although Nick spent the last hour trying to establish a plan on how to ask for the Russian's assistance, he was still searching for the right words. Finally he took a deep breath and started.

"Captain Rankow. On board the *Northern Explorer* are my, most-likely-pregnant fiancée, her father, four members of my team as well as more than thirty crew members. They're all being taken as hostages by eight terrorists. As far as we know, those terrorist plan to kill not only every citizen on Paulatuk, but also the complete crew and the officers of the research vessel. In order to do this they plan to release a significant amount of nerve gas. There's also an American as well as a Canadian politician involved in this situation. Their ultimate goal is to gain easy access to the oil fields up here. Besides that, the terrorists seem to follow another plan as well. Like I mentioned before, they're currently trying to recover the three nuclear Russian warheads from K9. Once they have them, I think it's safe to assume that they either want to sell them or want to use them in an act of terror themselves. In each single case, the plutonium would be traced back to Russia. I think we can all agree that this would seriously damage Russia's international reputation. It's my duty to get back on board the *Northern Explorer* to free my pregnant girlfriend, her father and my teammates. Once my team is complete we'll take control over the ship. But for that I would need your help."

Nick carefully watched Captain Rankow as Vasili translated. It seemed that Nick had touched a sensitive subject, but he was right. The plutonium would be traced back to Russia eventually; that was certain. It was obvious to Nick that Captain Rankow felt quite uncomfortable facing the fact that Russia could be held responsible as an accessory in three different nuclear terrorist attacks.

"What exactly is your plan? Do you want us to fight with you? That's not that easy. Technically we're not even here."

"I'm fully aware of that, Vasili. All I'm asking for is you to bring me back on board the research vessel with your little support submersible. Once I'm done I need you to pick up my girlfriend, her father, the remaining officers as well as me and my team."

"What about the rest of the crew?"

"There's a chance that the politicians have organized everything in a way that we'll look like the bad guys. That's the reason why I want those who know the truth to be safe. As far as I know the crew members don't know who's behind this whole situation. I don't want to risk getting lynched by them after they were locked up for five days. When the terrorist locked them up, they wore our coveralls and face masks. There's a great chance that the crew is convinced that we're behind all this."

"Captain Rankow wants to know how many people you bring on board our submarine, if you succeed."

"Between nine and eleven. All I want you to do is take me back to the ship, wait for us and take us back on board."

Vasili translated again and Captain Rankow spoke with his two officers for a few minutes before he looked back at Nick.

"Captain Rankow agrees. We'll get you back to surface, then we'll submerge and recover the nerve gas. We found pipeline ten days ago. We know where nerve gas is. We also take the warheads. They are ours anyway. We'll wait for you. You'll be done before sunrise. What else do you need?"

Nick took a deep breath.

"I would need either a black or dark grey coverall, some light combat boots or dark sneakers, a sharp knife and a gun. I don't have access to any weapons anymore."

Vasili translated again. Nick noticed that Captain Rankow took his time to think his request over. He finally replied.

"Captain wants to know what you'll say when people ask you where you got Russian gun from."

Nick looked around and shrugged his shoulders.

"I'm just going to tell everybody that I took over command of your Akula," he said jokingly to buy some time.

Vasili nodded and translated even before Nick could come up with a serious answer.

For a few seconds Captain Rankow and his officers looked at Nick motionless.

Then they all broke into laughter before he finally gave his approval. He also asked Vasili one more thing.

"Captain Rankow wants to know what's wrong with your grandparents. I don't understand why they are a fiasco."

"My grandparents are not a fiasco, Vasili. You're mixing the letters. I was talking about my fiancée, not a fiasco. She is my girlfriend and most likely pregnant. It has nothing to do with our grandparents."

At Vasilis expression Nick noticed that the Russian still didn't understand.

"A child. My girlfriend is most likely expecting a child."

Vasili looked at him appalled.

"Your girlfriend is still a child?"

"No, Vasili. She's not a child any more. She's expecting a child. A Baby," Nick explained and moved his arms as if he would sway a baby in its sleep.

"Oh, now I understand. A Baby!" Vasili finally said and translated again.

The Captain nodded once more and asked a last question.

"What about the submarine. Not this one. The other. What about K9?"

Nick looked at Captain Rankow.

"I can promise you that we'll never tell a soul about this wreck. No one from our unit will ever reveal the identity of K9 or your presence. We'll let them rest in peace."

Vasili translated and Nick was relieved to see that Captain Rankow believed him. The Russian nodded his agreement.

"When do you start?"

Nick looked at his watch. It was already late in the afternoon and it would be dark within the next thirty minutes.

"It would be best to start right now," the German said and looked at Captain Rankow.

"Dawei!" ordered Captain Rankow. Nick thanked him once again and followed Vasili out of the command center immediately.

Ottawa, Canadian Forces Maritime Command (MARCOM),
Thursday, October 13th

Brian Whittaker sat together with the Canadian Minister of Defence, the German and the Norwegian Ambassador as well as the commanding Officer of the Canadian Forces Maritime Command (MARCOM) at one table. Over the last ninety minutes the retired Admiral explained the facts and put almost all the details he had on the table. It was very important to him not to reveal the true identity of both Ariel Rashid and Shira Hadad. Besides that Brian was sure it could lead to some unnecessary and time-consuming discussions if the people at this meeting learned that there was a Russian nuclear long range submarine driving circles in their back yard as they spoke. Even the two ambassadors didn't know about those two details. The fact that a Russian Akula could simply follow a same size research vessel and travel from the Northern Sea over Iceland, all the way through the North-West passage without being detected from the NATO Sound and Surveillance system would be horrible news for their defense. Since Brian was convinced that this could distract this meeting from its original purpose, the British decided that it would be best not to mention it.

Once he finished his briefing he took a deep sip of his coffee and listened to both the German and the Norwegian Ambassador. They both backed him up and promised their support to shed some light in this matter.

Admiral Kerman exchanged some looks with Captain Lambert from the Maritime Forces Pacific (MARPAC) in Esquimalt, BC.

"Very well. First I want to tell you that I had no knowledge of this situation at hand and that I want to offer my apology in this. I tend to agree with your evaluation of the facts. Captain Lambert, I want you to send a reconnaissance plane up there at once. We have to get in contact with the ship. They have to establish radio communication and let's see if it's possible to get in contact with one of the German members of the expedition or the expedition leader himself. Try not to cause too much suspicion. I think we should also put a patrol boat of the Kingston Class and a frigate of the Halifax class on stand-by and let them prepare to set sail for Paulatuk immediately. We also have to alert a Joint Task Force 2 Assault Team and put them on stand-by as well."

"Yes, Sir," Captain Lambert replied and left the office to make some phone calls.

"How long do you think it'll be before we have visual contact with the research vessel?" Brian asked.

"If it's still at the same position then our reconnaissance plane will have visual contact with them within the next five and a half to six hours. With the two ships we're looking at, weather pending, around four to five days."

"Five days?" Brian asked surprised.

"Yes. Unfortunately we don't have military presence up there in the north. Trust me, I don't like that fact either, but we can't change it."

"How do you want to operate, if you have to?"

"Well, we have the opportunity to bring our JTF2 team by air within reach of their RIB's. I first want to have a situation report from my plane and I have to see what kind of intelligence the radio contact is going to give us. If we are not able to speak directly to members of your unit or if I suspect any illegal or terrorist activities up there, I'll send up the JTF2 team immediately. They'd be there around twelve to fourteen hours."

Brian nodded and took his Blackberry out of his pocket.

"I have the complete blue prints and schematics from the *Northern Explorer*. I think it wouldn't hurt if your boys have a look at them. It's a rather large vessel."

"I totally agree," Admiral Kerman replied and verified that the plans were forwarded to the right people.

"Very well. All we can do now is sit and wait," the Admiral finally commented and sat down.

Impatiently Brian paced the room. He didn't like the fact that they had to wait several hours now, but nobody could change that. Nevertheless he called his friend

Klaus Schwartze in London and informed him that help was finally on its way. All they could do now was pray that it was not too late.

On board the *Northern Explorer*, Amundsen Gulf, Darnley Bay, Thursday, October 13th

It was only late in the afternoon but it was already dark. The fact that thick clouds covered the sky raised the feeling of complete and utter darkness. The position lights were the only lights shining on deck. To conceal their precise location Chuck had turned off all lights on deck. There were only four people left from the Special Forces. Two of them were permanently locked away inside the Russian storage room and the other two were under his complete control. The crew was still locked up in one part of the ship. They followed the rules not to scream and not to send some Morse Codes by banging on the ships steel walls and floor. Chuck assumed they must have heard the shots when he executed the First Officer. The crew most likely feared for their life. Beside that they had access to more than enough food and drinking water and several washrooms. None of them knew about the fate they were about to face.

The Captain of the *Northern Explorer* was confined to the bridge together with his remaining officers. Only Astrid was allowed once in a while to leave the bridge to deliver food to his men and the two divers. Natascha was still in some sort of shock, at least that's what she looked like every time someone checked on her. If someone asked Chuck, he would probably say he was more worried about a military plane on a random flight path than he was about any activities from inside the ship. He checked his wristwatch and figured that Astrid was once more on her way to bring some food to the two remaining Norwegian divers as well as to Natascha and her father.

Since the early morning, Shira and Ariel didn't get anything else to eat any more. Chuck did not plan to execute them just yet, but their time was over. Ole-Einar's last dive with complete decompression went far better than Chuck expected. The next morning they could start at first sunlight to winch the warheads up to the ship. All three warheads were resting now just outside the wreck of the Russian U-Boat. The strong winch from the *Northern Explorer* would have no problems lifting them up. If everything continued as planned, they would be in their helicopters and on their way home within the next twenty-four hours. The deadly nerve gas would come to surface and kill most people in Paulatuk just hours after they left. Satisfied with his performance during this operation, Chuck sat inside the Captain's quarters and leaned back in a nice leather chair. When he heard footsteps in front of his door he looked up for a second. He recognized Astrid who always walked by on her usual routine.

Closely followed by Nelson, the young Norwegian radio operator walked through the ship carrying a basket with some sandwiches and some fruit. After she brought something to eat to the ship's bridge, Nelson followed her all the way down to the open deck where Brian Joice was. He was already preparing the steel cables for the next morning. The American also ordered a few sandwiches and something to drink over the radio and Astrid had no other choice but to obey, although it meant a long detour from her normal routine. As soon as Astrid left the relative warmth of the ships inner structure, she immediately felt the cold evening breeze. The temperature was just hovering above the freezing point. Without a windbreaker the cold air bit into her skin.

"Then go faster if you are cold," Nelson yelled at her when she started shivering.

Astrid saved a comment and followed the rail. Her shivers turned to violent convulsions as she turned her attention to not slip and fall over. Without the deck lights switched on, Astrid found it difficult to see where she was going. She knew the huge dark shadow in front of her was one of the containers for the little research submersibles that Natascha and her father used. Without paying too much attention to the container, she kept going, still followed closely by Nelson.

Without warning she saw a shadow in her peripherals, followed by sudden movement. When Astrid swung around on her heel, she only heard a death rattle. Nelson looked at her in disbelief, his eyes wide open. A deep cut appeared right through his throat. The person cloaked in black behind Nelson still pressed his hand on his mouth. In a final attempt, Nelson struggled to pry the hand off his mouth, but his eyes widened greater when the cloaked man stabbed him twice into his now unprotected back. One second later Nelson's lifeless body sank to the floor, his throat cut and his lung stabbed. Without hesitation the man in the black coverall pulled the knife out of Nelson's back.

Before Astrid could say something, Nick already pressed his hand on her mouth. He pulled her beside the container, out of the view from any potential onlookers.

"Relax. It's me. Nick. Do you recognize me?" Nick whispered calmly.

Astrid looked at him in disbelief and nodded.

"I'm going to take my hand off your mouth now, okay? Don't scream and just whisper."

Carefully Nick took his hand from Astrid's mouth and gave her some space to breathe.

"I thought you were dead!"

Nick shook his head.

"So did I. It's a long story, but I'm still alive and healthy. Where are the others?"

"Still in the same cabins."

"What about Ariel and Shira? Are they still in the Russian's storage room?"

"They were last evening, but I don't go there anymore, so I'm not sure."

"The Captain and his officers?"

"Still on the bridge."

"What about the monitors?"

"They're still using both of them. One is always sitting in front of them. They put them back in the radio room."

"Did someone else die while I was gone?"

"Not that I heard of," Astrid answered and shook her head hastily.

"Did the terrorists get some reinforcement?"

"No, but I was actually able to send a message to your headquarter with Ariel's laptop. Unfortunately I couldn't wait for an answer. We got called several times over the radio, but I had no choice. I always had to convince them that everything is fine."

"That's okay. You did great. How many of them are between here and the radio room?"

Astrid shook her head.

"No one. When I go back up I can turn the lights off behind me, if that's any help to you."

"That would be great. How many terrorists are on the bridge?"

"Most of the time there are two of them."

"Where are you going now?"

"First I have to bring that guy over there his sandwiches. After that I have to serve the other four before I go back to the bridge. What do you want me to do?"

"Nothing for now. Just follow your routine and be ready to send an emergency radio call if I tell you so, okay? And maybe turn the lights off behind you so I can get into the radio room undetected, okay?"

Astrid understood and nodded.

Nick looked around, but he didn't see any signs of danger.

"Do you know where the terrorists stay if they're not on their stations?"

"No, I don't. Sorry," Astrid whispered defeated and shook her head disappointedly.

"What about their leader? What about this Chuck?"

"He usually stays at the Captain's quarter."

Nick paused a moment to look around again before he continued. He stole a quick breath, "What about Natascha. How is she doing?"

She was the one who had been on his mind, and with this constant worry there was always a fear to ask about her state. He looked at Astrid closely, her face contorted deeply, her own concern for Natascha's wellbeing clearly evident. Nick felt a pierce jab him in his heart.

"Oh Nick. She's not doing very well. Like everybody, she thinks you're dead. They forced her to watch them pull you up. The helmet, the helmet came alone. We thought you died. There was no way for you to survive this. She had a complete breakdown after that. She's not doing any better. "

Although Nick had the strong urge to search for Natascha immediately and take her in his arms, he knew that other things had a higher priority. As long as Natascha was locked away in her cabin, she was in no immediate danger. Nicks first priority was to eliminate the person who was watching the monitors. After that he could free his friends.

"Okay, I suggest you keep going. Make sure they don't notice anything. Do you think you can lure the other guy over here when you call him?"

"I think so. Do you want me to?"

"Yes, just take your basket and go a few meters."

Astrid picked up the basket with the sandwiches and looked at Nelson's dead body that laid immediately in front of her. Trying not to touch him or his blood, the Norwegian took a couple steps towards Brian. The American was still working with the cables at the other end of the deck and had not noticed anything that just happened.

Once Astrid saw him moving against the white superstructure, she presented herself.

"Hello? It's me, Astrid. I have your sandwiches. Where are you? I can't see you?"

Astrid closed her eyes a little bit and she could see that Brian was coming towards her.

"Stay where you are. I'm coming over," Brian answered. He was proud about his excellent night vision and that he did not need much light. The last hour he worked in the dusk, but since he only straightened a cable he didn't need any light.

He was probably two meters away from Astrid when Nick covered Brian's mouth with his left hand. With all his strength Nick pulled Brian's head to his left side. The American showed the same reaction as Nelson and instinctively tried to grasp Nick's hand with his own. At the same moment Nick stabbed the knife twice into Brian's back, penetrating the lungs both times and Brian instinctively reached to the pain. Nick used this moment to immediately cut through Brian's unprotected throat, severing both his windpipe and artery. Only two seconds after the attack started, Brian sank lifelessly to the floor. Like Nelson, he was dead before Nick let go of him.

"Okay Astrid. Keep going and make sure they don't suspect anything. Can you at least try to tell Natascha that I'm okay and that I'm going to come for her later?"

"Oh," Astrid replied in a hurry, with recollection.

"Natascha's in a different cabin. She's one deck lower than before. I first have to bring something to eat to Ole-Einar, Olaf and her father. After that, someone still escorts me down to her. I don't know how to tell her. It's going to be difficult."

Nick looked around and thought for a while. Suddenly he had a smile on his face.

On board the Canadian *CF142 Arcturus*, over the Northwest Territories, Thursday, October 13th

Major Josh MacMillan turned the auto pilot on a couple hours ago and being bored as he was, he looked out the window into the darkness. The Northwest Territories stretched below him for thousands of square miles. Even if he would fly below the clouds, he would still be unable to see anything on the ground. That far up north there was simply no civilization to look at, nothing to distract them from their long flight. He and his crew got the call just a half an hour before their shift ended. If it had been just a few more minutes later, a different crew would have flown this trip.

The day was long already, but now it was even longer. They already spent all morning burning through many topics, talking about the latest news, sport results and the usual gossip. Besides that, Josh was also in a bad mood. Not only was he convinced that everybody was way too excited about this research vessel, he had absolutely no idea how he was suppose to fulfill his orders. If there was really a group of terrorist in control of a research vessel in such a remote area and if they didn't want to be seen, then it would be really difficult to see something even during the

Thin Ice

daylight. But Major MacMillan and his crew would only arrive in the area within a few hours. By then it would be completely dark. It would be difficult to see anything, and especially difficult to see if something was wrong. On top of that Josh knew he would not be back before late this evening and so he had to cancel the date with his fiancée. Today of all days, when they had their anniversary to celebrate he got a late call. Although she didn't say anything on the phone, Josh only knew too well that she was disappointed.

He turned his head around and checked his instruments. Everything was okay.

"Just buy her some flowers and surprise her. They all love flowers," Warrant Officer and radio operator Simon Clearwater suggested.

"No, she doesn't like flowers," Josh answered defeated.

"I have an idea," Major and co-pilot Erin Shields suggested from her seat. "Book a nice romantic getaway at that fancy new spa for next weekend and surprise her. The whole nine yards."

Josh looked at his co-pilot in disbelief. She could see that he didn't understand such language. Erin took a powdered cream-filled doughnut out of a brown paper bag and started eating it.

"Are you out of your mind? Do you have any idea how much that's going to cost me? It's not my fault we're flying up here. Not like I want to go anyway, there's the game on this Saturday."

Erin rolled her eyes and took another bite out of her doughnut.

"You men are all the same. Just because there's a game this weekend. This is the perfect way to show her how much she means to you. I really enjoyed it when my husband surprised me with it."

"Really? What did he do to invite you?" Simon asked seriously from his chair.

Erin threw him a sharp glare.

"Although you're obviously not one of them, there are some men who are romantic by nature. I was just lucky to get one of those really rare species. We women simply like spas."

Josh looked at his co-pilot again. Although he didn't understand the concept behind it, he could comprehend that female logic.

"Okay, I might give it a try. I can still record the game. Once you're done eating your doughnut you can tell me where you've been. But before that you can give me our ETA."

"Yes, Sir," Erin replied and brushed some powder sugar from her uniform. "Estimated time of arrival in T minus three hours and twenty-two minutes."

Josh rolled his eyes and looked outside the window again.

It's going to be a long night...

On board the *Northern Explorer*, Amundsen Gulf, Darnley Bay, Thursday, October 13th

Although Chuck took great care in the lighting details on the deck to reduce being spotted from the sky, all the necessary interior lights were turned on. The *Northern Explorer* should not appear to be abandoned just in case that a plane would fly over.

When Astrid stepped through the door to enter the ship, she first closed the door behind her and stopped. With her back leaning against the wall she took several deep breaths. It was only now that she realized her uncontrollable shivers was not only from the cold temperature. Just a few minutes ago she witnessed Nick, someone she knew and trusted, execute two people without hesitation. Astrid closed her eyes. She knew Nick didn't really have any other choice. Both terrorists would have executed him there and then if they would have seen him. The American's demonstrated their cold bloodedness several times already. The more Astrid thought about their general situation the less problems she had with Nick's actions.

Okay! Don't let them notice anything. Everything will be fine!

Astrid opened her eyes again and continued her routine. Steadily she walked up several stair cases and turned into the corridor where Ole-Einar, Olaf and Richard were kept hostage. Frank Garcia sat on a chair and looked up completely bored from his magazine when he noticed Astrid coming around the corner.

"Where is Nelson?"

The question hit her like a slap in the face. Since his murder she never thought about this. But, following Nick's orders, she went on as if nothing had happened.

"He's in the men's room. Stomach problems."

Frank thought about her answer for a moment and his hand reached for his radio. He paused as he looked back at her and returned his hand to the magazine. If he would call Nelson over the radio now, Chuck would hear it as well. His boss would definitely not be happy to learn that Astrid was walking around the ship without a personal escort. Frank decided to spare his friend the trouble and opened the door to Olaf's cabin. He turned on the light and used Astrid as shield in front of him when he entered the cabin.

"I don't want to hear a single word," he threatened them as always.

Astrid put her basket on the floor and took four sandwiches and a large plastic bottle of water out of it. Carefully she handed it to Olaf and winked at him with encouragement. Something she had not done in the last couple days.

She repeated the same procedure with Ole-Einar and Dr. Richard Weber. Satisfied with herself she turned back into the corridor and walked back the way she came.

"Stop. Where do you think you're going, alone?"

Scared to death Astrid turned around and looked at Frank.

"I still have to go to Natascha. Orders from Chuck. I have to bring her something to eat as well."

Frank looked past her and back at his watch. He wondered where Nelson was, but he didn't want to risk Chuck finding out that Astrid was walking through the ship alone. The American made sure that all three cabin doors were locked before he clipped the radio to his belt. He grabbed Astrid by her arm.

"Let's go. We got to hurry. Keep your mouth shut," he said and pushed her in front of him.

While Frank escorted Astrid downstairs, Ole-Einar and Olaf ate their sandwiches. Although they trusted Astrid with the goods, they always checked on what they were eating. Today she had prepared two sandwiches with cheese and two with liver

Thin Ice

sausage. Being hungry Ole-Einar picked up a liver sausage sandwich and became suspicious. Something seemed to be carved into the meat. He turned the sandwich so that he could read the message and almost choked at the last bite of the cheese sandwich in his mouth. Obviously Astrid used her finger nail to carve *Nick alive* into the sandwich. Excited about the news he picked up the second sandwich to find another note there. *On board -2* read this message, also carved with a finger nail. Curious, the Norwegian checked the last remaining cheese sandwich, but he didn't find a message on that one. He wondered how many more secret messages they might have consumed without knowing it. But the more he thought about it, the more he was convinced that this was Astrid's first attempt to communicate with them. Let alone because of the way she winked at them.

Carefully, Ole-Einar examined his remaining sandwiches again before he finally ate them. Because of Natascha's absence he and Olaf both suspected something must have happened to Nick, but obviously he was still fine and back on board without the terrorists knowing about it. The Norwegian had absolutely no idea how Nick could have managed it, but it seemed that he dodged this bullet. That would leave the remaining part of Astrid's message, which was *-2*. Ole-Einar knew that Nick would never be able to plan his actions so precise that he would free them in exactly two hours. Not when he was alone and had to rely on Astrid to deliver the message. So the message could only mean that Nick had already eliminated two of the mercenaries. In his mind Ole-Einar tried to come up with more scenarios, but that was the most likely one and he was convinced that the terrorists were down two men. The best part was that it didn't seem as if they noticed. With a smile on his face for the first time in days, he leaned back against the wall and closed his eyes.

Keep going, buddy. Just don't forget to get us out of here.

Inside the cabin next door Olaf came to the same conclusion, while Dr. Weber hungrily inhaled all his sandwiches without noticing the messages.

Finally Astrid stood in front of Natascha's cabin. She watched as Frank unlocked and opened the door. The light was still on and Natascha still sat in the same spot she was in hours before. When she noticed Astrid, she sadly looked up for a second before she stared at the corner again. Astrid's eyes filled with tears at this sight. Carefully she walked towards Natascha and put the basket on the floor. Slowly she took the remaining four sandwiches out and offered them to her German friend. Natascha looked at it briefly and slowly shook her head. She wasn't hungry and had not eaten in a long time now. Emotionless she looked back at the corner.

"Come on Natascha. You have to eat something. Please!" Astrid begged. It hurt to see Natascha suffering like that. At least she wanted to make sure that she read her message.

"I've seen you eating this for breakfast all the time. Come on, Angel!"

Suddenly Natascha's attention darted to Astrid. The shock, and horror, crossed her face as she stared deep into her Norwegian friend's eyes.

Before they could say another word, Frank took Astrid by her arm and escorted her back outside. While Natascha heard Frank lock the door again, her mind started spinning.

Angel! Only Nick called me an Angel!

She thought really hard but she was convinced that Nick never called her by this nickname when anyone else was around. Not even when it was only her father, Shira or Astrid. Since his friends still called him *Princess*, he always tried to avoid having them call her by a nickname as well. Natascha was also certain he never mentioned that nickname to Shira or Astrid. Why should he? How did Astrid know that Nick called her *Angel*? And even if Astrid knew about it, she would never say it for the pain it would cause her. Calling her something now that Nick had called her in privacy would be a new form of torture.

Natascha's mind spun with confusion.

What did she say about the breakfast?

Her eyes rested on the sandwiches. For breakfast she usually had some cereals with fruit or a bagel with jam, but she had never eaten liver sausage during this expedition. She was turning vegetarian and Astrid knew that. Her eyes rested on the two sandwiches with the liver sausage and she finally noticed the message.

Nick alive! and *Coming!*

Natascha picked up both sandwiches and her hands started to shake violently.

Her eyes filled with tears and she had to swallow hard. The sandwiches slowly fell from her hands as her inner confusion peaked.

That can't be. Nick is dead. I saw how he died. I have...Did you really see how he died?...Of course I did. I saw how they pulled the empty helmet and harness out of the water. Nobody can survive that!...Did you see his dead body?...No, I didn't see his body, but nobody can survive that. He would've had to take his gear off underwater and immediately enter a diving bell or a submersible with a pressurized lock and a pressure chamber. And I didn't see any of that...

Natascha's argument paused for a moment. Slowly her hands rose to her head and then her mouth. For a few seconds she concentrated really hard. Astrid would never deflect to the terrorists and play with Natascha's feelings like that. Not after what Chuck put her through during the last couple days. Besides that Natascha knew they were not alone done there.

It's unlikely, but the technology is there. Could it really be that the Russians...

Natascha closed her eyes again and didn't dare continue her thought. Overwhelmed with emotion she burst in tears again, but after a few minutes of brief pain returning a smile managed to burst across her face. It was the first time in five days.

Just a few meters away, and separated by only two steel walls, was Nick. At all costs, he had to avoid being detected by the mercenaries. The dead bodies from Nelson Singer and Brian Joice were no longer on board the ship. Nick put a weight belt around their hips and thrown them into the water where they sank immediately. The fact that he didn't know where the remaining terrorists were exactly was no help at all. Before he got rid of the dead bodies, he retrieved both their weapons and their radios. The radios were set to the same channel, but Nick still activated the call search function on one of them. He simply wanted to be prepared just in case they were switching channels at timed intervals. Until now, he did not hear any radio communication.

His first target was the radio room. He first had to eliminate the person watching the monitors. For everything else he needed to do, he relied on the support of his teammates. He simply could not free them as long as someone was watching the monitors. For a moment Nick thought to cut the main power as a distraction, but then he remembered that both the bridge and the radio room had their own emergency power supply. Within seconds their operation capability would be back to normal. He had no other choice but to take the radio room first. After that he would free Olaf and Ole-Einar, before he planned to take the bridge. Although he knew from Astrid that Natascha was kept one deck below Olaf and Ole-Einar, he still didn't know her exact cabin. There was simply not enough time to search each cabin, so he had to rely on Astrid's help for that. Nick knew this was anything but a perfect plan. Actually the longer he thought about it, the more lunatic the plan seemed to be. If just one terrorist noticed the radio room was no longer manned while he was on his way to his Norwegian friends, his entire plan would have gone up in smoke. If that was the case they would be waiting for him, firing with everything they had. Nick had gone over this again and again, but there was simply no way to free either Ariel and Shira, or his Norwegian friend's or Natascha without eliminating the monitors first. It was more wishful thinking, but Nick hoped the remaining terrorists would all be inside the ship. He couldn't imagine someone staying outside in these frigid temperatures if he didn't have to. So Nick decided to travel as much ground as possible outside. He remembered most parts of the main deck were under video surveillance, but during his time on the bridge he had never seen the staircases being monitored as well. Hoping this had not changed, he sneaked up the outer staircase.

In his right hand was the Sig Sauer he took from Nelson. The Russian gun was tugged in its holster on his coverall. He had two staircases left to the same deck level as the radio room. Like before, he kneeled down at the end of the first staircase and simply watched the deck in front of him. If someone was in the area, that person would have to walk directly towards Nick in order to see him. Nick waited for several minutes and since he did not hear anything over the radio, he carefully sneaked onto the deck. The young German scaled under the windows, avoiding detection. Although it was dark outside he didn't want to risk someone inside seeing his shadow. Successfully he reached the door and waited again.

A quick look through the window told him that no one was within the immediate area behind the door. Slowly and carefully he opened the door just a few centimeters and waited again. Finally he ducked inside, closed the door behind him and moved towards the dark corridor in front of him. He was glad he decided to enter the ship one deck below the radio room. The cold air rushing through the door when he entered could have given him away. The only light he could see were the ones at the staircase. The corridors all seemed to be dark.

Nick sneaked towards the brightly lit staircase and stopped a few meters short. He listened closely, but he could hear nothing that would indicate someone walking up or down the stairs. As close to the wall as possible and with his gun at the ready he entered the stairwell. The gun firmly followed his eyeline as he quickly looked downstairs, then upstairs. The only thing he could see was the beige colored rail and the white stairs. Nick spent some more time just listening, but he still didn't hear anything. Before he went on, he dried off his light Russian combat boots. He had to maintain his silence, squeaking boots on the metal stairs was too much of a risk.

He took one last quick look around and steadily moved upstairs, not without securing all directions permanently. He just realized how much he depended on the help of his teammates.

At the next half landing he could already see the corridor leading to the radio room and the bridge. Astrid had kept her word and turned the lights inside the corridor off. Nick was relieved when he noticed that she even closed the door to the bridge behind her. Slowly he walked up the last flight of stairs and took cover behind the door frame. Again he could not see anything suspicious. The only thing he saw was the door to the radio room was wide open.

Perfect. Couldn't be better.

Nick sneaked along the corridor until he reached the open door. He slowly leaned his head past the frame and took a quick look inside the room.

He didn't like what he saw at all. Although Robert Tyrell was alone inside the radio room, he sat on Astrid's chair and therefore around four meters away from the door. Not only that, but the monitors were right in front of him. So Nick would have to attack him head on over the table. Nick retreated silently and closed his eyes. It was physically impossible to overpower Robert Tyrell without him firing a shot or calling for help. Nick's brain worked feverishly, but he knew he could not stay here any longer. Carefully, he walked back the corridor and went towards the men's room. Without switching the lights on he slid inside and concealed himself behind the door.

His brain was still spinning but he did not come up with a new plan. A surprise attack was out of the question. It would automatically come with a lot of noise, something that must be avoided. While Nick was still trying to figure out what to do next, he heard some steps approach him from the corridor. He ducked behind the door and just seconds later someone entered the restroom. Robert Tyrell searched for the light switch with his hand and turned it on. He oriented himself and closed the door behind him. Before he could react he noticed the hand on his mouth. His head was pulled to the left side and he immediately felt the sharp pain concentrating on two points in his back. Trying to protect himself, he took his right hand off his attackers left and reached back. Next thing he saw was a shadow coming from the right side, immediately followed by a sharp pain inside his throat. Robert tried to fight against Nick, but as fast as the pain spread through his entire body, the same was for his energy leaving it as he fell effortlessly to the ground. Within seconds he was dead.

Nick turned the light off, opened the door and dragged Robert as fast as he could back to the radio room. Carefully he placed him in his original chair, but he turned him into a slightly different angle so that his back was now facing the door. Nick also adjusted the monitors to the new position and supported Robert's head with a simple ruler. After he took all the bullets out of Robert's gun, he placed it in the same position he saw it before. Beside the gun he even put Robert's radio. If someone walked by the radio room now, on first sight everything would look normal. Satisfied, Nick checked for a potential blood trail leading into the radio room. He surveyed the area one last time and his eyes rested on the communication controls. For a second he considered to radio for help, but immediately realized he would be screwed the moment someone would overhear him. There was also the risk that the radio operator at the other end could have some additional questions within a few minutes.

Nick scratched the idea from his head and found his eyes resting on Ariel's laptop, but his disappointment was great once he flipped it open. As Astrid told him, she turned the laptop off and Nick knew he would need Ariel's fingerprint to start it. Frustrated, he closed the laptop again. Since there was nothing else here, he closed the door behind him and sneaked back to the toilet. He cleaned up some blood and made his way back to the staircase. His next plan of action was to free his two Norwegian teammates and Natascha's father.

Without running into any complications Nick reached the respective deck. He peeked around the corner and noticed the bright light in the corridor. Nick waited for a few seconds and made sure that there was no danger coming from any side. It was almost certain that he would not be as lucky again as he was upstairs in the radio room. His other problem was that time was now running out. It was only a matter of minutes until someone would find Robert's dead body. Nevertheless Nick tried to prevent becoming careless. Like before, he leaned his head by the door frame and got a quick look down the corridor. At the other end sat Frank Garcia, reading a magazine. Nick estimated the distance to him at around five meters and pulled his head back. None of his guns had a silencer and he knew he would need a lot of luck if he wanted to do this without creating too much noise. Only one shot or one word over the radio from Frank and all hell would break loose. To make matters worse, Nick did not have any time to come up with a good plan. He settled his quickly beating heart with a slow exhale. He gathered his thoughts quickly and remembered his situation training. He spent endless hours preparing for this moment. He took one last quick look around the corner and sprinted towards Frank.

- 24 -

On board the Canadian *CF142 Arcturus*, over the Northwest Territories, Thursday, October 13th
By now Major MacMillan had successfully steered the military plane within thirty minutes to the *Northern Explorer*. Josh's mood was now much better than it was before. His co-pilot Erin Shields had told him more about the weekend at the Spa. The more he heard about it, the more he was convinced that his fiancée would forgive him the moment she would sip some champagne in the whirl-pool. He even marked down the name of the Spa on his navigation charts and was determined to call there as soon as possible. Even if this meant he would miss the game this weekend, he knew he had to do it. Satisfied with the world around him, he navigated the *Arcturus* to a lower altitude and pushed through the clouds. In the distance he could already see Paulatuk.

"Okay, let's find out what's going on up here in Santa Claus' backyard," Josh shouted over the noise of the four propeller engines and looked at his radio operator. Warrant Officer Simon Clearwater nodded and called the *Northern Explorer* over the radio. He had clear orders to call the ship on all frequencies until they answered or until they had visually checked the ship. In order to do that they wanted to take several pictures, some infrared images as well as some video. With such clear orders Warrant Officer Clearwater kept calling the *Northern Explorer*.

On board the *Northern Explorer*, Amundsen Gulf, Darnley Bay, Thursday, October 13th
Before Frank Garcia even noticed what was happening, Nick already covered the first three meters. With an explosion of adrenaline, Nick successfully swung his arms out and pulled Frank to the floor. Dazed, Frank looked around in shock, only spotting his gun and radio as they clacked to the ground beside him. He just turned his attention to his left when Nick's next attack burst towards him. Not a single sound escaped Frank's perplexed gaze as a fist contacted his face. The impact smacked his head back to the ground as it broke his nose instantly.

Stunned by the burning pain pulsing through him, Frank's eyes fluttered open struggling to find his assailant. Before he reached any matter of cognitive function, Frank cringed under the sharp pain that burned through his chest. His eyes dropped to the knife that protruded from his lungs. His lips opened, a scream reverberating from deep within, but Nick's hand quickly reached his mouth, muting his pain to a weak exhale of breath.

With wide eyes the American stared at the German, searching for an explanation he would never get. When Nick was convinced Frank no longer posed dangerous any more, he exhaled sharply. Frank was the fourth person he had executed this evening.

Even though it was his job, Nick never liked the thought of taking a life. These people were someone's brother, son and father. He shook his head sharply, these were not people. They were cold-blooded murderers that gambled with others lives like it was an honourable sport. They had no scruple killing others just to make a point.

"Sorry Frank, but you guys are messing with the wrong people," Nick whispered and closed the dead man's eyes. A gesture he had also performed with the other three. With a swift movement Nick got back on his feet and sat Frank back on his chair. He slightly turned the chair again so Frank's back would face the camera. With the set of keys from the American's belt, Nick could finally open the cabin doors.

"What the hell took you so long?" Ole-Einar asked, after giving Nick a hug.

"What kind of coverall is that? Where have you been?" Olaf asked surprised.

"Later. It's a rather long story. We're currently on our own. Ariel and Shira are most likely in the Russian storage room. I was able to eliminate all the members of the American expedition team but Jenna. One of the terrorists is also history. He's still sitting upstairs in front of the monitors, pretending to watch them. I had to take the radio room first because of the camera, but I'm not sure how long that cover will last," Nick whispered his explanation, while he opened the door to Richards cabin as swiftly as he could.

"Hurry up! We have to get away from the camera," Ole-Einar pushed his friends.

Without wasting any time, Nick grabbed Richard by the wrist, placed a hand over his mouth and pushed him down the corridor. Olaf followed close behind after relocking the cabin doors.

Ole-Einar secured the magazine tightly on Frank's lap, before he took his gun and radio. It just took them a few seconds to get out of the immediate danger zone and back under the protection of the dark corridors. Nick took a few moments to brief them on the situation.

"Oh my God," was all that Olaf could say.

"Well, you have to tell us that again when we have more time. What's your plan in the meantime?"

Nick handed Olaf one of his guns and one radio.

"Natascha is one deck below us, but besides the terrorists only Astrid knows exactly where she is. I think we should find her. Once we get her and her father off the ship we can take the bridge and..."

"Sorry to interrupt you Nick. But I think our priority should be getting Richard off this ship asap. If something goes wrong down the road, we have at least one person who knows the truth in safety. It'll take us less than five minutes to get him off the ship," Ole-Einar suggested quickly, eyeing Nick sharply.

Reluctant, Nick looked from Ole-Einar to Olaf, only to see he agreed with Ole-Einar. Nick knew the Norwegian had a very good point. This wasn't over yet and there were still three separate groups of hostages and Natascha. It was only a matter of time until the terrorists would find out what was happening.

Nick tried to push his priority to their suggestion, but it bothered him. He just wanted Natascha safe. He looked back at his teammates as they looked at him expectantly.

He knew they were dealing with highly trained and armed individuals who were former members of Special Forces. Nick's eyes drifted down the corridor. Ole-Einar made another very good argument, even if he didn't say it out loud. Natascha's father would not only slow them down significantly, he would also tie up one person for his permanent protection. It was a fact that he would be more of a problem than a help in the upcoming combat situations.

Reaching his resolve, Nick thought quickly. He plotted out their route, certain to avoid any unnecessary detection before taking action. He knew they would have to escort Richard off the ship. Hiding him anywhere would be too much of a risk. Finalizing his thoughts, Nick nodded his approval to his team.

"Okay, let's go," the German said and led the group down to the main deck.

The cold cross wind blew, biting at their exposed skin as they made their way through the ship. Together as a team they could move much faster and more efficiently than Nick could before. Checking around every corner and angle, the team moved swiftly, their guns following their sightline. Olaf and Nick secured their way up front, while Ole-Einar secured their back and their sides. Richard was in their middle, staying close to Nick.

When they walked by the storage room for the dive gear, they gave Richard the time to put on a dry-suit. If he would fall in the freezing water, he would at least be protected. Everybody was relieved Richard followed their instructions down to the letter. For a moment they feared he would insist on staying with them to free his daughter. Fortunately he surprised them all and followed Nick like a shadow to the rail.

"Okay Olaf, I think you can walk the last ten meters alone with Richard. We'll cover your back," Nick commented, pointing the way.

The Norwegian nodded. The last ten meters could be seen from the bridge and it was more difficult to spot just two instead of four people.

"Nick!" Natascha's father whispered, grabbing his arm just as he was turning around.

"Remember what you promised me! Please!"

Nick looked at Richard with shock. He was usually able to keep his expressive face under wraps while working in such situations, but Richard's expression reflected his desperation. Nick knew it was tearing his heart apart having to leave the ship his daughter was still kept hostage.

"I remember, Richard. Don't worry. We'll bring her back," Nick promised, attempting a higher level of certainty than he felt himself.

With tears running down his face, Natascha's father shook his hand before following Olaf over the rail.

Ole-Einar and Nick looked at each other and shook their heads.

"Do you hear that?"

"What?"

"That droning noise. Sounds like a huge propeller plane."

Nick could finally hear it himself and looked up into the sky. After a few seconds he spotted the position lights of a bigger plane. It was just below the clouds and flew towards them.

"It's too big for Paulatuk. Altitude is way too low and it is too slow for a normal passenger plane. Four propellers. That must be a Canadian military plane. Looks like they've noticed something," Ole-Einar laughed freely. His chuckle abruptly caught in his throat a few seconds later as their radios activated. They exchanged a hard glance as they listened to the chatter.

Jenna Mason and Martin Cunningham were on the bridge looking out through the large windows. The clouds made the night that much darker as they drifted over the moon, blanketing across the stars. It would be easy to recognize any object approaching them since no one could operate without lights in these conditions.

Jenna intently listened to the radio and a frown scrunched her forehead. The *Northern Explorer* had just been called by a military plane. Nervously she picked up the direct line to her brother in the Captain's quarters and alerted him to the news. Within a few seconds Chuck stood beside her on the bridge. He listened to the repeated message and knew it was the military. He tried to conceal his own nervousness, but it was clearly visible.

Only eighteen more hours! That's all we need. Why are they here? What do they know?

Chuck's thoughts raced quickly, refusing to cease. Feverishly he reflected on the last few days, determined to remember if something went wrong. The only chance that information could have made it off the ship was at the beginning of their mission. Chuck recalled the one guy talking on his cell phone when he and Jenna overpowered him. How much could he have told during that conversation? Chuck was certain the guy talked to his boss in London.

"We better answer them," Jenna recommended anxiously.

Even if they get suspicious, they need at least another twelve hours before they have some special troops up here. I don't think they're already on that plane. Even if we're done by then, they would have no issues tracking us down since we have to rely on the helicopters...

Chuck's anxiety increased with every passing moment. Between his thoughts, his sisters worrying gaze and the consistent call from the plane, Chuck struggled for a plan. He quickly paced the bridge. He knew answering them was inevitable, but he was still looking for the best solution.

"Okay Captain Rasmussen. I want you to pick up the radio and tell them everything is fine. No tricks!" Chuck ordered and pointed his gun at Astrid again.

Captain Rasmussen was tired, but he still nodded. The Norwegian knew very well the rules that Chuck installed.

The Captain walked slowly over to the radio, pressed the call button beckoning the Canadian military plane. The Canadian's replied right away and asked him if everything was all right. Like so many times before, Captain Rasmussen lied and convinced them that everything was fine.

"Would it be possible to talk to the expedition leader himself or to one of his German team members?"

Captain Rasmussen looked at Chuck, who hastily shook his head while Jenna more or less clung to her gun. She was much more nervous than her brother.

The Captain thought for a second before he answered.

"That would be negative. The expedition leader and the members of his team are currently not available. They just finished a deep dive and they're all in the decompression chamber as a precaution."

"Are you saying you had a diving accident on board? Do you need medical assistance?"

"That's a negative. No diving accident, I repeat, no diving accident. It's a simple precaution before they fly out tomorrow."

Chuck was satisfied and nodded towards the Captain. If Chuck did not know any better, he would have believed the Norwegian man. When he looked outside the window, he could already see the position lights of the military plane closing in fast.

"Okay. I could hear you loud and clear. No diving accident. Please inform the expedition leader that he has to contact his institute as soon as possible. It's very important."

"I'll make sure he will. Have a good flight. Out."

"Roger and out."

Chuck exhaled sharply. This would give him the additional time he needed. Satisfied he picked up his own radio and pressed the call button.

"Status report, please"

"Eagle four, everything is okay."

So there is no trouble at the storage room. Let's see how the other three are doing.

Chuck waited for a few moments, but the radio remained silent.

"This is eagle one. Everybody check in with status immediately."

Static.

No reply.

With a quick look at his sister, Chuck turned around and ran to the radio room. Carefully he opened the door just a little bit and he froze instantly. Robert was obviously dead. His head tilted to one side and Chuck could see the massive loss of blood at his neck. With a quick look at the monitor's Chuck knew Frank was also no longer alive. Without even checking Chuck knew both Norwegian's and the expedition leader had been freed. It seemed that the Russian storage room was the only place left under their control.

Chuck's hand rushed to his head. Not only did he just lose two men, he lost them silently, without a chance to fight back. Without wasting any more time, Chuck picked up his radio.

"Attention! We have intruders. The Norwegian's are free!" he screamed into the radio and ran back to the bridge. Before any word was spoken, he heard the shots.

"Martin! You're in command as long as I'm gone. We have to find them!" he shouted furiously, turning around to run down the corridor.

On the deck, Nick, Ole-Einar and Olaf listened to the radio and closed their eyes.

"Goddammit!" Nick cursed in a sharp whisper. Everything would be much more difficult now. Their enemy knew what was going on. He exchanged another glance with his friends, they all knew the crucial element of surprise was gone.

"Okay, what's our next move?" Nick asked and looked at Ole-Einar.

The Norwegian thought over the different scenarios.

"If I was them, I'd start hiding behind the hostages. They know Olaf and I are free and I assume they believe we had some help. They're most likely going to play their trumps."

"Ariel and Shira," Olaf added, concerned.

"Unlikely. By now they realize there are only four of them left. Ariel and Shira are at the other end of the ship. They're not going to risk getting them."

"Natascha!" Nick shouted in dismay.

"That's more likely. We should go and get Ariel and Shira. I assume their single guard is on his way to the bridge to get the new game plan."

Nick refused to agree with Ole-Einar's idea and reluctantly shook his head.

"What about Natascha?" he asked angrily.

"Nick! Try to think for a second, will you? It's going to be difficult now to free Natascha. They know we're coming for her. If we go after her now, chances are good that the fourth terrorist is sneaking up from behind. Besides, there are only three of us against four of them. If we get Ariel and Shira first we have the numbers on our side and nobody can intercept us from behind, since we're at the other end of the ship. Once we have Ariel and Shira, it'll be much easier to get Natascha and the bridge."

Nick thought for a second, he never thought he could be so stupid, so thoughtless. They needed to do what was good for the team, for the hostages. He gulped his emotions into check and apologized. Ole-Einar made complete sense.

"What about the plane? Do you think they're going to help us?" Olaf asked quickly.

All three looked up at the fast approaching military plane, but it was Nick who reacted. He took his Russian gun and aimed at the hull. He almost fired the whole magazine at the plane, which was now only about one hundred meters over the *Northern Explorer.*

"Well, I'm pretty sure they're going to do something now..." Nick trailed with wit. His teammates looked at him with shock, but knew he was right.

**On board the Canadian *CF142 Arcturus*, north off Paulatuk,
Thursday, October 13th**
Major Erin Shields just forwarded the whole radio traffic to MARCOM and Admiral Kerman when she explained they would fly over the research vessel at low altitude within the next few seconds.

She looked outside the window and confirmed that everything looked completely normal. Next thing she heard were multiple bullets hitting the hull of their plane.

"What the hell?" yelled Major Josh MacMillan as he pulled the heavy plane up immediately.

"They just shot at us!" radio operator Simon Clearwater shouted.

"Someone just fired several times at us, Sir!" Erin reported, taking a deep breath. "We could hear several hits. Doesn't look like anything is damaged. Will update once we get a damage report, Sir."

Erin Shields looked at her pilot, who already checked the instruments.

"Hydraulic...oil...fuel...electricity...Everything seems to be fine. Let's get out of range first. God knows what else they can fire with…"

Josh looked outside the window and turned the *Arcturus* around in a big loop. His eyes rested on the *Northern Explorer*. Despite the hostile action that just took place, she now rested peacefully on the water below him.

On board the *Northern Explorer*, Amundsen Gulf, Darnley Bay, Thursday, October 13th

Russell Greenstein guarded the door that separated Ariel and Shira from their freedom when he heard Chuck's message. He confirmed his status and wondered why nobody else called in. Shaking his head in disbelief he stood up and paced the corridor. He didn't mind working with those scientists, but he didn't trust them. They were not professionals like him and his friends. They were just greedy amateurs.

They probably fell asleep in the men's room or are waving at this stupid plane.

Although Russell had also heard the *CF142 Arcturus*, he refused to give it much thought. Still not receiving any radio contact from his teammates, he shook his head once more. It was only a second when he returned his attention to the device, a green LED blinking at him.

Finally. About time, he thought. But it wasn't eagle two or eagle three, it was Chuck's voice that he heard.

"Attention! We have intruders. The Norwegians are free!" he heard his boss yelling. Russell Greenstein spun around immediately and looked down the empty corridor.

Next thing he heard were several shots fired from the same weapon.

Damnnit! They really are free!

Russell had no way of knowing if the shots he just heard were fired from one of his men or from the Norwegians. Without hesitating, he walked back to the door. He reached to his vest and wedged a grenade between the lower bolt and the door. After he convinced himself that the trigger guard was tightly wedged in, he carefully removed the safety pin.

Should his two prisoners really be that lucky to pick the lock without the key, they would still have to open the locking bolts. The moment they would do that, the hand grenade would fall down, unsecured and activated. He smiled at the thought. His trap was fool proof and they would reach their inevitable end soon enough. They would blow themselves up the moment they stepped through the door.

Thin Ice

**Ottawa, Canadian Forces Maritime Command (MARCOM),
Thursday, October 13th**

Everybody inside the office threw anxious glances at each other, passing around their concern like a game of baseball. They carefully listened to Lieutenant Commander Erin Shields' situation report and were unable to muster words under the sudden shock.

In addition to the more or less questionable statement from Captain Rasmussen came the fact that someone just fired several bullets at a Canadian military plane. For Brian Whittaker it was enough to confirm his suspicion and he was already on his phone to inform his friend and colleague Klaus Schwartze in London.

While he spoke with Klaus, Brian noticed that Admiral Kerman just mobilized a JTF2 Assault Team. Their orders were to enter the *Northern Explorer* without using lethal force if possible and to take control over the vessel.

Just as Admiral Kerman and Brian finished their call, Major Erin Shields was back on the radio.

"Sir, I want to report we did not receive any serious damage. All systems are working normally. This is the situation: The research vessel is at it's reported location at anchor. It's position lights were all according to the regulations. As far as we could see, the deck looked like they were very active not too long ago. We were in no position to see if there were any people on deck. Besides that, we could not find anything unusual. As far as the radio contact goes, you heard as much as we did, Sir. Regarding the shooting, I want to say that we're certain we were hit by eight or ten bullets. As far as we know, they all hit our hull. We don't know if they hit anywhere else, but we'll check the video footage. The *Northern Explorer* was the only place the shots could've come from. Our radar did not show any other surface contacts. Judging by the low impact and the minimum damage, we assume someone shot at us with a small rifle or with a hand gun. In brief, all our systems are working fine. I repeat: All our systems are stable and working fine. Requesting permission to turn around. If there's some damage to our plane we don't know about, this is not the place to be, Sir."

"Permission granted. Get the hell out of there. Thank you," Admiral Kerman replied and ended the conversation.

"Okay, here's my question: If the Captain is really held hostage and if he has done everything they asked him to do, why in God's name did they shoot at us?" the Defence Minister asked and looked at everybody for any form of an answer.

Brian carefully watched as everybody shrugged their shoulders and looked at each other.

"I assume my boys are responsible for that," Brian finally admitted casually while he poured himself another cup of coffee.

"Excuse me? You really believe your own men are shooting at a Royal Canadian Air Force plane? Why the hell would they do that?" the Defence Minister demanded to know.

"To make sure we're coming back," Admiral Kerman answered for Brian and leaned back in his chair with success.

You finally seem to get it, Brian thought with a grin and added some milk and sugar to his coffee.

On board the *Northern Explorer*, Amundsen Gulf, Darnley Bay, Thursday, October 13th
Martin Cunningham stood on the bridge and just ordered Second Officer Mika Kankkunen to turn on all the flood lights on deck. They could hear the shots echo through the dark sky, but were unable to see where they came from. Martin cycled his aim from each individual, listening as Chuck gave new orders over his radio. On Martins command, Captain Rasmussen, Astrid and the remaining three officers had to lay down on their bellies, with their hands behind their head. Martin turned all the lights inside the bridge off and carefully looked through the window. His eyes wandered over the now brightly lit deck, but it was too dark to make anything out.

"Hey! You!" he shouted at the Second Officer, barking his orders.

"Turn on the surveillance cameras."

Without hesitating Second Officer Mika Kannkkunen walked over to the controls and flipped a row of several switches before he lay down again with the others.

Several color monitors sprang back to life. He looked at each monitor, noticing a lot of the footage covered the stern. They made it that much easier to control that area of the ship from the bridge. Tensed, Martin stared at the monitors, but he couldn't see any movement. His concentration was interrupted when his partner Russell Greenstein ran onto the bridge.

"What's the plan?" Russell asked, trying to catch his breath. His words came out in short gasps.

"Don't know yet. We have to ask Chuck. He'll be back in a minute. Someone helped the two Norwegians to escape. The old guy is also not in his cabin any more."

"What about the woman? Is she still in her cabin?"

Martin shrugged his shoulders and looked at the five people who lay between him and Jenna on the floor, fearing for their lives.

Ariel and Shira both stood in the storage room. A few moments ago they heard someone fire several shots from the same weapon and how their guard ran away shortly after that. They knew this was their only chance. Shira chewed on the plastic tie wraps that kept Ariel's hands together behind his back. It would take a while before she weakened them enough, but eventually it would work. There were no other options and Shira could feel her nerves pain with every bite. The light inside the storage room was not turned on and the Israeli had to act in complete darkness. They already searched every square centimeter in this room, but with their hands tied to their back, they didn't find anything. The American's thoroughly cleaned the room before they locked them up.

Shira focused intently on her task. She knew they were running out of time. Her thoughts travelled furiously through her brain, but she struggled to keep them focused. She refused to lose her motivation. After a little while Ariel finally noticed he could twist one hand a little more than before.

"Wait a second," he mentioned and shuffled forward from Shira. In a concentrated effort he managed to tear one of the tie wraps apart. The Israeli slowly took his arms in front of his body and massaged his wrists. He could feel the pain burn through his joints as his circulation returned. He stretched his arms in front of him, ignoring the pain with clenched teeth.

He shimmied towards the door, focusing on his balance since his ankles were still bound. He moved carefully but swiftly once he found his motion. His hands ran across the wall and finally found the light switch. With both his hands free it was no problem to turn it. The bright light cut through the darkness and both Ariel and Shira clenched their eyes shut, urging their eyes to adjust. Slowly they got used to the light again.

Ariel helped Shira out of her tie wraps and with free arms and hands it didn't take them too long to free their ankles as well. They hurriedly searched the storage room again, determined to find something useful. Their search was more effective than the last time as they managed to retrieve a piece of wire that someone used to fix a hinge in one of the cupboards. Shira took the wire and without wasting another second she started to work at the lock.

"Do you think you can pick it?"

Shira slowly shook her head.

"Not sure. It's certainly not the best tool for the job. It'll definitely take a while."

Her concentration peeked as she worked the wire in the hole. Just as she was about to make a little progress, there was a soft knock at the door. Shira immediately released the wire and took cover beside the door. She and Ariel looked at each other.

"Shira? Ariel? Are you in there?" they recognized Ole-Einar's voice instantly.

"Yes! How many are you?" Ariel asked as Shira continued to work on the lock again.

"Ole-Einar, Nick and Olaf. Oliver's dead. So are four of the scum bags. We just got flown over by a military plane at low altitude. Nick shot at them to get their attention. I think something's going to happen now sooner or later. The Professor is already off the ship and in safety."

"How is that possible?" Ariel asked through the door, surprised at how much had happened.

"The Russian submarine. Long story, but the good part of it is that they're here and on our side. Natascha is still locked up somewhere alone, the Captain and the officers are most likely on the bridge. The rest of the crew is, as far as we know, still locked up behind the welded doors. We want to get you out of there, but we don't have the keys. And there is also a...."

"I got it!" Shira shouted triumphantly, interrupting Ole-Einar as she placed her hands on the bolts that kept the door shut. The same moment she hurriedly pushed the door open, the unsecured hand grenade fell to the floor, a metallic scream heightened in their ears.

Ole-Einars large arms heavily pushed Nick and Olaf with all his strength into the Russian storage room. His four friends collided, falling to the floor as the huge Norwegian swung his foot to launch the grenade down the corridor. With another yell he dove into the room, crushing his four friends under his thick frame, as the deafening sound of the detonation chaotically filled the air.

Chuck immediately stopped once he heard the grenade go off. The deafening sound of it sent his adrenaline rushing through his thick veins.

On the bridge Russell Greenstein howled with excitement and picked up his radio.

"Eagle one, this is eagle four. Over."

"Eagle four, this is eagle one. What the hell was that?"

"That was the hand grenade I used to booby trap the door for our two guests. I'm on the bridge. Obviously they managed to free themselves, but they didn't get far..."

"Are you sure about this?" Chuck screamed into his radio.

"Come on, Chuck. You know it as well as I do. A fifteen meter long corridor, steel walls, steel ceiling and floor and all doors closed. The pressure wave itself killed everything inside that corridor. There is no way they're still alive."

"Did you see their dead bodies, did you see it on video?"

Russell hesitated before he answered.

"No, I haven't seen their dead bodies. But it isn't necessary, trust me. I know what I'm doing. They're both dead," he reassured Chuck, attempting to hone in his glee.

"Okay, I'm counting on you," Chuck finally replied, but Astrid couldn't hear him anymore. Like the other hostages, shock was clearly visible in her face. Ariel and Shira were dead.

Ole-Einar opened his eyes very slowly. All he could hear was a disturbing ringing sound in his ears. Painfully slow he rolled off his four friends and onto his back.

"Is anyone hurt?" Ariel asked immediately.

Shira answered in the negative and Nick and Olaf were also both more or less okay.

"Ole! Are you okay?" Ariel asked and kneeled beside his friend.

Ole-Einar closed his eyes for a second before he gave them the thumps-up. It was hard to hear his leader under the piercing sound. He knew he most likely suffered an ear trauma, but seemed to be all right. Since Ole-Einar was able to kick the hand grenade down the corridor, the complete shock wave went by the storage room itself. Inside the confinement of the corridor, the explosion was so powerful that the storage room door was a twisted sheet of metal that was torn off its hinges and now more than eight meters away.

"Hey Ole, can you say something?" Nick asked eagerly. He was as worried about his big Norwegian friend as everybody else.

"Tell that Israeli she better listen to me when I tell her there's a hand grenade in the door ready to blow her to bits. Like a child, she should keep her fingers off the door."

Shira sat up and used Ole-Einar's chest to push herself up.

"You could've told me that sooner. It turned out to be a valuable piece of information after all," the young Israeli snapped at him.

"Shira, he just saved our lives. Give it a rest," Ariel barked at her.

"What do you think? Can you walk?" Olaf asked his countryman and offered him a hand.

"Yes, I'm just a little dizzy. Was a little bit too much."

"What am I suppose to say? I was buried underneath three men." Shira complained.

"Yes, I think you really liked that," Ole-Einar shot back, immediately receiving a harsh look.

"Okay, enough of this," Ariel finally stopped them.

"We have to get out of here. Do you have any weapons?"

Nick handed Shira the remaining Sig Sauer, while he kept the Russian gun.

"What the hell are you wearing? Is that Russian?" Shira pointed out.

"The Russian *Akula*. Chapter two of a never-ending story. He didn't tell us the details either," Olaf commented matter-of-factly and led their group out of the storage room.

"Okay, let's find Natascha," Ariel ordered quickly, leading the way out the door..

Finally! Nick thought.

Natascha agitatedly paced inside her cabin. She didn't know what to think any more. After she had read Astrid's message she was actually happy at first, even euphoric, but then the reality sank back in. Natascha's mind simply refused to accept the possibility that Nick could still be alive. Too many things were against it.

While she walked nervously, her hope had a heated discussion with her sense for reality.

Okay, what is there against it? Nick's dive profile requires a long decompression. Without that decompression he's as good as dead.

Natascha swallowed hard at that thought, but she continued her discussion.

I saw first hand how they pulled up his empty helmet. Without a helmet he simply can't breathe. Not only that, he's also exposed to the extremely cold water temperature. He can't survive that either.

On the other hand we do know that there is a Russian nuclear submarine out there somewhere. They followed us through the whole Atlantic and all the way through the North-West Passage. Ole-Einar said it must be a hell of a skipper to stay so close to us all the time, that a certain warning system can't detect him. What if the Russians somehow knew about the terrorists and their plans? Chuck has detailed plans from the wreck. He must have gotten them from someone. What if they just came here to recover their property? It would make sense for them to recover their own missiles.

They let us do the work to get them out of the wreck and all they have to do is pick them up from the floor. But how are they going to do that?

They could have a little submersible with them. Something they can use to rescue sailors out of sunken submarines. With an air lock and everything. That would also mean that they would have a pressure chamber on board. But I haven't seen anything down there...Well, of course not. For one it's completely dark down there and two, they're most likely not going to look over our shoulders. They only have to be one hundred meters away and there's no way we can see them. They would still notice everything if they have the right gear. Technically it's really not that difficult.

Natascha was surprised how much she clung to that possibility, but she was simply tired of dealing with the thought that Nick was dead.

Besides, he definitely didn't want you to sit here and cry for days. He would want me to be strong and fight. No, actually he wanted to sit in the plane with me on our way home. That's what he wanted!

Natascha ceased her argument. With nothing else to think of, nothing else to occupy her time, it was hard to avoid the hope that Nick was alive. That he would save them. She wiped the tears from her eyes at the thought of their happy life together. A life that was swiftly taken away but suddenly given back with the hope that he was alive, that they would get out of this together. Her face scrunched as anohter round of tears escaped her. The uncertainty of his fate didn't really help her at all. She heard the shots and even a detonation and she knew that something was going on out there. Someone tried to get control over the ship and she could only hope that they were Nick and his friends. As if someone listened to her prayers, she heard someone unlock the door to her cabin.

Natascha was relieved, she knew he would finally come to get her. Her heart raced with speed, her joy escaping her with strong passion.

"Nick!" she shouted euphorically when the door finally opened.

"Almost." Chuck stated bluntly, pointing his gun at her. "Let's move and keep quiet."

- 25 -

Inside the bridge of the *Northern Explorer*, Amundsen Gulf, Darnley Bay, Thursday, October 13th

Russell Greenstein impatiently waited inside the bridge, taking a few steps to stop and think, only to do it again. He couldn't get Chuck's words out of his head. No, he did not see their bodies, after all he was on the bridge when it happened. Theoretically there was a slim chance that someone might have walked away from that blast alive. What if the others just tried to free them? If that was the case, there was a fair chance that all their enemies were dead by now. After all, they did not hear anything, or discover anything, from their enemies since the detonation. Against the odds Russell checked the monitor in the radio control room, but the camera in the corridor had not survived the explosion. He finally decided to head back to the Russian storage room to see if and how many casualties there were. Determined, he took one radio from the table, double-checked his gun and turned towards Martin.

"I'll have a look to see if the others are still alive. With a little bit of luck we're already rid of all of them."

Martin nodded his approval. He knew Russell was right. The chances that their enemies would first try to reunite their team were very big. If they had accidentally set the hand grenade off during that attempt, they were most likely not among the living any more.

"Be careful and keep radio contact. Don't do anything alone if you see something, okay?" Martin tried to warn him.

Russell nodded and walked off the bridge. He refused to be quiet as he ran down the stair case. Once he was on the deck, he stepped outside the door and grimaced. The cold and gusty wind bit into his skin and instead of looking ahead, Russell turned his head down and out of the wind. Steadily he walked along the rail, until he saw some movement right in front of him. Immediately he kneeled down and took cover. What he saw over his drawn pistol surprised him completely. He could clearly see the four men and the woman try to sneak over the deck under the cover of the blind spots provided by the container. Russell's face turned into a sharp scowl. Not only did the two survive the hand grenade, even the one guy who was believed to be dead was with them again. Russell was disgusted to see Nick again and crouched even closer to the little life raft that provided him cover. If he was detected right now he knew he was as good as dead. Pointing his gun at them with his right hand, the American used his left to carefully switch his radio off. Even the shortest radio message would give away his position. Russell carefully watched how the other group stopped for a second. They now stood behind the container and could not be seen from the bridge nor from one of the cameras. He knew he could not risk a shoot out with them. There was no chance for him to survive a direct confrontation with them. Sure, he would certainly be able to kill one, maybe two of them, but after that he would be history. There was no doubt in his mind that his enemies were well-trained with the weapons they were carrying. Taking a closer look, Russell noticed that the last guy in the group wasn't carrying a weapon at all. His original plan had been to go after the woman, but then he saw that she was armed. The group now concentrated on the bridge and the door leading to the inside of the ship. Russell was lucky they didn't pay any attention to the life raft he was hiding behind.

Russell watched as his enemies communicated with hand signals, not saying a word. One after the other, Nick and his friends covered the short distance from the container to the door, where they were once more invisible from both the bridge and the cameras. In the meantime Russell came up with another plan and he had to rely on perfect timing in order for it to work. The same moment the woman started to cover the open space, Russell stepped out of his cover and behind Ariel, who was now alone.

"Only one word and I blow your Goddamn brain out," Russell warned him bitterly, pressing his gun to the back of Ariel's head.

Natascha couldn't believe it. It was not Nick who came into her cabin, it was this monster again. Chuck grabbed her arm, but Natascha was determined to fight back. She pushed his arm away and tried to jab her finger in his eye, but she wasn't nearly fast enough. Chuck blocked her attack and hit her in the face with the palm of his hand. While Natascha's head spun around, she already tasted blood on her lips. Having a firm grip on Natascha's hair, Chuck pushed her outside the cabin and down the corridor. Using her as a shield at the next corner, he turned into the corridor that would bring them to the stair case.

"I don't want to hear a word, do you understand?" he whispered aggressively and yanked at her hair.

Hot waves of pain rushed through her as he tugged again at her lack of response. She hurriedly nodded her head as best she could. Natascha spat some blood out and abandoned herself to her faith. She was too scared to do anything and Chuck was simply too strong for her to even entertain the thought of overpowering him. Deeper and deeper he dragged her into the ships hull, his grip not letting up.

"Where are we going?" Natascha asked fearfully once they got closer to the engine room. She had never been here before.

"Somewhere where I have better control over you, where you can't do anything stupid," Chuck replied hotly and pushed her through the engine room.

Even though the *Northern Explorer* was at anchor, the main engines still produced enough heat and noise that it was difficult for Natascha to concentrate. The young German noticed how Chuck always looked back to make sure nobody followed them. Eventually they walked by a little control room. Chuck open the lexan door and pushed Natascha inside, before he locked the door. The moment he secured her, he ducked back out of sight. The trap was set.

Ariel froze. Slowly the Israeli rose his hands and watched Shira as she safely reached the other side. Looking back at Ariel, Shira immediately recognized his problem.

"Shooter behind Ariel," she called to her teammates, who all spun around, instantly aiming at Russell.

With a quick glance around the premises, Nick noticed they were only dealing with one person. He turned around immediately again to secure the door that led to the inside of the ship. He wanted to avoid the other three terrorists intercepting them from behind.

Although Russell was by himself against five of his opponents, he still felt in control. The four who were armed were almost eight meters away from him. He held the one unarmed hostile as a human shield.

"Just don't move. Stay where you are," Russell whispered and searched with his left hand for the radio. It was stuck in his pocket and for the fraction of a second Russell looked down. Ariel immediately noticed the slight change in the pressure of the gun pushed to the back of his head. Russell's inattentiveness was all that Ariel needed and he spun around. The former NAVY Seal was totally stunned by the surprise attack from the former close combat instructor from the Israeli special forces. Before Russell could even pull the trigger, Ariel's hand had already grabbed the gun and blocked the cock. At the same time the Israeli hit Russell twice on his throat, crushing the American's larynx, before his knee rammed just under Russell's Solar Plexus. His eyes grew wide with the sudden pain and a loud groan escaped him as he sank to the floor. Before Russell's knees touched the deck, Ariel already pushed the pressure point allowing him to retrieve his gun without any problems. The moment Russell was on his knees Ariel put his hands on Russell's chin and the back of his head and, with a sudden move, broke his neck. Less then two seconds had passed from the time Russell had looked at his radio until he was dead. Even to Ariel these moments always seemed the longest. The manipulation of adrenaline made the time warp in a way that the scene seemed a lot slower than real time.

Ariel took a deep breath as he made sure that Russell was really dead. He dragged the American's body underneath the life raft, before he joined his friends.

"Are you okay?" Ole-Einar whispered.

"Yes, everything's fine," the Israeli replied calmly and gazed through the door.

"Oh boy. Am I ever glad we always treated Shira well, never making a single rude comment to her," Nick commented and shook his head in disbelief. Like his friends he found Ariel's performance quiet impressive.

"Okay, just three more left," Ariel noted, ignoring Nick's comment.

"Where is Natascha?"

"According to Astrid she's on the same deck as our cabins were."

"Okay, let's go then."

With a quick look around the doorframe, Nick noticed the stair case was free. He carefully rounded the corner and took a step inside, immediately securing the stairs leading to the lower level of the ship, while his friends moved up. As soon as everybody was on the stairs, Olaf tapped Nick on his shoulders and he followed them up, still securing their backs and as close to the wall as possible. Once they reached the designated deck, Shira kept securing the stairs leading further up, while the rest quickly moved into the corridor. Once Nick passed the Israeli, he tapped her on the shoulder and she followed him around the corner and into the corridor. She just rounded the next corner and remained there to secure the corridor towards the stair case. Nobody could come from that direction without being detected by the young Israeli.

Nick turned around and closed in on his friends. To their surprise all the cabin doors were open and they noticed that their former cabins were thoroughly searched.

"That was to be expected," Ariel simply noted and walked further down the corridor.

"Nick, over here," Olaf called his friend and pointed at the last cabin.

Nick stepped inside the cabin. This was definitely the place where they had kept Natascha. Ole-Einar picked up a torn necklace and an engagement ring. He handed both items to Nick. Nick swallowed hard when he took them in his hands and looked at them as if they held all the answers.

"I can't see any blood in here. I'm pretty sure she's still alive," his Norwegian friend tried to reassure him.

Nick let his eyes wander through the cabin, looking for every possible clue suggestig Natascha's whereabouts or condition.

"Here's a little bit of blood," Ariel suddenly mentioned outside in the corridor.

Within seconds Nick stood beside him. Together they looked at some blood on the floor. Once they both kneeled down they noticed it was heavily mixed with saliva.

"It's saliva. They took her somewhere else."

Ariel slowly walked down the corridor, carefully examining the floor before he stopped at the T-junction. He examined the floor in both directions for the next few meters before he gave a short laugh.

"Shira! You have trained her very well," he laughed and pointed to the floor when Nick arrived beside him.

"That's definitely some blood mixed with saliva again. She left us a trail to follow," the Israeli explained with a hopeful smile.

"I'd prefer it if she'd use something else, but it will do," Nick mentioned and took a closer look at the blood when their radios chirped alive.

Jenna almost lost it. Not only did a military plane fly over them a few minutes ago, but also the hostages had escaped and half of their own men were dead. And if this was not enough to deal with, there was a detonation and she still didn't know if that was good or bad for them. The very person who was suppose to find out exactly what happened did not call in yet over the radio. Jenna looked at Martin and, judging by the expression on his face, knew that he thought the same.

Martin also didn't want to wait any longer. He didn't know where Chuck or Russell were. All he knew was that Robert and three other members of his team were dead. It was now no longer about recovering the nuclear warheads to sell them at the highest bidder on the black market. All that mattered now was a fast and efficient retreat without leaving any traces behind. The American took a quick glance at his watch. They had enough time before the nerve gas would rise to the surface and kill the first people in Paulatuk. Sure, they were out of the danger zone here, but they had to land in Paulatuk to pick up the other chopper with a greater range. It was only normal that he was nervous.

Jenna walked over to him.

"We have to kill them sooner rather than later. None of them must survive this, do you hear me?" she asked him hastily and pointed at the hostages who were still lying on the floor.

Martin knew that it was against their original plan, but there were many things that went wrong at this moment.

"We'll wait for Chuck. It's his decision," Martin claimed and picked his radio up.

"Russell, can you read me?"

No reply.

Martin walked over to the windows and looked down at the deck, but he couldn't see any sign of Russell.

"Russell, can you read me?"

Still no answer.

Martin knew that this could only mean that he fell to their enemies. His eyes rested on the hostages and after a few seconds a smile was on his face.

"Okay, listen up dirt bags! I know that you're listening. You have five minutes to come to the bridge. Your group will be complete and you must come without weapons. If you're not here within the next five minutes I'll start shooting the radio operator's knees. Every minute after that I'll shoot her in another joint. If she dies, I'll continue with the next hostage. It's your call. The clock is ticking."

Estate of US-Senator Jonathan Brown, Montana, USA,
Thursday, October 13th

The crackling fire inside the open fireplace filled the room with a comfortable warmth. But contrary to the soothing aroma of burning wood, US Senator Brown felt the atmosphere inside the room extremely hostile. His gut feelings told him that something had gone wrong. The more he listened to his instincts the more convinced he was. By now he was already certain that something did not go according to their plan. The fact that his British partner Gordon Ramshaw had mysteriously died while in the custody of the Scotland Yard was certainly helpful. However he still didn't know if, or how much, Gordon had told them. Jonathan had personally spoken to CIA Special Agent Abigail Sinclair, but the ambitious woman was convinced that Gordon had not told anything valuable to the British interrogators. According to her, Gordon was not only completely concentrated and mentally orientated, he also knew how to successfully put his interrogators on a wrong track. Despite Special Agent Sinclair's judgment, Jonathan was still not convinced. The British had something in their hands that made the local authorities nervous. By far the worst part was that he had not heard from Chuck in days. According to their plan, he should have been back now to cover his tracks. Whatever Jonathan Brown tried, he could not reach Chuck

Hogan. That was against their plan and it was a bad sign for Jonathan. He assumed the nerve gas accidentally rose to the surface and that Chuck and his men fell victim to their own trap. This would at least be the scenario that would be the most easiest to explain. After all, Chuck and his men were officially on board the research vessel. He could make the argument that they wanted to stay to shoot some extra footage for the next campaign. Besides that, it would save Jonathan a lot of money. Not that he cared about money, everything was paid from some black accounts funded by the government. It was simply that one money transaction less would also mean one less piece of evidence that someone could follow. Jonathan stared at the flames when his secretary Carl Miller interrupted his thoughts.

"I'm sorry to interrupt you, Sir. Pierre Dumont wants to talk to you."

Jonathan looked at his secretary and picked up the cordless phone from the table. He wondered why he had not heard it, but Carl Miller smiled.

"No, Sir. He's not on the phone. He's waiting outside in the entrance hall."

"What? He's here? Send him in."

Jonathan knew now that something was definitely wrong. It was the only reason why Pierre would bother him personally instead of calling him over the phone.

"What happened?" Jonathan asked the moment Pierre came into his study.

Pierre looked around quickly reassuring himself that no one else was in the room.

"There was a shooting several hours ago on board the *Northern Explorer*. MARCOM sent a reconnaissance plane up there, and they got shot at several times. At the moment there's an assault team of our Joint Task Force 2 on air transit to the research vessel. Their ETA is within a few hours. I couldn't risk telling you that over the phone."

"Goddammit!" Jonathan yelled and walked to the window.

Shooting at a military plane. That was indeed the fastest way to get some special forces on board. But why did they do that? Chuck was a professional. He and his men would never lose control and shoot at a military plane. They knew the consequences. That also meant that the nerve gas was not released yet. It would most likely rise to the surface while the Canadian assault team was on board the vessel. That would automatically put an end to the official version of their story that the German scientists carelessly released a gas pocket during their experiments.

"Okay! We have two major problems. First we have to come up with a new story. And second, we must know why our people shot at that plane."

"Jonathan, I'm not so sure if our men shot at them. Think about it. You know as well as I do that Chuck and his men are professionals. Yes, they are trigger happy once in a while, but still professionals. They would never do something like this, especially since they know that they would lose control over the boat to special forces within the next few hours. I contacted our Defence Minister and his office told me that the plane just had radio contact with the Captain immediately before the shooting. The Captain assured them that everything was okay, like he had done so many times before. I'm afraid that Chuck, for whatever reason, is still on board the ship and that he has no longer complete control over the situation. Remember, those British bodyguards are professionals, too. This can be dangerous for the two of us."

"This can be very dangerous for us, Pierre. Okay, worst case scenario that can happen to us is that the Canadian assault team take control over the ship and find Chuck and his men murdered. That would mean that the British bodyguards would've taken control over Chuck and in that case they would also have the Captain with his officers and a crew supporting their story. If that happens, we can shoot ourselves right away."

"That means we have to make sure that even if our men get executed, the British bodyguards will still look like the bad guys. And we have to make sure that our special forces still believe that, regardless of what everybody else on board the ship tells them and regardless of the evidence they find. Otherwise this complete project is purely academic."

Jonathan walked over to the fireplace and stared at the flames. Pierre was right.

"But how? How can we manage that?" he whispered.

"I think I got an idea, but I need your jet," Pierre replied and called for Carl, the secretary.

Inside the *Northern Explorer*, Amundsen Gulf, Darnley Bay, Thursday, October 13th

Ariel and Nick looked at each other. They both knew that with the bullets Martin used the hostages would not have a chance of survival. The tissue damage would be so severe that they would eventually bleed out under excruciating pain.

"Do they know how many we are?" Olaf asked.

"No, otherwise he would've mentioned the number. It doesn't matter anyway. Shira, you and Nick will go after Natascha. She left you a trail. Someone will be with her, so you got to be careful. Olaf, Ole-Einar, you two are with me. If one team succeeds, they must get the freed hostages off the ship first. Only then can they go and support the other team. Shira and I'll be the only ones using the radio, okay?"

Everybody nodded and both groups went on to pursue their missions. While Shira and Nick slowly moved downstairs inspecting the floor for Natascha's clues, Ariel and the two Norwegian's didn't lose any time getting to the bridge. For them, time was an issue and they knew they had some distance to cover. Without problems they reached the upper deck the bridge was located. Ole-Einar carefully sneaked up the last flight of stairs, kneeled down, rose his left hand and formed a fist. Just a few steps behind him were Ariel and Olaf, who secured their team to the back. The Israeli and the Norwegian both stopped as well and waited for Ole-Einar, who carefully watched the corridor leading to the bridge. He could easily see down the corridor and was even able to peak inside the bridge. While the bridge itself was almost in complete darkness, with the only light source coming from several LED gauges and monitors, the corridor was brightly lit. This meant it would be very difficult to get to the bridge undetected. Despite their time running out, the Norwegian kept watching and he noticed that both the doors to the radio room as well as to the washrooms were open. Both rooms could be another hiding place for one of the terrorists to fall into their backs. If time was not an issue he would spend some more minutes learning more details, but he knew Astrid did not have that time. The fact that the terrorists set them an ultimatum was a clear giveaway that they knew they were no longer in command. There could only be a total of three terrorists with the hostages, but it was more likely that there were only one or two. Ole-Einar signaled his teammates that he could not see what was going on in the bridge. His disadvantage was that he could only see a very small area. He had no way of finding out where exactly the hostages or the terrorists were. On the plus side, they knew that the terrorists had to be in a certain part of the bridge in order to see if Ole-Einar and his team would follow their orders and surrender. Ole-Einar strained his neck to see if there was a terrorist hiding somewhere in the radio room or in the washroom, when he heard their voices. It was obviously Jenna, who complained that Chuck was still gone. The second male voice answered her aggressively. This was all that Ole-Einar needed to know. Unless this was a trap, which he highly doubted, there would only be two terrorists on the bridge. Since he could not see them, it also meant that they could not see him. Ole-Einar pointed with his left index finger to his ear before he also stretched his middle finger out to signal his team mates that he heard two people.

Ariel tapped him on the shoulder twice to let him know he understood, before he whispered into the radio in hebrew. The Israeli knew the terrorists could hear the radio message he had just sent to Shira, but Ariel found it very unlikely they understood hebrew, especially the dialect he just used. Nevertheless he was careful enough not to give up their position. Once he got Shira's confirmation he tapped Ole-Einar once more on the shoulder. Ole-Einar nodded and swung his index finger in several circles. It was the signal to start their attack.

Deeper and deeper Shira and Nick followed the stairs down into the ships hull. Since they had searched the entire ship in Iceland and Halifax they had not penetrated the *Northern Explorer's* hull that deep. They both stopped for a second when they heard Ariel over the radio.

"Most likely only two terrorists on the bridge. One is most certainly with Natascha," Shira whispered and Nick nodded in affirmation. Shira confirmed their own position in her native hebrew dialect. Twice more they found Natascha's blood trail. Both times it was just after a corridor that led into a different part of the ship. Her trail led them definitely deeper into the hull. At the end of the last flight of stairs Nick quickly looked around the corner and down a short corridor. Like all other corridors this one was also brightly lit and empty. Nick quickly gazed upstairs before he sneaked into the corridor. Just after a few meters he found another blood drop, but he noticed the amount of blood was getting less and less.

Doesn't seem to be that bad, Nick thought and pointed the track out for Shira.

The Israeli nodded and followed Nick to the door, through which they could hear the muffled sounds of the engines. Nick switched the lights in the corridor off and nodded to Shira before he opened the door. Immediately they secured to both sides, but they did not get attacked. Shira was first to leave the protection of the steel door frame and ran under Nick's watchful eyes in to cover inside the engine room. Nothing happened.

Nick followed her and took cover on the other side. They both kneeled down, secured each other and checked the area in front of them without seeing anything suspicious. Shira pointed forward and they moved simultaneoulsy. After about ten meters they reached the next corner and Nick carefully peered around the steel wall. His heart raced instantly at the sight. It had been so long since he had seen her, and so much had happened since their last embrace. Just five meters in front of him was Natascha, locked up in a small control room. He easily resisted the urge to drop everything and run to her. The German was well aware this was a trap and he did not plan walking right into it. What he didn't know was that he was already right in the middle of it. The next moment a sharp pain pierced him, burning his side where Shira had just kicked him with all her strength.

- 26 -

Ottawa, Canadian Forces Maritime Command (MARCOM),
Thursday, October 13th
Admiral Kerman ordered something to eat for his guests. Brian was under the impression that the Admiral was embarrassed about not being informed about the situation and he was trying to make up for it now. They served Italian food and Brian noticed with a smile that it was the closest food to being politically neutral and both delicious and nutritious. Satisfied Brian used a napkin to wipe his lips clean and looked at his watch. The JTF2 assault team would need at least another three and a half hours before they would reach their general target area. From there they would rely on their fast RIB's for their last leg of the journey.

Goddammit. Why didn't this happen in England? We would have everything under control by now! He thought viciously several times, but he didn't speak his thoughts out loud. Admiral Kerman could have not acted any faster than he did, so Brian had to give him credit for that. All they could do now was sit and wait.

His thoughts were on the research vessel. The only explanation he had for the shooting, was that some of his men were able to operate and in possession of at least one weapon. Without knowing it, he shared Jonathan Brown's position in regards to Chuck's professionalism. There was no other explanation to make him believe his boys were not responsible for that firework. His thoughts were interrupted when a young adjutant knocked at the door and entered the room.

"Sir, you might want to have a look at this," the Captain said and showed a USB stick. With a few steps he was at a computer, where he inserted the stick in the respective port and activated a video file.

"We just received this information several minutes ago from the Central Intelligence Agency. It's some unedited video footage showing the visit from Senator Brown and MP Dumont on board the *Northern Explorer*. There seems to be a new development in the facts regarding the activities and their background on the ship."

Everybody noticed how the Captain distrustfully looked at Brian when he said that.

Together with Admiral Kerman and everybody else Brian stepped closer to the monitor. The video was standard quality, though there was no audio. It showed an obvious discussion between a man and a young woman. Another man stood close by and followed the discussion.

"The young woman is Natascha Kleinfeld. She's the daughter of the German expedition leader and the person our company was hired to protect. I don't know who the two men are," Brian explained.

"The person on the left is US Senator Jonathan Brown, Mr. Whittaker. I don't know the person in the middle," the Defence Minister added.

"Too bad there's no audio," Admiral Kerman noted. The discussion was getting heated and it was just seconds later that Natascha suddenly, and unexpectedly, rammed her knee into the Senator's groin. The video didn't show how they overpowered Natascha, it ended showing Senator Brown kneeling in agonizing pain.

"This behavior is unacceptable. She attacked the Senator for no good reason!" the Defence Minister yelled.

Both the Norwegian and the German Ambassador exchanged some worried looks. Brian turned his attention to the Admiral as he adressed him.

"What's your opinion on that? Do you have a reasonable explanation?"

"Well, it's too bad we can't hear what they were discussing," Brian started.

"You're not seriously trying to protect that lunatic, are you?" the Defence Minister yelled over the ringing of the phone.

Admiral Kerman's eyes rested on Brian as he walked over to the phone.

"I'm not trying to protect anyone. I just assume something must've happened prior the attack that led Ms. Kleinfeld to react the way she did. It would be very interesting to know why there's no audio on an official documentation footage for the media. What did the Senator say?" Brian asked everyone in the office.

"Why don't we ask him? He's on the phone. Conference call with our MP Pierre Dumont."

Now it was Brian's turn to be surprised. He watched as Admiral Kerman activated the speaker.

"Good Evening, Gentlemen. I am US Senator Jonathan Brown. I believe that there's a situation up north where you could need our input."

You God damned cur! Brian thought and fist angrily formed in his pocket.

Inside the engine rooms of the *Northern Explorer*, Amundsen Gulf, Darnley Bay, Thursday, October 13th

Shira put all her strength behind it when she kicked Nick and it was not a second too soon. Just about where Nick's head was a second ago, a fire axe hit the metal wall with a lot of force. With a loud *cloung* the weapon deflected from the wall. The energy behind this blow was so hard that Chuck almost lost his handling. Chuck still took advantage of his surprise attack and used the forward momentum to kick Shira's head. The Israeli was caught by surprise and had no chance to block or dodge the attack. Screaming out her pain, the young woman sagged to the floor unconscious while Chuck turned towards Nick again. Shira's kick had catapulted Nick against the wall, from where he fell to the floor. He immediately turned around and dodged Chuck's second strike by rolling on his side. His main priority was to get as much distance between him and the attacker.

The German's eyes darted from where he rolled and he could see his gun resting on the floor. Nick was unarmed and knew it was going to be a tough battle. Chuck could see the tension on his face as he looked to the gun. He wildly laughed as he closed in on him. He was holding the axe with both arms and he fainted several attacks. Nick noticed Chuck carried at least one gun in a holster, but it seemed that the American wanted to fight man against man.

Although Nick was not too enthusiastic to fight someone like Chuck as he carried a sharp axe, it still beat getting shot by him just six meters away. Given the circumstances, Nick was actually quite happy Chuck followed his emotions rather than his training. Looking around Nick searched for a weapon as Chuck continued towards him. Even though he was struggling to find anything, his eyes kept darting back to his gun. He could see he was getting further and further away from his gun, and the unconscious Shira.

"You're tough," Chuck laughed.

"Didn't expect to see you again. Your girlfriend was a bit worried for some time, but don't worry, I took care of her," he provoked Nick, hoping the German would get careless in his anger.

His training taught him well, he did not let him get under his skin. He was never tempted in such a trap before, but he knew he had to resist it. Although Chuck's words dug deep and he could feel the burning anger rise, he refused to let his emotions control his actions.

"Not sure if you even had to come back for her. She didn't seem to care about you that much," Chuck continued laughing and delivered a lightning fast strike with the axe.

Nick took another step back and still didn't fall for the provocations. He scanned the room again, he only had three more meters left before his back was against the wall. It was time for him to do something. Nick gazed past Chuck where Shira lay on the ground, still unconscious.

Chuck used this short span of Nick's inattention and delivered another blow with the axe, but Nick was ready for him. With a quick movement, Nick grabbed the axe and turned sideways, accelerating Chuck's forward momentum. Chuck staggered past Nick and rolled over his shoulder to control the energy. To Nick's surprise Chuck still had the axe in both hands when he got up. Immediately, the American initiated a staccato of blows and strokes. So far, Nick could avoid all of them, but he knew it would only be a matter of time before Chuck would hit him.

The American fainted another blow to Nick's upper body and kicked him in his abdomen. Nick yelled out in pain and sagged to his knee. He tried to roll out of the immediate danger zone, but it was too late. Chuck's next blow grazed him at the forehead. Nick could feel the handle scrape against his skin, gashing across his hairline swiftly. His head swooped with nausea, heat burning through him as the blood streamed down his face. The thick red substance dashed from his eyebrow to his cheek as the floor rushed towards him. Nick swooned to unconsciousness.

Ole-Einar swiftly moved down the corridor, closely followed by Ariel and Olaf. Halfway down to the bridge the Norwegian spotted some movement ahead of him.

"Cover," he yelled and dove together with Ariel into the radio room. Even before they rolled over the floor, they heard shots being fired and Olaf's painful yell behind them. Ole-Einar and Ariel both verified their condition, certain they were uninjured. The Israeli took cover behind the door frame and aimed at the open door to the bridge, but he couldn't see anything.

"Olaf, how bad are you hurt?" he calmly asked.

"Just got nicked at the shoulder. Nothing serious," the Norwegian replied from inside the washrooms.

"Nice try, you idiots! Listen up!" Martin Cunningham yelled at them from inside the bridge.

Ariel tried to see some more details, but the difference in the light was simply too great. He scanned the room for the switch but noticed it was located beside the door to the bridge and out of reach.

Before Martin said anything else, they could all hear Astrid's shriek of pain.

"You got ten seconds to come to the bridge. I know there are three of you. Hand above your heads, no weapons. Ten seconds...nine...eight..."

Ole-Einar shook his head and fired several times into the radio control desk and the computer station, immediately creating several short circuits. Sparks appeared everywhere and within the same second, the power was automatically cut from the corridor, the bridge and the radio room. They knew they had a maximum of five seconds before the emergency generators would kick in to restore the system. The three of them acted quickly, rushing to the bridge silently, fanning out. Being the last one to enter the bridge Olaf immediately turned all the light switches on. Although nothing happened right away, they knew the lights on the bridge would come on as soon as the emergency generators kicked in.

With a humming noise, the lights flickered back to life and blanketed the entire bridge with light. Both Ole-Einar and Olaf aimed at Jenna who quickly ducked behind the Second Officer and the control desk. Ariel had his gun locked on Martin, who used Astrid as a human shield. He nodded to them in appreciation.

"Not bad," Martin commented and looked in Ariel's eyes.

"You can still surrender. You know you don't stand a chance any more. Three of us against the two of you. You're the only survivors of your group. Surrender now and you will live," the Israeli demanded calmly and looked at Martin over his weapon.

"Surrender?" Martin yelled agitated and tightened his hold around Astrid's neck. "We have complete control! We know...," that was as far as Martin got. Realizing that Martin's actions were guided by his feelings, Ariel pulled the trigger twice. Astrid shrieked and felt the blood spatter in her face, warmly trickling down her cheek, but strangely she didn't feel any pain.

I'm dead, I'm dead, I'm dead, was all she thought, but the only thing she felt was Martin's grip slowly loosen as he sagged to the floor.

Jenna was more lucky. Since she was much smaller, the Second Officer provided much more cover than Astrid did for Martin. Ole-Einar only nicked her forehead, but it was enough for Mika Kankkunen to push her aside and duck for cover behind the control desk. Jenna screamed with pain and brought her weapon up, but her eyes were already covered with her own blood. Before she could wipe her eyes clear to fire, six more shots instantly echoed through the room. Fatally hit by all six bullets Jenna tumbled to the floor.

The whole shooting didn't take longer than three seconds and Astrid was still paralyzed with fear.

His weapon still raised Ariel walked past Astrid to check on Martin. There was no doubt that the American was dead. The Israeli looked up and his gaze met Ole-Einar, who just checked on Jenna. Four of the six bullets had hit the terrorist in her chest, one more in the head and the last one in her belly. Ole-Einar looked at Ariel and slowly shook his head.

"Okay, everything is under control. Is anyone hurt?" Ole-Einar finally explained and asked the crew, while Ariel wrapped his arms around Astrid.

The young Norwegian woman was obviously shocked and just stared at him.

"It's over, Astrid. Everything's fine. Nobody's going to hurt you any more," Ariel reassured her soothingly.

"You shot at me," the Norwegian stammered stunned.

Ariel looked up and his eyes wandered through the bridge. Captain Rasmussen, his Second Officer and the two Navigation Officers were obviously all right. While Ole-Einar took care of the Captain and his men, Olaf secured the door to the bridge. As far as they knew, Chuck was still alive and there was still the possibility that he could fall into their backs.

"You shot at me. I saw how you pointed that gun in my direction," Astrid muttered in her bewilderment.

"Astrid, I didn't shoot at you. I shot at him."

"You could've hit me. He was hiding behind me."

"I couldn't hit you. Not really," Ariel reassured again, a smile finally breaking across his lips. The Norwegian finally tried to wipe some blood out of her face.

"Let me take you to the washroom. You can clean up there. Olaf!"

The Norwegian nodded and entered the corridor to make sure that Chuck was not hiding somewhere.

Ariel escorted Astrid to the washrooms and helped her wash the blood out of her face and remove her blood covered sweater.

"Here, this is better," he said and offered her his own.

Still shaking Astrid put his sweater on, before she wrapped her arms around him and broke out in tears. Ariel just held her tight and stroke her hair, whispering to her that everything is going to be fine.

Ottawa, Canadian Forces Maritime Command (MARCOM), Thursday, October 13th

US Senator Jonathan Brown introduced himself once more and confirmed that he, together with his Canadian friend and MP Pierre Dumont, had indeed been on board the research vessel during the time in question.

"I must admit that our visit was partly altruistic. The Central Intelligence Agency had officially asked us if it would be possible for us to bring some of their agents under the cover of our official visit on board the *Northern Explorer*. We were accompanied to the ship by a group of four agents, who pretended to shoot a documentation about our travels. Once on board..."

"Just wait a second, Senator," Admiral Kerman interrupted. "Could you please explain to me under which authority you authorized a CIA mission on board a vessel within Canadian waters?"

"Admiral Kerman, I completely understand your apprehension, but you also know that the United States of America still firmly believes that the body of water in question is an official transit route in international waters. Canada has no jurisdictional powers over the United States within these waters. The vessel itself is Norwegian and on board that vessel was at the time of our presence a team of American scientists. My colleague can confirm that he was completely briefed into the situation and that he authorized all our actions."

"This is correct," Pierre Dumont added.

"Therefore I saw no reason to reject the CIA's request. On board the ship we were greeted by Captain Rasmussen as well as the German expedition leader. It was very obvious to us that the Captain was very reserved towards us, a fact that made me wonder why. During the course of the day we asked about some information in regards of this expedition and both the expedition leader as well as his daughter became very abusive and aggressive. I tried several times to explain to them that both the United States as well as Canada are not only large industrial nations but also leading when it comes to the protection of the environment. I also tried to explain to them that our own studies are based on facts and that they unfortunately produced a different result. They then insulted us in the most unpleasant way and it became quite apparent that the other members of their team were also very aggressive and radical. It was not possible to have a civilized conversation especially with the daughter of the expedition leader. She eventually attacked me unprovoked. I assume you've seen the video footage. The facts are speaking for themselves. It was only because of the fast actions of the bystanders, amongst them one CIA Agent, that her attacks could be stopped."

"You still didn't explain why the CIA wanted to be on board the ship," Admiral Kerman noted.

"The CIA gathered some intelligence that maybe the expedition leader Dr. Weber, but most likely his daughter Natascha Kleinfeld are so called eco-terrorists, who are planning some actions in this area that would significantly harm the local population."

"Excuse me? What did you just say?" Brian Whittaker interrupted Senator Brown.

"You heard correctly. There's obviously some evidence that the German expedition team is accompanied by some former members of military special forces, who are responsible for the successful completion of their action."

It took Brian all his willpower to control himself.

"Senator Brown. The former military staff that you are referring to are legal employees of my company *EuroSec Corporation*. After the expedition leader received several threats by mail, his institute hired us to provide the personal security detail. Our work was closely coordinated with the local authorities as well as the BKA and they all shared our evaluation of the situation. We could prevent an assassination attempt which had most likely been committed by former members of special forces with American nationality. In Iceland we were able to prevent a second assassination attempt. This time we also found out that the assassins were even too spineless to attack the expedition leader himself and that they went for his daughter instead. We made all those facts available to Scotland Yard as well as the German and Norwegian authorities, since our team members are of those nationalities."

"That's very interesting," Pierre Dumont commented.

"Mr. Whittaker, would you please be so kind and explain to me your official function in this situation?" the Canadian continued.

"Excuse me?" Brian asked the MP.

"Your position. What's the reason that you're here?"

Brian gave a quick summary of the reasons and did not hold back his frustration about the lack of Canadian support they received earlier, but he also praised Admiral Kerman's quick actions.

"Just to be sure: You assume your so-called unit actually attacked our military plane?" Pierre Dumont asked in disbelief.

Brian realized the direction this was going and it took him great effort not to yell at the Canadian politician.

"I never said that my men *attacked* your military plane. Foremost they wanted to alert the crew of the plane to the fact that something on board the *Northern Explorer* was, contrary to all declarations from Captain Rasmussen, wrong. They knew that the Canadian Forces would send some troops for on-board reconnaissance. It's safe to assume, that...."

"Mr. Whittaker," the Canadian interrupted. "Are you really trying to tell me that this attack on our plane was merely a way to contact them?"

"Yes, that is one way to..."

"May I ask why your men didn't use the radio, a satellite telephone or other official communication channels like in a civilized world?"

"I've already tried to explain to you that the bridge of the *Northern Explorer* was under a different command."

"Yes! The bridge is under the command of Captain Rasmussen, as all the radio messages have confirmed. Why didn't your people use flares? I'm sure they would have found some inside the life rafts."

"I assume they were in no position to access some flares in time."

"But they were certainly in a position to shoot, without any provocation, at an unarmed *Arcturus* from the Royal Canadian Air Force."

"I'm still convinced that my men just wanted to draw their attention..."

"Mr. Whittaker!" Pierre Dumont interrupted him now angrily and with a clearly raised voice.

"Did your men have any certainty that they could not put the plane and it's crew in danger when they shot not only once but several times at them? No, they didn't. Could they even recognize in complete darkness in which parts of the plane the bullets would hit? No, they most certainly could not. At the best case, your men carelessly jeopardized the life of eleven crew members. The plane was over arctic waters at the time of the attack, with water temperatures around the freezing point. Within hours there was no airport big enough to land in case of an emergency. A loss of oil, or a direct hit at their hydraulics or the electronics would've meant certain death for eleven Canadian military personnel. That doesn't look like a safe way to contact us at all."

"What does it look like to you?" Admiral Kerman wanted to know.

"It definitely looks to me like a terrorist attack on a Canadian military plane. I totally agree with Senator Brown and the CIA. I believe that there's a group of German terrorists up there preparing an attack against either Canada, the United States or maybe even both nations. Once our plane flew over them, they lost their nerve and deliberately attacked us."

Brian Whittaker shook his head and looked at Admiral Kerman.

"Admiral, you have seen the facts. Why should I be here, trying to get my boys out of there, if they're indeed planning a terrorist attack against your country?"

"Maybe so that you look innocent. I must agree that I tend to believe your arguments and the facts you presented, but until a few minutes ago I also didn't have any knowledge about the activities from the CIA."

"Admiral, you've seen the satellite images. One of the two dead people was an officer and obviously a member of the crew. I..."

"They already killed two people? Oh my God!" Senator Brown interrupted Brian.

"Mr. Senator, I really don't believe that my men killed those two people. I'm convinced that..."

"Mr. Whittaker! Your people also violently attacked a Canadian military plane. What other proof do you want?"

Brian could feel the noose around his neck slowly tightened.

"What other intelligence can the CIA provide in this matter?" Admiral Kerman demanded to know.

"I'll put you directly through to Special Agent Sinclair on the other line. She gathered some very valuable intelligence for us in London."

"Special Agent *Sinclair*?" Brian asked, caught with surprise. He remembered that Klaus held her responsible for Gordon Ramshaw's death.

"Admiral Kerman," MP Pierre Dumont addressed the Admiral without paying attention to Brian's comment.

"I'd like to fill you in on the latest intelligence that the CIA gathered in this development. After that I would like to discuss the several options that we have to proceed in this matter. I assume right that a JTF2 team is already on its way?" the Canadian politician continued.

"T minus three hours," Admiral Kerman confirmed.

"Perfect. Before we continue I want to suggest to exclude Mr. Brian Whittaker from this conversation. He's in no function that requires his presence, and I think it's safe to assume at this point and time that he has simply lost control over his men. The information I'm about to present are top secret, and I believe that you all agree, that it's in the best interest for the safety of both Canada and the United States that Mr. Whittaker is not going to be present any longer."

You're even to much of a coward to tell me that personally! Brian thought angrily. Without a word he rose from his chair and left the office. Once outside the room his rage burst into flames, he almost ran down the corridor, left the building and called a cab.

"Airport," he snarled at the driver while he called London from his Blackberry.

Inside the engine room of the *Northern Explorer*, Amundsen Gulf, Darnley Bay, Thursday, October 13th

Slowly Shira regained her consciousness. Carefully she looked around to orientate herself. She remembered the attack and despite the loud noise from the engines she could hear two people fighting close by, but she couldn't see anything. Nick and Chuck were obviously around the corner at the end of the corridor. The Israeli got on her knees, holding her head as it angrily pulsed with pain. She groaned under the spinning room that her eyes portrayed in front of her. Shira turned her attention to Natascha and could see her hammering with both fists on the lexan window of the tiny control room. She was just a few meters away and she decided to release Natascha first. If Shira and Nick should not make it out alive of this engine room for any reason, Natascha would still have a chance to get out and find Ariel and the others. Slowly and painfully Shira got on her feet and fought against the rising nausea, but after a few deep breaths she gained some measure of control over herself again. She carefully walked to the control room and unlocked the door. Natascha briefly wrapped her arms around and thanked her, but Shira immediately pushed her away and tried to localize the fight. She turned her senses to locate Nick and Chuck but she could neither see nor hear anything any more. It seemed as if the fight was over and Shira was concerned about the silence, despite the constant noise from the engines. Why did Nick not try to contact her if he defeated Chuck? Shira reached for her gun, but she noticed with horror that she must have lost it when she fell to the floor.

The Israeli whispered to Natascha to stay behind and follow her closely. Slowly they walked down the corridor. Just after two meters Chuck jumped out from behind a corner, holding Nick's Russian gun in his hand. The American was almost five meters away and Shira saw not only her own but also another gun tucked underneath his belt. With the distance between them, and Chuck already aiming at them, Shira knew she did not stand a chance and swallowed hard as Natascha stood beside her.

"Look at this. Who do we got here?" Chuck laughed, still aiming with Nick's gun at Shira, before he talked to Natascha.

"That's your friend's gun. I think you should know that. Remember the conversation we had inside that submersible? Back then I told you that I was the one who took the shot at you in Berlin. Remember that?" Chuck yelled.

Natascha nodded in fear and swallowed. She had no chance to escape this lunatic down here and, facing her certain death, panic rose deep inside her.

"I was also in Iceland. You managed to get away twice. That's a new record. You can be proud of yourself. Your only problem is that I usually finish for what I was paid for. I'm sorry, Natascha, but it's not personal," Chuck explained in a calm voice now, swinging the gun from Shira to Natascha and pulled the trigger.

"No!" Shira screamed before she threw herself on Natascha, throwing her to the ground. Before Natascha even hit the floor, the young German already noticed the blood on her hands and her abdomen.

- 27 -

Inside the bridge of the *Northern Explorer*, Amundsen Gulf, Darnley Bay, Thursday, October 13th

After approximately ten minutes Ariel walked back on the bridge, his arm tightly wrapped around Astrid. Usually he would have not spent that much time with her, but Astrid told him of the mental torture she endured during the last couple days each time Chuck threatened to cripple her. Ultimately, Ariel's first priority now was to get the Captain and his remaining officers safely off the ship as fast as possible.

"Olaf, you cover our six. Ole-Einar, you and I lead. Did you tell them?" the Israeli told his teammates immediately after he was back.

"Yes, I explained everything. We're ready."

Ariel walked over to the radio. Unfortunately the bullets went through Jenna's body and had completely destroyed the radio. Since Ole-Einar already destroyed the radio room itself earlier to cut the power, they were now cut off from everybody else.

Ole-Einar took Ariel to the side.

"Listen, Ariel. Why can't we just wait for the Canadian assault team? We have everything under control now."

Ariel shook his head.

"If the politicians are really involved or even behind all this, then I don't trust anybody. There's a realistic chance that someone somewhere thinks we're the bad guys. Especially after a Canadian military plane got shot at. We can still tell our side of the story from a different continent. Don't forget that the normal crew of this ship had been locked away by people wearing German coveralls and face masks. After all those days I highly doubt they would listen to or even like us."

"Yes, I could hear them when we looked for Natascha. At least they're still alive. Okay, let's go. You're the boss."

Ariel walked over to the radio room, picked up his laptop and put it in his little backpack, which was still underneath the table. With his laptop secured, he walked back onto the bridge and nodded towards the Captain.

"It's time to go, Captain Rasmussen."

"I'm not going to come. I'm staying with my ship and my crew. It's my responsibility," Captain Rasmussen stated in a way that left no room for doubt.

"I'm going to stay with my Captain. It's my duty as well," Second Officer Mika Kankkunen explained and even the two Navigation Officers insisted on staying.

Ariel respected their position and walked to the Captain.

Captain Rasmussen straightened himself and shook Ariel's hand.

"You and your men have saved ours and many others lives today. I want to thank you for that. We'll make sure the truth is told once the Canadian soldiers arrive."

The Israeli nodded.

"What are you going to do in the meantime?"

"Well, our long range radios are all destroyed. There's a slight chance that the terrorists have sabotaged our ship. We'll try to free our crew and examine the ship. We'll also repair the radio room, but it'll be some time. What about the warheads?"

"Don't mention them at all. The warheads are safe. You have to promise me that you'll not mention the Russian *Akula* nor the wreck of the Russian U-Boat under any circumstances. We can't even imagine the consequences and we already have enough problems the way things are at the moment. I want you to destroy all acoustic evidence from that *Akula*."

"We don't have any. As far as I know, the only audio recording is on Dr. Weber's and Natascha's computer. None of my men will ever mention either one of the submarines. We'll pull the anchor, retrieve the buoy and move the *Northern Explorer* away from this site before we set her adrift. I can guarantee you that no one will find this wreck."

"Very well then. I suggest you lock the door to the bridge from the inside until we confirm that the ship is safe. We'll leave this radio here with you. Only leave the bridge when we tell you, not a second before. Do you understand that?"

Captain Rasmussen nodded.

For a last time Ariel shook Captain Rasmussen's hand before he turned around to walk to Astrid. Carefully the Israeli put his arm around Astrid's shoulder and together with Olaf and Ole-Einar they left the bridge.

Behind them Second Officer Mika Kankkunen closed the door to the bridge. While Ariel and his friends didn't waste any time walking down the stairs, the Israeli tried several times to contact Nick and Shira, but he did not get an answer. After Ariel retrieved Prof Dr. Weber's laptop from his cabin, they stood just seconds later at the door that led them onto the deck.

"Ole-Einar, Olaf. You two make sure that Astrid gets off the ship safely. I'll see if I can find Nick and Shira down in the engine room. That's the only place where they don't have any radio contact. Once Astrid is safe, you will follow. Understood?"

Ole-Einar nodded and led Astrid through the door. The young Norwegian hesitated and looked back over her shoulder, her eyes resting on Ariel. He assured her with a smile that she could go with the two Norwegian. Slowly Astrid let them take her away, but she still kept looking at the Israeli. Ariel kept smiling at her, but as soon as Astrid was out of sight, he spun around and ran down the stairs as fast as he could.

Ottawa, Canadian Forces Maritime Command (MARCOM),
Thursday, October 13th

"Gentlemen, I don't question Mr. Whittaker's loyalty towards his employees, but I'm not sure if he's aware of all the facts. Special Agent Abigail Sinclair will now brief you in detail," Pierre Dumont finished.

"Thank you very much. Good evening Mr. Defence Minister, Mr. Ambassadors, Admiral. Our agency started investigating the members of this expedition several months ago. Some worrying facts about the German expedition team stood out during the course of our investigation. Please allow me a moment to give you some more background information for the better understanding on how they are connected to each other. You already learned that there are currently six people on board the *Northern Explorer* whose official job is to protect the daughter of the expedition leader, Ms. Kleinfeld. Those six people are indeed employed by Mr. Whittaker's company *EuroSec Corp*. Officially that company is a legit company. Their employees are without exception former members of different special forces from several European countries. Their main reason for them to work for *EuroSec Corp* was the significantly higher salary. At this point it's already clear that we're basically dealing with mercenaries, who do everything for money. Let's concentrate at the situation at our hands. Earlier this year during the month of May, the daughter from the German expedition leader had already contacted four of those six people over a period of several days in Norway. The meeting took place at a secluded cottage resort, although two of the four people have family homes within one hour. It's also remarkable that almost everybody choose different means of transportation to and from that meeting. Later on, on June ninth to be precise, the same six mercenaries who are now on the vessel met again at the weekend residence of one Gordon Ramshaw, just outside London. That would not be much of a surprise, given the fact that Mr. Ramshaw was one of the financial initiators of *EuroSec Corp*. However, we found it very interesting that Mr. Ramshaw had arranged for a money transfer over one million Euro to a non-traceable Swiss number account just shortly after that. Just one week later, one of the original four mercenaries from the meeting in Norway, met again with the daughter from the expedition leader. This time they chose a tiny Italian island as their meeting point. Although they left the island together, they arrived on different days to cover their tracks. The intelligence we gathered lets us assume that they discussed final details at that point. In the meantime her father and expedition leader Dr. Weber received so many threatening letters that his research institute felt pressured to hire personal protection detail. Strangely enough, the German Professor got assigned to exactly those six mercenaries from *EuroSec Corp*, which is, after all, a British company. During the second day of their protection detail, an event in Berlin on June twenty-fifth, someone fired a shot, which was dramatically caught by one of the mercenaries when he launched himself into the flight path of the projectile. Coincidentally this person was the only bodyguard wearing a protective vest."

"One moment, please. Are you actually trying to tell me that they shot at their own people? Why?" Admiral Kerman interrupted her.

"That's a very good question. We'll get to the answer in a few seconds. Now being convinced that their expedition leader and his daughter were in mortal danger, the institute decided to expand the protection detail for the complete duration of the expedition. Naturally the same group got the assignment and had now unrestricted access to the ship. Not only did they gain the trust of the Captain and his officers, they were also in charge of all security questions and they had complete control over all monitors and video-cameras on board the vessel, a fact that proved to be very helpful to them. It's also interesting that during the complete expedition absolutely nothing happened. There's not a single indication that her life was still in danger. It was only after almost all scientists had left the ship that the trouble started. We lost radio contact and the Captain was most likely forced to give false radio statements. When the ship deviated from it's filed navigation plan, it was most likely because they were in the final stages of preparation for their terrorist attack. Remember that at this point the only people beside the core crew on board the *Northern Explorer* were the expedition leader himself, his daughter as well as the six mercenaries, who were suppose to protect them. Once they saw the military plane, they panicked and attacked. I found Mr. Whittaker's explanation about the shooting very amusing, but unfortunately it's not very realistic. What Mr. Whittaker didn't tell us was not only the money transfer by Gordon Ramshaw, but also the facts how and why Mr. Gordon Ramshaw died so mysteriously while being in custody at Scotland Yard."

"But had it not been Mr. Whittaker who handed Gordon Ramshaw over to the authorities?"

"That's completely correct, Admiral. We suspect that Mr. Ramshaw had already been poisoned by that time. There are dozens of none traceable toxins out there that activate themselves hours after they were given, in which way ever. By handing Mr. Ramshaw over to Scotland Yard himself, Mr. Whittaker really took all the attention away from him. It is, however, very strange that Mr. Ramshaw died just hours later from a heart attack, despite the fact that a physician had attested him a clean bill of health upon the time of his arrest."

Everybody inside the office was silent and tried to process what Special Agent Sinclair had just told them. Abigail was very pleased with herself. By not mentioning Natascha's or Richard's name, she didn't give them the chance to see them as human persons. Abigail always mentioned them in connection with the word *terrorist*. Although she was dealing with both high ranking military personnel as well as politicians, these basic field tricks worked all the time. She gave them all the time they needed to digest this information, and, as she expected, it was Admiral Kerman who took the word after a while.

"Special Agent Sinclair. I can follow your argumentation, but I also see some logic in the facts presented to us by Brian Whittaker. Personally I would rather like him..."

"Mr. Whittaker did lie to you, Admiral," Special Agent Sinclair interrupted the commanding officer of MARCOM. She knew it was impolite and against protocol, but she could not let him raise some doubt and she decided that now was the perfect time to drop the bombshell.

"We're still not one hundred percent certain how Mr. Whittaker fits into the greater picture. There's the possibility that he simply lost control over the situation and his men and that he's trying to save as much as he can. There's also the slight chance that he's completely innocent, even though he had not been one hundred percent honest with us. Someone else could have poisoned Gordon Ramshaw. We have knowledge that a high ranking member of *EuroSec Corp* was at Scotland Yard for most of the time Gordon Ramshaw was alive. There is indeed the option that Brian Whittaker had been used by his own men as a cover. But we're certain about one thing: Brian

Whittaker knows more than he told you. Fact is that he would look pretty innocent by flying to Canada in person to drag the ambassadors of two nations first to the Defence Minister and after that to you, Admiral. But honestly I'm actually wondering why he only invited two ambassadors. We know for a fact that two of the six mercenaries are from the middle east."

Abigail paused for a few seconds, so that her words could sink in.

"From the middle east?" the Defence Minister asked in disbelief.

"According to our facts, yes. They can easily be out of any of those Arabic countries. You all know what they are capable of."

The Defence Minister and Admiral Kerman looked at each other. They were both stunned.

"Did you know about that?" Admiral Kerman asked the two ambassadors.

"No, we didn't know that. Mr. Whittaker never mentioned anything like that to us."

Special Agent Sinclair listened to the conversation and was satisfied. Contrary to her previous tactic she now used Brian Whittaker's name repeatedly to discredit his statements, so that this group would associate Brian as someone who was dishonest and could not be trusted. Abigail Sinclair finally continued to close the bag.

"I think it's safe to say that, under consideration of all the facts, those six members of an international terrorist cell, the German expedition leader and his daughter are a much bigger threat as our trusted and honorable Senator Jonathan Brown and PM Dumont, who are definitely no longer on board the vessel. Our team of CIA agents is still on board the *Northern Explorer* since they arrived with the Senator and the PM. Their mission is to gather more intelligence about the activities and the plans of this terrorist cell. Unfortunately we have no longer contact to them or the remaining four American Scientists, who only wanted to stay past their schedule departure time to meet with the Senator. I'm very satisfied to hear that special forces are on their way to the vessel, but I want to ask for a favor."

"Proceed," Admiral Kerman allowed her.

"Together with some of our own specialists we want to be the first ones to enter the ship. Your special forces can support us. We have reason to believe that they are planning to use some nerve gas, and I want to avoid that your men are running into a trap they can't see. We're equipped with special gas detectors and we're technically in a position to disarm pretty much anything they can come up with."

Admiral Kerman gazed at the Defence Minister, who silently nodded his approval.

"When could your team meet with our JTF2 assault team, Special Agent Sinclair?"

"I'm calling from a jet. Our ETA to Paulatuk is three hours."

"Our assault team will contact you once you arrive. I'm going to transfer you to our team leader. This whole thing can only work if you inform our team leader about everything you do. Can you agree to this?"

"Absolutely. I appreciate your trust, Admiral," Special Agent Sinclair ended the conversation.

"I think I'll get back to the embassy. This whole situation seems to be very complicated. Please keep us informed," the Norwegian Ambassador noted and rose from his chair. His German colleague followed his trail and shook Admiral Kerman's and the Defence Minister's hand. Together they expressed their gratitude for the support and the two ambassadors left the office together with their adjutants.

Admiral Kerman leaned back in his armchair, closed his eyes for a second and shook his head.

Inside the engine room of the *Northern Explorer*, Amundsen Gulf, Darnley Bay, Thursday, October 13th

Slowly Nick regained his consciousness. He moved his arms to push himself up and struggled to maintain position. He forced himself to his feet, fighting the pain that swooned over him. He realized he had only been unconscious for about a minute or two. While he held on to the wall for support with one hand, he wiped the blood out of his face with the other. He waited a few moments in a weak attempt to compose himself to a functioning degree. Looking down the corridor, he could see Chuck pick up his Russian gun before he rounded the corner. Nick dipped his head towards the floor as a wave of nausea crashed over him. He closed his eyes, focusing on taking a few deep breaths before he hurried as fast as he could down the corridor. Just before he reached the corner, he heard someone scream in panic as a loud shot broke above the engines chatter. Nick spun around the corner and stopped short for a second. His expression dropped quickly, his blood freezing in his veins as his eyes relayed the images to him. He refused to comprehend the series of images that made up a story, but couldn't shake the truth from it as his hand reached his head. Shira tried to use her own body to protect Natascha, who lay motionless on the floor, her belly covered with a pool of blood. Chuck re-cocked the gun as he held his aim at her, and fired again. He pulled the trigger for the second time with frustration, but knew the magazine was empty. Nick had sent all but one bullet into the hull of the Canadian plane.

"What the hell...?" Chuck cursed and threw the Russian gun away. With a swift movement he took the Sig Sauer out of it's holster and took aim.

With a loud bloodcurdling scream bearing the pain and anger that overcame him, Nick came over him. His right foot hit Chuck with the force of a baseball bat just below his chest. Chuck yelled up in pain, his hand releasing his weapon as it rushed to the pain as he curled against the wall, where he could barely remain on his feet. Nick immediately went after him and his next kick hit the side of Chuck's knee. With torn ligaments and a broken kneecap Chuck sagged to the ground, screaming in pain. He threw Nick a hateful gaze and reached for his remaining weapon. Nick's face scrunched devilishly as he let the rage overcome him, powering his strikes with more force than he knew he had. He consciously waited until Chuck moved his arm before he kicked him with all his strength just under the arm pit. Chuck's scream burst louder than the others, his shoulder slumping as it broke upon impact. Chuck fell on his back and Nick could see him reach for one of the weapons on the floor. Nick thought out his next action and motioned to implement it when a sudden shot surprised him. The bullet hit Chuck's abdomen, his final scream fading quickly as his last breath escaped him. Nick spun around and saw Natascha with one of Chuck's guns in her hands. She fired a second shot and this time she hit Chuck in the middle of his chest. Again and again Natascha angrily pulled the trigger, her hand shaking under the guns weight, until the magazine was empty. Slowly the young German lowered the Sig Sauer. With a hateful look she stared at Chuck, who had been hit by all seventeen bullets in his upper body and head. Natascha finally noticed Nick. He was real though she couldn't believe it. His hand brushed hers as he took the gun from her and threw it away. She looked into his eyes, though all they bore was high concern as they searched her face.

"Come here," he whispered and took her in his arms.

Natascha couldn't hold back any longer, the realization suddenly hitting her at full force, pushing the tears from deep within.

Nick suddenly noticed the blood on Natascha again and looked down at her.

"Are you injured? Did he hit you?"

Still unable to speak, Natascha shook her head and looked at Shira, who laid motionless on the ground a few meters away.

Nick's fright was unwavering as he looked to his Israeli friend and rushed towards her, her name the only word escaping his lips as he fell to his knees beside her, "Shira!"

Originally Ole-Einar and Olaf planned for Astrid to jump in the water three quarters of the way down the outside of the hull, like Dr. Weber did, but Astrid was so overcome with emotion they feared she would not be able to swim for too long. They acted quickly and brought her to the dive control room where Ole-Einar helped her in one of the dry-suits. It was way too big for her, but it didn't matter since it took the Norwegian only a minute to install new silicone seals at the wrists and neck. Olaf took the chance and used a first-aid kit to treat his shoulder. His plan was to get proper care once he was on the *Akula*, but for the moment, a temporary treatment to prevent an infection and to clean the wound had to do. After all, they still had to find Nick and the others. Astrid's whole body shivered uncontrollably, and this time it was not solely because of the fear. She repeatedly asked for Ariel.

"Ariel will follow us soon. He just has to take care of something. You're safe now, okay?" Ole-Einar calmly assured her.

Astrid nodded, but Ole-Einar knew she did not hear a single word he said.

The Norwegian helped her into the zodiac, which was then hoisted over the rail by the winch. Olaf operated the winch with the utmost care and lowered the zodiac into the water. Just a few seconds later Ole-Einar steered the inflatable around the *Northern Explorer*, where they were now protected from the choppy sea, and out of the cold wind. Using a large hammer, Ole-Einar banged at the hull and waited patiently.

Within minutes the little Russian support submersible broke through the surface right in front of them. Vasili, obviously the only German speaking member of the Russian crew, opened the outer hatch.

"Hurry! We not have much time. How much longer?"

"At the moment it's just one person. We go back to get the rest. All the terrorists are dead but one. It won't take much longer."

"Better not!" Vasili shouted.

"This not good place for us. Can bring up many, many questions we can not answer. Where's Nick?"

"Nick will be with us the next time we come," Ole-Einar replied and helped Astrid onto the submersible.

"This is Nick's fiasco? You are grandparent?"

"No, she's not a fiasco and she's not a grandparent. What are you talking about? Her name is Astrid."

"Not grandparent, sorry. Pregnant! That's what Nick said. Where is Nicks wife? She may be pregnant."

"What?" Ole-Einar yelled.

"Pregnant! Maybe Baby," Vasili explained and proudly showed the same arm movement as Nick did, when he tried to explain the word to Vasili.

"I know what pregnant means, Goddammit...I just didn't now that Natascha was..."

Ole-Einar didn't finish and waved his hand.

"It really doesn't matter now. I have to get back. You wait here for us, okay? We'll just be a couple more minutes," the Norwegian shouted over the noise of the wind and breaking waves.

"No problem," Vasili said and assisted Astrid through the hatch.

"We just underneath the surface. You just bang on big hull, we'll come. Russians will save your butt," Vasili commented calmly, but Ole-Einar was already gone.

Ariel was just meters away from the door that led to the engine room when he heard the shots. Carefully he opened the door and secured both sides before he rushed in, not stopping before the next corner. The Israeli gazed down the next corridor and lowered his weapon. His eyes first spotted Chuck, his blood covered body definitely lifeless. His eyes then darted up to Nick, his arms wrapped around Natascha as she crumbled in his strong arms, her tears shaking her shoulders. When Ariel's gaze met the second lifeless body on the floor, his face slowly twitched into fearful recognition. He could feel the sorrow rip through him, his mouth tightening with fear as he spotted his sister. The Israeli ran down the corridor and kneeled beside Shira just a second after Nick did.

"She's still alive," Nick noticed after he turned Shira on her back.

Against the odds the young Israeli was indeed still alive. She barely opened her eyes and looked at Nick and Natascha in agony. Shira tried to smile at them, but the pain turned her smile into a grimace.

"Stay calm, Shira. Everything's fine. The bullet passed right through," Ariel explained to her in hebrew.

In the meantime Natascha remembered the well organized first-aid kit in the little control room and brought it. Nick smiled at her and took several bags of blood-clotting material out.

"Here, you need those," Natascha told him and handed Nick a pair of surgical gloves. While Nick put the gloves on, Natascha carefully tore the bags open and waited until he generously cut off all the clothes around Shira's entry and exit wound. Next he took a spray bottle with disinfectant and looked Shira in the eyes.

"I'm sorry, but I have to do this. It's going to be painful now, okay?"

She could only nod weakly, but she still cried with a loud groan when Nick generously cleaned the wound. Satisfied with his handywork, he used a sterile pad to wipe Shira's belly dry and applied the blood-clotting powder before he placed another sterile pad over the wound and secured it with tape.

"Okay, we have to do the same procedure with the exit wound, all right? We have to turn you on your side."

Shira quickly closed her eyes and tried to nod, but most of her energy went into a painful scream when Nick disinfected the wound. After he finished the first aid treatment, he smiled at Shira.

"Okay, we just have to get you to a doctor now and you'll be as good as new. You were lucky it was a through and through. It doesn't look like any vital organs were affected, and your blood had a normal color."

Shira tried to smile and wanted to thank Nick, but she couldn't. She was too weak and the pain was too much to bear.

Fear quickly darted across his eyes and he looked at Natascha.

"Are you sure you weren't hit?" he asked, suddenly realizing that Natascha must have been behind Shira.

Without waiting for Natascha's response, Nick rose to his feet and pulled Natascha's sweater and shirt up. Relieved that there was no wound visible, he pulled his fiancée into his warm embrace again. It was only now that all the stress seemed to fall away from them.

"Oh, Angel, I'm so glad this is over and you're okay. I love you," he whispered in her ears, his voice choking on his words.

Natascha couldn't hold back her tears any longer and didn't fight the steady flow.

"I really thought you were dead. He forced me to turn off your air. I had to watch them pull up the empty helmet. I thought you died," Natascha sobbed barely understandable. They stood in the warm embrace, peace overcoming them for the first time in days. She suddenly let go of Nick.

"Don't you ever scare me like that again!" she told him with mock reprimand and gently punched him on his chest, laughing weakly.

Nick looked at her and took both the broken necklace and engagement ring out of his overall pocket and held it right in front of her.

"Found it on the floor. You're not getting rid of me that easy."

Natascha slowly retrieved both items. It was the only thing that got her through it all. The hope that Nick was alive, that they would be together. She embraced Nick again. "You will never get rid of me," she whispered to him softly.

"Never," Nick answered, but his weak smile faded with recollection.

"Did they do anything to you?"

The two seconds it took Natascha to form an answer felt like an eternity for Nick.

"No, they didn't. Besides two slaps to my face and a few pulled hairs, I'm fine."

Nick swallowed. His greatest fear did not come true.

"Okay, we have to take care of Shira now," the German said and turned towards the Israeli again.

"She saved my life," Natascha whispered and looked at Shira, who was supported by Ariel's arms.

"Yes, mine too," Nick replied and kneeled down beside Ariel again.

"Listen, Ariel. I could temporarily stop the bleeding, but we have to get Shira to a hospital as soon as possible. We don't know if one of the organs was hit. The projectile must have hit her hip-bone and deflected from there. She's also lost a large amount of blood. We have to go now."

Ariel handed Nick his radio and told him to inform the others that the last terrorist was dead.

Ariel picked up Shira with ease and walked down the corridor with her.

"I can give you a hand," Nick offered, assuming Shira's weight would take it's toll once they had to tackle the stairs.

"That won't be necessary. Just make sure all doors are open."

Without wasting another look at Chuck's dead body they all left the engine room. On their way up, Nick explained in a few short sentences how he was still alive. The groups astonishment was evident as they looked at Nick again, verifying he was still indeed alive.

Just a few minutes later they were greeted by Ole-Einar and Olaf on the deck as they waited for them.

"Okay. Nick, you take Natascha off this ship and bring her to her father. Ole-Einar and Olaf, you two go with him."

Nick and his team exchanged quick glances with each other before they looked at Ariel again. They really didn't like what Ariel just told them.

"What about you and Shira?" Ole-Einar asked carefully.

"We're not boarding this *Akula*," Ariel answered, raising his voice above the strong winds.

"Why? Are you insane?" Olaf yelled at his boss from the zodiac.

"I have several reasons for that. Firstly, I'll have to lay a false trail. In case you haven't thought about it, we can't simply vanish into thin air. Secondly, it's much better if we travel separately. That creates twice the work for anybody who wants to follow us. In case something happens to one group, there's still a second group on it's way who knows the truth."

"What about Shira? She needs professional medical attention as soon as possible," Natascha begged.

"You're right, she needs professional medical attention. She can't get that on board this *Akula*. It's a nuclear attack submarine, not a hospital. Besides that, my sister is a thorn in the flesh of some Russian politicians, and I'll not allow her to fall in their hands. I'll take Shira with me and you'll board this submarine now."

"She's your sister?" Natascha asked with complete surprise.

"Why didn't you tell us that?"

"There was no reason for it. Nick, you have to make sure you take Natascha's computer with you. Under no circumstances can we leave any acoustic files about the presence of the *Akula* behind. Natascha, except for your father's and your own laptop, are there any more recordings stored elsewhere?"

"No, not that I know of."

"Perfect, then let's go."

Together they walked towards the dive control room, where Nick picked Natascha's laptop up. After they all dressed up in a dry-suit or a survival suit, they approached the zodiac. Olaf climbed into it first, before he helped Natascha. Nick followed and Ole-Einar was was behind him.

"And you're sure you want to stay behind with your sister?"

"We're not going to stay behind, Olaf. We're just going somewhere else. And yes, I'm sure about it."

"How are you going to get her in the zodiac and launch it at the same time?" Nick yelled over the load sound of the outboard engines and the wind.

"You take care of Natascha. Besides Astrid, she and her father are the only civilians who know the truth. Contact Klaus or Brian as soon as you can. They'll arrange everything. Under no circumstances are you to contact either the Canadian or the American authorities. Understood?"

Natascha nodded at him and Ole-Einar pushed the zodiac away from the *Northern Explorer*.

They looked back and could see Ariel slowly walk away from the rail with Shira in his arms.

"Do you think she's going to make it?" Ole-Einar asked Nick.

"Difficult to say. It's a clean through and through, lot of blood loss and I assume the hip bone is cracked as well. I don't know how it looks on the inside. All I could do was disinfect the wound and stop the bleeding. She needs an emergency room and she needs it fast," Nick explained, while the Norwegian hammered at the hull. Within minutes the support submersible broke through the surface and the four of them swiftly climbed inside. Ole-Einar brought up the rear, secured the outer hatch and climbed down the ladder.

"Hatch secured," he shouted both in German and English.

"All on board finally?" Vasili wanted to know.

"All on board, yes," Nick nodded and watched Natascha embrace her father as he sat wrapped in blanket beside Astrid and cried.

Slowly the submersible disappeared beneath the surface and took on speed. Just an hour later it docked with a smacking noise at the Russian *Akula*. Compressed air pushed the water out of the air-lock and the engineer opened the lower escape hatch. They all followed him through the pressure chamber and climbed through the lower hatch and into the open outer auxiliary hatch of the *Akula* inside the Russian submarine.

"Welcome on board. No cruise ship, but much faster. Captain Rankow wants to see you. All of you. Now," Vasili greeted them once they were all inside the submarine.

Nick looked at Ole-Einar and followed Vasili. He turned back to his friends, formed Shira's name with his lips and shook his head. Ole-Einar barely nodded to tell him that he understood and Olaf told Astrid in Norwegian about their plan. Even Dr. Richard Weber understood.

Vasili led the group to the officers' mess, where they were already expected by Captain Rankow and two of his officers. The Captain looked at every individual seperately before he nodded at Vasili and spoke to him in Russian.

"Captain Rankow's asking if everybody is on board and if we can finally go home now."

"Yes," Nick answered.

"Very good. Captain Rankow also wants me to examine everybody who's hurt," Vasili continued and looked at both Nick and Olaf, who were both grateful.

"Can I ask a question?" Ole-Einar asked and Vasili nodded.

"What about the warheads? Could you successfully recover them?"

"Warheads are where they belong. No problem."

"What about the nerve gas?" Ole-Einar continued.

"Nerve gas neutralized. No problem."

"Are there going to be any certain precautions regarding our two women on board?"

Ole-Einar had not yet seen the female member of the Russian crew and was understandably concerned about both Natascha's and Astrid's safety on board.

Vasili shrugged his shoulders, translated for the Captain and listened to his explanation.

"We were on patrol to test support submersible. This not complete military crew. This also engineers and scientists. Some of them women. We give women pistol, so no problem. If they want, we can give them pistol, too," Vasili explained with a smile and winked a them.

"You can sleep in three free beds. No problem. Just have to take turns."

Ole-Einar expressed his gratitude towards the Captain, but Captain Rankow had a few more questions.

"You only six people. Plan was up to eleven people. Where are five?"

"Captain Rasmussen and his crew decided to stay on the research vessel," Nick explained.

"What will happen next on ship?"

"Well, we're actually convinced that within the next few hours Canadian Special Forces will take control over the *Northern Explorer*. It would be best for us to be as far away from the vessel as possible. We've already seen a Canadian military plane," Nick added.

"Yes. You have seen plane. And shot at plane. We hear everything," Vasili explained and kept listening to his Captain.

"Captain wants to know who shot at Canadian plane. Hopefully not one of you?"

"That actually would've been me," Nick answered and noticed the puzzled look on both Vasili's and Captain Rankow's face.

"You did not shoot with Russian gun, did you?"

Nick swallowed and grimaced.

"Idiota!" Captain Rankow cursed.

"Captain says that you're an idi..."

"Yes, Vasili, thank you. I know what the Captain just said. It was not that hard to understand."

Nick actually wasn't too concerned about the fact that he used the Russian gun to shoot at the *Arcturus*. That particular gun used the same ammunition as his Sig Sauer. What he was worried about was the fact that he forgot both the Sig Sauer and the Russian gun inside the engine room beside Chuck's body.

"Captain wants me to examine everybody who's injured, then you will eat."

Ole-Einar thanked the Russian Captain once more and together they followed Vasili. The Russian doctor showed them the only few toilets and showers on board the *Akula*, as well as their bunks. Vasili was very supportive to all their needs, but he also insisted in a very clear tone that they would have to stay out of several areas of the submarine. Ole-Einar assured him that this would not be a problem when they reached the medical compartment. Everybody received two sets of clothes, just simple pants and a thin sweater as well as an overall. It wasn't much, but they were fresh and clean items. Considering the circumstances of the last couple days, those clothes were much better than what they were wearing now. Natascha and Astrid immediately took a shower. Their clothes were still covered in blood and they both had the urge to wash the horror of the last couple days off their skin. Although Vasili promised them nothing would happen, Ole-Einar and Nick stood guard in front of the shower. They just wanted to make sure, but they worried for nothing. Once Natascha was finished, Nick escorted her to Vasili, but since she only suffered two slaps to her face and one fall to the deck, she was physically okay. Nick noticed she continued to hold his hand unusually tight and he was more concerned about how Natascha would mentally deal with the situation. While Vasili now examined the wound where Chuck hit him with the axe handle, Nick asked the Russian doctor if he could say something about Natascha's pregnancy.

"You're not sure if your fiasco is a grandparent or not?"

"*Pregnant*. It's *pregnant*, Vasili. And she is my *fiancée*, not a *fiasco*. You're still mixing the letters, and no, we're not sure."

"If pregnant, how far?"

Natascha looked at Nick.

"Eight or twelve weeks. We don't know exactly. We're not even sure."

"I cannot say yes or no. Grandparent not that common on Russian submarine, so I am no specialist for grandparent. You better go to doctor on land."

"When will we reach a safe harbor?" Natascha asked with anticipation while Vasili gave Nick a tetanus shot.

"That depends if Canadians can hear us or not, or by how much we have to avoid them. More concerned about Americans. If they want to destroy us, and they always do, then it will take longer, or..."

"Okay, okay, okay," Natascha interrupted Vasili and closed her eyes. She didn't need to hear about any more horror scenarios right now.

"Let's presume that everything goes fine. I mean, you followed us all they way through the Atlantic and the North-West Passage without being detected. So, how much longer?"

Vasili just closed Nick's wound with two stitches before he answered.

"Hm, maybe three weeks. And your ship did hear us. Now we cannot hide under loud noise from research vessel. We must be very careful, otherwise *bang!*"

"Thank you," Natascha said and rose from her chair unnerved.

"You're welcome," Vasili replied and winked at her, before he told Nick he was good to go.

Nick patted him on the shoulder and thanked him once more when he and Natascha walked by him on their way back.

Just minutes later their entire group sat together in the officers' mess, where Captain Rankow invited them to an unscheduled meal. Since Vasili was their only way to communicate between the two parties, the Captain insisted on his presence.

"Captain on his way, still on bridge. Wants to talk to Nick."

Nick looked at Ole-Einar.

"Vasili, I want you to know that Ole-Einar is our boss, not me."

"Don't care. One of you come with me."

The Norwegian rose from his chair and followed Vasili to the bridge, where Captain Rankow and his Second Officer stood behind the Sonar Officer. All three of them were obviously very concentrated and Ole-Einar remained at the entrance to the bridge.

Captain Rankow talked to Vasili for a few seconds and looked at him questioningly.

"Fast outboard engine from vessel in direction to land. One of your big zodiacs. Do you know what's happening?" Vasili asked the Norwegian.

Ole-Einar knew immediately that this could only be Ariel and Shira. Although he was surprised that Ariel left the *Northern Explorer* only now, he silently wished them all the best. To answer the Captain's question, he told him he had no idea what was going on.

Captain Rankow communicated with some different stations on the submarine, before he gave several orders, which were repeated by his First Officer. Obviously he ordered them to slightly increase their speed. Captain Rankow handed over his command to his First Officer and escorted Ole-Einar back to the officers' mess where he personally made sure that everybody was taken care of. Satisfied that this was the case, he let Vasili tell them he had to get back to the bridge to distance them from the *Northern Explorer.*

The moment Captain Rankow left the officers' mess and Ole-Einar sat down, the meal was served. Since none of them had eaten anything substantial for the last couple days, they emptied their plates, tempted to lick up the sauce that remained.

Thin Ice

Even Natascha didn't mind eating all the meat and sat as close to Nick as she could. They all discussed what happened during the last couple days and Nick told his story with great detail. It was only when he told them how he ran out of air and took his helmet off that he had to stop for a moment and comfort Natascha. He reassured her that it was not her fault. She still couldn't believe he survived. Remarkably none of them ever mentioned either Ariel or Shira in their stories. During a moment of silence they honored Oliver, who died for their cause at the wreck of the Russian U-Boat. They also took the time to thank Astrid for her creative way to deliver the important message on the sandwich, and that they were still hoping she had washed her hands before using her fingernails to carve the message. It was Dr. Weber, who had the last laugh when he admitted he was so hungry that he did not notice any of the messages and simply ate them all. After a few seconds of silence Ole-Einar looked at Nick.

"So, a little Russian bird chirped to me that you've successfully planted the seed of your pleasure root."

Natascha's face turned slightly red and she played with her ring, that she had fixed back to the necklace again.

"Come on, Natascha. You don't have to turn red. Don't be so shy. We could hear you one deck below," Olaf teased her.

"That's so not true. My bed didn't squeak," Natascha defended herself.

"It wasn't the bed we heard. I'm talking about you," Ole-Einar continued teasing from her opposite site.

"You're silly," Natascha snapped back and threw her napkin at him, before she started to laugh as well. She had not been teased by them for days and she wondered how she ever managed it before. She lost her witty remarks and couldn't wait for the day she'd have them back again.

"But yes, you're right. There is a slight chance that there's something growing in my garden. I might have a bun in my oven," she finally admitted. While everybody else was laughing, Natascha's eyes suddenly filled with tears. Abruptly she rose from her chair and rushed out of the officer's mess. The room fell silent as their eyes trailed after her. Nick followed her and found her just a few meters away.

Natascha was emotionally shattered and in tears. Her shoulders shook under her choking breath, she couldn't even speak.

"What happened, Angel?" Nick asked and wrapped his arm around her shoulder.

"What if I was really pregnant and everything in the last couple days was simply too much? What if something happened? I have to go to a hospital then. I have to see a doctor. I have to..."

"Natascha!" Nick interrupted her with an overpowering voice, looking at her eyes closely.

"You're doing great. You were incredibly strong during the last couple days. Stronger than anybody else. There's no problem. If you were pregnant before all this happened, then you're still pregnant now. You handled the attack from the polar bear without a problem and together we will handle this, okay? The last couple days are over and we're all safe. Everything's all right. I'm with you."

He embraced her and gently stroked her hair.

"Thanks," she whispered barely noticeable.

Ole-Einar and Olaf both walked out of the officers' mess and were suddenly behind them.

"Listen, Natascha," Ole-Einar started carefully.

"I want to apologize. I didn't mean to be rude, okay? I'm sorry. Is there something I can do for you?"

Natascha looked at the two Norwegians.

"I'm just not sure if I'm even pregnant. And if I was pregnant, I'm not sure if the last couple days changed any of that..."

The huge Norwegian wrapped his arms around the small woman, offering a hug. "Natascha, you are the strongest of us all. Everything will be fine. We'll take care of you."

"That's nice, Ole." Natascha admitted easily, then after a moment, "I really appreciate it, but can you please let go of me? I can't breathe," Natascha laughed.

Olaf also gave her a hug and Natascha thanked them both for being such great friends. She knew the last thing they wanted to do was hurt her, and after all, she laughed at their comments herself. Nick and Natascha followed them back to officers' mess, where they finished their meal.

"I think I'm ready for some serious sleep," Natascha finally said what everybody was thinking. On the short way to their bunks they met several Russians, who were all very friendly to them and after a few moments they found their designated bunks again. Natascha pulled the curtain to the side and looked at the tiny bed. Like all the other bunks, the mattress was barely one meter wide.

"Olaf and I can share a bunk. Olaf, you can take the first turn, you're injured," Ole-Einar commented.

"Dad and I can also share a bunk. Maybe we even fit in their together. We did that on the ship for one night," Natascha muttered, still looking at the mattress in front of her. Only after a few seconds she noticed that everybody stared at her.

"Okay, that means that Astrid and I will share the other bunk. If we get real close to each other, it might work," Nick teased his fiancée with a big smile.

"Oh...," Natascha suddenly noticed.

"Maybe we could...Astrid, would you mind, if you...," Natascha was too embarrassed now to ask Astrid if she would rather share a bunk with her father instead of her fiancé, but Astrid was so tired she didn't care.

"For a moment that sounded pretty good, but I can totally understand you probably can't sleep if your fiancé spends the night with me in such a small bed. Don't worry about it, I'm so tired I could sleep in the torpedo tube."

"Don't worry Astrid, I'll certainly leave the bunk for you, of course," Dr. Weber offered politely. The situation was getting longer and longer, increasing Natascha's embarrassment.

"That's too kind. Thank you very much, Dr. Weber," Astrid replied as she removed her clothes and was, like Olaf, fast asleep just five minutes later.

"You can have the bunk first. I'm going to stay up a little bit," Nick whispered and smiled at Natascha. He tried to look awake, but he was dead tired.

"Don't be stupid, Nick. You're as tired as I am. Come on," Natascha told him while she undressed to her underwear. Nick did the same, took his shirt off and climbed into the bunk first. Natascha followed him and closed the curtain. For a moment they both felt like they were in heaven. The last couple days had definitely taken their toll and none of them had barely any sleep. Natascha repositioned herself and found herself comfortably lying half on Nick. With her head resting on his shoulder she tiredly thanked him for coming back for her and she whispered how much she loved him. Seconds after she was fast asleep. For a while Nick watched his fiancée sleeping peacefully, a moment he would love to see forever. He turned the light switch off and immediately fell asleep.

- 28 -

**On board the *Northern Explorer*, Amundsen Gulf, Darnley Bay,
Friday, October 14th**

Under the cover of the dark night, the fast RIB's arrived at the *Northern Explorer* undetected. It was just after midnight when Abigail Sinclair led two other CIA special agents onto the deserted research vessel. The complete silence on deck of the vessel felt suspicious. She hoped they would be greeted by her fellow Americans. If not by them, then from the Germans or at least anybody. The fact that they didn't see any sign of life on deck made all her alarm bells ring. It would have been ideal if they only found the Americans. US Senator Jonathan Brown gave detailed instructions on what they had to do if they met any of the Germans. While the Canadian JTF2 team secured the deck, Abigail and the two special agents immediately penetrated the inside of the ship. The Canadian's would not enter inside the ship until she told them to do so. Abigail and her two friends ran upstairs and down the corridors of the next deck. On their search for survivors they opened all cabin doors and quickly looked inside, but they did not find anyone. On the next deck they could hear several muffled voices. Abigail's face scrunched as she saw the door to the conference room was welded shut to the frame.

"You're safe now. We'll free you in a few moments," CIA agent Sinclair shouted through the closed door to a relieved crew after they identified themselves.

A quick look told Abigail that someone already tried to force the door open, but the attempt failed. She ignored all the questions that were thrown at her through the closed door and continued her search. The next three decks were also abandoned. It was not before they reached the bridge that they heard voices again.

Abigail rose her hand and with their guns drawn they slowly walked onto the bridge.

"Ah, finally. You must be with the Canadian special forces," Captain Ramshaw greeted them, obviously relieved that help was finally there.

"This is my Second Officer Mika Kankkunen. Those two gentlemen are my Navigation Officers. Have you already freed my crew?"

"No, we're still working on that. Are there any more people roaming on the ship?"

"No, at least not that we know of. We tried to free the crew ourselves, but we had some issues with our tools. We're glad you're finally here," the Norwegian Captain explained.

"Were you able to send a radio or satellite message?" Abigail wanted to know.

"No, unfortunately all our communication devices got destroyed during a fight. We're trying to repair it, but it'll take some more time."

"What about the Americans? Where are they?" Abigail asked. Nobody on the bridge noticed that, although she had her weapon lowered, she had not holstered it.

"Thank God those damn terrorists are all dead. I've not seen their bodies, but I don't plan to see them either."

"Where are the German terrorists?" Abigail asked coldly.

"The German...what?" Captain Rasmussen asked irritated. "The German's were not the terrorists. The Americans were the terrorists. The Europeans helped us. You must be...," was all that Captain Rasmussen could say. He could barely hear the two *plops*, but he felt the two hollow point bullets bury in his chest. His eyes widened in shock as he looked at Special Agent Sinclair, who still gazed at him over the silencer of her gun. The last thing Captain Rasmussen saw was his Second Officer Mika Kankkunen taking bullets and sag to the floor beside him. Both Navigation Officers started alert but couldn't get far with the shock that overcame them. Their mouths dropped open as they stared at the dead body of their Captain, before they met the same fate as the Norwegian.

Emotionless Abigail lowered her gun and turned towards her two colleagues.

"Okay, let the Canadians search the ship. It's important they only search the vessel. You have to make it clear to them that we will secure all the evidence. Once you free the crew you can ask some initial questions. Make sure the crew is convinced they were locked up by the Germans. Don't let them have any doubt."

Without another word the two agents nodded and left the bridge. Abigail turned around and carefully examined the damage on the bridge. She found a lot of blood and several bullet holes from a fight that must have been, as far as she was concerned, pretty much one-sided, but there were no bodies. Her eyes looked at the control desks. There was no way the Captain or anyone else could have sent a message from this station or the radio room. With one thing less to worry about she reassured herself that the Captain and his three officers were indeed dead. Finally she walked over to the radio room and came to the same conclusion. Frustrated, she went back to the bridge and looked out the window.

Where the hell are the Germans? How did they escape?

On board the Russian nuclear long range attack Submarine, *Akula* Class, Beaufort Sea, Thursday, Friday, October 14th

It was the first time in several days that Natascha slept for so many hours without interruption or nightmares. The young German woman didn't even notice when Nick moved, although she was leaning on top of him. Nick also slept like a log, but a quick look at his watch told him that it was already late in the morning and he decided to get up. Carefully he looked at Natascha, her head still resting on his shoulder and her left reaching across his middle gripping his arm. Nick gently tried to pull his arm out without waking her up, but at the slightest movement Natascha's hand tightened. Although she was still asleep, she managed to continue her protest by crawling further on top of him. She didn't let go of him, and since Nick didn't want to wake her up, he waited for another thirty minutes until she woke up. Natascha smiled at him with sleepy eyes and stretched.

"Thank God," Nick muttered and took the chance not only to free his left arm from underneath her, but also to massage his right arm where her fingernails had dug into his skin.

"What happened? Did you hurt yourself?" Natascha asked him seriously noticing the red marks on his arm for the first time.

"You're seriously asking me if I hurt myself? You didn't want to let me go. Those are from your fingernails," Nick complained an showed her his arm. Natascha only shrugged her shoulders.

"You're right. I simply can't let you go."

"I was better off sharing a bed with Astrid," Nick whispered and got off bed as fast as he could, but not fast enough to escape Natascha's punches.

To their surprise they noticed Ole-Einar and Richard must have just gone to bed, and since they didn't want to wake them up they dressed as quietly as possible before they retreated to the mess for some breakfast. Nick thanked the Russians for the food and introduced Natascha, Astrid, Olaf and himself, before he asked Vasili if it would be possible to speak to Captain Rankow. Nick understandably knew the bridge was one of the areas they were denied access to, after all they were still on board a Russian nuclear long range attack submarine, which originally served not just peaceful purposes. The German knew and totally respected those rules and Vasili promised Nick, that Captain Rankow would see him in the officers' mess at the end of the shift.

When he finally met him later that day, Nick reassured the Captain that everything was fine and that they all slept for several hours. Nick also made sure to thank the Captain again for the food and the medical assistance.

"Vasili, can you please ask the Captain which course we're going and what he plans to do with us?"

The Russian doctor translated and together they watched Captain Rankow unroll a nautical chart. With his finger he pointed to their current position.

"Captain Rankow says we're now in Beaufort Sea. Can only drive with five knots. Otherwise too much noise and SOSUS* System can hear us. Not good if we are too loud. Many problems. We are, at the moment, over one hundred an twenty... how do say? Kilometers?"

"Yes, Kilometers," Natascha said and wondered why Vasili converted sea miles into kilometers. She knew what a sea mile was.

"We're now one hundred and twenty kilometers away from the ship. With a speed of five knots we make two hundred and forty kilometers per day. Canadian Navy still six days away with own ship, they won't find us. Course is north-north-west into polar sea. Next couple days travel with speed of only five knots, not very loud. After that we're behind polar sea and SOSUS no problem. Then we travel at least twenty knots, nine hundred and sixty kilometers a day. Maybe we go thirty knots, depends. Then only few more days to Severodvinsk. There you can go off submarine."

SOund and SUrveillance System: *Surveillance system from the NATO for early detection of marine traffic, especially submarine activity in the open ocean.*

Nick looked at the charts and thought for a few seconds.

"Did you tell anybody that we're on board?" Nick asked.

"Of course, we called CNN and BBC. They all waiting for you. Big parade and everything when we arrive," Vasili laughed and looked at Nick with amusement.

Nick apologized for his stupid question.

"We informed fleet command about you. No problem, we use code for everything."

"And they're okay with that?" Natascha asked suspiciously.

Vasili shrugged his shoulders.

"You found old Russian U-Boat with dead sailors. You promised not to tell anybody.

You found old Russian warheads. You did great favor to us. We're grateful."

Natascha nodded and looked at Nick.

"Three weeks," she said and rose from her chair. Nick waited until Natascha left the officers' mess before he looked at Vasili again.

"Vasili, can I ask you for a favor?"

The Russian doctor nodded with encouragement.

"Is there a chance that your fleet command could notify our company in London and tell them we're still alive? We all have families who are very worried."

Vasili translated for the Captain and told Nick that it shouldn't be a problem notifying them. He also told Nick how to prepare the message and what he was prohibited to include.

"There is something else, Vasili. I'm not sure if you know about it, but we lost a very good friend down there at the wreck. Is there a chance that you might have..."

The Russian doctor looked at Nick with sad eyes, before he placed a hand on his shoulder.

"Nick, we did see what happened, but there was nothing we could do. He's now in better world. We took him away from wreck, he can now rest in peace."

Without a word Nick wiped a tear from his eye and thanked Vasili, before he stood up. He thanked Captain Rankow again for all his help and left the officers' mess.

Estate of US-Senator Jonathan Brown, Montana, USA,
Monday, October 17th

Jonathan knew that the ambitious and enthusiastic young special agent Abigail Sinclair was loyal to him and his extra money. After all, Jonathan promised her a successful career if they would win the next elections. It turned out that Senator Brown had not been wrong in his opinion of the young field agent. When they had called her a couple days ago, she gladly took the opportunity to show her loyalty and flew north. As far as Jonathan and Pierre were concerned, there could only be two possible outcomes. Scenario number one was that every witness would die after the nerve gas released itself into the atmosphere, and they could present the public a well thoughtout, bullet proof story. Scenario number two was that Abigail Sinclair would successfully eliminate the expedition leader and his daughter along with their bodyguards and every other witness, so that she and the American scientists could be portrayed as heroes. Unfortunately neither the first nor the second scenario became reality and therefore Jonathan Brown and Pierre Dumont asked Abigail Sinclair to brief them personally. She sat in the comfortable chesterfield and watched the flames in the open fire place. Patiently they both listened to her report for the last hour. Abigail confirmed there were no witnesses and that the crew was still convinced that they were locked away by the Germans. Back at the ship she made sure that this part of their statement was well documented. The only problem was that there was no trace of the Germans and that the nerve gas obviously had not worked. There were only two possibilities for the Germans successful escape. Abigail Sinclair found one of the large RIB's stranded on the rough shoreline around two hundred kilometers west of the *Northern Explorer*. Their investigation led them to the conclusion that this could have been the maximum range at cruise speed. On the other side, there was also one helicopter missing and nobody knew where Nelson Singer, Jenna Mason and Brian Joice were. It was known, that at least Brian could pilot a helicopter.

"Maybe those three got cold feet and literally jumped ship. You found the helicopter in Paulatuk?"

"Yes, Sir. We found it at the airport. Must have flown in under the radar. They left it there and stole another helicopter with a far greater range. Flew out under the radar as well and has not been seen since. So we found one helicopter and lost another one."

"What about that zodiac?"

"Fact is, we found a blood soaked bandage underneath one of the seats. Definitely the blood of a woman and our lab confirmed that it's neither the blood from the German nor from the Norwegian radio operator. Both have a different blood type. The Israeli is the only other women we're not sure about where or even who she is. We don't have any information about her. We think the blood we found in the RIB is hers. Given the severity of her injuries she can't be far and she must have company."

"Why didn't they sink that zodiac? Or send it back to the open sea? They knew we would find it eventually."

"The tank was almost empty. They went as far as they could. Those new RIB's are practically unsinkable. They would've had to spend a lot of time trying to sink it. I assume they didn't want to waste their time with it, especially not when they knew we're after them."

"How far can they get?"

Abigail shrugged her shoulders.

"They have to transport a severely wounded person. Uneven terrain, cold climate. Not more than one mile per hour at best. I assume they're looking for some natives, where they can hide and care for the woman. The Canadian's are checking the area and all the bush pilots up there. Shouldn't take much longer."

"Are we still on schedule? We can't afford this backfiring on us."

"Absolutely. The video footage is finished and all the evidence is gathered. You can make your announcement as scheduled."

Jonathan Brown picked up his balloon glass with cognac and toasted her.

"I can see an interesting career in your near future. Now, let's get ready for round two."

Home Office and Operational Headquarters of *EuroSecCorporation*, London, Friday, October 21st

It was late afternoon and, like always, Klaus Schwartze sat behind his desk. In front of him was the message sent from the commander of the Russian submarine fleet. Klaus' employee Tatjana Volmatovja had been contacted by them and was flown to Russia to pick the message up personally. Klaus and Brian read the Russian letter together and they both learned the sad news that Oliver Schneider had not survived. Other than that, they didn't know where Ariel and Shira were and the Russian letter didn't provide any information regarding the two Israeli's. It was Klaus who respectfully performed the painful duty to inform General Rashid of the Israelian Mossad about the latest news about his children. A simple letter carried so much yet so little in some respects. It was a lot to process, and like that wasn't enough, even the official diplomatic relationship of Germany and Norway towards Canada suffered. Canada officially accused both nations for allowing eco-terrorists to participate in that questionable expedition and therefore endangering the safety and security of both the United States of America and Canada. As a direct result of that, Brian had to answer to almost every politician who thought to be of importance. Not only did it take a lot of Brian's valuable time, it also didn't help his mood. On the plus side they knew Inspector Conolly and Scotland Yard still supported their theory. Gordon Ramshaw's autopsy revealed that he died naturally from a stress induced heart attack.

Brian was still in his office. He still couldn't believe that Oliver was dead and was afraid he would never forget the emotional turmoil that beset his family upon sharing the news. Brian and Klaus only arrived a few hours ago from Germany after informing Oliver's family. Brian just started to read a report when his phone rang. The number in the display was blocked and the call was not put through by Brigitte.

"Brian Whittaker here," he growled into the phone, disgarding any manner of politeness.

"Good evening, Admiral. This is General Rashid."

Brian sat up straight and light flickered across his eyes.

"Good evening, General. Do you have any news?"

"Unfortunately, but they're not mine. Please turn on your TV and watch the American news. It's neither helpful nor nice for us, but it's definitely clever. Call me back."

With an uneasy feeling, Brian hooked up the phone and walked over to Klaus. Together they entered the conference room where Brigitte already turned on the TV. They could just see the announcement for the *Breaking News*.

"As we just learned today, there were some obvious terrorist activity on board a research vessel, called the Northern Explorer, *within Canadian waters in the North West Passage, just off the coast of the small community of Paulatuk. Investigations revealed that members of a group of German scientists under the guidance of expedition leader Dr. Richard Weber evidently prepared a terrorist attack inside*

Canadian waters. In a coordinated effort, investigators found nine dead bodies on board the research vessel, amongst them the bodies of the Norwegian Captain, his Second Officer of Finland, the two Norwegian Navigation Officers as well the body of an American scientist, who also took part in the expedition. A team of several American investigators, who worked undercover on board the research vessel, also fell victim to this tragedy. It's safe to assume, that the terrorists knew about the investigators. The American team leader, Chuck Hogan, was executed with seventeen shots. At the moment it's still unknown whether these killings happened before or after a Royal Canadian Air Force plane was shot at from the ship. Evidence found on board the ship clearly indicates who is responsible for those actions. Besides Chuck Hogan, whose body was barely recognizable after his brutal murder, investigators found the murder weapon. Finger prints pulled from the weapon match those of twenty-six year old Natascha Kleinfeld, the daughter of the expedition leader. Preliminary reports also confirm that the body of American team leader Chuck Hogan also shows several severe fractures, a clear indication that he endured the pain of physical torture before he was killed by Kleinfeld. Natascha Kleinfeld is armed and extremely dangerous. She's most likely in the company of several other armed and extremely dangerous people. A nation wide manhunt is in effect."

Without saying a word Klaus and Brian stared at the TV, where they could not only see pictures of the *Northern Explorer* being towed, but also of the completely damaged, blood soaked bridge as well as the bullet holes on the damaged hull of the plane. They even showed pictures of all the dead bodies and the destroyed radio room with its blood covered floor. Next were several images including close up facials of Natascha for almost thirty seconds, while they reported more about the former military background of Nick and the others.

"At this moment we don't have any knowledge about the whereabouts of Natascha Kleinfeld and the rest of the terrorist cell. According to some of the evidence, at least one woman in her company is severely wounded."

"Shira!" Klaus determined. He learned from the Russian memo that both Natascha and Astrid were not injured.

"It only seems like sheer luck that the political delegation of US Senator Jonathan Brown and Canadian MP Pierre Dumont, who visited the research vessel just days before the killings, escaped this tragedy. The following footage shows how US Senator Brown was physically attacked by Natascha Kleinfeld during their visit on board."

Klaus and Brian stared speechless at the screen, where they could see the same footage Brian viewed in Ottawa. Without a single sound, the message of the footage was clear. Following the short video clip were the interviews from the two pilots who confirmed that they feared for their life and that of their crew, when their plane got shot at. They even showed interviews from individual crew members of the *Northern Explorer*. Repeatedly they mentioned the horrible conditions under which they were kept hostage and every interview ended in the statement that the Germans had locked them away.

"Exclusively, we're now going live to Washington, where US Senator Jonathan

Brown and Canadian MP Pierre Dumont are meeting for the new energy talks and to talk about their experience on board the ship."

Together they listened for several minutes to the typical political and meaningless phrases, before somebody asked the two politicians the first question about the energy talks. Judging by the constant popping of the camera flashlights, Klaus and Brian assumed correctly that the two politicians gave their communiqué in the completely packed press office.

"Come on, ask him," Brian growled and as if one of the reporters heard him, she asked the first important question regarding the attack on his person on board the *Northern Explorer.*

US Senator Brown took his time before he answered. With a serious expression he made sure he established eye contact with as many reporters as possible before he told them in a low monotonous voice about the attack from the fanatic German woman. After, he praised the cooperation between Canada and the United States and expressed his sympathy for the families of the victims of this horrible terrorist attack. He also took the chance to once more emphasize the importance of effective anti-terror laws, since they were obviously and regrettably still the prime target of terrorist attacks.

"And there's the connection to September two-thousand-and-one," Klaus commented emotionless.

Knowing that the Senator now had the undivided attention of everybody in front of the TV, he finally made his big announcement.

Incidentally he mentioned the gigantic oil fields in the northern region and that they were most likely the target of the terrorist attack. He thanked once more the brave people who avoided a catastrophe, before he explained that their energy talks had secured enough oil for both the United States and Canada for the next twenty years. He promised the people a lower fuel price, a better economy, more jobs, more protection against terrorists and the continuation of the American Way of Life.

"When do they have elections?" Klaus asked ironically.

"Couple weeks."

US Senator Brown continued to tell everybody how important the fight against any terrorist and anybody else who threatened the American Way of Life was. He promised the nation that those who were responsible for the attack on the life-blood of North America would be held responsible. After Jonathan Brown finished his speech, the American news agency showed several interview with CIA military experts. They all attested Natascha and her friends a very brutal, cold-blooded course of action that was heavily detailed and planned with military precision. Promising more details and hoping for some new development in this case, the news announcer referred to a special show with Senator Brown later that day, before they continued with their normal news coverage.

Brigitte turned the TV off.

"We're so screwed!" Klaus summarized with exasperation.

Brian simply nodded, still staring at the blank TV.

"Okay, we have no time to lose," he finally said and rushed into his office.

"Our main priority is to find out what the hell is going on with Ariel and Shira. The injured woman they mentioned can only be Shira, the other two are on board that *Akula*. We must find out from Israel why our people on board that submarine did not mention Ariel and Shira, and we must also find out if Tel Aviv has heard anything from them. Gather the troops. We need three groups: A: What do they know in America and what facts do they have to prove it. B: Damage control and C: What is our next move. We also need Tatjana to fly to Russia immediately to contact the Russian. She has to convince them about our side of the story. I don't want them to kick our people out of their sub under the North Pole. Brigitte, there will most likely be a few hundred calls coming in within the next five minutes. I have absolutely no time for them, and I will pick up the phone only if it's the Queen or the Prime Minister."

Brigitte nodded and left for her office, while Klaus was already talking to General Rashid in Tel Aviv. Brian sat behind his desk and wrote all the information he just heard on the TV down on a sheet of paper. He knew Brigitte would bring him a written version of the interview as soon as it was available. Just after five minutes Brigitte opened the door to his office again.

"Phone call. Do you want to take it?"

"Brigitte, I told you the only calls I'd take are from the Queen or the Prime Minister."

"I know that," Brigitte replied seriously.

Brian closed his eyes for a second and picked up the phone.

On board the Russian nuclear long range attack Submarine, *Akula* Class, Northern Polar Sea, Monday, October 24th

Just two hundred meters below the new developing pack ice, the dark, iron hull of the Russian nuclear submarine glided silently through the cold waters of the polar sea.

The *Akula* was now more than one-thousand-three-hundred sea miles away from the closest ship of the Canadian Navy, but because of the extremely sensitive SOSUS System, they still didn't go faster than five knots. The six unscheduled passengers made themselves as comfortable as possible inside the confined space of the submarine and the politeness of their Russian hosts was better than ever. Dr. Richard Weber and Natascha had several interesting discussions with some of the Russian scientists. Only Astrid seemed to be a little bit lost. As much as Natascha tried, she preferred to stick with her countrymen Ole-Einar and Olaf, who fully supported her. It was very obvious how much Astrid missed Ariel.

Shortly after dinner Captain Rankow called Ole-Einar and Vasili to the officers' mess. Fifteen minutes later, they called Nick and the rest of their group as well. Horrified and utterly shocked, they all watched a recording of the news report on the little monitor. Once the clip ended, Natascha was stunned, her face was white as a sheet. She had just been declared an international terrorist and murderer by Senator Brown on international TV. Tears silently ran down her cheeks in the view of this injustice and she had difficulty breathing. She barely noticed the former republican President place an arm around Senator Brown's shoulder, before he congratulated him for his important role during the energy talks and his great

Thin Ice

courage he had demonstrated when facing that terrorist. As soon as the news showed once more the barely recognizable corpse of Chuck Hogan and one of her close-up facial shots immediately after, it struck Natascha that she was now one of the most wanted people in the world. She didn't even hear Senator Brown's negative review of environmental expeditions and prohibition of them taking place in American waters..

"Oh my God," Richard stammered and had to sit down.

Captain Rankow turned the monitor off and looked at each of his guests, before he gave a brief statement. Vasili nodded several times before he translated.

"We got message from England. Your company trusts you, but they're the only ones. Captain Rankow and crew, we also trust you."

"Thank you," Nick replied silently and, staring at the floor, put a hand on Natascha's shoulder.

"Once you're in Russia, you're company takes you home. There you are safe. Natascha, you have problem. You're wanted under international warrant," Vasili explained in a low and worried tone.

Completely shocked by this injustice, Natascha stared at the floor and nodded absent minded.

And for a moment I actually believed that everything would be okay, she thought.

"What now," she asked frightened and looked at Nick.

Nick didn't have an answer and looked at Ole-Einar.

"We'll find a solution. Don't worry. Everything will be okay," the Norwegian tried to support her. Natascha's energy burst in waves, heat igniting in her veins as fearful shivers assailed her spine provoking her to her feet, forcing herself in front of Ole-Einar's optimistic words.

"Okay? How the hell can it be okay? According to the worlds largest news I'm a mass murderer and an international terrorist! That Senator sent that monster after me, just to kill me! He followed me onto the ship! I drove with him along his stupid pipeline and I discovered his gas! He brought that monster onto the ship, and he killed Oliver! He forced me to shut Nick's air off and watch as they pulled up his empty helmet. I helplessly watched Oliver die just two meters in front of me because of him! I watched him execute the First Officer! Every five minutes he beat Astrid to the floor and stuck his gun into her knee! He killed Vitali! Down in the engine room he attacked Nick with an axe and shot at me and Shira! But no, according to the former President of the United States of Goddamn America and that lunatic politician, I just got promoted to one of the top ten enemies of their nation! I can't go back to Germany, I can't go to Great Britain and most likely I'll be on the run in Russia as well! So, what the hell is suppose to be okay with all that?" She yelled at Ole-Einar, her veins protruding from her neck in anger.

The silence in the room thundered in her ears. No one was able to say a word. One simple question, made of so few words, was impossible to answer. She swiftly turned around on her heel and rushed out of the officers' mess. Nick made motion to follow her, but Vasili held out his hand, begging him to stay.

"I'll see how she's doing," Richard whispered with a worrisome sigh and was happy Astrid offered her help.

Olaf, Ole-Einar and Nick stayed behind and sat down again.

"Nick, your girl friend is right. She can't go away. If they find her, no trial, she dead. She has problem," Vasili explained.

"Yes, I know, Vasili. She summed it up pretty good," Nick said in a worried tone, while Captain Rankow patted Vasili on his shoulder.

"Captain Rankow has question."

"Please."

"Who is Shira?"

Home Office and Operational Headquarters of *EuroSecCorporation*, London, Monday, October 24th

Brian Whittaker and Klaus Schwartze went over their notes once more, before they officially called an end to their briefing. All the members of their operation control were present and as soon as they divided into the three groups, they started work immediately. They all realized they couldn't do much against the well oiled and funded Central Intelligence Agency and the American oil lobbyists, but they had sworn not to go down without a fight. After all, they were satisfied that not only the British and the German's but also the Norwegian authorities still believed them. They promised to try to remain neutral, but they also made it very clear that they would have to arrest Natascha Kleinfeld at the first chance and that she would have to remain in custody until everything was cleared. Nobody wanted to promise that she would not be extradited to the United States of America. Klaus pushed his men to work even harder at this case. He also asked one group to find out what their legal options were to protect Natascha. Besides that, they provided protection detail for Natascha's mother, who suffered greatly after hearing the news.

Brian sorted his papers and he and Klaus rose from their chairs. While Klaus spoke to his wife, Brian walked into his office and, with never-before felt frustration, slammed the door shut. He looked at this desk and gave a shout.

Beside his desk a man stood with his back turned to him as he looked outside the window. He slowly turned around and looked directly at Brian.

"Great God! Ariel! How the hell did you get in here?"

On board the Russian nuclear long range Submarine, *Akula* Class, Northern Polar Sea, Monday, October 24th

"Excuse me?" Nick asked, although he had understood Vasili perfectly fine.

"Captain wants to know who Shira is," Vasili repeated his question.

"She was with us. She didn't make it," Olaf explained somberly.

"Vasili! Natascha has a huge problem," Nick stalled without offering anything new. Nick's mind raced around a potential solution, but so far he didn't come up with anything.

"Yes. She's very loud! *Akula* not loud enough for SOSUS. Natascha is! Would be very good if she's not that loud any more!" Vasili seriously said.

"Vasili, what's the range of your support submersible?" Nick wanted to know and his Russian friend asked Captain Rankow.

"It depends. On surface a total of four hundred sea miles. Below water, only twenty sea miles. Why?"

"A couple days ago you told me that Russia owes me a favor because of the nuclear warheads. Is that offer still good?"

Vasili hesitated and asked Captain Rankow.

"Captain says it depends. If small favor, then possible. Big favor maybe problem. We cannot help even more. We're not only in wrong part of the world, no, we also help terrorist escape crime. Not good for Russia."

Nick knew Vasili was right. They already did more than enough for them.

"Yes, I know all that. All I'm asking for is a little detour to drop me and Natascha off."

"Captain wants to know, how little that detour is."

Nick took a set of nautical charts, unrolled it on the table and pointed at a certain location.

"Here. I want the Captain to bring us within ten sea miles to this location. There Natascha and I will leave your submarine."

Captain Rankow took a closer look at the charts. He was more or less shocked by Nick's suggestion and spoke to Vasili for quite a while.

"Little detour is over two thousand sea miles. Why there?"

"To collect a favor, Vasili. To collect a favor."

Home Office and Operational Headquarters of *EuroSecCorporation*, London, Monday, October 24th

"It's not important how I got in here. The important thing is that I'm actually here," Ariel said and walked over to Brian to shake his hand. Brian turned to his closed door and yelled for Klaus.

Just seconds later, Klaus burst into Brian's office and was just as surprised as he was when he shook Ariel's hand.

"My apologies for not contacting you any sooner, but I didn't know how far this building is under surveillance," the Israeli apologized.

"I think we may have one or two friends left," Brian laughed and pointed at one of the chairs.

After they all sat down comfortably, Ariel told them in detail what had happened since the interrupted satellite phone call on board the *Northern Explorer*.

"Did you see yourself that the two politicians were involved?"

"No. At the time when Natascha and the Senator were back at the surface, we were already tied and locked up in one of the cabins. Natascha is, as far as I know, the only living person, who can connect both politicians directly to Chuck Hogan and his men. According to Natascha, the Senator himself told her they planned to release the nerve gas, so that the local community wouldn't protest against their oil plans. Shira and I were locked up in a different storage room at the other end of the vessel when they started the diving operations to recover the warheads. Nick and

Ole-Einar could only fill me in briefly. Oliver died during one of those dives and Nick would have met the same fate, if it wasn't for the Russians in that *Akula*. The Russians have their own support submersible attached to the *Akula*, with integrated pressure chamber and docking hatch. Nick could talk the Captain into helping him with a gun and a knife. Shortly after the Russians brought Nick back to the surface, they defused the nerve gas before they picked up the three Russian warheads, which were already outside the wreck. Nick had to execute four of the eight terrorists on board the ship before he could free Ole-Einar and Olaf. Together they freed Shira and myself. I had to kill another terrorist on our way to the bridge. Our plan was to split up. Together with Ole-Einar and Olaf, I could eliminate two more terrorists when we took command over the bridge, where Captain Rasmussen, the Second Officer, two Navigation Officers and Astrid, the radio operator, had been kept hostage. Nick and Shira found Natascha and Chuck in the engine room. During Nick's fight with Chuck, Natascha picked up a gun and shot him. When the American's locked up the crew, they were indeed wearing masks and the German coveralls, but Natascha is also the only witness to that. The only thing I've seen myself, was that Chuck Hogan and his team worked together with the group of American scientists. Everything else is based on the statements of those who are currently inside the Russian *Akula*."

"Is it true that Natascha literally executed Chuck Hogan, before she turned him into little pieces? What about that torture?"

"Fact is, Chuck used Natascha as bait for Nick. He also forced her to watch Oliver die and he forced her to turn Nick's air off. Inside the engine room, Chuck shot with Nick's gun at her, but Shira threw herself between the two and caught the bullet. Natascha was permanently under great physical and emotional stress. As far as I know, Nick and Chuck fought together, and Nick broke his shoulder, his knee and some of his ribs during that fight. When Natascha shot Chuck, I assume her emotions took over and she just couldn't stop. After all she went through, I don't blame her."

"What about that Canadian plane? Who shot at them?"

"Nick. He wanted to make sure they were coming back."

"How did you escape?"

"I used one of the RIB's. The rest was a lot of luck and a false trail."

"Did it work? Could you lose them?"

"As far as my sources tell me, yes. They're looking in a completely different direction."

"Do the Americans know about the Russians?"

"I can't imagine it. We took all necessary precautions to cover it, so that this won't change."

"Your father knows you're here?"

"Yes, I already briefed him."

"On TV they said that Chuck Hogan is CIA. What do you know?"

"Chuck and his men were professionals, but they were greedy and arrogant. I wouldn't be surprised to learn that the CIA hired them for several independent contracts. My father is working that angle. We also know that Senator Brown has excellent connections to the CIA."

"How did you get out of Canada?"

"After I was sure that I wasn't followed, I went directly to the Israelian embassy. From there I flew back to Israel under a different identity."

"Alone? Ariel, what happened to Shira? How bad is she wounded? Where is she?"

"Shira suffered a through and through at almost point blank range when she caught that bullet for Natascha. The projectile hit her hip bone and changed flight path, which saved Natascha's life. Unfortunately for Shira, she suffered severe tissue damage. Nick was able to disinfect the wound and to stop the bleeding for a short while, but my sister lost a lot of blood."

"How much blood?" Brian whispered uneasy.

Ariel slowly shook his head and looked at the floor, while tears filled the Israeli's eyes, his distraught voice caught in his throat.

"She lost too much blood. I had to leave her behind."

On board the Russian nuclear long range Submarine, *Akula* Class, Northern Polar Sea, Friday, November 4th

Captain Rankow carefully considered Nick's idea. In order to help him, he would have to maneuver the *Akula* once more within direct reach of the SOSUS system and far away from Russian territory. Nevertheless, it was Nick who helped them recover three lost nuclear warheads and Captain Rankow knew that Russia owed the young German that much. Technically he could call it even, since they saved his life and that of his friends, but Captain Rankow honored the way Nick and his team paid their respect to the Russian submarine wreck and the lost sailors. The Russian Captain did not inform his fleet command about the new possible route. Bottom line, it would only be a couple more days before they would be back home. The more he thought about this plan, the more he liked the challenge. He already fooled the US and Canadian Navy once when he steered his *Akula* under the coverage of the *Northern Explorer*'s noise all the way from Iceland to Canada and through the North-West Passage. During their retreat they also fooled the SOSUS System. Captain Rankow decided to grant Nick his favor and at times accelerated the *Akula* up to thirty knots before he reduced the speed down again to under five knots two days ago to be completely silent again. For now, the *Akula* was stationary and lay in one hundred and eighty meters on the muddy seafloor.

It was just after midnight and Natascha thought once more about Nicks plan. Although she was skeptical at the beginning, Ole-Einar and her father convinced her that Nick's idea was actually her best option. They did not mention that it was also their only option. Natascha's only comfort was that Nick stood to his word, that he would not leave her alone during this difficult time. The moment to part quickly approached them and Natascha embraced each of her friends and thanked them for everything. When it was her father's turn, she couldn't hold back her tears any longer.

"Tell Mom I love her, okay? Eventually everything will be fine, right?" Natascha sobbed, but Richard couldn't speak or offer her the solace she was looking for, that she needed from her loving father. He turned his head against hers as he helplessly submitted to his emotions.

"And tell *Rocky* not to worry, promise me?" Natascha tried to smile.

Richard nodded and kissed his daughter good-bye.

Natascha took a deep breath, wiped the tears from her face and smiled at her friends.

"I'm going to miss you all," she finally said and climbed through the hatch into the support submersible, out of view of her friends.

Nick's eyes followed her before he also turned to his friends. He wrapped his arms around everybody and thanked them for their help and support. He slowly approached Richard, his future father-in-law. Nick had never really thought about that before. Richard quickly pulled Nick into his arms.

"I want to thank you, Nick," he whispered almost inaudible.

"Without you, we would all be dead. You came back for us and you saved my daughter. I know you will, but just promise me once more you'll take care of her."

"Don't worry. I won't let anything happen to her," Nick promised and shook Richard's hand, before he disappeared inside the support submersible.

Ole-Einar followed him halfway in and placed a hand on his friend's shoulder.

"You take good care of her, okay? I have absolutely no idea why she chose you, but she's the best thing that could happen to you. You be careful!"

Nick swallowed the knot the filled his throat and smiled, while his eyes filled with tears.

"Don't worry Nick. You just take care of her. Once we're home, we'll take care of the rest. Nobody is going to find you."

The Norwegian raised his thumb and closed the hatch on his side. He could hear Nick do the same to the inner hatch and the green light turned red. Seconds later Ole-Einar could feel the pressure lock fill with sea water, and with a *plop* the little support submersible departed.

Nick and Natascha were gone.

About thirty minutes later the little support submersible floated silently at the flat surface. Although their navigation technology was almost as advanced as the *Akula's*, they surfaced to take a final visual bearing. The Captain of the little submersible leaned out of the top hatch and watched the lights of the coastal town on the horizon through his binoculars. Next he gazed up and was satisfied to see a cloud covered sky, which made for a completely dark night. Unless someone hit them, it would be literally impossible to detect them. Satisfied, he climbed back into the submersible and closed the hatch. Just minutes later the submersible glided twenty meters over the sea floor towards the coast. Nobody dared to break the silence on board the vessel during the two hour long trip. Their tensions were to high. Still worried, Natascha stared to the floor in front of her. She could feel the thick heavy weights returning. Not only her new title that weighed heavy on her mind but also the parting from her father. She felt like she had lost him on the research vessel, and to have him back for just a short time to be parted again made it difficult. It was now, more so than before, that the uncertainty of ever seeing her parents again dawned on her. The only comfort she had right now was the fact that Nick sat beside her holding her hand. During the last couple days he continuously promised her that everything would work out, but she knew him well enough to know that he only wanted to cheer her up. Nick had absolutely no way of knowing if his plan would work. He didn't even know where to start their search. And even if their search would end successful, it would all depend if the person would believe them over the Americans. But Natascha tried to be as optimistic as possible and relied on the impression she got when they first met.

While she was still lost in her thoughts, she noticed the submersible surfaced and stopped. She watched as the Captain climbed down from the top hatch again to talk to Vasili. Their Russian friend listened patiently, nodded satisfied, and finally looked at Nick and Natascha.

"Victor says everything is okay at the surface. Sea is flat, many clouds, but very cold. Coast approximately two hundred meters away. We can't get any closer. Behind coast you'll find road. Victor saw cars. You follow road to the east, then you should find your target in five kilometers."

Natascha took a deep breath and nodded towards Vasili before she rose from her seat. She and Nick first put some heavy thermo underwear on and finally two Russian dry-suits with integrated gloves and hoods. The fit wasn't perfect, but they only had to swim so they had to do. Vasili handed them a watertight bag with food and sneakers, before Natascha and Nick climbed up the ladder and out through the hatch onto the hull. Natascha thanked Vasili for his support and wished him well for the future.

Nick waited for Natascha to make some room, before he also turned to Vasili to shake his hand.

"Thank you very much, Vasili. You saved my life and you helped my friends. I'll never forget that."

"I'm the one to say thank you. Russia and you are even now. Good luck. Do Swidanja, Towaritsch," Vasili replied and clapped Nick on his shoulder.

Nick wanted to say something else, but he could hear Natascha already jump in the water.

"Do Swidanja, Vasili," whispered Nick, then jumped into the water and swam after his fiancée.

Vasili stayed on deck and watched the two until he couldn't see them anymore in the dark water and shook his head.

Let's hope that luck fortunes you, but in your position, you can't be picky. Good luck, my friend.

"Do Swidanja, Towaritsch. Do Swidanja," Vasili muttered to himself with a last gaze at the horizon, before he climbed down the ladder, sealing the hatch behind him. Within the next minute the little submersible dipped under the frigid surface.

- 29 -

Washington D.C., White House, USA, Wednesday, February 8th
US Senator Brown was a large step closer to his end goal, due to the positive news about the gigantic oil fields north of Canada and Alaska. This fact alone was beneficial, but in combination with the energy agreement between the two allies, America's insatiable demand for oil was secure for at least the next decade. Jonathan Brown personally entered the election campaign to support their candidate. He celebrated himself as a guardian of the American Way of Life, who barely escaped the attack from that German terrorist with his life, during a daring mission for his native country. Most American's liked that combination and they believed him. They believed in the recovery of their economy and that they could avoid the looming recession. They trusted him when he promised them that the middle class would have more money. But most important for the American's was the fact that he promised them low fuel prices and they would not have to follow any guidelines to stop global warming or even believe in these questionable theories. They believed him when he assured them that every American could do whatever he wanted to, and the rest of the world should be happy that America was there to make sure the world was a safer place. Based on those promises and a well lubricated PR campaign, the party around US Senator Jonathan Brown indeed won the presidential election and took over the White House. Although he never said it on TV, Jonathan Brown made sure that the party knew who they had to thank for this victory. With standing ovations, the new President officially named him his new Chief of Staff that Wednesday evening. Nobody held back congratulating and praising him during the following festivities, even his Canadian friend Pierre Dumont had traveled all the way down to Washington. Despite all the worship, Jonathan Brown did not forget who he had to thank for his success and he pulled his connections to lure Special Agent Abigail Sinclair away from the CIA. In a grand ceremony, he promoted her to his personal Chief of Security.

It was late in the evening when the festivities rounded up and he was able to retreat to his new office. Only Pierre Dumont and Abigail Sinclair were with him now, while his personal secretary Carl Miller made sure they were undisturbed for the next two hours. With all the arrangements in place, Carl finally joined them.

"Well, what a night. Do we have any news regarding that situation in the arctic?" Jonathan asked and looked at Abigail.

"No, our men covered the entire area back then. They even used helicopters with thermo cameras, but we didn't find anything."

"Do we at least know what happened to that second helicopter?"

"No, we still don't know where it is. We covered everything within it's range plus fifty per cent, but we came up empty handed. I had to dial back our efforts up there.

I'm afraid we've raised too much attention if we continue with the same number of people working this case."

"Do we have an idea where they most likely are?"

"Well, although we have no idea how they got out of there, we certainly know where the two Norwegian's and that radio operator are right now. The two guys are still commuting between London and Norway. It'll be very difficult to place enough evidence on them to get them extradited. However, I'm confident we're closing in on Natascha and that Nick guy. We're monitoring their parent's activities, and we do know their money transfers are going to Nick and Natascha. Unfortunately we have to wait until they come out of their hiding spot in order to snatch her. We're working on it."

"Okay. What else is new? Anything on those two Israeli's?"

"Well, it seems as if the two Israeli's fell off the face of the earth when everything happened. Like I said before, our search up there turned out empty. However, we received a report from the Coast Guard a few days ago about someone finding a female corpse that washed ashore inside the area in question. According to the first findings they suspect a bullet wound, but a positive identification will be difficult."

"Why? Isn't it too cold up there for a body to be that decomposed?"

"It's not the state of decomposition, Sir. Evidently she had been in the water for quite some time and it's more about what the animals did to her. However, I do know that her blood type is identical with the blood we found in the RIB. We'll know more once we have the results from the autopsy, but I believe we found the Israeli."

"That would be excellent news. I think it's even worth another televised press conference."

"With all due respect, Sir, but I suggest we wait a couple more months before we make this public. The media is still saturated from the elections and most people won't be that interested. In a few months that'll be a completely different story. That'll also give us enough time to figure out how to present the facts."

Reykjavik, Iceland, Saturday, June 9th
Natascha stood in the kitchen of their little house and cut some vegetables. Although there was still an international warrant out for her arrest, she could walk freely here in Iceland. The feeling Nick had in the *Akula* back then turned out to be true. After they had reached the coast late that November night, they hid the dry-suits and followed the coastal road eastward for about one hour before they reached a certain address and with that their destination. They waited until dawn and with the first sign of activity inside the house, Nick rang the bell. It was Bjorn's house, the son of the Icelandic Prime Minister, and although Björn wasn't entirely awake, he invited them in, where he introduced them to his young wife. Björn convinced them that he believed Natascha's innocence, although he admitted he was shocked when he saw the news. Their Icelandic friend mainly based his decision on Natascha's reaction, when she blamed herself for Bjorn's mishap with her own rebreather. Björn explained to them with laugh, that someone, who apologized as much as Natascha did, could never be a murderer. Nick and Natascha were both relieved that Björn trusted them. After he

explained their situation to his family, they treated them the same as the Russians did. The only question Nick didn't answer was how they got to Iceland in the first place. Nick asked them to trust him and promised to answer the question when the time was right. Björn also arranged a meeting with his mother, who carefully listened to Natascha's story. They were glad the Prime Minister also gave them the benefit of the doubt and that she promised to protect them for the time it took to go over all the evidence.

Two weeks after their arrival, Nick contacted Klaus Schwartze in London. Brian Whittaker and Scotland Yard Inspector Conolly personally flew to Reykjavik, where they presented all their evidence. The Icelandic Prime Minister as well as the police were finally convinced that Natascha had been framed and officially put her under their protection. That also meant that all the American requests for extradition were ignored, even though the American's threatened them with economic sanctions. Although Nick was still officially employed with *EuroSec Corp*, he worked part time at a local dive shop. Natascha worked at home for her father's institute. Although it was not much, it kept her busy. Due to her love for Nick and her parents annoyingly, persistent advice, she finally attended several cooking classes. It was no surprise to her, that she still had to deal with the consequences of her stress, but she planned to start dancing and diving soon, and she was certain this would be the best way for her to deal with it.

Natascha just cut another paprika, when Nick walked up and wrapped his arms her around her hips.

"Hello, Angel," he greeted her and brushed a kiss against her cheek.

She returned the caress, before she continued cutting the vegetables.

"How's my little assassin doing today?" Nick teased her.

Astonishingly, Natascha had no issue with that any more. Not only had they issued an international warrant for her arrest, they had also placed a reward on her. She was much more confident since she knew that not everybody believed the Americans and she still saw her actions against Chuck Hogan as self defense and poetic justice.

Natascha seductively looked at Nick and professional juggled the sharp kitchen knife in her hands.

"Your little assassin is doing wonderful today, but I think we have to change the one pipe at the geo-thermo-pump after all. I checked it this morning and it's still leaking."

Nick nodded and made a note. Their parents lent them some money and they bought a little house outside Reykjavik. It wasn't much, but it was theirs and they liked it. Brian Whittaker informed them that they were working closely together with the Mossad to clear their names. Nick knew right from the beginning that Brian and Klaus would do whatever they could, but they were no government agency. To have the support from the Israelian Mossad was a completely different story, and Nick was much more relieved now. Until the situation wasn't officially over, they would stay in Iceland and refrain making any travel plans.

"I think there's a car coming. Can you please go and check on Shira?" Natascha asked and put the paprika into the frying pan.

Thin Ice

While Natascha stirred the vegetables, Nick went into the bedroom and looked after their daughter.

With the birth of a completely healthy Shira Sarah Kleinfeld earlier that May, their little family was complete. She didn't even notice when he picked her up, and as with all babies, she always seemed to smile at her father.

"Yes, you're so right, my little angel. After all that you've seen in mommy's belly, you can only laugh about the rest. And your mommy's so famous," he whispered and picked her up. He carefully kissed her and walked back to the kitchen, where Natascha lightly kissed Shira's forehead. Incidentally they both looked at some of the photographs on their fridge. Besides numerous pictures of their daughter, there was also a picture of Shira Hadad. After Shira had saved both Nick's and Natascha's life back on the research vessel within the same ten minutes, they both knew their daughter's first name. Natascha's eyes still filled with tears when she looked at how the young Israeli laughed at them from the picture.

"Ah, Shira. I so wish you could still be here with us. I miss you," Natascha whispered, while Nick put an arm around her shoulder. For Natascha, Shira was more than just a bodyguard, the Israeli was like her best friend and sister. Both were still caught in their memories, when the door bell rang.

"I'll get it," Nick said and allowed Natascha enough time to wipe her tears.

"Hey, Björn. Good to see you. Come in," Nick greeted his new dive buddy.

"Thank you. Just wanted to check in and see if everything's okay."

Natascha walked over and greeted him with a hug.

"Nice to see you. Do you want to eat with us?"

"No, thank you, Natascha. I was just in the neighborhood and wanted to drop something off for you."

"For me? What is it?" Natascha asked curious.

Nick already interpreted Björn's wink and smiled as he led Natascha to the door.

"Oh my God!" Natascha shouted as she was attacked by a huge white dog.

"*Rocky*! Where did you come from?" she greeted her loyal Kuvasz, which by now had successfully thrown Natascha to the ground.

"Just picked him up from the quarantine. Everything is fine."

"Now I know where you always went in the mornings. I almost started to suspect another woman!" Natascha noted to Nick and rose back to her feet to play with her dog. Natascha fooled around like a little kid and Nick smiled as he watched his girl friend. It's been very rare to see her like this after the expedition.

Björn decided it was time for him to leave, wished them all the best and arranged for a dive with Nick before he left.

After dinner Natascha led *Rocky* to her daughter.

"Look at this! Your mistress had a puppy. You have to take really good care of her, okay?" she explained to her dog and let him sniff at the sleeping Shira from a safe distance.

"What is it? Why are you looking at me like that? Oh, you're disappointed she was the only one in the litter? Well, I'm still trying," Natascha continued her conversation with the dog, while Nick started the computer and checked a new e-mail from Brian Whittaker.

He only had to read the first two sentences for his good mood to change into sorrow.

"Natascha, come over for a second. Mail from Brian. They have some news."

With *Rocky* following her heel, Natascha walked over and looked at Nick.

"What's wrong? What did I do this time?"

"Brian said that the American's found a severely decomposed female body close to Paulatuk. According to the news reports the DNA matches the blood from the RIB. They also confirmed a through and through in the belly. They announced they found Shira. Will most likely be in all the news by tomorrow. Brian wants to give us a heads up."

Natascha stopped playing with her dog and put her free hand on Nick's shoulder.

"At least she can rest in peace now," she commented respectfully and looked at *Rocky*, who was still pulling the other end of his toy.

- 30 -

Estate of US-Senator Jonathan Brown, Montana, USA,
Tuesday, July 3rd

Chief of Staff Jonathan Brown had just come back from a long week at his office in the White House and was looking forward to two relaxing days without politics. He spent the holidays here at his estate to take a break from his daily work. A couple weeks ago he personally announced on television that they found the dead body of one of the terrorists. Jonathan claimed this event as another victory over terrorism. Although they were not able to confirm the identity of the woman due to the state her body was in, her DNA matched the blood from the zodiac. They couldn't even perform a dental record, not only because the dental structure on the corpse was no longer complete, but also they didn't have anything to match it against. As illogical that seemed to be, it was however, another clear indication that they found the Israeli woman. Beside that, Jonathan didn't care too much about it any more. All the contracts regarding the oil were signed and the only thing Natascha Kleinfeld had was an international warrant offering a high reward on her capture and a life confined to a volcanic rock in the North Atlantic. She had absolutely no evidence against him in her hands and she had to know that the CIA would snatch her the moment, she would leave Iceland.

Satisfied with the situation, Jonathan Brown walked to his living room and poured himself a generous whiskey. It was already after nine in the evening and his housekeeper had already left. Besides himself were only his secretary, Carl Miller, and Abigail Sinclair inside the estate.

Jonathan sat down in a leather couch and looked at the huge antique wall clock. In about thirty minutes a special visitor would come and serve him for the rest of the night. Since quite some time he trusted the service of a local escort ring. Discretion was a life saver in his business, but he didn't want to abstain from the service they offered. After all, he described himself as hard working and was convinced he deserved to use their service, especially since he paid for them.

Tonight he had another reason to be excited. The agent from the escort service promised him a new model, who would be perfect to satisfy his extraordinary wishes and Jonathan could barely wait to meet her.

He rose from his couch, emptied his drink and went upstairs to take a shower.

Just as he was finished, he could see the two bright car lights cutting through the darkness. Jonathan dressed into a satin morning robe and watched the large SUV drive up the driveway and stop in front of the door.

Like always, Carl Miller went outside to meet the model and Jonathan could see that she came alone, like all the other models before her. Even from his window Jonathan could see the endless long legs of this model, who followed Carl inside the house just seconds later. Jonathan went to his minibar and poured another drink.

Don't drink too much. Would be a shame, if it wouldn't last long, he told himself.

Within minutes he could hear the typical sound of high heels on the wooden stairs, followed by a soft knock at his door. Jonathan licked his lips.

"Come in," he told the model, his voice shaking anxiously, putting his glass down.

The door slowly opened and an oriental beauty stepped into the room.

The prostitute closed the door and turned towards her client.

"Hello, my name is Isis," she hissed seductively and placed her handbag on top of a drawer.

The sound of her voice itself was enough to arouse him and he asked the young woman to his bed. She couldn't be that old. He guessed she was barely twenty, most likely a student who had to sell her body to pay for university, but he didn't care about that. He only wanted to be in charge over her and her body, that's what he paid for. Anxiously the politician took his robe off and lay down on the large bed.

"Take your clothes off, but do it slowly," he told her.

If he would have not been so captivated by the seductive beauty as she ran her hand along her hourglass figure, he would have looked outside the window, his breath escaping his lips with utmost shock, irrevocable fear trembling through his veins.

With all his strength, the person clung to his horizontal position. Every muscle in his body burned it's own fire, but the man in the concealed ignored the pain. He heard the young woman step out of the SUV before a second person escorted her inside the house a few seconds later. Only two minutes after that the timer of the motion detector turned the lights off and everything went dark. This was what the man waited for. Under the cover of darkness and without making a sound, he lowered his body to the ground and rolled out from underneath the SUV and away from the house immediately. Hiding behind the SUV, the masked man in black clothes watched the estate with eagle eyes, soaking up every little detail from his new position. While he gave his muscles the chance to recover, he studied all the sensors for the motion detectors. With the sleekness of a cat he started moving parallel to the house without setting off a single motion detector.

Inside the huge log home Carl Miller sat on the couch in the living room and stared at the open fire place. Although it was early July, he still liked having a fire going, even if it was only to raise his mood. Lost in his thoughts he watched the flames lick up the side of the new log he added a moment ago. He looked at his watch. The prostitute usually stayed the whole night and wouldn't leave until early in the morning. Carl was not sure what to expect from the next day. Sometimes Jonathan noticed during those nights that his body was much older than he wanted it to be. If that was the case, he was usually in a very bad mood and he let everybody else feel it. On the other side, if he had a great night he was usually very friendly and generous. So Carl sat there and hoped for everybody, that his Boss would have the best night. He put his glass with orange juice back on the table and leaned back into the couch. His back barely touched the couch when an arm choked around his neck like a press. Instinctively Carl brought up both his hands and tried to loosen the chokehold, but he didn't stand a chance from his submissive position. He couldn't even scream for help as the arm around his neck completely eliminated the flow of blood and oxygen. His helpless cry came out in a weak wimper. In panic Carl looked up and saw two eyes watching him through the tight slits in the intruders facemask. Just before he passed out, Carl noticed the tiny object in his intruders hand, which now closed in at his face. It was something small, something like nasal spray. Without having the strength to resist, Carl helplessly watched the masked intruder injecting the content of this little white bottle in his nose. The last thing Carl noticed before he sagged to the couch, was the sharp pain that burned through his nose and down his throat in a roarous flaming fire.

Without saying a word the masked intruder let go of his victim and turned towards the door. It didn't look like Abigail Sinclair had noticed anything about this confrontation. Without making a noise, the intruder sneaked towards the door and stopped when he saw the light shining from underneath it. He carefully placed his ear against the wood to hear the typical sound of a shower and some music playing. Slowly and silently he opened the door, sneaked inside and closed it behind him. He noticed that the door to the adjoining bathroom was half open as the sound of the shower turned off. The intruder looked around and took cover beside the door frame while Abigail dried herself off. Not suspecting anything, Abigail sauntered back into her room without even noticing the intruder. She dropped her wet towel to the floor. She didn't care what her boss was doing upstairs with that young thing. He didn't pay her for moral advice and she didn't waste her time lecturing him. She stood in front of her closet and looked at her reflection in the mirror when she finally saw the sudden movement behind her. She spun around, but her scream never left her lips. The left hand of the intruder closed like a press around her neck. With her eyes widened in horror, Abigail looked on as the man pulled her to him. Abigail tried to fight back by viciously punching him, but he didn't show any reaction. He forced her with her back against the wall and, almost effortlessly, lifted her ten centimeters off the floor. The pressure on her throat became tighter and tighter and she grabbed her attackers arm with both her hands. With shock, the former CIA agent watched her attacker's right hand slowly come closer to her face. No longer able to fight back, Abigail could do nothing but witness the intruder spray the content of the little bottle into her nose. She didn't even feel the pain when she hit the floor. The intruder quickly kneeled down beside her and checked on her, before he rushed out of her room and upstairs to Jonathan.

Jonathan Brown felt like he was in heaven. The oriental beauty performed an incredible show and now Jonathan waited for the next part. He lay on his back, both ankles and his right wrist were already tied to the bed posts with leather straps. Isis just leaned over the politician and Jonathan almost lost it. He raised his head as high as he could to lick over her belly while she also tied his left arm to a bed post. Jonathan was now completely at her mercy. He was so excited he didn't even notice her fly off the bed and disappear into the bathroom, blowing him a seductive kiss. Jonathan followed her with his eyes. He wanted her, he wanted to be at her mercy, he was helpless to whatever she would do to him. Even the sound of the shower aroused him. Just a few minutes later Isis came out of the bathroom and she didn't even look at the politician. Her complete seductive behavior was gone and she dressed as fast as she could.

Jonathan Brown couldn't believe his eyes.

"Hey, what the hell are you doing? We're not done yet. I paid for the full night. Take your clothes off now, you bitch," he yelled at her, not realizing he wasn't exactly in a position to give such orders at the moment.

That had never happened to him before, and just now someone knocked at the door.

"What the hell is it?" Jonathan yelled. He had very clear rules that he must not be disturbed once he had company. He assumed it was Carl, but he didn't get an answer. Instead Isis rushed to the door and opened it. A masked man wearing a black coverall slowly came into the bedroom.

"I'll wait in the car," Isis whispered and ran out of the room and downstairs.

Jonathan almost panicked. He knew something must have happened to both Carl and Abigail inside his own house. It was the only logical explanation for there to be an intruder in his bedroom. Jonathan Brown looked down again and realized he was tied to his bed, completely helpless.

"Who the hell are you? What do you want?" Jonathan yelled at the intruder, trying to bear some level of power in the situation. Slowly the intruder took a revolver out of a pocket and a single bullet out of another. Almost as if he was bored, the intruder demonstratively loaded the single bullet. He looked at every detail in the room and spun the revolving breech.

"Money? Do you want money? I can give you money," Jonathan's righteous and powerful tone quickly turned to a stammer.

The intruder still held his silence and slowly moved closer to the bed. Without paying too much attention to Jonathan, he placed the barrel of the revolver on Jonathans knee and pulled the trigger.

The politician cried out loud, but neither the shot nor the pain materialized.

"For God's sake! Are you insane? There's a safe! Behind the painting! Please!" Jonathan begged nodding in the direction.

The intruder slowly turned around, walked to the picture and made sure it was not wired to an alarm system. Carefully the man placed the painting on the floor, leaning it against the wall before he looked at the safe. He picked his revolver back up and turned to Jonathan, looking at his other knee.

"It's open! You don't need the combination. It's open!" Jonathan yelled and hoped to God someone would come to his rescue.

The masked man shook his head in disbelief when he noticed the safe was indeed open. He never expected this to be that easy. Inside the safe he found several bundles of cash, which he ignored as much as the gun. Instead he was much more interested in a large brown envelope, which he took out and opened. Inside the envelope were a memory card for a video-camera as well as several personal notes and Swiss account numbers.

Horrified about what he just saw, Jonathan Brown swallowed hard. What this intruder was holding in his hands was much more valuable than the money and much more dangerous than the gun.

"Who the hell are you? What do you want? Listen! I give you money! Much more money like there is in the safe!" he begged with a shaking voice, his tears forming under the stress.

The man looked at him and, with a swift movement, took his mask off.

"I appreciate your kind offer, but I already have what I came for," Ariel said with a satisfied smile.

Jonathan Brown was completely shocked. His worst nightmare had just come true when he recognized Ariel. Of all the people it was the Israeli terrorist who stood in his bedroom. Not only that, but the Israeli held not only all of Jonathan notes about that certain case in his hands, but also the original audio-video footage about his confrontation with Natascha. That video footage was a complete confession and Jonathan literally handed it to Ariel. The Israeli looked at Jonathan for a long time. At first he had planned to tell him a couple things, but the image Ariel saw from the politician now was simply embarrassing. Ariel burst into laughter.

"What is it? I'll buy the envelope back. I can give you millions! I can..."

Lightning fast Ariel's hand closed around Jonathan Brown's throat. The laughter cut short in the quick movement.

"Don't talk as if you're still in control. You have no idea how many lives you've destroyed. You're nothing but dirt," the Israeli whispered and stood up again.

"So? What's your next move? Going to shoot me?" Jonathan asked after he had gained control over his heavy breathing, but Ariel didn't answer him.

Instead he took a smart phone out of his pocket and took several pictures of the notes and of Jonathan tied to the bed completely naked. He reached into Isis handbag that sat on the drawer and took out a video-camera. Jonathan swallowed again as Ariel punched a number into his phone.

"Good evening. Is this the news room? I have a story for you. Could you please send a crew to the estate of Chief of Staff Jonathan Brown? You'll find evidence that the former Senator and his Canadian colleague Pierre Dumont are the masterminds behind, and therefore responsible for, the terror attack that took place in the arctic on board the *Northern Explorer*. You'll find evidence that will explain the reason why the Senator ordered to kill an entire community with nerve gas back then to gain illegal access to cheap oil. If you want to ask the Chief of Staff some questions, feel free to do so. Currently he's naked and tied to his bedposts. I'll send you some pictures as proof."

Ariel placed the same call to four other news agencies.

"You God damn son of bitch! Why did you do that?" Jonathan Brown shrieked in panic.

"Because it's the truth," Ariel explained completely unimpressed and stepped closer to him. "You have approximately thirty minutes before the first news crew arrives. I'll take the originals with me, but I saw a nice fax machine downstairs. Every news agency will have copies of your notes as well as the video footage within the next fifteen minutes. I'll also upload them to the internet, just in case. I must say, your reception here is amazing," the Israeli noted as he used his smart phone to send the pictures. After all the files were sent, Ariel picked up the revolver again. Looking at Jonathan full of despise, the Israeli approached him again.

"Your two employees will wake up again within the next hour. I almost considered executing them, but it turned out they were no real threat to me and I'm not a monster. I gave them a little anesthetic cocktail. It's my favorite mixture. Not only will they patiently tell the truth to the reporters once they arrive, their memory of the last two hours will also be wiped clean, but I think the police is more interested in this other case anyway. I'll give you the chance to put an end to your miserable life," Ariel said and checked the revolver. He made sure that the single bullet was in the last chamber, so he would have enough time to leave the room.

"Oh, I almost forgot," Ariel said and patted the former Senator on his cheek. "Natascha asked me to say hello," the Israeli finally said and carefully placed the revolver in Jonathan Brown's hand before he rushed out of the room.

Seconds later the politician heard the typical confirmation sound of his fax machine. The next thing he heard was the SUV driving away with a high revving engine.

Jonathan cursed the Israeli and called himself an idiot for keeping those notes and the video. The politician yelled for Carl and Abigail as loud as he could, but he didn't get an answer. Finally Jonathan tried to think logically and calmed down a bit, but even after another half an hour, he didn't get a reaction when he called them. Jonathan tried several times to free himself, but the prostitute had secured the straps with additional knots and he couldn't even loosen them one bit. Those leather straps could only be loosened by two hands now. Jonathan started to think again. The information that was now in the hands of the Israeli was literally lethal for him. Every note, every phone call with Pierre Dumont, Chuck Hogan and Gordon Ramshaw was well documented and inside that envelope. Back then he had decided to keep them, just in case he needed some leverage on his business partners to black mail them. But the most important thing in the hands of the Israeli was the video footage of his confrontation with Natascha. Jonathan closed his eyes. Like it was yesterday, he remembered how he had yelled at Natascha Kleinfeld back on board that ship. He remembered in every detail what he had told her about their plan and all that in Chuck Hogan's presence. Not only was his own face clearly recognizable, the Chief of Staff knew, it would take the Mossad less than a day to match his voice from any of his public speeches to the voice on the video for a positive result. He knew his short career in the White House had come to an end. The government could probably hold the material back for twenty four hours, but once they saw it for themselves, it would be on every TV station in the world for the next forty eight hours. After that it wouldn't take much longer until he would be kicked out of the White House and his party. He really doubted he would even find a lucrative job in the private industry. Jonathan suddenly realized, that not only his career, but also his life was over. They would certainly press charges against him. Maybe he could strike a deal. Faced by the severity of the consequences he would have to deal with in the near future, he swallowed hard. Tears ran down his face when he noticed the first headlights coming up his driveway, shining through his bedroom window. The first news crew arrived.

"Oh my God!" he moaned, before he desperately shouted for Carl and Abigail again. When he still didn't get any reaction from them, he was close to a mental breakdown. His gaze fell to his left hand, at the revolver Ariel gave him. Panic rose inside him as he looked at the weapon. The cold hard metal chilled his fingertips as he lifted the heavy object. This was his only solution. It was cowardly, he knew that, but it was still his only option left. Carefully, so that he would not lose the revolver, he turned the chambers, loading the single bullet. The leather straps just allowed him enough movement to turn his hand towards his head. For the first time in his life, Jonathan Brown looked down the barrel of a gun and he knew, that his chance of survival was a solid zero. With closed eyes he turned his head away from the revolver, cried wretchedly and pulled the trigger.

Outside the estate of US-Senator Jonathan Brown, Montana, USA, Tuesday, July 3rd

Peter O'Sullivan, Erika Heynes and Josh MacKenzie were nervous. It was just before midnight and only half an hour ago their news agency had received an anonymous, non traceable call, claiming that Chief of Staff Jonathan Brown was responsible for the terrorist attack in the polar sea. Beside that, he would be tied to his bed naked, with nothing else but some copies of the evidence with him. First, the news agency thought it was one of the usual fake calls from some idiot to get attention, but the moment they received the pictures, their boss literally spilled his coffee all over his desk. Only thirty seconds after that, the three reporters where already in the large news van, rushing down the highway. If they would arrive at the estate first, then this could be their night. Peter just barely slowed down when he steered the huge van into the driveway. They hardly noticed the open gate when their tires skidded over the asphalt, but even Erika didn't complain. Every second was valuable at the moment. After a few hundred meters they were relieved and surprised to find out they were the first crew. Peter parked at the best spot right in front of the door, and before the van even came to a complete stop, all three of them were already outside.

"Okay, show time," Erika shouted and looked at the reflection of her face in a little mirror. They just turned towards the entrance door with all their gear when they heard the shot. All three of them stopped dead in their movement.

"Oh my God! Someone just fired a shot," Erika whispered.

They waited for a few seconds, but noting else happened.

"Maybe we should wait and call the police first?" Josh asked and let the camera sink.

"Are you out of your mind? It'll only take minutes, before other news crews arrive. We can get an exclusive tonight. This is our chance. We're going in there now," Erika snapped at them, darting to the door.

Upstairs in the bedroom Jonathan didn't understand what just happened. He clearly heard the shot, he even felt the burning hot gas on his face, but he was not dead. There was no way he could have missed at this short a distance. Desperately he looked at the wall, but he couldn't see a bullet hole, then he stared at the revolver and started laughing.

Ariel only loaded a blank round and Jonathan's attempted suicide at the same time as the arrival of the journalists was an even better confession. Still laughing, Jonathan could hear the journalists rush up the stairs, their breath coming in loud short gasps. He scratched his head with the end of the barrel as he awaited his fate.

Reykjavik, Iceland, Wednesday, July 4th
"Nick! You have to come to the living room! There's something new!" Natascha shouted anxiously.

As fast as he could, Nick rushed into their small living room and looked at Natascha, who pointed at their little TV.

A reporter by the name of Erika Heynes stood in front of Jonathan Brown's estate and commented on a series of video footage. It all started with the video shot by the camera in Isis' handbag and it ended with the video that showed Chief of Staff Jonathan Brown, Chuck Hogan, Natascha and sometimes even Jenna Mason on board the *Northern Explorer*. What was even more important was the original sound of the video. They could clearly hear the words that the former Senator had thrown at Natascha back then in anger.

"Well, I finally understand why you rammed your knee into his balls," Nick whispered.

The video footage was followed by close ups of several notes, which portrayed both Jonathan Brown and the Canadian Pierre Dumont as the masterminds behind this crime. The news reporter showed some video footage of their interview with a dazed Carl Miller, who generously confirmed not only the authenticity of the documents and the video footage, but also that his boss regularly invited prostitutes to his estate. His statement was confirmed by the interview with Abigail Sinclair, who was found naked inside the house. Suspicions quickly arose, but at the time, they weren't sure if or how she was involved in the sexual activities during that evening.

Natascha shook her head in disbelief. She was so relieved, tears ran down her face when she looked at Nick. The news reporter even mentioned the unsuccessful suicide attempt from Jonathan Brown and interpreted it as a confession.

"So far Jonathan Brown is denying any comment on what happened tonight at his hunting lodge. He only stated that earlier this evening, a masked man, which Jonathan Brown identified as one of the terrorists from the research vessel, forced entry into his house, where he overpowered and drugged his two employees. He also stated, that this was a set-up. An interesting story which unfortunately does not answer any of the many questions that came up this evening."

"Oh my God!" Natascha gasped and looked at Nick.

"That was Ariel. It must have been him," she said and shook her head still looking at Nick, before she turned to the TV again. With every word the news reporter spoke and with every picture they showed, a huge load fell off Natascha's mind.

"I told you I'm innocent!" Natascha finally laughed and punched Nick on his leg.

"Damnnit. I so hoped they'd raise the reward for your arrest a little bit more. Then I would've turned you in myself and retire on a nice Caribbean island," Nick teased and sat beside her.

Natascha turned her attention to their daughter as she lay in her lap and slept.

"Don't even listen to him, my little sunshine. Yes, I know, unfortunately he's your daddy. I can't believe it myself, but the important thing is that we're both healthy," she joked with Shira.

"Don't get too excited. You're not off the most wanted list yet, but I heard it's really nice and warm in Cuba," Nick mentioned in a serious tone.

"Can you believe this, my little angel? Daddy wants to take your mommy away and lock her up with many lonely men. He's some daddy, isn't he? Do you know what they would do with mommy? They would..."

"Okay, you win! Stop it," Nick interrupted her.

"I'm not turning you in. Don't worry," he added and stood up.

"There you see, my little sunshine. Your daddy still loves me."

"I didn't say that. I just don't want you to tell my daughter such horror stories."

Nick was surprised how fast and accurate Natascha could throw a pillow at him with their daughter in her lap.

Home Office and Operational Headquarters of *EuroSecCorporation*, London, Thursday, July 12th

It was the first time in almost a year that Nick drove onto the parking lot of *EuroSec Corp.*

"So, here we are," he mention and looked from the three storey building to Natascha, who sat on the passenger seat beside him.

She always wanted to know where Nick and his friends worked. As soon as they received confirmation that the international warrant for Natascha's arrest was lifted, they flew back to Germany and from there to London. The dog stayed with Björn for the couple days they were gone to visit their families. Nick took the baby stroller out of the trunk and unfolded it. Just as Natascha put their daughter into the stroller, Rolf Brengmann walked out of the building towards them.

Natascha never forgot that Rolf had caught a bullet for her back in Berlin and she happily wrapped her arms around him.

"Well, well, well, look who came to London," he greeted her.

"Rolf! It's so nice to see you!"

Rolf returned the gesture and lifted Natascha off the ground without any effort, before he clapped Nick on his shoulder.

"And how are you, your girl friend and my daughter doing?" he teased his old friend.

"Rolf," Natascha shouted and pretended to be shocked.

"I thought we agreed not to talk about that as long as Nick can hear us," she added whispering her tease.

"Yes, yes. Whatever. This child is both beautiful and intelligent. That means it can only be mine," Nick replied calmly.

They talked for a few more minutes, before Nick looked at this watch and pressed Natascha to come.

"We really got to go. They're already waiting," Nick said taking Natascha's hand.

"How long are you staying?"

"Just for the weekend, Rolf," Natascha answered.

"Perfect. Hey Nick, what do you think? You stay with my daughter at home, and I show Natascha London at night. I promise to bring her back at dawn."

"That sounds like fun. Can I go, please?" Natascha asked Nick with the most serious expression she could manage.

"Don't push it, or I'll insist for a paternity test," Nick countered and pushed the stroller towards the building, while Natascha walked with Rolf.

"Oh, Natascha. Can I ask you for a favor, please?" Rolf whispered and looked at the entrance Nick disappeared through.

"Sure. What is it?" Natascha asked, while she took the baby bag out of the car.

She noticed Rolf's gaze and saw the three women who just came out of the gym located on the ground floor of the building.

"Could you please pretend you're breaking up with me? One of the women there seems to like me. She's pretty hot, but I think she believes I'm in a relationship," Rolf explained in a low voice.

"You want me to do what?" Natascha laughed.

"You heard me. Come on, please. I owe you one if you play along," Rolf whispered and glanced at the three ladies, who now stood two cars down.

Natascha looked at them and it really seemed like Rolf was indeed attractive to one of the young women. At least she was following their conversation with great interest.

"You do realize this is pretty cheap?" Natascha turned to Rolf and whispered.

"Not really. Only if it doesn't work," he whispered back.

"Listen! I can't do this any more," he then suddenly shouted, surprising Natascha instantly.

"I know that you have a problem with my job," Rolf went on, satisfied the young woman was listening to their argument.

"It's not my fault, that I spent all that time with these rock stars," Rolf continued and made sure that the three women could hear him.

"I know that's your job, and you're right! I don't like it," Natascha shouted now with a serious expression on her face. Rolf was glad she played along.

"I know that you don't like it, honey, but this tour as head of security for the rock stars gets us a lot of money. Beside that, they're all my friends by now. I told you, that you could come, but you didn't want to, remember?" Rolf was really pleased to see, that the lady in question gave Natascha a really disapproving look.

Thin Ice

"Yes, I know you're making lots of money and that you're always driving all those fancy sports cars and big SUVs, but that's not the point," Natascha yelled at Rolf and pretended to be really upset.

"I simply can't believe you cheated on me!" she finally yelled at him so loud, that there was no doubt that the three ladies heard her.

Rolf was as stunned as the other women.

"Cheated? Natascha, what are you doing?" he whispered through his teeth barely audible and noticed the other women looking at him in disgust.

"Not only did you cheat on me, but with my own brother?" Natascha now almost screamed. While everybody was still frozen in shock, she winked at Rolf, turned around and rushed to the entrance door.

Although Rolf almost wanted to kill her right now, he had to give Natascha credit for setting him up like that. While the other three women got in their car and drove out of the parking lot without even looking at him, he had to smile. Slowly he turned around to take a last look at Natascha, who waved at him from the door and threw him a kiss.

Just moments later, the young German caught up with Nick and walked down the corridor inside *EuroSec Corp*. The walls were full of pictures of team members either during important events, on oil rigs or ships, or even with some celebrities. Natascha looked at each of those pictures with great interest. At the end of the corridor were two portraits in memory of Oliver Schneider and Shira Hadad. Nick stopped the baby stroller beside Natascha and took her hand. Together they looked at the portraits.

"They're new. Never seen them before," Nick explained.

"They both look good in this picture. I like them," Natascha commented and picked up her daughter to calm her down.

"Okay, we got to go. They're really waiting for us," Nick pressed on and turned around with the stroller.

He opened the door to the conference room and stopped with the stroller right in the middle of the door frame. He was as surprised as Natascha was.

"My apologies. I was under the impression that this would be a small, informal meeting," Nick apologized and looked into the faces of all the people.

"Slight change of plans. Nothing informal here anymore," Brian explained and came over to them. He and Klaus both congratulated Natascha and Nick on their child. While Klaus commented that Shira was literally living proof that his employees ignored company policies, Brian was more polite and offered them a seat. Nick and Natascha both sat into the comfortable leather chairs. Natascha rocked Shira in an attempt to calm her down.

"First I believe that introductions are in order. Natascha, left to Ariel are Sigrid Schneider, Sean MacLeod as well as Gunnar Eriksson. Like Ariel, they're all members of operation control and also act as team leaders from time to time. On my right you see General Rashid, who visits us from Israel, the German Ambassador, Inspector Conolly from Scotland Yard as well as the American Ambassador."

Natascha politely nodded at each person with an appreciating smile, but for the American Ambassador she had nothing more than a hateful look.

"It's okay, Natascha," Nick whispered and put his hand on her shoulder.

"There's absolutely no reason for concern. You're totally safe," Klaus promised her. Everybody inside the room noticed the hate and contempt that Natascha showed towards the American Ambassador. His eyes narrowed in sharp slits as she fixed her unwavering gaze on him.

"Well, I directly want to come to the purpose of this meeting. We all know the completely unfounded and appalling accusations you had to deal with the last couple months. Both the strength as well as the determination that you showed on board that vessel, especially during hours of great emotional pain, are unique and deserve the highest respect from all of us. As you know, this case took a serious turn towards reality and even the mighty American government couldn't hide the truth any longer."

Natascha laughed out loud, while she still looked at the American Ambassador in disgust. The diplomat took Brian's comment more personally than he wanted to and was clearly uncomfortable.

"Thanks to today's technology, we all know the material that was found in that lunatics house and that miraculously made it to the internet the same night. I think you'll be satisfied to hear that not only the Israeli and British, but also the German authorities verified the authenticity of the video footage shot on board the *Northern Explorer*. Furthermore, investigators from all three nations could also confirm independently that it's indeed the voice of former US Senator Jonathan Brown. Without knowing it, that idiot taped his own confession. The video was also enough evidence to prove that Chuck Hogan was his henchman. Together with the notes, the video also showed that Jenna Mason, who actually was Chuck Hogan's sister, as well as three other members of the American scientist team, were also involved in this matter. The authorities could also prove that Jonathan Brown was indeed the author of all those notes. The evidence at hand allows no other conclusion except that Jonathan Brown as well as the Canadian Pierre Dumont were the real masterminds behind these attacks. Unfortunately, Gordon Ramshaw, who had a great part in building this company, was also involved in this matter. Nevertheless we took the liberty and were so kind to inform the American authorities more than forty eight hours ago about the official findings. Of course they had to double check all that. As expected, the statement of Chief of Staff Brown regarding the intruder in his house was pursuitant, but since over ten reporters turned his place upside down before the police even arrived, nobody could find any evidence any more. Mr. Ambassador, would you please be so kind and officially inform Ms. Kleinfeld to which conclusion your great nation finally came?" Brian finished and looked, like everybody else, at the American diplomat.

Still uncomfortable, the ambassador looked from Brian to Natascha, who still stared at him in disgust.

"Ms. Kleinfeld, first I want to let you know that I feel incredibly sorry for what..."

"Save your sympathy and tell me what you want," Natascha interrupted him harshly.

"Natascha, please," Nick tried to calm her down. He noticed that Natascha was ready to explode any moment and decided to take Shira from her. It was quite obvious, that their daughter felt Natascha's emotions.

The American Ambassador looked to the ground and tried again.

"Very well. Our authorities examined all the evidence in this case and their final result is that you and your fiancé fell victim to a conspiracy in which you were portrayed as the scape goat. All the evidence clearly shows that all accusations against you and your friends are without substance and therefore void. As you already know, the international warrant for your arrest has been lifted several days ago."

The diplomat stopped for a moment and took a sealed envelope out of his attaché case. He closed the case and rose from his chair.

"In this envelope I also have an official apology from the President of the United States of America as well as the director of the Central Intelligence Agency."

The American Ambassador took his attaché case and walked around the desk to come to Natascha and Nick, who both rose from their seats.

Natascha was so disgusted by this person that she took a step back.

"I know that you hate me and I completely understand why. I only want you to know that I had nothing to do with this, and that I really am sorry that you had to endure all that stress and emotional pain."

"And yet here you are standing right in front of me, still working for that government and reminding me of that stress and emotional pain I had to endure," Natascha snapped at him bitterly, ignoring the envelope he offered her.

"I'm really sorry," the diplomat finally said and gave the envelope to Nick, before he left the conference room.

Without saying a word, Natascha waited until the door was closed again and took Shira back from Nick.

"Did we ever teach him a lesson, my little angel. He really thought he could crawl into our confidence, but he didn't know us," she told her daughter and carefully swayed her in her arms, while many present laughed.

"Natascha, you're officially an honorable member of the community. Although, I must admit, for a second I was worried you would beat him up. I just lost a case of expensive port wine to Brian," Klaus congratulated her, after she shook hands with the German Ambassador, who also left the conference room.

"I've never been anything else but an honorable member of the community. Most people just didn't know it," Natascha laughed. "I also have to admit that I thought for a second or two to kick him in his balls. If you want your wine back, I'm sure I can still catch up to him in the parking lot," Natascha added, after she was convinced the German diplomat had left.

"There's another thing I wanted to talk to you about, but we had to wait until the diplomats were gone. It's indeed about Jonathan Brown and Pierre Dumont," Brian mentioned, after he thanked Klaus for the expensive wine.

"What is it? They are cutting him a deal, aren't they?" Natascha asked, her voice turning cold again.

"Jonathan Brown found out the evidence against him is overwhelming. Two days ago he received a warning from a friend that the FBI was planning to arrest him, his secretary Carl Miller as well as his security detail, Abigail Sinclair, the next morning. On their way to his hunting lodge in the early morning, the FBI received a phone call that Brown's estate was burning. It took the FBI until the late afternoon, before they found four dead bodies in the remains. They were Jonathan Brown, Pierre Dumont, Abigail Sinclair and Carl Miller. All the evidence suggests they had an open fire in their fire place, before they damaged the gas line. Evidently all four of them committed suicide with Jonathan's gun just hours before the FBI would pick them up. So they're definitely not cutting a deal any more," Brian Whittaker explained with a wink and smiled at the young German.

For a few seconds Natascha and Nick were speechless. A sudden feeling of relief overwhelmed her and she wrapped her arms around Nick. With tears in her eyes she let go of him seconds later.

"I'm sorry, this is not very respectful," she apologized to all the people.

Ariel walked up to her with a smile and gave her a kiss on her cheek, before he hugged her.

"Look who it is, my little angel. He's your godfather. You know him. He's always so nice. Well, to be precise, he's always nice to us, and we don't even want to know where he was two nights ago. I'm sure he's still pretty tired from the long flight," Natascha shared her suspicion about Jonathan Brown's unnatural death and everybody started to laugh.

"Don't worry. I could sleep during the flight," Ariel assured her with a short laugh.

"Okay, let's see what the President had to say about all this," Brian mentioned and looked at Nick, who was still holding the letter in his hands.

Before anybody else could react, Natascha took the still sealed envelope out of her fiance's hand and fed it into a shredder beside the door without even opening it.

"Nothing that I'd believe them," she stated seriously, while everybody else stared at the thousands of pieces of fine confetti in disbelief.

For the next twenty minutes they kept talking and even the other members of *EuroSec Corp* stopped by to introduce themselves and to congratulate Nick and Natascha.

"Oh, by the way," Nick shouted over the chatter as Natascha put their daughter in the stroller.

"We almost forgot. Natascha and I are getting married this Saturday. It would be nice if all of you could make it."

The short moment of silence broke under an outburst of laughter and words of congratulations.

- 31 -

Reykjavik, Iceland, Monday, July 16th
It was not before late Monday afternoon when the little family flew back to Iceland. Although Nick and Natascha originally planned to have a little ceremony, they were relieved when both their parents agreed to cover the costs. They also convinced them that they deserved to have the ceremony they wanted to and to invite as many people as they liked. Grateful to their parents, they added a few more friends to their list, but they still kept it reasonably small. After an exhausting weekend, Nick and Natascha were glad to be back in Iceland. Their plan shifted from the wedding to relocating to London, where Nick would work for *EuroSec Corp* again. Natascha would still work on the computer, until their daughter would allow her to look for something else.

Once they were home, Natascha laid Shira down to sleep. When Nick came home minutes later with their dog, Natascha decided to take a shower. Tired and happy to be back home again, Nick sat down on the couch and turned their little TV on. The American news station just confirmed the suicide of Jonathan Brown and the others.

"Natascha, come over here. It's about them. It's interesting."

Just seconds later Natascha stood behind him, her hair dripping water all over the floor.

With great excitement they listened to the news reporter, her voice overlaying Natascha's picture once more.

"After careful examination of all available evidence, the authorities ultimately came to the conclusion that all accusations against Ms. Kleinfeld were unfounded. It was also ruled that Ms. Kleinfeld obviously fell victim to a well thought conspiracy and she was cleared of all charges against her. The international warrant for her arrest was lifted several days ago. During a meeting with Ms. Kleinfeld last Thursday in London, the American Ambassador officially expressed the deepest sympathies from the American government. The President of the United States, formerly one of the greatest supporters of Jonathan Brown, had personally written and signed a letter of apology. The envelope, which also included another written apology from the Central Intelligence Agency, was scheduled to be handed over to Ms. Kleinfeld by the American Ambassador during the Thursday meeting. We also got official information, that inside this sealed envelope was also a cheque over the total amount of twenty five million US Dollars to compensate Ms. Kleinfeld for the last couple months. So far it's not known how Ms. Kleinfeld reacted."

Nick turned the TV off and looked at his wife. His shock reflected her speechless jaw-dropped mouth. She still stared at the TV in disbelief, her eyes growing wider with thought.

"Do you think that's reason enough for a divorce?" Nick asked, breaking the momentary silence. He searched his wife's distraught complexion for an answer since she stood silent.

"I actually do still love you," Nick reassured Natascha, who had not moved or shown a reaction for almost two minutes.

"I mean, we could've really used the money, you know, moving to London and all that. But it is okay," Nick continued to tease his wife and smiled at her.

"Nick, I am so sorry!" Natascha finally whispered, still staring at the blank TV, her body tensed in its motionless position.

"How could I only be so arrogant," she loudly hissed at herself, pacing their living room with blistering heat.

Nick stood up and pulled her turned body into his arms, her back pressing into his chest as he ceased her agitated walk. He looked deep into her dark brown eyes as she looked up to him from their reflections in the mirror.

"It's okay, Natascha. We don't need their money. It's dirty money, you know that. We would've been unhappy with it, trust me. We're happy the way we are. We have a wonderful daughter and we both have jobs in London. We have enough money for the move," he tried to convince her.

"And you're really not mad at me?" she asked almost inaudible and looked at him, her eyes growing large, begging for his answer.

"No, how can I be mad at you? You're standing completely naked in front of me. How can I be mad?" Nick laughed in her ear.

"Oh, I didn't realize," Natascha replied matter-of-factly, and looked down at her, before she spun around. She gave Nick a long kiss, and his hands smoothly glided over her body.

"I'm still sorry. We could've donated twenty four million and kept one for us. That wouldn't have been that dirty," she regretfully admitted.

"Yes, it would've been the same. We would never have been happy with it."

Just as Nick believed he convinced her, the phone interruptively rang, beckoning their attention.

Natascha's eyes widened in shock, her joints individually tensing from head to toe. "You pick it up. That's my dad! He's going to disinherit me before he rips my head off!" Natascha whispered fearfully and didn't flinch a muscle.

Nick clapped her buttocks and walked over to pick up the phone. According to their display, there were now a total of three calls waiting.

"Okay, let's see. Who do you want me to talk to first? Your parents, my parents or London?" Nick asked looking at the numbers in the display.

"Take London first. Maybe they glued the cheque back together. That'll calm the other two down," Natascha helplessly hoped the impossible and closed her eyes. Nick picked up the phone to talk to Brigitte, who delivered him the bad news that all the shredded paper was already thrown away. Since he expected no difference, Nick was still very relaxed and turned towards Natascha.

"Well, Plan A didn't work out too well. Who's next?" he asked Natascha with a playful grin.

"Okay, your parents made a very reasonable impression on me. Too bad they're

Thin Ice

going to emancipate their disgraceful new daughter-in-law within the next five minutes."

Nick shook his head and activated the next line. He listened to his father for several minutes and hooked up the phone again.

"They told us not to worry about the lost money and promised to help, if necessary. They're concerned, but you heard what I told them. Nevertheless, my father insists that, for the future, you open all mail first before you destroy it."

With her hands leaning on the couch, Natascha nodded.

"You bet. Flyers, advertising, absolutely everything. Okay, now it's going to get difficult. Is that still my parents calling?" she asked desperately and pointed at the phone.

"Yes, persistently. They've been calling for exactly eight minutes and thirty two seconds. I mean, they hear the line is busy so they know we're here."

"Yeah, unfortunately for us they're not stupid. Not like their daughter. Okay, mom has most certainly already blotted my name from the family tree and is twisting a little, black-haired voodoo doll into a hedgehog with a gazillion needles. Dad's going to disinherit me for sure. Well, I can't blame him. After all, I gave a pretty impressive demonstration that I can't handle money..." Natascha sighed with fear, then suddenly straighted up, closed her eyes and took a couple deep breaths, "Okay, I'm ready. You can pick up now."

"You want *me* to pick up? They're your parents."

"Nick, if that ring on your finger has the slightest meaning to you, then please pick up the phone and pretend I'm not here. Tell them the dog ate me, but please, please, please, I beg you to protect me!" Natascha pleaded theatrically.

Nick frowned and finally picked up the phone again.

"Hello Richard...hello, no, I can't understand you if you're both shouting at the same time...yes, that's better, thank you...yes, we just got home, everything went well. Shira is fine...yes, we were back in time...I did see it on TV, Natascha just took a shower...yes, we heard it...no, the cheque is gone. I already spoke with London...no, I'm not mad at her...no, my parents were actually pretty relaxed. We don't want the money. It's dirty money...I know, Natascha had the same idea about donating some of it...no, we won't sue them...yes, I'll make sure Natascha doesn't touch the mail ever again, I promise... no, I don't want a divorce...of course I love her...she's here, she's standing right in front of me...yes, she's naked. She knew that would help...no, I don't think she wants to distract me that way, she was just taking a shower...yes, we'll be careful...thank you...Bye."

Nick finally put the cordless phone back on it's station and looked at Natascha.

"Oh, perfect. Not only do they think I'm completely financially incompetent, no, they also think I'm a hussy," Natascha moaned and her head sank.

"Well, you are standing here completely naked and you definitely have to make up for this," Nick teased her.

"I'm a decent girl," she glared at him.

"You shredded twenty five million dollars."

Natascha thought for a few seconds and played with her hair.

"Well, okay, I agree. You can decide tonight," she said shyly.

"Okay, but not only for tonight," Nick replied with a grin.

"Hey! Slow down. I'm not going to let you take me here on the coach because of that little trifle," Natascha answered and pretended to be appalled.

"No? Where can I take you?"

"You can take me in the bedroom, like a respectable newly wedded couple," Natascha smiled with a deep grin and turned around proudly, retreating to the bathroom to dry off.

**Approximately 20km west of Cape Kendall, Coronation Gulf,
Tuesday, July 17th**

The sun burned hot in the large blue cloudless sky as its rays beat through the window of the plane. It was the second time that the man flew beneath the radar that far north. On the horizon he finally saw some houses and started his descent. The pilot smiled silently at the sight of the little settlement and gently touched down a few minutes later. With the engines now idling down, he got out of the cockpit and greeted all the kids, who were already waiting for him. He opened the cargo compartment and took out several large bags. The kids swarmed around him like bees on honey, prohibiting him from doing anything before he gave them some sweets and toys from one of the bags. With the native children finally satisfied, he walked over to the adult as she waited for him and hugged her sincerely. He opened one of the bags and let the person have a look inside.

"Those are all the medication and vaccines you need. If you need something else, just let me know and I'll take care of it."

The adult woman thanked him warm-heartedly and helped carry one of the bags.

"You come with me. Everything okay. No more problem," she told the visitor.

In a caring way, she took him by his arm and led him to a distant house. The darkly dressed man watched the children, who ran around them shouting, and noticed the dogs persistently bark like they did in his first visit in October. The native woman pointed to the door, gesturing her guest to enter the house. Slowly the man opened the door and bend his head down as he stepped inside. It was so dark in the dimly lit room, he struggled to see. It took his eyes a little to adjust to the low lighting, but he could finally recognize the elderly woman in the nearby room. It was the same woman who had predicted Natascha's pregnancy back in September, after the polar bear incident. The woman looked at her guest and simply nodded encouragingly. The man had the feeling she was waiting for him for quite some time.

She pointed to the other side of the tiny room and her guests eyes fell to the bed. Ariel took a deep breath and with a sigh of relief, a smile spread across his tender lips.

Reykjavik, Iceland, Friday, July 20th

Natascha's laugh intensified as she sat on Nick, his hand resting on her soft skin. Nick grimaced under a deep growl that resounded in the room. His face was just centimeters away from the huge head of a dead serious Kuvasz. *Rocky*'s dark daring eyes stared at him angrily, his quivering lip turning up with a quick twitch.

"Natascha, tell your dog not to look at me like that. Just his hot breath is blistering my skin."

Natascha was still laughing when she patted *Rocky*'s head.

"It's okay, *Rocky*. I know I might have groaned a little bit, but that's not because I was in danger. Actually it was quite the opposite. You can get out of our bed now," Natascha said and burst out laughing again as her dog retreated from the room.

"Next time, the door will be closed," Nick demanded.

Natascha struggled to catch her breath.

"Sure, whatever you want. He's perfect for birth control, actually much better than the pill," Natascha roared with another fit of laughter, and Nick threw her a quizzical brow.

"Ah, this is so funny," the young German woman laughed, sat up and wiped a tear from her face.

"I have to go wash my hands. I'm going to have some water. Do you want something, too?" she asked and got out of bed.

"No, I'm fine, thank you," Nick answered and watched Natascha slide the bathrobe over her skin as she pulled it warmly around her. She turned towards him, a smile spreading from ear to ear and bit her lip, "Don't go anywhere, we're not done yet."

While Natascha left the bedroom, Nick laid back again and a deep chuckle escaped his smile. Still shaking his head, he could hear *Rocky* suddenly burst in another fit of barks. Just a few seconds after, Nick heard a car crawl up their driveway. The two headlights cut through the darkness and went out at the same time the engine did. Curious who their visitor might be, Nick got out of bed and jumped into a jogging suit. Although it wasn't that late in the evening, they still didn't expect any visitors.

"I'll get the door," Natascha called from the other end of their house. She turned the outdoor light on and opened the door. *Rocky* immediately ran outside barking loud, but almost immediately fell silent as he greeted their unexpected visitor. Based on *Rocky*'s reaction, Natascha knew it had to be a very good friend, but it was definitely not Björn. The man patted the huge white dog and finally walked over to Natascha as the passenger door of the car slowly opened.

"Ariel! It's you! What are you doing here? Is everything okay? Did something happen?" Natascha asked nervously and closed her bathrobe a little bit tighter in the cold evening wind.

"Who is it?" Nick asked, finally appearing beside Natascha.

"It's Ariel," Natascha answered and noticed that Nick kept his right hand concealed behind his back. Nick sighed in relief and took his gun back before he returned to the door to greet his boss. Natascha just unwrapped her arms from Ariel's shoulder when Nick finally shook his hand.

"Come in, it's chilly outside. Do you want to stay here tonight?" Natascha immediately asked, taking up her hospitable manner for her friend.

"Yes, if you don't mind. I just got back from a rather long trip. It'd be very nice if we could stay over night," Ariel thanked and stepped inside.

Nick led his friend and superior into the living room, while Natascha was still calling her dog back inside. *Rocky* stood beside the passenger door of the car, his tail wagging wildly.

"Ariel, did you bring someone we know?" Natascha asked the Israeli from the door, but Ariel just winked at her. Natascha's brow furrowed with wonder and perplexity. She had no idea who it could be. She returned her attention to the other guest who slowly approached the house. It was definitely a woman.

"Did you bring Astrid? Why didn't she walk with you?" Natascha asked, but she immediately knew this person could not be Astrid. *Rocky* never met her.

"It's a surprise," Ariel winked at Natascha again. Like his wife, Nick's curiosity peaked and he walked over to identify his guest, their surprise.

The woman walked into the light as if she was a mirage, a whimsy fantasy, a subject of an epiphany that wasn't supposed to exist, but did. Her figure slowly approached them, drifting under the weak outdoor light. Natascha recognized her instantly, but it wasn't, it couldn't, be true. Her heart stopped under the tension of unanswered questions, words, theories, the meaningless ideas that finally overcame her. Her thoughts stopped suddenly.

There was nothing.

She could feel her limbs fall numb with shock. She felt like she was floating between time and space, an ability that didn't exist. To go back in time, to envision everything they had been through, and here she was.

Natascha's lips twitched into a painful quiver as tears overwhelmed her. A stab pierced deep within her. She could feel the pain, the relief, the indescribable disbelief of the person who stood in front of her.

"Oh my God! This is not possible! Oh my God!" Natascha screamed, her words ripping through the lump that formed in her throat. Even Nick was completely speechless. He slightly shook his head, searching for the answers, the incredible details that didn't matter. She was here.

"Oh my God! Oh my God! Oh my God! You're alive, Shira, you're alive!" Natascha screamed and threw herself at her long lost friend, her sister.

Seconds passed like hours when Natascha finally broke their embrace and looked at her again, as if to reassure herself that she was here.

Shira smiled her same grin, and finally entered their loving home.

"Shalom!"

Epilogue

Though lies are easily formed, maintaining its worth as an illusive truth requires a skill that most are unable to possess. There was no doubt about Shira's fate as she sat in the Rehfeld's living room sharing the same food and drink with the newly weds. The Rehfeld's couldn't believe the truth that unveiled as Ariel explained.

To safe his sister's life, Ariel had faked her death. He knew Canadian physicians and hospitals were required, by law, to report bullet wounds to the authorities. Especially if the wounded person matched the description of a fugitive terrorist. Shortly after Nick and the others escaped on the Russian support submersible, Ariel brought his sister, unnoticed by the Captain or the crew, to the hospital ward. There he put her on an IV, a medical procedure that was part of his standard training for the Israeli close-combat forces.

With Shira's condition stabilized, Ariel took Jenna Mason's dead body and tied her in such a way to the RIB that her body would slip into the water after a few kilometers. To lay a false trail, he hid a bandage with Jenna's blood underneath the seats. To cover his own tracks, Ariel acted quickly and sunk the other dead bodies from the bridge and the radio room with weight belts. When he was ready to leave the ship with his sister, he sent off the RIB with only Jenna's body in it. As intended, she fell into the water after a few miles. Under the noise from the RIB's big twin outboard engines, Ariel used the helicopter to fly his sister to the only person he trusted: the elderly Inuvialuit who had predicted Natascha's pregnancy. Shira told Ariel about Natascha's conversation with the Inuvialuit woman and he remembered the approximate position. When he arrived, it seemed the Inuvialuit was already waiting for him, and she volunteered to care for Shira. After Ariel knew his sister would survive, he made his way to the Israelian embassy in Toronto. Under a new identity he traveled back to Tel Aviv to brief his father, before he continued his journey to London, where he officially informed Brian Whittaker and Klaus Schwartze of Shira's death. This was the only way to protect his sister and her location. He knew the Canadians would find and examine Jenna Mason's body sooner or later. Neither the Americans nor the Canadians could know Shira had suffered a through and through, but Ariel knew Brian Whittaker and Klaus Schwartze would independently recieve that information from Ole-Einar and the other survivors. Convinced that the body found by the Canadians was indeed Shira, Brian Whittaker arranged that the Israeli was officially declared dead. Ariel trusted that the American authorities would rely on the data of *foreign* people when they tried to identify Jenna Mason's body. Since the Americans concentrated their search on foreign people, they could not find a DNA or dental match and also officially declared Shira Hadad deceased.

Ariel kept his promise and supplied the Inuvialuit with much needed medication and vaccines, before he picked his sister up a few days ago. After visiting the Israelian embassy, Shira insisted on seeing Natascha and Nick first. Just a few days after her visit, Nick and his family moved back to London.

They knew their life was going to be different. It was the one thing they wanted in the beginning, but was sourly interrupted. They knew their life was going to be as normal as it could be. Nick reached for Natascha's hand.

Everything was okay.